Miller has elected to shame the devil and tell the truth, and his work is one of the bravest, richest and most consistent ventures in this domain since Jean-Jacques Rousseau. By its very nature such a task must transgress the narrow limits of what ordinary people regard as permissible; canons of taste, conventional ideas of beauty and propriety, they must be renovated in the light of his central objective—the search for truth. Often the result is shocking, terrifying; but then truth has always been a fierce oracle rather than a bleat or a whimper. But no one, I think, could read (as I have just done) through the whole length and breadth of his work without wonder and amazement—and finally without gratitude for what he has undertaken on behalf of us all. It isn't pretty, a lot of it, but then neither is real life. It goes right to the bone.

—Lawrence Durrell

THE ROSY CRUCIFIXION

HENRY MILLER

THE ROSY CRUCIFIXION
BOOK ONE

SEXUS

GROVE PRESS, INC.,   NEW YORK

Library of Congress Catalog Card Number: 65-23308

Sixteenth printing

MANUFACTURED IN THE UNITED STATES OF AMERICA

DISTRIBUTED BY RANDOM HOUSE, INC., NEW YORK

VOLUME ONE

It must have been a Thursday night when I met her for the first time—at the dance hall. I reported to work in the morning, after an hour or two's sleep, looking like a somnambulist. The day passed like a dream. After dinner I fell asleep on the couch and awoke fully dressed about six the next morning. I felt thoroughly refreshed, pure at heart, and obsessed with one idea—to have her at any cost. Walking through the park I debated what sort of flowers to send with the book I had promised her (*Winesburg, Ohio*). I was approaching my thirty-third year, the age of Christ crucified. A wholly new life lay before me, had I the courage to risk all. Actually there was nothing to risk : I was at the bottom rung of the ladder, a failure in every sense of the word.

It was a Saturday morning, then, and for me Saturday has always been the best day of the week. I come to life when others are dropping off with fatigue; my week begins with the Jewish day of rest. That this was to be the grand week of my life, to last for seven long years, I had no idea of course. I knew only that the day was auspicious and eventful. To make the fatal step, to throw everything to the dogs, is in itself an emancipation : the thought of consequences never entered my head. To make absolute, unconditional surrender to the woman one loves is to break every bond save the desire not to lose her, which is the most terrible bond of all.

I spent the morning borrowing right and left, dispatched the book and flowers, then sat down to write a long letter to be delivered by a special messenger. I told her that I would telephone her later in the afternoon. At noon I quit the office and went home. I was terribly restless, almost feverish with impatience. To wait until five o'clock was torture. I went again to the park, oblivious of everything as I walked blindly over the downs to the lake where the children were sailing their boats. In the distance a band was playing; it brought back memories of my childhood, stifled dreams, longings, regrets. A sultry, passionate rebellion filled my veins. I thought of certain great figures in the past, of all that they had accomplished at my age. What ambitions I may have had were gone; there was nothing I wanted to do except to put myself completely in her hands. Above everything else I wanted to hear her voice, know that she was still alive, that she had not already forgotten me. To be able to put a nickel in the slot every day of my life henceforth, to be able to hear her say hello, that and nothing more was the utmost I dared hope for. If she would promise me that much, and keep her promise, it wouldn't matter what happened.

Promptly at five o'clock I telephoned. A strangely sad, foreign voice informed me that she was not at home. I tried to find out when she would be home but I was cut off. The thought that she was out of reach drove me frantic. I telephoned my wife that I would not be home for dinner. She greeted the announcement in her usual disgusted way, as though she expected nothing more of me than disappointments and postponements. «Choke on it, you bitch,» I thought to myself as I hung up, «at least I know that I don't want you, any part of you, dead or alive.» An open trolley was coming along; without a thought of its direction I hopped aboard and made for the rear seat. I rode around for a couple of hours in a deep trance; when I came to I recognized an Arabian ice cream parlor near the water-front, got off, walked to the wharf and sat on a string-piece looking up at the humming fret-work of the Brooklyn Bridge. There were still several hours to kill before I dared venture to go to the dance hall. Gazing vacantly at the opposite shore my thoughts drifted ceaselessly, like a ship without a rudder.

When finally I picked myself up and staggered off I was like a man under an anaesthetic who has managed to slip away from the operating table. Everything looked familiar yet made no sense; it took ages to coordinate a few simple impressions which by ordinary reflex calculus would mean table, chair, building, person. Buildings emptied of their automatons are even more desolate than tombs; when the machines are left idle they create a void deeper than death itself. I was a ghost moving about in a vacuum. To sit down, to stop and light a cigarette, not to sit down, not to smoke, to think, or not to think, breathe or stop breathing, it was all one and the same. Drop dead and the man behind you walks over you; fire a revolver and another man fires at you; yell and you wake the dead who, oddly enough, also have powerful lungs. Traffic is now going East and West; in a minute it will be going North and South. Everything is proceeding blindly according to rule and nobody is getting anywhere. Lurch and stagger in and out, up and down, some dropping out like flies, others swarming in like gnats. Eat standing up, with slots, levers, greasy nickels, greasy cellophane, greasy appetite. Wipe your mouth, belch, pick your teeth, cock your hat, tramp, slide, stagger, whistle, blow your brains out. In the next life I will be a vulture feeding on rich carrion : I will perch on top of the tall buildings and dive like a shot the moment I

smell death. Now I am whistling a merry tune—the
epigastric regions are at peace. *Hello, Mara, how
are you?* And she will give me the enigmatic smile,
throwing her arms about me in warm embrace. This
will take place in a void under powerful Klieg lights
with three centimeters of privacy marking a mystic
circle about us.

I mount the steps and enter the arena, the grand
ball-room of the double-barrelled sex adepts, now
flooded with a warm boudoir glow. The phantoms
are waltzing in a sweet chewing gum haze, knees
slightly crooked, haunches taut, ankles swimming in
powdered sapphire. Between drum beats I hear the
ambulance clanging down below, then fire engines,
then police sirens. The waltz is perforated with
anguish, little bullet holes slipping over the cogs of
the mechanical piano which is drowned because it is
blocks away in a burning building without fire
escapes. She is not on the floor. She may be lying
in bed reading a book, she may be making love with
a prize-fighter, or she many be running like mad
through a field of stubble, one shoe on, one shoe off,
a man named Corn Cob pursuing her hotly. Wherever she is I am standing in complete darkness; her
absence blots me out.

I inquire of one of the girls if she knows when
Mara will arrive. *Mara?* Never heard of her. How
should she know anything about anybody since she's
only had the job an hour or so and is sweating like
a mare wrapped in six suits of woolen underwear
lined with fleece. Won't I offer her a dance—she'll
ask one of the other girls about this Mara. We
dance a few rounds of sweat and rose-water, the conversation running to corns and bunions and varicose
veins, the musicians peering through the boudoir mist
with jellied eyes, their faces spread in a frozen grin.
The girl over there, Florrie, she might be able to

tell me something about my friend. Florrie has a wide mouth and eyes of lapis lazuli; she's as cool as a geranium, having just come from an all-afternoon fucking fiesta. Does Florrie know if Mara will be coming soon? She doesn't think so... she doesn't think she'll come at all this evening. *Why?* She thinks she has a date with some one. Better ask the Greek—he knows everything.

The Greek says yes, Miss Mara will come... yes, just wait a while. I wait and wait. The girls are steaming, like sweating horses standing in a field of snow. Midnight. No sign of Mara. I move slowly, unwillingly, towards the door. A Porto Rican lad is buttoning his fly on the top step.

In the subway I test my eyesight reading the ads at the farther end of the car. I cross-examine my body to ascertain if I am exempt from any of the ailments which civilized man is heir to. Is my breath foul? Does my heart knock? Have I a fallen instep? Are my joints swollen with rheumatism? No sinus trouble? No pyorrhea? How about constipation? Or that tired feeling after lunch? No migraine, no acidosis, no intestinal catarrh, no lumbago, no floating bladder, no corns or bunions, no varicose veins? As far as I know I'm sound as a button, and yet... Well, the truth is I lack something, something vital...

I'm love-sick. Sick to death. A touch of dandruff and I'd succumb like a poisoned rat.

My body is heavy as lead when I throw it into bed. I pass immediately into the lowest depth of dream. This body, which has become a sarcophagus with stone handles, lies perfectly motionless; the dreamer rises out of it, like a vapor, to circumnavigate the world. The dreamer seeks vainly to find a form and shape that will fit his ethereal essence. Like a celestial tailor, he tries on one body after another, but

they are all misfits. Finally he is obliged to return
to his own body, to reassume the leaden mould, to
become a prisoner of the flesh, to carry on in torpor,
pain and ennui.

Sunday morning. I awaken fresh as a daisy. The
world lies before me, unconquered, unsullied, virgin
as the Arctic zones. I swallow a little bismuth and
chloride of lime to drive away the last leaden fumes
of inertia. I will go directly to her home, ring the
bell, and walk in. Here I am, take me—or stab me
to death. Stab the heart, stab the brain, stab the
lungs, the kidneys, the viscera, the eyes, the ears. If
only one organ be left alive you are doomed—doomed
to be mine, forever, in this world and the next and
all the worlds to come. I'm a desperado of love, a
scalper, a slayer. I'm insatiable. I eat hair, dirty
wax, dry blood clots, anything and everything you
call yours. Show me your father, with his kites, his
race horses, his free passes for the opera: I will eat
them all, swallow them alive. Where is the chair
you sit in, where is your favorite comb, your tooth-
brush, your nail file? Trot them out that I may
devour them at one gulp. You have a sister more
beautiful than yourself, you say. Show her to me—I
want to lick the flesh from her bones.

Riding towards the ocean, towards the marsh land
where a little house was built to hatch a little egg
which, after it had assumed the proper form, was
christened Mara. That one little drop escaping from
a man's penis should produce such staggering results!
I believe in God the Father, in Jesus Christ his only
begotten Son, in the blessed Virgin Mary, the Holy
Ghost, in Adam Cadmium, in chrome nickel, the
oxides and the mercurichromes, in water-fowls and
water-cress, in epileptoid seizures, in bubonic plagues,
in Devachan, in planetary conjunctions, in chicken
tracks and stick throwing, in revolutions, in stock

crashes, in wars, earthquakes, cyclones, in Kali Yuga
and in hula-hula. *I believe. I believe.* I believe
because not to believe is to become as lead, to lie
prone and rigid, forever inert, to waste away...

Looking out on the contemporary landscape.
Where are the beasts of the field, the crops, the ma-
nure, the roses that flower in the midst of corruption?
I see railroad tracks, gas stations, cement blocks, iron
girders, tall chimneys, automobile cemeteries, factories, warehouses, sweat shops, vacant lots. Not even
a goat in sight. I see it all clearly and distinctly : it
spells desolation, death, death everlasting. For thirty
years now I have worn the iron cross of ignominious
servitude, serving but not believing, working but
taking no wages, resting but knowing no peace. Why
should I believe that everything will suddenly change,
just having her, just loving and being loved?

Nothing will be changed except myself.

As I approach the house I see a woman in the
back-yard hanging up clothes. Her profile is turned
to me; it is undoubtedly the face of the woman with
the strange, foreign voice who answered the telephone.
I don't want to meet this woman, I don't want to
know who she is, I don't want to believe what I
suspect. I walk round the block and when I come
again to the door she is gone. Somehow my courage
too is gone.

I ring the bell hesitantly. Instantly the door is
yanked open and the figure of a tall, menacing young
man blocks the threshold. She is not in, can't say
when she'll be back, who are you, what do you want
of her? Then good-bye and bang! The door is
staring me in the face. Young man, you'll regret
this. One day I'll return with a shot-gun and blow
your testicles off... So that's it! Everybody on
guard, everybody tipped off, everybody trained to be
elusive and evasive. Miss Mara is never where she's

expected to be, nor does anybody know where she
might be expected to be. Miss Mara inhabits the
airs: volcanic ash blown hither and thither by the
Trade winds. Defeat and mystery for the first day of
the Sabbatical year. Gloomy Sunday amongst the
Gentiles, amongst the kith and kin of accidental birth.
Death to all Christian brethren! Death to the phoney status quo!

A few days passed without any sign of life from
her. In the kitchen, after my wife had retired, I
would sit and write voluminous letters to her. We
were living then in a morbidly respectable neighborhood, occupying the parlor floor and basement of a
lugubrious brown stone house. From time to time
I had tried to write but the gloom which my wife
created around her was too much for me. Only once
did I succeed in breaking the spell which she had
cast over the place; that was during a high fever
which lasted for several days when I refused to see a
doctor, refused to take any medicine, refused to take
any nourishment. In a corner of the room upstairs
I lay in a wide bed and fought off a delirium which
threatened to end in death. I had never really been
ill since childhood and the experience was delicious.
To make my way to the toilet was like staggering
through all the intricate passages of an ocean liner.
I lived several lives in the few days that it lasted.
That was my sole vacation in the sepulchre which is
called home. The only other place I could tolerate
was the kitchen. It was a sort of comfortable prison
cell and, like a prisoner, here I often sat alone late
into the night planning my escape. Here too my
friend Stanley sometimes joined me, croaking over my
misfortune and withering every hope with bitter and
malicious barbs.

It was here I wrote the maddest letters ever pen-
ned. Any one who thinks he is defeated, hopeless,

without resources, can take courage from me. I had
a scratchy pen, a bottle of ink and paper—my sole
weapons. I put down everything which came into
my head, whether it made sense or not. After I had
posted a letter I would go upstairs and lie down
beside my wife and, with eyes wide open, stare into
the darkness, as if trying to read my future. I said
to myself over and over that if a man, a sincere and
desperate man like myself, loves a woman with all
his heart, if he is ready to cut off his ears and mail
them to her, if he will take his heart's blood and
pump it out on paper, saturate her with his need and
longing, besiege her everlastingly, she cannot possibly
refuse him. The homeliest man, the weakest man,
the most undeserving man must triumph if he is willing to surrender his last drop of blood. No woman
can hold out against the gift of absolute love.

I went again to the dance hall and found a message waiting for me. The sight of her handwriting
made me tremble. It was brief and to the point.
She would meet me at Times Square, in front of the
drug store, at midnight the following day. I was to
please stop writing her to her home.

I had a little less than three dollars in my pocket
when we met. The greeting she gave me was cordial
and brisk. No mention of my visit to the house or
the letters or the gifts. Where would I like to go,
she asked after a few words. I hadn't the slightest
idea what to suggest. That she was standing there
in the flesh, speaking to me, looking at me, was an
event which I had not yet fully grasped. «Let's go
to Jimmy Kelly's place», she said, coming to my
rescue. She took me by the arm and walked me to
the curb where a cab was waiting for us. I sank
back into the seat, overwhelmed by her mere presence. I made no attempt to kiss her or even to hold

her hand. She had come—that was the paramount
thing. That was everything.

We remained until the early hours of the morning,
eating, drinking, dancing. We talked freely and un-
derstandingly. I knew no more about her, about her
real life, than I knew before, not because of any
secrecy on her part but rather because the moment
was too full and neither past nor future seemed
important.

When the bill came I almost dropped dead.

In order to stall for time I ordered more drinks.
When I confessed to her that I had only a couple of
dollars on me she suggested that I give them a check,
assuring me that since she was with me there would
be no question about its acceptance. I had to explain
that I owned no check book, that I possessed nothing
but my salary. In short, I made a full clearance.

While confessing this sad state of affairs to her an
idea had germinated in my crop. I excused myself
and went to the telephone booth. I called the main
office of the telegraph company and begged the night
manager, who was a friend of mine, to send a messenger to me immediately with a fifty dollar bill. It
was a lot of money for him to borrow from the till,
and he knew I wasn't any too reliable, but I gave
him a harrowing story, promising faithfully to return
it before the day was out.

The messenger turned out to be another good
friend of mine, old man Creighton, an ex-minister of
the gospel. He seemed indeed surprised to find me
in such a place at that hour. As I was signing the
sheet he asked me in a low voice if I was sure I
would have enough with the fifty. «I can lend you
something out of my own pocket», he added. «It
would be a pleasure to be of assistance to you.»

«How much can you spare?» I asked, thinking of
the task ahead of me in the morning.

«I can give you another twenty-five», he said readily.

I took it and thanked him warmly. I paid the bill, gave the waiter a generous tip, shook hands with the manager, the assistant manager, the bouncer, the hat check girl, the door man, and with a beggar who had his mitt out. We got into a cab and, as it wheeled around, Mara impulsively climbed over me and straddled me. We went into a blind fuck, with the cab lurching and careening, our teeth knocking, tongue bitten, and the juice pouring from her like hot soup. As we passed an open plaza on the other side of the river, just at daybreak, I caught the astonished glance of a cop as we sped by. «It's dawn, Mara,» I said, trying gently to disengage myself. «Wait, wait», she begged, panting and clutching at me furiously, and with that she went into a prolonged orgasm in which I thought she would rub my cock off. Finally she slid off and slumped back into her corner, her dress still up over her knees. I leaned over to embrace her again and as I did so I ran my hand up her wet cunt. She clung to me like a leech, wiggling her slippery ass around in a frenzy of abandon. I felt the hot juice trickling through my fingers. I had all four fingers up her crotch, stirring up the liquid moss which was tingling with electrical spasms. She had two or three orgasms and then sank back exhausted, smiling up at me weakly like a trapped doe.

After a time she got out her mirror and began powdering her face. Suddenly I observed a startled expression on her face, followed by a quick turn of the head. In another moment she was kneeling on the seat, staring out of the back window. «Some one's following us,» she said. «Don't look!» I was too weak and happy to give a damn. «Just a bit of hysteria,» I thought to myself, saying nothing but observing her attentively as she gave rapid, jerky orders to the driver to go this way and that, faster and faster. «*Please, please!*» she begged him, as though it were life and death. «Lady,» I heard him say, as if from far off, from some other dream vehicule. «I can't give her any more... I've got a wife and kid... I'm sorry.»

I took her hand and pressed it gently. She made an abortive gesture, as if to say—«You don't know... you don't know... this is terrible.» It was not the moment to ask her questions. Suddenly I had the realization that we were in danger. Suddenly I put two and two together, in my own crazy fashion. I reflected quickly... nobody is following us... that's all coke and laudanum... but somebody's after her, that's definite... she's committed a crime, a serious one, and maybe more than one... nothing she says adds up... I'm in a web of lies... I'm in love with a monster, the most gorgeous monster imaginable... I should quit her now, immediately, without a word of explanation... otherwise I'm doomed... she's fathomless, impenetrable... I might have known that the one woman in the world whom I can't live without is marked with mystery... get out at once... jump... save yourself!

I felt her hand on my leg, rousing me stealthily. Her face was relaxed, her eyes wide open, full, shining with innocence... «They've gone,» she said, «it's all right now.»

Nothing is right, I thought to myself. We're only beginning. Mara, Mara, where are you leading me? It's fateful, it's ominous, but I belong to you body and soul, and you will take me where you will, deliver me to my keeper, bruised, crushed, broken. For us there is no final understanding. I feel the ground slipping from under me...

My thoughts she was never able to penetrate,

neither then nor later. She probed deeper than thought: she read blindly, as if endowed with antennae. She knew that I was meant to destroy, that I would destroy her too in the end. She knew that whatever game she might pretend to play with me she had met her match. We were pulling up to the house. She drew close to me and, as though she had a switch inside her which she controlled at will, she turned on me the full incandescent radiance of her love. The driver had stopped the car. She told him to pull up the street a little farther and wait. We were facing one another, hands clasped, knees touching. A fire ran through our veins. We remained thus for several minutes, as in some ancient ceremony, the silence broken only by the purr of the motor.

«I'll call you to-morrow,» she said, leaning forward impulsively for a last embrace. And then in my ear she murmured—«I'm falling in love with the strangest man on earth. You frighten me, you're so gentle. Hold me tight... believe in me always... I feel almost as if I were with a god.»

Embracing her, trembling with the warmth of her passion, my mind jumped clear of the embrace, electrified by the tiny seed she had planted in me. Something that had been chained down, something that had struggled abortively to assert itself ever since I was a child and had brought my ego into the street for a glance around, now broke loose and went sky-rocketing into the blue. Some phenomenal new being was sprouting with alarming rapidity from the top of my head, from the double crown which was mine from birth.

After an hour or two's rest I got to the office which was already jammed with applicants. The telephones were ringing as usual. It seemed more than ever senseless to be passing my life away in the attempt to fill up a permanent leak. The officials of the cosmo-

coccic telegraph world had lost faith in me and I had
lost faith in the whole fantastic world which they
were uniting with wires, cables, pulleys, buzzers and
Christ only knows what. The only interest I displayed was in the pay check—and the much talked
of bonus which was due any day. I had one other
interest, a secret, diabolical one, and that was to work
off a grudge which I had against Spivak, the efficiency expert whom they had brought in from
another city expressly to spy on me.   As soon as
Spivak appeared on the scene, no matter in what
remote, outlying office, I was tipped off. I used to
lie awake nights thinking it out like a safe-cracker—
how I would trip him up and bring about his dismis-
sal. I made a vow that I would hang on to the job
until I had knifed him. It gave me pleasure to send
him phoney messages under false names in order to
give him a bum steer, covering him with ridicule and
causing endless confusion. I even had people write
him letters threatening his life. I would get Curley,
my chief stooge, to telephone him from time to time,
saying that his house was on fire or that his wife had
been taken to the hospital—anything that would
upset him and start him off on a fool's errand. I had
a gift for this underhanded sort of warfare. It was
a talent that had been developed since the tailoring
days. Whenever my father said to me—«Better cross
his name off the books, he'll never pay up!» I interpreted it very much as would a young Indian brave
if the old chief had handed him a prisoner and said—
«Bad pale face, give him the works!»   (I had a
thousand different ways of annoying a man without
running foul of the law. Some men, whom I disliked
on principle, I continued to plague long after they
had paid their petty debts. One man, whom I especially detested, died of an apoplectic fit upon receiving one of my anonymous insulting letters which

was smeared with cat shit, bird shit, dogshit and one or two other varieties, including the well-known human variety.) Spivak consequently was just my meat. I concentrated all my cosmococcic attention on the sole plan of annihilating him. When we met I was polite, deferential, apparently eager to cooperate with him in every way. Never lost my temper with him, though every word he uttered made my blood boil. I did everything possible to bolster his pride, inflate his ego, so that when the moment came to puncture the bag the noise would be heard far and wide.

Towards noon Mara telephoned. The conversation must have lasted a quarter of an hour. I thought she'd never hang up. She said she had been rereading my letters; some of them she had read aloud to her aunt, or rather parts of them. (Her aunt had said that I must be a poet. She was disturbed about the money I had borrowed. Would I be able to pay it back all right or should she try and borrow some? It was strange that I should be poor—I behaved like a rich man. But she was glad I was poor. Next time we would take a trolley ride somewhere. She didn't care about night clubs; she preferred a walk in the country or a stroll along the beach. The book was wonderful—she had only begun it this morning. Why didn't I try to write? She was sure I could write a great book. She had ideas for a book which she would tell me about when we met again. If I liked, she would introduce me to some writers she knew—they would be only too glad to help me...

She rambled on like that interminably. I was thrilled and worried at the same time. I had rather she put it down on paper. But she seldom wrote letters, so she said. *Why* I couldn't understand. Her fluency was marvellous. She would say things at random, intricate, flame-like, or slide off into a paren-

thetical limbo peppered with fireworks—admirable
linguistic feats which a practised writer might struggle for hours to achieve. And yet her letters—I remember the shock I received when I opened the first
one—were almost childlike.

Her words, however, produced an unexpected effect.
Instead of rushing out of the house immediately after
dinner that evening, as I usually did, I lay on the
couch in the dark and fell into a deep reverie.
«Why don't you try to write?» That was the phrase
which had stuck in my crop all day, which repeated
itself insistently, even as I was saying thank you to
my friend MacGregor for the ten-spot which I had
wrung from him after the most humiliating wheedl-
ing and cajoling.

In the darkness I began to work my way back to
the hub. I began to think of those most happy days
of childhood, the long Summer days when my mother
took me by the hand, led me over the fields to see
my little friends, Joey and Tony. As a child it was
impossible to penetrate the secret of that joy which
comes from a sense of superiority. That extra sense,
which enables one to participate and at the same
time to observe one's participation, appeared to me
to be the normal endowment of every one. That I
enjoyed everything more than other boys my age
I was unaware of. The discrepancy between myself
and others only dawned on me as I grew older.

To write, I meditated, must be an act devoid of
will. The word, like the deep ocean current, has to
float to the surface of its own impulse. A child has
no need to write, he is innocent. A man writes to
throw off the poison which he has accumulated because of his false way of life. He is trying to recapture his innocence, yet all he succeeds in doing (by
writing) is to inoculate the world with the virus of
his disillusionment. No man would set a word down

on paper if he had the courage to live out what he
believed in. His inspiration is deflected at the
source. If it is a world of truth, beauty and magic
that he desires to create, why does he put millions
of words between himself and the reality of that
world? Why does he defer action—unless it be that,
like other men, what he really desires is power, fame,
success. «Books are human actions in death,» said
Balzac. Yet, having perceived the truth, he deliberately surrendered the angel to the demon which possessed him.

A writer woos his public just as ingnominiously as
a politician or any other moutebank; he loves to
finger the great pulse, to prescribe like a physician,
to win a place for himself, to be recognized as a force,
to receive the full cup of adulation, even if it be de-
ferred a thousand years. He doesn't want a new
world which might be established immediately, because he knows it would never suit him. He wants
an impossible world in which he is the uncrowned
puppet ruler dominated by forces utterly beyond his
control. He is content to rule insidiously—in the
fictive world of symbols—because the very thought
of contact with rude and brutal realities frightens
him. True, he has a greater grasp of reality than
other men, but he makes no effort to impose that
higher reality on the world by force of example. He
is satisfied just to preach, to drag along in the wake
of disasters and catastrophes, a death-croaking pro-
phet always without honor, always stoned, always
shunned by those who, however unsuited for their
tasks, are ready and willing to assume responsibility
for the affairs of the world. The truly great writer
does not want to write: he wants the world to be a
place in which he can live the life of the imagination.
The first quivering word he puts to paper is the word
of the wounded angel: pain. The process of putting

down words is equivalent to giving oneself a narcotic.
Observing the growth of a book under his hands, the
author swells with delusions of grandeur. «I too am
a conqueror—perhaps the greatest conqueror of all!
My day is coming. I will enslave the world—by the
magic of words...»» Et cetera ad nauseam.

The little phrase—*Why don't you try to write?*—
involved me, as it had from the very beginning, in
a hopeless bog of confusion. I wanted to enchant but
not to enslave; I wanted a greater, richer life, but
not at the expense of others; I wanted to free the
imagination of all men at once because without the
support of the whole world, without a world imaginatively unified, the freedom of the imagination becomes a vice. I had no respect for writing *per se*
any more than I had for God *per se*. Nobody, no
principle, no idea has validity in itself. What is
valid is only that much—of anything, God included—
which is realized by all men in common. People are
always worried about the fate of the genius. I
never worried about the genius: genius takes care of
the genius in a man. My concern was always for the
nobody, the man who is lost in the shuffle, the man
who is so common, so ordinary, that his presence is
not even noticed. One genius does not inspire
another. All geniuses are leeches, so to speak. They
feed from the same source—the blood of life. The
most important thing for the genius is to make himself useless, to be absorbed in the common stream,
to become a fish again and not a freak of nature.
The only benefit, I reflected, which the act of writing
could offer me was to remove the differences which
separated me from my fellow-man. I definitely did
not want to become the artist, in the sense of becoming something strange, something apart and out of
the current of life.

The best thing about writing is not the actual labor

of putting word against word, brick upon brick, but
the preliminaries, the spade work, which is done in
silence, under any circumstances, in dream as well as
in the waking state. In short, the period of gestation.
No man ever puts down what he intended to say :
the original creation, which is taking place all the
time, whether one writes or doesn't write, belongs
to the primal flux : it has no dimensions, no form,
no time element. In this preliminary state, which is
creation and not birth, what disappears suffers no
destruction; something which was already there,
something imperishable, like memory, or matter, or
God, is summoned and in it one flings himself like
a twig into a torrent. Words, sentences, ideas, no
matter how subtle or ingenious, the maddest flights
of poetry, the most profound dreams, the most hallucinating visions, are but crude hieroglyphs chiselled
in pain and sorrow to commemorate an event which
is untransmissible. In an intelligently ordered world
there would be no need to make the unreasonable
attempt of putting such miraculous happenings down.
Indeed, it would make no sense, for if men only
stopped to realize it, who would be content with the
counterfeit when the real is at every one's beck and
call? Who would want to switch in and listen to
Beethoven, for example, when he might himself
experience the ecstatic harmonies which Beethoven
so desperately strove to register? A great work of
art, if it accomplishes anything, serves to remind us,
or let us say to set us dreaming, of all that is fluid
and intangible. Which is to say, *the universe*. It
cannot be understood; it can only be accepted or
rejected. If accepted we are revitalized; if rejected
we are diminished. Whatever it purports to be it is
not: it is always something more for which the last
word will never be said. It is all that we put into
it out of hunger for that which we deny every day

of our lives. If we accepted *ourselves* as completely,
the work of art, in fact *the whole world of art*, would
die of malnutrition. Every man Jack of us moves
without feet at least a few hours a day, when his
eyes are closed and his body prone. The art of
dreaming when wide awake will be in the power of
every man one day. Long before that books will
cease to exist, for when men are wide awake *and*
dreaming their powers of communication (with one
another and with the spirit that moves all men) will
be so enhanced as to make writing seem like the
harsh and raucous squawks of an idiot.

I think and know all this, lying in the dark
memory of a Summer's day, without having mastered,
or even half-heartedly attempted to master, the art
of the crude hieroglyph. Before ever I begin I am
disgusted with the efforts of the acknowledged masters. Without the ability of the knowledge to make
so much as a portal in the façade of the grand edifice, I criticize and lament the architecture itself. If
I were only a tiny brick in the vast cathedral of
this antiquated façade I would be infinitely happier;
I would have life, the life of the whole structure,
even as an infinitesimal part of it. But I am outside, a barbarian who cannot make even a crude
sketch, let alone a plan, of the edifice he dreams of
inhabiting. I dream a new blazingly magnificent
world which collapses as soon as the light is turned
on. A world that vanishes but does not die, for I
have only to become still again and stare wide-eyed
into the darkness and it reappears... There is then
a world in me which is utterly unlike any world I
know of. I do not think it is my exclusive property
—it is only the angle of my vision which is exclusive
in that it is unique. If I talk the language of my
unique vision nobody understands; the most colossal
edifice may be reared and yet remain invisible. The

thought of that haunts me. What good will it do to make an invisible temple?

Drifting with the flux—because of that little phrase. This is the sort of thinking that went on whenever the word writing came up. In ten years of sporadic efforts I had managed to write a million words or so. You might as well say—a million blades of grass. To call attention to this ragged lawn was humiliating. All my friends knew that I had the itch to write—that's what made me good company now and then: *the itch*. Ed Gavarni, for example, who was studying to become a priest: he would have a little gathering at his home expressly for my benefit, so that I could scratch myself in public and thus make the evening somewhat of an event. To prove his interest in the noble art he would drop around to see me at more or less regular intervals, bringing cold sandwiches, apples and beer. Sometimes he would have a pocketful of cigars. I was to fill my belly and spout. If he had had an ounce of talent he would never have dreamed of becoming a priest... There was Zabrowskie, the crack telegraph operator of the Cosmodemonic Telegraph Company of North America: he always examined my shoes, my hat, my overcoat, to see if they were in good condition. He had no time for reading, nor did he care what I wrote, nor did he believe I would ever get anywhere, but he liked to hear about it. He was interested in horses, mud-larks particularly. Listening to me was a harmless diversion and worth the price of a good lunch or a new hat, if needs be. It excited me to tell him stories because it was like talking to the man in the moon. He could interrupt the most subtle divagations by asking whether I preferred strawberry pie or cold pot cheese for dessert... There was Costigan, the knuckle-duster from Yorkville—another good stand-by and sensitive as an old sow. He once knew a writer for the Police Gazette; that made him eligible to seek the company of the elect. He had stories to tell me, stories that would sell, if I would come down off my perch and lend an ear. Costigan appealed to me in a strange way. He looked positively inert, a pimple-faced old sow with wiry bristles all over; he was so gentle, so tender, that if he had disguised himself as a woman you would never know that he was capable of shoving a guy against a wall and pummeling his brains out. He was the sort of tough egg who can sing falsetto and get up a fat collection to buy a funeral wreath. In the telegraph business he was considered to be a quiet, dependable clerk who had the company's interest at heart. In his off hours he was a holy terror, the scourge of the neighborhood. He had a wife whose maiden name was Tillie Jupiter; she was built like a cactus plant and gave plenty of rich milk. An evening with the two of them would set my mind to work like a poisoned arrow.

Of friends and supporters I must have had around fifty. Of the lot there were three of four who had some slight understanding of what I was trying to do. One of them, a composer named Larry Hunt, lived in a little town in Minnesota. We had once rented him a room and he had proceeded to fall in love with my wife—because I treated her so shamefully. But he liked me even better than my wife, and so, upon his return to the sticks, there began a correspondence which soon became voluminous. He was hinting now of coming back to New York for a little visit. I was hoping that he would come on and take the wife off my hands. Years ago, when we had just begun our unhappy affair, I had tried to palm her off on her old sweetheart, an up-State boy called Ronald. Ronald had come to New York to ask her hand in marriage. I use that high-flown phrase because he was the sort of fellow who could say a thing like that without looking foolish. Well, the three of us met and we had dinner together in a French restaurant. I saw from the way he looked at Maude that he cared more for her, and had more in common with her, than I would ever have. I liked him immensely; he was clean-cut, honest to the bone, kind, considerate, the type who would make what is called a good husband. Besides, he had waited for her a long time, something which she had forgotten, or she would never have taken up with a worthless son-of-a-bitch like myself who could do her no good... A strange thing happened that evening, something she would never forgive me for were she ever to learn of it. Instead of taking her home I went back to the hotel with her old sweetheart. I sat up all night with him trying to persuade him that he was the better man, telling him all sorts of rotten things about myself, things I had done to her and to others, pleading with him, begging him to claim her. I even went so far as to say that I knew she loved him, that she had admitted it to me. «She only took me because I happened to be around», I said. «She's really waiting for you to do something. Give yourself a break». But no, he wouldn't hear of it. It was like Gaston and Alphonse of the comic strip. Ridiculous, pathetic, altogether unreal. It was the sort of thing they still do in the movies and people pay to see it... Anyway, thinking of Larry Hunt's coming visit I knew I wouldn't repeat that line. My one fear was that he might have found another woman in the meantime. It would be hard to forgive him that.

There was one place (the *only* place in New York) that I enjoyed going to, particularly if I were in an exalted mood, and that was my friend Ulric's studio uptown. Ulric was a lecherous bird; his profession brought him in contact with stripteasers, cock-teasers, and all sorts of sexually bedeviled females. More than any of the glamorous lanky swans who walked into his place to undress I liked the colored maids whom he seemed to change frequently. To get them to pose for us was not an easy job. It was even more difficult, once we had persuaded them to try it, to get them to drape a leg over an arm-chair and expose a little salmon-colored meat. Ulric was full of lecherous designs, always thinking up ways to get his end in, as he put it. It was a way of emptying his mind of the slops he was commissioned to paint. (He was paid handsomely to make beautiful cans of soup, or corn on the cob, for the back covers of the magazines.) What he really wanted to do was to make cunts, rich, juicy cunts that you could plaster over the bath-room wall and so bring about a pleasant, agreeable bowel movement. He would have made them for nothing if some one had kept him in food and pin money. As I was saying a moment ago, he had an extraordinary flair for dark meat. When he had arranged the model in some out-landish position—bending over to pick up a hair-pin, or climbing a ladder to wash a spot off the wall —I would be given a pad and pencil and told off to some advantageous spot where, pretending to draw a human figure (something beyond my powers), I would feast my eyes on the choice anatomical portions offered me whilst covering the paper with bird-cages, checker-boards, pineapples and chicken tracks. After a brief rest we would elaborately aid the model to regain her original position. This necessitated some delicate manœuvering, such as lowering or raising the buttocks, lifting one foot a little higher, spreading the legs a little more, and so on. «I think that's about got it, Lucy», I can hear him say, as he deftly manipulated her into an obscene position. «Can you hold that now, Lucy?» And Lucy would let out a niggerish whine signifying that she was all set. «We won't keep you long, Lucy», he would say, giving me a sly wink. «Observe the longitudinal vagination», he would say to me, employing a high-falutin' jargon which Lucy found impossible to follow with her rabbit ears. Words like vagination had a pleasing, magical tintinnabulation for Lucy's ears. Meeting him in the street I heard her say to him one day—«Any vagination exercises to-day, Mister Ulric?»

I had more in common with Ulric than with any of my other friends. For me he represented Europe, its softening, civilizing influence. We would talk by the hour of this other world where art had some relation to life, where you could sit quietly in public watching the passing show and think your own thoughts. Would I ever get there? Would it be too late? How would I live? What language would I speak? When I thought about it realistically it seemed hopeless. Only hardy, adventurous spirits could realize such dreams. Ulric had done it—for a year— by dint of hard sacrifice. For ten years he had done the things he hated to do, in order to make his dream come true. Now the dreams was over and he was back where he had started. Farther back than ever, really, because he would never again be able to adapt himself to the treadmill. For Ulric it had been a Sabbatical leave: a dream which turns to gall and wormwood as the years roll by. I could never do as Ulric had done. I could never make a sacrifice of that sort, nor could I be content with a mere vacation however long or short it might be. My policy has always been to burn my bridges behind me. My face is always set toward the future. If I make a mistake it is fatal. When I am flung back I fall all the way back—to the very bottom.

My one safeguard is my resiliency. So far I have always bounced back. Sometimes the rebound has resembled a slow motion performance, but in the eyes of God speed has no particular significance.

It was in Ulric's studio not so many months ago that I had finished my first book—the book about the twelve messengers. I used to work in his brother's room where some short time previously a magazine editor, after reading a few pages of an unfinished story, informed me cold-bloodedly that I hadn't an ounce of talent, that I didn't know the first thing about writing—in short that I was a complete flop and the best thing to do, my lad, is to forget it, try to make an honest living. Another nincompoop who had written a highly successful book about Jesus-the-carpenter had told me the same thing. And if rejection slips mean anything there was simple corroboration to support the criticism of these discerning minds. «Who *are* these shits?» I used to say to Ulric. «Where do they get off to tell me these things? What have they done, except to prove that they know how to make money?»

Well, I was talking about Joey and Tony, my little friends. I was lying in the dark, a little twig floating in the Japanese current. I was getting back to simple abracadabra, the straw that makes bricks, the crude sketch, the temple which must take on flesh and blood and make itself manifest to all the world. I got up and put on a soft light. I felt calm and lucid, like a lotus opening up. No violent pacing back and forth, no tearing the hair out by the roots. I sank slowly into a chair by the table and with a pencil I began to write. I described in simple words how it felt to take my mother's hand and walk across the sun-lit fields, how it felt to see Joey and Tony rushing towards me with arms open, their faces beaming with joy. I put one brick upon another

like an honest brick-layer. Something of a vertical
nature was happening—not blades of grass shooting
up but something structural, something planned. I
didn't strain myself to finish it; I stopped when
I had said all I could. I read it over quietly, what
I had written. I was so moved that the tears came
to my eyes. It wasn't something to show an editor:
it was something to put away in a drawer, to keep
as a reminder of natural processes, as a promise of
fulfillment.

Every day we slaughter our finest impulses. That
is why we get a heart-ache when we read those lines
written by the hand of a master and recognize them
as our own, as the tender shoots which we stifled
because we lacked the faith to believe in our own
powers, our own criterion of truth and beauty.
Every man, when he gets quiet, when he becomes
desperately honest with himself, is capable of utter-
ing profound truths. We all derive from the same
source. There is no mystery about the origin of
things. We are all part of creation, all kings, all
poets, all musicians; we have only to open up, only
to discover what is already there.

What happened to me in writing about Joey and
Tony was tantamount to revelation. It was revealed
to me that I could say what I wanted to say—if I
thought of nothing else, if I concentrated upon that
exclusively—*and* if I were willing to bear the consequences which a pure act always involves.

2

Two or three days later I met Mara for the first
time in broad daylight. I was waiting for her in
the Long Island depot over in Brooklyn. It was

about six in the afternoon, daylight saving time,
which is a strange sun-lit rush hour that enlivens
even such a gloomy crypt as the waiting room of
the Long Island Railroad. I was standing near the
door when I spotted her crossing the car tracks
under the elevated line; the sunlight filtered through
the hideous structure, in shafts of powdered gold.
She had on a dotted Swiss dress which made her
full figure seem even more opulent; the breeze blew
lightly through her glossy black hair, teasing the
heavy chalk-white face like spray dashing against a
cliff. In that quick lithe stride, so sure, so alert, I
sensed the animal breaking through the flesh with
flowery grace and fragile beauty. This was her day-
time self, a fresh, healthy creature who dressed with
utter simplicity, and talked almost like a child.

We had decided to spend the evening at the beach.
I was afraid it would be too cool for her in that
light dress but she said she never felt the cold. We
were so frightfully happy that the words just babbled
out of our mouths. We had crowded together in the
motorman's compartment, our faces almost touching
and glowing with the fiery rays of the setting sun.
How different this ride over the roof-tops from the
lonely anxious one that Sunday morning when I set
out for her home! Was it possible that in such a
short span of time the world could take on such a
different hue?

That fiery sun going down in the West—what a
symbol of joy and warmth! It fired our hearts,
illumined our thoughts, magnetized our souls. Its
warmth would last far into the night, would flow
back from below the curved horizon in defiance of
the night. In this fiery blaze I handed her the
manuscript to read. I couldn't have chosen a more
favorable moment or a more favorable critic. It had
been conceived in darkness and it was being baptized

in light. As I watched her expression I had such
a strong feeling of exaltation that I felt as if I had
handed her a message from the Creator himself. I
didn't need to know her opinion, I could read it on
her face. For years I cherished this souvenir,
reviving it in those dark moments when I had
broken with every one, walking back and forth in a
lonely attic in a foreign city, reading the freshly
written pages and struggling to visualize on the faces
of all my coming readers this expression of unreserved
love and admiration. When people ask me if I have
a definite audience in mind when I sit down to write
I tell them no, I have no one in mind but, the truth
is that I have before me the image of a great crowd,
an anonymous crowd, in which perhaps I recognize
here and there a friendly face: in that crowd I see
accumulating the slow, burning warmth which was
once a single image: I see it spread, take fire, rise into
a great conflagration. (The only time a writer
receives his due reward is when some one comes to
him burning with this flame which he fanned in a
moment of solitude. Honest criticism means nothing:
what one wants is unrestrained passion, fire for fire.)
When one is trying to do something beyond his
known powers it is useless to seek the approval of
friends. Friends are at their best in moments of
defeat—at least that is my experience. Then they
either fail you utterly or they surpass themselves.
Sorrow is the great link—sorrow and misfortune.
But when you are testing your powers, when you are
trying to do something new, the best friend is apt to
prove a traitor. The very way he wishes you luck,
when you broach your chimerical ideas, is enough to
dishearten you. He believes in you only in so far
as he knows you; the possibility that you are greater
than you seem is disturbing, for friendship is founded
on mutuality. It is almost a law that when a man

embarks on a great adventure he must cut all ties.
He must take himself off to the wilderness, and when
he has wrestled it out with himself, he must return
and choose a disciple. It doesn't matter how poor in
quality the disciple may be: it matters only that he
believe implicitly. For a germ to sprout, some other
person, some one individual out of the crowd, has to
show faith. Artists, like great religious leaders, show
amazing perspicacity in this respect. They never
pick the likely one for their purpose, but always some
obscure, frequently ridiculous person.

What aborted me in my beginnings, what almost
proved to be a tragedy, was that I could find no one
who believed in me implicitly, either as a person or
as a writer. There was Mara, it is true, but Mara
was not a friend, hardly even another person, so
closely did we unite. I needed some one outside the
vicious circle of false admirers and envious denigra-
tors. I needed a man from the blue.

Ulric did his best to understand what had come
over me, but he hadn't it in him then to perceive
what I was destined to become. How can I forget
the way he received the news about Mara? It was
the day after we had gone to the beach. I had gone
to the office as usual in the morning, but by noon I
was so feverishly inspired that I took a trolley and
rode out into the country. Ideas were pouring into
my head. As fast as I jotted them down others came
crowding in. At last I reached that point where you
abandon all hope of remembering your brilliant
ideas and you simply surrender to the luxury of writing a book in your head. You know that you'll never
be able to recapture these ideas, not a single line of
all the tumultuous and marvellously dove-tailed
sentences which sift through your mind like sawdust
spilling through a hole. On such days you have for
company the best companion you will ever have—the

modest, defeated, plodding workaday self which has
a name and which can be identified in public registers
in case of accident or death. But the real self, the
one who has taken over the reins, is almost a stranger.
He is the one who is filled with ideas; he is the one
who is writing in the air; he is the one who, if you
become too fascinated with his exploits, will finally
expropriate the old, worn-out self, taking over your
name, your address, your wife, your past, your future.
Naturally, when you walk in on an old friend in this
euphoric state he doesn't wish to concede immediately
that you have another life, a life apart in which he
has no share. He says quite naively—«Feeling
rather high to-day, eh?» And you nod your head
almost shamefacedly.

«Look, Ulric,» I said, bursting in on him in the
midst of a Campbell's Soup design, «I've got to tell
you something, I'm bursting with it.»

«Sure, fire away,» he said, dipping his water color
brush in the big pot on the stool beside him. «You
don't mind if I go on with this bloody thing, do you?
I've got to finish it by tonight.»

I pretended I didn't mind but I was disconcerted.
I pitched my voice lower in order not to disturb him
too much. «You remember the girl I was telling you
about—the girl I met at the dance hall? Well I met
her again. We went to the beach together last
night...»

«How was it... *good going?*»

I could see from the way he slid his tongue over
his lips that he was priming himself for a juicy yarn.

«Listen, Ulric, do you know what it is to be in
love?»

He didn't even deign to look up in answer to this.
As he deftly mixed his colors in the tin tray he
mumbled something about being possessed with
normal instincts.

I went on unabashed. «Do you think you might meet a woman some day who would change your whole life?»

«I've met one or two who've tried—not with entire success, as you can see,» he responded.

«Shit! Drop that stuff a moment, will you? I want to tell you something... I want to tell you that I'm in love, madly in love. I know it sounds silly, but this is different—I've never been like this before. You wonder if she's a good piece of tail. Yes, magnificent. But I don't give a shit about that...»

«Oh, you don't? Well, that's something new.»

«Do you know what I did to-day?»

«You went to the Houston Street Burlesk maybe.»

«I went to the country. I was walking around like a madman....»

«What do you mean—has she given you the gate already?»

«No. She told me she loved me... I know, it sounds childish, doesn't it?»

«I wouldn't say that exactly. You might be temporarily deranged, that's all. Everybody acts a bit queer when he falls in love. In your case it's apt to last longer. I wish I didn't have this damned job on my hands—I might listen more feelingly. You couldn't come back a little later, could you? Perhaps we could eat together, yes?»

«All right, I'll come back in an hour or so. Don't run out on me, you bastard, because I haven't a cent on me.»

I blew down the stairs and headed for the park. I was riled. It was silly to get all steamed up before Ulric. Always cool as a cucumber, that guy. How can you make another person understand what is really happening inside you? If I were to break a leg he would drop everything. But if your heart is breaking with joy—well, it's a bit boring, don't you know. Tears are easier to put up with than joy. Joy is destructive: it makes others uncomfortable. «Weep and you weep alone»—what a lie that is! Weep and you will find a million crocodiles to weep with you. The world is forever weeping. The world is drenched in tears. Laughter, that's another thing. Laughter is momentary—it passes. But joy, joy is a kind of ecstatic bleeding, a disgraceful sort of super-contentment which overflows from every pore of your being. You can't make people joyous just by being joyous yourself. Joy has to be generated by oneself: it is or it isn't. Joy is founded on something too profound to be understood and communicated. To be joyous is to be a madman in a world of sad ghosts.

I couldn't remember ever seeing Ulric positively joyous. He could laugh readily enough, a good healthy laugh, too, but when he subsided he was always a bit below par. As for Stanley, the nearest semblance to mirth he could produce was a carbolic acid grin. There wasn't a soul I knew who was really gay inside, or even resilient. My friend Kronski, who was now an interne, would act as though he were alarmed if he found me in an effervescent mood. He spoke of joy and sadness as if they were pathological conditions—opposite poles in the manic-depressive cycle.

When I got back to the studio I found it crowded with friends of his who had arrived unexpectedly. They were what Ulric called fine young blades from the South. They had come up from Virginia and North Carolina in their trim racing cars and they had brought with them a few jugs of peach brandy. I didn't know any of them and I felt a bit uncomfortable at first, but after a drink or two I limbered up and began talking freely. To my amazement they seemed not to understand what I was talking about.

They excused their ignorance in a sly and embarrassing way by saying that they were just common
country folk who knew more about horses than
books. I wasn't aware of having mentioned any
books, but that was their way, as I soon discovered,
of telling me off. I was definitely an intellectual, say
what I would. And they were very definitely country
gentlemen, with boots and spurs. The situation was
getting rather tense, despite my efforts to talk their
language. And then of a sudden it became ridiculous,
owing to a stupid remark about Walt Whitman which
one of them had chosen to address to me. I had been
exalted for the better part of the day; the enforced
promenade had sobered me up somewhat, but with
the peach brandy flowing and the conversation all at
loose ends I had gradually become exhilarated again.
I was in a mood to combat these fine young blades
from the South, more particularly because what I had
on my chest to get off was being squelched by the
senseless hilarity. So when the cultured young gent
from Durham tried to cross swords with me about
my favorite American writer I was at him hammer
and tongs. As usual in such circumtances I overshot
the mark.

The place was in an uproar. Apparently they had
never seen any one so earnest about an unimportant
matter. Their laughter made me furious. I accused
them of being a bunch of drunken sots, of being idle
sons of bitches, ignorant, prejudiced, the product of
good for nothing whore-mongers, et cetera, et cetera.
A tall, lanky chap, who later became a famous movie
star, rose to his feet and threatened to crack me down.
Ulric came to the rescue in his suave, silky way, the
cups were filled to the brim and a truce declared.
At that moment the bell rang and a good-looking
young woman made her way in. She was presented
to me as the wife of somebody or other whom the

others all seemed to know and to be very solicitous about. I got Ulric to one side to find out what it was all about. «She's got a paralytic husband,» he confided. «Nurses him night and day. Drops in now and then to have a little drink—it's getting too much for her, I guess.»

I stood apart and sized her up. She looked like one of those over-sexed females who, while playing the role of the martyr, manage somehow to get their needs satisfied. She had hardly gotten seated when two other females buzzed in, one of them quite decidedly a trollop, the other just somebody's wife, and rather rusty and shopworn at that. I was hungry as a bear and getting fantastically tight. With the arrival of the women I completely lost my combativeness. I thought of only two things—food and sex. I went to the can and absent-mindedly left the door unlocked. I had backed up a bit because of a slow poisonous hard'on which the brandy had induced and, as I stood thus, pecker in hand and aiming at the bowl in a high curve, the door suddenly opened. It was Irene, the paralytic's wife. She made a smothered exclamation and started to close the door, but for some reason, perhaps because I seemed utterly calm and nonchalant, she stood at the door-sill and while I finished my piss, she talked to me as though nothing unusual were happening. «Quite a performance,» she said, as I shook the last few drops out. «Do you always back up that way?» I caught her by the hand and pulled her in, locking the door with the other hand. «No, please don't do that,» she begged, looking thoroughly frightened. «Just one moment,» I whispered, my cock brushing against her dress. I fastened my lips to her red mouth. «Please, please,» she begged, trying to squirm out of my embrace. «You'll disgrace me.» I knew I had to let her go. I worked fast and furiously. «I'll let you go,» I said, «just one more kiss.» With that I backed her against the door and, without even bothering to lift her dress, I stabbed her again and again, shooting a heavy load all over her black silk front.

My absence wasn't even noticed. The Southern boys were clustered around the other two females, doing their best to get them cock-eyed in short order. Ulric asked me slyly if I had seen anything of Irene.

«I think she's gone to the bathroom,» I said.

«*How was it?*» he said. «Are you still in love?»

I gave him a wry smile.

«Why don't you bring your friend around some night,» he went on. «I can always find a pretext to get Irene over. We can take turns at giving her consolation, *what?*»

«Listen,» I said, «lend me a dollar, will you? I've got to eat, I'm famished.»

Ulric always had a way of looking bewildered, nonplussed, when you asked him for money. I had to take him short like that or he'd edge out of it in that smooth, irresistible way he had of refusing. «Come on,» I said, taking him by the arm, «this is no time to fumble and stammer.» We went to the hall where he furtively slipped me a bill. Just as we were approaching the door Irene came out of the bathroom. «What, you're not going, are you?» she asked, coming up to me and slipping her arms in ours. «Yes, he's got to hurry off now,» said Ulric, «but he's promised to come back later.» And with this we put our arms around her and smothered her with kisses.

«When am I going to see you again?» said Irene. «I may not be here when you return. I'd like to have a talk with you.»

«Just a talk?» said Ulric.

«Well, you know....» she said, finishing it off with a lascivious laugh.

The laugh got me in the scrotum. I got hold of

her again and pushing her into a corner I put my
hand on her cunt, which was blazing, and slid my
tongue down her throat.

«Why do you run away now?» she murmured.
«Why don't you stay?»

Ulric stepped in to get his share. «Don't worry
about *him*,» he said, fastening on her like a leech.
«That bird doesn't need any consolation. He's got
more than he can handle.»

As I slipped out I caught a last imploring signal
from Irene, her back bent almost in half, her dress up
above her knees, Ulric's hand creeping up her leg and
fastening on her warm cunt. «Whew! what a bitch!»
I mumbled, as I slid down the stairs. I was faint
with hunger. I wanted a steak smothered in onions
and a schooner of beer.

I ate in the back of a saloon on Sixth Avenue, not
far from Ulric's place. I had what I wanted and was
still ten cents to the good. I felt genial and expansive,
in a mood to accept anything. My mood must have
been written on my face because, as I stood a moment
at the doorway to take in the scene, a man airing a
dog saluted me in friendly fashion. I thought he had
mistaken me for some one else, something which
frequently happens to me, but no, he was just
friendlily inclined, perhaps in the same glowing mood
as myself. We exchanged a few words and presently
I was walking along with him and the dog. He said
he lived nearby and that if I cared to join him in a
friendly drink I might accompany him to his
apartment. The few words we had exchanged
convinced me that he was sensitive, cultured gentleman
of the old school. As a matter of fact he intimated,
almost in the next breath, that he had just returned
from Europe where he had been living for a number
of years. As we reached his apartment he was relating
a story about an affair he had had with a countess

in Florence. He seemed to take it for granted that I knew Europe. He treated me as if I were an artist.

The apartment was rather sumptuous. He immediately brought out a beautiful box of excellent Havana cigars and asked me what I prefered to drink. I took a whisky and settled down in a luxurious armchair. I had the feeling that this man would be putting money in my hand before long. He listened to me as though he believed every word I uttered. Suddenly he ventured to ask if I were not a writer? *Why?* Well, from the way I looked around, the way I stood, the expression about the mouth—little things, undefinable, a general impression of sensitivity and curiosity.

«*And you?*» I asked, «what do *you* do?»

He made a deprecatory gesture, as though to say. I'm nothing any more. «I *was* a painter once, a poor one, too. I don't do anything now. I try to enjoy myself.»

That set me off. The words just fell out of me, like hot shot. I told him where I stood, how messy things were, how things were happening nevertheless, what grand hopes I had, what a life lay before me if I could only take hold of it, squeeze it, marshall it, conquer it. I lied a bit. It was impossible to admit to him, this stranger who had come to my rescue out of a clear sky, that I was a total failure.

What had I written thus far?

Why, several books, some poems, a batch of short stories. I rattled on at top speed so as not to be caught in trivial questions of fact. About the new book I had begun—that was to be something magnificent. There were over forty characters in it. I had made a great chart on my wall, a sort of map of the book—he must see it some time. Did he remember Kirillov, that character in one of Dostoievski's works, who had shot or hanged himself because

he was too happy? That was me all over. I was
going to shoot everybody off—out of sheer happiness...
To-day for example, if he could only have seen me a
few hours ago. Completely mad. Rolling in the grass
by the side of a brook; chewing mouthsful of grass;
scratching myself like a dog; yelling at the top of my
lungs; doing handsprings; even got down on my knees
and prayed, not to ask for something, but to give
thanks, thanks for being alive, for being able to
breathe the air.... *Wasn't it wonderful just to
breathe?*

I went on to relate little episodes out of my
telegraphic life: the crooks I had to deal with, the
pathological liars, the perverts, the shell-shocked
bums sitting in the lodging houses, the slimy,
hypocritical charity workers, the diseases of the poor,
the runaway boys who disappear from the face of the
earth, the whores who try to muscle in and work the
office buildings, the cracked pots, the epileptics, the
orphans, the reformatory lads, the ex-convicts, the
nymphomaniacs.

His mouth hung open like a hinge, his eyes were
popping out of his head; he looked for all the world
like a good-natured toad that had been hit with a
rock. *Have another drink?*

Sure! What was I saying? Oh yes... in the middle
of the book I would explode. Why not? There
were plenty of writers who could drag a thing out to
the end without letting go of the reins; what we
needed was a man, like myself for instance, who
didn't give a fuck what happened. Dostoievski
hadn't gone quite far enough. I was for straight
gibberish. One should go cuckoo! People have had
enough of plot and character. Plot and character
don't make life. Life isn't in the upper storey: life
is here now, any time you say the word, any time you

let rip. Life is four-hundred and forty horsepower
in a two-cylinder engine...

He interrupted me here. «Well, I must say that
you certainly seem to have it... I wish I could read
one of your books».

«You will,» I said, carried away by internal
combustion. «I'll send you one in a day or two.»

There was a knock at the door. As he got up to
open it he explained that he had been expecting some
one. He begged me not to be disturbed, it was merely
a charming friend of his.

A gorgeously beautiful woman stood in the doorway.
I rose to greet her. She looked Italian. Possibly the
countess he had spoken of earlier.

«Sylvia,» he said, «it's too bad you didn't come a
little sooner. I've just been listening to the most
wonderful stories. This young man is a writer. I
want you to know him.»

She came close and put out her two hands for me
to grasp. «I am sure you must be a very good
writer,» she said. «You have suffered, I can see that.»

«He's had the most extraordinary life, Sylvia. I
feel as though I haven't even begun to live. And
what do you suppose he's doing for a living?»

She turned to me as if to say that she preferred to
hear it from my own lips. I was confused. I had not
been prepared to meet such a stunning creature, so
full of assurance, so poised, and so thoroughly natural.
I wanted to get up and place my hands on her hips,
hold her thus and say something very simple, very
honest, as one human being to another. Her eyes
were velvety and moist; dark, round eyes that
glistened with sympathy and warmth. Could she be
in love with this man who was so much older? From
what city did she come and out of what world? To
say even two words to her I felt that I had to have
some clue. A mistake would be fatal.

She semed to divine my dilemma. «Won't some one offer me a drink?» she asked, looking first at him and then at me. «Port, I think», she added, addressing herself to me.

«But you never take anything!» said my host. And he rose to help me. The three of us were standing close together, Sylvia with empty glass upraised. «I am very glad things have turned out this way,» he said. «I couldn't have brought together two people more opposite in every way than you two. I am sure you will understand one another.»

My head was spinning as she raised the glass to her lips. I knew that this was the preliminary to some strange adventure. I had a strong intuition that he would presently find some excuse to leave us alone for a while and that without a word being said, she would pass into my arms. I felt too that I would never see either of them again.

In fact, it happened precisely as I had imagined. In less than five minutes from the time she arrived my host announced that he had a very important errand to run and begged us to excuse him for a little while. He had hardly closed the door when she came over to me and sat herself in my lap, saying as she did so—«He will not be back to-night. Now we may talk.» I was more frightened than startled by these words. All sorts of ideas flashed through my mind. I was even more taken aback when she added after a pause—«And what about me, am I just a pretty woman, perhaps his mistress? What do you think my life is like?»

«I think you're a very dangerous person,» I answered spontaneously and with truthfulness. «I wouldn't be surprised if you were a famous spy.»

«You have strong intuitions,» she said. «No, I am not a spy, but....»

«Well, if you were you wouldn't tell me, I know

that. I really don't want to know about your life. Do you know what I'm wondering? I'm wondering what you want of me. I feel as if I were in a trap.»

«That's unkind of you. Now you're imagining things. If we did want something of you we would have to know you better, wouldn't we?» A moment's silence, then suddenly: «Are you sure you want to be nothing more than a writer?»

«What do you mean?» I retorted quickly.

«Just that. I know you *are* a writer... but you could also be other things. You're the sort of person who could do anything he chose to do, isn't that so?»

I'm afraid it's just the contrary,» I replied. «So far everything I've tackled has ended disastrously. I'm not even sure that I'm a writer, at this moment.»

She rose from my lap and lit herself a cigarette. «You couldn't possibly be a failure,» she said, after a moment's hesitation in which she seemed to be collecting herself to make some important revelation. «The trouble with you,» she said slowly and deliberately, «is that you've never set yourself a task worthy of your powers. You need bigger problems, bigger difficulties. You don't function properly until you're hard pressed. I don't know what you're doing but I'm certain that your present life is not suited to you. You were meant to lead a dangerous life; you can take greater risks than others because.... well, you probably know it yourself.... because you are protected.»

«*Protected?* I don't understand,» I blurted out.

«Oh yes you do,» she answered quietly. «All your life you've been protected. Just think a moment.... Haven't you been near death several times.... haven't you always found some one to help you, some stranger usually, just when you thought all was lost? Haven't you committed several crimes already, crimes which nobody would suspect you of? Aren't you right now in the midst of a very dangerous passion, an affair which, if you weren't born under a lucky star, might lead you to ruin? I know that you're in love. I know that you're ready to do anything in order to satisfy this passion.... You look at me strangely... you wonder how I know. I have no special gifts— except the ability to read human beings at a glance. Look, a few moments ago you were waiting eagerly for me to come to you. You knew that I would throw myself in your arms as soon as he left. I did. But you were paralyzed—a little frightened of me, shall I say? *Why?* What could I do to you? You have no money, no power, no influence. What could you expect me to ask of you?» She paused, then added: «Shall I tell you the truth?»»

I nodded helplessly.

«You were afraid that if I did ask you to do something for me you would not be able to refuse. You were perplexed because, being in love with one woman, you already felt yourself the potential victim of another. It isn't a woman you need—it is an instrument to liberate yourself. You crave a more adventurous life, you want to break your chains. Whoever the woman is you love I pity her. To you she will appear to be the stronger, but that is only because you doubt yourself. *You* are the stronger. You will always be stronger—because you can think only of yourself, of your destiny. If you were just a little stronger I would fear for you. You might make a dangerous fanatic. But that is not your fate. You're too sane, too healthy. You love life even more than your own self. You are confused, because whomsoever or whatever you give yourself to is never enough for you—isn't that true? Nobody can hold you for long: you are always looking beyond the object of your love, looking for something you will never find. You will have to look inside yourself

if you ever hope to free yourself of torment. You
make friends easily, I'm sure. And yet there is no
one whom you can really call your friend. You are
alone. You will always be alone. You want too
much, more than life can offer...»

«Wait a moment, please,» I interrupted. «Why
have you chosen to tell me all this?»

She paused a moment, as if hesitating to answer
this directly. «I suppose I am merely answering a
question in my own mind,» she said. «To-night I
must make a grave decision; I leave in the morning
on a long journey. When I saw you I said to myself
—this may be the man who can help me. But I was
wrong. I have nothing to ask of you... You may
put your arms around me, if you like... if you are
not afraid of me.»

I walked over to her, clasped her tightly and kissed
her. I drew my lips away and looked into her eyes,
my arms still about her waist.

«What is it you see?» she said, gently disengaging
herself.

I moved away from her and looked at her steadily,
for several moments, before answering. «*What do
I see?* Nothing. Absolutely nothing. To look into
your eyes is like looking into a dark mirror.»

«You're disturbed. What is it?»

«What you said about me—it frightens me... So
I'm no help to you, is that it?»

«You have helped, in a way,» she replied. «You
always help, indirectly. You can't help radiating
energy, and that is something. People lean on you,
but you don't know why. You even hate them for
it, though you act as though you were kind and truly
sympathetic. When I came here to-night I was a bit
shaken inwardly; I had lost that confidence I usually
have. I looked at you and I saw... what do you
think?»

«A man flushed with his own ego, I suppose.»

«I saw an animal! I felt that you would devour me, if I were to let myself go. And for a moment or two I felt that I wanted to let myself go. You wanted to take me, throw me down on the carpet. To have me that way wouldn't have satisfied you, would it? You saw in me something you had never observed in another woman. You saw the mask which is your own.» She paused for just a second. «You don't dare to reveal your real self, nor do I. That much we have in common. I live dangerously, not because I am strong, but because I know how to make use of others' strength. I am afraid not to do the things I do because if I were to stop I would collapse. You read nothing in my eyes because there is nothing to read. I have nothing to give you, as I told you a moment ago. You look only for your prey, your victims on whom you fatten. Yes, to be a writer is probably the best thing for you. If you were to act out your thoughts you would probably become a criminal. You have always the choice of going two ways. It is not the moral sense which deters you from going the wrong way—it is your instinct to do only that which will serve you best in the long run. You don't know why it is you abandon your brilliant projects; you think it is weakness, fear, dubiety, but it isn't. You have the instincts of the animal; you make everything subservient to the desire to live. You would not hesitate to take me against my will, even if you knew you were in a trap. The man trap you are not afraid of, but the other trap, the trap which would set your feet in the wrong direction, that you are wary of. And you are right.» Again she paused. «Yes, you did me a great service. If I had not met you to-night I would have given in to my doubts.»

«Then you *are* about to do something dangerous,»
I said.

She shrugged her shoulders. «Who knows what
is dangerous? To doubt, that is dangerous. You will
have a much more dangerous time of it than I. And
you will cause a lot of harm to others in defending
yourself from your own fears and doubts. You are
not even sure at this moment that you will go back
to the woman you love. I have poisoned your mind.
You would drop her like that if you were sure that
you could do what you wanted without her aid. But
you will need her and you will call it love. You will
always fall back on that excuse when you are sucking the life out of a woman.»

«That is where you are wrong, » I interrupted
with some heat. «It's me who gets sucked dry, not
the woman.»

«That is your way of deceiving yourself. Because
the woman can never give you what you want you
make yourself out to be a martyr. A woman wants
love and you're incapable of giving love. If you
were a lower type of man you would be a monster;
but you will convert your frustration into something
useful. Yes, by all means go on writing. Art can
transform the hideous into the beautiful. Better a
monstrous book than a monstrous life. Art is painful, tedious, softening. If you don't die in the
attempt, your work may transform you into a
sociable, charitable human being. You are big
enough not to be satisfied with mere fame, I can see
that. Probably, when you have lived enough, you
will discover that there is something beyond what
you now call life. You may yet live to live for
others. That depends on what use you make of your
intelligence.» (We looked at one another keenly.)
«For you are not as intelligent as you think you are.
That is your weakness, your overweening intellectual

pride. If you rely exclusively on that you defeat
yourself. You have all the feminine virtues, but you
are ashamed to acknowledge them to yourself. You
think because you are strong sexually that you are
a virile man, but you are more of a woman than a
man. Your sexual virility is only the sign of a greater
power which you haven't begun to use. Don't try
to prove yourself a man by exploiting your powers
of seduction. Women are not fooled by that sort
of strength and charm. Women, even when they
are subjugated mentally, are always master of the
situation. A woman may be enslaved, sexually, and
yet dominate the man. You will have a harder time
than other men because to dominate another doesn't
interest you. You will always be trying to dominate
yourself; the woman you love will only be an instrument for you to practise on... »

Here she broke off. I saw that she expected me
to go.

«Oh, by the way,» she said, as I was making my
adieu, «the gentleman asked me to give you this»—
and she handed me a sealed envelope. «He's probably explained why he couldn't make a better
excuse for leaving so mysteriously.» I took the
envelope and shook hands with her. If she had
suddenly said: «Run! run for your life!» I would
have done so without question. I was completely
mystified, knowing neither why I had come nor why
I was leaving. I had been whisked into it on the
crest of a strange elation the origin of which now
seemed remote and of little concern to me. From
noon to midnight I had gone full circle.

I opened the envelope in the street. It contained
a twenty dollar bill enclosed in a sheet of paper on
which was written «Good Luck to you!» I was not
altogether surprised. I had expected something of
the sort when first I laid eyes on him...

A few days after this episode I wrote a story called
«Free Fantasia» which I brought to Ulric and read
aloud to him. It was written blindly, without
thought of beginning or end. I had just one fixed
image in mind throughout, and that was of swinging
Japanese lanterns. *The pièce de résistance* was a
kick in the slats which I gave the heroine in the
act of submission. This gesture, which was aimed
at Mara, was more of a surprise to me than it could
possibly be to the reader. Ulric thought the writing
quite remarkable but confessed he couldn't make
head nor tail of it. He wanted me to show it to
Irene whom he was expecting later. She had a perverted streak in her, he said. She had returned to
the studio with him late that night, after the others
had gone, and she had almost bled him to death.
Three times ought to be enough to satisfy any woman, he thought, but this one could keep it up all
night. «The bitch can't stop coming,» he said. «No
wonder her husband's a paralytic—she must have
twisted the cock off him.»

I told him what had occurred the other night when
I left the party abruptly. He shook his head from
side to side, saying—«By God, those things never
happen to *me*. If anybody but you were to tell me
a story like that I wouldn't believe it. Your whole
life seems to be made up of just such incidents.
Now why is that, can you tell me? Don't laugh at
me, I know it sounds foolish to ask such a question.
I know too that I'm a rather cagey bird. You seem
to lay yourself wide open—I suppose that's the secret
of it. And you're more curious about people than
I will ever be. I get bored too easily—it's a fault,
I admit. So often you tell me of the wonderful time
you've had—*after* I've left. But I'm sure nothing
like you relate would happen to me even if I were
to sit up all night... Another thing about you that

gets me is that you always find a character interesting whom most of us would ignore. You have a way of opening them up, of making them reveal themselves. I haven't got the patience for it... But tell me honestly now, aren't you just a bit sorry that you didn't get your end in with what's her name?»

«Sylvia, you mean?»

«Yes. You say she was a Loulou. Don't you think you could have stayed another five minutes and had what was coming to you?»

«Yes, I suppose so...»

«You're a funny fellow. I suppose you mean to say that you got something more by not staying, is that it?»

«I don't know. Perhaps I did, perhaps not. To tell you the truth, I forgot all about fucking her by the time I was ready to leave. You can't fuck every woman you run into, can you? If you ask me, I was fucked good and proper. What more could I hope to get out of her if I had gone through with it? Maybe she'd have given me a dose of clap. Maybe I would have disappointed her. Listen, I don't worry too much if I lose a piece of tail now and then. You seem to be keeping some kind of fuck-ledger. That's why you don't loosen up with me, you bugger, you. I have to work on you like a dentist to extract a measly buck from you; I go round the corner and a stranger whom I speak to just a few minutes leaves a twenty dollar bill for me on the mantelpiece. How do you explain *that?*»

«You don't explain it,» said Ulric, making a wry grin. «That's why things never happen to me, I guess... But I do want to say this,»» he continued. getting up from his seat and frowning over his own cussedness, «whenever you find yourself in a real pinch you can always rely on me. You see, I don't worry much about your privations usually because

I know you well enough to realize that you'll always find a way out, even if I happen to let you down.»

«You sure have a lot of confidence in my ability, I must say.»

«I don't mean to be callous when I say a thing like that. You see, if I were in your boots I'd be so depressed that I wouldn't be able to ask a friend for help—I'd be ashamed of myself. But you come running up here with a grin, saying—'I must have this... I must have that.' You don't act as if you needed help desperately.»

«What the hell,» I said, «do you want me to get down on my knees and beg for it?»

«No, not that, of course. I'm talking like a damned fool again. But you make people envious of you, even when you say you're desperate. You make people refuse you sometimes because you take it for granted that they *should* help you, don't you see?»

«No, Ulric, I don't see. But it's all right. To-night I'm taking you to dinner.»

«And to-morrow you'll be asking me for carfare.»

«Well, is there any harm in that?»

«No, it's just cock-eyed,» and he laughed. «Ever since I know you, and I know you a long while, you've been hitting me up—for nickels, dimes, quarters, dollar bills.... why once you tried to bludgeon me for fifty dollars, do you remember? And I always keep saying no to you, isn't that so? But it doesn't make any difference to you apparently. And we're still good friends. But sometimes I wonder what the hell you really think of me. It can't be very flattering.»

«Why, I can answer that right now, Ulric,» I said blithely: «You're....»

«No, don't tell me now. Save it! I don't want to hear the truth just yet.»

We went to dinner down in Chinatown and on

the way home Ulric slipped me a ten dollar bill, just to prove to me that his heart was in the right place. In the park we sat down and had a long talk about the future. Finally he said to me what so many of my friends had already told me—that he had no hopes for himself but that he was confident I would break loose and do something startling. He added very truthfully that he didn't think I had even begun to express myself, as a writer. «You don't write like you talk,» he said. «You seem to be afraid of revealing yourself. If you ever open up and tell the truth it will be like Niagara Falls. Let me tell you honestly—I don't know any writer in America who has greater gifts than you. I've always believed in you—and I will even if you prove to be a failure. You're not a failure in life, that I know, though it's the craziest life I've ever known of. I wouldn't have time to paint a stroke if I did all the things you do in a day.»

I left him, feeling as I often did, that I had probably underestimated his friendship. I don't know what I expected of my friends. The truth is I was so dissatisfied with myself; with my abortive efforts, that nothing or nobody seemed right to me. If I were in a jam I would be sure to pick the most unresponsive individual, just to have the satisfaction of wiping him off my list. I knew full well that in sacrificing one old friend I would have three new ones by the morrow. It was touching, too, to run across one of these discarded friends later on and find that he bore me no hatred, that he was eager and willing to resume the old ties, usually by way of a lavish meal and an offer to lend me a few dollars. In the back of my head there was always the intention of surprising my friends one day by paying off all debts. Nights I would often lull myself to sleep by adding up the score. Even at this date it

was already a huge sum, one that could only be
settled by the advent of some unexpected stroke of
fortune. Perhaps one day some unheard-of relative
would die and leave me a legacy, five or ten thousand
dollars, whereupon I would immediately go to the
nearest telegraph office and dispatch a string of
money orders to all and sundry. It would have to
be done by telegraph because if I were to keep the
money in my pocket more than a few hours it would
vanish in some foolish, unexpected way.

I went to bed that night dreaming of a legacy.
In the morning the first thing I heard was that the
bonus had been declared—we might have the dough
before the day was over. Everybody was in a state
of agitation. The burning question was—*how much?*
Towards four in the afternoon it arrived. I was
handed something like 350 dollars. The first man
I took care of was McGovern, the old flunkey who
guarded the door. (Fifty dollars on account.) I
looked over the list. There were eight or ten I could
take care of immediately—brothers of the cosmo
coccic world who had been kind to me. The rest
would have to wait until another day—including the
wife whom I had decided to lie to about the bonus.

Ten minutes after I had received the money I was
arranging to throw a little spread at the Crow's Nest
where I had decided to make the pay-off. I checked
up the list again to make sure I had not overlooked
any of the essential ones. They were a curious lot,
my benefactors. There was Zabrowskie, the crack
telegrapher, Costigan, the knuckle-duster, Hymie
Laubscher, the switch-board operator, O'Mara, my
old crony whom I had made my assistant, Steve Romero from the main office, little Curley, my stooge,
Maxie Schnadig, an old stand-by, Kronski, the interne,
and Ulric of course... oh yes, and MacGregor, whom
I was paying back merely as a good investment.

All told I would have to shell out about three hundred dollars—250 dollars in debts and a possible fifty for the banquet. That would leave me flat broke, which was normal. If there were a five spot left over I'd probably go to the dance hall and see Mara.

As I say, it was an incongruous group I had gathered together, and the only way to unite them in fellowship was to make merry. First of course I paid them off. That was better than the best hors d'œuvre. Cocktails followed promptly and then we fell to. It was a staggering meal I had ordered and there was plenty to wash it down with. Kronski, who was not used to liquor, got tipsy almost immediately. Had to go out and stick a finger down his throat long before we came to the roast duckling. When he rejoined us he was pale as a ghost: his face had the hue of a frog's belly, a dead frog floating on the scum of a stinking swamp. Ulric thought he was a rum bird—had never met a type like that before. Kronski, on the other hand, took a violent dislike to Ulric, asking me on the side why I had invited a polite fart like that. MacGregor positively detested little Curley—couldn't understand how I could be friendly with such a venomous little crook. O'Mara and Costigan seemed to be getting along best of all; they fell into a lengthy discussion about the relative merits of Joe Gans and Jack Johnson. Hymie Laubscher was trying to get a hot tip from Zabrowskie who made it a point never to give tips because of his position.

In the midst of it a Swedish friend of mine named Lundberg happened to walk in. He was another one I owed money to but he never pressed me to pay up. I invited him to join us and, taking Zabrowskie aside, I borrowed back a ten spot in order to settle accounts with the new arrival. From him I learned

that my old friend Larry Hunt was in town and eager
to see me. «Get him here,» I urged Lundberg.
«The more the merrier.»

While the festivities were in full swing, after we
had sung «Meet Me To-Night in Dreamland» and
«Some of These Days,» I noticed two Italian boys at
a nearby table who seemed eager to be in the fun.
I went over to them and asked them if they would
like to join us. One of them was a musician and the
other was a prize-fighter, it appeared. I introduced
them and then made a place for them between
Costigan and O'Mara. Lundberg had gone out to telephone Larry Hunt.

How he had gotten on to such a subject on such
an occasion I don't know, but for some reason or
other Ulric had gotten it into his head to make me
an elaborate speech about Uccello. The Italian boy,
the musician, pricked up his ears. MacGregor turned
away disgustedly to talk to Kronski about impotency,
a subject which the latter delighted to explore if he
thought he could make his listener uncomfortable
thereby. I noticed that the Italian was impressed by
Ulric's glib flow. He would have given his right
arm to be able to speak English like that. He was
also flattered to think that we were talking so enthu-
siastically about one of his own race. I drew him
out a bit and, realizing that he was getting drunk on
language, I got exalted and went off into a mad flight
about the wonders of the English tongue. Curley and
O'Mara turned to listen and then Zabrowskie came
round to our end of the table and drew up a chair,
followed by Lundberg who informed me quickly that
he hadn't been able to get hold of Hunt. The Italian
was in such a state of excitement that he ordered
cognac for everybody. We stood up and clinked
glasses. Arturo, that was his name, insisted on giving
a toast—in Italian. He sat down and said with great

fervor that he had lived in America ten years and
had never heard the English language spoken like
this. He said he would never be able to master it
now. He wanted to know if we talked this way ordinarily. He went on like this, piling one compliment
upon another, until we were all so infected with a
love of the English language that we all wanted to
make speeches. Finally I got so drunk on it that I
stood up and, downing a stiff drink at one gulp, I
launched into a frenzied speech which lasted for
fifteen minutes or more. The Italian kept wagging
his head from side to side, as if to signify that he
couldn't stand another word, that he would burst.
I fastened my eye on him and drowned him with
words. It must have been a mad and glorious speech
because every now and then there was a salvo of
applause from the surrounding tables. I heard
Kronski murmuring to some one that I was in a fine
state of euphoria, a word which touched me off anew.
Euphoria! I paused the fraction of a second while
some one filled my glass and then I was off, down
the stretch, a gay mud-lark flinging words in every
direction. I had never in my life attempted to make
a speech. If some one had interrupted me and told
me I was making a wonderful speech I would have
been dumbfounded. I was out on my feet, in the
language of the ring. The only thing I had in mind
was the Italian's hunger for that marvelous English
which he would never be able to master. I hadn't
the slightest idea what I was talking about. I didn't
have to use my brain—I simply stuck a long, snake-
like tongue into a cornucopia and with a felicitous
flip I spooled it off.

The speech ended in an ovation. Some of the
guests at the other tables came over and felicitated
me. The Italian, Arturo, was in tears. I felt as if I
had unwittingly let off a bomb. I was embarrassed

and not a little frightened by this unexpected display of oratory. I wanted to get out of the place, get off by myself and feel what had happened. Presently I made an excuse and, taking the manager aside, I told him I had to leave. After footing the bill I found I had about three dollars left over. I decided to beat it without saying a word to anybody. They could sit there till Kingdom Come—I had had enough of it.

I started walking uptown. Soon I was on Broadway. At Thirty-Fourth Street I quickened my pace. It was decided—I would go to the dance hall. At Forty-Second Street I had to elbow my way through the pack. The crowd excited me: there was always the danger of running into some one and getting diverted from one's goal. Soon I was standing in front of the joint, a little out of breath and wondering if it were the right thing to do. At the Palace opposite, Thomas Burke of the Covent Garden Opera was being featured as the headliner. The name «Covent Garden» stuck in my crop as I turned to ascend the stairs. *London*—it would be swell to take her to London. I must ask her if she would like to hear Thomas Burke...

She was dancing with a young-looking old man as I entered. I watched her a few minutes before she espied me. Dragging her partner by the hand she came over to me with a radiant flush. «I want you to meet an old friend of mine,» she said, presenting me to the white-haired Mr. Carruthers. We greeted one another cordially and stood chatting for several minutes. Then Florrie came along and whisked Carruthers off.

«He seems like a fine chap, «I said. «One of your admirers, I suppose?»

«He's been very good to me—he nursed me when

I was ill. You mustn't make him jealous. He likes to pretend that he's in love with me.»

«To pretend?» I said.

«Let's dance», she said. «I'll tell you about him some other time.»

While we were dancing she took the rose she was wearing and stuck it in my buttonhole. «You must have been enjoying yourself to-night,» she said, getting a whiff of the booze. A birthday party, I explained, leading her towards the balcony to have a few words with her in private.

«Do you think you could get away to-morrow night —go to the theatre with me?»

She squeezed my arm by way of assent. «You look more beautiful than ever to-night,» I said, holding her close.

«Be careful what you do,» she murmured, looking stealthily over her shoulder. «We mustn't stay here long. I can't explain it now but you see, Carruthers is very jealous and I can't afford to make him angry Here he comes now... I'll leave you.»

I purposely refrained from looking round though I was dying to study Carruthers more closely. I hung over the flimsy iron rail of the balcony and became absorbed in the sea of faces below. Even from this low height the crowd took on that dehumanized appearance which comes with weight and number. If there were not this thing called language there would be little to differentiate this maelstrom of flesh from other forms of animal life. Even that, even the divine gift of speech, hardly served to make a distinction. What was their talk? Could one call it language? Birds and dogs have a language too, probably just as adequate as that of the mob. Language only begins at the point where communication is endangered. Everything these people are saying to one another, everything they read, everything they regulate their lives by is meaningless. Between this hour and a thousand other hours in a thousand different pasts there is no fundamental difference. In the ebb and tide of planetary life this stream goes the way of all other streams past and future. A minute ago she was using the word jealous. A queer word, especially when you are looking at a mob, when you see the haphazard mating, when you realize that those who are now locked arm in arm will most likely be separated a little while hence. I didn't give a fuck how many men were in love with her as long as I was included in the circle. I felt sorry for Carruthers, sorry that he should be a victim of jealousy. I had never been jealous in my life. Maybe I had never cared enough. The one woman I had desperately wanted I had relinquished of my own free will. To have a woman, to have anything, as a matter of fact, is nothing: it's the living with a person that matters, or the living with possessions. Can you go on forever being in love with persons or things? She could just as well admit that Carruthers was madly in love with her—what difference would it make in my love? If a woman is capable of inspiring love in one man she must be capable of inspiring it in others. To love or be loved is no crime. The really criminal thing is to make a person believe that he or she is the only you could ever love.

I went inside. She was dancing with some one else. Carruthers was standing alone in a corner. Impelled by a desire to give him a little consolation I went up to him and engaged him in conversation. If he were in the throes of jealousy he certainly didn't show it. He treated me rather cavalierly, I thought. I wondered was he really jealous or was she only trying to make me think that in order to conceal something else. The illness she had spoken of—if it were so serious then it was strange that she hadn't mentioned it before. The way she had alluded to it made me think it was a fairly recent event. He had nursed her. *Where?* Not at her home surely. Another little item came to mind: she had strongly urged me never to write to her at her home. *Why?* Maybe she had no home. That woman in the yard hanging up clothes—that was not her mother, she said. Who was it then? It might have been a neighbor, she tried to insinuate. She was touchy about the subject of her mother. It was her aunt who read my letters, not her mother. And the young man who answered the door—was he her brother? She said he was, but he certainly didn't resemble her. And where was her father all day, now that he was no longer breeding race horses or flying kites from the roof? She evidently didn't like her mother very much. She had even let out a broad hint once that she wasn't sure whether it was her mother.

«Mara's a strange girl, isn't she?» I said to Carruthers after a lull in our rather brittle conversation.

He gave a short shrill laugh and, as though to put me at ease about her, replied: «She's just a child, you know. And of course you can't believe a word she says.»

«Yes, that's just the impression she gives me,» said I.

«She hasn't a thing on her mind except having a good time,» said Carruthers.

Just then Mara came along. Carruthers wanted to dance with her. «But I promised this one to *him,*» she said, taking my hand.

«No, that's all right, dance with him! I've got to go anyway. I'll see you soon, I hope.» I sailed out before she had a chance to protest.

The following evening I was at the theatre ahead of time. I bought seats down front. There were several other favorites of mine on the program, among

them Trixie Friganza, Joe Jackson, and Roy Barnes.
It must have been an all-star bill.

I waited half an hour beyond the appointed time
and still no sign of her. I was so eager to see the
show I decided not to wait any longer. Just as I was
wondering what to do with the extra ticket a rather
handsome Negro passed me to approach the box office.
I intercepted him to inquire if he wouldn't accept my
ticket. He seemed surprised when I refused to
accept money from him. «I thought you were a
speculator,» he said.

After the intermission Thomas Burke appeared before the footlights. He made a tremendous impression
upon me, for reasons which I shall never be able
to fathom. A number of curious coincidences are
connected with his name and with the song which he
sang that night—«Roses of Picardy.» Let me jump
seven years from the moment the night before when
I stood hesitantly at the foot of the steps leading to
the dance hall....

Covent Garden. It is to Covent Garden I go a few
hours after landing in London, and to the girl I single
out to dance with I offer a rose from the flower
market. I had intended to go direct to Spain, but
circumstances obliged me to go straight to London.
A Jewish insurance agent from Bagdad, of all places,
is the one to lead me to the Covent Garden Opera
which has been converted into a dance hall for the
time being. The day before leaving London I pay a
visit to an English astrologer who lives near the Cry-
stal Palace. We have to pass through another man's
property in order to get to his house. As we are
walking through the grounds he informs me casually
that the place belongs to Thomas Burke, the author
of *Limehouse Nights*. The next time I attempt to go
to London, unsuccessfully, I return to Paris via Picardy
and in travelling through that smiling land I stand

up and weep with joy. Suddenly, recalling the
disappointments, the frustrations, the hopes turned to
despair, I realized for the first time the meaning of
«voyage». She had made the first journey possible
and the second one inevitable. We were never to see
each other again. I was free in a wholly new sense—
free to become the endless voyager. If any one thing
may be said to be accountable for the passion which
seized me and which held me in its grip for seven
long years then it is Thomas Burke's rendering of
this sentimental ditty. Only the night before I had
been commiserating Carruthers. Now, listening to
the song, I was suddenly stricken with fear and
jealousy. It was about the one rose that dies not,
the rose that one keeps in one's heart. As I listened
to the words I had a premonition that I would lose
her. I would lose her because I loved her too much,
that was how the fear shaped itself. Carruthers,
despite his nonchalance, had put a drop of poison in
my veins. Carruthers had brought her roses; she had
given me the rose he had pinned to her waist. The
house is bursting with applause. They are throwing
roses on the stage. He is going to give an encore.
It is the same song—«Roses of Picardy». It is the
same phrase which he is coming to now, the words
which stab me and leave me desolate—«but there is
one rose that dies not in Picardy... 'tis the rose that
I keep in my heart!» I can't stand it any longer, I
rush out. I rush across the street and bound up the
steps to the dance hall.

She's on the floor, dancing with a dark-skinned
fellow who is holding her close. As soon as the dance
is out I rush over to her. «Where were you?» I ask.
«What was the matter? Why didn't you come?»

She seemed surprised that I should be so upset over
such a trivial thing. *What had kept her?* Oh, it
was nothing at all. She had been out late, a rather

wild party... not with Carruthers... he had left shortly
after me. No, it was Florrie who had organized the
party. Florrie and Hannah—did I remember them?
(*Did remember them?* Florrie the nymphomaniac
and Hannah the drunken sot. How could I forget
them?) Yes, there had been a lot to drink and somebody had asked her to do the split and she had tried...
well, and she had hurt herself a bit. That was all.
I should have realized that something had happened
to her. She wasn't the sort who made dates and
broke them—just like that.

«When did you get here?» I asked, remarking to
myself that she seemed quite intact, unusually cool
and collected, in fact.

She had come just a few minutes ago. What
difference did it make? Her friend Jerry. an ex-
pugilist who was now studying law, had taken her to
dinner. He had been at the party last night and had
been kind enough to see her home. She would see
me Saturday afternoon in the Village—at the Pagoda
Tea Room. Dr. Tao. who ran the place, was a good
friend of hers. She would like me to meet him. He
was a poet.

I said I would wait around for her and take her
home, by subway this time if she didn't mind. She
begged me not to bother—I would get home so late
and so on. I insisted. I could see that she wasn't
too pleased. In fact she was plainly annoyed. In a
moment she excused herself to go to the dressing
room. That meant a telephone call, I was certain.
Again I wondered if she really lived at this place she
called home.

She reappeared with a good-natured smile. saying
that the manager had offered to let her off early.
We might go at once, if we liked. First we were to
have a bite somewhere. On the way to the restaurant.
and all through the meal. she kept up a rapid-fire

talk about the manager and his little kindnesses. He was a Greek with a tender heart. It was extraordinary what he had done for some of the girls. How did she mean? Like what? Well, like Florrie, for instance. The time Florrie had had an abortion—that was before she met her doctor friend. Nick had paid for everything; he had even sent her to the country for a few weeks. And Hannah, who had had all her teeth extracted... Well, Nick had presented her with a lovely set of false teeth.

And Nick, what was he getting for all his trouble, I inquired blandly.

«Nobody knows anything about Nick,» she continued. «He never makes any overtures to the girls. He's too busy with his affairs. He runs a gambling joint uptown, he plays the stock market, he owns a bath house at Coney Island, he has an interest in a restaurant somewhere... he's too busy to think about such things.»

«You seem to be one of the favored ones,» I said. «You come and go as you please.»

«Nick thinks the world of me,» she said. «Perhaps because I attract a different type of man than the other girls.»

«Wouldn't you like to do something else for a living?» I asked abruptly. «You're not meant for this sort of thing—that's why you're such a success. I guess. Isn't there something else you'd rather do, tell me?»

Her smile indicated how naive my question was. «You don't think I do this because I like it, do you? I do it because I earn more money than I could elsewhere. I have a lot of responsibilities. It doesn't matter what I do—I must earn a certain amount of money each week. But don't let's talk about that, it's too painful. I know what you're thinking about, but you're wrong. Everybody treats me like a queen.

The other girls are stupid. I use my intelligence.
You notice that my admirers are mostly old men...»
   «Like Jerry, you mean?»
   «Oh Jerry, he's an old friend. Jerry doesn't count.»
   I dropped the subject. Better not to inquire too
deeply. There was one little thing that bothered me
however, and I broached it as gently as I could.
Why did she waste time on such trollops as Florrie
and Hannah?
   She laughed. Why, they were her best friends.
They would do anything for her, they worshipped
her. One has to have some one he can rely on in a
pinch. Why, Hannah would hock her false teeth for
her if she asked her to. Speaking of friends, there
was a wonderful girl she would like to introduce me
to some day—quite another type, almost aristocratic.
Lola was her name. She had a little colored blood
in her, but it was scarcely noticeable. Yes, Lola was
a very dear friend. She was sure I would like her.
   «Why not make a date?» I suggested promptly.
«We could meet at my friend Ulric's studio. I've
wanted you to meet him too.»
   She thought that would be excellent. Couldn't say
when it would be, though, as Lola was always going
off on trips. But she would try to make it soon.
Lola was the mistress of some rich shoe manufacturer:
she wasn't always free. But it would be good to have
Lola—she had a racing car. Perhaps we could drive
out into the country and stay the night somewhere.
Lola had a way about her. She was just a little too
haughty, in fact. But that was because of her colored
blood. I mustn't let on that I knew anything about
that. And as for my friend Ulric—I wasn't to breathe
a word of that to him.
   «But he likes colored girls. He'll be crazy about
Lola.»
   «But Lola doesn't want to be liked for that reason.»

said Mara. «You'll see—she's very pale and very attractive. Nobody would suspect that she had a drop of colored blood in her.»

«Well, I hope she's not *too* proper.»

«You don't need to worry about that,» said Mara promptly. «Once she forgets herself she's very gay. It won't be a dull evening, I assure you.»

We had a bit of a walk from the subway station to her home. Along the way we stopped under a tree and started to mush it up. I had my hand up her dress and she was fumbling with my fly. We were leaning against the tree trunk. It was late and not a a soul in sight. I could have laid her out on the sidewalk for all it mattered.

She had just got my pecker out and was opening her legs for me to ram it home when suddenly from the branches above a huge black cat pounced on us, screaming as if in heat. We nearly dropped dead with fright, but the cat was even more frightened since its claws had gotten caught in my coat. In my panic I beat the hell out of it and in return was badly clawed and bitten. Mara was trembling like a leaf. We walked into a vacant lot and lay on the grass. Mara was fearful I might get an infection. She would sneak home and come back with some iodine and what not. I was to lie there and wait for her.

It was a warm night and I lay back full length looking up at the stars. A woman passed but didn't notice me lying there. My cock was hanging out and beginning to stir again with the warm breeze. By the time Mara returned it was quivering and jumping. She kneeled beside me with the bandages and the iodine. My cock was staring her in the face. She bent over and gobbled it greedily. I pushed the things aside and pulled her over me. When I had shot my bolt she kept right on coming, one orgasm after another, until I thought it would never stop.

We lay back and rested awhile in the warm breeze.
After a while she sat up and applied the iodine.
We lit our cigarettes and sat there talking quietly.
Finally we decided to go. I walked her to the door
of her home and as we stood there embracing one
another she grabbed me impulsively and whisked
me off. «I can't let you go yet,» she said. And
with that she flung herself on me, kissing me passionately and reaching into my fly with murderous
accuracy. This time we didn't bother to look for a
vacant patch of ground, but collapsed right on the
sidewalk under a big tree. The sidewalk wasn't too
comfortable—I had to pull out and move over a few
feet where there was a bit of soft earth. There was
a little puddle near her elbow and I was for taking
it out again and moving over another inch or so,
but when I tried to draw it out she got frantic.
«Don't ever take it out again,» she begged, «it drives
me crazy. Fuck me, fuck me!» I held out on her
a long while. As before, she came again and again,
squealing and grunting like a stuck pig. Her mouth
seemed to have grown bigger, wider, utterly lascivious; her eyes were turning over, as if she were
going into an epilectic fit. I took it out a moment
to cool it off. She put her hand in the puddle
beside her and sprinkled a few drops of water over
it. That felt marvelous. The next moment she was
on her hands and knees, begging me to give it to
her assways. I got behind her on all fours; she
reached her hand under and grabbing my cock she
slipped it in. It went right in to the womb. She
gave a little groan of pain and pleasure mixed. «It's
gotten bigger,» she said, squirming her ass around.
«Put it in again all the way... go ahead, I don't care
if it hurts,» and with that she backed up on me
with a wild lurch. I had such a cold-blooded erection
that I thought I'd never be able to come. Besides,

not worrying about losing it, I was able to watch the performance like a spectator. I would draw it almost out and roll the tip of it around the silky, soppy petals, then plunge it in and leave in there like a stopper. I had my two hands around her pelvis, pulling and pushing her at will. «Do it, do it,» she begged, «or I'll go mad!» That got me. I began to work on her like a plunger, in and out full length without a let-up, she going Oh—Ah, Oh —Ah! and then bango! I went off like a whale.

We brushed ourselves off and started back towards the house once again. At the corner she stopped dead in her tracks and, turning round to face me squarely, she said with a smile that was almost ugly —«*And now for the dirt!*»

I looked at her in amazement. «What do you mean? What are you talking about?»

«I mean,» she said, never relinquishing that strange grimace, «that I need fifty dollars. I must have it tomorrow. *I must. I must....* Now do you see why I didn't want you to take me home?»

«Why did you hesitate to ask me for it? Don't you think I can raise fifty dollars if you need it badly?»

«But I need it at once. Can you get a sum like that by noon? Don't ask me what it's for—it's urgent, very urgent. Do you think you can do it? Will you promise?»

«Why of course I can,» I answered, wondering as I said so where in hell I would get it in such quick time.

«You're wonderful,» she said, seizing my two hands and squeezing them warmly. «I do hate to ask you. I know you have no money. I'm always asking for money—that seems to be all I can do—get money for others. I hate it, but there's nothing else to do. You trust me, don't you? I'll give it back to you in a week.»

«Don't talk that way, Mara. I don't want it back.
If you're in need I want you to tell me. I may be
poor but I can raise money too now and then. I
wish I could do more. I wish I could take you out
of that damned place—I don't like seeing you there.»

«Don't talk about that now, please. Go home and
get some sleep. Meet me at twelve-thirty to-morrow
in front of the drug store at Times Square. That's
where we met before, you remember? God, I didn't
know then how much you would mean to me. I
took you for a millionaire. You won't disappoint
me to-morrow—you're sure?»»

«I'm sure, Mara.»

Money always has to be raised in jig time and
paid back at regular stipulated intervals, either by
promises or in cash. I think I could raise a million
dollars if I were given enough time, and by that
I don't mean sidereal time but the ordinary clock
time of days, months, years. To raise money quickly,
however, even carfare, is the most difficult task one
can set me. From the time I left school I have
begged and borrowed almost continuously. I've
often spent a whole day trying to raise a dime; at
other times I've had fat bills thrust into my hand
without even opening my mouth. I don't know any
more about the art of borrowing now than I did
when I started. I know there are certain people
whom you must never, not under any circumstances,
ask for help. There are others again who will refuse
you ninety-nine times and yield on the hundredth,
and perhaps never again refuse you. There are some
whom you reserve for the real emergency, knowing
that you can rely on them, and when the emergency
comes and you go to them you are cruelly deceived.
There isn't a soul on earth who can be relied on
absolutely. For a quick, generous touch the man

you met only recently, the one who scarcely knows
you, is usually a pretty safe bet. Old friends are the
worst: they are heartless and incorrigible. Women,
too, as a rule, are usually callous and indifferent.
Now and then you think of some one you know
would come across, if you persisted, but the thought
of the prying and prodding is so disagreeable that
you wipe him out of your mind. The old are often,
like that, probably because of bitter experience .

To borrow successfully one has to be a mono-
maniac on the subject, as with everything else. If
you can give yourself up to it, as with Yoga exercises,
that is to say, whole-heartedly, without squeamish-
ness or reservations of any kind, you can live your
whole life without earning an honest penny. Naturally the price is too great. In a pinch the best single
quality is desperation. The best course is the unusual one. It is easier, for example, to borrow from
one who is your inferior than from an equal or from
one who is above you. It's also very important to
be willing to compromise yourself, not to speak of
lowering yourself, which is a *sine qua non*. The
man who borrows is always a culprit, always a
potential thief. Nobody ever gets back what he lent,
even if the sum is paid with interest. The man
who exacts his pound of flesh is always short-changed,
even if by nothing more than rancor or hatred.
Borrowing is a positive thing, lending negative. To
be a borrower may be uncomfortable, but it is also
exhilarating, instructive, life-like. The borrower
pities the lender, though he must often put up with
his insults and injuries.

Fundamentally borrower and lender are one and
the same. That is why no amount of philosophizing
can eradicate the evil. They are made for one another,
just as man and woman are made for each other.
No matter how fantastic the need, no matter how

crazy the terms, there will always be a man to lend
an ear, to fork up the necessary. A good borrower
goes about his task like a good criminal. His first
principle is never to expect something for nothing.
He doesn't want to know how to get the money on
the least terms but exactly the contrary. When the
right men meet there is a minimum of talk. They
take each other at face value, as we say. The ideal
lender is the realist who knows that to-morrow the
situation may be reversed and the borrower become
the lender.

There was only one person I knew who could see
it in the right light and that was my father. He
was the one I always held in reserve for the crucial
moment. And he was the only one I never failed
to pay back. Not only did he never refuse me but
he inspired me to give to others in the same way.
Every time I borrowed from him I became a better
lender—or I should say giver, because I've never
insisted on being repaid. There is only one way
to repay kindnesses and that is to be kind in turn
to those who come to you in distress. To repay a
debt is utterly unnecessary, so far as the cosmic book-
keeping is concerned. (All others forms of book-
keeping are wasteful and anachronistic.) «Neither
a borrower nor a lender be,» said the good Shakespeare, voicing a wish-fulfillment out of his Utopian
dream life. For men on earth, borrowing and lending is not only essential but should be increased to
outlandish proportions. The fellow who is really
practical is the fool who looks neither to the left
nor the right, who gives without question and asks
unblushingly.

To make it short, I went to my old man and without beating about the bush I asked him for fifty
dollars. To my surprise he didn't have that much
in the bank but he informed me quickly that he

could borrow it from one of the other tailors. I asked him if he would be good enough to do that for me and he said sure, of course, just a minute.

«I'll give it back to you in a week or so,» I said, as I was saying good-bye.

«Don't worry about that,» he replied, «any time will do. I hope everything's all right with you otherwise.»

At twelve-thirty sharp I handed Mara the money. She ran off at once, promising to meet me the next day in the garden of the Pagoda Tea Room. I thought it a good day to make a little touch for myself and so I trotted off to Costigan's office to ask for a five spot. He was out, but one of the clerks, suspecting the nature of my errand, volunteered to help me out. He said he wanted to thank me for what I had done for his cousin. *Cousin?* I couldn't think who his cousin might be. «Don't you remember the boy you took to the psychiatric clinic?» he said. «He was a runaway boy from Kentucky—his father was a tailor, remember? You telegraphed his father that you would take care of the boy until he arrived. That was my cousin.»

I remembered that lad very well. He wanted to be an actor—his glands were out of order. At the clinic they said he was an incipient criminal. .He had stolen some clothes belonging to a buddy of his while at the Newsboy's Home. He was a fine lad, more of a poet than an actor. If *his* glands were out of order then mine were completely disorganized. He had given the psychiatrist a kick in the balls for his pains—that's why they had tried to make him out a criminal. When I heard about it I laughed my head off. He should have used a black-jack on that sadistic jake of a psychiatrist.... Anyway, it was a pleasant surprise to find I had an

unknown friend in the wardrobe attendant. Nice,
too, to hear him say I could have more any time
I was in need of a little change. In the street I
bumped into an ex-wardrobe attendant now working
as a messenger. He insisted on giving me two tickets
for a ball to be run under the auspices of the Magicians and Conjurors' Association of New York City
of which he was the president. «I wish you could
get me a wardrobe attendant's job again,» he said.
«I have so many things to attend to now since I'm
president of the Association that I can't do justice
to the messenger work. Besides, my wife is going to
have another baby soon. Why don't you come up
to see us—I have some new tricks to show you. The
little boy is learning to be a ventriloquist; I'm going
to put him on the stage in a year or so. We have
to make a living somehow. You know, magic doesn't
pay very much. And I'm getting too old to run my
feet down too much. I was cut out for the professional life. You understand my personal capabilities and idiosyncrasies. If you come to the ball
I'm going to introduce you to the great Thurston—
he's promised to be there. I've got to go now—
I've got a death message to deliver.»

*You understand my personal capabilities and idio-
syncrasies.* I stood at the corner and wrote it down
on the back of an envelope. Seventeen years ago.
Here it is. Fuchs was his name. Gerhardt Fuchs
of FU Office. Same name as that of the «hundski»
picker in Glendale where Joey and Tony lived.
Used to meet this other Fuchs coming through the
cemetery grounds, a sack of dog, bird and cat shit
over his shoulder. Brought it to a perfumery house
somewhere. Always smelt like a skunk. A foul,
evil-minded bugger, one the original tribe of blind
Hessians. Fuchs and Kunz—two obscene birds who
could be seen drinking every night in Laubscher's

Beer Garden near the Fresh Pond Road. Kunz was
tubercular, a dermatologist by profession. They
talked a bird and skin language over their stinking
pots of beer. Ridgewood was their Mecca (1). Never
spoke English unless they had to. Germany was
their God and the Kaiser His spokesman. Well, bad
'cess to them! May they die like dirty umlauts—
if they haven't already. Funny, though, to find a
pair of inseparable twins with names like that. *Idio-
syncratic*, I should say....

3

And now it's Saturday afternoon, the sun's out
bright and strong, and I'm sipping some pale Chinese tea in Dr. Wuchee Hachee Tao's garden. He's
just handed me a long poem about Mother written
on fire-cracker paper. He looks like a superior type
of man—not very communicable either. I'd like to
ask him something about the original Tao but it so
happens that at this point in time, retrogressively
speaking, I haven't yet read the Tao Teh Ching.
If I had read it I wouldn't need to ask him any
questions—nor in all probability would I be sitting
in his garden waiting for a woman named Mara.
Had I been intelligent enough to have read that most
illustrious and most elliptical piece of ancient wisdom
I would have been spared a great many woes that
befell me and which I am now about to relate.

As I sit in the garden, B. C. 17, I have utterly
different thoughts than these. To be quite honest,

---

(1) A German-American quarter in Brooklyn.

I can't recall a single one at this moment. I vaguely
remember that I didn't like the poem about Mother
—it struck me as being sheer crap. And what's
more, I didn't like the Chink who wrote it— I remember that very distinctly. I know too that I was
getting furious because it was beginning to look like
another stand-up. (Had I imbibed a bit of Tao I
would not have lost my temper. I would have sat
there as contented as a cow, thankful that the sun
was out and grateful to be alive.) To-day as I write
this there is no sun and no Mara and, though I have
not yet become a contented cow, I feel very much
alive and at peace with the world.

I hear the telephone ringing inside. A slatfaced
Chink, probably a professor of philosophy, tells me
in chopstick language that a lady wishes to speak
to me on the telephone. It's Mara, and to believe
her she's only just getting out of bed. Has a hang-
over, she informs me. So has Florrie. The two of
them are sleeping it off in a hotel nearby. *What
hotel?* She doesn't want to say. Just wait a half
hour and she'll doll herself up. I dont feel like
waiting another half hour. I'm in a bad mood.
First it's the split and then it's a hang-over. And
who else is in bed with her, I want to know. Couldn't
possibly be a man whose name begins with a C, no?
She doesn't like that. She doesn't allow anybody
to talk to her that way. Well, I'm talking that way,
do you hear? Tell me where you are and I'll be
up to see you in a jiffy. If you don't want to say
then to hell with you. I'm sick of.... *Hello, hello!
Mara!*

No answer. Well, that must have touched her to
the quick. Florrie, that's the little bitch who's
responsible for it. Florrie and her itchy fur-lined
muff. What are you to think when all you ever hear
about a girl is that she can't find a prick big enough

to suit her? To look at her you'd think a good
fuck would knock the slats out of her. About 103 in
her stocking feet. A hundred and three pounds of
insatiable flesh. A booze artist to boot. An Irish
slut. A sluttee, if you ask me. Putting on a stage
accent as if to pretend that she'd once been a Zieg-
feld Follies girl.

A week rolls by and no word from Mara. Then
out of the blue a telephone call. She sounds depressed. Could I meet her for dinner somewhere,
she wants to talk to me about something very important. There's a gravity in her voice which I haven't
detected before.

In the Village, as I'm hurrying to keep the appointment, who should I run into but Kronski. I try to
wave him off but it's no go.

«What's the great hurry?» he asks with that bland,
sardonic grin he always summons at the wrong
moment.

I explain to him that I have a date.

«Are you going to eat?»

«Yes, I'm going to eat, but alone,» I say pointedly.

«Oh no you're not, Mister Miller. You need company, I can see that. You're not in such fine fettle
to-day.... You look worried. It's not a woman, I
hope?»

«Listen, Kronski, I'm going to meet somebody and
I don't want you around.»

«Now, *Mister* Miller, how can you talk that way
to an old friend? I insist on accompanying you.
I'm going to buy the meal—you can't resist that,
can you?»

I laughed in spite of myself. «All right, shit, tag
along then. Maybe I'll need your help. You're no
good to me except in a pinch. Listen, don't start
any funny work. I'm going to introduce you to the
woman I'm in love with. She probably won't like

your looks, but I want you to méet her anyway.
Some day I'll marry her and, since I can't seem to
get rid of you, she might as well begin to tolerate you
now as later. I have a hunch you won't like her.»

«This sounds very serious, *Mister* Miller. I'll have
to take steps to protect you.»

«If you start meddling I'll crown you,» I answered,
laughing savagely. «About this person I'm in dead
earnest. You never saw me that way before, did
you? You can't believe it, eh? Well, just watch
me. Tell you how earnest I am.... if you get in my
way I'll murder you in cold blood.»

To my surprise Mara was already at the restaurant.
She had chosen a lonely table in a dark corner.
«Mara,» I said, «this is an old friend, Dr. Kronski.
He insisted on coming along. I hope you don't
mind.» To my astonishment she greeted him cordially. As for, Kronski, the moment he laid eyes on
her he dropped his leer and banter. Even more
impressive was his silence. Usually, when I presented
him to a female, he became garrulous and made a
sort of fluttering noise with his invisible wings.

Mara too was unusually calm; her voice sounded
soothing and hypnotic.

We had scarcely given the order and exchanged
a few polite words when Kronski, looking at Mara
steadily and appealingly, said: «Something has happened, something tragic, it seems to me. If you'd
rather have me go I'll leave right now. To tell the
truth, I'd prefer to stay. Perhaps I can be of help.
I'm a friend of this guy and I'd like to be a friend
of yours. I mean it sincerely.»

Rather touching, this. Mara, visibly moved, responded warmly.

«By all means stay,» she said, extending her hand
cross the table in token of trust and confidence.
«You make it easier for me to talk being here. I've

heard a lot about you, but I don't think your friend did you justice,» and she looked up at me reprovingly, then smiled warmly.

«No,» said I quickly, «it's true I never do give an honest picture of him.» I turned to him. «You know, Kronski, you have about the most unlovely character imaginable and yet...»

«Come, come,» he said, making a wry grimace, «don't begin that Dostoievski line with me. I'm your evil genius, you were going to say. Yes, I do have some queer diabolical influence over you, but I'm not confused about you as you are about me. I sincerely like you. I'd do anything you asked if I thought you meant it—even if it brought harm to some one I dearly loved. I put you above every one I know, *why* I can't say, because you certainly don't deserve it. Right now I'll confess I feel sad. I see that you love each other and I think you're meant for each other, but....»

«You're thinking that it won't be so hot for Mara, that's it, eh?»»

«I can't say yet,» he said, with alarming seriousness. «I see only this, that you've both met your match.»

«So you think I'd really be worthy of him?» said Mara very humbly.

I looked at her in amazement. I never suspected that she could say a thing like that to a stranger.

Her words fired Kronski. «Worthy of *him?*» he sneered. «Is he worthy of *you?* that's the question. What has he ever done to make a woman feel worthy of him? He hasn't begun to function yet—he's in a torpor. If I were you I wouldn't put an ounce of faith in him. He isn't even a good friend, let alone a lover or a husband. Poor Mara, don't worry your head about such things. Make him do something for you, spur him on, drive him nuts if you have to,

but make him open up! If I were to give you an
honest piece of advice, knowing him and loving him
as I do, it would be this: lacerate him, punish him,
goad him to the last ditch! Otherwise you're lost—
he'll devour you. Not that he's a bad sort, not
because he means harm... oh no! he does it out of
kindness. He almost makes you believe that he has
your own interest at heart when he sinks his hooks
into you. He can tear you apart with a smile and
tell you·that he's doing it for your own good. *He's*
the diabolical one, not me. I pretend, but he means
everything he does. He's the cruelest bastard that ever
walked on two legs—and what's queer about it is this,
that you love him because he is cruel, or perhaps
because he's honest about it. He warns you in
advance when he's going to strike. He tells you it
smilingly. And when it's over he picks you up and
brushes you off tenderly, asks you did he hurt you
very much and so on—like an angel. *The bastard!*»

«Of course I don't know him as well as you do,»
said Mara quietly, «but I must confess he's never
revealed that side of his nature to me—not yet, at
any rate. I only know him to be gentle and good.
I hope to act so that he'll always be that way with
me. I not only love him, I believe in him as a person.
I would sacrifice everything to make him happy....»

«But you're not very happy right now, are you?»
said Kronski, as though ignoring her words. «Tell
me, what has he done to make you—?»

«He hasn't done anything,» she said spiritedly.
«He doesn't know what's bothering me.»

«Well, can you tell *me*?» said Kronski, altering
his voice and moistening his eyes so that he resembled
a piteous, friendly little whelp.

«Don't press her,» I said, «she'll tell us in due
time.» I was looking at Kronski as I spoke. His
expression suddenly changed. He turned his head

away. I looked at Mara and there were tears in her eyes; they began to flow copiously. In a moment she excused herself and went to the washroom. Kronski looked at me with a wan dead smile, the look of the sick clam expiring in moonlight.

«Don't take it so tragically,» I said. «She's brave sort, she'll pull out of it.»

«That's what *you* say! You don't suffer. You get emotional and you call it suffering. That girl's in trouble, can't you see? She wants you to do something for her—not just wait till it passes. If *you* don't pump her *I* will. This time you've got a real woman. And a real woman, Mister Miller, expects something of a man—not just words and gestures. If she wants you to run away with her, to leave your wife, your child, your job, I'd say do it. Listen to her and not to your own selfish promptings!» He slumped back in his seat and picked his teeth. After a pause—«And you met her in a dance hall? Well, I must congratulate you for having the sense to recognize the genuine article. That girl can make something of you, if you'll let her. If it's not too late, I mean. You're pretty far gone, you know. Another year with that wife of yours and you're finished.» He spat on the floor in disgust. «You have luck. You get things without working for them. I work like a son of a bitch and the moment I turn my back everything crumbles.»

«That's because I'm a Goy,» I said jestingly.

«You're no Goy. You're a black Jew. You're one of those fascinating Gentiles that every Jew wants to shine up to. You're.... Oh, good you mentioned that. Mara is a Jewess, of course? Come now, don't pretend you don't know. Hasn't she told you yet?»

That Mara should be a Jewess sounded so highly preposterous I simply laughed in his face.

«You want me to prove it to you, is that it?»

«I don't care what she is,» I said, «but I'm sure she's not Jewish.»

«What is she then? You don't call that a pure Aryan, I hope?»

«I never asked her,» I replied. «You ask her if you like.»

«I won't ask her,» said Kronski, «because she might lie to me in front of you—but I'll tell you whether I'm right or not the next time I see you. I guess I can tell a Jew when I see one.»

«You thought I was a Jew you first met me.»

He laughed outright at this. «*So you really believed that?* Haw haw! Well, that's pretty good. You poor sap, I told you that just to flatter you. If you had a drop of Jewish blood in you I'd lynch you, out of respect for my people. *You a Jew?...* Well, well....» He rolled his head from side to side with tears in his eyes. «First of all a Jew is smart,» he began again, «and you, you're certainly not smart. And a Jew is *honest*—get that! Are *you* honest? Have you got an ounce of truth in you? And a Jew *feels*. A Jew is always humble, even when he's arrogant.... Here comes Mara now. Let's drop the subject.»

«You were talking about me, weren't you?» said Mara, as she sat down. «Why don't you go on? I don't mind.»

«You're wrong,» said Kronski, «we weren't talking about you at all...»

«He's a liar,» I broke in. «We *were* talking about you, only we didn't get very far. I wish, Mara, you'd tell him about your family—the things you told me, I mean.»

Her face clouded up. «Why should you be concerned about my family?» she said, with an ill-disguised show of irritation. «My family is thoroughly uninteresting.»

«I don't believe it,» said Kronski blankly. «I think you're concealing something.»

The look that passed between them gave me a jolt. It was as if she had given him the signal to proceed cautiously. They understood one another in some subterranean fashion, in a way which excluded me. The image of the woman in the backyard of her home came vividly to my mind. That woman was no neighbor, as she had tried to insinuate. Could it have been her step-mother? I tried to recall what she had told me about her real mother but immediately became lost in the complicated maze she had woven about this obviously painful subject.

«What is it you'd like to know about my family?» she said, turning to me.

«I don't want to ask you anything that would make you uncomfortable,» I said, «but if it isn't indiscreet would you mind telling us about your step-mother?»

«Where did your step-mother come from?» asked Kronski.

«From Vienna,» said Mara.

«And you, were you born in Vienna too?»

«No, I was born in Roumania, in a little mountain village. I may have some Gypsy blood in me.»

«You mean your mother was a Gypsy?»

«Yes, there's a story to that effect. My father is said to have run away with her on the eve of his marriage to my step-mother. That's why my mother hates me, I guess. I'm the black sheep of the family.»

«And you adore your father, I suppose?»

«I worship him. He's like me. The others are strangers to me—we haven't anything in common.»

«And you support the family, is that it?» said Kronski.

«Who told you that? I see, so that's what you were talking about when...»

«No, Mara, nobody told me. I can see it in your

face. You're making a sacrifice of yourself—that's why you're unhappy.»

«I won't deny it,» she said. «It's for my father I'm doing it. He's an invalid, he can't work any more.»

«What's the matter with your brothers?»

«Nothing. Just lazy. I spoiled them. You see, I ran away when I was sixteen; I couldn't stand the life at home. I stayed away a year; when I returned I found them in misery. They're helpless. I'm the only one who has any initiative.»

«And you support the entire family?»

«I try to,» she said. «Sometimes I want to give up—it's too big a burden. But I can't. If I were to walk out they would starve to death.»

«Nonsense,» said Kronski heatedly. «That's the very thing you ought to do.»

«But I can't—not while my father is alive. I'd do anything, I'd prostitue myself, rather than see him in want.»

«And they'd let you do it, too,» said Kronski. «Look, Mara, you've put yourself in a false position. You can't assume all the responsibility. Let the others take care of themselves. Take your father away—we'll help you to look after him. He doesn't know how you get the money, does he? You haven't told him that you work in a dance hall, have you?»

«No, I haven't. He thinks I'm in the theatre. But my mother knows.»

«And she doesn't care?»

«*Care?*» said Mara, with a bitter smile. «She wouldn't care what I did so long as I keep the house together. She says I'm no good. Calls me a whore. I'm just like my mother, she says.»

I interrupted. «Mara,» I said, «I had no idea it was as bad as this. Kronski's right, you've got to extricate yourself. Why don't you do as he suggests—

leave the family and take your father along with you?»

«I'd love to,» she said, «but my father would never leave my mother. She's got a hold over him—she's made a child of him.»

«But if he knew what you were doing?»

«He'll never know. I won't let anybody tell him. My mother threatened to tell him once: I told her I'd kill her if she did.» She smiled bitterly. «Do you know what my mother said? She said I had been trying to poison her.»

At this point Kronski suggested that we continue the conversation uptown at the home of a friend of his who was away. He said we could spend the night there if we liked. In the subway his mood changed; he became again the leering, bantering, diabolical, pale-faced toad that he usually was. This meant that he considered himself seductive, felt empowered to ogle the attractive looking females. The perspiration was pouring down his face, wilting his collar. His talk became hectic, scattered, altogether without continuity. In his distorted way he was trying to create an atmosphere of drama; he flapped his arms loosely, like a demented bat caught between two powerful search-lights.

To my disgust Mara appeared to be amused by this spectacle. «He's quite mad, your friend,» she said, «but I like him.»

Kronski overheard the remark. He grinned tragically and the perspiration began flowing more freely. The more he grinned, the more he clowned and aped it, the more melancholy he looked. He never wanted anybody to think him sad. He was Kronski, the big, vital, healthy, jovial, negligent, reckless, carefree fellow who solved everybody's problems. He could talk for hours on end—for days, if you had the courage to listen to him. He awoke talking, plunging immediately into hair-splitting arguments, always about the fate of the world, about its bio-chemical nature, its astro-physical constitution, its politico-economic configuration. The world was in a disastrous state: he knew, because he was always amassing facts about the shortage of wheat or the shortage of petroleum, or making researches into the condition of the Soviet Army or the condition of our arsenals and fortifications. He would say, as if it were a fact beyond dispute, that the soldiers of the Soviet Army could not make war this winter because they had only so many overcoats, so many shoes, etc. He talked about carbohydrates, fats, sugar, etc. He talked about world supplies as though he were running the world. He knew more about international law than the most famous authority on the subject. There wasn't any subject under the sun about which he did not appear to have a complete and exhaustive knowledge. As yet he was only an interne in a city hospital, but in a few years he would be a celebrated surgeon or psychiatrist, or perhaps something else, he didn't know yet what he would elect to be. «Why don't you decide to become President of the United States?» his friends would inquire ironically. «Because I'm not a half-wit,» he would answer, making a sour puss. «You think I couldn't become President if I wanted to? Listen, you don't think it takes brains to become President of the United States, do you? No, I want a real job. I want to help people, I don't want to bamboozle them. If I were to take this country over I'd clean house from top to bottom. To begin with I'd have guys like you castrated....» He'd go on this way for an hour or two, cleaning up the world, putting the big house in order, paving the way for the brotherhood of man and the empire of free thought. Every day of his life he went over the affairs of the world with a fine comb, cleaning out the lice that made men's thinking lousy. One day he'd be all heated up about the condition of the slaves on the Gold Coast, quoting you the price of bullion on the half-shell or some other fabulous statistical concoction which inadvertently made men hate one another and created superfluous jobs for spineless, weak-chested men on financial dope sheets, thus adding to the burden of intangible political economies. Another day he'd be up in arms about chromium or permanganate, because Germany perhaps or Roumania had cornered the market on something or other which would make it difficult for the surgeons in the Soviet Army to operate when the big day arrived. Or he would have just garnered the latest dope on a new and startling pest which would soon reduce the civilized world to anarchy unless we acted at once and with the greatest wisdom. How the world staggered along day after day without Dr. Kronski's guidance was a mystery which he never cleared up. Dr. Kronski was never in doubt about his analyses of world conditions. Depressions, panics, floods, revolutions, plagues, all these phenomena were manifesting themselves simply to corroborate his judgment. Calamities and catastrophes made him gleeful; he croaked and chortled like the world toad in embryo. How were things going with him personally—nobody ever asked him that question. Personally it was no go. He was chopping up arms and legs for the moment, since nobody had the perspicacity to ask anything better of him. His first wife had died because of a medical blunder and his second wife would soon be going crazy, if he knew what he were talking about. He could plan the most wonderful model houses for the New Republic of Mankind but oddly enough he couldn't keep his own little nest free of bedbugs and other vermin, and because of his preoccupation with world events, setting things to right in Africa, Guadaloupe, Singapore, and so on, his own place was always just a trifle upset, that is to say, dishes unwashed, beds unmade, furniture falling apart, butter running rancid, toilet stopped up, tubs leaking, dirty combs lying on the table and in general a pleasing, wretched, mildly insane state of dilapidation which manifested itself in the person of Dr. Kronski personally in the form of dandruff, eczema, boils, blisters, fallen arches, warts, wens, halitosis, indigestion and other minor disorders, none of them serious because once the world order was established everything pertaining to the past would disappear and man would shine forth in a new skin like a new-born lamb.

The friend whose house he was taking us to was an artist, he informed us. Being a friend of the great Dr. Kronski that meant an uncommon artist, one who would be recognized only when the millenium had been ushered in. His friend was both a painter and a musician—equally great in both realms. The music we wouldn't be able to hear, owing to his friend's absence, but we would be able to see his paintings— some of them, that is, because the great bulk of them he had destroyed. If it weren't for Kronski he would have destroyed everything. I inquired casually what his friend was doing at the moment. He was running a model farm for defective children in the wilds of Canada. Kronski had organized the movement himself but was too busy thinking things out to bother with the practical details of management. Besides, his friend was a consumptive, and he would have to remain up there forever most likely. Kronski telegraphed him now and then to advise him about this and that. It was only a beginning—soon he would empty the hospitals and asylums of their inmates, prove to the world that the poor can take care of the poor and the weak the weak and the crippled the crippled and the defective the defective.

«Is that one of your friend's paintings?» I asked, as he switched on the light and a huge vomit of yellowish green bile leaped out from the wall.

«That's one of his early things,» said Kronski. «He keeps it for sentimental reasons. I've put his best things away in storage. But here's a little one that gives you some idea of what he can do.» He looked at it with pride, as if it were the work of his own off-spring. «It's marvelous, isn't it?»

«Terrible,» I said. «He has a shit complex; he must have been born in the gutter, in a pool of stale horse piss on a sullen day in February near a gas house.»

«You *would* say that,» said Kronski vengefully. «You don't know an honest painter when you see one. You admire the revolutionaries of yesterday. You're a Romantic.»

«Your friend may be revolutionary but he's no painter,» I insisted. «He hasn't any love in him; he just hates, and what's more he can't even paint what he hates. He's fog-eyed. You say he's a consumptive: I say he's bilious. He stinks, your friend, and so does his place. Why don't you open the windows? It smells as though a dog had died here.»

«Guinea pigs, you mean. I've been using the place as a laboratory, that's why it stinks a bit. Your nose is too sensitive, Mister Miller. You're an aesthete.»

«Is there anything to drink here?» I asked.

There wasn't, of course, but Kronski offered to run out and get something. «Bring something strong,» I said, «this place makes you retch. No wonder the poor bastard got consumptive.»

Kronski trotted off rather sheepishly, I looked at Mara. «What do you think? Will we wait for him or shall we beat it?»

«You're very unkind. No, let's wait. I'd like to hear him talk some more—he's interesting. And he

really thinks a lot of you. I can see that by the
way he looks at you.»

«He's only interesting the first time,» I said.
«Frankly, he bores me stiff. I've been listening to
this stuff for years. It's sheer crap. He may be
intelligent but he's got a screw loose somewhere.
He'll commit suicide one day, mark my words.
Besides, he brings bad luck. Whenever I meet that
guy things turn out wrong. He carries death around
with him, don't you feel that? If he isn't croaking
he's gibbering like an ape. How can you be friends
with a guy like that? He wants you to be a friend
of his sorrow. What's eating him I don't know. He's
worried about the world. I don't give a shit about
the world. I can't make the world right, neither can
he... neither can anybody. Why doesn't he try to
live? The world mightn't be so bad if we tried to
enjoy ourselves a little more. No, he riles me.»

Kronski came back with some vile liquor he
claimed was all he could find at that hour. He
seldom drank more than a thimbleful himself so it
didn't make much difference to him whether we
poisoned ourselves or not. He hoped it would poison
us, he said. He was depressed. He seemed to have
settled in for an all-night depression. Mara, like an
idiot, felt sorry for him. He stretched out on the
sofa and lay his head in her lap. He began another
line, a weird one—the impersonal sorrow of the
world. It was not argument and invective as before
but a chant, a dictaphone chant addressed to the
millions of unhappy creatures throughout the world.
Dr. Kronski always played this tune in the dark, his
head on some woman's lap, his hand dragging the
carpet.

His head nestling in her lap like a swollen viper,
the words sieved through Kronski's mouth like gas
escaping through a half-opened cock. It was the

weird of the irreducible human atom, the sub-soul
wandering in the cellar of collective misery. Dr.
Kronski ceased to exist: only the pain and torment
remained, functioning as positive and negative
electrons in the vast atomic vacuum of a lost personality. In this state of abeyance not even the miraculous Sovietization of the world could rouse a spark
of enthusiasm in him. What spoke were the nerves,
the ductless glands, the spleen, the liver, the kidneys,
the little blood vessels lying close to the surface of the
skin. The skin itself was just a bag in which were
loosely collected a rather messy outfit of bones,
muscles, sinews, blood, fat, lymph, bile, urine, dung,
and so on. Germs were stewing around in this stinking bag of guts; the germs would win out no matter
how brilliantly that cage of dull gray matter called
the brain functioned. The body was in hostage to
Death, and Dr. Kronski, so vital in the X-ray world
of statistics, was just a louse to be cracked under a
dirty nail when it came time to surrender his shell.
It never occurred to Dr. Kronski, in these fits of
genito-urinary depression, that there might be a view
of the universe in which death assumed another
aspect. He had disembowelled, dissected and
chopped to bits so many corpses that death had come
to mean something very concrete—a piece of cold
meat lying on the mortuary slab, so to say. The
light went out and the machine stopped, and after a
time it would stink. *Voilà*, it was as plain and simple
as that. In death the loveliest creature imaginable
was just another piece of extraordinary cold plumb-
ing. He had looked at his wife, just after the
gangrene had set in; she might have been a codfish,
he intimated, for all the attractiveness she displayed.
The thought of the pain she was suffering was
overruled by the knowledge of what was going on
inside that body. Death had already made his entry

and his work was fascinating to behold. Death is always present, he asserted. Death lurks in dark corners, waiting for the opportune moment to raise his head and strike. That is the only real bond we have, he said—the constant presence of death in all of us always.

Mara was quite taken in by all this. She stroked his hair and purred softly as the steady stream of singing gas parted from his thick bloodless lips. I was more annoyed by her evident sympathy for the sufferer than by the monotony of his weird. The image of Kronski huddled up like a sick goat struck me as distinctly comical. He had swallowed too many empty tin cans. He had nourished himself on discarded automobile parts. He was a walking cemetery of facts and figures. He was dying of statistical indigestion.

«Do you know what you ought to do?» I said quietly. «You ought to kill yourself—now, tonight. You haven't anything to live for—why kid yourself? We'll leave you in a little while and you just do away with yourself. You're a smart alec, you must know a way to do it without making too much of a mess. Really, I think you owe it to the world. As it is, you're only making a nuisance of yourself.»

These words had an almost electrical effect upon the suffering Dr. Kronski. He actually bounded to his feet in one porpoise-like movement. He clapped his hands and danced a few steps with the grave of a spavined pachyderm. He was ecstatic, in the way that a sewer digger becomes ecstatic when he learns that his wife has given birth to another brat.

«So you want me to get rid of myself, Mister Miller, that's it, eh? What's the great hurry? You're jealous of me, are you? Well, I'm going to disappoint you this time. I'm going to stay alive and make you miserable. I'm going to torture you. One day you're going to come to me and beg me to give you something to put you out of harm's way. You're going to beg me on your knees and I'm going to refuse you.»

«You're crazy,» I said, stroking him under the chin.

«Oh no I'm not!» he answered, patting my bald knob. «I'm just a neurotic, like all Jews. I won't ever kill myself, don't fool yourself. I'll be at your funeral and I'll be laughing at you. Maybe you won't have a funeral. Maybe you'll be so in debt to me that you'll have to will me your body when you die. Mister Miller, when I start carving you up there won't be a crumb left over.»

He reached for a paper knife on the piano and placed the point of it on my diaphragm. He traced an imaginary line of incision and flourished the knife before my eyes.

«That's how I'll begin,» he said, «*in your guts.* First I'll let out all that romantic nonsense which makes you think you lead a charmed life; then I'll skin you like a snake so as to get at your calm, peaceful nerves and make them quiver and jump; you'll be more alive under the knife than you are right now; you'll look queer with one leg on and one leg off and your head sitting on my mantelpiece with your mouth fixed in a perpetual grin.»

He turned to Mara. «Do you think you'll still be in love with him when I dress him for the laboratory?»

I turned my back on him and went to the window. It was a typical back view in the Bronx: wooden fences, clothes poles, wash lines, mangy grass plots, serial tenement houses, fire escapes, et cetera. Figures prowled back and forth before the windows in all states of attire. They were getting ready to retire in order to go through with the morrow's meaningless humdrum. One out of a hundred thousand might escape the general doom; as for the rest it would be an act of mercy if some one came in the night and slit their throats while they slept. To believe that these wretched victims had it in them to create a new world was sheer insanity. I thought of Kronski's second wife, the one who would eventually go crazy. She was from these parts. Her father ran a stationery stone; the mother lay in bed all day nursing a cancerous womb. Her youngest brother had the sleeping sickness, another was paralyzed, and the oldest one was a mental defective. An intelligently ordered state would have put the whole family out of commission and the house with it...

I spat out of the window in disgust.

Kronski was standing beside me, his arm around Mara's waist. «Why not jump it?» I said, throwing my hat out the window.

«What, and make a mess for the neighbors to mop up? No sir, not me. Mister Miller, it seems to me that you're the one who's anxious to commit suicide. Why don't *you* jump?»

«I'm willing,» I said, «provided you jump with me. Let me show how easy it is. Here, give me your hand...»

«Oh, stop it!» said Mara. «You're behaving like children. I thought you two were going to help me solve *my* problem. I've got *real* worries.»

«There are no solutions,» said Kronski glumly. It's impossible to help your father because he doesn't want to be helped. He wants to die.»

«But I want to live,» said Mara. «I refuse to be a drudge.»

«That's what everybody says, but it doesn't help. Until we overthrow this rotten capitalistic system there'll be no solution to...»

«That's all rot,» Mara broke in. «Do you think

I'm going to wait for the revolution in order to live my life? Something has to be done now. If I can't solve it any other way I'll become a whore—an intelligent one, of course».

«There are no intelligent whores,» said Kronski. «To prostitute the body is a sign of feeble intelligence. Why don't you use your brains? You'd have a better time of it if you became a spy. *Now that's an idea!* I think I could dig up something for you along those lines. I have some pretty good connections in the Party. Of course, you'd have to give up the idea of living with this bird,» and he jerked his thumb in my direction. «But a dame like you,» and he eyed her gloating from head to foot, «could take her pick. How would you like to pose as a countess or a princess?» he added. «A hundred a week and all expenses paid... not so bad, what?»

«I make more than that now,» said Mara, «without the risk of being shot.»

«*What?*» we both exclaimed at once.

She laughed. «You think that's big money, do you? I need much more than that. If I wanted to I could marry a millionaire to-morrow; I've had several offers already.»

«Why don't you marry one and divorce him quickly,» said Kronski. «You could marry one after another and become a millionairess yourself. *Where's your brains?* You don't mean to tell me you have scruples about such things?»

Mara didn't know quite how to answer this. All she could think to say was that it was obscene to marry an old derelict for his money.

«And you think you could be a whore!» he said scornfully. «You're as bad as this guy here—he's corrupted by bourgeois morality too. Listen, why don't you train him as your pimp? You'd make a fine romantic couple in the underworld of sex. Do that! Maybe I can bring you some trade now and then.»

«Dr. Kronski,» I said, giving him the bland and amiable smile, «I think we'll be taking leave of you now. This has been a most pleasant and instructive evening, I assure you. When Mara gets her first dose of syphilis I'll be sure to call on you for your expert services. I think you've solved all our problems with admirable finesse. When you send your wife to the asylum come and spend a little time with us—it will be jolly to have you around, you're inspiring and entertaining, to say the least.»

«Don't go yet,» he begged, «I want to talk to you seriously.» He turned to Mara. «Just how much do you need immediately? I could lend you three hundred dollars, if that would help. I'd have to have it back in six months, because it isn't mine. Listen, don't run off now. Let him go—I want to tell you a few things.»

Mara looked at me as if to ask whether this was just talk on his part.

«Don't ask his advice,» said Kronski. «I'm sincere with you. I like you and I want to do something for you.» He turned round on me gruffly: «Go on, go home, will you? I'm not going to rape her.»

«Shall I go?» I asked.

«Yes, please do,» said Mara. «Only why did the idiot wait so long to tell me this?»

I had my doubts about the three hundred dollars but I left anyway. In the subway, faced with the broken-down night riders of the big city, I fell into a deep introspection, such as comes over the hero in modern novels. Like them, I asked myself useless questions, posed problems that didn't exist, made plans for the future which would never materialize, doubted everything, including my own existence. For the modern hero thought leads nowhere; his brain is

a collender in which he washes the soggy vegetables
of the mind. He says to himself that he is in love
and he sits in the moving underground trying to run
like a sewer. He beguiles himself with pleasant
thoughts. For example this one: he is probably
kneeling on the floor, stroking her knees: he is
working his sweaty ham-like paw slowly upwards over
the cool flesh: he is telling her in glutinous language
how unique she is; there never was any three hundred
dollars but if he can get it in, if he can get her to
open her legs a little more, he'll try to raise something; while she is sliding her twat closer and closer,
hoping that he'll just be satisfied to suck her off and
not make her go the whole hog, she tells herself that
it's no betrayal because she warned all and sundry
with explicit frankness that if she had to do it she'd
do it and she *must* do something. God help her, it's
very real and very urgent: she can get away with this
easily enough because nobody knows how many times
she's let herself be fucked for a little loose change;
she's got a good excuse, not wanting her father to
die like a dog; he's got his head between her legs
now, his tongue is hot; she slips down lower and puts
a leg around his neck; the juice is flowing and she
feels hornier than she ever felt; is he going to
tantalize her all night? She takes his head in her
hands and runs her fingers through his greasy hair;
she presses her cunt against his mouth; she feels it
coming, she squirms and wriggles, she gasps, she pulls
his hair. *Where are you?* she screams to herself.
Give me that fat prick! She pulls frantically at his
collar, yanks him off his knees; in the dark her hand
slips like an eel into the bulging fly, cups the fat
swollen balls, traces with thumb and finger the stiff
chicken neck of the penis where it dives into the
unknown; he's slow and heavy and he pants like a
walrus; she raises her legs high, slings them round

his neck. Get it in, you fuss-pot! Not there—*here!*
She puts her fist around it and leads it to the stable.
Oh, that's good. Oh! Oh! Oh God, it's good this
way, keep it in, hold it, hold it. Get it in deeper,
push it in all the way... there, that's it, that's it. Oh,
Oh! He's trying to hold it. He's trying to think of
two things at once. Three hundred dollars... three
greenbacks. Who'll give it to me? Jesus, that feels
marvelous. Jesus, hold that now! Hold it! He's
feeling and thinking at the same time. He feels a
little clam without a shell opening and closing, a
thirsty flower clamping the end of his prick. Don't
move now, he says to himself. Just watch it with
closed eyes. Count one two three four. Don't move,
you bastard, or I'll spill it. Do that again! Jesus,
what a cunt! He feels for her boobies, rips the dress
open, laps a nipple greedily. Don't move now, just
suck, that's it, like that. Easy now, easy! Jesus, if
we could only lie like this all night. Oh Jesus, it's
coming. Move, you bitch! Give it to me... faster,
faster. Oh, Ah, Sis, Boom, Blam!

Our hero opens his eyes and becomes himself again
—that is to say, the man known herein as myself, who
refuses to believe what his mind tells him. They are
probably having a long talk, I say to myself, drawing
a curtain over the pleasant substitution. She
wouldn't think of letting a greasy, sweaty incubus
like that touch her. He probably tried to kiss her
but she knows how to take care of herself all right.
Wonder if Maude's still awake? Feeling horny
myself. Walking towards the house I open my fly
and let my pecker out. Maude's cunt. She can
certainly fuck when she's a mind to. Get her half
asleep, her blinders off. Just lay there quiet like,
snuggle up spoon fashion. I put the key in the lock
and shove the iron gate. Cold iron against a quivering
prick. Must sneak up on her, slip it to her while

she's dreaming. I slip quietly upstairs and shuffle
out of my clothes. I can hear her turning over,
getting ready in her sleep to turn her warm ass on
me. I slide gently into bed and cup myself around
her. She's pretending to be out, dead to the world.
Not too fast or she'll wake up. Must do it in my
sleep like or she'll be insulted. I've got the tip of it
in the loose hairs. She's lying terribly still. She
wants it, the bitch, but she won't let on. All right,
play dead dog! I move her a little, just a wee bit.
She responds like a water-soaked log. She's going to
lie heavy like that and pretend she's asleep. Yes,
I've got it half in. I have to move her around like
a hoist, but she's movable and everything's smoothly
oiled. It's wonderful to fuck your own wife as if she
were a dead horse. You know every ripple in the
silken lining; you can take your time and think about
anything you like. The body is hers but the cunt's
yours. The cunt and the prick, they're married, by
crikey, no matter if the bodies are going different
ways. In the morning the two bodies will face each
other and make small change; they will act as if they
were independent, as if the penis and the other thing
were only to make water with. Being sound asleep
she doesn't mind how I joggle her. I've got one of
those dumb, senseless hard-ons, like my prick was
just a rubber hose and no nozzle to it. With the tips
of my fingers I can move her at will. I shoot a load
into her and leave it in, the thick rubber hose, I mean.
She's opening and closing like a flower. It's agony,
but the right kind of agony. Flower says: Stay there,
sonny boy! Flower talks like a drunken sponge.
Flower says: I do take this piece of meat to cherish
until I wake. And what says the body, the independent hoist moving on ball-bearings? Body is
wounded and humiliated. Body lost its name and
address temporarily. Body would like to cut prick

off and keep it like a kangaroo, forever. Maude is
not this body lying ass skyward, the helpless victim
of a rubber hose. Maude, if the author were God
and not her husband, sees herself standing prissily
on a green lawn, holding a beautiful red parasol.
There are beautiful gray doves pecking at her shoes.
These lovely doves, as she thinks them to be, are
saying in their koochkoo way, what a gracious, bounti-
ful creature you are. They make white shit all the
while, but being doves sent from heaven above, the
white part is only angel cake and shit is a bad word
which man invented when he put on clothes and
civilized himself. If she should squint her eye while
saying benediction over God's little pigeons she would
see a shameless hussy offering a naked man the hind
part of her body, just like a cow or a mare in the
field. She doesn't want to think of this woman,
especially in such a disgraceful posture. She tries
to keep the green grass around her and the parasol
open. How lovely to stand naked in the pure
sunlight conversing with an imaginary friend! Maude
is talking very elegantly now, as if dressed all in
white and the church bells tolling: she is in her own
private corner of the universe, a nun-like creature
telling off the Psalms in Moon (1). She stoops to
stroke the head of a dove, so soft and feathery, so
warm with love, a piece of blood wrapped in velvet.
The sun is shining brilliantly and now, oh how good
it is, it is warming her cool hinder parts. Like a
merciful angel she spreads her legs apart: the dove
flutters between her legs, the wings brush lightly
against the marble arch. The little dove is fluttering
madly; she must squeeze his soft little head between
her legs. Still Sunday and not a soul in this corner
of the universe. Maude is talking to Maude. She is

---

(1) «Moon» is cipher language for the blind.

saying that if a bull came along and mounted her she would not budge an inch. It feels good, doesn't it, Maude, she whispers to herself. It feels so good. Why don't I come here every day and stand this way? Really, Maude, this is wonderful. You take off all your clothes and stand in the grass; you bend over to feed the pigeons and the bull climbs up over the hill and puts his terrible long thing inside you. Oh God, but it's terribly good to have it this way. The clean green grass, the smell of his warm hide, that long, smooth thing he moves in and out—O God, I want him to fuck me like he would a cow. O God, I want to fuck and fuck and fuck...

4

The following evening my old friend Stanley drops in to see me. Maude detests Stanley, and with good reason, because every time he looks her way he blows her down with a silent curse. His look says very clearly—«If I had that bitch in my place I'd take the axe to her and hew her down.» Stanley is full of submerged hatreds. He looks as gaunt and wiry now as he did when he came out of the cavalry at Fort Oglethorpe years ago. What he's looking for is something to murder. He'd murder me, his best friend, if he could get away with it. He's foul on the world, green all the way back to the bile with accumulated hatred and vengeance. What he comes around for is to make sure that I am not making any progress, that I'm sinking deeper and deeper. «You'll never get anywhere,» he says. «You're like me— you're weak, you have no ambition.» We have one

ambition in common, which we make light of: to
write. There was more hope for us fifteen years ago,
when we were writing letters to one another. Fort
Oglethorpe was a good place for Stanley; it made him
a drunkard, a gambler, a thief. It made his letters
interesting. They were never about the army life
but about exotic, romantic writers whom he tried to
imitate when he wrote. Stanley should never have
come back North; he should have gotten off the train
at Chickamauga, wrapped himself in tobacco leaves
and cowdung, and taken himself a squaw. Instead
he came back North to the funeral parlor, found
himself a fat Polish wench with fertile ovaries,
saddled himself with a brood of little Poles, and
tried in vain to write standing up over the kitchen
tubs. Stanley rarely talked about anything in the
present; he preferred to spin incredible yarns about
the men he loved and admired in the army.

Stanley had all the bad traits of the Poles. He
was vain, vitriolic, violent, generous in a false way,
romantic as a brokendown hack, loyal as a fool and
deeply treacherous to boot. Above all, he was simply
corroded with envy and jealousy.

There is one thing I like about the Poles—their
language. Polish, when it is spoken by intelligent
people, puts me in ecstasy. The sound of the
language evokes strange images in which there is
always a greensward of fine spiked grass in which
hornets and snakes play a great part. I remember
days long back when Stanley would invite me to visit
his relatives; he used to make me carry a roll of
music because he wanted to show me off to these rich
relatives. I remember this atmosphere well because
in the presence of these smooth-tongued, overly
polite, pretentious and thoroughly false Poles I always
felt miserably uncomfortable. But when they spoke
to one another, sometimes in French, sometimes in

Polish, I sat back and watched them fascinatedly. They made strange Polish grimaces, altogether unlike our relatives who were stupid barbarians at bottom. The Poles were like standing snakes fitted up with collars of hornets. I never knew what they were talking about but it always seemed to me as if they were politely assassinating some one. They were all fitted up with sabres and broad-swords which they held in their teeth or brandished fiercely in a thundering charge. They never swerved from the path but rode rough-shod over women and children, spiking them with long pikes beribboned with blood-red pennants. All this, of course, in the drawing-room over a glass of strong tea, the men in butter-colored gloves, the women dangling their silly lorgnettes. The women were always ravishingly beautiful, the blonde houri type garnered centuries ago during the Crusades. They hissed their long polychromatic words through tiny, sensual mouths whose lips were softs as geraniums. These furious sorties with adders and rose petals made an intoxicating sort of music, a steel-stringed zithery slipper-gibber which could also register anomalous sounds like sobs and falling jets of water.

On the way home we always rode through dreary, sombre patches of land studded with gas tanks, smoking chimneys, grain elevators, car barns and other bio-chemical emulsions of our glorious civilization. The way home bore in on me the fact that I was just a shit, another piece of stinking offal like the burning garbage piles in the vacant lots. All the way in there would be the acrid stench of burning chemicals, burning refuse, burning offal. The Poles were a race apart and their language clung to me like smoking ruins from a past I had never known. How was I to guess, then, that one day I would be riding through their outlandish world in a

train filled with Jews who shivered with fear when
ever a Pole addressed them? Yes, I would be having
a fight in French (me the little shit from Brooklyn)
with a Polish nobleman—because I couldn't bear to
see these Jews cowering in fear. I would be traveling
to the estate of a Polish count to watch him paint
maudlin pictures for the Salon d'Automne. How was
I to imagine such an eventuality, riding through the
swamp lands with my savage, bile-ridden friend
Stanley? How could I believe that, weak and lacking
ambition, I should one day tear myself away, learn
a new language, learn a new way of living, like it,
lose myself, sever all ties, look back on this which I
am riding through as if it were a night-mare told by
an idiot in a railway station on a bitter cold night
when you change trains in a trance?

On this particular night little Curley happened to
drop in. Maude had no use for Curley either, apart
from the thrill he gave her when he slyly caressed
her bottom as she stooped to put the meat in the
oven. Curley always thought he did these things
without any one noticing him; Maude always let
people do these things to her as if they happened by
accident; Stanley always made it very clear that he
saw nothing, but under the table you could distinctly
observe him pouring nitric acid over his rusty brass
knuckles. Myself, I noticed everything, even the new
cracks in the plaster wall which I stared at so intensely
when alone that, if I were given time, I could read
back at top speed, without missing a comma or a dash,
the whole history of the human race leading up to
the particular square inch of plaster on which my
eyes were focused.

This particular night it is warm outdoors and the
grass is velvety. There is no reason to stay indoors
and silently murder one another. Maude is eager for
us to evacuate; we are polluting the sanctuary.

Besides, she is going to menstruate in a day or two
and that makes her more than ever weepy, miserable
and despondent. The best thing would be for me to
step outdoors and accidentally walk into a fast truck;
that would be such a marvelous relief to her that it
seems incredible to me now why I never did a little
thing like that to oblige her. Many a night she must
have sat alone and prayed that I would come back
to her on a stretcher. She was the sort of woman
who, if a thing like that were to occur, would say
very frankly—«Thank God, he's done it at last!»

We walked to the park and lay flat on our backs
in the short grass. The sky was friendly and peaceful,
a bowl without limits; I felt strangely at ease,
detached, serene as a sage. To my surprise, Stanley
was whistling a different tune. He was saying that
I owed it to myself to make a break, that as a friend
of mine he was going to help me do what I couldn't
do alone.

«You leave it to me,» he muttered, «I'll fix it for
you. But don't come to me afterwards and say that
you regret it,» he added.

How was he going to fix it? I demanded.

That was none of my business, he gave me to
understand. «You're desperate, aren't you? You
want to get rid of her, that's all, isn't that so?»

I shook my head and smiled, smiled because it
seemed utterly preposterous that Stanley, of all
people, could be so confident of arranging such a
decisive coup. He acted as if he had plotted it all
out a long time ago, as if he had merely been waiting
for the opportune moment to broach the subject.
He wanted to know more about Mara—was I
absolutely sure of her?

«Now about the kid,» he said, in his usual cold-
blooded way, «that's going to be tough on you. But
you'll forget about her after a time. You were never

meant to be a father. Only, don't come to me and
ask me to fix it up again, understand? When I do
this job it's going to be settled once and for all. I
don't believe in half-way measures. Now, if I were
you I'd go to Texas or some place like that. Don't
ever come back here! You've got to start all over
again, as if you were just beginning your life. You
can do it, if you want to. *I can't. I'm trapped.*
That's why I want to help you. I'm not doing this
for your sake—I'm doing it because it's what I'd like
to do myself. You can forget me too while you're
at it. I'd forget everybody if I were in your boots.»

Curley was fascinated. Wanted to know immediately if he couldn't go with me.

«Don't take him along, whatever you do!» Stanley
blurted savagely. «He's no good—he'd be in the way,
that's all. Besides, he's not to be trusted.»

Curley was hurt and he showed it.

«Listen, don't rub it in,» I said. «I know he's no
good, but what the hell...»

«I don't mince matters,» said Stanley bluntly. «As
far as I'm concerned, I don't want to see him ever
again. He can go away and die for all I care. You're
soft—that's why you're in such a lousy mess. I
haven't any friends, you know that. I don't want
any. I don't do anything for anybody out of pity.
If he's hurt it's too bad, but he'll have to swallow it
as best he can. I'm talking seriously. I mean
business.»

«How do I know I can trust you to handle this
right?»

«You don't have to trust me. One day—I won't
say when—it'll happen. You won't know how it
happened. You'll get the surprise of your life. And
you won't be able to change your mind because it'll
be too late. You'll be free whether you like it or
not—that's all I can tell you. It's the last thing I'll

do for you—after that you take care of yourself. Don't write me that you're starving because I won't pay any attention to you. Sink or swim, that's the size of it.»

He got up and brushed himself off. «I'm going,» he said. «It's settled then?»

«O. K.,» I said.

«Give us a quarter,» he said, as he was about to walk off.

I didn't have a quarter on me. I turned to Curley. He nodded, to indicate he understood, but made no move to hand it over.

«Give it to him, will you,» I said, «I'll return it to you when we get home.»

«*To him?*» said Curley, looking at Stanley contemptuously. «Let him beg for it!»

Stanley turned his back and walked off. He had the loping gait of a cowboy. Even from the back he looked like a thug.

«The dirty bastard!» mumbled Curley. «I could stick a knife in him.»

«I almost hate him myself,» said I. «He'll wither and die before he softens. I don't know why he's doing this for me—it's not like him.»

«How do you know what he's going to do? How can you trust a guy like that?»

«Curley,» I said, «he wants to do me a favor. Something tells me it's going to be unpleasant, but I don't see any other way out. You're just a kid. You don't know what it's all about. I feel relieved somehow. It's a turn in the road.»

«Reminds me of my father,» said Curley bitterly. «I hate him, hate his guts. I'd like to see the two of them hanging from the same post: I'd like to burn them up, the dirty bastards.»

A few days later I was sitting in Ulric's studio

waiting for Mara to arrive with her friend Lola Jackson. Ulric had never met Mara.

«You think she's good stuff, eh?» he was saying, meaning Lola. «We won't have to stand on too much ceremony, what?»

These feelers which Ulric always put out amused me highly. He liked to be guaranteed that the evening would not be entirely wasted. He was never certain of me when it came to women or friends; in his humble opinion I was just a wee bit too reckless.

However, the moment he laid eyes on them he felt reassured. In fact, he was bowled over. He took me aside almost at once to congratulate me on my taste.

Lola Jackson was a queer girl. She had only one defect—the knowledge that she was not pure white. That made her rather difficult to handle, at least in the preliminary stages. A little too intent upon impressing us with her culture and breeding. After a couple of drinks she unlimbered enough to show us how supple her body was. Her dress was too long for some of the stunts she was eager to demonstrate. We suggested that she take it off, which she did, revealing a stunning figure which showed to advantage in a pair of sheer silk hose, a brassiere and pale blue panties. Mara decided to follow suit. Presently we urged them to dispense with the brassieres. There was a huge divan on which the four of us huddled in a promiscuous embrace. We turned the lights down and put on a record. Lola thought it too warm to keep anything on except the silk stockings.

We had about a square yard of space in which to dance flesh to flesh. Just as we had changed partners, just as the tip of my cock had buried itself in Lola's dark petals, the phone rang. It was Hymie Laub-

scher telling me in a grave and urgent voice that
the messengers had declared a strike. «You'd better
be on hand early to-morrow morning, H. M.,» he
said. «No telling what will happen. I wouldn't
have bothered you if it hadn't been for Spivak.
He's on your trail. He says you ought to have
known that the boys were going on strike. He's
hired a fleet of taxi cabs already. There's going to
be hell to-morrow.»

«Don't let him know you got in touch with me,»
I said. «I'll be there bright and early.»

«*Are you having a good time?*» piped Hymie. «No
chance of my horning in on the party, is there?»

«I'm afraid not, Hymie. If you're looking for
something I can recommend you one up at I. Q.
office—you know, the one with the big teats. She
goes off duty at midnight.»

Hymie was trying to tell me something about his
wife's operation. I couldn't make it out because
Lola had slipped up alongside me and was petting
my cock. I hung up in the midst of it and pretended
to explain to Lola what the message was about. I
knew Mara would be on my heels in a moment.

I had just gotten it half way in, Lola's back bent
almost in half, and still talking about the messenger
boys, when I heard Ulric and Mara stirring. I pulled
away and picking up the phone I called a number
at random. To my astonishment a woman's voice
answered sleepily—«Is that you, dear? I've just
been dreaming about you.» I said *Yes?* She went
on, as if still half asleep: «Do hurry home, won't
you dear? I've been waiting and waiting. Tell me
you love me...»

«I'll make it as quick as I can, *Maude*,» I said, in
my own clear natural voice. «The messengers are
on strike. I wish you'd call...»

«*What's that?* What are you saying? What *is* this?» came the woman's startled voice.

«I said rush a few waybills (1) up to D.T. office and ask Costigan to...» The phone clicked.

The three of them were lying on the divan. I could smell them in the dark. «I hope you don't have to go,» said Ulric in a smothered voice. Lola was lying over him, her arms around his neck. I reached between her legs and caught hold of Ulric's pecker. I was on my knees, in a good position to tackle Lola from the rear should Mara suddenly decide to go to the lavatory. Lola raised herself a bit and sank down on Ulric's prick with a savage grunt. Mara was tugging at me. We lay down on the floor beside the divan and went to it. In the midst of it the hall door opened, the light was suddenly switched on, and there stood Ulric's brother with a woman. They were a bit drunk and had apparently returned at an early hour to do a bit of quite fucking on their own.

«Don't let *us* stop you,» said Ned, standing in the doorway inspecting the scene as if it were an every day affair. Suddenly he pointed to his brother and shouted—«Holy Smokes! What's happened? You're bleeding!»

We all looked at Ulric's bleeding cock: from the navel down to his knees he was a mass of blood. It was rather embarrassing for Lola.

«I'm sorry, » she said, the blood dripping down her thighs, «I didn't think it would be so soon.»

«That's all right,» said Ulric, «what's a little blood between bouts?»

I went with him to the lavatory, pausing a moment on the way to be presented to his brother's · girl.

---

(1) Messengers, relayed from their own office to another to help out when there is a shortage.

She was pretty far gone. I held out my mitt to
shake hands and in reaching for it she accidentally
made a pass for my prick. That made everybody
feel a little easier.

«A great work-out,» said Ulric, washing himself
assiduously. «Do you think I might take another
crack at it? I mean, there's no particular harm
getting a little blood on the end of your cock, is
there? I feel as though I'd like to have another go
at it, what say?»

«It's good for the health,» I said cheerily. «Wish
I could swap places with you.»»

«I wouldn't be averse to that at all,» said he, sliding his tongue lecherously over his lower lip. «Do
you think you can manage it?»

« Not to-night,» I said. «I'm going now. I've got
to be fresh and spruce to morrow.»

«Are you going to take Mara with you?»

«I sure am. Tell her to come in here a minute,
will you?»

When Mara opened the door I was powdering my
cock. We fell into a clutch at once.

«What about trying it in the tub?»

I turned the warm water on and threw in a bar
of soap. I soaped her crotch with tingling fingers.
By this time my prick was like an electric eel. The
warm water felt delicious. I was chewing her lips,
her ears, her hair. Her eyes sparkled as if she had
been struck by a fistful of stars. Every part of her
was smooth nad satiny and her breasts were ready
to burst. We got out and, letting her straddle me,
I sat on the edge of the tub. We were dripping
wet. I reached for a towel with one hand and dried
her a bit down the front. We lay down on the bath
mat and she slung her legs around my neck. I moved
her around like one of those legless toys which
illustrate the principle of gravity.

118 *THE ROSY CRUCIFIXION*

Two nights later I was in a depressed mood. I was lying on the couch in the dark, my thoughts shifting rapidly from Mara to the bloody, futile telegraph life. Maude had come over to say something to me and I had made the mistake of running my hand carelessly up her dress as she stood there complaining about something or other. She had walked off insulted. I hadn't been thinking about fucking her—I just did it naturally, like you'd stroke a cat. When she was awake you couldn't touch her that way. She never took a fuck on the wing, as it were. She thought fucking had something to do with love: carnal love, perhaps. A lot of water had passed under the bridge since the days when I first knew her, when I used to twirl her around on the end of my cock sitting on the piano stool. Now she acted like a cook preparing a difficult menu. She would make up her mind deliberately, letting me know in her sly, repressed way that the time had come for it. Maybe that's what she had come for a moment ago, though it was certainly odd the way she begged for it. Anyway I didn't give a fuck whether she wanted it or not. Suddenly, though, thinking of Stanley's words, I began to have a yen for her. «Get in your last licks,» I kept saying to myself. Well, maybe I'd go up and tackle her in her pseudo-sleep. Spivak came to mind. He was watching me like a hawk the last few days. My hatred for the telegraph life was concentrated in my hatred for him. He was the bloody cosmococcus in person. Must polish him off somehow before they fire me. I kept thinking how I could lure him to a dark wharf and have some obliging friend push him overboard. I thought of Stanley. Stanley would relish a job like that....

How long was he going to keep me on tenterhooks? I wondered. And what form would it take, this

abrupt deliverance? I could see Mara coming to
meet me at the station. We'd start a new life together, righto! What sort of life I didn't dare think.
Maybe Kronski would raise another three hundred
dollars. And those millionaires she talked about,
they ought to be good for something. I began
thinking in thousands—a thousand for her old man,
a thousand for travelling expenses, a thousand to
tide us over for a few months. Once in Texas, or
some God-forsaken place like that, I'd have more
confidence. I'd stop off at newspaper offices with
her—she always made a good impression—and I'd
ask permission to write a little sketch. I'd walk in
on business men and show them how to write their
ads. In hotel lobbies I'd be sure to meet up with
a friendly soul, some one who would give me a break.
The country was so big, so many lonely people, so
many generous souls ready to give, if only they met
the right individual. I would be sincere and forthright. Say we get to Mississippi, some old ramshackle
hotel. A man walks up to me out of the darkness
and asks me how I feel. A guy just aching for a
little chat. I'd introduce him to Mara. We'd saunter
out arm in arm and stroll about in the moonlight,
the trees strangled with lianas, the magnolias rotting
on the floor of the earth, the air humid, sultry, making things rot—and men too. To him I'd be a fresh
breeze from the North. I'd be honest, sincere,
almost humble. Would put my cards on the table
immediately. There you are, man, there's the situation. I love this place. I want to stay here all my
life. That would scare him off a little, because you
don't start talking that way to a Southerner straight
off. *What's your game?* Then I'd speak up again,
soft and distant, like a clarinet with a wet sponge
plugging the bell. I'd give him a little melody out
of the cold North, a sort of chill factory whistle on

a frosty morning. Mister man, I don't like the cold.
No sir! I want to do some honest work, anything
to keep alive. *Can I talk straight?* You won't think
I'm cracked, will you? It's lonely up there in the
North. Yes sir, we go blue with fright and loneliness. Live in little rooms, eat with knives and
forks, carry watches, liver pills, bread crumbs, saus-
ages. Don't know where we're at up there, *honest*,
Mister. We're frightened to death we'll say something, something real. Don't sleep.... not really.
Thrash around all night praying for the world to
end. We don't believe in anything: we hate everybody, we poison one another. Everything so tight
and solid, everything riveted with cruel hot irons.
Don't make a thing with our hands. Sell. Buy and
sell. Buy and sell, that's all, Mister....

I could visualize the old gentleman distinctly as
he stood under a droopy tree mopping his feverish
brow. He wouldn't run away from me, like others
had. I wouldn't let him! I'd hold him spell-
bound—the whole night long, if I felt like it. Make
him give us a cool wing in the big house near the
bayou. The darkie would appear with a tray, serving mint juleps. We would be adopted. «*This is
your home, son; stay as long as you like.*» No desire
to play tricks on a man like that. No, if a man
treated me that way I'd be faithful to him, to the
bitter end....

It was all so real I felt I had to tell Mara about
it right away. I went to the kitchen and began a
letter. «Dear Mara—All our problems are solved....»
I went on as though it were all clear and definitive.
Mara looked different to me now. I saw myself
standing under the big trees talking to her in a
way that surprised me. We were walking arm in
arm through the thick growths, conversing like
human beings. There was a big yellow moon out

and the dogs were yapping at our heels. It seemed
to me we were married and the blood ran deep and
still between us. She would be craving a pair of
swans for the little lake in back of the house. No
money talk, no Neon lights, no chop suey. How
wonderful just to breathe naturally, to never hurry,
never get anywhere, never do anything important—
except live! She thought so too. She had changed,
Mara. Her body had grown fuller, heavier; she
moved slowly, talked calmly, became silent for long
periods, all so real and natural like. Should she
wander off by herself I felt certain she would come
back unchanged, smelling sweeter, moving more
sure-footedly...

«Do you get it, Mara? Do you see how it will be?»
There I was, putting it all down so honestly,
almost weeping with the sheer wonder of it, when
I heard Maude paddling slip-slop through the hall.
I gathered the sheets together and folded them. I
put my fist over them and waited for her to say
something.

«Who are you writing to?» she asked—just as
direct and sure as that.

«To some one I know,» I answered calmly.

«A woman, I suppose?»

«Yes, a woman. A girl, to be more exact.» I
said it heavily, solemnly, still thick with the trance,
the image of her under the big trees, the two swans
floating aimlessly on the unruffled lake. If you
want to know, I thought to myself, I will tell you.
I don't see why I should lie any more. I don't hate
you, as I once did. I wish you could love as I do
—it would make it so much easier. I don't want
to hurt you. I just want you to let me be.

«You're in love with her. You don't need to
answer—I know it's so.»

«Yes, that's true—I *am* in love. I found some one I really love.»

«Maybe you'll treat her better than you did me.»

«I hope so,» I said, still calm, still hoping she'd hear me through to the end. «We never really loved each other, Maude, that's the truth, isn't it?»

«You never had any respect for me—as a human being,» she replied. «You insult me in front of your friends; you run around with other women; you don't even show any interest in your child.»

«Maude, I wish just for once that you wouldn't talk that way. I wish we could talk about it without bitterness.»

«*You* can—because you're happy. You've found a new toy.»

«It isn't that, Maude. Listen, supposing all the things you say are true—what difference does it make *now?* Supposing we were on a boat and it was sinking...»

«I don't see why we have to suppose things. You're going to take up with some one else and I'm going to be left with all the drudgery, all the responsibilities.»

«I know,» I said, looking at her with genuine tenderness. «I want you to try to forgive me for that—can you? What good would it do to stay? We wouldn't ever learn to love each other. Can't we part friends? I don't mean to leave you in the lurch. I'm going to try to do my share—I mean it.»

«That's easy to say. You're always promising things you can't fulfill. You'll forget us the moment you walk out of this house. *I know you.* I can't afford to be generous with you. You deceived me bitterly, from the very beginning. You've been selfish, utterly selfish. I never thought it possible for a human being to become so cruel, so callous, so thoroughly inhuman. Why, I hardly recognize you now. It's the first time you've acted like a...»

«Maude, it's cruel what I'm going to say, but I have to say it. I want you to understand something. Maybe I had to go through this with you in order to learn how to treat a woman. It isn't altogether my fault—fate had something to do with it too. You see, the moment I set eyes on her I knew...»

«Where did you meet her?» said Maude, her feminine curiosity suddenly getting the better of her.

«In a dance hall. She's a taxi girl. Sounds bad, I know. But if you saw her...»

«I don't want to see her. I don't want to hear anything more about her. I just wondered.» She gave me a quick pitying look. «And you think she's the woman who will make you happy?»

«You call her a woman—she's not, she's just a young girl.»

«So much the worse. Oh, what a fool you are!»

«Maude, it's not like you think, not at all. You mustn't judge, really. How can you pretend to know? And in any case I don't care. I've made up my mind.»

At this she hung her head. She looked indescribably sad and weary, like a human wreck hanging from a meat hook. I looked down at the floor, unable to bear the sight of her face.

We sat like that a full few minutes, neither of us daring to look up. I heard a sniffle and as I looked up I saw her face quivering with pain. She put her rams forward on the table and, weeping and sobbing, she flung her head down, pressing her face against the table. I had watched her weep many times but this was the most ghastly, unresisting sort of surrender. It unnerved me. I stood over her and put my hand on her shoulder. I tried to say something but the words stuck in my throat. Not knowing what to do I rubbed my hand over her hair, caressed it sadly, and distantly too, as thought it were the head of a strange, wounded animal I had come upon in the dark.

«Come, come,» I managed to gurgle, «this won't do any good.»

Her sobs redoubled. I knew I had said the wrong thing. I couldn't help myself. No matter what she were to do—even if she were to kill herself—I couldn't change the situation. I had expected tears. I had also half expected to do this very thing— stroke her hair as she wept and say the wrong thing. My mind was on the goal. Is she would get through with it and go to bed I could sit down and finish the letter. I could add a postscript about cauterizing the wound. I could say with honest joy and sorrow mixed—«It's over.»

That's what was going on in my mind as I stroked her hair. I was never further from her. While I felt the quivering gasps of her body I also felt pleasure at thinking how serene she would be a week hence when I had gone. «You will be feeling like a new woman,» I thought to myself. «And now you are going through all this anguish—it's right and natural, of course, and I don't blame you for it— only get done with it!» I must have given her a shake to punctuate the thought, for at that instant she suddenly sat erect and, looking at me with wild, hopeless, tear-stained eyes, she flung her arms around me and pulled me to her in a frantic, maudlin em- brace. «You won't leave me yet, will you?» she sobbed, kissing me with salty, hungry lips. «Put your arms around me, please. Hold me tight. God, I feel so lost!» She was kissing me with a passion I had never felt in her before. She was putting body and soul into it—and all the sorrow that stood between us. I slid my hands under her arms-pits and raised her gently to her feet. We were as close as lovers could be, swaying as only the human animal can sway when he is given utterly to another. Her kimono slipped pone and she was naked underneath. I slid my hand down the small of her back, over her plump buttocks, wedged my fingers deep into the big crack, pressing her against me, chewing her lips, biting her ear lobes, her neck, licking her eyes, the roots of ther hair. She got limp and heavy, closing her eyes, closing her mind. She sagged as though she were going to drop to the floor. I caught her up and carried her through the hall, up the flight of stairs, threw her on the bed. I fell over her, as if stupefied, and let her rip my things off. I lay on my back like a dead man, the only thing alive being my prick. I felt her mouth closing over it and the sock on my left foot slowly slipping off. I ran my fingers through her long hair, slid them round under her breast, moulded her bread basket which was soft and rubbery like. She was making some sort of wheeling motion in the dark. Her legs came down over my shoulders and her crotch was up against my lips. I slid her ass over my head, like you'd raise a pail of milk to slake a lazy thirst, and I drank and chewed and guzzled like a buzzard. She was so deep in heat that her teeth were clamped dangerously around the head of my cock. In that frantic, teary passion she had worked herself up to I had a fear that she might sink her teeth in deep, bite the end of it clean off. I had to tickle her to make her relax her jaws. It was fast, clean work after that—no tears, no love business, no promise me this and that. *Put me on the fucking block and fuck!* that's what she was asking for. I went at it with cold-blooded fury. This might be the very last fuck. Already she was a stranger to me. We were committing adultery, the passionate, incestuous kind which the Bible loves to talk about. Abraham went

into Sarah or Leander and he *knew* her. (Strange
italicizations in the English Bible.) But the way
those horny old patriarchs tackled their young and
old wives, sisters, cows and sheep, was very knowing.
They must have gone in head first, with all the cunning and skill of aged lechers. I felt like Isaac
fornicating with a rabbit in the temple. She was a
white rabbit with long ears. She had Easter eggs
inside her and she would drop them one by one in
a basket. I took a long think inside her, studying
every crevice, every slit and tear, every soft, round
bump that had swollen to the size of a shrivelled
oyster. She moved over and took a rest, reading it
like Braille (New York Point) with her inquisitive
fingers. She crouched on all fours like a she animal,
quivering and whinnying with undisguised pleasure.
Not a human word out of her, not a sign that she
knew any language except this block-and-tackle-
subgum-one-ton-blow-the-whistle sort. The gentleman
from Mississipi had completely faded out: he had
slipped back into the swampy limbo which forms the
permanent floor of the continents. One swan
remained, an octaroon with ruby duck lips fastened
to a pale blue head. Soon we'd be in clover, the
blow-off, with plums and apricots falling from the sky.
The last push, the drag of choked, white-hot ashes,
and then two logs lying side by side waiting for the
axe. Fine finish. Royal flush. I *knew* her and she
knew me. Spring will come again and Summer and
Winter. She will sway in somebody else's arms, go
into a blind fuck, whinny, blow off, do the crouch
and sag—but not with me. I've done my duty, given
her the last rites. I closed my eyes and played dead
to the world. Yes, we would learn to live a new life,
Mara and I. I must get up early and hide the letter
in my coat pocket. It's strange sometimes how you
wind up affairs. You always think you're going to

put the last word in the ledger with a broad flourish; you never think of the automaton who closes the account while you sleep. It's all the strictest kind of double-entry. It gives you the creeps, it's all so nicely calculated.

The axe is falling. Last ruminations. Honeymoon Express and all aboard: Memphis, Chattanooga, Nashville, Chickamauga. Past snowy fields of cotton... alligators yawning in the mud... the last apricot is rotting on the lawn... the moon is full, the ditch is deep. the earth is black, black, black.

VOLUME TWO

5

The next morning it was like after a storm—
breakfast as usual, a touch for carfare, a dash for the
subway, a promise to take her to the movies after
dinner. For her it was probably just a bad dream
which she would do her best to forget during the
course of the day. For me it was a step towards
deliverance. No mention of the subject was ever
made again. But it was there all the time and it
made things easier between us. What she thought I
don't know, but what I thought was very clear and
definite. Every time I assented to one of her
requests or demands I said to myself: «Fine, is that
all you want of me? I'll do anything you like
except give you the illusion that I am going to live
the rest of my life with you.»

She was inclined now to be more lenient with
herself when it came to satisfying her bestial nature.
I often wondered what she told herself in making
excuses to herself for these extra-nuptial, pre- or post-
morganatic bouts. Certainly she put her heart and
soul into them. She was a better fucker now than in
the early days when she used to put a pillow under
her ass and try to kiss the ceiling. She was fucking
with desperation, I guess. Fuck for fuck's sake and
the devil take the hindmost.

A week had passed and I hadn't seen Mara. Maude
had asked me to take her to a theatre in New York,
a theatre just opposite the dance hall. I sat

throughout the performance thinking of Mara so close
and yet so far away. I thought of her so insistently
and unremittingly that as we were leaving the theatre
I gave voice to an impulse which I was powerless to
quelch. «How would you like to go up there?» I
said, pointing to the dance hall, «and meet her?» It
was a cruel thing to say and I felt sorry for her the
moment it left my mouth. She looked at me, Maude,
as if I had struck her with my fist. I apologized at
once and, taking her by the arm, I led her quickly
away in the opposite direction, saying as I did so—
«It was just an idea. I didn't mean to hurt you.
I thought you might be curious, that's all.» She made
no answer. I made no further efforts to smooth the
thing over. In the subway she slipped her arm in
mine and let it rest there, as if to say—«I understand,
you were just tactless and thoughtless, as usual.» On
the way home we stopped off at her favorite ice
cream parlor and there, over a plate of French ice
cream which she doted on, she unlimbered sufficiently
to eke out a thin conversation about domestic trifles,
a sign that she had dismissed the incident from her
mind. The French ice cream, which she regarded as
a luxury, combined with the opening of a fresh
wound, had the effect of making her amorous.
Instead of undressing upstairs in the bed-room, as she
did ordinarily, she went to the bathroom which
adjoined the kitchen and, leaving the door open, she
took off her things one by one, leisurely, studiedly,
almost like a strip-teaser, calling me in finally as she
was combing out her hair to show me a blue mark on
her thigh. She was standing there naked except for
her shoes and stockings, her hair flowing luxuriantly
down her back.

I examined the mark carefully, as I knew she
wanted me to, touching her lightly here and there
to see if there were any other tender spots which she

might have overlooked; at the same time I kept up a
running fire of solicitous queries in a calm, matter of
fact voice which enabled her to prime herself for a
cold-blooded fuck without admitting to herself that
that was what she was doing. If I said to her, as
I did, in the calm, dull, professional voice of the
M.D.—«I think you'd better lie on the table in the
kitchen where I can examine you better»—she would
do so without the least coaxing, spreading her legs
wide apart and letting me insert a finger without a
qualm, because now by this time she remembered that
since a fall which she had had some time ago there
was a little bump inside her, at least so she thought;
it worried her, this bump; perhaps if I would put my
finger in ever so gently she could track it down, and
so on and so forth. Nor did it appear to disturb her
in the least when I suggested that she lie there a
moment, on the table, while I removed my clothes
because it was getting too warm for me in the kitchen,
next to the red hot stove, *and so on and so forth.*
And so I removed my things, all but my socks and
shoes, and with an erection fit to break a plate I
stepped blandly forth and resumed operations. Or
rather, I in turn had now become aware of things
past, such as bumps, bruises, spots, warts, birthmarks
et cetera, and would she kindly give *me* the once
over while we were at it, and then we would go to
bed because it was getting late and I didn't want to
tire her out.

Strangely enough she wasn't tired at all, she
confessed, getting down from the table and solicitously squeezing my cock and then my balls and
then the root of my cock, all with such firm, discreet
and delicate manipulations that I almost gave her a
squirt in the eye. After that she was curious to see
how much taller I was than she, so first we stood
back to back and then front to front; even then,

when it was jumping between her legs like a fire-
cracker, she pretended to be thinking of feet and
inches, saying that she ought to take her shoes off
because her heels were high, *and so on and so forth.*
And so I made her sit down on the kitchen chair and
slowly I pulled off her shoes and stockings, and she,
as I politely rendered her service, thoughtfully stroked
my cock, which was difficult to do being in the
position she was, but I graciously abetted her strategy
by moving in closer and hoisting her legs up in the
air at a right angle; then, without any more ado I
lifted her up by the hind quarters, shoved it in to
the hilt and carried her into the next room where
I tumbled her on to the couch, sank it in again and
went at it with sound and fury, she doing the same
and begging me in the most candid, non-professional,
non-casual language to hold it, to make it last, to
keep it in forever, and then as an after-thought to
wait a minute while she slipped out and turned over,
raising herself on her knees, her head sunk low, her
ass wriggling frantically, her thick gurgling voice
saying in the English language openly and admittedly
to herself for her own ears to hear and to recognize:
«Get it in all the way... please, please do... *I'm
horny.*»

Yes, on occasion she could trot out a word like
that, a vulgar word that would have made her curl
up with horror and indignation if she were in her
right senses, but now after the little pleasantries,
after the vaginal exploration by finger, after the
weight lifting and measuring contest, after the comparison of bruises, marks, bumps and what not, after
the delicately casual manipulation of prick and
scrotum, after the delicious French ice cream and the
thoughtless faux pas outside the theatre, to say nothing of all that had transpired in her imagination since
the cruel avowal a few nights ago, a word like «hor-

ny» was just the right and proper word to indicate
the temperature of the Bessemer steel furnace which
she had made of her inflamed cunt. It was the
signal to give her the works and spare nothing. It
meant something like this:—«No matter what I was
this afternoon or yesterday, no matter what I think
I am or how I detest you, no matter what you do
with that thing to-morrow or the day after, now I
want it and I want everything that goes with it: I
wish it were bigger and fatter and longer and juicier:
I wish you would break it off and leave it in there:
I don't care how many women you've fucked, I want
you to fuck *me*, fuck my cunt, fuck my ass off, fuck
and fuck and fuck. *I'm horny*, do you hear? I'm
so horny I could bite it off. Shove it in all the way,
harder, harder, break your big prick off and leave it
in there. *I'm horny*, I tell you...»

Usually after these bouts I awoke depressed. Looking at her with her clothes on and that grim, tight,
caustic, everyday expression about her mouth, studying her at the breakfast table, indifferently, not
having anything else to look at, I wondered sometimes
why I didn't take her for a walk some evening and
just push her off the end of a pier. I began to look
forward like a drowning man to that solution which
Stanley had promised and of which as yet there was
not the least sign. To cap it all I had written a
letter to Mara saying that we had to find a way out
soon or I would commit suicide. It must have been
a maudlin letter because when she telephoned me she
said it was imperative to see me immediately. This
shortly after lunch on one of those hectic days when
everything seemed to go wrong. The office was
jammed with applicants and even if I had had five
tongues and five pairs of arms and twenty-five telephones instead of three at my elbow, I could never
have hired as many applicants as were needed to fill

the sudden and inexplicable vacuum which had come about overnight. I tried to put Mara off until the evening but she would not be put off. I agreed to meet her for a few minutes at an address which she gave me, the apartment of a friend of hers, she said, where we would be undisturbed. It was in the Village.

I left a mob of applicants hanging at the rail, promising Hymie who was frantically telephoning for «waybills» that I'd be back in a few minutes. I jumped into a cab at the corner and got out in front of a doll's house with a miniature garden in front. Mara came to the door in a light mauve dress under which she was nude. She flung her arms around me and kissed me passionately.

«A wonderful little nest, this,» I said, holding her off to take a better look at the place.

«Yes, isn't it?» she said. «It belongs to Carruthers. He lives down the street with his wife; this is just a little den which he uses now and then. I sleep here sometimes when it's too late to go home».

I said nothing. I turned to look at the books— the walls were solidly lined with them. Out of the corner of my eye I saw Mara snatch something from the wall—seemed like a sheet of wrapping paper.

«What's that?» I said, not really curious but pretending to be.

«It's nothing,» she answered. «Just a sketch of his which he asked me to destroy».

«Let's see it!»

«You don't want to look at it—it's worthless»—and she started to crumple it up.

«Let's see it anyway,» I said, grasping her arm and snatching the paper from her hand. I opened it up and saw to my amazement that it was a caricature of myself with a dagger through the heart.

«I told you he was jealous,» she said. «It doesn't

mean anything—he was drunk when he did it. He's
been drinking a great deal lately. I have to watch
him like a hawk. He's just a big child, you know.
You mustn't think he hates you—he acts that way
with everybody who shows the least sign of interest
in me.»

«He's married, you said. What's the matter—
doesn't he get along with his wife?»

«She's an invalid,» said Mara, almost solemnly.

«In a wheel chair?»

«No-o-o, not exactly,» she replied, a faint irrepressible smile suffusing her lips. «Oh, why talk about
that now? What differences does it make? You
know I'm not in love with him. I told you once that
he had been very kind to me; now it's my turn to
look after *him*—he needs some one to steady him.»

«So you sleep here now and then—while he stays
with his invalid wife, is that it?»

«He sleeps here too sometimes: there are two cots,
if you notice. Oh, please,» she begged, «don't let's
talk about *him*. There's nothing for you to worry
about, can't you see, can't you believe me?» She
came close to me, put her arms around me. Without
ado I lifted her up and carried her over to the
couch. I pulled her dress up and, opening wide her
legs, I slipped my tongue into her crack. In a
moment she had me over her. When she had gotten
my cock out she took her two hands and opened her
cunt for me to slip it in. Almost at once she had
an orgasm, then another, and another. She got up
and washed herself quickly. As soon as she had
finished I followed suit. When I came out of the
bathroom she was lying on the couch with a cigarette
to her lips. I sat there a few minutes with my hand
between her legs, talking quietly to her.

«I've got to get back to the office,» I said, «and we
haven't had a chance to talk.»

«Don't go yet,» she begged, sitting upright and
putting her hand affectionately over my prick. I put
my arm around her and kissed her long and passionately. She had her fingers in my fly again and was
reaching for my prick when suddenly we heard some
one fumbling at the door knob.

«It's him,» she said, jumping quickly to her feet
and making for the door. «Stay where you are, it's
all right,» she threw out quickly as she glided
forward to meet him. I hadn't time to button my
fly. I stood up and casually straightened it out as
she flew into his arms with some silly joyous
exclamation.

«I've got a visitor,» she said. «I asked him to
come. He's leaving in a few minutes.»

«Hello,» he said, coming forward to greet me with
hand out and an amiable smile on his lips. He
showed no unusual surprise. In fact, he seemed
much more affable than he did the night I first met
him at the dance hall.

«You don't have to go this instant, do you?» said
he, undoing a bundle which he had brought with
him. «You might have a little drink first, won't
you? Which do you prefer—Scotch or Rye?»

Before I could say yes or no Mara had slipped out
to get some ice. I stood with my back partially
turned to him as he busied himself with the bottles
and, pretending to be interested in a book on the
shelf before me, I stealthily buttoned my fly.

«I hope you don't mind the looks of the place,»
he said. «This is just a little retreat, a hide-out,
where I can meet Mara and her little friends. She
looks cute in that dress, don't you think?»

«Yes,» I said, «it is rather attractive.»

«Nothing much there,» he said, nodding towards
the book shelves. «The good ones are all over at the
house.»

«Seems like quite a fine collection,» I said, glad to be able to divert the conversation to this ground.

«You're a writer, I understand—or so Mara tells me.»

«Not really,» I replied. «I'd like to be. You're probably one yourself, aren't you?»

He laughed. «Oh,» he said deprecatingly, as he measured out the drinks, «we all begin that way, I guess. I've scribbled a few things in my time—poems mostly. ˙ ˙ I don't seem to be able to do anything any more, except drink.»

Mara returned with the ice. «Come here,» he said, putting the ice on the table and throwing an arm around her waist, «you haven't kissed me yet.» She held her head up and cooly received the slobbery kiss which he planted on her lips.

«I couldn't stand it at the office any longer,» he said, squirting the fizz water into the glasses. «I don't know why I go to the damned place—there's nothing for me to do except look important and sign my name to silly papers.» He took a long swallow. Then, motioning to me to take a seat, he flung himself into the big Morris chair. «Ah, that's better,» he grunted, like a tired business man, though obviously he hadn't done a stroke of work. He beckoned to Mara. «Sit here a minute,» he said, patting the arm of the chair. «I want to talk to you. I've got good news for you.»

It was a highly interesting scene to witness after what had taken place just a few minutes ago. I wondered for a moment whether he were putting on an act for my benefit. He tried to pull her head down to give her another slobbery kiss but she resisted, saying—«Oh come, you're acting silly. Put that drink down, *please*. You'll be drunk in a moment and then there'll be no talking to you.»

She put her arm over his shoulder and ran her fingers through his hair.

«You see what a tyrant she is,» he said, turning to me. «God help the poor sap who marries her! Here I rush home to give her a piece of good news and...»

«Well, what is it?» Mara interrupted. «Why don't you come out with it?»

«Give me a chance and I'll tell you,» said Carruther, patting her rump affectionately. «By the way,» turning to me, «won't you pour yourself another drink? Pour me one too—that is, if you can get her permission. I have nothing to say around here. I'm just a general nuisance.»

This sort of banter and cross-fire promised to continue indefinitely. I had made up my mind that it was too late to go back to the office—the afternoon was shot. The second drink had put me in the mood to stay and see it through. Mara wasn't drinking, I noticed. I felt that she wanted me to leave. The good news got sidetracked, then forgotten. Or perhaps he had told her on the sly—he seemed to have dismissed the subject too abruptly. Perhaps while she was begging him to spill the news she had pinched his arm warningly. (Yes, what is the good news? And that pinch telling him not to dare blurt it out in front of me.) I was all at sea. I sat on the other couch and discreetly turned up the cover to see if there were any sheets on it. There weren't. Later I would hear the truth about the matter. We had a long way to go yet.

Carruthers was indeed a drunkard—a pleasant, sociable one too. One of those who drink and sober up at intervals. One of those who never think of food. One of those who have an uncanny memory, who observe everything with an eagle's eye and yet seem to be unconscious, sunk, dead to the world.

«Where's that drawing of mine?» he asked

suddenly, out of the blue, looking steadily at the spot on the wall where it had been hung.

«I took it down,» said Mara.

«So I see,» he snarled, but not too disagreeably. «I wanted to show it to your friend here.»

«He's already seen it,» said Mara.

«Oh, he has? Well then, it's all right. Then we're not concealing anything from him, are we? I don't want him to have any illusions about me. You know that if *I* can't have you I won't let anybody else have you, isn't that so? Otherwise everything's fine. Oh, by the way, I saw your friend Valerie yesterday. She wants to move in here—just for a week or two. I told her I'd have to speak to you about it—you're running the place.»

«It's your place,» said Mara testily, «you can do as you please. Only, if she comes in I move out. I have a place of my own to live in; I only come here to look after you, to prevent you from drinking yourself to death.»

«It's funny,» he said, turning to me, «how those two girls detest each other. On my word, Valerie is an adorable creature. She hasn't an ounce of brains, it's true, but then that's no great drawback; she has everything else a man wants. You know, I kept her for a year or more; we got along splendidly too—until this one came along,» and he nodded his head in Mara's direction. «Between you and me I think she's jealous of Valerie. You should meet her—you will if you stick around long enough. I have a hunch she's going to drop in before the day's over.»

Mara laughed in a way I had never heard her laugh before. It was a mean, ugly laugh. «That nit-wit,» she said scornfully, «why she can't even look at a man without getting into trouble. She's a walking abortion...»

«You mean your friend Florrie,» said Carruthers
with a stupid fixed grin.

«I wish you'd leave her name out of this,» said
Mara angrily.

«You've met Florrie, haven't you?» asked Carruthers, ignoring the remark. «Did you ever see a
more lascivious little bitch than that? And Mara is
trying to make a lady of her...» He burst out laughing. «It's strange, the trollops she picks up. Roberta
—that was another wild one for you. Always had to
ride around in limousines. Had a floating kidney,
she said, but what it really was... well, between
ourselves, she was just a lazy bum. But Mara had to
take her under her wing, after I kicked her out, and
nurse her. Really, Mara, for an intelligent girl, as
you pretend you are, you do behave like a fool
sometimes. Unless»—and he looked up at the ceiling
meditatively—«there's something else to it. You
never know»—still gazing at the ceiling—«what
makes two women stick together. Birds of a feather
flock together, that's the old saying. Still, it's strange.
I know Valerie, I know Florrie, I know this one, I
know them all—and yet, if you were to press me, I
don't know anything about them, not a thing. It's
another generation than the one I was brought up
with; they're like another species of animal. To
begin with, they have no moral sense, none of them.
They refuse to be house-broken; it's like living in a
menagerie. You come home and find a stranger lying
in your bed—and you excuse yourself for intruding.
Or they'll ask you for money in order to take a boy
friend to a hotel for the night. And if they get into
trouble you have to find a doctor for them. It's
exciting but some times it's a damned nuisance too.
It would be easier to keep rabbits, *what!*»

«That's the way he talks when he's drunk,» said

Mara, trying to laugh it off. «Go on, tell him some more about us. I'm sure he enjoys it.»

I wasn't so sure that he was drunk. He was one of those men who talk loosely drunk or sober, who say even more fantastic things, in fact, when they are sober. Embittered, disillusioned men, usually, who act as if nothing could surprise them any more; at bottom however, thoroughly sentimental, soaking their bruised emotional system in alcohol in order not to burst into tears at some unexpected moment. Women find them particularly charming because they never make any demands, never show any real jealousy, though outwardly they may go through all the motions. Often, as with Carruthers, they are saddled with crippled, thwarted wives, creatures whom out of weakness (which they call pity or loyalty) they allow themselves to be burdened with for life. To judge from his talk, Carruthers had no difficulty in finding attractive young women to share his love-nest. Sometimes there were two or three living with him at the same time. He probably had to make a show of jealousy, of possessiveness, in order not to be made an utter fool of. As for his wife, as I found out later, she was an invalid only to this extent— that her hymen was still intact. For years Carruthers had endured it like a martyr. But suddenly, when he realized that he was getting on in years, he had begun tearing around like a college boy. And then he had taken to drink. Why? Had he found that he was already too old to satisfy a healthy young girl? Had he suddenly regretted his years of abstinence? Mara, who had vouchsafed this information, was of course purposely vague and clinical about the subject. She did admit, however, that she had often slept with him on the same couch, leaving me to infer that obviously he never dreamed of molesting her. And then in the next breath adding that of course the

other girls were only too pleased to sleep with him;
the implication was, of course, that he only «molested»
those who liked to be molested. That there was any
particular reason why Mara should not want to be
molested I couldn't see. Or was I supposed to think
that he wouldn't molest a girl who had his welfare
so much at heart? We had quite a ticklish wrangle
about it as I was taking leave of her. It had been a
crazy day and night. I had gotten tight and had
fallen asleep on the floor. This was before dinner,
and the reason for it was that I was famished.
According to Mara, Carruthers had grown quite
incensed over my conduct; she had had quite a time
dissuading him from breaking a bottle over my head.
In order to mollify him she had lain down with him
on the couch for a while. She didn't say whether
he had tried to «molest» her or not. Anyway he had
only taken a cat nap; when he awoke he was hungry,
wanted to eat right away. During his sleep he had
forgotten that he had a visitor; seeing me lying on
the floor sound asleep he had become angry again.
Then they had gone out together and had a good
meal; on the way home she had induced him to buy
a few sandwiches for me and some coffee. I
remembered the sandwiches and the coffee—it was
like an interlude during a blackout. Carruthers had
forgotten about me with Valerie's arrival. That I
remembered too, though dimly. I remembered seeing
a beautiful young girl enter and fling her arms about
Carruthers. I remembered being handed a drink and
falling back again into a torpor. And then? Well
then, as Mara explained it, there had been a little
tiff between herself and Valerie. And Carruthers had
gotten blind drunk, had staggered out into the street
and disappeared.

«But you were sitting on his lap when I woke up!»
I said.

Yes, that was so, she admitted, but only after she had been out searching for him, wandering all through the Village, and finally picking him up on the steps of a church and bringing him home in a taxi.

«You must certainly think a lot of him to go to all that trouble.»

She didn't deny it. She was tired of going all over that ground again with me.

So that was how the evening had passed. And Valerie? Valerie had left in a huff, after smashing an expensive vase. And what was that bread knife doing alongside me, I wanted to know. *That?* Oh, that was some more of Carruther's tomfoolery. Pretending that he was going to cut my heart out. She hadn't even bothered to take the knife out of his hand. He was harmless, Carruthers. Wouldn't hurt a fly. Just the same, I thought to myself, it would have been wiser to wake me up. What else had happened, I wondered. Christ only knows what went on during the blackout. If she could let me put the blocks to her, knowing that Carruthers was apt to walk in at any moment, surely, she could let him «molest» her a few minutes (if only to pacify him), seeing that I was in a deep trance and would never be any the wiser.

However, it was now four in the morning and Carruthers was sound asleep on the couch. We were standing in a doorway on Sixth Avenue trying to come to some understanding. I was insisting that she let me take her home; she was trying to make me understand that it was too late.

«But I've taken you home before at an even later hour.» I was determined not to let her return to Carruthers' den.

«You don't understand,» she pleaded. «I haven't been home for several weeks. All my things are there.»

«Then you're living with him. Why didn't you say that in the first place?»

«I'm *not* living with him. I'm only staying there temporarily until I find a place to live. I'm not going back home any more. I had a bad quarrel with my mother. I walked out. Told them I'd never come back again.»

«And your father—what did he say?»

«He wasn't there when it happened. I know he must be heart-broken, but I couldn't stand it any longer.»

«I'm sorry,» I said, «if that's how it is. I suppose you're broke too. Let me walk you back—you must be fagged out.»

We started walking through the empty streets. She stopped suddenly and threw her arms around me. «You trust me, don't you?» she said, looking at me with tears in her eyes.

«Of course I do. But I wish you would find another place to stay. I can always dig up the price of a room. Why don't you let *me* help you?»

«Oh, I won't be needing any help now,» she said brightly. «Why, I almost forgot to tell you the good news! Yes, I'm going away for a few weeks—to the country. Carruthers is sending me to his cabin up in the North woods. The three of us are going— Florrie, Hannah Bell and myself. It'll be a real vacation. Maybe you can join us? You'll try, won't you? *Aren't you glad?*» She stopped to give me a kiss. «You see, he's not a bad sort,» she added. «He's not coming up himself. He wants to give us a treat. Now if he were in love with me, as you seem to think, wouldn't he want to go up there with me alone? He doesn't like *you*, that I admit. He's afraid of you—you're too serious. After all, you've got to expect him to have some feelings. If his wife were dead he'd undoubtedly ask me to marry him—

not because he's in love with me but because he wants
to protect me. *Do you see now?*»

«No,» I said, «I don't see. But it's all right. You
certainly need a vacation; I hope you'll enjoy yourself
there. As for Carruthers, no matter what you say
about him, I don't like him and I don't trust him.
And I'm not at all sure that he's acting from such
generous motives as you describe. I hope he croaks,
that's all, and if I could give him a drop of poison
I'd do it—without a qualm.»

«I'm going to write you every day,» she said, as
we stood at the door saying farewell.

«Mara, listen,» I said, drawing her close to me and
murmuring the words in her ear. «I had a lot to
tell you today and it's all gone up in smoke.»

«I know, I know,» she said feverishly.

«Maybe things will change when you're gone,» I
continued. «Something's got to happen soon—we
can't go on this way forever.»

«That's what I'm thinking too,» she said softly,
snuggling against me affectionately. «I hate this life.
I want to think it out when I'm up there and alone.
I don't know how I ever got into this mess.»

«Good,» I said, «maybe we'll get somewhere then.
You'll write, that's a promise?»

«Of course I will... *every day*,» she said, as she
turned to go.

I stood there a moment after she had turned in,
wondering whether I was a fool to let her go, wondering if it wouldn't be better to drag her out and just
smash a way through, wife or no wife, job or no job.
I walked off, still debating it in my mind, but my
feet dragging me towards home.

6

Well, she was off to the North woods. Just arrived, in fact. Those two pole cats had accompanied her and everything was just ducky. There were two wonderful backwoodsmen who looked after them, cooked their meals, showed them how to shoot the rapids, played the guitar and the harmonica for them on the back porch at night when the stars came out, and so on—all crammed on the back of a picture post-card showing the wonderful pine cones which drop from the pine trees up in Maine.

I immediately went round to Carruther's den to see if he were still in town. He was there all right and quite surprised, and not any too pleased, to see me. I pretended that I had come to borrow a book which had caught my fancy the other evening. He informed me dryly that he had given up the practise of lending out books long ago. He was thoroughly sober and obviously determined to freeze me out as quickly as possible. I noticed, as I was taking leave, that he had tacked up the picture of me with the dagger through the heart. He noticed that I had noticed it but made no reference to it.

I felt somewhat humiliated but vastly relieved just the same. For once she had told me the truth! I was so overjoyed that I rushed to the public library, buying a pad and an envelope on the way, and sat there till closing time writing her a huge letter. I told her to telegraph me—couldn't wait to receive word by mail. After mailing the letter I wrote out a long telegram and dispatched it to her. Two days later, not having heard from her, I sent another

telegram, a longer one, and after I had dispatched it
I sat down in the lobby of the Mc Alpin Hotel and
wrote her an even more voluminous letter than the
first one. The next day I received a short letter,
warm, affectionate, almost childish. No mention of
the first telegram. That made me quite frantic.
Perhaps she had given me a phoney address. But
why would she do that? Anyway, better telegraph
again! Demand full address and nearest telephone.
Had she received the second telegram and both letters?
«Keep a sharp lookout for mail and future telegrams.
Write often. Telegraph when possible. Advise when
returning. I love you. I'm mad about you. The
Cabinet Minister speaking.»

The «Cabinet Minister» must have done the trick.
Soon there came a telegram for Glahn the Hunter,
followed by a letter signed Victoria (1). God was
looking over her shoulder as she wrote. She had seen
a deer and she had followed it through the woods and
had lost her way. The backwoodsmen had found her
and carried her home. They were wonderfully simple
fellows, and Hannah and Florrie had fallen in love
with them. That is, they went canoeing with them
and sometimes slept in the woods with them all night.
She was coming back in a week or ten days. She
couldn't bear staying away from me longer than that.
Then this: «I am coming back to you, I want to be
your wife.» Just as simple as that, the way she put
it. I thought it marvelous. I loved her all the more
for being so direct, so simple, so frank and honest.
I wrote her three letters in a row, moving from place
to place, as I shuffled about in a delirium of ecstasy.

On fever hooks waiting for her return. She had
said she'd be back Friday night. Would telephone
me at Ulric's studio soon as she hit town. Friday

_____

(1) All characters from Knut Hamsun's books.

night came and I sat there until two in the morning
waiting for her phone call. Ulric, always skeptical,
said maybe she meant the following Friday. I went
home thoroughly dejected but certain I would hear
from her in the morning. Next day I telephoned
Ulric several times to inquire if he had had any word
from her. He was bored, thoroughly disinterested,
almost a little ashamed of me, I felt. At noon, as I
was leaving the office, I ran into MacGregor and his
wife sporting a new car. We hadn't seen each other
for months. He insisted on my having lunch with
them. I tried to get out of it but couldn't. «What's
the matter with you,» he said, «you're not yourself.
A woman again, I suppose. Jesus, when will you ever
learn to take care of yourself?»

During the lunch he informed me that they had
decided to take a ride out on Long Island, perhaps
spend the night there somewhere. Why couldn't I
come along? I said I had made a date with
Ulric. «That's all right,» he said, «bring your friend
Ulric along. I haven't much use for him, but if it'll
make you any happier, sure we'll pick up, why not?»
I tried to tell him that Ulric might not be so eager
to join us. He wouldn't listen. «Hell' come,» he
said, «you leave that to me. We'll go out to Montauk
Point or Shelter Island and just lie around and take
it easy—it'll do you good. As for that Jane you're
worrying about, why forget it! If she likes you she'll
come round by herself. Treat 'em rough, that's what
I always say, eh Tess?» and with that he gave his
wife a dig in the ribs that knocked the breath out
of her.

Tess Molloy was what you'd call a good-natured
Irish slob. She was about the homeliest woman I've
ever seen, broad in the beam, pock-marked, her hair
scant and stringy (she was getting bald), but jolly
and indolent, always ready to fight at the drop of the

hat. MacGregor had married her for purely practical reasons. They had never pretended to be in love with one another. There was scarcely even an animal affection between them since, as he had readily explained to me shortly after their marriage, sex didn't mean a thing to her. She didn't mind being diddled now and then, but she got no pleasure from it. «*Are you through?*» she would ask every now and then. If he took too long a time over it she would ask him to fetch her a drink or bring her something to eat. «I got so damned sore at her once that I brought her the newspaper to read. 'Now go ahead and read,' I says to her, 'and see that you don't miss the comic strip!'»

I thought we'd have a hard time persuading Ulric to come along. He had only met MacGregor a few times and each time he had shaken his head as though to say—«It beats me!» To my surprise Ulric greeted MacGregor quite cordially. He had just been promised a fat check for a new can of beans he was to do next week and he was in a mood to lay off work for a while. He had just been out to get himself a few bottles of liquor. There had been no phone call from Mara, of course. There wouldn't be any, not for a week or two, thought Ulric. *Have a drink!*

MacGregor was impressed by a magazine cover that Ulric had just finished. It was a picture of a man with a golf bag just setting out for the greens. Mac Gregor found it extremely life-like. «I didn't know you were that good,» he said with his customary tactlessness. «What do you get for a job like that, if I may ask?» Ulric told him. His respect deepened. Meanwhile his wife had spied a water color which she liked. «Did *you* do that?» she asked. Ulric nodded. «I'd like to buy it,» she said. «How much do you want for it?» Ulric said he would be glad to *give* it to her when it was finished. «*It's not finished yet, you mean?*» she screamed. «It looks finished to me. I don't care, I'll take it anyway, just as it is. Will you take twenty dollars for it?»

«Now listen, you fathead,» said MacGregor, giving her a playful ox-like poke on the jaw which knocked the glass out of her hand, «the man says it ain't finished yet; what do you want to do, make a liar out of him?»

«I'm not saying it's finished,» she said, «and I didn't call him a liar. I like it just as it is and I want to buy it.»

«Well, buy it then, by Jesus, and get done with it!»

«No, really, I couldn't let you take it in that condition,» said Ulric. «Besides, it's not good enough to sell—it's just a sketch.»

«That doesn't matter,» said Tess Molloy, «I want it. I'll give you thirty dollars for it.»

«You just said twenty a minute ago,» put in Mac Gregor. «What's the matter with you, are you nuts? Didn't you ever buy a picture before? Listen, Ulric, you'd better let her have it or else we'll never get started. I'd like to do a little fishing before the day's over, what do you say? Of course this bird»—indicating me with his thumb—«doesn't like fishing; he wants to sit and mope, dream about love, study the sky and that kind of crap. Come on, let's get going. Yeah, that's right, take a bottle along—we might want a swig of it before we get there.»

Tess took the water color from the wall and left a twenty dollar bill on the desk.

«Better take it with you,» warned MacGregor. «No telling who may break in while we're gone.»

After we had gone a block or so it occurred to me that I ought to have left a note for Mara on the door-bell. «Oh, fuck that idea!» said MacGregor. «Give her something to worry about—they like that. *Eh Toots?*» and again he poked his wife in the ribs.

«If you poke me again like that,» said she, «I'll wrap this bottle around your neck. I mean it too.»

«*She means it*,» he said, glancing back at us with a bright nickel-plated sort of smile. «You can't prod her *too much*, can you Toots? Yep, she's got a good disposition—otherwise she'd never have stood me as long as she has, ain't that right, kid?»

«Oh, shut up! Look where you're driving. We don't want this car smashed up like the other one.»

«*We* don't?» he yelled. «Jesus, I like that. And who, may I ask, ran into the milk truck on the Hempstead Turnpike in broad daylight?»

«Oh, forget it!»

They kept it up like that until way past Jamaïca. Suddenly he quit pestering and nagging her and, looking though the mirror, he began talking to us about his conception of art and life. It was all right, he thought, to go in for that sort of thing—meaning pictures and all that humbug—provided one had the talent for it. A good artist was worth his money, that was his opinion. The proof was that he got it, if you noticed. Anybody who was any good always got recognition, that's what he wanted to say. Wasn't that so? Ulric said he thought so too. Not always, of course, but generally speaking. Of course, there were fellows like Gauguin, MacGregor went on, and Christ knows they were good artists, but then there was some strange quirk in them, something antisocial, if you wanted to call it that, which prevented them from being recognized immediately. You couldn't blame the public for that, could you? Some people were born unlucky, that's how he saw it. Now take himself, for instance. He wasn't an artist, to be sure, but then he wasn't a dud either. In his way he was as good as the next fellow, maybe just a little bit better. And yet, just to prove how uncertain everything could be, nothing he had put his hand

to had turned out right. Sometimes a little shyster
had gotten the better of him. And why? Because
he, MacGregor, wouldn't stoop to doing certain things.
There are things you just don't do, he insisted. No
sir! and he banged the wheel emphatically. But
that's the way they play the game, and they get away
with it too. But not forever! Ah no!

«Now you take Maxfield Parrish,» he continued.
«I suppose he doesn't count, but just the same he gives
'em what they want. While a guy like Gauguin has
to struggle for a crust of bread—and even when he's
dead they spit in his eye. It's a queer game, art. I
suppose it's like everything else—you do it because
you like it, that's about the size of it, what? Now
you take that bastard sitting alongside of you—yeah
you!» he said, grinning at me through the mirror—
«he thinks we ought to support him, nurse him along
until he writes his masterpiece. He never thinks that
he might look for a job meanwhile. Oh no, he
wouldn't soil his lily-white hands that way. He's an
artist. Well, maybe he is, for all I know. But he's
got to prove it first, am I right? Did anybody support
me because I thought I was a lawyer? It's all right
to have dreams—we all like to dream—but somebody
has to pay the rent.»

We had just passed a duck farm. «Now that's
what I'd like,» said MacGregor. «I'd like nothing
better than to settle down and raise ducks. Why
don't I? Because I've got sense enough to know
that I don't know anything about ducks. You can't
just dream them up—you've got to raise them! Now
Henry there, if he took it into his head to raise ducks,
he'd just move out here and dream about it. First
he'd ask me to lend him some money, of course.
He's got that much sense, I must admit. He knows
that you have to *buy* them before you can raise them.
So, when he wants something, say a duck now, he

just blandly says 'Give me some money, I want to buy a duck!' Now that's what I call impractical. That's dreaming.... *How did I get my money?* Did I pick it off a bush? When I tell him to get out and hustle for it he gets sore. He thinks I'm against him. Is that right—or am I slandering you?» and he gave me another nickel-plated grin through the mirror.

«It's O.K.,» I said. «Don't take it to heart.»

«Take it to heart? Do you hear that? Jesus, if you think I lay awake nights worrying about you, you're sadly mistaken. I'm trying to set you right, that's all. I'm trying to put a little sense into your thick head. Of course I know you don't want to raise ducks, but you must admit you do get some crazy notions now and then. Jesus, I hope you don't forget the time you tried to sell me a Jewish Encyclopaedia. Imagine, he wanted me to sign for a set so that he could get his commission, and then I was to return it after a while—just like that. I was to give them some cock-and-bull story which he had trumped up on the spur of the moment. That's the sort of genius he has for business. And me a lawyer! Can you see me signing my name to a phoney proposition like that? No, by Jesus, I'd have more respect for him if he had told me he wanted to raise ducks. I can understand a guy wanting to raise ducks. But to try and palm off a Jewish Encyclopaedia on your best friend—that's raw, to say nothing of it being illegal and untenable. *That's another thing*—he thinks the law is all rot. I don't believe in it,' he says, as if his believing or not believing made any difference. And as soon as he's in trouble he comes hot-footing it to me. 'Do something,' he says, 'you know how to handle these things.' It's just a game to him. He could live without law, so he thinks, but I'll be damned if he isn't in trouble all the time. And of course, as to paying me for my trouble, or just for

the time I put in on him, that never enters his bean.
I should do those little things for him out of
friendship. You see what I mean?»

Nobody said anything.

We drove along in silence for a while. We passed
more duck farms. I asked myself how long it would
take to go crazy if one bought a duck and settled
down on Long Island with it. Walt Whitman was
born here somewhere. I no sooner thought of his
name than, like buying the duck, I wanted to visit
his birthplace.

«What about visiting Walt Whitman's birthplace?»
I said aloud.

«*What?*» yelled MacGregor.

«Walt Whitman!» I yelled. «He was born somewhere on Long Island. Let's go there.»

«Do you know where?» shouted MacGregor.

«No, but we could ask some one.»

«Oh, the hell with that! I thought you knew
where. These people out here wouldn't know who
Walt Whitman was. I wouldn't have known myself
only you talk about him so goddamn much. He was
a bit queer, wasn't he? Didn't you tell me he was
in love with a bus driver? Or was he a nigger lover?
I can't remember any more.»

«Maybe it was both,» said Ulric, uncorking the
bottle.

We were passing through a town. «Jesus, but I
seem to know *this* place!» said MacGregor. «Where
in hell are we?» He pulled up to the curb and
hailed a pedestrian. «Hey, what's the name of this
burg?» The man told him. «Can you beat that?»
he said. «I thought I recognized the dump. Jesus,
what a beautiful dose of clap I got here once! I
wonder if I could find the house. I'd just like to
drive by and see if that cute little bitch is sitting on
the verandah. God, the prettiest little trick you ever

laid eyes on—a little angel, you'd say. And could she fuck! One of those excitable little bitches, always in heat—you know, always throwing it up to you, rubbing it in your face. I drove out here in a pouring rain to keep a date with her. Everything just fine. Her husband was away on a trip and she was just itching for a piece of tail.... I'm trying to think now where I picked her up. I know this, that I had a hell of a time persuading her to let me visit her. Well, anyway, I had a wonderful time—never got out of bed for two days. Never got up to wash even—*that was the trouble.* Jesus, I swear if you saw that face alongside of you on the pillow you'd think you were getting the Virgin Mary. She could come about nine times without stopping. And then she'd say—'Do it again, once more... I feel *depraved.*' That was a funny one, eh? I don't think she knew what the word meant. Anyway, a few days later it began to itch and then it got red and swollen. I couldn't believe I was getting the clap. I thought maybe a flea had bitten me. Then the pus began to run. Boy, fleas don't make pus. Well, I went round to the family doctor. That's a beauty,' he said, where did you get it?' I told him. 'Better have a blood test,' he said, 'it might be syphilis.'»

«That's enough of that,» groaned Tess. «Can't you talk about something pleasant for a change?»

«Well,» says MacGregor, in answer to that, «you've got to admit I've been pretty clean since I know you, *right?*»

«You better had,» she answered, «or it wouldn't be healthy for you.»

«She's always afraid I'm going to bring her a present,» said MacGregor, grinning through the mirror again. «Listen Toots, *everybody* gets a dose some time or other. You can be thankful I got it before I met you—isn't that right, Ulric?»

«Oh yeah?» snapped Tess. Another long wrangle
might have ensued had we not come to a hamlet
which MacGregor thought would be a good stopping
place. He had an idea he would like to go crabbing.
Besides, there was a road house nearby which served
good food, if he remembered rightly. He bundled
us all out. «Want to take a leak? Come on!» We
left Tess standing at the roadside like a torn umbrella and went indoors to empty our bladders. He
got us both by the arm. «Confidentially,» he said,
«we ought to stick around here for the evening.
There's a fast crowd comes here; if you'd like to
dance and have a drink or two, why this is the
place. I won't tell her we're staying just yet—
might get the wind up. We'll go down to the beach
first and loll around. When you get hungry just say
so and then I'll suddenly remember the road house
—get me?»

We strolled down to the beach. It was almost
deserted. MacGregor bought a pocketful of cigars,
lit one, took off his shoes and socks and waded
around in the water smoking a fat cigar. «It's great,
isn't it?» he said. «You've got to be a kid once in
a while.» He made his wife take her shoes and
stockings off. She waddled into the water like a
hairy duck. Ulric sprawled out on the sand and
took a nap. I lay there watching MacGregor and
his wife at their clumsy antics. I wondered if Mara
had arrived and what she would think when she
found I was not there. I wanted to get back as
quick as possible. I didn't give a fuck about the
road house and the fast ponies who came there to
dance. I had a feeling that she was back, that she
was sitting on Ulric's doorstep waiting for me. I
wanted to get married again, that's what I wanted.
What had ever induced me to come out here to this
God-forsaken place? I hated Long Island, always

had. MacGregor and his ducks! The thought of it drove me mad. If I were to own a duck I would call it MacGregor, tie it to a lamp post and shoot it with a 48 calibre revolver. I'd shoot it until it was dead and then pole-axe it. His ducks! *Fuck a duck!* I said to myself. *Fuck everything!*

We went to the roadhouse just the same. If I had thought to demur I forgot it. I had reached a state of indifference born of despair. I let myself drift with the current. And, as always happens when you relent and allow yourself to be borne along by the clashing wills of others, something occurred which we didn't bargain for.

We had finished eating and we were having a third or fourth drink; the place was cosily filled, everybody was in a good mood. Suddenly, at a table nearby, a young man rose to his feet with a glass in hand and addressed the house. He wasn't drunk, he was just in a pleasant state of euphoria, as Dr. Kronski would put it. He was explaining quietly and easily that he had taken the liberty of calling attention to himself and his wife, to whom he raised his glass, because it was the first anniversary of their wedding, and because they felt so good about it that they wanted everybody to know it and to share their happiness. He said he didn't want to bore us by making a speech, that he had never made a speech in his life, and that he wasn't trying to make a speech now, but he just had to let everybody know how good he felt and how good his wife felt, that maybe he'd never feel this way again all his life. He said he was just a nobody, that he worked for a living and didn't make much money (nobody did any more), but he knew one thing and that was that he was happy, and he was happy because he had found the woman he loved, and he still loved her just as much as ever, though they were now married

a whole year. (He smiled.) He said he wasn't
ashamed to admit it before the whole world. He
said he couldn't help telling us all about it, even
if it bored us, because when you're very happy you
want others to share you happiness. He said he
thought it wonderful that there could be such happiness when there were so many things wrong with
the world, but that perhaps there would be more
happiness if people confessed their happiness to one
another instead of waiting to confide in one another
only when they were sorrowful and sad. He said
he wanted to see everybody looking happy, that
even if we were all strangers one to another, we
were united this evening with him and his wife and
if we would share their great joy with them it would
make them still happier.

He was so completely carried away by this idea
that everybody should participate in their joy that
he went on talking for twenty minutes or more,
roaming from one thing to another like a man sitting
at the piano and improvising. He hadn't a doubt
in the world that we were all his friends, that we
would listen to him in peace until he had had his
say. Nothing he said sounded ridiculous, however
sentimental his words may have been. He was
utterly sincere, utterly genuine, and utterly possessed by the realization that to be happy is the greatest
boon on earth. It wasn't courage which had made
him get up and address us, for obviously the thought
of getting to his feet and delivering a long extempora-
neous speech was as much of a surprise to him as
it was to us. He was for the moment, and without
knowing it, of course, on the way to becoming an
Evangelist, that curious phenomenon of American
life which has never been adequately explained. The
men who have been touched by a vision, by an unknown voice, by an irresistible inner prompting—

and there have been thousands upon thousands of them in our country—what must have been the sense of isolation in which they dwelled, and for how long, to suddenly rise up, as if out of a deep trance, and create for themselves a new identity, a new image of the world, a new God, a new heaven? We are accustomed to think of ourselves as a great democratic body, linked by common ties of blood and language, united indissolubly by all the modes of communication which the ingenuity of man can possibly devise; we wear the same clothes, eat the same diet, read the same newspapers, alike in everything but name, weight and number; we are the most collectivized people in the world, barring certain primitive peoples whom we consider backward in their development. And yet— yet despite all the outward evidences of being close-knit, inter-related, neighborly, good-humored, helpful, sympathetic, almost brotherly, we are a lonely people, a morbid, crazed herd thrashing about in zealous frenzy, trying to forget that we are not what we think we are, not really united, not really devoted to one another, not really listening, not really anything, just digits shuffled about by some unseen hand in a calculation which doesn't concern us. Suddenly now and then some one comes awake, comes undone, as it were, from the meaningless glue in which we are stuck— the rigmarole which we call the everyday life and which is not life but a trance-like suspension above the great stream of life—and this person who, because he no longer subscribes to the general pattern seems to us quite mad, finds himself invested with strange and almost terrifying powers, finds that he can wean countless thousands from the fold, cut them loose from their moorings, stand them on their heads, fill them with joy, or madness, make them forsake, their own kith and kin, renounce their call-

ing, change their character, their physiognomy, their
very soul.   And what is the nature of this overpowering seduction, this madness, this «temporary
derangement,» as we love to call it? What else if
not the hope of finding joy and peace? Every
Evangelist uses a different language but they are all
talking about the same thing. (To stop seeking, to
stop struggling, to stop climbing on top of one another, to stop thrashing about in the pursuit of vain
and vacillating goals.) In the twinkle of an eye it
comes, the great secret which arrests the outer motion,
which tranquilizes the spirit, which equilibrates,
which brings serenity and poise, and illumines the
visage with a steady, quiet flame that never dies.
In their efforts to communicate the secret they become a nuisance to us, true. We shun them because
we feel that they look upon us condescendingly; we
can't bear to think that we are not the equal of any
one, however superior he may seem to be. But we
are not equals; we are mostly inferior, vastly inferior, inferior particularly to those who are quiet and
contained, who are simple in their ways, and un-
shakeable in their beliefs. We resent what is steady
and anchored, what is impervious to our blandish-
ments, our logic, our collectivized cud of principles,
our antiquated forms of allegiance.

A little more happiness, I thought to myself as
I listened to him, and he'd become what is called
a dangerous man. Dangerous, because to be permanently happy would be to set the world on fire.
To make the world laugh is one thing; to make it
happy is quite another. Nobody has ever succeeded
in doing it. The great figures, those who have
influenced the world for good or evil, have always
been tragic figures. Even St. Francis of Assisi was
a tormented being. And the Buddha, with his
obession to eliminate suffering, well he was not

precisely a happy man. He was beyond that, if
you like: he was serene, and when he died, so it
is related, his whole body glowed as if the very
marrow were afire.

And yet, as an experiment, as a preliminary (if
you like) to that more wondrous state to which the
holy men attain, it seems to me that it would be
worth the attempt to make the whole world happy.
I know that the very word (happiness) has come to
have an odious ring, in America particularly; it
sounds witless and shitless; it has an empty ring;
it is the ideal of the weak and the infirm. It is a
word borrowed from the Anglo-Saxons, and distorted
by us into something altogether senseless. One is
ashamed to use it seriously. But there is no good
reason why it should be thus. Happiness is as legitimate as sorrow, and everybody, except those emancipated souls who in their wisdom have found something better, or bigger, desires to be happy and
would, if he could (if he only knew how!), sacrifice
everything to attain it.

I liked the young man's speech, inane as it might
appear on close scrutiny. Everybody liked it.
Everybody liked him and his wife. Everybody felt
better, more communicative, more relaxed, more
liberated. It was as if he had given us all a shot
in the arm. People spoke to one another across the
tables, or got up and shook hands, or clapped one
another on the back. Yes, if you happened to be
a very serious person, concerned with the fate of the
world, dedicated to some high purpose (such as
improving the conditions of the working classes or
lowering the rate of illiteracy among the native
born), perhaps this little incident would seem to
have assumed a thoroughly exaggerated importance.
An open, universal display of unfeigned happiness
gives some people an uncomfortable feeling; there

are some people who prefer to be happy privately,
who consider a public demonstration of their joy
immodest or slightly obscene. Or perhaps they are
simply so locked up in themselves that they can't
understand communion or communication. At any
rate, there were no such tender souls among us; it
was an average crowd made up of ordinary people,
ordinary people who owned cars, that is to say.
Some of them were downright rich and some were
not so rich, but none of them were starving, none
of them were epileptic, none of them were Moham-
medan or Negroid or just plain white trash. They
were ordinary, in the ordinary sense of the word.
They were like millions of other American people,
that is to say, without distinction, without airs, without any great purpose. Suddenly, when he had
finished, they seemed to realize that they were all
just like one another, no better no worse, and throwing off the petty restraints which kept them segreg-
ated in little groups, they rose indistinctively and
began mingling with one another. Soon the drinks
began to flow and they were singing, and then they
began to dance, and they danced differently than
they would have before; some got up and danced
who hadn't shaken a leg for years, some danced with
their own wives; some danced alone, giddy, intoxicated with their own grace and freedom; some sang as
they danced; some just beamed good-naturedly at
every one whose glance they happened to encounter.
It was astonishing what an effect a simple, open
declaration of joy could bring about. His words
were nothing in themselves, just plain ordinary words
which any one could summon at a moment's notice.
MacGregor, always sceptical, always striving to detect
the flaw, was of the opinion that he was really a very
clever young fellow, perhaps a theatrical figure, and
that he had been deliberately simple, deliberately

naif, in order to create an effect. Still, he couldn't deny that the speech had put him in a good mood. He simply wanted to let us know that he wasn't being taken in so easily. It made him feel better, so he pretended, to know that he hadn't been duped, even if he had enjoyed the performance thoroughly.

I felt sorry for him if what he said were true. Nobody can feel better than the man who is completely taken in. To be intelligent may be a boon, but to be completely trusting, gullible to the point of idiocy, to surrender without reservation, is one of the supreme joys of life.

Well, we all felt so good that we decided to go back to town and not stay overnight as we had planned. We sang at the top of our lungs all the way in. Even Tess sang, off-key it's true, but lustily and without restraint. MacGregor had never heard her sing before; she had always been like a reindeer, as far as the vocal apparatus was concerned. Her speech was limited, restricted to coarse grunts, punctuated by groans of approval or disapproval. I had the queer presentiment that, in the throes of this extraordinary expansiveness, she might take it into her head to burst out singing (later on) instead of making the usual request for a glass of water or an apple or a ham sandwich. I could visualize the expression on MacGregor's face, were she to absent-mindedly pull off a stunt like that. His look would register incredible amazement («*What next, b'Jesus?*») but at the same time it would suggest—«Go on, keep it up, try a falsetto for a change!» He liked people to do unheard of things. He liked to be able to think that there were certain vile, almost incredible things people could do that he had never imagined. He liked to think that there was nothing too vile, too scabrous, too ignominious for the human being to perpetrate on or against his fellow-man.

He boasted of having an open mind, a mind receptive
to any alleged form of stupidity, cruelty, treachery
or perversity. He went on the assumption that
every one was at heart a mean, callous, selfish, bas-
tardly son of a bitch, a fact which was proven by
the miraculously limited number of cases which
came to public attention through the law-courts. If
every one could be spied on, trailed, hounded, sur-
veilled, cross-examined, nailed down, forced to confess, why in his honest opinion, we would all be
in jail. And the most notorious offenders, to take
his word for it, were the judges, the ministers of
state, the public wardens, the members of the clergy,
the educators, the charitable workers. As for his
own profession, he had met one or two in his life
who were scrupulously honest, whose word could be
depended on; the rest, which included practically
the whole profession, were lower than the lowest
criminals, the scum of the earth, the shittiest dregs
of humanity that ever stood on two legs. No, he
wasn't being taken in by any horse shit these birds
handed out for general consumption. He didn't
know why he was honest and truthful himself; it
certainly didn't pay. He was just made that way,
he guessed. Besides, he had other foibles, and here
he would add up all the faults which he had, or
admitted he had, or imagined he had, and a for-
midable list it made, so that when he had finished
one was tempted to ask why he bothered to retain
the other two virtues of truthfulness and honesty.

  «*So you're still thinking about her?*» he popped
suddenly, turning his head slightly and twisting the
words out of the corner of his mouth. «Well, I feel
sorry for you. I suppose nothing will do but to
marry her. You certainly are a glutton for punishment. And what will you live on—have you thought
of that? You know you're not going to keep this

job very much longer—they must be wise to you by
this time. It's a wonder to me they didn't fire you
long ago. It certainly is a record for you— how
long is it now, *three years?* I can remember when
three days was a long time. Of course if she's the
right kind of girl you won't have to worry about
keeping a job—*she'll keep you.* That would be
ideal, wouldn't it? Then you could write those
masterpieces you're always promising us. I think,
by Jesus, that's why you're so eager to get rid of
your wife: she's on to you, she keeps your nose to
the grind-stone. God, how it must gripe you to get
up every morning and go to work! How do you
do it, will you tell me? You used to be too damned
lazy to get up for a meal.. Listen, Ulric, I've seen
that bastard stay in bed for three days hand-running.
Nothing the matter with him—just couldn't bear the
thought of facing the world. Love sick, sometimes.
Or just suicidal. That's something he used to like
—to threaten us with suicide. (He looked at me
through the mirror.) «*You forget those days, don't
you?*» Now he wants to live... I don't know why...
nothing's changed... everything's just as lousy as
ever. Now he talks of giving something to the world
—a masterpiece, no less. He couldn't just give us
an ordinary book *that would sell.* Oh no, not him!
It's got to be unique, something unheard of. Well,
I'm waiting. I don't say you won't do it, and I don't
say you will. I'm just waiting. Meanwhile the rest
of us have to go on making a living. We can't take
a lifetime trying to turn out a masterpiece.» (He
paused for breath.) «You know, sometimes I feel
as though I'd like to turn out a book myself—just
to prove to this guy that you don't have to make
a monkey of yourself to do a trick like that. I
think if I wanted to I could do a book in six months
—on the side, without neglecting my practice. I

don't say that it would be a prize-winner. I never boasted of being an *artist*. What gets me about this bird is that he's so damned sure he's an artist. He's certain that he's infinitely superior to a Hergesheimer, let's say, or a Dreiser—and yet he hasn't a damned thing to show for it. He wants us to take it on faith. He gets ruffled if you ask him to show you something tangible like a manuscript. Can you picture me trying to impress a judge with the fact that I'm a capable lawyer without having even taken a degree? I know that you can't wave a diploma in front of some one's eyes to prove that you're a writer, but just the same you could wave a manuscript, couldn't you? He says he's written several books already—well then, where are they? Has anybody ever seen them?»

Here Ulric interrupted to put in a word for me. I was sitting back in my soft seat chuckling. I enjoyed these tirades of MacGregor's

«Well, all right,» said MacGregor, «if you say you've seen a manuscript I'll take your word for it. He never shows me anything, the bastard. I suppose he hasn't any respect for my judgment. All I know is, to listen to him talk you'd think he was a genius. Mention any author—nobody suits him. Even Anatole France is no good. He must be aiming pretty high if he's going to make these birds take a back seat. To my way of thinking, a man like Joseph Conrad is not only an artist but a master. He thinks Conrad is over-rated. Melville, he tells me, is infinitely superior. And then, by Jesus, do you know what he admits to me one day? *That he never read Melville!* But that doesn't make any difference, he says. How are you going to reason with a guy like that? I haven't read Melville either, but I'm damned if I'll believe that he's better than Conrad—not till I've read him anyway.»

«Well,» said Ulric, «maybe he's not so crazy at that. Lots of people who've never seen a Giotto are fairly certain that he's better than Maxfield Parrish, for example.»

«That's different,» said MacGregor. «There's no question about the value of Giotto's work, nor of Conrad's either. Melville, from what I can gather, is pretty much of a dark horse. This generation may find him superior to Conrad, but then again he may fade out like a comet in a hundred or two hundred years. He was almost extinct when they rediscovered him recently.»

«And what makes you think that Conrad's fame won't fade in a hundred or two hundred years?» said Ulric.

«Because there's nothing dubious about it. It rests on solid achievement. He's *universally* liked, tranlated into dozens of languages already. The same is true of Jack London or O'Henry, decidedly inferior writers but decidedly lasting, if I know what I'm talking about. Quality isn't everything. Popularity is just as important as quality. As far as staying power goes, the writer who pleases the greatest number—assuming he has *some* quality and isn't just a hack—is certain of outlasting the higher, purer type of writer. Most everybody can read Conrad; not everybody can read Melville. And when you come to a unique case, such as Lewis Carroll, why I'll wager that, as far as English-speaking peoples go, he'll outlast Shakespeare...»

He went on after a moment's reflection: « Now painting is a little different, to my way of thinking. It takes more to appreciate a good painting than to appreciate a good book. People seem to think that because they know how to read and write they can tell a good book from a bad one. Even writers, good writers, I mean, aren't in agreement about what is good and what is bad. Neither are painters about paintings, for that matter. And yet I have the notion that in general painters are more in accord about the merits or lack of merit in the work of well-known painters than writers are with respect to writing. Only a half-assed painter would deny the value of Cézanne's work, for instance. But take the case of Dickens or of Henry James, and see what astounding differences of opinion there are among capable writers and critics as to their respective merits. If there were a writer to-day as bizarre in his realm as Picasso is in his you'd soon see what I'm driving at. Even if they don't like his work, most people who know anything about art agree that Picasso is a great genius. Now take Joyce, who's fairly eccentric as a writer, has he gained anything like the prestige of Picasso? Except for a scholarly few, except for the snobs who try to keep up with everything, his reputation, such as it is to-day, stands largely on the fact that he's a freak. His genius is admitted, I agree, but it's tainted, so to speak. Picasso commands respect, even if he isn't always understood. But Joyce is something of a butt: his fame increases precisely because he *can't* be generally understood. He's accepted as a freak, a phenomenon, like the Cardiff giant... And another thing, while I'm at it—no matter how daring the painter of genius may be, he's far more quickly assimilated than a writer of the same calibre. At the most, it takes thirty or forty years for a revolutionary painter to be accepted; it takes a writer centuries sometimes. To come back to Melville—what I meant was this: it took him sixty or seventy years, say, to make the grade. We don't know yet whether he'll stick it out; he may fall into the discard in another two or three generations. He's holding on by his teeth and only in spots, as it were. Conrad's dug in with toes and fingers; he's got roots already, everywhere; that's something you can't easily wave aside. As to whether he deserved it, that's another thing. I think if the truth were known, we'd find that lots of men were killed off or forgotten who deserved to be kept alive. It's hard to prove, I know, but I feel that there's some truth in what I say. You have only to look around you in every day life to observe the same thing happening everywhere. I know myself, in my own field, dozens of men who deserve to be on the Supreme Court bench; they lost out, they're finished, but what does it prove? Does it prove that they wouldn't have been better than the old fluffs whom we've got sitting on the bench now? There can only be one President of the United States elected every four years; does it mean that the man who happened to get elected (usually unfairly) is better than the ones who were defeated or than thousands of unknown men who never even dreamed of running for office? No, it seems to me that more often than not the ones who get the place of honor turn out to have been the least deserving. The deserving ones often take a back seat, either out of modesty or out of self-respect. Lincoln never wanted to become President of the United States; it was forced on him. He was practically rail-roaded in, by Christ. Fortunately he turned out to be the right man—but it could just as well have been otherwise. He wasn't chosen because he was the right man. Quite the contrary. Well shit, I'm getting off the track. I don't know what the hell started me off...»

He stopped just long enough to light a fresh cigar, then went on again.

«There's just one more thing I'd like to say. I know now what started me off. It's this—I feel sorry for the guy who's born a writer. That's why I razz this bird so much; I try to discourage him because I

know what he's up against. If he's really any good
he's cooked. A painter can knock out a half dozen
paintings in a year—so I'm told. But a writer—why
sometimes it takes him ten years to do a book, and if
it's good, as I say, it takes another ten years to find
a publisher for it, and after that you've got to allow
at least fifteen to twenty years before it's recognized
by the public. It's almost a lifetime—for one book,
mind you. How's he going to live meanwhile? Well,
he lives like a dog usually. A panhandler leads a
royal life by comparison. Nobody would undertake
such a career if he knew what lay in store for him.
To me the whole thing is cock-eyed. I say flatly that
it's not worth it. Art was never meant to be produced
this way. The point is that art is a luxury nowadays.
I could get along without ever reading a book or
looking at a painting. We've got too many other
things—we don't need books and paintings. Music
yes—music we'll always need. Not good music
necessarily—but music. Nobody writes good music
anymore anyway... The way I see it, the world is
going to the dogs. You don't need much intelligence
to get along, as things go. In fact, the less intelligence you have the better off you are. We've got
it so arranged now that things are brought to you on
a platter. All you need to know is how to do one
little thing passably well; you join a union, you do
as little work as possible, and you get pensioned off
when you come of age. If you had any aesthetic
leanings you wouldn't be able to go through the
stupid routine year in and year out. Art makes you
restless, dissatisfied. Our industrial system can't
afford to let that happen—so they offer you soothing
little substitutes to make you forget that you're a
human being. Soon there won't be any art at all,
I tell you. You'll have to pay people to go to a
museum or listen to a concert. I don't say it'll go on

like that forever. No, just when they've got it down
pat, everything running smooth as a whistle, nobody
squawking any more, nobody restless or dissatisfied,
the thing'll collapse. Man wasn't intended to be a
machine. The funny thing about all these Utopian
systems of government is that they're always promising to make man free—but first they try to make him
run like an eight-day clock. They ask the individual
to become a slave in order to establish freedom for
mankind. It's rum logic. I don't say that the
present system is any better. As a matter of fact, it
would be difficult to imagine anything worse than
what we've got now. But I know it's not going to be
improved by giving up what little rights we now have.
I don't think we want more rights—I think we want
larger ideas. Jesus, when I see what lawyers and
judges are trying to preserve it makes me puke. The
law hasn't any relation to human needs; it's a racket
carried on by a syndicate of parasites. Just take up
a law-book and read a passage (anywhere) aloud. It
sounds insane, if you're in your right senses. It *is*
insane, by God, I *know* it! But Jesus, if I begin to
question the law I've got to question other things too.
I'd go off my nut if I looked at things with a clear
eye. You can't do it—not if you want to keep in
step. You've got to squint as you go along; you've
got to pretend that it makes sense; you've got to let
people suppose that you know what you're doing.
But nobody knows what he's doing! We don't get
up in the morning and *think* what we're about. No
sir! We get up in a fog and shuffle through a dark
tunnel with a hang-over. We play the game. We
know it's a dirty lousy fake but we can't help it—
there's no choice. We're born into a certain set-up,
we're conditioned to it: we can tinker with it a little
here and there, like you would with a leaky boat, but
there's no making it over, there's no time for it,

you've got to get to port, or you imagine you have to.
We'll never get there, of course. The boat'll go
down first, take my word for it... Now if I were
Henry here, if I felt as sure as he does that I was an
artist, do you think I'd bother to prove it to the
world? *Not me!* I wouldn't put a line down on
paper; I'd just think my thoughts, dream my dreams,
and let it go at that. I'd take any kind of job,
anything that would keep me alive, and I'd say to
the world: «Fuck you, Jack, you're not putting
anything over on *me!* You ain't making me starve
to prove that I'm an artist. No siree—I know what
I know and nobody can tell me different.» I'd just
worm my way through life, doing just as little as
possible and enjoying myself just as much as possible.
If I had good, rich, juicy ideas I'd enjoy them all
to myself. I wouldn't try to ram them down people
throats. I'd act dumb most of the time. I'd be a yes
man, a rubber stamp. I'd let them walk over me if
they wanted to. Just so long as I knew in my heart
and soul that I really was somebody. I'd retire right
in the midst of life; I wouldn't wait till I was old and
decrepit, until they had first hammered the shit out
of me and then salved me with the Nobel Prize... I
know this sounds a bit cock-eyed. I know that ideas
have to be given form and substance. But I'm
talking about knowing and being rather than doing.
After all, you only become something in order to *be*
it—there wouldn't be any fun in just becoming all
the time, would there? Well, supposing you say to
yourself—the hell with becoming an artist, I know I
am one, I'll just *be* it—*what then?* What does it
mean, to be an artist? Does it mean that you have
to write books or make pictures? That's secondary,
I take it—that's the mere evidence of the fact that
you *are one*.... Supposing, Henry, you had written
the greatest book ever written and you lost the

manuscript just after you had completed it? And supposing nobody knew that you had been writing this great book, not even your closest friend? In that case you'd be just where I am who haven't put a stroke on paper, wouldn't you? If we were both to die suddenly, at that point, the world would never know that either of us was an artist. I would have had a good time of it and you would have wasted your whole life.»

At this point Ulric couldn't stand it any longer. «It's just the contrary,» he protested. «An artist doesn't enjoy life by evading his task. You're the one who would be wasting his life. Art isn't a solo performance; it's a symphony in the dark with millions of participants and millions of listeners. The enjoyment of a beautiful thought is nothing to the joy of giving it expression—*permanent* expression. In fact, it's almost a sheer impossibility to refrain from giving expression to a great thought. We're only instruments of a greater power. We're creators by permission, by grace, as it were. No one creates alone, of and by himself. An artist is an instrument that registers something already existent, something which belongs to the whole world and which, if he *is* an artist, he is compelled to give back to the world. To keep one's beautiful ideas to oneself would be like being a virtuoso and sitting in an orchestra with hands folded. *You couldn't do it!* As for that illustration you gave, of an author losing his life's work in manuscript, why I'd compare such a person to a wonderful musician who had been playing with the orchestra all the time, only in another room, where nobody heard him. But that wouldn't make him any the less a participant, nor would it rob him of the pleasure to be hand in following the orchestra leader or hearing the music which his instrument gave forth. The greatest mistake you

make is in thinking that enjoyment is something
unearned, that if you know you can play the fiddle,
well it's just the same as playing it. It's so silly that
I don't know why I bother to discuss it. As for the
reward, you're always confusing recognition with
reward. They're two different things. Even if you
don't get paid for what you do, you at least have the
satisfaction of doing. It's a pity that we lay such
emphasis on being paid for our labors—it really
isn't necessary, and nobody knows it better than the
artist. The reason why he has such a miserable time
of it is because he elects to do his work gratuitously.
He forgets, as you say, that he has to live. But that's
really a blessing. It's much better to be preoccupied
with wonderful ideas than with the next meal, or the
rent, or a pair of new shoes. Of course when you get
to the point where you must eat, and you haven't
anything to eat, then to eat becomes an obsession.
But the difference between an artist and the ordinary
individual is that when the artist does get a meal he
immediately falls back into his own limitless world,
and while he's in that world he's a king, whereas
your ordinary duffer is just a filling station with nothing in between but dust and smoke. And even
supposing you're not an ordinary chap, but a wealthy
individual, one who can indulge his tastes, his whims,
his appetites: do you suppose for one minute that a
millionaire enjoys food or wine or women like a
hungry artist does? To enjoy anything you have to
make yourself ready to receive it; it implies a certain
control, discipline, *chastity*, I might even say. Above
all, it implies desire, and desire is something you
have to nourish by right living. I'm speaking now
as if I were an artist, and I'm not really, I'm just a
commercial illustrator, but I do know enough about
it to say that I envy the man who has the courage to
be an artist—I envy him because I know that he's

infinitely richer than any other kind of human being.
He's richer because he spends himself, because he
gives *himself* all the time, and not just labor or
money or gifts. You couldn't possibly be an artist,
in the first place, because you lack faith. You
couldn't possibly have beautiful ideas because you kill
them off in advance. You deny what it takes to make
beauty, which is love, love of life itself, love of life
for its own sake. You see the flaw, the worm, in
everything. An artist, even when he detects a flaw,
makes it into something flawless, if I may put it that
way. He doesn't try to pretend that a worm is a
flower or an angel, but he incorporates the worm into
something bigger. He knows that the world isn't
full or worms, even if he sees a million or a billion
of them. You see a tiny worm and you say—«Look,
see how rotten everything is!» You can't see beyond
the worm... Well, excuse me, I didn't mean to put
it so caustically or so personally. But I hope you
see what I'm driving at....»

«That's quite all right,» said MacGregor briskly
and cheerily. «It's good to have the other fellow's
opinion once in a while. Maybe you're right. Maybe
I am unduly pessimistic. But that's how I'm built.
I think I'd be a lot happier if I could see it your
way—but I can't. Besides, I must confess I've really
never met a good artist. It would be a pleasure to
talk to one some time.»

«Well,» said Ulric, «you've been talking to one
all your life without knowing it. How are you going
to recognize a good artist when you meet one if you
can't recognize one in your friend here?»

«I'm glad you said that,» piped MacGregor. «And
now that you've pushed me to the ropes I'll admit I
do think he's an artist. I've always thought so. As
for listening to him, well I do that too, and quite
seriously. But then I also have my doubts. You

see, if I listened to him long enough he'd undermine
me. I know he's right, but it's like I told you before
—if you want to get along, if you want to live, you
just can't permit yourself such thoughts. Sure he's
right! I'd change places with him any day, the lucky
dog. What have I got for all my struggles? I'm a
lawyer. *So what?* I might just as well be a piece
of shit. Sure, you bet I'd like to change places.
Only I'm not an artist, as you said. I guess the
trouble with me is that I can't swallow the fact that
I'm just another nobody...»

7

Back in town I found a note on Ulric's bell, from
Mara. She had arrived shortly after we left. Had
been sitting on the steps waiting for me, waiting for
hours, if I were to believe her words. A postcript
informed me that she was off to Rockaway with her
two friends. I was to call her there as soon as
I could.

I arrived at dusk and found her waiting for me at
the station; she was in a bathing suit over which she
had thrown a mackintosh. Florrie and Hannah were
sleeping it off again at the hotel; Hannah had lost her
beautiful new set of false teeth and was in a state
of nervous prostration. Florrie, she said, was going
back to the woods again; she had fallen hard for Bill,
one of the backwoodsmen. But first she had to have
an abortion performed. It was nothing—not for
Florrie anyway. The only thing that bothered her
was that she seemed to grow larger down there with
each abortion; soon she wouldn't be able to take on
anything but niggers.

She led me to another hotel where we were to pass the night together. We sat talking awhile in the lugubrious dining room over a glass of beer. She looked queer in that mackintosh—like a person who's been driven out of the house by fire in the middle of the night. We were itching to get to bed but in order not to arouse suspicion we had to pretend to be in no great hurry. I had lost all sense of place: it seemed as if we had made a rendezvous in a dark room by the Atlantic Ocean in the wake of an exodus. Two or three other couples slipped in noiselessly, sipped their drinks, and chatted furtively in subdued whispers. A man walked through with a bloody meat cleaver, holding a decapitated chicken by the legs; the blood dripped on to the floor, leaving a zigzag trail—like the passage of a drunken whore who is menstruating freely.

Finally we were shown to a cell at the end of a long corridor. It was like the terminus of a bad dream, or the missing half of a Chirico painting. The corridor formed the axis of two wholly unrelated worlds; if you were to go left instead of right you might never find your way back again. We undressed and fell on the iron cot in a sexual sweat. We went at it like a pair of wrestlers who have been left to untangle themselves in an empty arena after the lights are out and the crowd dispersed. Mara was struggling frantically to bring on an orgasm. She had somehow become detached from her sexual apparatus; it was night and she was lost in the dark; her movements were those of a dreamer desperately struggling to re-enter the body which had begun the act of surrender. I got up to wash myself, to cool it off with a little cold water. There was no sink in the room. In the yellow light of an almost extinct bulb I saw myself in a cracked mirror; I had the expression of a Jack the Ripper looking for a straw hat in

a pisspot. Mara lay prone on the bed, panting and
sweating; she had the appearance of a battered
odalisque made of jagged pieces of mica. I slipped
into my trousers and staggered through the funnel-
like corridor in search of the wash-room. A bald-
headed man, stripped to the waist, stood before a
marble basin washing his trunk and arm-pits. I
waited patiently until he had finished. He snorted
like a walrus in performing his ablutions; when he
had done he opened a can of talcum powder and
sprinkled it generously over his torso which was
creased and caked like an elephant's hide.

When I returned I found Mara smoking a cigarette
and playing with herself. She was burning up with
desire. We went at it again, trying it dog-fashion
this time, but still it was no go. The room began to
heave and bulge, the walls were sweating, the mattress
which was made of straw was almost touching the
floor. The performance began to take on all the
aspects and proportions of a bad dream. From the
end of the corridor came the broken wheeze of an
asthmatic; it sounded like the tail end of a gale
whizzing through a corrugated rat hole.

Just as she was about to come we heard some one
fumbling at the door. I slid off her and poked my
head out. It was a drunk trying to find his room.
A few minutes later, when I went to the wash-room
to give my cock another cool spritz-bath, he was still
looking for his room. The transoms were all open
and from them come a stertorous cacophany which
resembled the Epiphany of John the locust-eater.
When I returned to resume the ordeal my cock felt
as if it were made of old rubber bands. I had absolutely no more feeling at that end; it was like pushing
a piece of stiff suet down a drain-pipe. What's more,
there wasn't another charge left in the battery; if
anything was to happen now it would be in the

nature of gall and leathery worms or a drop of pus in a solution of thin pot cheese. What surprised me was that it continued to stand up like a hammer; it had lost all the appearance of a sexual implement; it looked disgustingly like a cheap gadget from the five and ten cent store, like a bright-colored piece of fishing tackle minus the bait. And on this bright and slippery gadget Mara twisted like an eel. She wasn't any longer a woman in heat, she wasn't even a woman; she was just a mass of undefinable contours wriggling and squirming like a piece of fresh bait seen upside down through a convex mirror in a rough sea.

I had long ceased to be interested in her contortions; except for the part of me that was in her I was as cool as a cucumber and remote as the dog star. It was like a long distance death message concerning some one whom you had forgotten long ago. All I was waiting for was to feel that incredibly aborted explosion of wet stars which drop back to the floor of the womb like dead snails.

Towards dawn, Eastern Standard Time, I saw by that frozen condensed milk expression about the jaw that it was happening. Her face went through all the metamorphoses of early uterine life, only in reverse. With the last dying spark it collapsed like a punctured bag, the eyes and nostrils smoking like toasted acorns in a slightly wrinkled lake of pale skin. I fell off her and dove straight into a coma which ended towards evening with a knock on the door and fresh towels. I looked out the window and saw a collection of tar-covered roofs spotted here and there with doves of taupe. From the ocean front came the boom of surf followed by a frying pan symphony of exasperated sheet metal cooling off in a drizzle at 139 degrees Centigrade. The hotel was droning and purring like a fat and moribund swamp

fly in the solitude of a pine forest. Along the axis of
the corridor there had been a further sag and recess
during the interim. The Grade A world to the left
was all sealed and boarded, like those colossal bath
houses along the boardwalk which, in the off season,
curl up on themselves and expire in gasps through
endless chinks and slats. The other nameless world
to the right had already been chewed off by a trip-
hammer, the work doubtless of some maniac who had
endeavored to justify his existence as a day laborer.
Underfoot it was slimy and slippery, as if an army of
zippered seals had been weaving it back and forth to
the wash-room all day long. Here and there an open
door revealed the presence of grotesquely plastic
water nymphs who had managed to squeeze their
mammiferous trundles of avoirdupois into sylph-like
fish nets made of spun glass and ribbons of wet clay.
The last roses of Summer were fading away into
goiterous udders with arms and legs. Soon the
epidemic would be over and the ocean would resume
its air of gelatinous grandeur, of mucilaginous dignity,
of sullen and spiteful solitude.

We stretched ourselves out in the hollow of a
suppurating sand dune next to a bed of waving stink
weed on the lee side of a macadamized road over
which the emissaries of progress and enlightenment
were rolling along with that familiar and soothing
clatter which accompanies the smooth locomotion of
spitting and farting contraptions of tin woven
together by steel knitting needles. The sun was
setting in the West as usual, not in splendor and
radiance however but in disgust, like a gorgeous
omelette engulfed by clouds of snot and phlegm. It
was the ideal setting for love, such as the drug stores
sell or rent between the covers of a handy pocket
edition. I took off my shoes and leisurely deposited
my big toe in the first notch of Mara's crotch. Her

head was pointed south, mine north; we pillowed them on folded hands, our bodies relaxed and floating effortlessly in the magnetic drift, like two enormous twigs suspended on the surface of a gasoline lake. A visitor from the Renaissance, coming upon us unexpectedly, might well have assumed that we had become dislodged from a painting depicting the violent end of the mangy retinue of a sybaritic Doge. We were lying at the edge of a world in ruins, the composition being a rather precipitate study of prespective and foreshortening in which our prostrated figures served as a picaresque detail.

The conversation was thoroughly desultory, spluttering out with a dull thud like a bullet encountering muscle and sinew. We weren't talking, we were simply parking our sexual implements in the free parking void of anthropoid chewing gum machines on the edge of a gasoline oasis. Night would fall poetically over the scene, like a shot of ptomaine poison wrapped in a rotten tomato. Hannah would find her false teeth behind the mechanical piano; Florrie would appropriate a rusty can-opener with which to start the blood flowing.

The wet sand clung to our bodies with the tenacity of fresh-laid wall-paper. From the factories and hospitals nearby came the ingratiating aroma of exhausted chemicals, of hair soaked in pipi, of useless organs plucked out alive and left to rot slowly through an eternity in sealed vessels labelled with great care and veneration. A brief twilight sleep in the arms of Morpheus the Danubian dachshund.

When I got back to town Maude inquired in her polite fish-like way if I had had a pleasant holiday. She remarked that I looked rather haggard. She added that she was thinking of taking a little vacation herself; she had received an invitation from an old

convent friend to pass a few days at her home in the
country. I thought it an excellent idea.

Two days later I accompanied her and the child
to the station. She asked me if I wouldn't care to
ride part of the way with them. I saw no reason
why I shouldn't. Besides I thought maybe she had
something of importance to tell me. I boarded the
train and rode some distance into the country, talking about things of no consequence and wondering
all the time when she would come out with it.
Nothing happened. I finally got off the train and
waved good-bye. «Say good-bye to daddy,» she urged
the child. «You won't see him again for several
weeks.» Bye bye! Bye bye! I waved good-
naturedly, like any suburban papa seeing his wife and
child off. Several weeks, she had said. That would
be excellent. I walked up and down the platform
waiting for the train and pondering on all the things
I would do in her absence. Mara would be delighted.
It would be like having a private honeymoon: we
could do a million wonderful things in a stretch of
several weeks.

The following day I awoke with a frightful ear-
ache. I telephoned Mara and urged her to meet me
at the doctor's office. The doctor was one of the
wife's demonic friends. He had almost murdered
the child once with his mediaeval instruments of
torture. Now it was my turn. I left Mara to sit it
out on a bench near the entrance to the park.

The doctor seemed delighted to see me; engaging
me in a pseudo-literary discussion, he put his instruments up to boil. Then he tested out an electrically
run glass cage which looked like a transparent ticker
but which was actually some devilish sort of inhuman
blood-sucking contraption which he intended to try
out as a parting fillip.

So many doctors had tinkered with my ear that

I was quite a veteran by this time. Each fresh irruption meant that the dead bone was drawing closer and closer to the brain. Finally there would be a grand conjunction, the mastoid would become like a wild mustang, there would be a concert of silver saws and silver mallets, and I would be shipped home with my face twisted to one side like a haemoplagic rhapsodist.

«You don't hear any more with that ear, of course?» said he, plunging a hot wire into the very core of my skull without a word of warning.

«No, not at all,» I answered, almost sliding off the seat with pain.

«Now this is going to hurt a bit,» said he, manipulating a diabolical-looking fish-hook.

It went on like that, each operation a little more painful than the last, until I was so beside myself with pain that I wanted to kick him in the guts. Still there remained the electrical cage: that was to irrigate the canals, extract the last iota of pus, and send me out into the street rearing like a bronco.

«It's a nasty business,» he said, lighting a cigarette in order to give me a breathing spell. «I wouldn't want to go through with it myself. If it get any worse you'd better let me operate on you.»

I settled down for the irrigation. He inserted the nozzle and turned on the switch. It felt as though he were irrigating my brain with a solution of prussic acid. The pus was coming out and with it a thin stream of blood. The pain was excruciating.

«Does it really hurt as much as that?» he exclaimed seeing that I had become white as a sheet.

«It hurts worse than that,» I said. «If you don't stop soon I'll smash it. I'd rather have triple mastoids and look like a demented frog.»

He pulled the nozzle out and with it the lining of

my ear, of my cerebellum, of one kidney and the marrow of my coccyx.

«A fine job,» said I.   «When do I come again?»

He thought it best to come to-morrow—just to see how it was progressing.

Mara had a fright when she saw me. She wanted to take me home at once and nurse me. I was so used up I couldn't stand having anyone near me. Hurriedly I said good-bye.   «Meet me to-morrow!»

I staggered home like a drunk and fell on the couch, into a deep drugged sleep. When I awoke it was dawning. I felt excellent. I got up and went for a stroll through the park. The swans were coming to life: their mastoids were non-existent.

When pain lets up life seems grand, even without money or friends or high ambitions. Just to breathe easily, to walk without a sudden spasm or twitch. Swans are very beautiful then. Trees too. Even automobiles. Life moves along on roller skates; the earth is pregnant and constantly churning up new magnetic fields of space. See how the wind bends the tiny blades of grass! Each little blade is sentient; everything responds. If the earth itself were in pain we could do nothing about it. The planets never have an ear-ache; they are immune, though bearing within them untold pain and suffering.

For once I was at the office ahead of time. I worked like a Trojan without feeling the slightest fatigue. At the appointed time I met Mara. She would sit again on the park bench, in the same spot.

This time the doctor merely took a look at the ear, picked away a fresh scab, swabbed it with a soothing ointment, and plugged it up. «Looks fine,» he mumbled, «come back in a week.»

We were in good spirits, Mara and I. We had dinner in a road house and with it some Chianti. It was a balmy evening, just made for a stroll over the downs. After a time we lay down in the grass and gazed up at the stars. «Do you think she'll really stay away several weeks?» asked Mara.

It seemed too good to be true.

«Maybe she'll never come back,» I said. «Maybe that's what she wanted to tell me when she asked me to ride part of the way with her. Maybe she lost her nerve at the last minute.»

Mara didn't think she was the sort to make a sacrifice like that. It didn't matter anyway. For a while we could be happy, could forget that she existed.

«I wish we could get away from this country altogether,» said Mara. «I wish we could go to some other country, somewhere where nobody knows us.»

I agreed that that would be ideal. «We'll do it eventually,» I said. «There isn't a soul here whom I care about. My whole life has been meaningless— until you came along.»

«Let's go and row in the lake,» said Mara suddenly. We got up and sauntered over to the boats. Too late, the boats were all padlocked. We started strolling aimlessly along a path by the water; soon we came to a little rest house built out over the water. It was deserted. I sat down on the rough bench and Mara seated herself on my lap. She had on the stiff dotted Swiss dress which I liked so much. Underneath it not a stich. She got off my lap a moment and lifting her dress she straddled me. We had a wonderful close-knit fuck. When it was over we sat for a while without unhitching, just silently chewing one another's lips and ears.

Then we got up and, at the edge of the lake, we washed ourselves with our handkerchiefs. I was just drying my cock with the tail of my shirt when Mara suddenly grasped my arm and pointed to something moving behind a bush. All I could see was a gleam of something bright. I quickly buttoned up my pants

and taking Mara by the arm we regained the gravel
path and started slowly walking in the opposite
direction.

«It was a cop, I'm sure,» said Mara.   «They do that,
the dirty perverts. They're always hiding in the
bushes spying on people.»

In a moment, sure enough, we heard the heavy
tread of a thick-witted Mick.

«Just a minute, you two,» he said, «where do you
think you're going?»

«What do you mean?» said, I pretending to be
annoyed.   «We're taking a walk, can't you see?»

«It's about time you took a walk,» he said. I've a
good mind to walk you back to the station with me.
What do you think this is—a stud farm?»

I pretended I didn't know what he was talking
about.   Being a Mick, that enraged him.

«None of your lip,» said he.   «Better get that dame
out of here before I run you in.»

«She's my wife.»

«So.... *your wife*, is it?   Well now, ain't that nice?
Just doing a little billing and cooing, eh?   Washing
your private parts in public too—I'll be damned if I
ever saw the likes of it. Now don't be in too great
a hurry.   You're guilty of a grave offense, me lad,
and if this *is* your wife she's in for it too.»

«Look here, you don't mean to say....»

«What's your name?» he demanded cutting me
short, and making to reach for his little note book.

I told him.

«And where do you live?»

I told him.

«And *her* name?»

«The same as mine—she's my wife, I told you.»

«So you did.» he said, with a dirty leer.   «All right.
Now then, what do you do for a living?   *Are you
working?*»

I pulled out my wallet and showed him the Cosmodemonic pass which I always carried and which entitled me to ride free of charge on all subway, elevated and street car lines of the city of Greater New York. He scratched his head at this and tilted his cap back on his head. «So you're the employment manager, are you? That's a pretty responsible position for a young man like you.» Heavy pause. «I suppose you'd like to keep your job a little longer, wouldn't you?»

Suddenly I had visions of seeing my name plastered in headlines over the morning papers. A fine story the reporters could make of it if they wanted to. It was time to do something.

«Look here, Officer,» says I, «let's talk the thing over quietly. «I live nearby—why don't you walk over to the house with me? Maybe my wife and I were a little reckless—we're not married very long. We shouldn't have carried on like that in a public place, but it was dark and there was nobody around....»

«Well, there might be a way of fixing it,» says he. «You don't want to lose your job, do you?»

«No, I don't,» says I, wondering at the same time how much I had in my pocket and whether he would sneeze at it or not.

Mara was fumbling in her bag.

«Now don't be in such a hurry, lady. You know you can't bribe an officer of the law. By the way, what church do you go to, if I'm not too inquisitive?»

I answered quickly, giving the name of the Catholic church on our corner.

«Then you're one of Father O'Malley's boys! Well, why didn't you tell me that in the first place? Shure, you wouldn't want to disgrace the parish now, would you?»

I told him it would kill me were Father O'Malley to hear of it.

«And you were married in Father O'Malley's church?»

«Yes, fath... I mean Officer. We were married last April.»

I was trying to count the bills in my pocket without extracting them. It seemed as if there were only three or four bucks. I was wondering how much Mara might have. The cop had started walking and we fell in with him. Presently he stopped short. He pointed ahead with his club. And with his club in the air and his head slightly averted, he began a slow monologue about a coming novena to Our Lady of the Flying Buttress or something of the sort, saying as he held out his left hand that the shortest way out of the park was straight ahead and mind you, be on on your good behavior and so forth.

Mara and I hastily stuffed a few bills in his hand and, thanking him for his kindness, we lit out like a bolt.

«I think you'd better come home with me,» I said. «If it wasn't enough we gave him he may be coming to pay us a visit. I don't trust these dirty bastards.... Father O'Malley, *shit!*»

We hurried home and locked ourselves in. Mara was still trembling. I dug up a little port wine which was hidden away in a cupboard.

«The thing to happen now,» I said, as I downed a glassful, «is for Maude to come back and surprise us.»

«She wouldn't do that, would she?»

«Christ only knows what she might do.»

«I think we'd better sleep down here,» said Mara. «I wouldn't like to sleep in her bed.»

We finished the wine and got undressed. Mara came out of the bath rom in Maude's silk kimono. It gave me a start to see her in Maude's outfit. «I'm your wife, am I not?» she said, putting her arms around me. It gave me a thrill to hear her say that. She walked about the room examining the things.

«Where do you write?» she asked. «At that little table?»

I nodded.

«You ought to have a big table and a room of your own. How can you write here?»

«I have a big desk upstairs.»»

«Where? In the bed room?»

«No, in the parlor. It's wonderfully lugubrious up there—would you like to see it?»

«No,» she said quickly, «I'd rather not go up there. I'll always think of you as sitting here in this corner by the window.... Is this where you wrote me all those letters?»

«No,» I said, «I wrote you from the kitchen,»

«Show me,» she said. «Show me just where you sat. I want to see how you looked.»

I took her by the hand and led her back to the kitchen. I sat down and pretended I was writing her a letter. She bent over me and putting her lips to the table she kissed the spot encircled by my arms.

«I never dreamt I would see your home,» she said. «It's strange to see the place which is to have such an effect upon your life. It's a holy place. I wish we could take this table with us and this chair—everything—even the stove. I wish we could move the whole room and build it into our own home. It belongs to us, this room.»

We went to bed on the divan in the basement. It was a warm night and we went to sleep in the raw. About seven in the morning, as we lay entwined in each other's arms, the rolling doors were violently pushed open and there stood my darling wife, the landlord who lived upstairs, and his daughter. In flagrant delectation we were caught. I sprang out of bed stark naked. Holding a towel which was on the

chair beside the couch I flung it around me and
waited for the verdict. Maude motioned to her
witness to step in and take a look at Mara who was
lying there holding a sheet over her bosom.

«I'll ask you to please get this woman out of here
as quickly as possible,» said Maude, and with that she
turned on her heel and went upstairs with her
witnesses.

Had she been sleeping upstairs in our own bed all
night? If so, why had she waited until morning?

«Take it easy, Mara. The goose is cooked now.
We may as well stay and have breakfast.»

I dressed hurriedly and ran out to get some bacon
and eggs.

«God, I don't see how you can take it so calmly,»
she said, sitting at the table with a cigarette to her
lips, watching me prepare the breakfast. «Haven't
you any feelings?»

«Sure I have. My feeling is that everything has
worked out splendidly. *I'm free*, do you realize that?»

What are you going to do now?»

«I'm going to work, for one thing. This evening
I'll go to Ulric's place—you might meet me there. I
have an idea my friend Stanley is behind all this.
We'll see.»

At the office I sent a telegram to Stanley to meet
me at Ulric's that evening. During the day I had a
telephone call from Maude suggesting that I find
myself a room. She said she would get the divorce
as soon as possible. No comments upon the situation
just a pure business-like statement. I was to let her
know when I wished to call for my things.

Ulric took it rather gravely. It meant a change of
life and all changes were serious to him. Mara on
the other hand was thoroughly in possession of herself
and already looking forward to the new life. It
remained to see how Stanley would take it.

Presently the bell rang and there he was, sinister-looking as usual and drunk as a pope. I hadn't seen him that way for years. He had decided that it was an event of the first importance and that it should be celebrated. As far as getting any details from him was concerned it was absolutely impossible. «I told you I'd fix it for you,» he said. «You walked into it like a fly into a web. I had it figured out to a T. I didn't ask you any questions, did I? I knew just what you'd do.»

He took a swig from a flask which he was carrying in his inside coat pocket. He didn't even bother to remove his hat. I could see him now as he must have looked when at Fort Oglethorpe. He was the sort of fellow I would have given a wide berth, seeing him in that state.

The telephone rang. It was Dr. Kronski asking for *Mister* Miller. «Congratulations!» he shouted. «I'm coming over there to see you in a few minutes. I have something to tell you.»

«By the way,» I said, «do you know anybody who has an extra room to let?»

«That's just what I was going to talk to you about. I've got a place all picked out for you—up in the Bronx. It's a friend of mine—he's a doctor. You can have a whole wing of the house to yourself. Why don't you take Mara with you? You'll like it there. He's got a billiard room on the ground floor, and a good library, and....»

«Is he Jewish?» I asked.

«*Is he?* He's a Zionist, an anarchist, a Talmudist and an abortionist. A damned fine chap—and if you're in need of help he'll give you his shirt. I was just around to your house—that's how I found out. Your wife seems to be tickled to death. She'll live pretty comfortably on the alimony you'll have to pay her.»

I told Mara what he had said. We decided to have a look at the place immediately. Stanley had disappeared. Ulric thought he might have gone to the bathroom.

I went to the bathroom and knocked. No answer. I pushed the door open. Stanley was lying in the tub fully dressed, his hat over his eye, the empty bottle in his hand. I left him lying there.

«He's gone, I guess,» I shouted to Ulric as we sailed out.

VOLUME THREE

8

The Bronx! We had been promised a whole wing of
the house—a turkey wing, with feathers and goose
pimples thrown in. Kronski's idea of a haven.

It was a suicidal period which began with
cockroaches and hot pastrami sandwiches and ended
à la Newberg in a cubby-hole on Riverside Drive
where Mrs. Kronski the Second began her thankless
task of illustrating a vast cycloramic appendix to the
insanities.

It was under Kronski's influence that Mara decided
to change her name again—from Mara to Mona.
There were other, more significant changes which also
had their origin here in the purlieus of the Bronx.

We had come in the night to Dr. Onirifick's hide-
out. A light snow had fallen and the colored panes
of glass in the front door were covered with a mantle
of pure white. It was just the sort of place I had
imagined Kronski *would* select for our «honeymoon».
Even the cockroaches, which began scurrying up and
down the walls as soon as we turned on the lights,
seemed familiar—and ordained. The billiard table
which stood in a corner of the room was at first
disconcerting, but when Dr. Onirifick's little boy
casually opened his fly and began to make pipi
against the leg of the table everything seemed quite
as it should be.

The front door opened directly on to our room
which was equipped with a billiard table, as I say, a

large brass bedstead with eiderdown quilts, a writing
desk, a grand piano, a hobby horse, a fire place, a
cracked mirror covered with fly-specks, two cuspidors
and a settee. There were in all no less than eight
windows in our room. Two of them had shades
which could be pulled down about two-thirds of the
way; the others were absolutely bare and festooned
with cobwebs. It was very jolly. No one ever rang
the bell or knocked first; every one walked in unan-
nounced and found his way about as best he could.
It was «a room with a view» both inside and out.

Here we began our life together. A most auspicious
début! The only thing lacking was a sink in which
we could urinate to the sound of running water. A
harp might have come in handy, too, especially on
those droll occasions when the members of Dr.
Onirifick's family, tired of sitting in the laundry
downstairs, would waddle up to our room like auks
and penguins and watch us in complete silence as we
ate or bathed or made love or combed the lice out
of one another's hair. What language they spoke we
never knew. They were as mute as the reindeer and
nothing could frighten or astound them, not even the
sight of a mangy foetus.

Dr. Onirifick was always very busy. Children's
diseases was his specialty, but the only children we
ever noticed during our stay were embryonic ones
which he chopped into fine pieces and threw down the
drains. He had three children of his own. They
were all three super-normal, and on this account were
allowed to behave as they pleased. The youngest,
about five years of age and already a wizard at
algebra, was definitely on his way to becoming a
pyromaniac as well as a super-mathematician. Twice
he had set fire to the house. His latest exploit
revealed a more ingenious turn of mind: it was to set
fire to a perambulator containing a tender infant and

then push the perambulator downhill towards a congested traffic lane.

Yes, a jolly place to begin life anew. There was Ghompal, an ex-messenger whom Kronski had salvaged from the Cosmodemonic Telegraph Company when that institution began to weed out its non-Caucasian employees. Ghompal, being of Dravidian stock and dark as sin, had been one of the first to get the gate. He was a tender soul, extremely modest, humble, loyal and self-sacrificing—almost painfully so. Dr. Onirifick cheerfully made a place for him in his vast household—as a glorified chimney-sweep. Where Ghompal ate and slept was a mystery. He moved about noiselessly in the performance of his duties, effacing himself, when he deemed it necessary, with the celerity of a ghost. Kronski prided himself on having rescued in the person of this outcast a scholar of the first water. «He's writing a history of the world,» he told us impressively. He omitted mentioning that, in addition to his duties as secretary, nurse, chamber-maid, dish-washer and errand boy, Ghompal also stoked the furnace, hauled the ashes, shoveled the snow, papered the walls and painted the spare rooms.

Nobody attempted to wrestle with the problem of roaches. There were millions of them hidden away beneath the mouldings, the woodwork, the wall-paper. One had only to turn on the light and they streamed out in double, triple file, column after column, from walls, ceiling, floor, crannies, crevices—veritable armies of them parading, deploying, manœuvering, as if obeying the commands of some unseen super-roach of a drill-master. At first it was disgusting, then nauseating, and finally, as with the other strange, disturbing phenomena which distinguished Dr. Onirifick's household, their presence among us was accepted by all and sundry as inevitable.

The piano was completely out of tune. Kronski's wife, a timid, mouse-like creature whose mouth seemed to be curled in a perpetual deprecatory smile, used to sit and practise the scales on this instrument, oblivious apparently of the hideous dissonances which her nimble fingers produced. To hear her play the Barcarolle, for example, was excruciating. She seemed not to hear the sour notes, the jangled chords; she played with an expression of utter serenity, her soul enrapt, her senses numbed and bewitched. It was a venomous composure which deceived no one, not even herself, for the moment her fingers ceased wandering she became what in truth she was—a petty, mean, spiteful, malevolent little bitch.

It was curious to see the way in which Kronski pretended to have found a jewel in this second wife. It would have been pathetic, not to say tragic, were he not such a ridiculous figure. He cavorted about her like a porpoise attempting to be elfish. Her digs and barbs served only to galvanize the ponderous, awkward figure in which was hidden a hyper-sensitive soul. He writhed and twisted like a wounded dolphin, the saliva dripping from his mouth, the sweat pouring from his brow and flooding his all too liquid eyes. It was a horrible charade he gave us on these occasions; though one pitied him one had to laugh, to laugh until the tears came to one's eyes.

If Curley were around he would turn on Curley savagely, in the very midst of his antics, and vent his spleen. He had a loathing for Curley that was inexplicable. Whether it was envy or jealousy which provoked these uncontrollable rages, whatever it was, Kronski would, in these moments, act like a man possessed. Like a huge cat, he would circle around poor Curley, taunting him, baiting him, stinging him with rebukes, slanders, insults, until he was actually foaming at the mouth.

«Why don't you do something, say something?» he would sneer. «Put up your dukes! Give me a crack, why don't you? You're yeller, aren't you? You're just a worm, a cad, a stooge.»

Curley would leer at him with a contemptuous smile, saying not a word, but poised and ready to strike should Kronski lose all control.

Nobody understood why these ugly scenes took place. Ghompal especially. He had evidently never witnessed such situations in his native land. They left him pained, wounded, shocked. Kronski felt this keenly, loathing himself even more than he loathed Curley. The more he fell in Gomphal's estimation the harder he strove to ingratiate himself with the Hindu.

«There's a really fine soul,» he would say to us. «I would do anything for Ghompal—*anything.*»

There were lots of things he might have done to alleviate the latter's burdens, but Kronski gave the impression that when the time came he would do something magnificent. Until then nothing less would satisfy him. He hated to see any one lend Ghompal a helping hand. «Trying to salve your conscience, eh?» he would snarl. «Why don't you put your arms around him and kiss him? Afraid of contamination, is that it?»

Once, just to make him uncomfortable, I did exactly that. I walked up to Ghompal and, putting my arms around him, I kissed him on the brow. Kronski looked at us shamefacedly. Every one knew that Ghompal had syphilis.

There was Dr. Onirifick himself, of course, a presence which made itself felt throughout the house, rather than a human being. What went on in that office of his on the second floor? None of us really knew. Kronski, in his elaborate, melodramatic way, gave crude imaginative pictures of abortion and

seduction, bloody jig-saw puzzles which only a
monster could put together. On the few occasions
when we met, Dr. Onirifick impressed me as being
nothing more than a mild, good-hearted man with a
smattering of learning and a deep interest in music.
Only for a few minutes did I see him lose his poise,
and that altogether justifiable. I had been reading
a book by Hilaire Belloc dealing with the persecution
of the Jew throughout the centuries. It was like
waving a red flag in front of him to even mention
the book and I immediately regretted the blunder.
In diabolical fashion Kronski tried to widen the
breach. «Why are we harboring this snake in the
grass?» he seemed to say, arching his eyebrows and
twitching and squirming in his customary way. Dr.
Onirifick, however, passed it off by treating me as if
I were merely another gullible idiot who had fallen
for the arch casuistry of a diseased Catholic mind.

«He was upset to-night,» Kronski volunteered after
the doctor had retired. «You see, he's after that
twelve-year old niece of his and his wife is on to him.
She's threatening to turn him over to the district
attorney if he doesn't stop running after the girl.
She's jealous as the devil and I don't blame her.
Besides, she hates to think of the abortions that are
pulled off every day, right under her nose, polluting
her home, as it were. She swears there's something
wrong with him. There's something wrong with her
too, if you notice. If you ask me, I think she's afraid
he'll cut her open some night. She looks at his hands
all the time, as if he always came to her fresh from
a murder.»

He paused a moment to let these observations sink
in. «There's something else preying on her mind,»
he resumed. «The daughter is growing up... she'll
be a young woman before long. Well, with a husband
like that you can see what's bothering her. It's not

just the idea of incest—horrible enough—but the
further thought, that... that he'll come to her some
night with bloody hands... the hands that murdered
the life in her own daughter's womb... Complicated,
what? But not impossible. Not with that guy!
such a fine fellow. A sensitive, delicate chap, really.
She's right. And what makes it worse is that he's
Almost Christ-like. You can't talk to him about the
sex mania because he won't admit a word you say.
He pretends to be absolutely innocent. But he's in
deep. Some day the police will come and take him
away—there'll be a hell of a stink, you'll see...»

That Dr. Onirifick had made it possible for Kronski
to pursue his medical studies I knew. And that
Kronski had to find some extraordinary way of paying
Dr. Onirifick back I was also aware of. Nothing
would suit him better than to have his friend
disintegrate completely. Then Kronski would come
to the rescue in magnificent fashion. He would do
something wholly unexpected, something no man had
ever done for another. That was how his mind
worked. Meanwhile, by spreading rumors, by
slandering and maligning his friend, by undermining
him, he was only hastening a downfall which was
inevitable. He was positively itching to get to work
on his friend, to rehabilitate him, to repay him
superabundantly for the kindness he had shown him
in putting him through college. He would pull the
house down about his friend's ears in order to rescue
him from the ruins. A curious attitude. A sort of
perverted Galahad. A meddler. A super-meddler.
Always doing his damndest to make things go from
bad to worse so that at the last ditch he, Kronski,
might step in and magically transform the situation.
Even so, it was not gratitude he desired but
recognition, recognition of superior powers, recognition of his uniqueness.

While he was still an interne I used to visit him occasionally at the hospital where he was serving his time. We used to play billiards with the other internes. I only visited the hospital when I was in a desperate mood, when I wanted a meal or the loan of a few dollars. I hated the atmosphere of the place; I loathed his associates, their manners, their conversation, their very aims even. The great healing art meant nothing to them; they were looking for a snug berth, that was all. Most of them had as little flair for medicine as a politician has for statesmanship. They didn't even have that fundamental prerequisite of the healer—the love of human kind. They were callous, heartless, utterly self-centered, utterly disinterested in anything but their own advancement. They were worse boors than the butchers in the slaughter-house.

Kronski was thoroughly at home in this environment. He knew more than the others, could out-talk them, out-smart them, out-shout them. He was a better billiard player, a better crap-shooter, a better chess player, a better everything. He knew it all and he loved to spew it forth, parade up and down in his own vomit.

Naturally he was heartily detested. Of a gregarious nature he managed, despite his obnoxious traits, to keep himself surrounded by his kind. Had he been obliged to live alone he would have fallen apart. He knew that he was not wanted: nobody ever sought him out except to ask a favor of him. Alone, the realization of his plight must have caused him bitter moments. It was difficult to know how he really appraised himself because in the presence of others he was all gusto, merriment, bluster, bravado, grandeur and grandiloquence. He behaved as though he were rehearsing a part before an invisible mirror. How he loved himself! Yes, and what loathing there was behind that façade, that amour-propre! «I smell bad!» that's what he must have said to himself every night when alone in his room. «But I'll do something magnificent yet... just watch!»

At intervals there came moods of dejection. He was a pitiful object then—something quite inhuman, something not of the animal world but of the vegetable kingdom. He would plop himself down somewhere and let himself rot. In this condition tumors sprouted from him, as from some gigantic mouldy potato left to perish in the dark. Nothing could stir him from his lethargy. Wherever he was put he would stay, inert, brooding incessantly, as though the world were coming to an end.

As far as one could make out he had no personal problems. He was a monster who had emerged from the vegetable kingdom without passing through the animal stage. His body, almost insentient, was invested with a mind which ruled him like a tyrant. His emotional life was a mush which he ladled out like a drunken Cossak. There was something almost anthropophagous about his tenderness; he demanded not the promptings and stirrings of the heart but the heart itself, and with it, if possible, the gizzard, the liver, the pancreas and other tender, edible portions of the human organism. In his exalted moments he seemed not only eager to devour the object of his tenderness but to invite the other to devour him also. His mouth would wreath itself in a veritable mandibular ecstasy; he would work himself up until the very soul of him came forth in a spongy ectoplasmic substance. It was a horrible state of affection, terrifying because it knew no bounds. It was a depersonalized glut or slop, a hang-over from some archaic condition of ecstasy—the residual memory of crabs and snakes, of their pro-

longed copulations in the protoplasmic slime of ages
long forgotten.

And now, in Cockroach Hall, as we called it, there
was preparing itself a delicious sexual omelette which
we were all to savour, each in his own particular
way.   There was something intestinal about the
atmosphere of the establishment, for it was an
establishment more than a home. It was the clinic
of love, so to speak, where embryos sprouted like
weeds and, like weeds, were pulled up by the roots
or chopped down with the scythe.

How the employment manager of the great Cosmodemonic Telegraph Company had ever allowed himself to be ensnared and trapped in this blood-soaked
den of sex surpasses understanding. The moment
I got off the train at the elevated station and started
descending the stairs into the heart of the Bronx
I became a different person. It was a walk of a
few blocks to Dr. Onirifick's establishment, just
sufficient to disorient me, to give me time to slip
into the role of the sensitive genius, the romantic
poet, the happy mystic who had found his true love
and who was ready to die for her.

There was a frightful discordance between this
new inner state of being and the physical atmosphere
of the neighborhood through which I had to plunge
each night. Everywhere the grim, monotonous walls
loomed up; behind them lived families whose whole
life centered about a job. Industrious, patient,
ambitious slaves whose one aim was emancipation.
In the interim putting up with anything; oblivious
of discomfort, immune to ugliness. Heroic little
souls whose very obsession to liberate themselves
from the thralldom of work served only to magnify
the squalor and the misery of their lives.

What proof had I that poverty could bear another
face? Only the dim, fuzzy memory of my child-

hood in the 14th Ward, Brooklyn. The memory of a child who had been sheltered, who had been given every opportunity, who had known nothing but joy and freedom—until he was ten years of age.

Why had I made that blunder in talking to Dr. Onirifick? I had not intended to talk about the Jews that evening—I had intended to talk about *The Path to Rome*. That was the book of Belloc's which had really set me on fire. A sensitive man, a scholar, a man for whom the history of Europe was a living memory, he had decided to walk from Paris to Rome with nothing but a knapsack and a stout walking stick. And he did. En route, all those things happened which always happen en route. It was my first understanding of the difference between process and goal, my first awareness of the truth that the goal of life is the living of it. How I envied Hilaire Belloc his adventure! Even to this day I can see in the corner of his pages the little pencil sketches he made of walls and spires, of turrets and bastions. I have only to think of the title of his book and I am sitting in the fields again, or standing on a quaint medieval bridge, or snoozing beside a quiet canal in the heart of France. I never dreamed that it would be possible for me to see that land, to walk through those fields, stand on those same bridges, follow those same canals. That could never happen to *me!* I was doomed.

When I think now of the ruse by which I was liberated, when I think that I was released from this prison because the one I loved wanted to get rid of me, what a sad, baffled, mystifying smile comes over my features. How confused and intricate everything is! We are grateful to those who stab us in the back; we run away from those who would help us; we congratulate ourselves on our good luck, never dreaming that our good luck may be a quagmire

from which it will be impossible to extricate ourselves. We run forward with head turned; we rush
blindly into the trap. We never escape, except into
a cul de sac.

I am walking through the Bronx, five or six blocks,
just time and space enough to twist myself into a
corkscrew. Mona will be there waiting for me.
She will embrace me warmly, as if we had never
embraced before. We will have only a couple of
hours together and then she will leave—to go to
the dance hall where she still works as a taxi girl.
I will be sound asleep when she returns at three or
four in the morning. She will pout and fret if I
don't awaken, if I don't throw my arms around her
passionately and tell her I love her. She has so
much to tell me each night and there is no time to
tell it. Mornings, when I leave, she is sound asleep.
We come and go like railroad trains. This is the
beginning of our life together.

I love her, heart and soul. She is everything to
me. And yet she is nothing like the women I
dreamed of, like those ideal creatures whom I worshipped as a boy. She corresponds to nothing I had
conceived out of my own depths. She is a totally
new image, something foreign, something which
Fate whirled across my path from some unknown
sphere. As I look at her, as I get to love her morsel
by morsel, I find that the totality of her escapes me.
My love adds up like a sum, but she, the one I am
seeking with desperate, hungry love, escapes like an
elixir. She is completely mine, almost slavishly so,
but I do not possess her. It is I who am possessed.
I am possessed by a love such as was never offered
me before—an engulfing love, a total love, a love
of my very toe-nails and the dirt beneath them—
and yet my hands are forever fluttering, forever
grasping and clutching, seizing nothing.

Coming home one evening, I observed out of the corner of my eye of those soft, sensuous creatures of the ghetto who seem to emerge from the pages of the Old Testament. She was one of the Jewesses whose name must be Ruth or Esther. Or perhaps *Miriam*.

Miriam, yes! That was the name I was searching for. Why was that name so wonderful to me? How could such a simple appellation evoke such powerful emotions? I kept asking myself this question.

Miriam is the name of names. If I could mould all women into the perfect ideal, if I could give this ideal all the qualities I seek in woman, her name would be Miriam.

I had forgotten completely the lovely creature who inspired these reflections. I was on the track of something, and as my pace quickened, as my heart thumped more madly, I suddenly recalled the face, the voice, the figure, the gestures of the Miriam I knew as a boy of twelve. Miriam Painter, she called herself. Only fifteen or sixteen, but full-blown, radiantly alive, flagrant as a flower and—untouchable. She was not a Jewess, nor did she even remotely suggest the memory of those legendary creatures of the Old Testament. (Or perhaps I had not then read the Old Testament.) She was the young woman with long chestnut hair, with frank, open eyes and rather generous mouth who greeted me cordially whenever we met on the street. Always at ease, always giving herself, always radiant with health and good nature; withal wise, sympathetic, full of understanding. With her it was unnecessary to make awkward overtures: she always came towards me beaming with this secret inner joy, always welling over. She swallowed me up and carried me along; she enfolded me like a mother, warmed me like a mistress, dispatched me like a fairy. I never had an impure thought about her: never desired her, never craved for a caress. I loved her so deeply, so completely, that each time I met her it was like being born again. All I demanded was that she should remain alive, be of this earth, be somewhere, anywhere, in this world, and never die. I hoped for nothing, I wanted nothing of her. Her mere existence was all-sufficing. Yes, I used to run into the house, hide myself away, and thank God aloud for having sent Miriam to this earth of ours. What a miracle! And what a blessed thing to love like this!

I don't know how long this went on. I haven't the slightest idea whether she was aware of my adoration or not. What matter? I was in love, with love. To love! To surrender absolutely, to prostrate oneself before the divine image, to die a thousand imaginary deaths, to annihilate every trace of self, to find the whole universe embodied and enshrined in the living image of another! Adolescent, we say. Rot! This is the germ of the future life, the seed which we hide away, which we bury deep within us, which we smother and stifle and do our utmost to destroy as we advance from one experience to another and flutter and flounder and lose our way.

By the time I meet the second ideal—Una Gifford —I am already diseased. Only fifteen years of age and the canker is gnawing at my vitals. How explain it? Miriam had dropped out of my life, not dramatically, but quietly, unostentatiously. She simply disappeared, was seen no more. I didn't even realize what it meant. I didn't think about it. People came and went; objects appeared and disappeared. I was in the flux, like the others, and it was all natural even if inexplicable. I was beginning to read, to read too much. I was turning inward, closing in on myself, as flowers close up in the night.

Una Gifford brings nothing but pain and anguish. I want her, I need her, I can't live without her. She says neither Yes or No, for the simple reason that I have not the courage to put the question to her. I will be sixteen shortly and we are both still in school—we are only going to graduate next year. How can a girl your own age, to whom you only nod or stare at, be the woman without whom life is impossible? How can you dream of marriage before you have crossed the threshold of life? But if I had eloped with Una Gifford then, at the age of fifteen, if I had married her and had ten children by her, it would have been right, dead right. What matter if I became something utterly different, if I sank down to the bottom rung? What matter if it meant premature old age? I had a need for her which was never answered, and that need was like a wound which grew and grew until it became a gaping hole. As life went on, as that desperate need grew more intense, I dragged everything into the hole and murdered it.

I was not aware, when I first knew Mona, how much she needed me. Nor did I realize how great a transformation she had made of her life, her habits, her background, her antecedents, in order to offer me that ideal image of herself which she all too quickly suspected that I had created. She had changed everything—her name, her birthplace, her mother, her upbringing, her friends, her tastes, even her desires. It was characteristic of her that she should want to change my name too, which she did. I was now Val, the diminutive of Valentine which I had always been ashamed of—it seemed like a sissy's name—but now that it issued from her lips it sounded like the name which suited me. Nobody else called me Val, though they heard Mona repeat it endlessly. To my friends I was what I always had been; they were not hypnotized by a mere change of name.

Of transformations.... I remember vividly the first night we passed at Dr. Onirifick's place. We had taken a shower together, shuddering at the sight of the myriads of roaches which infested the bathroom. We got into bed beneath the eiderdown quilt. We had had an ecstatic fuck in this strange public room filled with bizarre objects. We were drawn very close together that night. I had separated from my wife and she had separated from her parents. We hardly knew why we had accepted to live in this outlandish house; in our proper senses neither of us would have dreamed of choosing such a setting. But we were not in our right senses. We were feverish to begin a new life, and we felt guilty, both of us, for the crimes we had committed in order to embark on the great adventure. Mona felt it more than I, in the beginning. She felt that she had been responsible for the break. It was the child which I had left behind, not my wife, whom she felt sorry for. It preyed on her mind. With it was the fear, no doubt, that I would wake up one day and realize that I had made a mistake. She struggled to make herself indispensable, to love me with such devotion, such complete self-sacrifice, that the past would be annihilated. She didn't do it deliberately. She wasn't even aware of what she was doing. But she clung to me desperately, so desperately that when I think of it now the tears come to my eyes. Because it was unnecessary: I needed her even more than she needed me.

And so, as we were falling off to sleep that night, as she rolled over to turn her back on me, the cover slipped off and I became aware, from the animal-like crouch she had assumed, of the massive quality of her back. I ran my two hands over her flesh,

caressed her back as one would caress the flanks of
a lioness. It was curious that I had never been
aware of her superb back. We had slept together
many times and we had fallen asleep in all sorts of
postures, but I had noticed nothing. Now, in this
huge bed which seemed to float in the wan light of
the big room, her back became engraved in my
memory. I had no definite thoughts about it—just
vague pleasure sensations of the strength and the
vitality that was in her. *One who could support the
world on her back!* I didn't formulate anything so
definite as that, but it was there, the thought, in
some vague, obscure region of my consciousness. In
my finger-tips more likely.

Under the shower I had teased her about her
tummy, which was growing rather generous, and I
realized at once that she was extremely sensitive
about her figure. But I was not critical of her
opulent flesh—I was delighted to discover it. It
carried a promise, I thought. And then, under my
very eyes, this body which had been so generously
endowed began to shrink. The inner torture was
beginning to take its toll. At the same time the
fire that was in her began to burn more brightly.
Her flesh was consumed by the passion that ravaged
her. Her strong, columnar neck, the part of her body
which I most admired, grew slenderer and slenderer,
until the head seemed like a giant peony swaying
on its fragile stem.

«You're not ill?» I would ask, alarmed by this
swift transformation.

«Of course not!» she would say. «I'm reducing.»

«But you're carrying it too far, Mona.»

«I was like this as a girl,» she would answer.
«It's natural for me to be thin.»

«But I don't want you to grow thin. I don't want

you to change. Look at your neck—do you want
to have a scrawny neck?»

«My neck isn't scrawny,» she would say, jumping
up to look at herself in the mirror.

«I didn't say it was, Mona... but it may get that
way if you keep on in this reckless fashion.»

«Please Val, don't talk about it. You don't understand....»

«Mona, don't talk that way. I'm not criticizing
you. I only want to protect you.»

«You don't like me this way... is that it?»

«Mona, I like you *any* way. I love you. I adore
you. But please be reasonable. I'm afraid you're
going to fade away, evaporate in thin air. I don't
want you to get ill...»

«Don't be silly, Val. I never felt better in my
life.»

«By the way,» she added, «are you going to see
the little one this Saturday?» She would never
mention either my wife or the child by name. Also,
she preferred to think that I was visiting only the
child on these weekly expeditions to Brooklyn.

I said I thought I would go... why, was there any
reason not to?

«No, no!» she said, jerking her head strangely
and turning away to look for something in the bureau
drawer.

I stood behind her, as she was leaning over, and
clasped my arms around her waist.

«Mona, tell me something... Does it hurt you very
much when I go over there? Tell me honestly.
Because if it does, I'll stop going. It has to come
to an end some day anyway.»

«You know I don't want you to stop. Have I ever
said anything against it?»

«No-o-o,» I said, lowering my head and gazing

intently at the carpet. «No-o-o, you never say anything. But sometimes I wish you would...»

«Why do you say that?» she cried sharply. She looked almost indignant. «Haven't you a right to see your own daughter? I would do it, if I were in your place.» She paused a moment and then, unable to control herself, she blurted out: «I would never have left her if she had been mine. I wouldn't have given her up, not for anything!»

«Mona! What are you saying. What does this mean?»

«Just that. I don't know how you can do it. I'm not worth such a sacrifice. Nobody is.»

«Let's drop it,» I said. «We're going to say things we don't mean. I tell you, I don't regret anything. It was no sacrifice, understand that. I wanted you and I got you. I'm happy. I could forget everybody if it were necessary. You're the whole world to me, and you know it.»

I seized her and pulled her to me. A tear rolled down her cheek.

«Listen, Val, I don't ask you to give up anything, but...»

«But what?»

«Couldn't you meet me once in a while at night when I quit work?»

«At two in the morning?»

«I know... it *is* an ungodly hour.... but I feel terribly lonely when I leave the dance hall. Especially after dancing with all those men, all those stupid, horrible creatures who mean nothing to me. I come home and you're asleep. What have I got?»

«Don't say that, *please*. Yes, of course I'll meet you—now and then.»

«Couldn't you take a nap after dinner and...»

«Sure I could. Why didn't you tell me sooner? It was selfish of me not to think of that.»

«You're not selfish, Val.»

«I am too... Listen, supposing I ride down with you this evening? I'll come back, take a snooze, and meet you at closing time.»

«You're sure it won't be too tiring?»

«No, Mona, it'll be wonderful.»

On the way home, however, I began to realize what it would mean to arrange my hours thus. At two o'clock we would catch a bite somewhere. An hour's ride on the elevated. In bed Mona would chat a while before going to sleep. It would be almost five o'clock by that time and by seven I would have to be up again ready for work.

I got into the habit of changing my clothes every evening, in preparation for the rendezvous at the dance hall. Not that I went every evening—no, but I went as often as possible. Changing into old clothes—a khaki shirt, a pair of moccasins, sporting one of the canes which Mona had filched from Carruthers—my romantic self asserted itself. I led two lives: one at the Cosmodemonic Telegraph Company and another with Mona. Sometimes Florrie joined us at the restaurant. She had found a new lover, a German doctor who, from all accounts, must have possessed an enormous tool. He was the only man who could satisfy her, that she made clear. This frail-looking creature with a typical Irish mug, the Broadway type par excellence, who would have suspected that between her legs there was a gash big enough to hide a sledge hammer—or that she liked women as well as men? She liked anything that had to do with sex. The gash was now rooted in her mind. It kept spreading and spreading until there was no room, in mind or gash, for anything but a superhuman prick.

One evening, after I had taken Mona to work, I started wandering through the side streets. I

thought perhaps I would go to a cinema and meet
Mona after the performance. As I passed a doorway
I heard someone call my name. I turned round and
in the hallway, as though hiding from some one,
stood Florrie and Hannah Bell. We went across the
street to have a drink. The girls acted nervous and
fidgety. They said they would have to leave in a
few minutes—they were just having a drink to be
sociable. I had never been alone with them before
and they were uneasy, as if afraid of revealing things
I ought not to know. Quite innocently I took
Florrie's hand which was lying in her lap and
squeezed it, to reassure her—of what I don't know.
To my amazement she squeezed it warmly and then,
bending forward as if to say something confidential
to Hannah, she unloosed her grip and fumbled in
my fly. A that moment a man walked in whom they
greeted effusively. I was introduced as a friend.
Monahan was the man's name. «He's a detective,»
said Florrie, giving me a melting look. The man
had hardly taken a seat when Florrie jumped up
and seizing Hannah's arm whisked her out of the
place. At the door she waved good-bye. They ran
across the street, in the direction of the doorway
where they had been hiding.

«A strange way to act,» said Monahan. «What'll
you have?» he asked, calling the waiter over. I
ordered another whisky and looked at him blankly.
I didn't relish the idea of being left with a detective
on my hands. Monahan however was in a different
frame of mind; he seemed happy to have found
some one to talk to. Observing the cane and the
sloppy attire he at once came to the conclusion that
I was an artist of some sort.

«You're dressed like an artist» (meaning a painter)
«but you're not an artist. Your hands are too delicate.» He seized my hands and examined them

quickly. «You're not a musician either,» he added.
«Well, there's only one thing left—you're a writer!»

I nodded, half amused, half irritated. He was the
type of Irishman whose directness antagonizes me.
I could foresee the inevitable challenging *Why?*
Why not? How come? What do you mean? As
always, I began by being bland and indulgent. I
agreed with him. But he didn't want me to agree
with him—he wanted to argue.

I had hardly said a word and yet in the space of
a few minutes he was insulting me and at the same
time telling me how much he liked me.

«You're just the sort of chap I wanted to meet,» he
said, ordering more drinks. «You know more than
I do, but you won't talk. I'm not good enough for
you, I'm a low-brow. That's where you're wrong!
Maybe I know a lot of things you don't suspect.
Maybe I can tell you a few things. *Why don't you
ask me something?*»

What was I to say? There wasn't anything I
wanted to know—from him, at least. I wanted to
get up and go—without offending him. I didn't
want to be jerked back into my seat by that long
hairy arm and be slobbered over and grilled and
argued with and insulted. Besides, I was feeling a
little woozy. I was thinking of Florrie and how
strangely she had behaved—and I could still feel her
hand fumbling in my fly.

«You don't seem to be all there,» he said. «I
thought writers were quick on the trigger, always
there with the bright repartee. What's the matter—
don't you want to be sociable? Maybe you don't like
my mug? *Listen*»—and he laid his heavy hand on
my arm—«get this straight... I'm your friend, see!
I want to have a talk with you. You're going to tell
me things... all the things I don't know. You're going
to wise me up. Maybe I won't get it all at once, but

I'm going to listen. We're not going to leave here until we get this settled, see what I mean?» With this he gave me one of those strange Irish smiles, a mélange of warmth, sincerity, perplexity and violence. It meant that he was going to get what he wanted out of me or lay me out flat. For some inexplicable reason he was convinced that I had something which he sorely needed, some clue to the riddle of life, which, even if he couldn't grasp it entirely, would serve him in good stead.

By this time I was almost in a panic. It was precisely the sort of situation that I am incapable of dealing with. I could have murdered the bastard in cold blood.

A mental uppercut, that's what he wanted of me. He was tired of beating the piss out of the other fellow—he wanted some one to go to work on *him*.

I decided to go at it directly, to deflate him with one piercing lunge and then trust to my wits.

«You want me to talk frankly, is that it?» I gave him an ingenuous smile.

«Sure, sure,» he retorted. «Fire away! I can take it.»

«Well, to begin with,» says I, still offering the bland, reassuring smile, «you're just a louse and you know it. You're afraid of something, what it is I don't know yet, but we'll get to it. With me you pretend that you're a low-brow, a nobody, but to yourself you pretend that you're smart, a big shot, a tough guy. You're not afraid of a thing, are you? That's all shit and you know it. You're full of fear. You say you can take it. *Take what? A sock in the jaw?* Of course you can, with a cement mug like yours. But can you stand the truth?»

He gave me a hard, glittery smile. His face, violently flushed, indicated that he was doing his utmost to control himself. He wanted to say «Yes,

go on!» but the words choked him. He just nodded
and turned on the electric smile.

«You've beaten up many a rat with your bare
hands, haven't you? Somebody held the guy down
and you went at him until he screamed blue murder.
You wrung a confession out of him and then you
dusted yourself off and poured a few drinks down
your throat. He was a rat and he deserved what he
got. But you're a bigger rat, and that's what's eating
you up. You like to hurt people. You probably
pulled the wings off flies when you were a kid.
Somebody hurt you once and you can't forget it.»
(I could feel him wince at this.) «You go to church
regularly and you confess, but you don't tell the truth.
You tell half-truths. You never tell the Father what
a lousy stinking son of a bitch you really are. You
tell him about your little sins. You never tell him
what pleasure you get beating up defenceless guys
who never did you any harm. And of course you
always put a generous donation in the box. *Hush
money!* As if that could quiet your conscience!
Everybody says what a swell guy you are—except the
poor bastards whom you track down and beat the piss
out of. You tell yourself that it's your job, you have
to be that way or else... It's hard for you to figure
out just what else you could do if you ever lost your
job, isn't that so? What assets have you? What do
you know? What are you good for? Sure, you
might make a street-cleaner or a garbage collector,
though I doubt that you have the guts for it. But
you don't know anything useful, do you? You don't
read, you don't associate with any but your own kind.
Your sole interest is politics. Very important,
politics! Never know when you may need a friend.
Might murder the wrong guy some day, and then
what? Why, then you'd want somebody to lie for
you, somebody who'd go to the bat for you—some

low-down worm like yourself who hasn't a shred of
manhood or a spark or decency in him. And in
return you'd do *him* a good turn some day—I mean
you'd bump some one off some time, if he asked
you to.»

I paused for just a second.

«If you really want to know what I think, I'd say
you've murdered a dozen innocent guys already. I'd
say that you've got a wad in your pocket that would
choke a horse. I'd say that you've got something on
your conscience—and you came here to drown it.
I'd say that you know why those girls got up suddenly
and ran across the street. I'd say that if we knew
all about you you might be eligible for the electric
chair...»

Completely out of breath, I stopped and
mechanically rubbed my jaw, as if surprised to find
it still intact. Monahan, unable to hold himself in
any longer, burst out with an alarming guffaw.

«You're crazy,» he said, «crazy as a bedbug, but
I like you. Go on, talk some more. Say the worst
you know—I want to hear it.» And with that he
called the waiter over and ordered another round.
«You're right about one thing,» he added, «I have
got a wad in my pocket. *Want to see it?*» He fished
out a roll of greenbacks, flipped them under my nose,
like a cardsharper. «Go on now, give it to me...!»

The sight of the money derailed me. My one
thought was how to separate him from some of his
ill-gained boodle.

«It *was* a bit crazy, all that stuff I just handed
you,» I began, adopting another tone. «I'm surprised
you didn't haul off and crack me. My nerves are on
edge, I guess... »

«Don't have to tell *me*,» said Monahan.

I adopted a still more conciliatory tone. «Let me
tell you something about myself,» I continued in an

even voice, and in a few brief strokes I outlined my
position in the Cosmodemonic skating rink, my
relationship with O'Rourke, the company detective,
my ambition to be a writer, my visits to the psycho-
pathic ward, and so on. Just enough to let him
know that I was not a dreamer. The mention of
O'Rourke's name impressed him. O'Rourke's brother
(as I well knew) was Monahan's boss and he stood in
awe of him.

«And you pal around with O'Rourke?»

«He's a great friend of mine,» said I. «A man I
respect. He's almost a father to me. I learned
something about human nature from him. O'Rourke's
a big man doing a small job. He belongs somewhere
else, where I don't know. However, he seems satisfied
to be where he is, though he's working himself to
death. What galls me is that he isn't appreciated.»

I went on in this vein, extolling O'Rourke's virtues,
indicating none too subtly the comparison between
O'Rourke's methods and those of the ordinary flat-
foot.

My words were producing the effect intended.
Monahan was visibly wilting, softening like a sponge.

«You've got me wrong,» he finally burst out. «I've
got as big a heart as the next guy, only I don't show
it. You can't go around exposing yourself—not on
this job. We ain't all like O'Rourke, I'll grant you,
but we're human, b'Jesus! You're an idealist, that's
what's the matter with you. You want perfection...»
He gave me a strange look, mumbled to himself.
Then he continued in a clear, calm voice: « The
more you talk the more I like you. You've got
something I once had. I was ashamed of it then...
you know, afraid of being a sissy or something. Life
hasn't spoiled you—that's what I like about you
You know what it's like and yet it doesn't make you
sour or mean. You said some pretty nasty things a

while back, and to tell you the truth, I *was* going to take a swing at you. *Why didn't I?* Because you weren't talking to *me:* you were aiming at all the guys like me who got off the track somewhere. You sound personal, but you ain't. You're talking to the world all the time. You should have been a preacher, do you realize that? You and O'Rourke, you're a good team. I mean it. We guys have a job to do and we don't get any fun out of it; you guys work for the pleasure of it. And what's more... well, never mind... Look, give me your hand...» He reached for my free hand and grasped it in a vice. «*You see*», (I winced as he applied the pressure) «I could squeeze your hand to a pulp. I wouldn't have to make a pass at you. I could just sit like this, talking to you, looking straight at you, and crush your hand to a pulp. That's the strength I have.»

He relaxed his grip and I withdrew my hand quickly. It felt numb, paralyzed.

«There's nothing to that, you see,» he went on. «That's dumb brute strength; you've got another kind of strength which I lack. You could make mince meat of me with that tongue of yours. You've got a brain.» He looked away, as if absent-minded. «How is your hand?» he said, dreamy-like. «I didn't hurt you, did I?»

I felt it with my other hand. It was limp and useless.

«It's all right, I guess.»

He looked me through and through, then laughingly he burst out: «I'm hungry. Let's eat something.»

We went downstairs and inspected the kitchen first. He wanted me to see how clean everything was: went about picking up carving knives and cleavers, holding them up to the light for me to examine and admire.

«I had to chop a guy down with one of these

once.» He brandished a cleaver. «Split him in two, clean as a whistle.»

Taking my arm affectionately he led me back upstairs. «Henry,» says he, «we're going to be pals. You're going to tell me more about yourself—and you're going to let me help you. You've got a wife—very beautiful too.» I gave an involuntary jerk. He tightened his grip on my arm and led me to the table.

«Henry, let's talk straight for a change. I know a thing or two, even if I don't look it.» *Pause.* «Get your wife out of that joint!»

I was just about to say «What joint?» when he resumed: « A guy can get mixed up in all sorts of things and come out clean—sometimes. But a woman's different. You don't like to see her working there, with those dizzy fluffs, do you? Find out what's keeping her there. Don't get sore now... I'm not trying to hurt your feelings. I don't know anything about your wife—that is, any more than I've heard...»

«She's not my wife,» I blurted out.

«Well, whatever she is to you,» he said smoothly, as if that were quite an unimportant detail, «get her out of that joint! I'm telling you like a friend. I know what I'm talking about.»

I began to put two and two together, rapidly, fitfully. My mind shifted back to Florrie and Hannah, to their sudden exit. Was there going to be a raid, a shake-up—or a shake-down? Was he trying to warn me?

He must have divined what was going on in my head, for the next thing out of his mouth was this: «If she has to have a job let me try to find her something. She could do something else, couldn't she? An attractive girl like her...»

«Let's drop it,» I said, «and thanks for the tip.»

For a while we ate in silence. Then, apropos of

nothing, Monahan took out the fat wad of greenbacks
and peeled off two fifty dollar bills. He placed them
beside my plate. «Take them,» he said «and put
'em in your pocket. Let her try the theatre, why
don't you?» He lowered his head to shovel a forkful
of spaghetti into his mouth. I picked up the bills and
quietly shoved them into my trousers pocket.

As soon as I could free myself I set off to meet
Mona in front of the dance hall. I was in a strange
mood.

My head was spinning a bit as I rolled merrily
along towards Broadway. I was determined to be
cheerful, though something told me I had reason to
be otherwise. The meal and the few parting shots
that Monahan had succeeded in driving home had
sobered me up somewhat. I felt large and luxuriant,
in a mood to enjoy my own thoughts. *Euphoric*, as
Kronski would say. To me that always meant being
happy for no reason. Just being happy, knowing
you're happy, and staying happy no matter what any
one says or does. It wasn't alcoholic joy; the whis-
kies may have precipitated the mood, but nothing
more. It wasn't some underneath self that was
cropping out—it was rather an overhead self, if I
might put it that way. With each step I took the
fumes of the liquor evaporated; my mind was growing
almost frighteningly clear.

As I passed a theatre a glancing look at a bill-
board brought back a familiar face. I knew who it
was, the name and everything, and I was astonished
but—well, to put it truthfully, I was so much more
astonished by what was going on inside me that I
hadn't time or room to be astonished by something
that had happened to some one else. I would come
back to *her* later, when the euphoria had passed

away. And just as I was promising myself that, who
did I run into head on but my old friend Bill Woodruff.

Hello hello, how are you, yes fine, long time since
I saw you, what are you doing, how's the wife, see
you again some time, yes I'm in a hurry, sure I'll
come up, so long, good-bye... it went like that, rat-a-
tat-tat. Two solid bodies colliding in space at the
wrong time, rubbing surfaces together, exchanging
souvenirs, plugging in wrong numbers, promising and
re-promising, forgetting, parting, remembering again...
hurried, mechanical, meaningless, and what the hell
does it all add up to?

After ten years he looked just the same, Woodruff.
I wanted to take a look at myself in the mirror—
quick. *Ten years!* And he wanted all the news in a
nut-shell. Dumb bastard! A sentimentalist. *Ten
years.* I ran back through the years, down a long
twisted funnel of a corridor with distorted mirrors on
either side. I got right to that spot in time and
space where I had Woodruff fixed in my mind the
way I would always see him, even in the next world.
He was pinned there, as if he were a winged specimen
under the microscope. That was where he revolved
helplessly on his axis. And that's where *she* comes
in—the one whose picture flashed through my brain
as I passed the theatre. She was the one he was
crazy about, the girl he couldn't live without, and
everybody had to help him woo her, even his mother
and father, even his cluck of a Prussian brother-in-
law whose guts he hated.

Ida Verlaine. Born to fit the name. She was just
exactly the way her name sounded—pretty, vain,
theatrical, faithless, spoiled, pampered, petted. Beautiful as a Dresden doll, only she had raven tresses and
a Javanese slant to her soul. If she had a soul at
all! Lived entirely in the body, in her senses, her

desires—and she directed the show, the body show, with her tyrannical little will which poor Woodruff translated as some monumental force of character.

Ida, Ida.... He used to chew our ears off about her. She was delicate in a perverse way, like one of Cranach's nudes. The body very fair, the hair very black, the soul tilted backwards, like a stone becoming dislodged from its Egyptian setting. They had disgraceful scenes during the courtship; Woodruff would often leave her in tears. The next day he would send her orchids or a beautiful lavellier or a gigantic box of chocolates. Ida swallowed everything, like a pythoness. She was heartless and insatiable.

Eventually he prevailed on her to marry him. He must have bribed her, for it was obvious that she despised him. He built a beautiful little love nest which was far beyond his means, bought her the clothes and other things she craved, took her to the theatre several nights a week, stuffed her with sweets, sat by her side and held her hand when she was having her menstrual pains, consulted a specialist if she had a cough, and in general played the fond, doting husband.

The more he did for her the less she cared for him. She was a monster from head to toe. Little by little it leaked out that she was frigid. None of us believed it of course, except Woodruff. He was to have the same experience later, with his second wife, and if he had lived long enough he would have had it with the third and fourth wives. With Ida his infatuation was so great that, if she had lost her legs, I don't think it would have altered his affection in the least—in fact, he would only have loved her the more.

For all his faults Woodruff was keen on friendship. There were at least six of us whom he had taken to his bosom and whom he trusted implicitly.

I was one of them—his oldest friend, as a matter of
fact. I had the privilege of walking in and out of
his home at will; I could eat, sleep, bathe, shave there
I was one of the family.

From the very beginning I disliked Ida, not because
of her behavior towards Woodruff, but instinctively
Ida in turn was uneasy in my presence. She didn't
quite know what to make of me. I never criticized
her nor did I ever flatter her; I acted as though she
were the wife of my friend, and nothing more. She
wasn't satisfied with such an attitude, naturally. She
wanted to bring me under her spell, make me walk
the tight-rope, as she had done with Woodruff and
her other suitors. Oddly enough, I was never more
immune to a woman's charms. I just didn't give a
fuck for her, as a person, though I often wondered
what she might be like as a piece of fuck, so to speak.
I wondered about it in a detached way, but somehow
it got across to her, got under her skin.

Sometimes, after passing the night at their home.
she would complain aloud that she didn't want to be
left alone with me. Woodruff would be standing at
the door, ready to go to work, and she pretending to
be worried. I'd be lying in bed waiting for her to
bring me my breakfast. And Woodruff saying to
her: «Don't talk that way, Ida. He's not going to
harm you—I'd trust him with my life.»

Sometimes I'd burst out laughing and yell: «Don't
worry, Ida, I'm not going to rape you. I'm impotent.»

«*You impotent?*» she'd scream with pretended
hysteria. «You're not impotent. You're a lecher.»

«Bring him his breakfast!» Woodruff would say,
and off to work he'd go.

She hated the thought of waiting on me in bed.
She didn't do it for her husband and she couldn't
see why she should do it for me. To take breakfast in
bed was something I never did, except at Woodruff's

place. I did it expressly to annoy and humiliate her.

«Why don't you get up and come to the table?» she would say.

«I can't—I've got an erection.»

«Oh, stop talking about that thing. Can't you think of anything but sex?»

Her words implied that sex was horrible, nasty, simply odious to her, but her manner indicated quite the oposite. She was a lascivious bitch, frigid only because she had the heart of a whore. If I ran my hand up her leg when she put the tray on my lap she would say: «Are you satisfied? Take a good feel while you're at it. I wish Bill could see you, see what a loyal friend he has.»

«Why don't you tell him?» says I one day.

«He wouldn't believe me, the simp. He'd think I was trying to make him jealous.»

I would ask her to prepare the bath for me. She would pretend to demur but she would do it just the same. One day, while I was seated in the tub soaping myself, I noticed that she had forgotten the towels. «Ida,» I called, «bring me some towels!» She walked into the bathroom and handed me them. She had on a silk bathrobe and a pair of silk hose. As she stooped over the tub to put the towels on the rack her bathrobe slid open. I slid to my knees and buried my head in her muff. It happened so quickly that she didn't have time to rebel, or even to pretend to rebel. In a moment I had her in the tub, stockings and all. I slipped the bathrobe off and threw it on the floor. I left the stockings on—it made her more lascivious looking, more the Cranach type. I lay back and pulled her on top of me. She was just like a bitch in heat, biting me all over, panting, gasping, wriggling like a worm on the hook. As we were drying ourselves she bent over and began nibbling at my prick. I sat on the edge of the tub and she kneeled at my feet gobbling it. After a while I made her stand up, bend over; then I let her have it from the rear. She had a small juicy cunt which fitted me like a glove. I bit the nape of her neck, the lobes of her ears, the sensitive spot on her shoulder, and as I pulled away I left the mark of my teeth on her beautiful white ass. Not a word spoken. When we had finished she went to her room and began dressing. I heard her humming softly to herself. I was quite amazed that she was capable of expressing her tenderness that way.

From that day on she only waited for Woodruff to go in order to throw herself on me.

«Aren't you afraid he might come back unexpectedly and find you in bed with me?» I asked once.

«He wouldn't believe his eyes. He'd think we were fooling.»

«He wouldn't think we were fooling if he felt this,» and I gave her a jolt that made her gasp.

«God, if he only knew how to take me! He's too eager. He takes it out like a broomstick and shoves it in before I've had a chance to feel anything. I just lie there and let him work it off—it's over in a jiffy. But with you I get hot before you even touch me. It's because you don't care, I suppose. You don't really like me, do you?»

«I like *this*,» said I, giving her a stiff jab. «I like your cunt, Ida... it's the best thing about you.»

«You dog,» she said. «I ought to hate you for that.»

«Why don't you hate me, then?»

«Oh, don't talk about it,» she murmured cuddling closer and working herself up to a lather. «Just keep it there and hold me tight. Here, bite my breast... not too hard... *there*, that's it.» She reached for my hands and pressed my fingers into her crack.

«Go on, do it, do it!» she muttered, her eyes rolling, her breath coming short.

A little later, at lunch: «Do you have to run off now? Can't you stay a little longer?»

«You want another crack at it, is that it?»

«Can't you put it more delicately? God, if Bill ever heard you say that!»

I got up and pushed her chair back. I took her leg and swung it over the arm of the chair.

«You never wear any undies, do you? You're a slut, do you know it?»

I pulled her dress up and made her sit that way while I finished my coffee.

«Play with it a bit while I finish this.»

«You're filthy,» she said, but she did as I told her.

«Take your two fingers and open it up. I like the color of it. It's like coral inside. Just like your ears. You say he's got a terrific wang, Bill. I don't know how he ever gets it in there.» With this I reached for a candle on the dresser at my side and I handed it to her.

«Let's see if you can get it in all the way.»

She spread the other leg over the other arm of the chair and began to work it in. She was looking at herself intently, her lips parted as if on the verge of an orgasm. She began to move back and forth, then rolled her ass around. I pushed her chair back farther, got down on my knees, and watched.

«You can make me do anything, you dirty devil.»

«You like it, don't you?»

She was on the point of coming off. I pulled the candle out and slipped three fingers inside her twat.

«Is it big enough for you?» She pulled my head close and bit my lips.

I stood up and unbuttoned my fly. In a jiffy she had it out and in her mouth. Gobble, gobble, like a hungry buzzard. I came in her mouth.

«God,» she said, choking and sputtering, «I never did that before.» She ran to the bathroom, as if she had swallowed poison.

I went inside and flung myself on the bed. I lit a cigarette and waited for her to join me. I knew it was going to be a long drawn-out affair.

She came back in the silk bathrobe, nothing underneath. «Take your things off,» she said, pulling back the covers and diving in. We lay there fondling each other, her cunt sopping wet.

«You smell wonderful,» I said. «What did you do?»

She pulled my hand away and put it to my nostrils.

«Not bad,» I said, «what is it?»

«Guess!»

She got up impulsively, went to the bathroom and came back with a small bottle of perfume. She spilt some into her hand and rubbed my genitals with it; then she sprinkled a few drops on the pubic hairs. It stung like fire. I grabbed the bottle and soused her with it all over, from head to foot. Then I began licking her arm-pits, chewed the hair over her cunt, and slid my tongue like a snake down the curve of her thighs. She bobbed up and down as if she were having convulsions. It went on like this until I had such an erection that even after I shot a wad into her it stayed up like a hammer. That excited her terribly. She wanted to try all sorts of positions and she did. She had several orgasms in succession and almost fainted in the process. I laid her on a small table and when she was on the verge of exploding I picked her up and walked around the room with her; then I took it out and made her walk on her hands, holding her by the thighs, letting it slip out now and then to excite her still more.

Her lips were chewed to a frazzle and she was full of marks, some green, some blue. I had a strange taste in my mouth, of fish glue and Chanel 976 1/2. My cock looked like a bruised rubber hose; it hung between my legs, extended an inch or two beyond its normal length and swollen beyond recognition. When I got to the street I felt weak in the knees. I went to the drug store and swallowed a couple of malted milks. A royal bit of fucking, thought I to myself, wondering how I'd act when I met Woodruff again.

Things happened to Woodruff in quick succession. First of all he lost his job at the bank. Then Ida ran off with one of his best friends. When he discovered that she had been sleeping with the fellow for a year before she ran off, he grew so despondent that he went on a bat which lasted for a year. After that he was knocked down by a car and his brain trepanned. Then his sister went crazy, setting fire to the house and burning her own children alive.

He couldn't understand why these things should happen to him, Bill Woodruff, who had never done anybody any harm.

Now and then I would run into him on Broadway and we would have a little chat standing on a street corner. He never gave any hint that he suspected me of having tinkered with his beloved Ida. He spoke of her bitterly now, as a thankless slut who had never showed a spark of feeling. But it was evident he still loved her. However, he had taken up with another girl, a manicurist, not so attractive as Ida, but loyal and trustworthy, as he put it. «I want you to meet her some time,» said he. I promised I would—some time. And then, as I was parting from him, I said: «What did become of Ida, do you know?»

«She's on the stage,» he said. «Where she belongs,

I guess. They must have taken her on her looks—
she never had any talent that I could see.»

Ida Verlaine. I was still thinking of her and of
those free and easy days in the past as I took up
my post at the entrance to the dance hall. I had a
few minutes to kill. I had forgotten about the money
in my pocket. I was still riveted to the past. Wondered whether I would stop by the theatre one day
and have a look at Ida from the third row front.
Or go up to her dressing room and have a little
tête-à-tête while she made up. I wondered if her
body were still as white as ever. Her black hair
was long then and hung over her shoulders. She
really was a bewitching piece of cunt. Pure cunt,
that's what she was. And Woodruff so bewildered
by it all, so innocent, so worshipful. I remember
his saying once that he used to kiss her ass every
night, to show her what a devoted slave he was. It's
a wonder she didn't pee on him ever. He deserved
that, the imbecile!

And then I thought of something which made me
laugh. Men always think that to own a big cock
is one of life's greatest boons. They think you have
only to shake it at a woman and she's yours. Well,
if anybody had a big cock it was Bill Woodruff.
It was a veritable horse cock. I remember the first
time I saw it—I could scarcely believe my eyes. Ida
should have been his slave, if all that stuff about
big cocks be true. It impressed her all right all
right, but the wrong way. She was scared stiff. It
froze her up. And the more he pushed and plugged,
the smaller she grew. He might just as well have
fucked her between the teats, or in the arm-pits.
She would have enjoyed that more, no doubt about
it. Woodruff never had such ideas, though. He
would have thought them degrading. You can't ask
the woman you idolize to let you fuck her between

the teats. How he got his nookie I never inquired.
But that ass-licking ritual made me smile. It's tough
to be crazy about a woman and then find that nature
has played you a mean trick.

Ida Verlaine. I had a hunch I'd be looking her
up soon. It wouldn't be the same smooth-fitting cunt
any more, no use kidding oneself. By this time it
had been well reamed, if I knew Ida. Still, if there
was any juice left, if her ass had that smooth, slippery feel, it would be worth having another go at it.

I began to have an erection thinking about her.

I waited around for a half hour or more, but no
sign of Mona. I decided to go upstairs and inquire.
Learned that she had gone home early—with a sick
headache.

9

It was only the next evening, after dinner, that
I found out why she had left the dance hall early.
She had received a message from home and had
rushed out to see her parents. I didn't press her
to talk, knowing how secretive she was about this
other life. For some reason, however, she was
anxious to get it off her chest. As usual, she circled
about with mysterious swoops. It was difficult to
make head or tail of her story. All I could gather
was that they were in distress—and by «they» she
meant the whole family, including her three brothers,
and her sister-in-law.

«Do they all live under the same roof?» I asked
innocently.

«That's neither here nor there,» she said, strangely
irritated.

I said nothing for a while. Then I ventured to ask about her sister whom she had once told me was even more beautiful than herself—«only very normal», as she put it.

«Didn't you say she was married?»

«Yes, of course she is. What's that got to do with it?»

«With what?» I asked, getting a little peeved now myself.

«Well, what are we talking about?»»

I laughed. «That's what I want to know. What is it? What *are* you trying to tell me?»

«You don't listen. *My sister*—I suppose you don't believe I have a sister?»

«Why do you say that? Of course I believe you. Only I can't believe she's more beautiful than you.»

«Well she is, believe it or not,» she snapped. «I despise her. It's not jealousy, if that's what you're thinking. I despise her because she has no imagination. She sees what's happening and she doesn't lift a finger. She's absolutely selfish.»

«I suppose,» I began gently, «that it's the same old problem—they want your help. Well, maybe I....»

«*You!* What can *you* do? Please, Val, don't start talking that way.» She laughed hysterically. «God, it reminds me of my brothers. They all make suggestions—and nobody does anything.»

«But, Mona, I'm not talking in the air. I...»

She turned on me almost fiercely. «You've got your wife and daughter to look after, haven't you? I don't want to hear anything about your help. This is *my* problem. Only I don't know why I have to do everything alone. The boys could do something if they wanted to. God, I supported them for years. I've supported the whole family—and now they're asking more of me. I can't do any more. It isn't fair...»

There was a silence and then she continued. «My father is a sick man—I don't expect anything of him. Besides, he's the only one I care about. If it weren't for him I'd turn my back on them—I'd walk off and leave them flat.»

«Well, what about your brothers?» I asked. What's holding them back?»

«Nothing but laziness,» she said. «I've spoiled them. I led them to believe that they were helpless.»

«Do you mean that nobody is working—not any of them?»

«Oh yes, now and then one of them gets a job for a few weeks and then quits for some silly reason. They know I'll always be there to rescue them.»

«I can't go on living this way!» she burst out. «I won't let them destroy my life. I want to be with you—and they're pulling me away. They don't care what I do so long as I bring them money. Money, money. God, how I hate to hear the word! »

«But Mona,» I said gently, «I've got some money for you. Yes, I have. Look!»

I extracted the two fifty dollar bills and placed them in her hand.

To my amazement she began to laugh, a weird, three-pronged laugh which became more and more uncontrollable. I put my arms around her. «Easy, Mona, easy... you're terribly upset.»

The tears came to her eyes. «I can't help it, Val,» she said weakly, «it reminds me so much of my father. He used to do the same thing. Just when everything was blackest he would turn up with flowers or some crazy gift. You're just like him. You're dreamers, both of you. That's why I love you.» She flung her arms around me passionately and began to sob. «Don't tell me where you got it,» she muttered. «I don't care. I don't care if you stole it. I'd steal for you, you know that, don't you?

Val, they don't deserve the money. I want you to buy something for yourself—. *Or*», she added impulsively, «get something for the little one. Get something beautiful, something wonderful— that she'll always remember.»

«Val,» she said, trying to collect herself, «you trust me, don't you? You won't ever ask me things I can't answer, will you? Promise me!»

We were seated in the big arm chair. I held her in my lap, smoothing down her hair by way of answer.

«You see, Val, if you hadn't come along, I don't know what would have happened to me. Until I met you I felt—well, almost as if my life didn't belong to me. I didn't care what I did, if only they would leave me in peace. I can't bear to have them ask for things. I feel humiliated. They're all helpless, every one of them. Except my sister. She could do things—she's a very practical, level-headed sort. But she wants to play the lady. 'It's enough to have one wild one in the family,' she says, meaning me. I've disgraced them, that's what she thinks. And she wants to punish me, by making me submit to more and more indignities. She takes a fiendish delight in seeing me bring the money that no one lifts a finger to raise. She makes all sorts of foul insinuations. I could kill her. And my father doesn't seem to realize the situation at all. He thinks she's sweet—*angelic*. He wouldn't let her make the least sacrifice—she's too delicate to be exposed to the brutal contamination of the world. Besides, she's a wife and a mother. But *I*....» Her eyes became filled with tears again. «I don't know what they think I'm made of. *I'm strong*, that's all they think. I can stand anything. I'm the wild one. God, sometimes I think they're insane, the whole pack of them. Where do they think I get the money? They don't care... *they don't dare to ask.*»

«Will your father ever get well?» I asked after a long silence.

«I don't know, Val.»

«If he were dead,» she added, «I'd never go near the others again. They could starve to death, I wouldn't move a muscle.»

«You know,» she said, «you don't resemble him at all, physically, and yet you're so much alike. You're weak and tender, like him. But you weren't spoiled, as he was. You know how to take care of yourself, when you want to—but he never learned. He was always helpless. My mother sucked the blood out of him. She treated him like she treats me. Anything to have her own way.... I wish you could meet him—before he dies. I've often dreamed of it.»

«We probably will meet some day,» said I, though I didn't think it at all likely.

«You'd adore him, Val. He has such a wonderful sense of humor. He's a great story teller, too. I think he would have been a writer, if he hadn't married my mother.»

She got up and began to make her toilette, still talking in a fond way about her father and the life he had known in Vienna and other places. It was getting time to leave for the dance hall.

Suddenly she turned abruptly away from the mirror and said: «Val, why don't you write in your spare time? You always wanted to write—why don't you do it? You don't need to call for me so often. You know, I'd much rather come home and find you working at the typewriter. You aren't to stay at that job all your life, are you?»

She came over to me and put her arms around me. «Let me sit in your lap,» she said. Listen, dear Val... you mustn't sacrifice yourself for me. It's bad enough

that one of us does it. I want you to free yourself.
I *know* you're a writer—and I don't care how long
it takes until you become known. I want to help
you... *Val*, you're not listening.» She nudged me
gently. «What are you thinking of?»

«Oh, nothing,» I said. «I was just dreaming.»

«Val, do something, *please!* Don't let's go on this
way. Look at this place! How did we ever get
here? What are we doing here? We're a little mad
too, you and I. Val, do start in—*to-night*, yes? I
like you when you're moody. I like to think that
you have thoughts about other things. I like it
when you say crazy things. I wish I could think
that way. I'd give anything to be a writer. To
have a mind, to dream, to get lost in other people's
problems, to think of something else beside work
and money.... You remember that story you wrote
for me once—about Tony and Joey? Why don't
you write something for me again? Just for *me*.
Val, we must try to do something... we *must* find a
way out. Do you hear?»

I had heard only too well. Her words were running in my head like a refrain.

I jumped up, as if to brush the cobwebs away.
I caught her by the waist and held her at arm's
length. «Mona, things are going to be different soon.
Very soon. I *feel* it.... Let me walk you to the
station—I need a breath of air.»

I could see that she was slightly disappointed; she
had hoped for something more positive.

«Mona,» I said, as we walked rapidly down the
street, «one doesn't change all at once, like that!
I do want to write, yes, I'm sure of it. But I've got
to collect myself. I don't ask to have it easy, but
I need a little tranquillity. I can't switch from one
thing to another so easily. I hate my job just as
much as you hate yours. And I don't want another

job: I want a complete break. I want to be with myself for a while, see how it feels. I hardly know myself, living the way I do. I'm engulfed. I know all about others—and nothing about myself. I know only that I *feel*. I feel too much. I'm drained dry. I wish I could have days, weeks, months, just to think. Now I think from moment to moment. It's a luxury, *to think*.»

She squeezed my hand, as if to tell me she understood.

«When I get back to the house I'm going to sit down and try to think. Maybe I'll fall asleep. It seems as though I were geared up only for action. I've become a machine.»

«Do you know what I think sometimes?» I went on. «I think that if I had two or three quiet days of just sheer thinking I'd upset everything. Fundamentally everything is cock-eyed. It's that way because we don't dare to let ourselves think. I ought to go the office one day and blow out Spivak's brains. That's the first step....»

We had come to the elevated station.

«Don't think about such things just now,» she said. «Sit down and dream. Dream something wonderful for me. Don't think about those ugly little people. Think of *us!*»

She ran up the steps lightly, waving good-bye.

I was strolling leisurely back to the house, dreaming of another, richer life, when suddenly I remembered, or thought I remembered, her leaving the two fifty dollar bills on the mantelpiece under the vase filled with artificial flowers. I could see them sticking out half-way, just as she had placed them. I broke into a trot. I knew that if Kronski saw them he would filch them. He would do it not because he was dishonest but to torture me.

As I drew near the house I thought of Crazy Shel-

don. I even began to imitate his way of speaking,
though I was out of breath from running. I was
laughing to myself as I opened the door.

The room was empty and the money was gone.
I knew it would be thus. I sat down and laughed
again. Why hadn't I said anything to Mona about
Monahan? Why hadn't I mentioned anything to
her about the theatre? Usually I spilled things out
immediately, but this time something had held me
back, some instinctive distrust of Monahan's intentions.

I was on the point of calling up the dance hall
to see if by chance Mona had taken the money without my noticing it. I got up to go to the telephone
but on the way I changed my mind. The impulse
seized me to explore the house a bit. I wandered
to the rear of the house and descended the stairs.
After a few steps I came upon a large room with
blinding lights in which the laundry was drying.
There was a bench along one wall, as in a school
room, and on it sat an old man with a white beard
and a velvet skull cap. He was bent forward, his
head resting on the back of his hand, supported by
a cane. He seemed to be gazing blankly into space.

He gave a sign of recognition with his eyes; his
body remained immobile. I had seen many members
of the family but never him. I greeted him in
German, thinking he would prefer that to English
which no one seemed to speak in this queer house.

«You can talk English if you like,» he said, in
a thick accent. He gazed straight ahead into space,
as before.

«Am I disturbing you?»

«Not at all.»

I thought I ought to tell him who I was. «My
name is...»

«And I,» said he, without waiting to hear my name,

«am Dr. Onirifick's father. He never told you about me, I suppose?»

«No,» I said, «he never did. But then I hardly ever see him.»

«He's a very busy man. Too busy perhaps....»

«But he will be punished one day,» he continued. «One must not murder, not even the unborn. It is better here—there is peace.»

«Wouldn't you like me to put out some of the lights?» I asked, hoping to divert his thoughts to some other subject.

«There should be light,» he answered. «More light... more light. He works in darkness up there. He is too proud. He works for the devil. It is better here with the wet clothes.» He was silent for a moment. There was the sound of drops of water falling from the wet garments. I gave a shudder. I thought of the blood dripping from Dr. Onirifick's hands. «Yes, drops of blood,» said the old man, as if reading my thoughts. «He is a butcher. He gives his mind to death. This is the greatest darkness of the human mind—killing what is struggling to be born. Even animals one should not kill, except in sacrifice. My son knows everything—but he doesn't know that murder is the greatest sin. There is light here... great light... and *he* sits up there in darkness. His father sits in the cellar, praying for him, and *he* is up there butchering, butchering. Everywhere there is blood. The house is polluted. It is better here with the wash. I would wash the money too, if I could. This is the only clean room in the house. And the light is good. Light. Light. We must open their eyes so that they can see. Man must not work in darkness. The mind must be clear, the mind must know what it is doing.»

I said nothing. I listened respectfully, hynoptized by the droning words, the blinding light. The old

man had the face and manners of a patrician; the
toga he wore and the velvet skull cap accentuated
his lofty air. His fine sensitive hands were those of
a surgeon; the blue veins stood out like quicksilver.
In his overlighted dungeon he sat like a court
physician who been banished from his native land.
He reminded me vividly of certain celebrated physi-
cians who had flourished at the court of Spain during
the time of the Moors. There was a silvery, musical
quality about him; his spirit was clean and it radiated from every pore of his being.

Presently I heard the patter of slippered feet. It
was Ghompal arriving with a bowl of hot milk.
Immediately the old man's expression altered. He
leaned back against the wall and looked at Ghompal
with warmth and tenderness.

«This is my son, my true son,» he said, turning
his full gaze upon me.

I exchanged a few words with Ghompal as he held
the bowl to the old man's lips. It was a pleasure
to watch the Hindu. No matter how menial the
task he performed it with dignity. The more humble
the service the more ennobled he became. He
seemed never to be embarrassed or humiliated.
Neither did he efface himself. He remained always
the same, always completely and uniquely himself.
I tried to -imagine what Kronski would look like
performing such a service.

Ghompal left the room for a few moments to
return with a pair of warm bedroom slippers. He
knelt at the old man's feet and, as he performed this
rite, the old man gently stroked Ghompal's head.

«You are one of the sons of light», said the old
man, lifting Gompal's head back and looking into
his eyes with a steady clear gaze. Ghompal returned
the old man's gaze with the same clear liquescent
light. They seemed to flood each other's being—

two reservoirs of liquid light spilling over in a purifying exchange. Suddenly I realized that the blinding light which streamed from the unshaded electric bulbs was as nothing in comparison to this emanation of light which had passed between the two. Perhaps the old man was unaware of this yellow, artificial light which man had invented; perhaps the room was illuminated by this flood-light which came from his soul. Even now, though they had ceased gazing into one another's eyes, the room was appreciably lighter than before. It was like the after-glow of a fiery sunset, a supernal, empyrean luminosity.

I stole back to the living room to await Ghompal. He had something to tell me. I found Kronski seated in the arm-chair reading one of my books. He was ostensibly calmer, quieter than usual, not subdued but *settled* in some queer, undisciplined way.

«Hullo! I didn't know you were home,» he said, startled by my unexpected presence. «I was just glancing at some of your junk.» He threw the book aside. It was *The Hill of Dreams* (1).

Before he had a chance to resume his habitual banter Ghompal entered. He walked towards me holding the money in his hand. I took it with a smile, thanked him, and put it in my pocket. To Kronski it appeared that I was borrowing from Ghompal. He was irritated—more than that—*indignant*.

«Jesus, do you have to borrow from *him?*» he blurted out.

Ghompal spoke up at once, but Kronski cut him short.

«You don't have to lie for him. I know his tricks.»

Ghompal spoke up again, quietly, convincingly. «Mr. Miller doesn't play tricks with me,» he said.

«All right, you win,» said Kronski. «But Jesus,

---

(1) By Arthur Macken.

don't make an angel of him. I know he's been good
to you—and to all your comrades on the messenger
force—but that's not because he has a good heart...
He's taken a fancy to you Hindus because you're
queer fish, *see?*»

Ghompal smiled at him indulgently, as if he understood the aberrations of a sick mind.

Kronski reacted testily to this smile of Ghompal's.
«Don't give me that commiserating smile,» he screech-
ed. «I'm not a wretched outcast. I'm a doctor of
medecine. I'm a...»

«You're still a child,» said Ghompal quietly and
firmly. «Anybody with a little intelligence can
become a doctor...»

At this Kronski sneered vehemently. «They can,
eh? Just like that, hah? Just like rolling off a
log—» He looked around as if searching for a place
to spit.

«In India we say...», and Ghompal began one of
those child-like stories which are devastating to the
analytical-minded person. He had a little story for
every situation, Ghompal. I relished them hugely;
they were like simple, homeopathic remedies, little
pellets of truth garbed in some inocuous clok. You
could never forget them afterwards, that was what I
liked about these yarns. *W*e write fat books to
expound a simple idea; the Oriental tells a simple,
pointed story which lodges in your brain like a
diamond. The story he was narrating was about a
glow-worm that had been bruised by the naked foot
of an absent-minded philosopher. Kronski detested
anecdotes in which lower forms of life communicated
with higher beings, such as man, on an intellectual
level. He felt it to be a personal humiliation, an
invidious aspersion.

In spite of himself he had to smile at the conclusion of the tale. Besides, he was already repentant

of his crude behavior. He had a profound respect
for Ghompal. It nettled him that he had been
obliged to turn sharply on Ghompal when he meant
merely to crush me. So, still smiling, he inquired in
in a kindly voice about Ghose, one of the Hindus who
had returned to India some months ago.

Ghose had died of dysentery shortly after arriving
in India, Ghompal informed him.

«That's lousy,» said Kronski, shaking his head
despairingly, as if to imply that it was hopeless to
combat conditions in a country like India. Then,
turning to me, with a sad flicker of a smile: «You
remember Ghose, don't you? The fat, chubby little
guy, like a squatting Buddha.»

I nodded. «I should say I do remember him.
Didn't I raise the money for him to go back to India?»

«Ghose was a saint,» said Kronski vehemently.

A mild flicker of a frown came over Ghompal's face.
«No, not a *saint*,» he said. «We have many men in
India who...»

«I know what you're going to say,» Kronski broke
in. «Just the same, to *me* Ghose was a saint.
Dysentery! Good Christ! it's like the Middle Ages...
worse than that!» And he launched into a terrifying
description of the diseases which still flourished in
India. And from disease to poverty and from poverty
to superstition and from these to slavery, degradation,
despair, indifference, hopelessness. India was just a
vast, rotting sepulchre, a charnel house dominated by
conniving British exploiters in league with demented
and perfidious rajahs and maharajahs. Not a word
about the architecture, the music, the learning, the
religion, the philosophies, the beautiful physionomies,
the grace and delicacy of the women, the colorful
garments, the pungent odors, the tinkling bells, the
great gongs, the gorgeous landscapes, the riot of
flowers, the incessant processions, the clash of tongues,

races, types, the fermentation and pullulation amidst
death and corruption. Statistically correct as always,
he succeeded only in presenting the negative half of
the picture. India was bleeding to death, true. But
the part of her that was alive was resplendent in a
way that Kronski could never appreciate. He never
once mentioned a city by name, never differentiated
between Agra and Delhi, Lahore and Mysore, Darjeel-
ling and Karachi, Bombay and Calcutta, Benares
and Colombo. Parsee, Jain, Hindu, Buddhist—they
were all one, all miserable victims of oppression, all
rotting slowly under a murderous sun to make an
imperialist holiday.

Between him and Ghompal there now ensued a
discussion to which I only half listened. Each time
I heard the name of a city I went on an emotional
jag. The very mention of such words as Bengal,
Gujurati, Malabar Coast, Kali-ghat, Nepal, Kashmir,
Sikh, Bhagavad-Gita, Upanishads, raga, stupa, prav-
ritti, sudra, paranirvana, chela, guru, Hounaman,
Siva was sufficient to put me in a trance for the rest
of the evening. How could a man condemned to lead
the restricted life of a physician in a cold, brutal city
like New York dare to talk about setting in order a
continent of half a billion souls whose problems were
so vast, so multiform, as to stagger the imagination
of India's own great pundits? No wonder he was
attracted to the saintly characters whom he had made
contact with in the infernal regions of the most
Cosmococcic Corporation of America. These «boys»,
as Ghompal called them (they ranged from twenty-
three to thirty-five years of age) were like picked
warriors, like chosen disciples. The hardships they
had endured, first in getting to America, then
struggling to keep body and soul together while
finishing their studies, then finding the means to
return, then renouncing everything in order to devote

themselves to the advancement of their people—
well, no American, no white American, any way,
could brag of anything comparable. When now and
then one of these «boys» went astray, became the
lap-dog of some society woman or the slave of some
ravishing dancer, I felt like rejoicing. It did me
good to hear of Hindu boy lolling on soft cushions,
eating rich foods, wearing diamond rings, dancing at
night clubs, driving cars, seducing yong virgins, and
so on. I recalled a cultured yong Parsee who had
run off with some languorous middle-aged woman of
dubious reputation; I remembered the malicious
stories that were spread about him, the demorali-
zation that he brought about among the less disciplined ones. It was grand. I followed his career
with avidity, lapping up the dregs, imaginatively, as
he moved from sphere to sphere. And then one day,
when I was lying ill in the morgue which my wife
had made of my room, he came to see me, bringing
flowers and fruit and books, and he sat by my bed
and held my hand, talked to me of India, of the
wondrous life he had known as a child, of the miseries
he had endured subsequently, of the humiliations
inflicted upon him by Americans, of his hunger for
life, a large life, a rich life, a splendorous life, and
how he had grabbed the opportunity when it came and
found it empty, empty of everything but clothes,
jewels, money, women. He was giving it all up, he
confided. He would go back to his people, suffer
with them, raise them up if he could, and if not, die
with them, die as they died, in the street, naked,
homeless, shunned, despised, stepped on, walked over,
spat upon, a bundle of bones which even the vultures
would find it difficult to feast on. He would do this
not out of guilt, remorse or repentance but because
India in rags, India festering like a maggot, India
starving, India writhing under the heel of the con-

queror, meant more to him than all the comforts,
opportunities and advantages of a heartless country
like America. He was a Parsee, I say, and his family
had been rich once; he had known a happy childoood
at least. But there were other Hindus who had been
reared in forest and field, who had lived what to us
would seem an animal existence. How these obscure,
shy individuals ever surmounted the stupendous
obstacles which confronted them from day to day
remains a mystery to me to this day. With them, at
any rate, I travelled the roads that lead from village
to town and town to city; with them I listened to the
songs of simple folk, the tales of elderly men, the
prayers of the devout, the admonitions of the gurus,
the legends of the story tellers, the music of the street
players, the wails and lamentations of the mourners.
Through their eyes I saw the desolation wreaked
upon a great people. But I saw also that there are
qualities which survive the greatest desolation. In
their faces, as they related their experiences, I saw
reflected the gentleness, the humility, the reverence,
the devotion, the faith, the truthfulness and the
integrity of those millions whose destiny baffles and
disturbs us. They die like flies and they are reborn;
they increase and multiply; they offer up prayers
and sacrifices, they resist not, and yet no foreign devil
can extirpate them from the soil which they nourish
with their own impoverished carcasses. They are of
all kinds, all conditions, all shades, all tongues, all
cults; they shoot up like weeds and are trampled
down like weeds. To lift the curtain upon even the
tiniest segment of this seething life leaves the mind
reeling with incertitude. Some are like hard-cut
gems, some like rare flowers, some like monuments,
some like blazing images of the divine, some like
disembodied minds, some like rotting vegetables: side
by side they move in an endless, confused throng.

In the midst of these reflections Kronski reminded me in a loud voice that he had run into Sheldon. «He wanted to pay you a visit, the blinking idiot, but I put him off... I think he wanted to lend you some money».

Crazy Sheldon! Curious that I should have thought of him on my way home. Money, yes... I had had a hunch Sheldon would be lending me money again. I had no idea what I owed him. I never expected to pay him back—neither did he. I took what he offered because it made him happy. He was as mad as a hare, but cunning and wily, practical withal. He had fastened himself to me like a leech, for some obscure reason of his own which I never even tried to fathom.

What fascinated me about Sheldon were the grimaces he made. And the way he gurgled when he spoke. It was as though an invisible hand were strangling him. To be sure, he had had some terrible experiences—in that murderous ghetto of Cracow where he was reared. There was one incident I would never forget: it had occured during a pogrom just before his escape from Poland. He had rushed home in a panic during the butchering which was taking place in the street to find the room full of soldiers. His sister, who was pregnant, was lying on the floor, violated by one soldier after another. His mother and father, their arms trussed behind them, were compëlled to watch this horrible performance. Sheldon completely beside himself, had thrown himself on the soldiers and was cut down with a sabre. When he came to his mother and father were dead; his sister's body was lying naked beside them, her belly ripped open and stuffed with straw.

We were walking through Tompkins Park the night he first related this story to me. (He repeated it a number of times subsequently, always in exactly the

same way, even down to the words he used. And
each time my hair stood on end and a cold shiver
ran down my spine.) But that first evening, on
concluding the story, I observed a queer change come
over him. He was making those grimaces which I
mentioned. It was as if he were trying to whistle
and couldn't. His eyes, which were unusually small,
sandy, inflamed, shrank to the size of two B.B. bullets.
There was nothing to be seen between the lids but
two burning pupils which bored clean through me.
I had the most uncanny feeling when, grasping my
arm and bringing his face close to mine, he began
making a choking, gurgling sound which finally culminated in a noise very much like a peanut whistle.
His emotions were so overpowering that for a few
minutes, the while clutching me feverishly and
pressing his face close to mine, there issued from his
throat no recognizable human sound, nothing in the
faintest resembling what we call speech. But what
a language it was, this gurgling, hissing, choking,
whistling frenzy! I couldn't turn my face away, even
if I had wanted to; nor could I break his grip,
because he had me in a vise. I wondered how long
it would last, and would he throw a fit afterwards.
But no!—when the emotion had subsided he began
to talk in a calm, low voice, in a most matter of fact
tone, indeed, quite as if nothing had occurred. We
had resumed our stride and were making for the
other end of the park. He was talking about the
jewels which he had so cleverly swallowed, the value
that had been put upon them, the way the emeralds
and the rubies sparkled, how economically he lived,
the insurance policies he sold in his spare time, and
other seemingly unrelated facts and incidents.

He related these things, as I say, in an unnaturally
subdued vein, in an almost monotonous tone of voice,
except that, now and then, when he came to the end

of a sentence, he would raise his voice and end unintentionally on an interrogation point Meanwhile, however, his manner was undergoing a drastic change. He was becoming, as best I can explain it, lynx-like. All that he was narrating seemed directed towards some invisible presence. He was only using me, as a listener, so it seemed, to make known in a sly, insinuating fashion things which this «other» person, present but invisible, might construe in his or her own way. «Sheldon is not a fool,» he was saying in this oblique, glancing language. «Sheldon has not forgotten certain little tricks which were played on him. Sheldon is behaving like a gentleman now, very *comme il faut*, but he is not asleep... no, Sheldon is always on the *qui vive*. Sheldon can play the fox when he needs to. Sheldon can wear nice clothes, like everybody else, and behave *most* courteously. Sheldon is amiable, always ready to be of service. Sheldon is kind to little children, *even to Polish children*. Sheldon does not ask for anything. Sheldon is very quiet, very calm, very well-behaved... BUT BEWARE!!!» And then to my surprise Sheldon whistled... a long, clear whistle which was intended, I have no doubt, as a warning to the invisible one. *Beware the day!* It was as clear as that, his whistle. *Beware*, because Sheldon is preparing something super-diabolical, something which the clumsy brain of a Polak could never imagine or invent. Sheldon has not been idle all these years...

The money lending had come about quite naturally. It began that evening over a cup of coffe. As usual I had only five or ten cents in my pocket and was therefore obliged to let Sheldon take the check. The idea of the employment manager being without spending money was so inconceivable to Sheldon that for a moment I feared he would pawn all his jewels.

«Five dollars will be enough, Sheldon,» said I, «if you insist on lending me something.»

An expression of disgust came over Sheldon's face. «Oh no, oh no-O-O!» he exclaimed in a shrill, grating voice which rose almost to a whistle, «Sheldon will never give five dollars. No-oo, Mr, Miller, Sheldon will give *fifty* dollars!»

And by God, with that he did fish out fifty dollars, in fives and singles. Again he put on his lynx-like air, looking beyond me as he doled the money out, and mumbling something between his teeth about showing some one what sort of man he, Sheldon, was.

«But Sheldon, I'll be broke again to-morrow,» I said, pausing to see what effect this would produce.

Sheldon smiled—a cagey, cunning smile, as if he were sharing some great secret with me.

«Then Sheldon will give you another fifty dollars to-morrow,» he said, bringing the words out with a queer hissing effect.

«I have no idea when you will get the money back,» I then informed him.

In answer to this Sheldon produced three greasy bank books from his inside pocket. The deposits totalled over two thousand dollars. From his vest pockets he extracted a few rings whose stones glittered like the authentic thing.

«This is nothing,» he said. «Sheldon is not telling all.»

This was the beginning of our relationship, a rather strange one for the employment manager of a cosmococcic corporation. I wondered sometimes if other employment managers enjoyed these advantages. When I met with them occasionally at luncheons I felt more like a messenger boy than a personnel manager. I could never muster that dignity and self-importance in which they appeared to be perpetually enshrouded. They never seemed to look

me in the eye when I spoke, but always at my baggy
trousers, my run-down shoes, my torn, soiled shirt or
the holes in my hat. If I told them an innocent
little story they made so much of it that I was
embarrassed. They were tremendously impressed, for
example, when I told them about a certain messenger
in the Broad Street office who, while waiting for his
calls, would read Dante, Homer and Thomas Aquinas
in the original. They didn't wait to hear that he
had been a professor once in a university in Bologna,
that he had tried to commit suicide because he had
lost his wife and three children in a railroad accident,
that he had lost his memory and had arrived in
America with another man's passport, and that only
after he had been working as a messenger for six
months had he recovered his identity. That he had
found the work agreeable, that he preferred to remain
a messenger, that he wished to remain unknown—
these things would have sounded too fantastic for
their ears. All they could seize and marvel at was
the fact that a «messenger», in uniform, was able to
read the classics in the original. Now and then I
would borrow a ten spot from one of them, after relating one of these amusing incidents, never intending
to repay of course. I felt compelled to extract some
little token from them—for my services as entertainer.
And what hemming and hawing they resorted to
before coughing up these trivial sums! What a contrast to the easy touches I made among the «goofy»
messengers!

Reflections of this order always excited me to the
breaking point. Ten minutes of introspective reverie
and I was bursting to write a book. I thought of
Mona. If only for her sake I ought to begin. And
where would I begin? In this room which was like
the lobby of an insane asylum? Begin with Kronski
looking over my shoulder?

Somewhere I had read recently about an abandoned
city of Burma, the ancient capital of a region where.
in the compass of a hundred miles, there once flourished eight thousand thriving temples. The whole
area was now empty of inhabitants, had been so for
a thousand years or more. Only a few lone priests,
probably half-crazed, were now to be found among the
empty temples. Serpents and bats and owls infested
the sacred edifices; at night the jackals howled
amidst the ruins.

Why should this picture of desolation cause me
such painful depression? Why should eight thousand
empty, ruined temples awaken such anguish? People
die, races disappear, religions fade away: it is in the
order of things. But that something of beauty should
remain, and be powerless to affect, powerless to
attract us, was an enigma which weighed me down.
For I had not even begun to build! In my mind
I saw my own temples in ruins, before even one brick
had been laid upon another. In some freakish way
I and the goofy messengers who were to aid me were
prowling about the abandoned places of the spirit
like the jackals which howled at night. We wandered amidst the halls of an ethereal edifice, a dream
stupa, which would be abandoned before it could
take earthly shape. In Burma the invader had been
responsibile for driving the spirit of man into the
ground. It had happened over and over in the
history of man and it was explicable. But what
prevented us, the dreamers of this continent, from
giving form and substance to our fabulous edifices?
The race of visionary architects was as good as
extinct. The genius of man had been canalized and
directed into other channels. So it was said. I could
not accept it. I have looked at the separate stones,
the girders, the portals, the windows which even in
buildings are like the eyes of the soul; I have looked

at them as I have looked at separate pages of these books, and I have seen one architecture informing the lives of our people, be it in book, in law, in stone, in custom; I saw that it was created (seen first in the mind) then objectified, given light, air and space, given purpose and significance, given a rhythm which would rise and fall, a growth from seed to flourishing tree, a decline from shrivelled leaf and branch to seed again, and a compost to nourish the seed. I saw this continent as other continents before and after: creations in every sense of the word, including the very catastrophes which would make their existence forgotten...

After Kronski and Ghompal had retired I felt so wide awake, so stimulated by the thoughts which which were racing through my head that I felt impelled to go for a long walk. As I was putting on my things I looked at myself in the mirror. I made that whistling grimace of Sheldon's and felicitated myself on my powers of mimicry. Once upon a time I had thought I might make a good clown. There was a chap in school who passed as my twin brother; we were very close to one another and later, when we had graduated, we formed a club of twelve which we called the Xerxes Society. We two possessed all the initiative—the others were just so much slag and driftwood. In desperation sometimes George Marshall and I would perform for the others. an impromptu clowning which kept the others in stitches. Later I used to think of these moments as having quite a tragic quality. The dependency of the others was really pathetic: it was a foretaste of the general inertia and apathy which I was to encounter all through life. Thinking of George Marshall, I began to make more faces; I did it so well that I began to get a little frightened of myself. For, suddenly I remembered the day when for the

first time in my life I looked into the mirror and
realized that I was gazing at a stranger. It was after
I had been to the theatre with George Marshall and
MacGregor. George Marshall had said something
that night which disturbed me profoundly. I was
angry with him for his stupidity, but I couldn't deny
that he had put his finger on a sore spot. He had
said something which made me realize that our
twinship was over, that in fact we would become
enemies henceforth. And he was right, though the
reasons he had given were false. From that day
forth I began to ridicule my bosom friend George
Marshall. I wanted to be the opposite of him in
every way. It was like the splitting of a chromosome.

George Marshall remained in the world, with it,
of it; he took root and grew like a tree, and there
was no doubt but that he had found his place and
with it a relatively full measure of happiness. But
as I looked in the mirror that night, disowning my
own image, I knew that what George Marshall had
predicted about my future was only superficially
correct. George Marshall had never really understood me; the moment he suspected I was *different*
he had renounced me.

I was still looking at myself as these memories
flitted through my head. My face had grown sad
and thoughtful. I was no longer looking at my
image but at the image of a memory of myself at
another moment—when sitting on a stoop one night
listening to a Hindu «boy» named Tawde. Tawde
too had said something that night which had provoked in me a profound disturbance. But Tawde had
said it as a friend. He was holding my hand, the
way Hindus do. A passer-by looking at us might
have thought we were making love. Tawde was
trying to make me see things in a different light.
What baffled him was that I was «good at heart»

and yet... I was creating sorrow all about me.
Tawde wanted me to be true to myself, that self
which he recognized and accepted as my «true» self.
He seemed to have no awareness of the complexity
of my nature, or if he did he attached no importance to it. He didn't understand why I should be
dissatisfied with my position in life, particularly
when I was doing so much good. That one could
be thoroughly disgusted with being a mere instrument of good was unthinkable to him. He didn't
realize that I was only a blind instrument, that I
was merely obeying the law of inertia, and that I
hated inertia even if it meant doing good.

I left Tawde that night in a state of despair. I
loathed the thought of being surrounded by dumb
clucks who would hold my hand and comfort me
in order to keep me in chains. A sinister gayety
came over me as I drew farther away from him;
instead of going home I went instinctively to the
furnished room where the waitress lived with whom
I was carrying on a romantic affair. She came to
the door in her night shirt, begging me not to go
upstairs with her because of the hour. We went inside, in the hallway, and leaned against the radiator
to keep warm. In a few minutes I had it out and
was giving it to her as best I could in that strained
position. She was trembling with fear and pleasure.
When it was over she reproached me for being in-
considerate. «Why do you do these things?» she
whispered, snuggled close against me. I ran off,
leaving her standing at the foot of the stairs with
a bewildered expression. As I raced through the
street a phrase repeated itself over and over: «Which
is the true self?»

It was this phrase which accompanied me now,
racing through the morbid streets of the Bronx. Why
was I racing? What was driving me on at this pace?

I slowed down, as if to let the demon overtake me...

If you persist in throttling your impulses you end by becoming a clot of phlegm. You finally spit out a gob which completely drains you and which you only realize years later was not a gob of spit but your inmost self. If you lose that you will always race through dark streets like a madman pursued by phantoms. You will always be able to say with perfect sincerity: «I don't know what I want to do in life.» You can push yourself clean through the filament of life and come out at the wrong end of the telescope, seeing everything beyond you, out of grasp, and diabolically twisted. From then on the game's up. Whichever direction you take you will find yourself in a hall of mirrors; you will race like a madman, searching for an exit, to find that you are surrounded only by distorted images of your own sweet self.

What I disliked most in George Marshall, in Kronski, in Tawde and the incalculable hosts which they represented, was their surface seriousness. The truly serious person is gay, almost nonchalant. I despised people who, because they lacked their own proper ballast, took on the problems of the world. The man who is forever disturbed about the condition of humanity either has no problems of his own or has refused to face them. I am speaking of the great majority, not of the emancipated few who, having thought things through, are privileged to identify themselves with all humanity and thus enjoy that greatest of all luxuries: service.

There was another thing I heartily disbelieved in —*work*. Work, it seemed to me even at the threshold of life, is an activity reserved for the dullard. It is the very opposite of creation, which is play, and which just because it has no raison d'être other than itself is the supreme motivating power in life. Has any one ever said that God created the universe in order to provide work for Himself? By a chain of circumstances having nothing to do with reason or intelligence I had become like the others—a drudge. I had the comfortless excuse that by my labors I was supporting a wife and child. That it was a flimsy excuse I knew, because if I were to drop dead on the morrow they would go on living somehow or other. To stop everything, and play at being myself, why not? The part of me which was given up to work, which enabled my wife and child to live in the manner they unthinkingly demanded, this part of me which kept the wheel turning—a completely fatuous, egocentric notion!—was the least part of me. I gave nothing to the world in fulfilling the function of breadwinner; the world exacted its tribute of me, that was all.

The world would only begin to get something of value from me the moment I stopped being a serious member of society and became—*myself*. The State, the nation, the united nations of the world, were nothing but one great aggregation of individuals who repeated the mistakes of their forefathers. They were caught in the wheel from birth and they kept at it till death—and this treadmill they tried to dignify by calling it «life». If you asked any one to explain or define life, what was the be all and the end all, you got a blank look for answer. Life was something which philosophers dealt with in books that no one read. Those in the thick of life, «the plugs in harness,» had no time for such idle questions. «*You've got to eat, haven't you?*» This query, which was supposed to be a stop-gap, and which had already been answered, if not in the absolute negative at least in a disturbingly relative negative by those who knew, was a clue to all the other questions which followed in a veritable Eucli-

dian suite. From the little reading I had done I had
observed that the men who were most *in* life, who
were moulding life, who were life itself, ate little,
slept little, owned little or nothing. They had no
illusions about duty, or the perpetuation of their
kith and kin, or the preservation of the State. They
were interested in truth and in truth alone. They
recognized only one kind of activity—*creation*. Nobody could command their services because they had
of their own pledged themselves to give all. They
gave gratuitously, because that is the only way to
give. This was the way of life which appealed to
me: it made sound sense. It *was* life—not the simulacrum which those about me worshipped.

I had understood all this—with my mind at the
very brink of manhood. But there was a great
comedy of life to be gone through before this vision
of reality could become the motivating force. The
tremendous hunger for life which others sensed in
me acted like a magnet; it attracted those who needed
my particular kind of hunger. The hunger was
magnified a thousand times. It was as if those who
clung to me (like iron filings) became sensitized and
attracted others in turn. Sensation ripens into experience and experience engenders experience.

What I secretly longed for was to disentangle myself of all those lives which had woven themselves
into the pattern of my own life and were making
my destiny a part of theirs. To shake myself free
of these accumulating experiences which were mine
only by force of inertia required a violent effort.
Now and then I lunged and tore at the net, but only
to become more enmeshed. My liberation seemed to
involve pain and suffering to those near and dear
to me. Every move I made for my own private good
brought about reproach and condemnation. I was
a traitor a thousand times over. I had lost even

the right to become ill—because «they» needed me. I wasn't *allowed* to remain inactive. Had I died I think they would have galvanized my corpse into a semblance of life.

«I stood before a mirror and said fearfully: ' I want to see how I look in the mirror with my eyes closed.'»

These words of Richter's, when I first came upon them, made and indescribable commotion in me. As did the following, which seems almost like a corollary of the above—from Novalis:

«The seat of the soul is where inner world and outer world touch each other. For nobody knows himself, if he is only himself and not also another one at the same time.»

«To take possession of one's transcendental I, to be the I of one's I, at the same time,» as Novalis expressed it again.

There is a time when ideas tyrannize over one, when one is just a hapless victim of an other's thoughts. This «possession» by another seems to occur in periods of depersonalization, when the warring selves come unglued, as it were. Normally one is impervious to ideas; they come and go, are accepted or rejected, put on like shirts, taken off like dirty socks. But in those periods which we call crises, when the mind sunders and splinters like a diamond under the blows of a sledge-hammer, these innocent ideas of a dreamer take hold, lodge in the crevices of the brain, and by some subtle process of infiltration bring about a definite, irrevocable alteration of the personality. Outwardly no great change takes place; the individual affected does not suddenly behave differently; on the contrary, he may behave in more «normal» fashion than before. This seeming normality assumes more and more the quality of a protective device. From surface deception

he passes to inner deception. With each new crisis,
however, he becomes more strongly aware of a
change which is no change, but rather an intensifica-
tion of something hidden deep within. Now when
he closes his eyes he can really look at himself. He
no longer sees a mask. He sees without seeing, to
be exact. Vision without sight, a fluid grasp of
intangibles: the merging of sight and sound: the
heart of the web. Here stream the distant personalities which evade the crude contact of the senses:
here the overtones of recognition discreetly lap
against one another in bright, vibrant harmonies.
There is no language employed, no outlines deline-
ated.

When a ship founders it settles slowly; the spars,
the masts, the rigging float away. On the ocean
floor of death the bleeding hull bedecks itself with
jewels; remorselessly the anatomic life begins. What
was ship becomes the nameless indestructible.

Like ships, men founder time and again. Only
memory saves them from complete dispersion. Poets
drop their stitches in the loom, straws for drowning
men to grasp as they sink into extinction. Ghosts
climb back on watery stairs, make imaginary ascents,
vertiginous drops, memorize numbers, dates, events,
in passing from gas to liquid and back again. There
is no brain capable of registering the changing
changes. Nothing happens in the brain, except the
gradual rust and detrition of the cells. But in the
minds, worlds unclassified, undenominated, unassimil-
ated, form, break, unite, dissolve and harmonize
ceaselessly. In the mind-world ideas are the indestructible elements which form the jewelled constellations of the interior life. We move within their
orbits, freely if we follow their intricate patterns,
enslaved or possessed if we try to subjugate them.

Everything external is but a reflection projected by the mind machine.

Creation is the eternal play which takes place at the border-line; it is spontaneous and compulsive, obedient to law. One removes from the mirror and the curtain rises. *Séance permanente.* Only madmen are excluded. Only those who «have lost their mind,» as we say. For these never cease to dream that they are dreaming. They stood before the mirror with eyes open and fell sound asleep; they sealed their shadow in the tomb of memory. In them the stars collapse to form what Hugo called «a blinding menagerie of suns which, through love, make themselves the poodles and the Newfoundlands of immensity.»

The creative life! Ascension. Passing beyond oneself. Rocketing out into the blue, grasping at flying ladders, mounting, soaring, lifting the world up by the scalp, rousing the angels from their ethereal lairs, drowning in stellar depths, clinging to the tails of comets. Nietzsche had written of it ecstatically —and then swooned forward into the mirror to die in root and flower. «Stairs and contradictory stairs,» he wrote, and then suddenly there was no longer any bottom; the mind, like a splintered diamond, was pulverized by the hammer-blows of truth.

There was a time when I acted as my father's keeper. I was left alone for long hours, cooped up in the little booth which we used as an office. While he was drinking with his cronies I was feeding from the bottle of creative life. My companions were the free spirits, the overlords of the soul. The young man sitting there in the mingy yellow light became completely unhinged; he lived in the crevices of great thoughts, crouched like a hermit in the barren folds of a lofty mountain range. From truth he passed to imagination and from imagination to in-

vention. At this last portal, through which there is
no return, fear beset him. To venture farther was
to wander alone, to rely wholly upon oneself.

The purpose of discipline is to promote freedom.
But freedom leads to infinity and infinity is terrifying. Then arose the comforting thought of stopping
at the brink, of setting down in words the mysteries
of impulsion, compulsion, propulsion, of bathing the
senses in human odors. To become utterly human,
the compassionate fiend incarnate, the locksmith of
the great door leading beyond and away and forever
isolate....

Men founder like ships. Children also. There
are children who settle to the bottom at the age of
nine, carrying with them the secret of their betrayal.
There are perfidious monsters who look at you with
the bland, innocent eyes of youth; their crimes are
unregistered, because we have no names for them.

Why do lovely faces haunt us so? Do extraordinary flowers have evil roots?

Studying her morsel by morsel, feet, hands, hair,
lips, ears, breasts, travelling from navel to mouth
and from mouth to eyes, the woman I fell upon,
clawed, bit, suffocated with kisses, the woman who
had been Mara and was now Mona, who had been
and would be other names, other persons, other
assemblages of appendages, was no more accessible,
penetrable, than a cool statue in a forgotten garden
of a lost continent. At nine or earlier, with a
revolver that was never intended to go off, she might
have pressed a swooning trigger and fallen like a
dead swan from the heights of her dream. It might
well have been that way, for in the flesh she was
dispersed, in the mind she was as dust blown hither
and thither. In her heart a bell tolled, but what it
signified no one knew. Her image corresponded to
nothing that I had formed in my heart. She had

intruded it, slipped it like thinnest gauze between the crevices of the brain in a moment of lesion. And when the wound closed the imprint had remained, like a frail leaf traced upon a stone.

Haunting nights when, filled with creation, I saw nothing but her eyes and in those eyes, rising like bubbling pools of lava, phantoms came to the surface, faded, vanished, reappeared, bringing dread, apprehension, fear, mystery. A being constantly pursued, a hidden flower whose scent the blood-hounds never picked up. Behind the phantoms, peering through the jungle brush, stood a shrinking child who seemed to offer herself lasciviously. Then the swan dive, slow, as in motion pictures, and snow-flakes falling with the falling body, and then phantoms and more phantoms, the eyes becoming eyes again, burning like lignite, then glowing like embers, then soft like flowers; then nose, mouth, cheeks, ears looming out of chaos, heavy as the moon, a mask unrolling, flesh taking form, face, feature.

Night after night, from words to dreams, to flesh, to phantoms. Possession and depossession. The flowers of the moon, the broad-backed palms of jungle growth, the baying of blood-hounds, the frail white body of a child, the lava bubbles, the rallitando of the snow-flakes, the floorless bottom where smoke blooms into flesh. And what is flesh but moon? and what is moon but night? Night is longing, longing, longing, beyond all endurance.

«Think of *us!*» she said that night when she turned and flew up the steps rapidly. And it was as if I could think of nothing else. We two and the stairs ascending infinitely. Then «contradictory stairs»: the stairs in my father's office, the stairs leading to crime, to madness, to the portals of invention. How *could* I think of anything else?

Creation. To create the legend in which I could fit the key which would open her soul.

A woman trying to deliver her secret. A desperate woman, seeking through love to unite herself with herself. Before the immensity of mystery one stands like a centipede that feels the ground slipping beneath its feet. Every door that opens leads to a greater void. One must swim like a star in the trackless ocean of time. One must have the patience of radium buried beneath a Himalayan peak.

It is about twenty years now since I began the study of the photogenic soul; in that time I have conducted hundreds of experiments. The result is that I know a little more—about myself. I think it must be very much the same with the political leader or the military genius. One discovers nothing about the secrets of the universe; at the best one learns something about the nature of destiny.

In the beginning one wants to approach every problem directly. The more direct and insistent the approach, the more quickly and surely one succeeds in getting caught in the web. No one is more helpless than the heroic individual. And no one can produce more tragedy and confusion than such a type. Flashing his sword above the Gordian knot, he promises speedy deliverance. A delusion which ends in an ocean of blood.

The creative artist has something in common with the hero. Though functioning on another plane, he too believes that he has solutions to offer. He gives his life to accomplish imaginary triumphs. At the conclusion of every grand experiment, whether by statesman, warrior, poet or philosopher, the problems of life present the same enigmatic complexion. The happiest peoples, it is said, are those which have no history. Those which have a history, those which have made history, seem only to have emphasized through their accomplishments the eternality of struggle. These disappear too, eventually, just as those who made no effort, who were content merely to live and to enjoy.

The creative individual (in wrestling with his medium) is supposed to experience a joy which balances, if it does not outweight, the pain and anguish which accompany the struggle to express himself. He lives in his work, we say. But this unique kind of life varies extremely with the individual. It is only in the measure that he is aware of more life, the life abundant, that he may be said to live in his work. If there is no realization there is no purpose or advantage in substituting the imaginative life for the purely adventurous one of reality. Every one who lifts himself above the activities of the daily round does so not only in the hope of enlarging his field of experience, or even of enriching it, but of quickening it. Only in this sense does struggle have any meaning. Accept this view, and the distinction between failure and success is nil. And this is what every great artist comes to learn en route—that the process in which he is involved has to do with another dimension of life, that by identifying himself with this process he *augments* life. In this view of things he is permanently removed—and protected—from that insidious death which seems to triumph all about him. He divines that the great secret will never be apprehended but incorporated in his very substance. He has to make himself a part of the mystery, live *in* it as well as with it. Acceptance is the solution: it is an art, not an egotistical performance on the part of the intellect. Through art then, one finally establishes contact with reality: that is the great discovery. Here all is play and invention; there is no solid foothold from which to launch the projectiles which will pierce the miasma of folly, ignorance and greed. The world has *not* to be put in order: the world *is* order incarnate. It is for us to put ourselves in unison with this order, to know what is the world order in contradistinction to the wishful-thinking orders which we seek to impose on one another. The power which we long to possess, in order to establish the good, the true and the beautiful, would prove to be, if we could have it, but the means of destroying one another. It is fortunate that we are powerless. We have first to acquire vision, then discipline and forbearance. Until we have the humility to acknowledge the existence of a vision beyond our own, until we have faith and trust in superior powers, the blind must lead the blind. The men who believe that work and brains will accomplish everything must ever be deceived by the quixotic and unforeseen turn of events. They are the ones who are perpetually disappointed; no longer able to blame the gods, or God, they turn on their fellow-men and vent their impotent rage by crying «Treason! Stupidity!» and other hollow terms.

The great joy of the artist is to become aware of a higher order of things, to recognize by the compulsive and spontaneous manipulation of his own impulses the resemblance between human creation and what is called «divine» creation. In works of fantasy the existence of law manifesting itself through order is even more apparent han in other works of art. Nothing is less mad, less chaotic, than a work of fantasy. Such a creation, which is nothing less than pure invention, pervades all levels, creating, like water, its own level. The endless interpretations which are offered up contribute nothing, except to heighten the signifiance of what is seemingly unintelligible. This unintelligibility somehow makes profound sense. Every one is affected, including those who pretend not to be affected. Something is present, in works of fantasy, which can only be likened to an elixir. This mysterious element, often referred to as «pure nonsense», brings with it the flavor and the aroma of that larger and utterly impenetrable world in which we and all the heavenly bodies have their being. The term nonsense is one of the most baffling words in our vocabulary. It has a negative quality only, like death. Nobody can explain nonsense: it can only be demonstrated. To add, moreover, that sense and nonsense are interchangeable is only to labor the point. Nonsense belongs to other worlds, other dimensions, and the gesture with which we put it from us at times, the finality with which we dismiss it, testifies to its disturbing nature. Whatever we cannot include within our narrow framework of comprehension we reject. Thus profundity and nonsense may be seen to have certain unsuspected affinities.

Why did I not launch into sheer nonsense immediately? Because, like others, I was afraid of it. And deeper than that was the fact that, far from situating myself in a beyond, I was caught in the very heart of the web. I had survived my own destructive school of Dadaism: I had progressed, if that is the word, from scholar to critic to pole-axer. My literary experiments lay in ruins, like the cities of old which were sacked by the vandals. I wanted to build, but the materials were unreliable and the plans had not even become blueprints. If the substance of art is the human soul, then I must confess that with dead souls I could visualize nothing germinating under my hand.

To be caught in a glut of dramatic episodes, to be ceaselessly participating, means among other things that one is unaware of the outlines of that bigger drama of which human activity is but a small part.

The act of writing puts a stop to one kind of activity in order to release another. When a monk, prayerfully meditating, walks slowly and silently down the hall of a temple, and thus walking sets in motion one prayerwheel after another, he gives a living illustration of the act of sitting down to write. The mind of the writer, no longer preoccupied with observing and knowing, wanders meditatively amidst a world of forms which are set spinning by a mere brush of his wings. No tyrant, this, wreaking his will upon the subjugated minions of his ill-gotten kingdom. An explorer, rather, calling to life the slumbering entities of his dream. The act of dreaming, like a draught of fresh air in an abandoned house, situates the furniture of the mind in a new ambiance. The chairs and tables collaborate; an effluvia is given off, a game is begun.

To ask the purpose of this game, how it is related to life, is idle. As well ask the Creator why volcanos? why hurricanes? since obviously they contribute nothing but disaster. But, since disasters are disastrous only for those who are engulfed in them, whereas they can be illuminating for those who survive and study them, so it is in the creative world. The dreamer who returns from his voyage, if he is not shipwrecked en route, may and usually does convert the collapse of his tenuous fabric into other stuff. For a child the pricking of a bubble may offer nothing but astonishment and delight. The student of illusions and mirages may react differently. A scientist may bring to a bubble the emotional wealth of a world of thought. The same phenomenon which causes the child to scream with delight may give birth, in the mind of an earnest experimenter, to a dazzling vision of truth. In the artist these contrasting reactions seem to combine or merge, producing that ultimate one, the great catalyzer called *realiza-*

tion. Seeing, knowing, discovering, enjoying—these faculties or powers are pale and lifeless without realization. The artist's game is to move over into reality. It is to see beyond the mere «disaster» which the picture of a lost battlefield renders to the naked eye. For, since the beginning of time the picture which the world has presented to the naked human eye can hardly seem anything but a hideous battle ground of lost causes. It has been so and will be so until man ceases to regard himself as the mere seat of conflict. Until he takes up the task of becoming the «I of his I».

10

Saturdays I usually quit work at noon, lunching either with Hymie Laubscher and Romero or with O'Rourke and O'Mara. Sometimes Curley joined us, or George Miltiades, a Greek poet and scholar, who was one of the messenger force. Now and then O'Mara would invite Irma and Dolores to joins us; they had worked their way up from humble secretaries in the Cosmococcic employment bureau to buyers in a big department store on Fifth Avenue. The meal usually stretched out until three of four in the afternoon. Then, with dragging feet, I would wend my way over to Brooklyn to pay my weekly visit to Maude and the little one.

As the snow was still on the ground we were no longer able to take our walks through the park. Maude was generally attired in a negligee and bathrobe; her long hair hung loosely, almost to her waist. The rooms were super-heated and encumbered with

furniture. She usually kept a box of candy near
the couch where she reclined.

The greetings we exchanged would make one think
we were old friends. Sometimes the child was not
there when I arrived, having gone to a neighbor's
house to play with one of her little friends.

«She waited for you until three o'clock,» Maude
would say, with an air of mild reproach, but secretly
thrilled that it had turned out thus.

I would explain that my work had detained me
at the office. To this she would give me a look
which signified—«I know your excuses. Why don't
you think up something different?»

«How is your friend Dolores?» she would ask
abruptly. «Or,» giving me a sharp look, «isn't she
your friend any more?»

A question like this was meant as a gentle insinua-
tion that she hoped I was not deceiving the other
woman (Mona) as I had her. She would never mention Mona's name, of course, nor would I. She
would say «she» or «her» in a way that was un-
mistakably clear as to whom she meant.

There was also, in these questions, an overtone of
deeper implications. Since the divorce proceedings
were only in the preliminary stages, since the rupture
had not yet been definitely created by law, there was
no telling what might happen in the meantime. We
were no longer enemies, at least. There was always
the child between us—a strong bond. And, until she
could arrange her life differently, they were both
dependent on me. She would like to have known
more about my life with Mona, whether it was going
as smoothly as we had expected or not, but pride
prevented her fom inquiring too openly. She
doubtless reasoned to herself that the seven years we
had lived together constituted a not altogether negligible factor in this now seemingly tenuous situation.

One false move on Mona's part and I would fall back into the old pattern. It behoved her to make the most of this strange new friendship which we had established. It might prepare the ground for another and deeper relationship.

I felt sorry for her sometimes when this unexpressed hope manifested itself only too clearly. There was never the slightest fear on my part that I would sink back into the old pattern of conjugal life. Should anything happen to Mona—the only threat of separation I could think of was death—I would certainly never resume a life with Maude. It was much more plausible that I should turn to some one like Irma or Dolores, or even Monica, the little waitress from the Greek restaurant.

«Why don't you come over here and sit beside me—I won't bite you.»

Her voice seemed to come from far away. Often it happened that when we were left alone, Maude and I, my mind would wander off. As now, for example, I would often respond in a semi-trance, the body obedient to her wishes but the rest of me absent. A brief struggle of wills always ensued, a struggle rather between her will and my absence of will. I had no desire to tickle her erotic fancies; I was there to kill a few hours and be off without opening any fresh wounds. Usually, however, my hand would absent-mindedly stray over her voluptuous form. There was nothing more to it at first than the involuntary caress that one would give a pet. But little by little she would make me aware that she was responding with concealed pleasure; then, just when she had succeeded in riveting my attention upon her body, she would make some abrupt move to break the connection.

«Remember, *I'm not your wife any more!*»

She loved to hurl that at me, knowing that it

would incite me to renewed efforts, knowing that it
would focus my mind, as well as my fingers, upon the
forbidden object: *herself*. These taunts served
another purpose too—they roused an awareness of
her power to offer or deny. She always seemed to be
saying with her body: «To have this you can't ignore
me.» The idea that I could be satisfied with her
body only was a most humiliating one for her. «I'd
give you more than any woman could offer,» she
seemed to say, «if only you *looked* at me, if only you
saw *me*, the real me.» She knew only too well that
I looked beyond her, that the dislocation between
our centers was far more real, far more dangerous,
now than it had ever been. She knew too that there
was no other way of reaching me than through the
body.

It's a curious fact that a body, however familiar it
may be to sight and touch, can become eloquently
mysterious once we feel that the owner of it has
become elusive or evasive. I remember the renewed
zest with which I explored Maude's body after I
learned that she had been to see a doctor for a
vaginal examination. What gave spice to the
situation was that the doctor in question had been
an old suitor of hers, one of those suitors whom she
had never mentioned. Out of the blue one day she
announced that she had been to his office, that she
had had a fall one day which she had told me nothing
about, and, having lately run into her old sweetheart,
whom she knew she could trust (!), she had decided
to let him examine her.

«You just walked in on him and asked to be
examined?»

«No, not quite like that.» She had to laugh herself
at this.

«Well, what did happen exactly?»

I was curious to know whether he had found her

improved or otherwise in the interval of five or six
years which had elapsed. Hadn't he made any
advances? He was married, of course, she had
already informed me of that. But he was also extremely handsome, a magnetic personality, she had taken
pains to let me know.

«Well, how did it feel to get on the table and
spread your legs open—before your old sweetheart?»

She tried to make me understand that she had
grown absolutely frigid, that Dr. Hilary, or whatever
the devil his name was, had urged her to relax, that
he had reminded her that he was acting as a
physician, and so on and so forth.

«Did you succeed in relaxing—finally?»

Again she laughed, one of those tantalizing laughs
which she always produced when she had to speak
of «shameful» things.

«Well, what did he do?» I pressed.

«Oh, nothing much, really. He just explored the
vagina (she wouldn't say *my* vagina!) with his finger.
He had a rubber over his finger of course.» She
added this as though to absolve herself of any
suspicion that the procedure might have been anything more than a perfunctory one.

«He thought I had filled out beautifully,» she
volunteered, to my surprise.

«Oh, he did, did he? He gave you a thorough
examination, then?»

The recollection of this little incident had been
stirred by a remark she had just dropped. She said
she had been worried about the old pain which had
reappeared recently. She redescribed the fall which
she had years ago when she believed, mistakenly, that
she had injured her pelvis. She spoke with such
seriousness that when she took my hand and placed
it above her cunt, just at the ridge of the Mons Venus,

I thought the gesture one of complete innocence.
She had a thick growth of hair there, a genuine rose
bush which, if the fingers strayed within striking
distance of it, immediately stood on end, stiffened like
a brush.   It was one of those bushy things which are
maddening to touch through a film of silk or velvet.
Often, in the early days, when she wore attractive
flimsy things, when she acted coquettish and seductive,
I used to make a grab for it and hold on to it while
standing in some public place, the lobby of a theatre,
or an elevated station.   She used to get furious with
me.   But, standing close to her, blocking the sight of
my groping hand, I would continue to hold on to it,
saying: «Nobody can see what I'm doing. Don't
move!» And I would continue talking to her, my
hand buried in her muff, she hypnotized with fear.
In the theatre, as soon as the lights were lowered,
she would always spread her legs apart and let me
fool with her.   She thought nothing of it then to
open my fly and play with my cock throughout the
performance.

Her cunt still held a thrill. I was conscious of it
now, my hand resting warmly on the edge of her
thick sporran. She kept up a continuous flow of
talk in order to postpone that embarrassing moment
of silence when there would be nothing but the
pressure of my hand and the tacit admission that she
wished it to remain there.

As though vitally interested in what she was
relating, I suddenly reminded her of the stepfather
whom she had lost. As I anticipated, she thrilled
immediately to the suggestion. Excited by the very
mention of the name, she placed her hand over mine
and pressed it warmly. That my own hand slipped a
little farther down, that the fingers became entangled
in the thick hairs, she seemed not to mind at all—for
the moment. She carried on about him gushingly.

quite like a school-girl. As my fingers twined and untwined I felt a double passion stirring in me. Years ago, when I first used to call on her, I was violently jealous of this step-father. She was then a woman of twenty-two or three, her figure full-blown, mature in every sense of the word; to see her sitting on his lap before the window, at dusk, talking to him in a low, caressing voice, used to infuriate me. «I love him,» she would say, as though that excused her behavior, for with her the word love always meant something pure, something divorced from carnal pleasure. It was in Summer that these scenes occured, and I, who was only waiting for the old duffer to release her, was all too conscious of the warm naked flesh beneath the filmy, gauze-like dress she wore. She might just as well have sat naked in his arms, it seemed to me. I was always conscious of the weight of her in his arms, of the way she settled down on him, her thighs rippling, her generous crack anchored firmly over his fly. I was certain that, however pure the old man's love for her was, he must have been aware of the luscious fruit he was holding in his arms. Only a corpse could have been impervious to the sap and the heat generated by that warm body. Moreover, the better I knew her, the more I thought it natural for her to offer her body in this furtive, libidinous way. An incestuous relationship was not beyond her; if she had to be «violated» she would prefer that it be done by the father she loved; the fact that he was not her real father, but the one she had chosen, simplified the situation, if indeed she ever permitted herself to think about such things openly. It was this damned, perverted relationship which had made it so difficult for me to bring her out into any clear, open sexual relationship in those days. She expected of me a love which I was unable to give her. She wanted me to fondle her like a child, whisper sweet nothings in her ear, pet her, pamper her, humor her. She wanted me to embrace and caress her in some absurd, incestuous way. She didn't want to admit that she had a cunt and I a prick. She wanted love talk and silent, furtive pressures, explorations with the hands. I was too forthright, too brutal, for her liking.

After she had had a taste of the real thing she was nearly beside herself—with passion, rage, shame, humiliation, and what not. She evidently had never thought it would be so enjoyable, nor so disgusting. What was disgusting—to her—was the abandonment. To think that there was something hanging between a man's legs which could make her forget herself completely was exasperating to her. She did so want to be independent—when not just a child. She didn't want the in between realm, the surrender, the fusion, the exchange. She wanted to keep that little tight core of self which was hidden away in her breast and only allow herself the legitimate pleasure of surrendering the body. That body and soul could not be separated, especially in the sex act, was a source of the most profound irritation. She always behaved as if, having abandoned her cunt to the exploration of the penis, she had lost something, some little particle of her abysmal self, some element which could never be replaced. The more she fought against it the more complete was her abandon. No woman can fuck as savagely as the hysterical woman who has made her mind frigid.

Playing now with the stiff, wiry hairs of that bush of hers, letting a finger stray down occasionally to the tip of her cunt, my thoughts roamed vagrantly deep into the past. I had almost the feeling that I was her chosen father, that I was playing with this lascivious daughter in the hynoptic dusk of an over-heated room. Everything was false and deep and real at the same time. If I were to act as she wished, act the part of the tender, understanding lover, there would be no doubt of the reward. She would devour me in passionate surrender. Only keep up the pretences and she would open those thighs of hers with a volcanic ardor.

«Let me see if it hurts inside,» I whispered, withdrawing my hand and deftly slipping it under the filmy thift and up her cunt. The juices were oozing from her; her legs slipped farther apart, responsive to the slightest pressure of my hand.

«There... does it hurt *there?*» I asked, piercing deep within her.

Her eyes were half closed. She gave a meaningless nod, signifying neither yes nor no. I slipped two more fingers inside her cunt and quietly stretched my length beside her. I put an arm under her head and drew her gently to me, my fingers still deftly churning the juices that were seeping from her.

She lay still, absolutely passive, her mind thoroughly absorbed in the play of my fingers. I took her hand and slid it into my fly which came unbuttoned magically. She grasped my prick firmly and gently, caressing it with a practised touch. I stole a quick glance at her and saw an expression almost of bliss on her countenance. This was what she loved, this blind, tactile exchange of emotions. If she could only really fall asleep now and let herself be fucked, pretend that she had no watchful, waking part in it... just give herself completely and yet be innocent... what bliss that would be! She liked to fuck with the inner cunt, lying absolutely still, as in a trance. With semaphores erect, distended, jubilant, twitching, tickling, sucking, clinging, she could fuck to her heart's content, fuck till the last drop of juice was exhausted.

It was imperative now not to make a false move,

not to puncture the thin skin which she was still
spinning, like a cocoon, about her naked, carnal
self. To make the transfer from finger to prick
required the adroitness of a mesmerist. The deadly
pleasure had to be increased most gradually, as
though it were a poison to which the body became
only gradually accustomed. She would have to be
fucked through the veil of the cocoon, just as years
ago, in order to take her, I had to violate her through
her nightgown.... A devilish thought came to my
mind, as my cock twitched with delight under her
skillful caresses. I thought of her sitting on her step-
father's lap, in the gloaming, her crack glued to his
fly as always. I wondered what the expression on
her face would have been had she suddenly felt that
glow-worm of his penetrating her dreamy cunt; if,
while murmuring her perverse litany of adolescent
love in his ears, if, unconscious of the fact her gauze-
like dress no longer covered her fleshy buttocks, this
unmentionable thing which was hidden between his
legs suddenly stood bolt upright and climbed inside
her, exploding like a water pistol. I looked at her to
see if she could read my thoughts, exploring the
folds and crevices of her inflamed cunt meanwhile
with bold, aggressive palps. Her eyes were tightly
closed, her lips parted lasciviously; the lower part of
her body began to squirm and twist, as if trying to
free itself from a net. Gently I removed her hand
from my cock, at the same time gingerly lifting a leg
and slinging it over me. For a few moments I let
my cock jump and quiver at the mouth of her crack,
letting it slide from front to rear and back again, as
if it were a flexible rubber toy. An idiotic refrain
was repeating itself in my head: «What is this I
hold over thy head—*fine or super-fine?*» I continued
this little game for a tantalizing spell, now and then
nosing the head of my prick in an inch or so, then

running it up against the tip of her cunt and letting it nestle down in her dewy bush. All of a sudden she gave a gasp and with eyes wide open she swung full round; balanced on hands and knees, she strove frantically to catch my prick with her slimy trap. I put my two hands around her buttocks, the fingers doing a glissando along the inner edge of her swollen cunt, and opening it like you would a torn rubber ball, I placed my cock at the vulnerable point and waited for her to bear down. For a moment I thought she had suddenly changed her mind. Her head, which had been hanging loosely, the eyes helplessly following the frantic movements of her cunt, now thrust itself up taut, the gaze suddenly shifted to some point above my head. An expression of utter selfish pleasure filled the full, roving orbs, and as she began to rotate her ass, my prick only half inside her, she began to chew her underlip. With that I slid a trifle lower and pulling her down with all my force I jabbed it in up to the hilt, so deep that she gave a groan and her head fell forward on the pillow. At this moment, when I could have taken a carrot and shoved it around inside her for all the difference it would have made, there came a loud knock at the door. We were both so startled that our hearts almost stopped beating. As usual, she recovered first. Tearing herself from me, she ran to the door.

«Who's there?» she asked.

«It's only me,» came the timid, quaking voice which I recognized immediately.

«Oh, it's *you!* Why didn't you say so? What is it?»

«I only wanted to know,» came the faint, dragging voice with a slowness which was exasperating, «if Henry was there?»

«Yes, of course he's here,» snapped Maude, pulling

herself together. «Oh, Melanie,» she said, as if the latter were torturing her, «is that all you wanted to know? Couldn't you...?»

«There's a telephone call for Henry,» said poor old Melanie. And then even more slowly, as if she were just able to get that much more out of her system: «I... think... it's important.»

«All right,» I yelled, getting up from the couch and buttoning my fly, «I'll be right there!»

When I picked up the receiver I got quite a shock. It was Curley telephoning from Cockroach Hall. He couldn't tell me what it was, he said, but I was to get home as fast as I could.

«Don't talk that way,» I said, «tell me the truth. What's happened? Is it Mona?»

«Yes,» he said, «but she'll be all right in a little while.»

«She's not dead then?»

«No, but it was a close call. Hurry up...», and with that he hung up.

In the hall I ran into Melanie, her bosom half exposed, limping along with melancholy satisfaction. She gave me an understanding look, one of pity, envy and reproach combined.

«I wouldn't have disturbed you, you know»—her voice drawled painfully upward—«if they hadn't said it was important. Dear me,» and she started dragging her body towards the stairs, «there's so much to do. When you're young....»

I didn't wait to hear her out. I ran downstairs and almost into Maude's arms.

«What is it?» she asked solicitously. Then, since I didn't answer immediately, she added: «Did something happen.... to... to *her?*»

«Nothing serious, I hope,» said I, fumbling about for my coat and hat.

«Must you go right away? I mean....»

There was more than anxiety in Maude's voice; there was a hint of disappointment, a faint suggestion of disapproval.

«I didn't turn the light on,» she continued, moving towards the lamp as if to switch it on, «because I was afraid Melanie might come down with you.» She fussed a little with her bathrobe, as if to bring my mind back to the subject which was uppermost in her mind.

I suddenly realized that it was cruel to run off without a little show of tenderness.

«I've really got to run,» I said, dropping my hat and coat and moving swiftly to her side. «I hate to leave you now... like this,» and taking the hand which was about to light the lamp, I drew her to me and embraced her. She offered no resistance. On the contrary, she put her head back and offered her lips. In a moment my tongue was in her mouth and her body, limp and warm, was pressing convulsively against mine. («Hurry, hurry!» came Curley's words.) «I'll make it quick,» I said to myself, not caring now whether I made a rash move or not. I slipped my hand under her gown and plunged the fingers into her crotch. To my surprise she reached for my fly, opened it, and took out my prick. I backed her against the wall and let her place my prick against her cunt. She was all aflame now, conscious of every move she made, deliberate and imperious. She handled my prick as if it were here own private property.

It was awkward trying to get at it bolt upright. «Let's lie here,» she whispered, sinking to her knees and dragging me down likewise.

«You'll catch cold,» I said, as she feverishly attempted to slide out of her things.

«I don't care,» she said, pulling my pants down and pulling me to her recklessly. «Oh God,» she

groaned, chewing her lips again and squeezing my
balls as I slowly inserted my prick. «Oh God, give it
to me... put it all the way in!» and she gasped and
groaned with pleasure.

Not wishing to jump up immediately and make
a grab for my hat and coat I rested there on top of
her, my prick still inside her and stiff as a ramrod.
She was like a ripe fruit inside and the pulp seemed
to be breathing. Soon I felt the two little flags
fluttering; it was like a flower swaying, and the
caress of the petals was tantalizing. They were
moving uncontrollably, not with hard, convulsive
jerks, but like silken flags responding to a breeze.
And then it was as though she suddenly assumed the
control: with the walls of her cunt she became a soft
lemon squeezer inside, plucking and clutching at will,
almost as if she had grown an invisible hand.

Lying absolutely still, I surrendered myself to these
artful manipulations. («Hurry, hurry!» But I
recalled very clearly now that he had said she wasn't
dead.) I could always summon a taxi; a few minutes
more or less wouldn't matter. Nobody would ever
imagine that I had stayed behind for this.

(Take your pleasure while it lasts.... Take your
pleasure....)

She knew now that I wouldn't run. She knew that
she could draw it out as long as she pleased, especially
lying quiet this way, fucking only with that inner
cunt, fucking with a mindless mind.

I put my mouth to hers and began to fuck with
my tongue. She could do the most amazing things
with her tongue, things I had forgotten she knew.
Sometimes she slid it into my throat as though to
let me swallow it, then withdrew it tantalizingly to
concentrate on the signalling below. Once I pulled
my prick out all the way, to give it a breath of air, but
she reached for it greedily and slipped it back in

again, thrusting herself forward so that it would touch bottom. Now I drew it out just to the tip of her cunt and, like a dog with a moist nose, I sniffed at it with the tip of my pecker. This little game was too much for her; she began to come, a long drawn-out orgasm that exploded softly like a five-pointed star. I was in such a cold-blooded state of control that as she went through her spasms I poked it around inside her like a demon, up, sideways, down, in, out again, plunging, rearing, jabbing, snorting, and absolutely certain that I wouldn't come until I was damned good and ready.

And now she did something she had never done before. Moving with furious abandon, biting my lips, my throat, my ears, repeating like a crazed automaton, «Go on, give it to me, go on, give it, go on, Oh God, give it, give to me!» she went from one orgasm to another, pushing, thrusting, raising herself, rolling her ass, lifting her legs and twining them round my neck, groaning, grunting, squealing like a pig, and then suddenly, thoroughly exhausted, begging me to finish her off, begging me to shoot. «Shoot it, shoot it... I'll go mad.» Lying there like a sack of oats, panting, sweating, utterly helpless, utterly played out that she was, I slowly and deliberately rammed my cock back and forth, and when I had enjoyed the chopped sirloin, the mashed potatoes, the grazy and all the spices, I shot a wad into the mouth of her womb that jolted her like an electric charge.

In the subway I tried to prepare myself for the ordeal ahead. Somehow I felt certain that Mona was not in danger. To tell the truth, the news was not altogether a shock; I had been expecting an outburst of some sort for weeks. A woman can't go

on pretending that she is indifferent when her whole
future is in jeopardy. Particularly a woman who
feels guilty. While I didn't doubt that she had made
an effort to do something desperate, I knew also that
her instincts would prevent her from accomplishing
her end. What I feared more than anything was
that she might have bungled the job. My curiosity
was aroused. What had she done? How had she
gone about it? Had she planned it knowing that
Curley would come to the rescue? I hoped, in some
strange, perverted way, that her story would sound
convincing; I didn't want to hear some preposterous,
outlandish tale which in my unsettled condition
would cause me to burst out into hysterical laughter.
I wanted to be able to listen with a straight face—
to look sorrowful and sympathetic because I *felt*
sorrowful and sympathetic. Drama always affected
me strangely, always aroused the sense of the ridiculous, especially when motivated by love. Perhaps
that was why, in moments of desperation, I could
always laugh at myself. The moment I made the
decision to act I became another person—the actor.
And of course I always overplayed the part. I suppose that at bottom this queer behavior was based on
an incurable dislike for deception. Even though it
meant saving my own skin, I hated to take people in.
To break down a woman's resistance, to make her
love you, to awaken her jealousy, to win her back—it
went against the grain to accomplish these things by
even the unconscious use of legitimate methods.
There was no triumph or satisfaction in it for me
unless the woman surrendered voluntarily. I was
always a bad suitor. I became discouraged easily,
not because I doubted my own powers but because I
distrusted them. I wanted the woman to come to
me. I wanted *her* to make the advances. No danger
of her becoming too bold! The more recklessly she

gave herself the more I admired her. I hated virgins and shrinking violets. *La femme fatale!*—that was my ideal.

How we hate to admit that we would like nothing better than to be the slave! Slave and master at the same time! For even in love the slave is always the master in disguise. The man who must conquer the woman, subjugate her, bend her to his will, form her according to his desires—is he not the slave of his slave? How easy it is, in this relationship, for the woman to upset the balance of power! The mere threat of self-dependence, on the woman's part, and the gallant despot is seized with vertigo. But if they are able to throw themselves at one another recklessly, concealing nothing, surrendering all, if they admit to one another their interdependence, do they not enjoy a great and unsuspected freedom? The man who admits to himself that he is a coward has made a step towards conquering his fear; but the man who frankly admits it to every one, who asks that you recognize it in him and make allowance for it in dealing with him, is on the way to becoming a hero. Such a man is often surprised, when the crucial test comes, to find that he knows no fear. Having lost the fear of regarding himself as a coward he is one no longer: only the demonstration is needed to prove the metamorphosis. It is the same in love. The man who admits not only to himself but to his fellowmen, and even to the woman he adores, that he can be twisted around a woman's finger, that he is helpless where the other sex is concerned, usually discovers that he is the more powerful of the two. Nothing breaks a woman down more quickly than complete surrender. A woman is prepared to resist, to be laid siege to: she has been trained to behave that way. When she meets no resistance she falls headlong into the trap. To be able to give oneself wholly and

completely is the greatest luxury that life affords.
Real love only begins at this point of dissolution.
The personal life is altogether based on dependence,
mutual dependence. Society is the aggregate of
persons all interdependent. There is another richer
life beyond the pale of society, beyond the personal,
but there is no knowing it, no attainment possible,
without first traversing the heights and depths of the
personal jungle. To become the great lover, the
magnetiser and catalyzer, the blinding focus and
inspiration of the world, one has to first experience
the profound wisdom of being an utter fool. The
man whose greatness of heart leads him to folly and
ruin is to a woman irresistible. To the woman who
loves, that is to say. As to those who ask merely to
be loved, who seek only their own reflection in the
mirror, no love however great, will ever satisfy them.
In a world so hungry for love it is no wonder that
men and women are blinded by the glamour and
glitter of their own reflected egos. No wonder that
the revolver shot is the last summons. No wonder
that the grinding wheels of the subway express,
though they cut the body to pieces, fail to precipitate
the elixir of love. In the egocentric prism the
helpless victim is walled in by the very light which
he refracts. The ego dies in its own glass cage...

My thoughts were running crab-wise. Melanie's
image popped up suddenly. She was always there,
like a fleshy tumor. Something bestial and angelic
about her. Always limping along, dragging her
words, droning, drooling, her enormous melancholy
eyes hanging like hot coals in their sockets. She was
one of those beautiful hypochondriacs who, in becoming unsexed, take on the mysterious sensual qualities
of the creatures which fill the Apocalyptic menagerie
of William Blake. She was extremely absent-minded,
not about the usual trivialities of routine life, but

about her body. It was not at all unusual for her
to roam about the house, doing the chores which
never ended, with her full milk-white teats exposed.
Maude was always berating her, always furious about
Melanie's indecencies, as she called them. But Melanie was as innocent as an insane otter. And if the
word otter seems odd it is because it is so appropriate.
With Melanie all sorts of absurd images always leaped
into my mind. She was only «mildly» insane, so to
speak. The more her mental faculties dribbled away
the more obsessive her body became. Her mind had
sunk down into the flesh and, if she was awkward
and doddering in her movements, it was because she
was thinking with this fleshy body and not her brain.
Whatever sex there was in her seemed to have become
distributed throuhout the body; it wasn't localized
any more, neither between her legs nor elsewhere.
She had no sense of shame. The hair on her cunt,
if she happened to expose it at the breakfast table
while serving us, was undifferentiated from her toe
nails or her bellybutton. I am sure that had I ever
absent-mindedly touched her cunt, while reaching for
the coffee-pot, she would have reacted no differently
than if I had touched her arm. Often, when I was
taking a bath, she would open the door unconcernedly
and hang the towels on the rack over the tub, excus-
ing herself in a weak, self-effacing way, but never
making the slightest attempt to avert her eyes.
Sometimes, on such occasions, she would stand and
talk to me a few moments—about her pets or her
bunions or the menu for the morrow—looking at me
with absolute candor, never in the least embarrassed.
Though she was old and had white hair her flesh
was alive, almost revoltingly alive for one her age.
Naturally now and then I got an erection lying there
in the tub with her looking on unabashed and talking
utter gibberish. Once or twice Maude had come

upon us unawares. She was horrified, of course.
«You must be crazy,» she said to Melanie. «Oh
dear,» the latter replied, «what a fuss you make!
I'm sure Henry doesn't mind,» and she would smile
that melancholy, wistful smile of the hypochondriac.
Then she would shuffle off to her room which Maude
had selected for her to live in. Wherever we lived
Melanie's room was always exactly the same. It was
a room where Dementia was caged and imprisoned.
Always the parrot in its cage, always a mangy poodle,
always the same daguerrotypes, always the sewing
machine, always the brass bedstead and the old-
fashioned trunk. A disorderly room which to Melanie seemed like Paradise. A room filled with shrill
barks, with squawks punctuated by caressing mur-
murs, coaxings, cooings, jumbled phrases, squeals of
affection. Sometimes, in passing the open door, I
would catch her sitting on the bed clad only in her
chemise, the parrot perched on her crooked hand,
the dog nibbling at the bait between her legs.
«Hello,» she would say, looking up at me with blank,
bland innocence. «It's a beautiful day to-day, isn't
it?» And perhaps she would push the dog away, not
because of shame or embarassment, but because he
was tickling her with his diabolically cunning little
moist tongue.

Sometimes I stole into her room on the quiet, just
to snoop around. I was curious about Melanie, about
the letters she received, the books she read, and so
on. Nothing was hidden away in her room. Neither
was anything ever fully consumed. There was always
a little water in the saucer under the bed, always
some halfnibbled crackers lying on the trunk or a
piece of cake which she had bitten into and forgotten
to finish. Sometimes an open book lay on the bed,
the page held open by a torn slipper. Bulwer-
Lytton was one of her authors, apparently, also Rider

Haggard. She seemed to be interested in magic, in the black art more particularly. There was a pamphlet about Mesmerism which betrayed evidences of having been well thumbed. The most amazing discovery, tucked away in one of the bureau drawers, was of a rubber instrument which had only one use, unless Melanie in her cracked way had intended it for some wholly innocent usage. Whether Melanie sometimes whiled away a pleasant hour with this object, as did the nuns of old, or whether she had bought it in a junk shop and hidden it away for some unsuspected use some time or other in the course of her never-ending life, was a mystery to me. It was not difficult for me to picture her lying on the filthy quilt clad in her torn chemise, poking this thing in and out of her twat in absent-minded glee. I could even picture the dog licking the juice that slowly trickled between her legs. And the parrot squawking insanely, perhaps repeating some idiotic phrase which Melanie had taught it, such as, «Ever so easy, dearie!» or «Get a move on now, get a move on!»

A queer one, Melanie, and even though her wits had flown, she understood in a primitive, almost cannibalistic way that sex was everywhere, like food and water and sleep and bunions. It used to exasperate me that Maude kept up such unnecessary pretences when Melanie was around. If we lay on the couch after dinner, to enjoy a quiet little fuck in the dark, Maude would suddenly jump up and switch on a soft light—so that Melanie wouldn't suspect what we were up to, or that she wouldn't intrude absent-mindedly to hand us a letter which she had forgotten to give us at breakfast. I used to enjoy the thought of Melanie breaking in on us (say just as Maude is climbing over me), breaking in on us to hand me a letter, and me taking the letter with a smile and a thank you, and Melanie standing there a moment to

say some little nothing about the hot water being
too hot or asking Maude if she wanted eggs for the
morning or some head cheese. It would have given
me a great kick to pull off a stunt like that on Maude.
But Maude could never admit to herself that Melanie knew we had intercourse together. Regarding
her either as an idiot or wholly daft, she had made
herself believe that people like Melanie never thought
of sex. Her step-father had had no sex life with this
demented creature, that she was certain of. She
wouldn't go into it, why she was so certain, but she
was positive of it, and the way she dismissed the
subject indicated all too clearly that she thought a
crime had been done her step-father. One would
almost think, to follow her, that Melanie had
deliberately addled her pate in order to deprive the
step-father of his sexual due.

Melanie had a soft spot in her heart for me, always
took my part when I quarreled with Maude, and
never once that I can remember made any attempt
to reproach me for my flagrant misbehavior. It was
that way from the very beginning. Maude used to
try to keep her out of sight, in the early days. Melanie was something she was deeply ashamed of—a
walking reminder, it would seem, of the family taint.
Melanie seemed not to notice the difference between
good and bad people; she had only one guiding
principle, an immediate response to kindness. And
so, when she discovered that I was not trying to run
away from her as soon as she opened her trap, when
she found that I could listen to her prattle and not
become distraught, like Maude, when she found that
I enjoyed food and beer and wine, especially cheeses
and bolognas, she was willing to be my slave. I held
the most wonderful moronic conversations with her
some times when Maude was absent—usually in the
kitchen with a bottle of beer between us and perhaps

a little liverwurst and a bit of Liederkranz on the side. Giving her free rein as I would on such occasions, I caught remarkable glimpses of her not uninteresting past. «They» seemed to have hailed from some indolent, semi-constipated region where the Wurzburger flows. The women were always getting caught and the men were always going to jail for some trivial reason. It was a sort of Sunday School picnic atmosphere with kegs of beer, pumpernickel sandwiches, taffeta petticoats, lace drawers and stray goats fucking contentedly on the greensward. Sometimes I had a mind to ask her if she had ever let herself be fucked by a Shetland pony. If Melanie thought you sincerely wanted to know, she would answer a question like that without the least to do. You could pass from a question like that to a query about the communion service without modulating. There was no censor standing on her subliminal threshold; messengers came and went without the least formality.

It was wonderful to see how she took up the little Jap who was our star boarder. Tori Takekuchi was his name, and a delightful, gracious, princely little chap he was. He had taken the situation in at a glance, despite his inadequate grasp of the language. Of course, being a Jap, it was easy for him to smile and beam at Melanie when she posted herself at his door-sill and prattled like a cracked nannygoat. He smiled the same way at us, even when we informed him of a grave catastrophe. I think he would have given the same smile had I told him that I was going to die in a few minutes. Of course Melanie knew that Orientals smile in this inscrutable way, but she thought Mr. T's smile—that was how she called him always, «Mr T.»—was particularly engaging. She thought he was like a doll. So clean and tidy too! Never left a crumb of dirt behind him.

When we got more intimate, and I must say that
we all became very intimate before a month or two
was out, Mr. T. began bringing girls to his room.
He had, to be sure, discreetly taken me aside one
day and asked if he might be permitted to bring a
young lady home occasionally, offering the flimsy
excuse (with a broad grin) that he had business to
transact. I used his excuse to obtain Maude's
consent. I pretended that the little bugger was so
unattractive that it couldn't possibly be anything but
business which would bring a pretty American girl
to his room. Maude consented reluctantly, torn between the desire to keep up appearances with the
neighbors and the fear of losing a generous boarder
whose money we needed.

I wasn't home when the first intruder stepped
across the threshold, but I heard about it the next
day—heard that she was «terribly cute». It was Melanie who spilled the beans. She was so glad that he
had found a little friend—like himself.

«But she's not a friend,» Maude put in cere-
moniously.

«Oh well,» drawled Melanie, «maybe it's just
business... but she was awfully cute. He has to have
a girl, just like any one else.»

A few weeks later Mr. T. had switched to another
girl. This one wasn't so «cute». She was a good
head taller than him, built like a panther, and quite
obviously not there to talk business.

I congratulated him the next morning at table,
asking him point blank where he had picked up such
a blazing beauty.

«Dance hall.» said Mr. T., baring his yellow fangs
most amiably, then bursting into a girlish giggle.

«Very intelligent, yes?» I queried, just to keep
the ball rolling.

«Oh yes, her very intelligent, her very good girl.»

«Look out she doesn't give you a dose of clap,» says I, calmly swallowing my coffee.

I thought Maude would fall off the chair. How could I talk that way to Mr. T.? It was insulting as well as disgusting, she wanted me to know.

Mr. T. looked puzzled. He hadn't yet learned the word *clap*. He was smiling, of course, and why shouldn't he? He didn't give a fuck what we said so long as we allowed him to do as he pleased.

Out of politeness I volunteered a definition. *Headache*, I explained.

He laughed uproariously at this. Very good joke. Yes, he understood. He understood nothing, the little prick, but it was polite to let him think he understood. Then I smiled too, a banjo smile, which made Mr. T. giggle some more, rinse his fingers in the water tumbler, belch and throw his napkin on the floor.

I must confess that he had good taste, Mr. T. No doubt he was generous with his money. They made my mouth water, some of them. To him I don't think their beauty meant very much; he probably was more interested in their weight, the texture of their skin, and above all, in their cleanliness. He had all kinds—red heads, blondes, brunettes, short, tall, plump, lithe ones—quite as if he had drawn them from a grab bag. He was buying cunt—and that was all there was to it. At the same time he was learning a little more English. («How you say this...?» «What that called?» «You like bon-bons, yes?») He was good at making gifts—it was an art with him. I often thought, when I saw him taking a girl to his room, heard him giggle and stammer in that fuckee-wuckee way of the Japs, how much better off the girls were to have got hold of Mr. T. than some young American college boy out on a spree. I felt sure, too, that Mr. T. always got his money's worth. («You turn over, please.» «You suck now, yes?») Compared to the artists in his own country, these dumb American bitches must have cut a sorrowful figure in Mr. T.'s eyes. I remembered O'Mara's description of his visits to the bordels in Japan. They were like opium dreams, to hear him tell. The emphasis was placed on the preliminaries, apparently. There was music, incense, baths, massages, caresses, a full orchestration of seduction and enchantment, making the final consumation a thing of unbearable ecstasy. «Just like dolls,» O'Mara would say. «And so gentle, so loving. They bewitch you.» And then he would go into raptures about the tricks they had up their sleeves. They seemed to have a manual of fuck which began where ours left off. And all this in an ambiance of delicacy, as though fucking was *the* spiritual art, the vestibule to heaven.

Mr. T. had to make the most of it in his furnished room, fortunate indeed if he could find a piece of punk to burn. Whether he enjoyed himself or not was hard to tell, because to all questions he invariably answered: «Very good.» Now and then, coming in late, I caught him going to the bath room after one of his sessions with an American cunt. He always went to the bathroom in straw slippers and kimono, a short kimono which just about covered his prick. Maude thought it was shocking, his running around in that rig, but Melanie thought it suited him to a T. «They all run around like that,» she said, knowing not a damned thing about it, but always ready to take the other person's side.

«Good time, Mr. T.?» I would smile.

«Very good, very good,» and then a giggle. Perhaps he would scratch his balls while baring his teeth in a grin. «Water hot, yes?» In the bathroom he would go through his endless ablutions.

If he surmised that Maude were asleep he would sometimes beckon with his finger, signifying that he had something to show me. I would follow him to his room.

«I come in, yes?» he would say, frightening the girl out of her wits. «This Mr. Miller, my friend of mine... this Miss Slith.» They were always Smith, Brown or Jones, I noticed. He probably never bothered to ask their real names .

Some of the girls were of surprising calibre, I must say. «Cute, isn't he?» they would often say. Whereupon Mr. T. would go over to the girl, as you would approach a figure in a shop window, and lift her dress. «Her very beautiful, yes?» And he'd proceed to inspect her twat as if he had bought stock in it.

«Here, you little devil, you can't do that!» the girl would say.

«*You go now, yes?*» That was Mr. T's way of dispatching them. It sounded crude as hell, coming from a little yellow belly. But Mr. T. was unaware of being indelicate. He had given her a good fuck, he had licked her ass, he had paid her in honest coin and given her a little gift into the bargain... *what more*, for Christ's sake? «*You go now, yes?*» And he would half close his eyes, look utterly wooden and disinterested, leaving not the least doubt in the girl's mind, that the speedier she left the healthier it would be for her.

«Next time *you try!* Her very small..» Here he would grin, making a little gesture with his fingers to show me how smooth it went. «Japanese girl sometimes very big. This country big girl small. Very good.» He would lick his chops after a remark like this. Then, as if to make the most of the occasion, he would take a tooth-pick and, while picking his teeth, he would look for the words he had written down in his little note book. «*This mean*

what? He would show me a word like «precarious»
or «unearthly.» «Now I teach you Japanese word
—*OHIO!* That mean Good Morning!» A broad
grin. Still picking his teeth, or else examining
his toes.

«Japanese very simple. All words pronounce same
way,» and he would rattle off a string of words,
giggling as he did so, probably because what they
meant were «shit-heel,» «white bugger,» «foreign
fool,» and so on. I didn't give a shit what the words
meant, since I had no intention of making a serious
study of Japanese. What I was more interested in
was his technique of picking up white women. To
hear him, it was all very simple. Of course, many
of the girls were recommended from one Jap to another. And many of these same girls must have made
a speciality of Japs, knowing that they were clean
and generous. Hump for the Japs, that's what they
were, and a profitable business it was. There was
class to the Japs. They had cars of their own,
dressed well, ate in good restaurants, and so on.
Now a Chink was different. Chinks were white-
slavers. But a Jap you could trust. And so on. I
could follow their reasoning perfectly. What they
appreciated most were the little gifts the Japs made
them. Americans never thought of giving gifts, not
usually. A guy had to be a sap to piss away his
money on a gift for a whore.

I don't know why my mind reverted to the amiable
Mr. T. It's a devil of a long ride to the Bronx, and
if you let your mind go you can write a book between
Borough Hall and Tremont. Besides, despite the
exhaustive bout with Maude, one of those slow,
creepy erections was coming on. It's a commonplace
observation but true just the same—the more you
fuck, the more you want to fuck, and the better you
do fuck! When you overdo it your cock seems to

get more flexible: it hangs limp, but on the alert, as it were. You only have to brush your hand over your fly and it responds. For days you can walk around with a rubber truncheon dangling between your legs. Women seem to sense it, too.

Nown and then I tried to fix my mind on Mona, to set my face in plastic sorrow, but it wouldn't last. I felt too damned good, too relaxed, too carefree. Horrible as it sounds, I thought more of the fuck I anticipated pulling off once I soothed her down. I smelled my fingers to make sure I had scoured them properly. In doing so a rather comical image of Maude assailed me. I had left her lying on the floor, exhausted, and had rushed to the bathroom to tidy myself up. As i was scrubbing my cock she opens the door. Wants to take a douche immediately always fearful of getting caught. I tell her to go ahead, not to mind me. She peels off her things, fastens the hose to the gas jet, and lies on the bath mat, her legs running up the wall.

«Can I help you?» says I, drying my cock and sprinkling some of her excellent sachet powder over it.

«Do you mind?» says she, wiggling her ass so that her legs will stand up straighter.

«Open it up a bit,» I urge, taking the nozzle in readiness to insert it.

She did as I told her, pulling her gash open with all her fingers. I bent over and examined it leisurely. It was a dark, liverish color and the lips were rather exaggerated. I took them, between my fingers and rubbed them gently together, like you would two velvety petals. She looked so helpless lying with her ass propped against the wall and her legs sticking up straight, like the hands of a compass, that I had to chuckle.

«Please don't fool now,» she begged, as if the delay

of a few seconds might mean an abortion. «I thought you were in such a hurry.»

«I am,» I replied, «but Jesus, when I look at this thing I get horny again.»

I inserted the nozzle. The water began running out of her, over the floor. I threw some towels down to soak it up. When she stood up I took the soap and wash rag and scrubbed her cunt for her. I soaped her well, inside and out—a delicious tactile sensation which was mutual.

It felt silkier than ever now, her cunt, and I whooshed my fingers in and out, like you'd strum a banjo. I had one of those half-hearted, swollen erections which makes a cock look even more murderous than when full blown. It was hanging out of my fly, brushing her thigh. She was still naked. I began to dry her off. To do so comfortably I sat on the edge of the tub, my cock gradually stiffening and making spasmodic leaps at her. As I pulled her close, to dry her flanks, she looked down at it with a hungry, despairing look, fascinated and yet half-ashamed of herself for acting the glutton. Finally she could stand it no longer. She got to her knees impulsively and took it in her mouth. I ran my fingers through her hair, caressed the shell of her ears, the nape of her neck, caught her teats and massaged them gently, lingering over the nipples until they stood out taut. She had unfastened her mouth and was licking it now as if it were a stick of candy. «Listen,» said I, murmuring the words in her ear, «we won't go through it again but just let me put it in a few moments and then I'll go. It's too good to stop all of a sudden. I won't come, I promise...» She looked at me imploringly, as if to say «Can I believe you? Yes, I do want it. Yes, yes, only don't knock me up, will you?»

I pulled her to her feet, turned her around like

a dummy, placed her hands on the edge of the tub, and raised her bum just a trifle. «Let's do it this way for a change,» I murmured, not inserting my cock immediately, but rubbing it up and down her crack from behind.

«You won't come, will you?» she begged, craning her neck around and giving me a wild, imploring look through the mirror over the washstand. «I'm wide open...»

That «wide open» brought out all the lust in me. «You bloody bitch,» says I to myself, «that's just what I want. I'm going to piss in your palatial womb!» And with that I let it slip in slowly, little by little, moving it from right to left, grazing the pockets and lining of her wide-open cunt until I felt the mouth of her womb; there I wedged it good and solid, soldering it to her as if I intended to leave it in for good. «Oh, oh!» she groaned. «Don't move, please.... just hold it!» I held it all right, even when that rear end began revolving like a pin-wheel.

«Can you still hold it?» she murmured huskily, trying again to look round and catching her reflection in the mirror.

«I can hold it,» I said, not making the slightest movement, knowing that that would encourage her to unleash all her tricks.

«It feels wonderful,» she said, her head falling limp, as if it had become unhinged. «You're bigger now, do you know it? It is tight enough for you? I'm terribly opened up.»

«It's all right,» I said. «It fits marvelously. Listen, don't move any more... just clutch it... you know how....»

She tried but somehow it wouldn't perform, her little lemon squeezer. I withdrew abruptly, without warning. «Let's lie down... *here*,» I said, pulling her away and placing a dry towel under her. My cock was glistening with juice and hard as a pole. It hardly seemed to be a prick any more: it was like an instrument I had attached, an erection made flesh. She lay prone, looking at it with terror and joy, wondering what next it might think to do— yes, quite as if *it* were deciding things and not me or her.

«It's cruel of me to keep you,» she said, as I socked it in swiftly. The suction created a smacking sound, like wet farts.

«Jesus, now I'm going to fuck you good and proper. Don't worry, I won't come... I haven't got a drop left. Move all you want... jerk it up and down... that's it, rub it around, go on, do it... fuck your guts out!»

«Shhh!» she whispered, putting her hand to my mouth. I bent forward and bit into her neck, long and deep; I bit her ears, her lips. I pulled out again, for one tantalizing second, and bit the hair over her cunt, caught the two little lips up and slid them between my teeth.

«Put it in, put it in!» she begged, her lips slavering, her hand reaching for my prick and placing it back in again. «Oh God, I'm going to come... I can't hold it any more. Oh, oh....» and she went into a spasm, slapping it up against me with such fury, such abandon, that she looked like a crazed animal. I pulled out without coming, my prick shiny, glistening, straight as a ramrod. Slowly she rose to her feet. Insisted on washing it for me, patted it admiringly, tenderly, as if it had been found tried and true. «You must run,» she said, holding my prick between her two hands, the towel wrapped around it. And then, dropping the towel and looking away— «I hope she's all right. Tell her so, will you?»

Yes, I had to smile thinking of this last minute scene. «*Tell her so...*» That extra fuck had softened her up. I thought of a book I had read which told of rather strange experiments with carnivorous animals—lions, tigers, panthers. Seems that when these ferocious beasts were kept well-fed— over-fed, indeed—one could put gentle creatures in the same cage with them and they would never molest them. The lion attacked only out of hunger. He was not perpetually murderous. That was the gist of it....

And Maude... Having satisfied herself to her heart's content, she had probably realized for the first time that it was useless to harbor a grudge against the other woman. If, she may have told herself, if it were possible to be fucked like that whenever she wished, it wouldn't matter what claims the other one had on me. Perhaps it entered her mind for the first time that possession is nothing if you can't surrender yourself. Perhaps she even went so far as to think that it might be better this way —having me protect her and fuck her and not having to get angry with me because of jealous fears. If the other one could hold on to me, if the other one could keep me from running around with every little slut that came accross my path, if together they could share me, tacitly of course and without embarrassment and confusion, perhaps after all it might be better than the old arrangement. Yes, to be fucked that way, fucked without fear of being betrayed, to be fucking your own husband who is now your friend (and perhaps a lover again), to be taking what you want of him, calling him when you need him, sharing a warm, passionate secret with him, reliving the old fucks, learning new ones, stealing and yet not stealing, but giving oneself with pleasure and abandon, growing younger again, losing nothing except a conventional tie... yes, it might be ever so much better.

I'm sure something of this sort had been running through her head, had spread its aureole about her.

I could see her, in my mind's eye, languorously brushing her hair, feeling her breasts, examining the marks of my teeth on her neck, hoping Melanie would not notice them but not caring too deeply whether she did or not. Not caring greatly any more whether Melanie overheard things or not. Asking herself wistfully perhaps how it had ever come about that she had lost me. Knowing now that if she had to live her life all over again she would never act as she had, never worry about useless things. So foolish to worry about what the other woman may be doing! What matter if a man did let his feet stray now and then? She had locked herself up, put a cage around herself; she had pretended she had no desires, pretended she dare not fuck—because we weren't man and wife any longer. What a terrible humiliation! Wanting it dreadfully, longing for it, almost begging for it like a dog—and there it was all the time, waiting for her. Who cared whether it was right or not? Wasn't this wonderful stolen hour better than anything she had ever known? *Guilt?* She had never felt less guilty in her life. Even if the «other one» had died meanwhile she couldn't feel bad about it.

I was so certain of what had been going on in her mind that I made a mental note to ask her about it next time we met. Of course next time she might be her old self again—that was only too possible with Maude. Besides, it wouldn't do to let her see that I was too interested—that might only stir up the poison. The thing to do would be to keep it on an impersonal level. No sense in letting her relapse into her old ways. Just walk in with a cheery greeting, ask a few questions, send the kid out to play, move in close, quietly, firmly take out my prick and put it in her hand. Make sure the room was not too bright. No nonsense! Just walk up to her and, while asking how things are going, slip a hand up her dress and start the juice flowing.

That extra last minute fuck had done wonders for me too. Always, when one digs down into the reservoir, when one summons the last ounce, so to speak, one is amazed to discover that there is a boundless source of energy to be drawn on. It had happened to me before, but I had never given it serious attention. Staying up all night and going to work without sleep had a similar effect upon me; or the converse, staying in bed long past the period of recuperation, forcing myself to rest when I no longer needed rest. To break a habit, establish a new rhythm—simple devices, long known to the ancients. It never failed. Break down the old pattern, the worn-out connections, and the spirit breaks loose, establishes new polarities, creates new tensions, bequeaths new vitality.

Yes, I observed with the keenest pleasure now how my mind was sparking, how it radiated in every direction. This was the sort of ebullience and élan I prayed for when I felt the desire to write. I used to sit down and wait for this to happen. But it never did happen—not this way. It happened afterwards, sometimes, when I had left the machine and gone for a walk. Yes, suddenly it would come on, like an attack, pellmell, from every direction, a veritable inundation, an avalanche—and there I was, helpless, miles away from the typewriter, not a piece of paper in my pocket. Sometimes I would start for the house on the trot, not running too fast because then it would peter out, but easy like, just as in fucking—when you tell yourself to take it easy, don't think about it, that's it, in and out, cool detached, trying to pretend to yourself that it's your prick that's fucking and not you. Exactly the same procedure. Jog along, steady, hold it, don't think

about the typewriter or how far it is to the house,
just easy, steady like, that's it...

Rehearsing these odd moments of inspiration I
suddenly recalled a moment when I was on my way
to the burlesque theatre, «The Gayety», at Lorimer
Street and Broadway. (I was riding the elevated
line.) Just about two stations before my destination
the attack came on. This was a very important
attack because for the first time in my life I was
cognizant of the fact that it was what is called «a
flood of inspiration.» I knew then, in the space of
a few moments, that something was happening to me
which apparently did not happen to everyone. It
had come without warning, for no reason that I could
possibly think of. Perhaps just because my mind
had become a perfect blank, because I had sunk
back, deep into myself, content to drift. I recall
vividly how the exterior world brightened suddenly,
how like a flash the mechanism of my brain began
to function with awesome smoothness and rapidity,
thoughts telescoping one another, images succeeding
and obliterating one another, in their frantic desire
to register themselves. That Broadway (1) which I
hated so, especially from the elevated line (affording
me a «superior» view, a downward look upon life,
people, buildings, activities), this Broadway had
suddenly undergone a metamorphosis. It wasn't
that it became ideal or beautiful or unreal; on the
contrary, it became terribly real, terribly vivid. But
it had acquired a new orientation; it was situated in
the heart of the world, and this world which I now
seemed able to take in with one grasp had meaning.
Before, Broadway had stuck out like an eye-sore,
all ugliness and confusion; now it fell back into its
proper place, an integral part of the world, neither

_____

(1) Broadway, **Brooklyn**.

good nor bad, neither ugly nor beautiful: *it simply belonged.* It was there like a rusty nail in a log thrown up on a deserted beach during a wintry storm. I can't express it better. You walk along the beach, the air is tangy, your spirits are high, you think clearly—not always brilliantly—but *clearly.* Then the log, a phenomenal part of the substantial world: it lies there, full of experience, full of mystery. Some man hammered that nail in somewhere, sometime, somehow. There was a reason for doing it. He was making a ship for other men to sail in. Building ships was his life-work—and his own destiny as well as the destiny of his children went into every stroke of the hammer. Now the log lies there, and the nail is rusty, but Christ, it's more than just a rusty nail—or else everything is crazy and meaningless... That's how it was with Broadway. Hams in the window, and the dreary windows of the glaziers, with lumps of putty on the counter making greasy stains in the coarse paper. Strange how man evolves through the ages—from *pithecanthropus erectus* to a gray-faced glazier handling a brittle substance called glass which for millions of years nobody, not even the magicians of old, had even dreamed of. I could see the street slowly sinking, fading out in time: time which passes like lead or evaporates like steam. The buildings collapsed; the boards, bricks, mortar, glass, nails, hams, putty, paper, everything receded into the great laboratory. A new race of men walking the earth (over this very same ground), knowing nothing of our existence, not caring about the past nor able to comprehend it, even were it possible to revive it. In the crevices of the earth bugs crawling about, as they had for billions of years: clinging stubbornly to their pattern, contributing nothing to evolution, defying it seemingly. They had witnessed, in their generation, every race of man tread the earth

—and they had survived all the cataclysms, all the
historical smash-ups. Down in Mexico, certain crawling bugs were a delicacy to the palate. There were
men, still alive and walking the earth, separated not
by tremendous physical distances but by mental and
spiritual chasms, who took ants and fried them, and,
while they rolled their tongues around with satisfaction, music played and it was a different music from
ours. And like that, over all the wide earth, in the
same moment of time, such vastly different things
were happening, not only on land but in the air and
deep in the sea.

Then came Lorimer Street station. I got out
automatically, but I was powerless to move towards
the stairs. I was caught in the fiery flux, fixed there
just as definitely as if I had been speared by a fisher-
man. All those currents I had let loose were swirling
about me, engulfing me, sucking me down into the
whirlpool. I had to stand there like that, transfixed,
for possibly three or four minutes, thought it seemed
much longer. People passed as in a dream. Another train pulled in and left. Then a man bumped
into me, rushing towards the stairs, and I heard him
excuse himself, but his voice came from far away.
In jostling me he had swung me round just a little.
Not that I was conscious of his rudeness, no... but
suddenly I saw my image in the slot machine where
the chewing gum was racked up. Of course it wasn't
so, but I had the illusion of catching up with myself
—as though I had caught the tail-end of the re-instal-
lation of my old self, the familiar everyday person
looking out at me from behind my own eyes. It
made me just a little jittery, as it would any one if,
coming out of a reverie, he should suddenly see the
tail of a comet streaking across the heavens, erasing
itself as it passed across the retina. I stood there
gazing at my own image, the seizure gone now but

the after effect settling in. A more sober exaltation making itself felt. *To be drunk!* Christ, it seemed so feeble compared to this! (An after-glow, nothing more.) I was intoxicated now—but a moment ago I had been inspired. A moment ago I had known what it was to pass beyond joy. A moment ago I had forgotten absolutely who I was: I had spread myself over the whole earth. Had it been more intense perhaps I would have passed over that thin line which separates the sane from the insane. I might have achieved depersonalization, drowned myself in the ocean of immensity. Slowly I made towards the stairs, descended, crossed the street, bought a ticket, and entered the theatre. The curtain was just going up. It opened on a world even more weird than the hallucinating one I had just eased out of. It was utterly unreal—utterly, utterly so. Even the music, so painfully familiar, seemed foreign to my ears. I could hardly differentiate between the living bodies cavorting before my eyes and the glitter and paste of the scenery; they seemed made of the same substance, a gray slag infused with a low voltage of the vital current. How mechanically they flung themselves about! How absolutely tinny were their voices! I looked around, looked up at the tiers of boxes, the plush cords slung between the brass posts, the puppets seated there one above another, all gazing towards the stage, all expressionless, all made of one substance: *clay,* common clay. It was a shadow world, awesomely fixed. All glued together—scenery, spectators, performers, curtain, music, smoke—in a dreary, meaningless pall. Of a sudden I became itchy, so itchy that it was like a thousand fleas biting me at once. I wanted to yell. I wanted to yell something that would shock them out of this awesome trance. (*Shit! Hot shit!* And every one would jump to his feet, the curtain would

come tumbling down, the usher would grab me by
the collar and give me the bum's rush.) But I
couldn't make a sound. My throat was like sand-
paper. The itchiness passed and then I grew hot and
feverish. Thought I would suffocate. Jesus, but I
was bored. Bored as never before. I realized that
nothing would happen. Nothing *could* happen, not
even if I were to throw a bomb. They were dead,
stinking dead, that's what. They were sitting in their
own stinking shit, steaming in it.... I couldn't stand
it another second. I bolted.

In the street everything appeared gray and normal
again. A most depressing normality. People trund-
led along like spindled vegetables. They resembled
the things they ate. And what they ate made shit.
Nothing more. *Phew!*

In the light of that previous experience on the
elevated train I realized that a new element was
manifesting itself, one which had portentous significance. This element was awareness. I knew now
what was happening to me, and in a measure I could
control the explosion. Something lost, something
gained. If there was no longer the same intensity
as in that early «attack» neither was there the help-
lessness which had accompanied it. It was like being
in an aeroplane racing through the clouds at phenomenal speed and, though unable to shut off the
motor, discovering with joyous surprise that you
could at any rate manage the controls.

Swung out of my accustomed orbit, I nevertheless had sufficient balance to observe my bearings.
The way I now saw things was the way I would
write about them one day. Immediately questions
assailed me, like slings and darts from angry gods.
Would I remember? Would I be able, on a sheet
of paper, to exfoliate in all directions at once? Was
it the purpose of art to stagger from fit to fit, leaving

a bloody haemorrhage in one's wake? Was one merely to report the «dictation»—like a faithful *chela* obeying the telepathic behest of his Master? Did creation begin, as with the earth itself, in the fiery bubble of inchoate magma, or was it necessary that the crust first cool?

Rather frantically I excluded all but the question of remembrance. It was hopeless to think of reproducing a mental cloud-burst. I could merely try to retain certain definite clues, transform them into mnemonic touch-stones. To find the vein again was the all-important—not how much gold I could mine. My task was to develop a mnemonic index to my inspirational atlas. Even the hardiest adventurer scarcely deludes himself that he will be able to cover every square foot of earth on this mysterious globe. Indeed, the true adventurer must come to realize, long before he has come to the end of his wanderings, that there is something stupid about the mere accumulation of wonderful experiences.

I thought of Melanie whom normally, were I planning a book of my life, I would never have bothered to include. How had she managed to inject herself when ordinarily I scarcely gave her a thought? What was the significance of this intrusion? What had she to contribute? Two touchstones fell immediately into my lap. Melanie? Why yes, remember always «beauty» and «insanity.» And why should I remember beauty and insanity? Then there came to mind these words: «varieties of flesh.» This was followed by the most subtle divagations on the relation between flesh, beauty and insanity. What was beautiful in Melanie derived from her angelic nature; what was insane in her derived from the flesh. The fleshly and the angelic had parted ways, and Melanie, as inexplicably beautiful as a crumbling statue, was slowly expiring on the frontier. (There

were hysterical types who also succeeded in isolating
the flesh, giving it thereby a peculiar life of its own.
But with them it was always possible to plug in the
fuse, to restore the current, to put the mind in control again.   They kept a shutter in the mind which,
like the asbestos curtain in the theatre, could be
unrolled in case of fire or as indication that another
act had come to an end.)   Melanie was like some
strange naked creature, half-human, half-divine,
whose whole time was spent in vainly trying to climb
from the orchestra pit to the stage.   In her case it
made little difference whether the show was on or
off, whether it was a rehearsal, an entr'acte, or a
silent empty house.   She clambered about with the
repulsive seductiveness of the insane in their nakedness.   The angels may wear tiaras or brown derbies,
according to their whims, if we are to believe the
vagaries of certain visionaries, but they have never
been described as insane.   Neither has their nakedness ever been a provocation to lust.   But Melanie
could be as ridiculous as a Swedenborgian angel and
as provocative as a ewe in heat to the sight of a
lonely shepherd.   Her white hair served only to
enhance the rippling allure of her flesh; her eyes
were jet black, her bosom firm and full, her haunch
like a magnetic field.   But the more one reflected
on her beauty the more obscene her insanity appeared.   She gave the illusion of moving about naked,
of inviting you to finger her so that she might laugh
in that low, eerie way which the demented have of
registering their unpredictable reactions.   She haunted me like a danger signal glimpsed from a train
window at night when one suddenly wonders if the
engineer is awake or asleep.   Just as one wonders in
such moments, too paralyzed with fear to move or
speak, what the precise nature of the catastrophe
will be, so in thinking of Melanie's insane beauty

I often gave myself up to ecstatic dreams of flesh, the varieties I had known and explored and the varieties 'yet to be discovered. To embark unrestrainedly on carnal adventures awakens the sense of danger. I had experienced more than once the terror and the fascination which the pervert knows when in the crowded subway he submits to the compulsion of stroking a tempting ass or squeezing the seductive teat which lies within reach of his fingers.

The element of awareness acted not only as a partial control, enabling me to move with imaginative feet from one escalator to another, but it served a more important purpose still—it stimulated the desire to commence the work of creation. That Melanie whom I had heretofore ignored, whom I had regarded as a mere cipher in the complicated sum of experiences, could prove such a rich vein, opened my eyes. It was not Melanie at all, as a matter of fact, but those word-clots («beauty,» «insanity,» «varieties of flesh») which I felt the need to explore and clothe in sumptuous style. Even if it took years to do so, I would remember this train of fabulation, capture its secret, expose it on paper. How many hundred women had I pursued, followed like a lost dog, in order to study some mysterious trait—a pair of eyes set far apart, a head hewn out of quartz, a haunch that seemed to live its own life, a voice as melodious as the warble of a bird, a cataract of hair falling like spun-glass, a torso invested with the flexibility of rubber.... Whenever the beauty of the female becomes irresistible it is traceable to a single quality. This quality, often a physical defect, can assume such unreal proportions that in the mind of the possessor her staggering beauty is nil. The excessively attractive bust can become a double-headed maggot that bores into the brain and becomes a

mysterious watery tumor; the tempting overfull lips
can grow in the depths of the skull like a double
vagina, bringing on that most difficult of all diseases
to cure: melancholia. (There are beautiful women
who almost never stand before the mirror nude,
women who, when they think of the magnetic power
which the body wields, become terrified and shrink
into themselves, fearful that even the odor which
they give off will betray them. There are others
who, standing before the mirror, can scarcely restrain
themselves from rushing outdoors stark naked and
offering themselves to the first comer.)

Varieties of flesh.... Before sleep, just as the eyelids close down over the retina and the unbidden
images begin their nocturnal parade... That woman
in the subway whom you followed into the street: a
nameless phantom now suddenly reappearing, advancing towards you with lithe, vigorous loins. Reminds
you of someone, someone just like that, only with
a different face. (But the face was never important!) You have the memory of the ripple and flash
of loins just as strong as you have somewhere in your
brain the image of the bull you saw when a child:
the bull in the act of mounting a cow. Images come
and go, and always it is some particular part of the
body which stands out, some identification mark.
Names—names fade out. The endearing phrases—
they too fade out. Even the voice, that which was
so potent, so undoing, so altogether personal—that too
has a way of vanishing, of becoming lost in all the
other voices. But the body lives on, and the eyes,
and the fingers of the eyes, remember. They come
and go, the unknown, unnamed, mingling as freely
with the others as if they were an integral part of
one's life. With the unknown ones comes the
remembrance of certain days, certain hours, the
voluptuous way they eased into a blank moment of

lassitude. You remember just how the tall one in
a mauve silk dress stood that afternoon, when the
sun beat down with smouldering warmth, and gazed
entranced at the play of water in the fountain. You
remember exactly the way your hunger expressed
itself at the time—sharp, quick, like a knife-blade
between the shoulders, then dying away almost as
quickly, but in such pleasurable smoke, like a deep
nostalgic whiff. And then another one rises up,
heavy, stolid, with the porous skin of sand-stone;
with her everything is centered in the head, the head
which does not fit the body, the head which is
volcanic, still filled with eruption. They come and
go like that, clear, precise, trailing the ambiance of
the collision, radiating their instantaneous effects.
All kinds, all tempered by texture, weather, mood:
metallic ones, marble figurines, translucent shadowy
ones, flowerlike ones, svelte animals covered with
pelts of suede, trapeze artists, silver sheets of water
rising in human form and bending like Venetian glass.
Leisurely you undress them, examine them under the
microscope, bid them sway, bend, flex the knees, roll
over, spread their legs. You talk to them, now that
your lips are unsealed. What were you doing that
day? Do you always wear your hair like that?
What were you going to tell me when you stared at
me that way? Could I ask you to turn around?
That's it. Now cup your breasts with two hands.
Yes, I could have thrown myself on you that day.
I could have fucked you right on the sidewalk, and
people stepping all over us. I could have fucked you
into the ground, buried you there near the lake
where you were sitting with legs crossed. You knew
I was watching you. Tell me... tell me because
nobody will ever know... what were you thinking then,
that very moment? Why did you keep your legs
crossed? You knew I was waiting for you to open

them. You wanted to open them, didn't you? Tell
me the truth! It was warm and you had nothing on
under your dress. You had come down from your
perch to get a bit of air, hoping that something
would happen. You didn't much care what happened, did you? You wandered around by the lake,
waiting for it to get dark. You wanted some one to
look at you, some one whose eyes would undress you,
some one who would rivet his gaze on that warm,
moist spot between your legs...

You spool it off like that, a million feet to the
roll. And all the time, shifting the eyes from one
to another with kaleidoscopic fury, what gets under
your skin is the inexplicable nature of attraction.
The mysterious law of attraction! A secret buried
as deep in the isolated parts as in the mysterious
whole.

The irresistible creature of the other sex is a
monster in process of becoming a flower. Feminine
beauty is a ceaseless creation, a ceaseless revolution
about a defect (often imaginary) which causes the
whole being to gyrate heavenward.

11

«*She tried to poison herself!*»

Those were the words that greeted me on opening
the door of Dr. Onirifick's establishment. It was
Curley who made the announcement, smothering his
words under the rattle of the door-knob.

A glance over his shoulder told me that she was
asleep. Kronski had taken care of her. He had
requested that nothing be said to Dr. Onirifick
about it.

«I smelled the chloroform as soon as I came in,» Curley explained. «She was seated in the chair, huddled up, as if she had had a stroke.»

«I thought maybe it was an abortion...» he added, looking a little sheepish.

«Why did she do it, did she say?»

Curley hemmed and hawed.

«Come on, don't be silly. What was it—jealousy?»

He wasn't sure. All he knew was what she blabbed on coming to. She had repeated over and over that she couldn't stand it any longer.

«Stand what?» I asked.

«Your seeing your wife, I suppose. She said she had picked the receiver up to telephone you. She felt that something was wrong.»

«How did she put it exactly, do you remember?»

«Yes, she talked a lot of nonsense about being betrayed. She said it wasn't the child you went to see but your wife. She said you were weak, that when she was not with you you were capable of doing anything...»

I looked at him in astonishment. «She really said that? You're not putting it on, are you?»

Curley pretended not to hear. He went on to speak of Kronski, how well he had behaved.

«I didn't think he could lie so cleverly,» said Curley.

«Lie? How do you mean?»

«The way he talked about you. You should have heard it. God, it was almost as if he were making love to her. He said such wonderful things about you that she began to weep and sob like a child.»

«Imagine,» he continued, «telling her that you were the most loyal, faithful fellow in the world! Saying that you had changed completely since you knew her—that no woman could tempt you!»

Here Curley couldn't restrain a sickly grin.

«Well it's true,» I said, almost angrily. «Kronski was telling the truth.»

«That you love her so much you...»

«And what makes you think I don't?»

«Because I know you. You'll never change.»

I sat down near the bed and looked at her. Curley moved about restlessly. I could feel the anger in him smouldering. I knew what was at the bottom of it.

«She's quite all right now, I suppose?» I inquired after a time.

«How do I know, she's not *my* wife.» The words flashed back like the gleam of a knife.

«What's the matter with you, Curley? Are you jealous of Kronski? Or are you jealous of *me?* You can hold her hand and pet her when she wakes up. You know me...»

«Damned right I do!» came Curley's sullen reply. «You should have been here holding her hand yourself. You're never there when any one wants you. I suppose you were holding Maude's hand— now that she doesn't want you any more. I remember how you treated her. I thought it funny then—I was too young to know better. And I remember Dolores too...»

«Easy!» I whispered, motioning with my head towards the prostrate figure.

«She won't wake up so soon, don't worry.»

«All right... now what about Dolores?» I said, lowering my voice. «Just what did I do to Dolores that hurt you so?»

He could say nothing for a moment. He was simply bursting with scorn and contempt. Finally he blurted it out.

«You ruin them! You destroy something in them, that's all I can say.»

«You mean that after we broke up you tried to hook Dolores and she wouldn't have you?»

«Before or after—what difference does it make,» he snarled. «I know how she felt—she used to spill it out to me. Even when she hated you she couldn't see me. She used me for a pillow. She wept all over me, as if I were made of Christ knows what... You used to sail out after those sessions in the back room beaming all over. Little Curley was left to lick up the crumbs. Little Curley would tidy things up for you. You never thought what happened when the door closed on you, did you?»

«No-o-o,» I drawled, smiling at him tauntingly. «What did happen? You tell me.»

It's always interesting to learn what does really happen when the door closes behind you. I was ready to sit back and listen with ears cocked.

«Of course,» I ventured, to stimulate him further, «you tried to make the most of the situation.»

«If you want to know,» he replied with brutal frankness, «yes, I did. Even if it was a wet deck! I encouraged her to weep, because then I could put my arms around her. And finally I managed it. I didn't do so bad either, considering the disadvantage I was under. I can tell you a few things about your beautiful Dolores...»

I nodded. «Let's hear everything. It sounds exciting.»

«What you probably don't know is the way she acts when she gets a weeping spell. You missed something.»

I tried to give him free rein, concealing my emotions behind a mask of disinterested tolerance. Curiously enough, in spite of his desire to wound me, he found it difficult to tell his story coherently, or even to take advantage of the opportunity I had given him. The more he talked the more sorry he

became for himself. He couldn't get away from his
own sense of frustration. He wanted to besmirch her,
and being able to obtain my approval added spice
to the procedure. He thought I too would enjoy this
profanation of an old idol.

«So you never really did get your end in?» I
threw him a consoling glance. «Too bad, because
she certainly was a good piece of hump...If I had only
known about it I might have helped you. You
should have said something. I thought you were too
callow to feel that way about her. Naturally I
suspected that you put your arms around her when
my back was turned. I didn't give you credit,
though, for taking your cock out and trying to shove
it in. No, I thought you were too worshipful for
that. Jesus, you were only a kid then. How old
were you—sixteen, seventeen? I should have remembered about your aunt. But that was different. She
raped *you*, wasn't that it?»

I lit a cigarette and settled back in the arm chair.
«You know, Curley, this makes me wonder a bit...»
«You mean about Maude? I never tried
anything...»
«No, I don't mean that. I don't give a damn what
you tried or didn't try...»
«I think you ought to be going soon,» I added.
«When she comes to I'll want to talk to her. It's
lucky you came when you did. H'm! I suppose I
ought to thank you.»
Curley gathered up his things. «By the way,» he
said, «her heart's not so good. And there's something else wrong with her too... Kronski will tell
you.»
I went to the door with him. We shook hands. I
felt impelled to say something.
«Listen, I don't hold it against you about Dolores,
but... but don't be dropping in here when I'm away,

see! You can worship her all you want—from a distance. I don't want any of this damned monkey business, do you understand?»

He gave me a murderous look and strode sullenly off. I had never spoken that way to him before and I regretted it, not because I had wounded him but because I suddenly realized that I had put an idea into his head. Now he would think himself dangerous; he wouldn't be happy until he had tested his powers.

Dolores! Well, I had learned nothing of any consequence. Still, there was something about it I didn't like. Dolores was soft. Too yielding to suit me. There was a time when I had been on the point of asking her to marry me. I recalled what it was that had prevented me from making such a blunder. It was that I knew she would say yes, weakly, because she was mentally still a virgin, unable to resist the pressure of a stiff cock. *That*— her weak yes, to be followed by a lifetime of blubbering regrets. Instead of helping me to forget, she would be a constant mute reminder of the crime I intended to commit. (The crime of leaving my wife.) God knows, part of me was soft as a sponge. I didn't need any one to cultivate that side of me! She was really disgusting, Dolores. Her eyes glowed with such adolescent fervor as she watched me pouring balm over the maimed and wounded. Yes, I could see her clearly now. She was like a nurse attending a physician. She wanted to mother all those poor bastards I was killing myself to aid in one way or another. She wanted only to slave all day by my side. Then offer her little cunt—as a reward, as a mark of approbation. What the hell did she know about love? She was just a puppy. I felt sorry for Curley.

Kronski had told the truth! That's what I kept

repeating to myself as I sat beside the bed and waited for her to return to life. She was not dead, thank God. Merely asleep. She looked as though she were floating in luminol.

It was so unusual for me to play the role of the bereaved one that I became fascinated by the thought of how I would act if she were actually to die now before my eyes. Supposing she were never to open her eyes again? Supposing she passed from this deep trance into death? I tried to concentrate on that thought. I wanted desperately to know how I would feel if she were to die. I tried to imagine that I was a fresh widower, that I had not even called the undertaker.

First of all, however, I got up to put my ear to her mouth. Yes, she was still breathing. I pulled the chair close to the foot of the bed and concentrated as best I could on death—*her death*. No extraordinary emotions manifested themselves. To be truthful, I forgot about my supposed personal loss and became absorbed in a rather blissful contemplation of the desirability of death. I began to think about my own death, and how I would enjoy it. The prone figure lying there, hardly breathing, floating in the wake of a drug like a small boat attached to the stern of a vessel, was myself. I had wanted to die and now I was dying. I was no longer aware of this world but not yet in the other one. I was passing slowly out to sea, drowning without pain of suffocation. My thoughts were neither of the world I was leaving nor of the one I was approaching. In fact, there was nothing comparable to thought going on. Nor was it dreaming. It was more like a diaspora; the knot was unravelling, the self was dribbling away. There wasn't even a self any more: I was the smoke from a good cigar, and like smoke I was vanishing in thin air, and what was left of the cigar was crumbling to dust and dissolution.

I gave a start. The wrong tack. I relaxed and gazed at her less fixedly. Why should I think about her death?

Then it came to me: only if she were dead could I love her the way I imagined I loved her!

«Still the actor! You did love her once, but you were so pleased with yourself to think that you could love another beside yourself that you forgot about her almost immediatly. You've been watching yourself make love. You drove her to this in order to feel again. To lose her would be to find her again.»

I pinched myself, as if to convince myself that I was capable of feeling.

«Yes, you are not made of wood. You have feelings—but they're misdirected. Your heart works spasmodically. You're grateful to those who make your heart bleed; you don't suffer for them, you suffer in order to enjoy the luxury of suffering. You haven't begun to suffer yet; you're only suffering vicariously.»

There was some truth in what I was telling myself. Ever since I had entered the room I had been preoccupied with how I should act, how I should express my feelings. As for that last minute business with Maude—that was excusable. My feelings had switched, that was all. Fate had tricked me. Maude, pfui! I didn't give a fuck about her. I couldn't remember when she had ever stirred any real feeling in me. What a cruel piece of irony it would be if Mona were to discover the truth! How could I ever explain such a dilemma? At the very moment I am betraying her, as she divined, Kronski is telling her how faithful and devoted I am. And Kronski was right! But Kronski must have suspected, when he was telling her the truth, that it was built on a lie.

He was affirming his faith in me because he himself
wanted to believe in me. Kronski was no fool. And
he was probably a far better friend than I had ever
estimated him to be. If only he didn't show such
eagerness to reach into my guts! If only he would
quit driving me into the open.

Curley's remark returned to plague me. Kronski
had behaved so wonderfully—as if he were making
love to her! Why was it that I always got a thrill
when I thought of some one making love to her?
Jealous? I was quite willing to be made jealous if
only I could witness this power she had of making
others love her. My ideal—it gave me quite a shock
to formulate it!—was that of a woman who had the
world at her feet. If I thought there were men
impervious to her charms I would deliberately aid
her to ensnare them. The more lovers she garnered
the greater my own personal triumph. Because she
did love *me*, that there was no doubt about. Had
she not singled me out from all the others, I who
had so little to offer her?

I was weak, she had told Curley. Yes, but so was
she. I was weak as regards women in general; she
was weak as regards the one she loved. She wanted
my love to be focused on her exclusively, even in
thought.

Oddly enough, I *was* beginning to focus on her
exclusively, in my own weak way. If she had not
brought her weakness to my attention I would have
discovered for myself, with each new adventure,
that there was only one person in the world for me—
and that it was her. But now, having placed it
before my mind dramatically, I would always be
haunted by the thought of the power I exercised over
her. I might be tempted to prove it, even against
the grain.

I dismissed this train of thought—violently. That

wasn't at all how I wanted things to be. I did love her exclusively, only her, and nothing on earth would make me swerve.

I began to review the evolution of this love. *Evolution?* There had been no evolution. It had been instantaneous. Why, and I was amazed to think that I should adduce this proof, why, even the fact my first gesture had been one of rejection was proof of the fact that I recognized the attraction. I had said no to her instinctively, because of fear. I went all over that scene in the dance hall the evening I walked out on my old life. She was coming towards me, from the center of the floor. I had cast a quick glance to either side of me, hardly believing it possible that she had singled *me* out. And then a panic, though I was dying to throw myself into her arms. Had I not shaken my head vigorously? No! No! Almost insultingly. At the same time I was shaken by the fear that even if I were to stand there forever she would never again cast an eye in my direction. Then I knew I wanted her, that I would pursue her relentlessly even if she had no use for me. I left the rail and went over to the corner to smoke. Trembling from head to foot. I kept my back to the dance floor, not daring to look at her. Jealous already, jealous of whomever it might be that she would choose for the next partner...

(It was wonderful to recapture those moments. Now, by God, I was feeling again....)

Yes, after a time I had picked myself up and returned to the rail, pressed on all sides by a pack of hungry wolves. She was dancing. She danced several dances in succession, with the same man. Not close, like the other girls, but airily, looking up into the man's face, smiling, laughing, talking. It was plain that he meant nothing to her.

Then came my turn. She *had* deigned to notice

me after all! She seemed not at all displeased with
me; on the contrary, she behaved as though she were
going out of her way to be pleasant. And so, in a
swoon, I had let her carry me round the floor. And
then again, and again, and again. And even before
I ventured to draw her into conversation I knew I
would never leave the place without her.

We danced and danced, and when we were tired
of dancing we sat in a corner and talked, and for
every minute I talked or danced a clock ticked off the
dollard and cents. How rich I was that night! What
a delicious sensation it was to peel off dollar after
dollar recklessly! I acted like a millionaire because
I *was* a millionaire. For the first time in my life I
knew what it was to be wealthy, to be a Mogul, a
Rajah, a Maharajah. I was giving my soul away—
not bartering it, as did Faust, but pissing it away.

There had been that strange conversation about
Strindberg, which was to run through our life like a
silver thread. I was always going to reread *Miss
Julie*, because of what she said that night, but I
never did—and probably never would.

Then I waited for her in the street, on Broadway,
and as she came towards me this second time she
took complete possession of me. In the booth, at
Chin Lee's, she became still another person. She
became—and this was really the secret of her irresistible charm—*she became vague.*

I didn't frame it thus to myself, but as I sat
blindly groping through the smoke of her words, I
knew that I would fling myself like a madman into
every gap in her story. She was spinning a web too
delicate, too tenuous, to support the weight of my
prying thoughts. Another woman acting thus would
have aroused my suspicions. I would have branded
her a skilful liar. This one was not lying. She was

embroidering. She was stitching—and now and then she dropped a stitch.

Here a thought flitted through my head which had never formulated itself before. It was one of those larval thoughts which scud through the mind like a thin moon through mutton chops. *She has been doing this always!* Yes, it had probably occured to me at the time, but I had dismissed it instantly. The way she leaned over, the weight of her resting on one arm, the hand, the right hand, moving like a needle—yes, at that moment, and again several times later, an image had flashed through my mind, but I had had no time, or rather she had given me no time, to track it down. But now it was clear. Who was it that «had been doing it always»? *Fate.* There were three of them, and there was something sinister about them. They lived in a twilight and they spun a web: one of them had assumed this posture, had shifted her weight, had looked into the camera with hand poised, then resumed that endless stitching, spinning, weaving, that silent talk which weaves in and out of the spoken web of words.

A shuttle moving back and forth, a bobbin ceaselessly bobbing. Now and then a dropped stitch... Like the man who lifted her dress. He was standing on the stoop saying good-night. Silence. He blows his brains out.... Or the father flying his kites on the roof. He comes flying down out of the sky, like a violet angel of Chagall's. He walks between his race horses, holding one on either side, by the bridle. Silence. The Stradivarius is missing....

We are on the beach and the moon is scudding through the clouds. But before that we were sitting close together in the motorman's box in the elevated train. I had been telling her the story of Tony and Joey. I had just written it—perhaps because of her, because of the effect of certain vaguenesses. She had thrown me back suddenly on myself, made loneliness seem delectable. She had stirred those grape-like bunches of emotion which were strung like a garland on the skeleton of my ego. She had revived the boy, the boy who ran through the fields to greet his little friends. There was never any actor then! That boy ran alone. That boy ran to throw himself into the arms of Joey and Tony... Why did she look at me so intently when I told her the story of Joey and Tony? There was a terrible brightness in her face, that I can never forget. Now I think I know what it was. I think I had stopped her—stopped that incessant spinning and weaving. There was gratitude in her eyes, as well as love and admiration. I had stopped the machine and she had risen like a vapor, for just a few minutes. That terribly bright look was the nimbus of her liberated self.

Then sexual plunges. Submerging that cloud of vapor. Like trying to hold smoke under water. Peeling off layer after layer of darkness in the dark. Another kind of gratitude. A bit horrible, though. As if I had taught her the prescribed way to commit hari-kiri.... That utterly inexplicable night at Rockaway Beach—in the Doctor Caligari hotel and bathing establishment. Running back and forth to the lavatory. Swooping down on her, scooping it out, piercing her... plunging, plunging, as if I had become a gorilla with knife in hand and were slashing the Sleeping Beauty to life. The next—morning—or was it afternoon? Lying on the beach with our toes in one another's crotch. Like two Surrealist objects demonstrating a hazardous *rencontre*.

And then Dr. Tao, his poem printed on fire-cracker paper. Encysted in the mind, because she had failed to meet me in the garden as she promised. I was holding it in my hand while talking to her over the telephone. Some of the gold had rubbed off and

clung to my fingers. She was still in bed—with that
slut Florrie. They had drunk too much the night
before. Yes, she had stood on a table—*where?*
somewhere!—and had tried to do the split. And she
had hurt herself. But I was too furious to care
whether she had hurt herself or not. She was alive,
wasn't she, and she had failed to show up. And
perhaps Florrie was lying there beside her, as she
pretended, and perhaps it wasn't Florrie but that guy
Carruthers. Yes, that old fool who was so kind and
thoughtful, but who had still enough gumption in
him to stick daggers in people's portaits.

A desolating thought suddenly assailed me. The
danger form Carruthers was past. Carruthers had
helped her. Others had helped her before him no
doubt... But this was the thought: if I had not
come that night to the dance hall with a wad in my
pocket, if I had had just enough for a few dances,
what then? And putting aside that first grand occasion, what about that other time in the empty lot?
(«*And now for the dirt..!*») Supposing I had failed
her then? But I couldn't have failed her, that was
just it. She must have realized that or she would
never have risked it.....

In cold-blooded honesty I was forced nevertheless,
to concede that those few miraculous sums I had
managed to produce at the right moment had been
an important factor. They had helped her to believe
that she could rely on me.

I wiped the slate clean. Damn it, if one were to
interrogate Fate that way everything could be
explained by what you had to eat for breakfast.
Providence puts opportunities in your path: they can
be translated as money, luck, youth, vitality, a
thousand different things. If the attraction isn't
there nothing can be made of even the most golden
opportunity. It was because I would do anything for

her that so many opportunities were afforded 'me. *Money*, shit! Money had nothing to do with it. So much anfractuosity, or defectuosity, or impecuniosity! It was like the definition of hysteria in Dr. Onirifick's library: «an undue permeability of the psychical diaphragm.»

No, I wasn't going to get off into these complicated eddies. I closed my eyes to sink back into that other clear stream which ran on and on like a silver thread. In some quiet part of me there was a legend which she had nourished. It was of a tree, just as in the Bible, and beneath it stood the woman called Eve with an apple in her hand. Here it ran like a clear stream, all that really constituted my life. Here there was feeling, from bank to bank.

What was I getting at—*here where the subterranean stream ran clear?* Why that image of the Tree of Life? Why was it so exhilarating to retaste the poisonous apple, to kneel in supplication at the feet of a woman in the Bible? Why was the Mona Lisa's smile the most mysterious of all human experssions? And why should I transpose this smile of the Renaissance to the lips of an Eve whom I had known only as an engraving?

There was something which hung on the fringe of memory, some enigmatic smile which expressed serenity, beatitude, beneficence. But there was also a poison, a distillation which exuded from that mystifying smile. And this poison I had quaffed and it had blurred the memory. There had been a day when I had accepted something in exchange for something; on that day a strange bifurcation had taken place.

In vain I ransacked my brain. However, I was able to recall this much. On a certain day in Spring I met her in the Rose Room of a large hotel. She had arranged to meet me there in order to show me

a dress she had bought. I had come ahead of time
and after a few restless moments I had fallen into
a trance. It was her voice which brought me to.
She had spoken my name and the voice had passed
through me, like smoke through gauze. She *was*
ravishing, appearing suddenly like that before my
yes. I was still coming out of the mist. As she sat
down I rose slowly, still moving through a fog, and
knelt at her feet, mumbling something about the
radiance of her beauty. For a full few minutes she
made no effort to rouse me. She held my two hands
in hers and smiled down at me, that effulgent,
luminous smile which spreads like a halo and then
vanishes, never to reappear again. It was the seraphic
smile of peace and benediction. It was given in a
public place wherein we found ourselves alone. It
was a sacrament, and the hour, the day, the place
were recorded in letters of gold in the book of the
legend which lay at the foot of the Tree of Life.
Thenceforth we who had united were joined by an
invisible being. Never again were we to be alone.
Never again would come that hush, that finality—
until death perhaps. Something had been given,
something received. For a few timeless moments we
had stood at the gates of Paradise—then we were
driven forth and that starry effulgence was shattered.
Like tongues of lightning it vanished in a thousand
different directions.

There is a theory that when a planet, like our earth
for example, has manifested every form of life, when
it has fulfilled itself to the point of exhaustion, it
crumbles to bits and is dispersed like star dust
throughout the universe. It does not roll on like a
dead moon, but explodes, and in the space of a few
minutes there is not a trace of it visible in the
heavens. In marine life we have a similar effect.
It is called implosion. When an amphibian accus-

tomed to the black depths rises above a certain level, when the pressure to which it adapts itself is lifted, the body blows apart, implodes in a million directions. Are we not familiar with this spectacle in the human being also? The Norsemen who went berserk, the Malay who runs amok—are these not examples of implosion and explosion? When the cup is full it runs over. But when the cup and that which it contains are one substance, what then?

There are moments when the elixir of life rises to such over-brimming splendor that the soul spills over. In the seraphic smile of the Madonnas the soul is seen to flood the psyche. The moon of the face becomes full; the equation is perfect. A minute, a half-minute, *a second later*, the miracle has passed. Something intangible, something inexplicable, was given out—and received. In the life of a human being it may happen that the moon never comes to the full. In the lives of some human beings it would seem, indeed, that the only mysterious phenomenon observable is that of perpetual eclipse. In the case of those afflicted with genius, whatever the form it may take, we are almost frightened to observe that there is nothing but a continuous waxing and waning of the moon. Rarer still are the anomalous ones who, having come to the full, are so terrified by the wonder of it that they spend the rest of their lives endeavoring to stifle that which gave them birth and being. The war of the mind is the story of the soul-split. When the moon was at full there were those who could not accept the dim death of diminution; they tried to hang full-blown in the zenith of their own heaven. They tried to arrest the action of the law which was manifesting itself through them, through their own birth and death, in fulfillment and transfiguration. Caught between the tides they were sundered; the soul departed the body, leaving the simulacrum of a divided self to fight it out in the mind. Blasted by their own radiance they live forever the futile quest of beauty, truth and harmony. Depossessed of their own effulgence they seek to possess the soul and spirit of those to whom they are attracted. They catch every beam of light; they reflect with every facet of their hungry being. Instantly illumined, when the light is directed towards them, they are also as speedily extinguished. The more intense the light which is cast upon them the more dazzling—*and blinding*—they appear. Especially dangerous are they to the radiant ones; it is always towards these bright and inexhaustible luminaries that they are most passionately drawn....

She lay in an argent light, the lips slightly parted in a mysterious smile. Her body seemed extraordinarily light, as if floating in the distilled vapors of a drug. The glow which always emanated from her flesh was still there, but it was detached, suspended all about her, hovering over her like some rare condensation waiting to be reabsorbed by the flesh.

A strange idea took possession of me, as I lost myself in contemplation. Was it mad to think that in trying to extinguish herself she had discovered that she already was extinct? Had death rolled back on her, refusing to be cheated? Was that strange glow, which was collecting about her like the breath on a mirror, the reflection of another death?

She was always so intensely alive. Supernaturally alive, one might say. She never rested, except in sleep. And her sleep was that of a stone.

«Don't you ever dream?» I had asked her once.

She couldn't remember—it was so long ago since she had had a dream.

«But everybody dreams,» I insisted. «You make no effort to remember, that's all.»

Soon thereafter she made known to me in a too obviously casual way that she was beginning to dream again. They were extraordinary dreams. Utterly different from her talk. At first she pretended to be shy about revealing them, but then, when she saw from my queries how remarkable they were, she elaborated at great length.

One day, in recounting one of them to Kronski, giving it to him as my own and pretending that I was perplexed and mystified, I was dumbfounded to hear him say: «There's nothing original about that, *Mister* Miller! Are you trying to trip me up?»

«Trip you up?» I repeated with genuine atonishment.

«It might sound original to a writer,» he sneered, «but to a psychologist it's phoney. You can't invent dreams like you can stories, you know. Dreams have their mark of authenticity just as stories do.»

I allowed him to demolish the dream and admitted, to shut him up, that I *had* invented it.

A few days later, browsing through Dr. Onirifick's library, I came across a ponderous tome dealing with depersonalization. Skimming the pages I found an envelope with my own name and address on the back of it. It was just the flap of the envelope, but the hand writing was indubitably my own. There was only one explanation: it had been left there by Mona.

The pages which I raced through like an ant-eater were devoted to the dreams recorded by a psychiatrist. The dreams were the walking dreams of a somnambulist, with a dimorphic personality. I found myself following them with a disturbing sense of familiarity. I recognized them only in spots.

Finally I became so absorbed that I made notes

of the recognizable fragments. **Where the other elements had come from I would discover** in due time. I yanked out a number of books, searching for place-mark, but found none.

The process, however, I had caught on to. She had extracted only the most dramatic elements—and then joined them together. It made no difference to her that one fragment was the dream of a sixteen year old female and another fragment the dream of a male drug addict.

I thought it a good idea to put the piece of torn envelope in another section of the book before returning it to the shelf.

A half hour later I had a still better idea. I took down the book, consulted my notes, and then carefully underlined the fragmentary passages she had plagiarized. I realized, of course, that with her I might never hear the truth of the matter till years later—perhaps never. But I was content to wait.

A depressing thought followed in the wake of this reflection. If she could fake her dream life, what about her waking life? If I were to begin investigating her past... The enormity of that task was in itself enough to dissuade me from any immediate attempt in that direction. However, one could always prick up his ears. That was not a cheerful thought either. One can't go through life with ears cocked. Curiously enough, I had no more than told myself this when I recalled the way she had dismissed a certain subject. It was strange how she had succeeded in making me forget that little item. In disabusing me of the idea that I had caught a glimpse of her mother in the backyard, on my first inspection of her home precincts, she had skilfully buried the suspicion by dwelling with artful sincerity on the traits and qualities of the woman I had imagined to be her mother, the woman she insisted

must have been her aunt. It was such a commonplace ruse of the liar that I was annoyed at myself,
thinking back on it, to have been taken in so easily.
This at least was something I could investigate in
the near future. I was so positive that I was right
that I almost decided to forego te mechanical task
of corroboration. It would be more enjoyable, I
thought to myself, not to go there just yet, but to
trap her by some clever verbal manœuvering. If I
could develop the art of laying traps it would save
a lot of useless footwork.

Above all, I concluded, it was imperative never to
let her suspect that I was on to her lies. Why was
that so imperative? I asked myself almost immediately. To have the pleasure of uncovering more
and more untruths? *Was that a pleasure?* And
then another question popped into my head. If you
were married to a dipsomaniac, would you pretend
that the mania for alcohol was perfectly harmless?
Would you keep up the pretence that everything
was lovely in order to study the effects of this particular vice upon the person of the one you loved?

If there were any legitimacy in abetting the appetites of curiosity then it were better to get at the
root of the thing, to discover *why* she lied so flagrantly. The effects of this malady were not altogether obvious to me—yet. A little thought and I
should have perceived instantly that this first and
most disastrous effect is—alienation. The shock of
detection, which the discovery of the first lie brings,
has almost the same emotional outlines as the shock
which accompanies the knowledge that one is confronted by an insane person. Treachery, the fear
of it, has its roots in the universal fear of loss of
personality. It must have required aeons of time
for humanity to raise truth to such a supreme level,
to make it the fulcrum, as it were, of individuality.

The moral aspect was merely a concomitant, a cover-all for some deeper, almost forgotten purpose. That *histoire* should be story, lie and history all in one, was of a significance not to be despised. And that a story, given out as the invention of a creative artist, should be regarded as the most effective material for getting at the truth about its author, was also significant. Lies can only be imbedded in truth. They have no separate existence; they have a symbiotic relationship with truth. A good lie reveals more than the truth can ever reveal. To the one, that is, who seeks truth. To such a person there could never be cause for anger or recrimination when confronted with the lie. Not even pain, because all would be patent, naked and revelatory.

I was quite amazed to discern the lengths to which such philosophic detachment could bring me. I made a note to resume the experiment again. It might bear fruit.

VOLUME FOUR

12

I had just left Clancy's office. Clancy was the general manager of the Cosmodemonic Cocksucking Corporation. He was the Cocksucker in Chief, so to speak. He said «Sir» to his inferiors as well as his superiors.

My respect for Clancy had touched zero. For over six months I had avoided calling on him, though it had been understood between us that I was to drop in once a month or so—to have a little chat. To-day he had summoned me to his office. He had expressed disappointment in me. He had virtually intimated that I had failed him.

The poor cluck! If I hadn't been so disgusted I might have felt sorry for him. He was in a spot, I could see that. But he had angled to put himself in that spot for twenty years or more.

Clancy's model of behavior was the soldier, the man who can take orders and give them, if necessary. Blind obedience was his motto. Clearly I was a poor soldier. I had been an excellent tool so long as I had been given a free hand, but now that the reins were being tightened he was chagrined to learn that I was not responsive to the behests of those to whom he himself, Clancy, the General Manager, had to bow deferentially. He was pained to hear that I had been insulting to one of Mr. Twilliger's henchmen. Twilliger was the vice-president, a man with

a heart of cement who had risen from the ranks, just
as Clancy himself had.

I had swallowed such a lot of shit in that brief
interview with my superior that I was regurgitating.
The conversation had terminated on a most unpleasant note, to wit, that I was to learn to cooperate
with Mr. Spivak who had now definitely become
Mr. Twilliger's go-between.

How can you cooperate with a rat? Especially
with a rat whose sole function is to spy on you?

Spivak's entrance upon the scene, I reflected, as
I stepped into a bar to have a drink, had only pre-
ceded by a few months my resolution to walk out
on the old life. His coming had precipitated that
event, or conspired to bring it about, I now felt. The
turning point in my cosmococcic life had come at
the moment of plenitude. Just when I had put everything in order, when the machine was working like
a clock, Twilliger had summoned Spivak from another city and installed him as an efficiency expert.
And Spivak had taken the pulse of the cosmococcic
machine and found that it was beating too slowly.

Since that fatal day they had moved me around
like a chess piece. As if to threaten me, they had
first changed my quarters to the main office. Twilliger had his sanctum in the same building, about
fifteen floors above me. No shenanigans now, as in
the old messenger bureau with the dressing booths
in the rear and the zinc-covered table, where now and
then I had knocked off a fugitive piece of tail. I
was in an airless cage now, surrounded by infernal
contraptions that buzzed and rang and gleamed every
time a client put in a call for a messenger. In a
space just big enough for a double desk and a chair
on either side (for the applicants), I had to sweat
and shout at the top of my lungs to make myself
heard. Three times, in the course of a few months,

I had lost my voice. Each time I reported to the company doctor upstairs. Each time he shook his head in perplexity.

«Say Ah!»

«Ah!»

«Say E-e-e-e!»

«E-e-e-e!»

He'd shove a smooth stick, like a suds duster, down my throat.

«Open your mouth wide.»

I'd open it wide as I could. He'd swab it out, spray it if he felt like it.

«Feel better now?»

I'd to say yes but the best I could do was to give him a vocable piece of phlegm. *Ooogh!*

«There's nothing wrong with your throat that I can see,» he would say. «Come back in a few days and I'll have another look. It may be the weather.»

It never occurred to him to ask what I did with my throat all day long. And of course, once I realized that to lose my voice was to enjoy a few day's vacation, I felt that it was just as well to leave him in ignorance of the cause of my affliction.

Spivak however suspected that I was malingering. I enjoyed talking to him in an almost inaudible whisper long after I had recovered my voice.

«What did you say?» he would rasp.

Choosing the moment when the din was at its height I would repeat some highly unimportant piece of information in the same inaudible whisper.

«Oh *that!*» he would say, highly irritated, exasperated that I made not the slightest effort to strain my voice.

«When do you think you'll get your voice back?»

«I don't know,» I would say, looking him straight in the eye and letting my voice die out.

Then he would talk to the call clerk, pump him

behind my back to find out if I were putting it on.
As soon as he had gone I would resume my natural
tone of voice. If the telephone rang, however, I
would have my assistant answer it. «Mr. Miller can't
use the phone—his voice is gone.» I kept that up
in order to foil Spivak. It was just like him to leave
my office, go out the front door, step into a booth
and ring me up. He would have been jubilant to
catch me off guard.

It was all such a lot of shit, though. Child's play.
In every big corporation these games go on. It's
the only outlet for one's human side. It's like civilization. Everything geared up to function smoothly
in order to destroy it with a little bon-fire. Just
when your impulses have been given a shine, a mani-
cure and a tailor-made suit, a rifle is stuck in your
hand and in six lessons you're expected to learn the
art of sticking a bayonet through a sack of wheat.
It's bewildering, to say the least. And if there's no
panic, no war, no revolution, you go on rising from
one cock-sucking vantage point to another until you
become the Big Prick himself and blow your brains
out.

I swallowed another drink and took a glance at
the big clock on the Metropolitan Tower. Funny
that that clock had inspired the one and only poem
I had ever written. That was shortly after they had
moved me uptown from the main office. The tower
framed itself in the window from which I looked out
on to the street. In front of me sat Valeska. It was
because of Valeska that I had written the poem. I
recalled the excitement that had come over me the
Sunday morning I began the poem. It was unbelievable—a poem. I had to call Valeska on the telephone and tell her the good news. A couple of
months later she was dead.

That was one time, however, that Curley had

managed to get his end in. I had learned that only recently. Seems he used to take her to the beach. He did it, by God, in the water, standing up. The first time, that is. Afterwards it was just fuck, fuck, fuck—in the car, in the bath room, along the water-front, on the excursion boat.

In the midst of these pleasant reminiscences I saw a tall figure dressed in uniform passing the window. I ran out and hailed him.

«I don't know whether I ought to come in, Mr. Miller. I'm on duty, you know.»

«That doesn't matter. Come in a minute and have one drink with me. I'm glad to see you.»

It was Colonel Sheridan, the head of the messenger brigade which Spivak had organized. Sheridan was from Arizona. He had come to me in search of work and I had put him on the night force. I liked Sheridan. He was one of the few dozen clean souls I had raked in among all the thousands I had put to work on the messenger force. Everybody liked him, even that piece of animated cement, Twilliger.

Sheridan was absolutely guileless. He had been born in a clean environment, had been given no more education than he needed, which was very little, and had no ambition except to be what he was, which was a plain, simple, ordinary individual accepting life as he found it. He was one in a million, so far as my observation of human nature went.

I inquired how he was getting on as drill-master. He said it was discouraging. He was disappointed—the boys showed no spirit, no interest in military training.

«Mr. Miller,» he exclaimed, «I never met such boys in all my life. They have no sense of honor...»

I burst out laughing. No honor, God!

«Sheridan,» I said, «haven't you learned yet that you're dealing with the scum of the earth? Besides, boys aren't born with a sense of honor. City boys especially. These boys are incipient gangsters. Have you ever been to the Mayor's office? Have you seen the crowd that hangs out there? Those are grown-up messenger boys. If you were to put them behind the bars you wouldn't be able to tell the difference between them and the real convicts. The whole god-damned city is made up of nothing but crooks and gangsters. That's what a city is—a breeding place for crime.»

Sheridan gave me a puzzled look.

«But you're not like that, Mr. Miller,» he said, grinning sheepishly.

I had to laugh again. «I know, Sheridan. I'm one of the exceptions. I'm just killing time here. Some day I'm going out to Arizona, or some place where it's quiet and empty. I've told you, haven't I, that I went to Arizona years ago? I wish I had had the sense to stay there... Tell me, what was it you did back there... you weren't a sheep-herder, were you?»

It was Sheridan's turn to smile. «No, Mr. Miller, I told you, don't you remember, that I was a barber.»

«A barber!»

«Yes,» said Sheridan, «and a darned good one too.»

«But you know how to ride, don't you? You didn't spend your life in a barber shop, I hope?»

«Oh no,» he answered quickly. «I did a little of everything, I guess. I've earned my own living ever since I was seven.»

«What made you come to New York?»

«I wanted to see what it was like in a big city. I had been to Denver and L.A.,—and Chicago too. Everybody kept telling me I had to see New York, so I decided I would. I tell you, Mr. Miller, New

York is a fine place—but I don't like the people... I don't understand their ways, I guess.»

«You mean the way they shove you around?»

«Yes, and the way they lie and cheat. Even the women here are different. I can't seem to find a girl I like.»

«You're too good, Sheridan. You don't know how to treat them.»

«I know it, Mr. Miller.» He dropped his head. He acted shy as a faun.

You know,» he began falteringly, «I guess there is something wrong with me. They laugh behind my back—everybody does, even the youngsters. Maybe it's the way I talk.»»

«You can't be too gentle with the boys, Sheridan,» I put in. «I warned you—be rough with them! Give 'em a cuffing once in a while. Swear at them. Don't let them think you're soft. If you do, they'll walk all over you.»

He looked up softly and held out his hand. «See that? That's where a boy bit me the other day. Can you imagine that?»

«What did you do to him?»

Sheridan looked down at his feet again. «I sent him home,» he said.

«That's all? You just sent him home? You didn't give him a thrashing?»

He was silent. After a few moments he spoke, quietly and with simple dignity.

«I don't believe in punishment, Mr. Miller. If a man hits me I never strike back. I try to talk to him, find out what's wrong with him. You see, I was knocked around a lot as a kid. I didn't have an easy time of it...»

He stopped dead, shifted his weight from one foot to the other.

I always wanted to tell you something,» he resumed, summoning all his courage. «You're the only man I could tell this to, Mr. Miller. I know I can trust you...»

Again a pause. I waited attentively, wondering what it was he was trying to get off his chest.

«When I came to the telegraph company,» he continued, «I didn't have a dime in my pocket. You remember that, Mr. Miller... you had to help me out. And I appreciate everything you did for me.»

Pause.

«I said a while back that I came to New York to see the big city. That's only half-true. I was running away from something. You see, Mr. Miller, I was very much in love back there. I had a woman who meant everything to me. She understood me, and I understood her. But she was married to my brother. I didn't want to steal her from my brother, but I couldn't live without her...»

«Did your brother know that you were in love with her?»

«Not at first,» said Sheridan. «But after a time he couldn't help but notice it. You see, we all lived together. He owned the barber shop and I helped him. We were doing first-rate too.»

Another awkward pause.

«The trouble all started one day, a Sunday it was, when we went on a picnic. We had been in love all the time, but we hadn't done anything. I didn't want to hurt my brother, as I told you. Anyway, it happened. We were sleeping outdoors and she was lying between us. I woke up all of a sudden and felt her hand on me. She was wide awake, staring at me with big eyes. She bent over and kissed me on the mouth. And right there, with my brother lying beside us, I took her.»

«Have another drink,» I urged.

«I guess I will,» said Sheridan. «Thank you.»

He continued in his slow, hesitant way, very delicate about it all, and obviously genuinely disturbed.
I liked the way he talked about his brother. It was
almost as if he were talking about himself.

«Well, to make it short, Mr. Miller, one day he
went plumb crazy with jealousy—he came after me
with the razor. You see that scar?» He turned his
head slightly to one side. «That's where I caught
it, trying to dodge him. If I hadn't ducked he would
have sliced the side of my face off, I guess.»

Sheridan slowly sipped his drink, looking thoughtfully into the soaped mirror before him.

«I calmed him down finally,» he said. «He was
frightened of course when he saw the blood running
down my neck and my ear almost hanging off. And
then, Mr. Miller, a terrible thing happened. He
began to cry, just like a boy. He told me he was no
good, and I knew that wasn't so. He said he oughtn't
to have married Ella—that was her name. He said
he would get divorced, go away somewhere, start all
over again—and that *I* should marry Ella. He
begged me to say I would. He even tried to lend me
some money. He wanted to go away immediately...
said he couldn't stand it any longer. Of course I
wouldn't hear of it. I begged him not to say anything
to Ella. I said I would take a little trip myself, to
let things blow over. He wouldn't hear of that... but
finally, after I showed him that that was the only
sensible thing to do, he agreed to let me go....»

«And that's how you came to New York?»

«Yes, but that's not all. You see, I tried to do the
right thing. You would have done the same, if it
had been *your* brother, wouldn't you? I did all I
could...»

«Well,» I said, «and what's worrying you now?»

He stared vacant-eyed at the mirror.

«*Ella*,» he said, after a long pause. «She ran away

from him. At first she didn't know where I was.
I sent them a postcard now and then, from this place
and that, but never gave my address. The other day
I got a letter from my brother, saying she had written
him—from Texas. Begged him to give her my
address. Said if she didn't hear from me soon she
would commit suicide.»

«Did you write her?»

«No,» he said, «I haven't written her yet. I don't
know quite what to do.»

«But for Christ's sake, you love her, don't you?
And she loves you. And your brother—he wouldn't
object. What the devil are you waiting for?»

«I don't want to steal my brother's wife. Besides,
I know she does love him. She loves the two of us—
that's the size of it.»

It was my turn to be astonished again. I gave a
low whistle. «So that's it!» I chortled. «Well,
that's different.»

«Yes,» said Sheridan rapidly, «she loves the two of
us equally well. She didn't run away from him
because she hated him or because she wanted me.
She wants me, yes. But she ran away to make him
do something, make him find me and bring me back.»

«Does he know that?» I asked, having a faint
suspicion that Sheridan might have imagined things.

«Yes, he knows it and he's willnig to live that way,
if that's what she wants. I think he'd feel better,
too, if it could be arranged that way.»

«Well?» I said. «What now? What are your
plans?»

«I don't know. I can't think. What would
you do in my place? I've told you everything,
Mr. Miller.»

And then, as if to himself: «A man can't hold out
forever. I know it's wrong to live like that... but if
I don't do something quick maybe Ella will do away

with herself. I wouldn't want that. I'd do anything to prevent that.»

«Look, Sheridan... your brother was jealous before. But he's gotten over that, I imagine. He wants her back just as much as you do. *Now*... did you ever think whether you'd be jealous of your brother— *eventually?* It's not easy to share the woman you love with some one else, even your own brother. You know that, don't you?»

Sheridan showed no hesitation in responding to this.

«I've thought all that out, Mr. Miller. I know *I* wouldn't be the jealous one. And I'm not worried about my brother either. We understand each other. It's Ella. I wonder sometimes if she really knows her own mind. The three of us grew up together, you see. That's why we were able to live together so peacefully.... *until*.... well, that was only natural, wasn't it? But if I go back now, and we share her openly, she might begin to care for us differently. This thing has broken up the happy family. And soon people will begin to notice things. It's a small world back there, and our people don't do those things. I don't know what would happen after a time...»

He paused again and fiddled with his glass.

«There's another thing I thought of, Mr. Miller... Supposing she has a child. We may never know which of us was the father of it. Oh, I've thought it out from every angle. It's not easy to decide.»

«No,» I agreed, «it isn't. I'm stumped, Sheridan. I'll have to think about it.»

«Thanks, Mr. Miller. I know you'll help me, if you can. I think I ought to run along now. Spivak will be looking for me. Good-bye, Mr. Miller,» and he darted off.

When I got back to the office I was informed that
Clancy had telephoned. He had asked for the apli-
cation of a messenger I had hired recently—a woman.

«What's up?» I inquired. «What did *she* do?»

Nobody could offer any precise information.

«Well, where was she working?»

I found that we had sent her to one of the mid
town office buildings. Her name was Nina Andrews.
Hymie had made a note of all the details. He had
already telephoned the manager of the office where
the girl worked, but couldn't glean a thing. The
manager, a young woman herself, was of the
impression that the girl was satisfactory in every way.

I decided I had better call Clancy and get it over
with. His voice was gruff and irritable. Mr. Twilliger had evidently raked him over the coals. And
now it was my turn.

«But what has she done?» I asked in all innocence.

«*What has she done?*» Clancy's voice echoed
furiously. «Mr. Miller, haven't I warned you time
and again that we want only refined young women
on our messenger force?»

«Yes sir,» I had to say, cursing him under my
breath for the dumb cluck he was .

«Mr. Miller,» and his voice took on a devastating
solemnity, «the woman who calls herself Nina
Andrews is nothing but a common prostitute. She
was reported to us by one of our important clients.
He told Mr. Twilliger that she tried to solicit him.
Mr. Twilliger is going to make an investigation. He
suspects that we may have other undesirable females
on our staff. I needn't tell you, Mr. Miller, that this
is a very serious matter. A very serious matter. I
trust that you will know how to cope with the
situation. You will give me a report in a day or
two—is that clear?» He hung up.

I sat there trying to recall the young woman in question.

«Where is she now?» I asked.

«She was sent home,» said Hymie.

«Send her a telegram,» I said, «and ask her to give me a ring. I want to talk to her.»

I waited around until seven o'clock hoping she would telephone. O'Rourke had just come in. I had an idea. Maybe I would ask O'Rourke...

The telephone rang. It was Nina Andrews. She had a very pleasant voice, one that aroused my sympathies immediately.

«I'm sorry I couldn't call you sooner,» she said. «I was out all afternoon.»

«Miss Andrews,» I said, «I wonder if you'd do me a favor. I'd like to drop up to your place for a few minutes and have a little chat with you.»

«Oh, I don't want the job back,» she said in a cheery tone. «I've found another one already—a much better one. It was kind of you to...»

«Miss Andrews,» I insisted, «I *would* like to see you just the same—just for a few minutes. Would you mind?»

«No, no, not at all. Why come up, of course. I merely wanted to spare you the trouble...»

«Well thank you... I'll be there in a few minutes.»

I went over to O'Rourke and explained the case to him in a few brief words. «Maybe you'd like to come along,» I said. «You know, I don't believe that girl is a whore. I'm beginning to remember her now. I think I know...»

We hopped into a cab and drove uptown to Seventy-Second street where she lived. It was a typical old-fashioned rooming house. She lived on the fourth floor back.

She was a little startled to see O'Rourke with me.

But not frightened—a point in her favor I thought
to myself.

«I didn't know you would bring a friend,» she said,
looking at me with frank blue eyes. «You'll have to
excuse the appearance of the place.»

«Don't worry about that, Miss Andrews.» It was
O'Rourke who spoke. «Nina is the name, isn't it?»

«Yes,» she said. «Why?»

«It's a pretty name,» he said. «One doesn't hear it
much any more. You're not of Spanish descent by
any chance, are you?»

«Oh no, not Spanish,» she said, very bright and
quick, and in an altogether disarming tone. «My
mother was Danish, and my father is English. Why,
do I look Spanish?»

O'Rourke smiled. «To be honest, Miss Andrews...
Miss Nina... may I call you that?... no, you don't look
at all Spanish. But Nina is a Spanish name, isn't it?»

«Won't you sit down?» she said, adjusting the
pillows on the divan. And then, in a perfectly
natural tone of voice: «I suppose you heard that I
was fired? Just like that! Not a word of explanation. But they gave me two weeks' pay—*and* I've just
landed a better job. So it isn't so terrible, is it?»

I was glad now that I had brought O'Rourke along.
If I had come alone I would have left without more
ado. I was absolutely convinced, at this point, that
the girl was innocent.

The girl. She had given her age as 25 on the
application blank, but it was obvious that she wasn't
a day over nineteen. She looked like a girl who had
been brought up in the country. A bewitching little
creature, and very alert.

O'Rourke had evidently been making a similar
appraisal. When he lifted his voice it was apparent
that he was thinking only how to spare her unnecessary unpleasantness.

«Miss Nina,» he said, speaking like a father, «Mr. Miller asked me to come along. I'm the night inspector, you know. There's been some misunderstanding with one of our clients, one of the clients served by your office. Perhaps you will recall the name—The Brooks Insurance Agency. Do you remember that name, Miss Nina? Think, because maybe you can help us.»

«Of course I know the name,» she responded with alacrity. «Room 715, Mr. Harcourt. Yes, I know him very well. I know his son too.»

O'Rourke immediately pricked up his ears.

«You know his son?» he repeated.

«Why yes. We were sweethearts. We come from the same town.» She mentioned a little town up State. «You could hardly call it a town, I guess.» She gave a bright little laugh.

«I see,» said O'Rourke, lingering over his words to draw her on.

«Now I understand why I was fired,» she said. «He doesn't think I'm good enough for his son, this Mr. Harcourt. But I didn't think he hated me that much.»

As she rattled on I recalled more and more clearly the circumstances of her first visit to the employment bureau. One detail stood out clearly. She had specifically requested, when filling out the application blank, that she be sent to a certain office building. It was not an unusual request; applicants often gave their preference for certain localities for one reason or another. But I remembered now the smile she had given me when thanking me for the courtesy I had shown her.

«Miss Andrews,» I said, «didn't you ask me to send you to the Heckscher Building when you applied for the job?»

«Of course I did,» she replied. «I wanted to be

near John. I knew his father was trying to keep us apart. That's why I left home.»

«Mr. Harcourt tried to ridicule me at first,» she added. «I mean when I first delivered telegrams to his office. But I didn't care. Neither did John.»

«Well,» said O'Rourke, «so you don't mind too much losing your job? Because, if you'd like to have it back, I think Mr. Miller could arrange if for you.» He glanced in my direction.

«Oh, I don't really want it back,» she said breathlessly. «I've found a *much* better job—and it's in the same building!»

The three of us burst out laughing.

O'Rourke and I rose to go. «You're a musician, aren't you?» asked O'Rourke.

She blushed. «Why yes... why, how did you know? I'm a violinist. That's another reason, of course, why I decided to come to New York. I hope to give a recital here some day—perhaps in Town Hall. It's thrilling to be in a big city like this, isn't it?» She giggled like a school-girl.

«It is wonderful to live in a place like New York,» said O'Rourke, his voice suddenly dropping to a more serious register. «I hope you will have all the success you are looking for...» He paused, a heavy pause, and then taking her two hands in his, he placed himself squarely in front of her and said:

«Let me suggest something to you, may I?»

«Why of course!» said Miss Andrews, reddening slightly.

«Well then, when you give your first concert at Town Hall, let us say, I would suggest that you use your real name. Marjorie Blair sounds just as good as Nina Andrews... *don't you think?* Well,» and without pausing to observe the effect of this retort, he said, grasping my arm and turning towards the door, «I think we should be getting along. Good luck, Miss Blair. Good-bye!»

«I'll be damned,» I said, when we got to the street.

«She's a fine little girl, isn't she?» said O'Rourke, dragging me along. «Clancy called me in this afternoon... showed me the application. I've got all the dope on her. She's absolutely O.K.»

«But the name?» I said. «Why did she change her name?»

«Oh *that*, that's nothing,» said O'Rourke. «Young people find it exciting to change their name sometimes.... It's lucky she doesn't know what Mr. Harcourt told Mr. Twilliger, eh? We'd have a nice case on our hands, if that ever leaked out.»

«By the way,» he added, as though it were of no importance, «when I make my report to Twilliger, I'll say that she was going on twenty-two. You won't mind that, will you? They suspected, you see, that she was under age. Or course you can't check every one's age. Still, you have to be careful. You understand, of course....»

«Of course,» I said, «and it's damned good of you to cover me up.»

We walked in silence for a few moments, keeping our eyes open for a restaurant.

«Wasn't Harcourt taking a big risk in giving Twilliger a story like that?»

O'Rourke didn't answer at once.

«It makes me furious,» I said. «Damn him, he almost lost me my job too, do you realize that?»

«Harcourt's case is more complicated,» said O'Rourke slowly. «I'm telling you this in strict confidence, you understand. We're not going to say anything to Mr. Harcourt. In my report I'll inform Mr. Twilliger that the case has been satisfactorily dealt with. I'll explain that Mr. Harcourt was in error as to the girl's character, that she *immediately*

found another position, and recommend that the
matter be dropped.... Mr. Harcourt, as I suppose you
have already gathered, is a close friend of Twilliger's.
Everything the girl said was true, to be sure, and
she's a fine little girl too, I like her. But there's one
thing she omitted to tell us—naturally. Mr. Harcourt
had her dismissed because he's jealous of his son...
You wonder how I learned that so quickly? Well,
we have our way of learning things. I could tell you
a lot more about this Harcourt, if you'd care to
hear it.»

I was about to say «Yes, I would,» when he
abruptly changed the subject.

«You met a chap named Monahan recently, I
understand.»

I felt as if he had given me a jolt.

«Yes, Monahan... of course. Why, did your brother
tell you?»

«You know, of course,» O'Rourke continued in his
easy, suave way, «what Monahan's job is, don't you?
His assignment, I mean?»

I mumbled some answer, pretending that I knew
more than I did, and waited impatiently for him to
continue.

«Well, it's curious in this racket,» he went on,
«how things connect up. Miss Nina Andrews didn't
go immediately to the messenger bureau in search of
that job, when she got to New York. Like all young
girls, she was attracted to the bright lights. She's
young, intelligent, and knows how to take care of
herself. I don't think she's quite as innocent as she
looks, to be candid with you. *Knowing Harcourt*,
that is. But that's none of my business.... Anyway,
to make it short, Mr. Miller, her first job was that
of a taxi girl in a dance hall. You may know the
one...» He looked directly ahead of him as he said
this. «Yes, the very place that Monahan has his

eye on. It's run by a Greek. Nice chap too. Absolutely on the level, I should say. But there are other individuals hanging around who would bear looking into more closely. Especially when a pretty little thing like Nina Andrews walks in—with those red cheeks and that demure country-like manner.»

I was hoping I would hear more about Monahan when again he switched the subject.

«Funny thing about Harcourt. Shows you how careful you have to be when you begin checking up on things...»

«What do you mean?» said I, wondering what he was going to blurt out next.

«Well, just this,» said O'Rourke, measuring his words. «Harcourt has a whole string of dance halls here in New York, and in other places too. The insurance agency is just a blind. That's why he's breaking his son in. He isn't interested in the insurance game. Harcourt's one passion is young girls—the younger the better. Of course, I don't know this, Mr. Miller, but I wouldn't be surprised if he had already tried to seduce Miss Andrews—or Marjorie Blair, to use her right name. If anything had happened between them Miss Andrews wouldn't be apt to tell any one, would she? Least of all the young man she's in love with. She's only nineteen now, but she probably looked the same at sixteen. She's a country girl, don't forget. They start in early sometimes—you know, red, warm blood.»

He stopped, as if to study the restaurant which, unknown to me, he had been gently and slowly leading me to.

«Not such a bad place, this. Shall we try it? Oh, just a minute, before we go in... *About Harcourt....* The girl, of course, doesn't suspect that he has anything to do with dance halls. That was just a coincidence, her walking into that place. You know the one I mean, don't you? Just opposite...»

«Yes, I know it,» I said, a little annoyed with him for practising these sly digs on me. «I have a friend working there,» I added. And you know damned well what I mean, I thought to myself.

I was wondering how much Monahan might have revealed to him. I wondered too, suddenly, if Monahan hadn't known O'Rourke for many a year. How they liked to put on these little acts, these expressions of surprise, of ignorance, of amazement, and so on. I suppose they can't help it. They're like cashiers who say «thank you!» in their sleep.

And then, as I waited for him to continue, another suspicion entered my mind. Maybe those two fifty dollar bills that Monahan had dropped came from O'Rourke's pocket. I was almost certain of it. Unless.... but I dismissed the following flash—it was too far-fetched. Unless, I couldn't help repeating to myself, the money had come from Harcourt's pocket. It was a fat roll of bills he had flashed on me that night. Detectives don't usually walk around with huge sums of money in their pockets. Anyway, if Monahan had shaken Harcourt down (or perhaps the Greek!) O'Rourke wouldn't know about it.

I was routed out of these interior speculations by an even more startling remark of O'Rourke's. We were in the hallway, just about to enter the restaurant, when I distinctly heard him saying:

«In that particular dance hall it's almost impossible for a girl to get a job without sleeping with Harcourt first. A least, that's what Monahan tells me.»

«Of course there's nothing irregular about that,» he continued, allowing a moment's pause for the observation to sink in.

We took seats at a table in the far corner of the restaurant, where we could talk without fear of being overheard. I noticed O'Rourke glancing about with his habitual keen, all-encompassing yet thoroughly unobtrusive gaze. He did it instinctively, just as an interior decorator takes in the furnishings of a room, including the pattern of the wall-paper.

«But the fact that Miss Marjorie Blair had taken the job under another name almost led him to commit an indiscretion.»

«God, yes», I exclaimed. «I never thought of that!»

«It was fortunate for him that he had taken the precaution to ask for her photograph first....»

I couldn't help interrupting him.«I must say that you learned a devil of a lot in a short time.»

«A pure accident,» said O'Rourke modestly. «I bumped into Monahan on my way out of Clancy's office.»

«Yes, but how did you manage to put two and two together so quickly? I persisted. «You didn't know when you met Monahan that the girl had been working in a dance hall. I don't see how the devil you just fell on to that piece of information.»

«I didn't,» said O'Rourke. «I extracted it from Harcourt. You see, while talking to Monahan... he was talking about his assignment—and about you, incidentally... yes, he said he liked you very much... he wants to see you again, by the way... you should get in touch with him... well, anyway, as I was saying, I had a hunch to go and telephone Harcourt. I asked him a few routine questions—among them where had the girl worked before, if he knew. He said she had worked in a dance hall. He said it as if to say: 'She's just a little tart.' When I went back to the table I just took a flier and asked Monahan if he knew a girl named Andrews—at the dance hall. I didn't even know then which dance hall. And then, to my surprise, after I had explained the case, he began telling me about Harcourt. So there you are.

It's simple, isn't it? I tell you, everything connects up in this racket. You play your hunch, you throw out a feeler—and sometimes it tumbles right into your lap.»

«I'll be damned,» was all I could say .

O'Rourke was studying the menu. I looked at it distractedly, unable to decide what I wanted to eat. All I could think of was Harcourt. So Harcourt fucked them all! Jesus Christ, I was furious. I wanted more than ever to do something about it. Maybe Monahan was the man; maybe he was already laying his traps.

I ordered something at random and sat looking disconsolately at the diners.

«What's the matter?» said O'Rourke. «You look depressed.»

«I am,» I answered. «It's nothing. It'll pass.»

Throughout the meal I only half listened to O'Rourke's talk. I kept thinking of Mona. I wondered what she would say if I were to mention Harcourt's name. That son of a bitch! Fucking everything in sight and then, b'Jesus, almost fucking me out of a job! The gall of him! Well, another clue to work on. Things were happening fast....

It took several hours for me to break away from O'Rourke. When he wanted to hold you he could tell one story after another, gliding from one to another with the most dexterous ingenuity. I was always exhausted after spending an evening with him. It exhausted me just to listen, because with every sentence he let fall I watched like a bird of prey for my opening. Besides, there were always long interruptions in the stories, demanding regressions, recapitulations and all manner of acrobatics. Sometimes he'd keep me waiting a half hour or more in a telegraph office while, with that patience which exasperated me, he laboriously went through the files

in search of some trivial detail. And always, before
resuming his story, he would make a long, windy
detour, as we went from one office to another,
concerning the clerk or the manager or the telegrapher
in the office we had just left. His memory was
prodigious. In the hundred or more branch offices
scattered throughout the city he knew all the clerks
by name, the record of their progress from one job
to another, one office to another, and thousands of
intimate details about their family life. Not only
did he know the present staff—he knew the ghosts
who had occupied their places before them. In
addition he knew many of the messengers, both of
the night and the day shifts. He was especially
devoted to the old fellows, some of whom had served
the company almost as many years as O'Rourke
himself.

I had learned a great deal from these nocturnal
inspections, things which I doubted that Clancy
himself knew. More than a few of the clerks, I
discovered through the course of these rounds with
O'Rourke, had been guilty of embezzlement at one
time or another in their seedy, cosmococcic career.
O'Rourke had his own way of dealing with these
cases. Relying upon the good judgment which his
long experience had given him, he often took amazing
liberties in dealing with these unfortunate individuals.
Half the cases, I am certain, never became known to
any one but O'Rourke. Where he had confidence in
the man he would allow him to make restitution little
by little, making it clear, of course, that the matter
was to remain a secret between them. There was at
times a twofold purpose in this benevolence. By
handling the incident in this irregular way not only
was the company certain of retrieving all that had
been stolen but, because of his gratitude, the victim
could henceforth be relied upon to act as a sort of

stool pigeon. He could be made to squeal and
squawk when occasion arose. Many a time, in the
beginning, when I wondered why O'Rourke was
taking such an interest in certain rat-like characters,
I discovered that they were of the lost tribe whom
O'Rourke had converted to useful instruments. In
fact, I learned one thing about O'Rourke which
explained everything, so far as his mysterious
behavior was concerned: that was that every one to
whom he gave the least time or attention had some
importance in the scheme of his cosmococcic life.

Though he gave the illusion of running rings
around himself, though he often acted like a fool
and an ignoramus, though he seemed to be doing
nothing more than wasting time, actually everything
he said or did had a vital bearing on the work in
hand. Moreover, there was never just one case which
occupied him exclusively. He had a hundred strings
to his lyre. No case was ever too hopeless for him
to drop. The company might have scratched it off
the record—but not O'Rourke. He had the infinite
patience of an artist, and with it the conviction that
time was on his side. There didn't seem to be any
phase of life with which he had not familiarized
himself. Though, speaking of the artist, I must
admit that perhaps in that realm he was least sure
of himself. He could stand and look at the work of
a *pompier* in a department store window with dewy
eyes. His knowledge of literature was almost nil.
But if, for example, I should happen to relate the
story of Raskolnikov, as Dostoievski unfolded it for
us, I could be certain of reaping the most penetrating
observations. And what it was indeed that made me
cherish his friendship, was the kinship he had,
humanly and spiritually, with such writers as
Dostoievski. His acquaintance with the underworld
had softened and broadened him. He was a detective

because of his extraordinary interest in and sympathy with his fellow-man. He never caused a man unnecessary pain. He always gave his man the wide benefit of the doubt. He never held a grudge against any one, no matter what the man had done. He sought to understand, to fathom their motives, even when they were of the basest. Above all, he was to be relied upon absolutely. His word, once given, was adhered to at any cost. Neither could he be bribed. I can't possibly imagine what temptation one could put before him to deflect him from the performance of his duty. A further point in his favor, in my opinion, was that he was totally lacking in ambition. He hadn't the slightest desire to be anything other than he was. He gave himself body and soul to his task, knowing that it was a thankless one, knowing that he was being used and abused by a heartless, soulless organization. But, as he himself had more than once remarked, whatever the attitude of the company might be was none of his concern. Nor did it matter to him that, in the event of retirement, they should undo everything be had labored to build up. Having no illusions, he nevertheless gave his utmost to all who made demands upon him.

He was a unique being, O'Rourke. He disturbed me profoundly sometimes. I don't think I've ever known any one before or since who made me feel quite so transparent as he did. Nor do I ever remember any one who so abstemiously withheld giving advice or criticism. He was the only man I've ever known who made me realize what it means to be tolerant, what it means to respect the other person's liberty. It's curious, now that I reflect on it, how deeply he symbolized the Law. Not the petty spirit of law which man uses for his own ends, but the inscrutable cosmic law which never ceases to work, which is implacable and just, and thus ultimately the most merciful.

As I lay in bed wide awake, I would, after an evening such as this one, often ask myself what O'Rourke would do if he were in my boots. In endeavoring to make the transposition it had occurred to me more than once that I knew nothing about O'Rourke's private life. Absolutely nothing. Not that he was evasive—I couldn't say that. It was just a blank. Somehow the subject never came up.

I don't know why I thought so, but I had the feeling that in some period long past he had suffered a great deception. A frustrated love, perhaps.

Whatever it was, he had not been soured by it. He had foundered and then recovered. But his life had been irreparably altered. Putting all the little pieces together, putting on one side the man I knew, and on the other side the man whom I caught glimpses of now and then (when he was in a reminiscent mood), comparing them one with the other, it was impossible to deny that they were two quite different beings. All those rugged, sterling qualities which O'Rourke possessed were like protective devices, worn not outwardly but inwardly. From the world he had little or nothing to fear. He was in it and of it, totally. But against the decrees of Fate he was powerless.

It was strange, I thought to myself as I closed my eyes, that the man I should owe so much to must remain forever a sealed book. I could only learn from his behavior and example.

A wave of tenderness swept over me. I understood O'Rourke in a bigger way than I had before. I understood everything more clearly. I understood for the first time what it really means to be «delicate».

13

There are days when the return to life is painful and distressing. One leaves the realm of sleep against one's will. Nothing has happened, except an awareness that the deeper and truer reality belongs to the world of the unconscious.

Thus one morning I opened my eyes involuntarily, struggling frantically to fall back into that condition of bliss in which dream had wrapped me. So chagrined was I to find myself awake that I was on the point of tears. I closed my eyes and tried to sink back again into the world from which I had been so cruelly ejected. It was useless. I tried every device I had ever heard of but I could no more accomplish the trick than one can stop a bullet in flight and restore it to the empty chamber of a revolver.

What remained, however, was the aura of the dream: in that I lingered voluptuously. Some deep purpose had been fulfilled, but before I had been given time to read the significance of it the slate had been sponged and I was thrust out, out into a world whose one solution for everything is death.

There were only a few tangible shreds left in my hand and, as with those crumbs which the poor are supposed to gather from the tables of the rich, I clung to them greedily. But the crumbs dropped from the table of sleep are like the meagre facts in a crime whose solution must ever remain a mystery. Those dripping images which, in the act of awakening, one spirits across the threshold like a mystic smuggler, have a way of undergoing the most heart-

rending transformations on the hither side. They
melt like ice cream on a sultry day in August. And
yet, as they merge toward the inchoate magma which
is the very stuff of the soul, some blurred knot of
remembrance keeps alive—*forever*, it would seem—
the dim and velvety outline of a palpable, sentient
continuum wherein they move and have, not their
being, but reality. Reality! That which embraces,
sustains and exalts life. It is in this stream that one
craves to return and remain forever immersed.

What remained then of that inextinguishable world
from which I awakened one morning full of tender
wounds that had been so skillfully staunched in the
night? The face of the one I had loved and lost!
Una Gifford. Not the Una I had known, but a Una
whom years of pain and separation had magnified
into a frightening loveliness. Her face had become
like a heavy flower caught in darkness; it seemed
transfixed by its own suffused glow. All those
memories of her which I had jealously preserved and
which had been lightly tamped down, like fine tobacco under the finger of a pipe smoker, had suddenly
brought about a spontaneously combustible beautifica-
tion. The pallor of her skin was heightened by the
marble glow which the smouldering embers of memory awakened. The head turned slowly on the
almost indistinguishable stem. The lips were parted
in thirst; they were extraordinarily vivid and vulnerable. It seemed like the detached head of a dreamer
seeking with eyes sealed to receive the hungry lips
of one summoned from some remote place. And,
like the convolvulutions of exotic plants which writhe
and lash in the night, our lips with endless searching
finally met, closed and sealed the wound which until
then had bled unceasingly. It was a kiss that
drowned the memory of every pain; it staunched
and healed the wound. An endless time it lasted, a

forgotten period, as between two unremembered dreams. And then, as though the folds of night had gently come between us, we were apart and gazing at each other, penetrating the flowing veils of darkness with a single hypnotic stare. Just as previously the wet lips had been glued together—like fluffy, fragile petals tossed by a storm—so now the eyes were joined, welded by the electric current of long withheld recognition. In neither instance did there seem to be the least operation of the mental faculties: all was mindless and unwilled. It was like the union of two magnets, of their dull gray termini; the ever searching parts had at last come together. In this still, charged coalescence another sensation gradually made itself known: the sound of our ancient voice. A single voice which spoke and answered simultaneously: a two-pronged note which sounded at first like interrogation but which always died away like the pleasurable lapping of a wave. It was difficult to realize at first that this monologue was really the marriage of two distinct voices; it was like the play of two fountains sending and receiving from the same source and with the same gush.

Then everything was suddenly interrupted, a shift as of wet sand slipping from the upper bank, a deep dark substance suddenly scooped out, leaving a thin deceptive crust of gleaming white on which the unwary foot would tread and crash to doom.

An interim of little deaths, all painless, as though the senses were so many organ stops and a hand, invisible and beneficient, had absent-mindedly choked off the air.

Now she is reading aloud—familiar passages from a book which I must have read. She is lying on her stomach, her elbows bent, her head cupped in the two palms. It is the profile of her face which she gives me and the white opacity of the flesh is gloved and fragrant. The lips are like bruised geraniums, two perfectly hinged petals that open and close. The words are melodiously disguised; they issue from a sound box made of duveteen.

It is only when I recognize that they are my own words, words that were never put on paper but written in the head, that I notice she is not reading to me but to a young man lying beside her. He lies on his back and looks up into her face with the attentiveness of a devotee. There are just the two of them, and the world has no existence for them. It is not a matter of space which separates me from them but a world chasm. There is no longer any possibility of communication; they float in space on a lotus leaf. We are cut off. I try desperately to send a message across the void, to let her know at least that the enchanting words are from the embryonic book of my life. But she is out of bounds. The reading continues and her ecstasy mounts. I am lost and forgotten.

Then, for just a flash, she turns her full face towards me, the eyes revealing no sign of recognition. The eyes are turned inward, as though in deep meditation. The fullness of the face is gone; the contours of the skull become pronounced. She is still beautiful, but it is no longer the allure of star and flesh; it is the phantasmal beauty of the smothered soul emerging with crest and dye from the prism of death. A fleeting cloud of remembrance passes over the empty map of her sharp features. She who was alive, incarnate, a tormented flower in the crevice of memory, now vanishes like smoke from the empire of sleep. Whether she had died in sleep, perchance in dream, or whether I myself had died and found her on the other side, asleep and dreaming, I could not tell. For an interminable instant of time our paths had crossed, the union had been consummated, the wound of the past had been healed. Incarnate or discarnate, we were now wheeling off into space, each to his own orbit, each accompanied by his own music. Time, with its endless trail of pain, sorrow and separation, had folded up; we were again in the timeless blue, distant one from another, but no longer separated. We were wheeling like the constellations, wheeling in the obedient meadows of the stars. There was nothing but the soundless chime of starry beams, the bright collisions of floating feathers churning with scintillating brilliance in the fiery sound track of the angelic realms.

I knew then that I had found bliss, and that bliss is the world, or state of the world, where creation reigns. I knew another thing, that if it were merely a dream it would end, and if it were not a dream...

My eyes were open and I was in a room, the same room in whice I had gone to bed the night before.

Others would be content to call it a dream. But what is a dream? Who experienced what? And where and when?

I was drugged by the vanished splendors of the phantasmal voyage. I could neither return nor depart. I lay abed with eyes lightly closed and reviewed the procession of hypnagogic images which passed like ghostly sentinels from station to station along the tenuous frontier of sleep. Recollections of other waking images crowded in, leaving dark stains across the bright track made by the passage of the autochtonous ghosts. There was the Una to whom I had waved goodbye one Summer's day, the Una on whom I had turned my back, the Una whose eyes had followed me down the street, and at the corner when I turned I had felt those eyes piercing through me—and I knew that no matter where I went or how much I would try to forget, those two beseeching eyes would be forever buried between my shoulder blades.

There was another Una who showed me her bedroom
—years later when we met by chance on the street
in front of her house. A changed Una, who
blossomed only in dream. The Una who belonged
to another man, the Una surrounded by the spawn
of wedlock. A recurrent dream, this pleasant, trivial,
comforting. It recurred obsessively in a configuration almost mathematically exact. Guided by my
double, George Marshall, I would stand in front of
her house and, like a Peeping Tom, I would wait
for her to come out of the house with sleeves rolled
up and take a breath of air. She was never aware of
our presence, though we were there as large as life
and only a few feet away from her. That meant that
I was privileged to observe her at leisure, even to
discuss her points with my companion and guide.
She always looked the same—the matron in full
bloom. I would have my fill of her and then quietly
take my leave. It would be dark and I would make
a desperate effort to remember the name of the street
which somehow I never could find unaided. But at
the corner, looking for the street sign, the darkness
would become a thick pall of black. I knew that
then George Marshall would take my arm and say,
as he always did, «Don't worry, *I* know where it is...
I'll bring you back again some day.» And then
George Marshall, my very double, my friend and
traitor, would suddenly give me the slip, and I would
be left to stumble about in the grimy purlieus of
some odious quarter which reeked of crime and vice.
   From bar to bar I would wander, always looked
on askance, always insulted and humiliated, often
pummeled and kicked about like a sack of oats.
Time after time I would find myself flat on the
pavement, the blood trickling from mouth and ears,
my hands cut to ribbons, my body one great welter
of bruises and contusions. It was a terrible price

I always had to pay for the privilege of watching her take a breath of air. But it was worth it! And when in my dreams I saw George Marshall approaching, when I heard the promise which his reassuring words of greeting always contained, my heart would begin to pound furiously and I would hasten my steps to arrive in front of her house at just the right moment. Strange that I could never find my way alone. Strange that George Marshall had to be the one to lead me to her, for George Marshall had never seen in her anything more than a pleasing bundle of flesh. But George Marshall, tied to me by an invisible cord, had been the silent witness of a drama which his unbelieving eyes had repudiated. And so in dream George Marshall could look again with eyes of wonder; he too could find a certain contentment in rediscovering the junction where our ways had parted.

Suddenly now I remembered something I had completely forgotten. I opened wide my eyes as if to stare across the stretch of distant past and capture the angle of an empty vision. I see the back yard. as it was during the long winter, the black boughs of the elm trees laced in ince, the ground hard and barren, the sky splotched with zinc and laudanum. I am the prisoner in the house of mis-placed love. I am August Angst growing a melancholy beard. I am a drone whose sole function is to shoot spermatozoa into the cuspidor of anguish. I pull off orgasms with zygomatic fury. I bite the beard which covers her mouth like moss. I chew fat pieces out of my own melancholy and spit them out like roaches.

All through the winter it goes on like this—until the day when I come home and find her lying on the bed in a pool of blood. In the dresser the doctor has left the body of the seven month tooth-ache wrapped in a towel. It is like a homunculus, the skin a dark red, and it has hair and nails. It lies breathless in the drawer of the dresser, a life yanked out of darkness and thrust back into darkness. It has no name, nor has it been loved, nor will it be mourned. It was pulled up by the roots, and if it shrieked no one heard. What life it had was lived and lost in sleep. Its death was only a further, deeper plunge into that sleep from which it never awakened.

I am standing at the window, gazing vacantly across the bleak yard at the window opposite. A form flits vaguely to and fro. Following it with a vacant stare a faint remembrance stirs, flickers, then gutters out. I am left to wallow in the morass of swamp-filled vagaries. I stand sullen and upright, like Rigor Mortis himself. I am the King of Silicon and my realm includes all that is tarnished and corroded.

Carlotta lies cross-wise on the bed, her feet dangling over the edge. She will lie that way until the doctor comes and rouses her back to life. The landlady will come and change the sheets. The body will be disposed of in the usual way. We will be told to move, the room will be fumigated, the crime will be unrecorded. We will find another place with a bed, a stove, a chest of drawers. We will go through the same routine of eating, sleeping, breeding, and burying. August Angst will give way to Tracy le Crêvecœur. He will be an Arabian Knight with a penis of cool jade. He will eat nothing but spices and condiments and he will spill his seed recklessly. He will dismount, fold his penis like a jack-knife, and take his place with the other emptied studs.

That form flitting to and fro—it was Una Gifford. Weeks later, after Carlotta and I had moved to another flat, we met on the street in front of her house. I went upstairs with her and perhaps I stayed a half hour, perhaps longer, but all I can remember of that visit is that she brought me to the bedroom and showed me the bed, their bed in which a child had already been born.

Not long thereafter I managed to escape from Carlotta's devouring clutches. Towards the end I had been carrying on with Maude. When we were married about three months a most unexpected meeting occurred. I had gone to the cinema alone one night. That is, I had bought my ticket and entered the theatre. I had to wait a few moments in the rear of the house until a seat could be found. In the subdued light an usherette approached me carrying a flash light. It was Carlotta. «Harry!» she said, giving a little cry like a wounded doe. She was too overpowered to say much. She kept looking at me, listening with eyes grown large and moist. I quickly whitered under this steady, silent accusation. «I'll find you a seat,» she said at last, and as she ushered me to a place she murmured in my ear: «I'll try to join you later.»

I kept my eyes riveted on the screen but my thoughts were travelling like wild-fire. It might have been hours that I sat thus, my brain reeling with recollections. Suddenly I was aware of her sliding into the seat beside me, grasping my arm. Quickly she slid her hand over mine and as she squeezed it I looked at her and saw the tears rolling down her cheeks. «God, Harry, it's been so long,» she whispered, and with that her hand travelled to my leg and grasped it fervently just above the knee. Instantly I did the same, and we sat thus for some time, our lips sealed, our eyes staring blankly at the flickering screen.

Presently a wave of passion swept over us and our hands groped frantically for the burning flesh. We

had hardly finished the quest when the picture came
to an end and the lights were turned on.

«I'll take you home,» I said, as we stumbled out
into the aisle. My voice was thick and hoarse, my
throat dry, my lips parched. She put her arm in
mine, rolled her thigh against mine. We staggered
towards the exit. In the lobby she stopped a moment
to powder her face. She had not changed greatly;
the eyes had grown larger, more sorrowful. They
were brilliant and haunting. A mauve dress of some
clinging, film-like material showed her figure to
advantage. I looked at her feet and suddenly recalled that they had always been tiny and supple,
the nimble feet of one who would never grow old.

In the cab I started to tell her what had happened
since I ran away, but she put her hand over my
mouth and in a low husky voice she begged me not
to tell her until we got home. Then, still holding
her hand over my mouth, she said: «You're married,
aren't you?» I nodded. «I knew it,» she murmured,
and then she withdrew her hand.

The next moment she flung her arms about me.
Kissing me wildly, she sobbed the words out—«Harry,
Harry, you should never have treated me that way.
You could have told me everything... everything.
You were terribly cruel, Harry. You killed every-
thing.»

I held her close, pulling her leg up over mine and
swiftly running my hand up her leg until it settled
in her crotch. The cab stopped suddenly and we
disentangled ourselves. I followed her up the stoop
tremblingly, knowing not what to expect once we
were inside. As the house door closed behind
us she whispered in my ear that I was to move
silently. «You mustn't let Georgie hear you. He's
very ill... he's dying, I'm afraid.»

The hall was in pitch darkness. I had to hold

her hand as she let me up the two long winding
flights of stairs to the attic where she and her son
were finishing their days.

She turned on a dim light and with forefinger to
her lips she indicated the couch. Then she stood
with her ear to the door of the adjoining room and
listened intently to make certain that Georgie was
asleep. Finally she tiptoed to my side and sat herself gingerly on the edge of the couch. «Be careful,» she whispered, «it squeaks.»

I was so bewildered that I neither whispered nor
moved a muscle. What Georgie would do if he were
to find me sitting there I did'nt dare to think. So
he was dying, at last. A horrible end. And here
we were, sitting like guilty mummies in a poverty-
stricken garret. And yet, I reflected, it was perhaps
fortunate that this little scene could only be played
in a muffled key. God knows what terrible words
of reproach she might have hurled at me had she
been able to speak out.

«Put out the light!» I begged in mute pantomime.
As she rose to obey I pointed to the floor, signifying
that I would stretch myself out beside the couch.
It was some moments before she joined me on the
floor. She was standing in a corner stealthily remov-
ing her things. I watched her by the faint light
which stole through the windows. As she reached
for a wrap to throw about her naked figure I quickly
unbuttoned my fly.

It was difficult to move without making a sound.
She seemed terrified of the thought that Georgie
might hear us. I understood that he had conve-
niently saddled me with the responsibility for his
suffering. I understood that she had silently ac-
quiesced and that her terror now was a recoil from
the ultimate horror of betrayal.

To move without breathing, to entwine ourselves

like two corkscrews, to fuck with a passion such as
we had never experienced before and yet not make
a sound, required a skill and patience which would
have been admirable to dwell on were it not for the
fact that something else was going on which affected
me profoundly... She was weeping without tears.
I could hear it gurgling inside her, like a toilet box
which won't stop running. And though she had
begged me in a frightened whisper not to come, that
she couldn't wash because of the noise, because of
Georgie in the next room, though I knew that she
was the sort who gets caught just by looking at her,
and that if she were caught it would go hard with
her, still, and perhaps more because of the silent
weeping, more because I wanted to put an end to
the gurgling, I came again and again. She too passed from one orgasm to another, knowing each time
that I would shoot a wad into her womb, but unable to help herself. Never once did I take my cock
out. I would wait quietly for the answering needle
bath, jam it tight like a cartridge, and then go off
into the electrically moist darkness of a mouth with
the soft lips of an artichoke. There was something
fiendishly detached about it, almost as if I were a
pyromaniac sitting in a comfortable chair in my own
house which I had set fire to with my own hand,
knowing that I would not budge until the very chair
I sat in would begin to sizzle and roast my ass.

When eventually I go to the landing outside and
stood embracing her for the last time, she whispered
that she needed money for the rent, begged me to
bring it to her on the morrow. And then, as I was
about to descend the stairs, she pulled me back, her
lips glued to my ear. «He won't last another week!»
These words came to me as if through an amplifier.
Even to-day, as I repeat them to myself, I can hear
the soft whistling rush of air that accompanied the

sound of her almost inaudible voice. It was as if my ear were a dandelion and each little thistle an antenna which caught the message and relayed it to the roof of my brain where it exploded with the dull splash of a howitzer. «He won't last another week!» I said it all the way home, a thousand times or more. And every time I commenced this refrain I saw a photogenic image of fright—the head of a woman sawed off by the frame of the picture just below the scalp. I saw it always the same—a face looming out of darkness, the upper part of the head caught as if in a trap door. A face with a calcium glow about it, suspended by its own dream-like effort above an indistinguishable mass of writhing creatures such as infest the swampy regions of the mind's dark fears. And then I saw Georgie being born—just as she had related it to me once. Born on the floor of the outhouse where she had locked herself in to escape the hands of his father who was blind with drink. I saw her lying huddled on the floor and Georgie between her legs. Lying that way until the moon flooded them with mysterious platinum waves. How she loved Georgie! How she clung to him! Nothing was too good for her Georgie. Then north on the night train with her little black sheep. Starving herself to feed Georgie, selling herself in order to put Georgie through school. Everything for Georgie. «You were crying,» I would say, catching her unawares. «What is it—has he been treating you badly again?» There wasn't any good in Georgie: he was full of black pus. «Hum that tune,» he would say sometimes, the three of us sitting in the dark. And they would begin to hum and croon, and after a time Georgie would come over to her, put his arms around her, and weep like a child. «I'm no god-damned good,» he would say, over and over. And then he would cough and the

coughing never stopped. Like hers, his eyes were
large and black; they peered out from his hollowed
face like two burning holes. Then he went away—
to a ranch—and I thought maybe he would get well
again. A lung was punctured, and when that healed
the other one was punctured. And before the doctors had finished their experiments I was like a
bundle of malignant tumors, rearing to explode, to
break the chains, to kill his mother if necessary,
anything, anything, only no more heartaches, no
more misery, no more silent suffering. When had
I ever truly loved her? *When?* I couldn't think.
I had been searching for a cosy womb and I had
been caught in the out-house, had locked myself in,
had watched the moon come and go, had seen one
bloody pulp after another fall from between her legs.
Phoebus! Yes, that was the place! Near the Old
Soldiers' Home. And he, the father and seducer,
was safely behind the bars in Fortress Monroe. He
was. And then, when no one any longer mentioned
his name, he was a corpse lying in a coffin a few
blocks away and before I ever realized that they had
shipped his body north, she had buried him—with
military honors! Christ! What all can happen
behind one's back—while you're out for a walk or
going to the library to look up an important book!
One lung, two lungs, an abortion, a still-birth, milk
legs, no work, boarders, hauling ash cans, hocking
bicycles, sitting on the roof watching pigeons: these
phantasmal objects and events fill the screen, then
pass like smoke, are forgotten, buried, thrown in the
ash can like rotted tumors, *until....* two lips pressed
against the waxen ear explode with a deafening
dandelion roar, whereupon August Angst, Tracy le
Crêvecœur and Rigor Mortis sail slantwise through
the roof of the brain to hang suspended in a sky
shimmering with ultra-violet.

The day after this episode I do not go back to her with the money, nor do I appear ten days later at the funeral. But about three weeks later I feel compelled to unburden myself to Maude. Of course I say nothing about the whispering fuck on the floor that night, but I do confess to escorting her to her rooms. To another woman I might have confessed everything, but not to Maude. As it is, with only a thimbleful spilled out, she's already as stiff as a frightened mare. She's not listening any more—just waiting for me to conclude so that she can say with absolute finality—NO!

To be fair to her, it was a bit mad to expect her to consent to my suggestion. It would be a rare woman who would say yes. What did I want her to do? Why, to invite Carlotta to live with us. Yes, finally I had come to the extraordinary conclusion that the only decent thing to do would be to ask Carlotta to share her life with us. I was trying to make it plain to Maude that I had never loved Carlotta, that I had only pitied her, and that therefore I owed her something. Queer masculine logic! Dingo! Absolutely dingo. But I believed every word I uttered. Carlotta would come and take a room and live her own life. We would treat her graciously, like a fallen queen. It must have sounded terribly hollow and false to Maude. But as I listened to the reverberations of my own voice I had the distinct sensation of hearing those sound waves quell the horrible gurgle of the toilet box. Since Maude had already made up her mind, since no one was listening except myself, since the words bounced back like egg plants ricocheting against a gourd, I continued with my transmission, growing more and more earnest, more and more convinced, more and more determined to have my way. One wave on top of another, one rhythm against another: quell against beat, surge against

gush, confession against compulsion, ocean against
brook. Beat it down, sink it, drown it, drive it
below the earth, set a mountain on top of it! I went
on and on, con amore, con furioso, con connecti-
busque, con aboulia, con aesthesia, con Silesia... And
all the while she listened like a rock, fire-proofing
her little camisoled heart, her tin cracker-box, her
meat-loafed gizzard, her fumigated womb.

The answer was No! Yesterday, to-day, to-morrow
—NO! Positively no! Her whole physical, mental,
moral and spiritual development had brought her to
that great moment when she could answer triumph-
antly: NO! Positively No!

If she had only said to me: «Listen, you can't ask
me to do a thing like that! It's mad, don't you see?
How would we get along, the three of us? I know
you'd like to help her—so would I... but———»

If she had spoken that way I would have gone to
the mirror, taken a long cool look at myself, laughed
like a broken hinge and agreed that it was utterly
mad. Not that only, but more... I would have given
her credit for really desiring to do something which
I knew her meagre spirit was incapable of imagining.
Yes, I'd have chalked up a white mark for her and
topped it off with a quiet insane fuck à la Huysmans.
I'd have taken her on my lap, as her father in heaven
used to do, and cooing and billing, and pretending
that 986 plus 2 makes minus 69 I'd have delicately
lifted her organdy cover-all, and put the fire out with
an ethereal fire extinguisher.

However, and instead of which, pissing in vain
against a wall of fire-proofed sheet metal, I got so
infuriated that I burst out of the house in the middle
of the night and started walking to Coney Island.
The weather was mild and when I got to the boardwalk I sat down on a ramp and began to laugh. I
got to thinking of Stanley, of the night I met him

after his release from Fort Oglethorpe, of the open barouche we hired and the beer bottles piled up on the seat opposite. After four years in the cavalry Stanley was a man of iron. He was tough inside and out, as only a Pole can be. He would have bitten my ear off, if I had dared him to, and perhaps spat it in my face. He had a couple of hundred dollars in his pocket and he wanted to spend it all that night. And before the night was over I remember that we had just enough between us to share a room together in some broken-down hotel near Borough Hall. I remember too that he was so stinking drunk that he wouldn't get out of bed to relieve his bladder—just turned over and pissed a steady stream against the wall.

The next day I was still furious. And the following day and the day after. That NO! was eating me up. It would take a thousand Yes-es to bury it. Nothing vital occupied me at the time. I was making a pretense of earning a living by selling a shelf of books which were supposed to contain «the world's best literature». I hadn't yet sunk to the encyclopaedia stage. The rat who had put me on to the game had hypnotized me. I sold everything in a post-hypnotic trance. Sometimes I awoke with bright ideas, that's to say, slightly criminal or definitely hallucinatory. Anyway, still hopping mad, still furious, I awoke one day with that NO! still reverberating in my ears. I was eating breakfast when I suddenly recalled that I had never canvased cousin Julie. Maude's cousin Julie. Julie was married now, just long enough, I figured, to want a change of rhythm. Julie would be my first call. I'd take it easy, pop in just a little before lunch, sell her a set of books, have a good meal, get my end in and then go to a movie.

Julie lived at the upper end of Manhattan in a

wall-papered incubator. Her husband was a dope, as
near as I could make out. That's to say he was a
perfectly normal specimen who earned an honest
living and voted the Republican or Democratic ticket
according to mood. Julie was a good-natured slob
who never read anything more disturbing than the
Saturday Evening Post. She was just a piece of ass,
with about enough intelligence to realize that after
a fuck you have to take a douche and if that doesn't
work then a darning needle. She had done it so
often, the darning needle stunt, that she was an adept
at it. She could bring on a haemorrhage even if it
had been an immaculate conception. Her main idea
was to enjoy herself like a drunken weasel and get it
out of her system as quick as possible. She wouldn't
flinch at using a chisel or a monkey wrench, if she
thought either would do the trick.

I was a bit flabbergasted when she came to the
door. I hadn't thought of the change a year or so
can work in a female, nor had I thought how most
females look at eleven in the morning when they are
not expecting visitors. To be cruelly exact, she looked like a cold meat loaf that had been spattered
with catsup and put back in the ice box. The Julie
I had last seen was a dream by comparison. I had
to make some rapid transpositions to adjust myself
to the situation.

Naturally I was more in the mood to sell than to
fuck. Before very long, however, I realized that to
sell, I would have to fuck. Julie just couldn't
understand what the hell had come over me—to walk
in on her and try to dump a load of books on her.
I couldn't tell her it would improve her mind because
she had no mind, and she knew it and wasn't the
least embarrassed to admit it.

She left me alone for a few minutes in order to
primp herself up. I began reading the prospectus.

I found it so interesting that I almost sold myself a set of books. I was reading a fragment about Coleridge, what a wonderful mind he had, (and I had always thought him a bag of shit!), when I felt her coming towards me. It was so interesting, the passage, that I excused myself without looking up and continued reading. She knelt behind me, on the couch, and began reading over my shoulder. I felt her sloshy boobs joggling me but I was too intent on pursuing the ramifications of Coleridge's amazing mind to let her vegetable appendages disturb me.

Suddenly the beautifully bound prospectus went flying out of my hand.

«What are you reading that crap for?» she cried, swinging me around and holding me by the elbows. «I don't understand a word of it, and neither do you, I'll bet. What's the matter with you—can't you find yourself a job?»

A witless-shitless sort of grin slowly spread over her face. She looked like a Teutonic angel doing a real think. I got up, recovered the prospectus, and asked what about lunch.

«Jesus, I like your crust,» said she. «What the hell do you think I am anyway?»

Here I had to pretend that I was only joking, but after putting my hand down her bosom and twiddling the nipple of her right teat a while, I defly brought the conversation back to the subject of food.

«Listen, you've changed,» she said. «I don't like the way you talk—or act.» Here she firmly stuck her teat back, as if it were a ball of wet socks going into a laundry bag. «Listen, I'm a married woman, do you realize that? Do you know what Mike would do to you if he caught you acting this way?»

«You're a bit changed yourself,» said I, rising to my feet and sniffing the air in search of provender. All I wanted now was food. I don't know why, but

I had made up my mind that she would dish me up
a good meal—that was the least she could do for me,
lop-sided moron that she was.

The only way to get anything out of her was to
handle her. I had to pretend to get passionate
mauling the cheeks of her tumorous ass. And yet
not too passionate, because that would mean a quick
fuck and maybe no lunch. If the meal were good
I might do a hit and run job—that's what I was thinking to myself as I foozled around.

«Jesus Christ, all right, I'll get you a meal,» she
blurted out, reading my thoughts like a blind book-
worm.

«Fine,» I almost shouted. «What have you got?»

«Come and see for yourself,» she answered, dragging me to the kitchen and opening the icebox.

I saw ham, potato salad, sardines, cold beets, rice
pudding, apple sauce, frankfurters, pickles, celery
stalks, cream cheese and a special dish of puke with
mayonnaise on it which I knew I didn't want.

«Let's bring it all out,» I suggested. «And have
you any beer?»

«Yeah, and I got mustard too,» she snarled.

«Any bread?»

She gave me a look of clean disgust. I quickly
yanked the things out of the ice-box and set them on
the table.

«Better make some coffee too,» I said.

«I suppose you'd like some whipped cream with it,
wouldn't you? You know, I feel like poisoning you.
Jesus, if you're hard up you could ask me to lend you
some money... you oughtn't to come here and try to
sell me a lot of crap. If you'd been a little nicer I'd
have asked you out to lunch. I've got tickets for
the theatre. We could have had a good time... I
might even have bought the fool books. Mike isn't a
bad guy. He'd have bought the books even if we had

no intention of reading them. *If he thought you need help....* You walk in and treat me as if I were dirt. What did I ever do to you? I don't get it. Don't laugh! I'm serious. I don't know why I should take this from *you*. Who the hell do you think you are?»

She slammed a dish down in front of me. Then she turned on her heel and went to the kitchen. I was left there with all the food heaped up in front of me.

«Come, come, don't take it like that!» I said, shoveling a forkful into my mouth. «You know I didn't mean anything personal.» (The word personal struck me as being highly incongruous, but I knew she'd like it.)

«Personal or not, I'm not joining you,» she retorted. «You can eat your fill and get out. I'll make you some coffee. I don't want to ever see you again. You're disgusting.»

I put the knife and fork down and went into the kitchen. The things were cold anyway, so it wouldn't matter if I did spend a few minutes soothing her feelings.

«I'm sorry, Julie,» I said, trying to put my arm around her. She brushed me away angrily. «You see,» and I began to put some feeling into my words, «Maude and I don't get along very well. We had a bad quarrel this morning. I must be out of sorts....»

«Is that any reason to take it out on *me*?»

«No, it isn't. I don't know, I was desperate this morning. That's why I came to see *you*. And then, when I started in to work on you... to sell you the books... I felt ashamed of myself. I wouldn't have let you take the books even if you had pretended you wanted them....»

«I know what's the matter with you,» she said. «You were disappointed in my looks. *I've changed,* that's what's the matter. And you're a bad loser. You want to take it out on me—but it's your own fault. You've got a good-looking wife... why don't you stick to her? Everybody has quarrels—you're not the only two in the world. Do I run off to somebody else's husband when things go wrong? Where the hell would that get us? Mike's no angel to live with... nobody is, I guess. You act like a spoiled child. What do you think life is, *a wet dream?*»

This speech couldn't be laughed off. I had to beg her to sit down and eat with me, give me a chance to explain myself. Reluctantly she consented.

It was a long drawn-out story I unfolded, as I polished off one plate after another. She seemed so impressed by my sincerity that I began to toy with the idea of re-introducing the world's best literature. I had to skate very delicately because this time it would have to look as if I were doing *her* a favor. I was trying to jockey myself into the position of letting her help me. At the same time I was wondering if it were worth it, if perhaps it wouldn't be more pleasant to go to the matinee.

She was just getting back to normal, getting friendly and trusting. The coffee was excellent, and I had just finished the second cup when I felt a bowel movement coming on. I excused myself and went to the bathroom. There I enjoyed the luxury of a thorough evacuation. I pulled the chain and sat there a few moments, a bit dreamy and a bit lecherous too, when suddenly I realized that I was getting a sitz bath. I pulled the chain again. The water started to over-flow between my legs on to the floor. I jumped up, dried my ass with a towel, buttoned my trousers and looked frantically up at the toilet box. I tried everything I could think of but the water kept rising and flowing over—and with it came one or two healthy turds and a mess of toilet paper.

In a panic I called Julie. Through a crack in the door I begged her to tell me what to do.

«Let me in, I'll fix it,» said she.

«Tell *me*,» I begged, «I'll do it. You can't come in yet.»

«I can't explain,» said Julie, «you'll have to let me in.»

There was no help for it, I had to open the door. I was never more embarrassed in my life. The floor was one ungodly mess. Julie, however, went to work with dispatch, as though it were an everyday affair. In a jiffy the water had stopped running; it only remained to clean up the mess.

«Listen, you get out now,» I begged. «Let me handle this. Have you got a dust-pan—and a mop?»

«*You* get out!» said she. «I'll take care of it.» And with that she pushed me out and closed the door.

I waited on pins and needles for her to come out. Then a real funk took hold of me. There was only one thing to do—escape as fast as possible.

I fidgeted a few moments, listening first on one foot, then the other, not daring to make a peep. I knew I'd never be able to face her. I looked around, measured the distance to the door, listened intently for just a second, then grabbed my things and tiptoed out.

It was an elevator apartment, but I didn't wait for the elevator. I skipped down the stairs, three steps at a time, as though the devil himself were pursuing me.

The first thing I did was to go to a restaurant and wash my hands thoroughly. There was a machine which, by inserting a coin, squirted perfume over you. I helped myself to a few squirts and sallied out into the bright sunshine. I walked aimlessly for a while, contrasting the beautiful weather with my uncomfortable state of mind.

Soon I found myself walking near the river. A

few yards ahead was a little park, or at least a strip
of grass and some benches. I took a seat and began
to ruminate. In less than no time my thoughts had
reverted to Coleridge. It was a relief to let the mind
dwell on problems purely aesthetic.

Absent-mindedly I opened the prospectus and began
rereading the fragment which had so absorbed me—
prior to the horrible fiasco at Julie's. I skipped from
one item to another. At the back of the prospectus
there were maps and charts and reproductions of
ancient writings found on tablets and monuments in
various parts of the world. I came upon «the mysterious writing» of the Uighurs who had once overrun
Europe from the over-flowing well of Central Asia.
I read of cities which had been lifted heavenward
twelve and thirteen thousand feet when the mountain
ranges began to form; I read about Solon's discourse
with Plato and about the 70,000 year old glyphs
found in Tibet which hinted all too clearly of the
existence of now unknown continents. I came upon
the sources of Pythagoras' conceptions and read with
sadness of the destruction of the great library at
Alexandria. Certain Mayan tablets reminded me
vividly of the canvases of Paul Klee. The writings of
the ancients, their symbols, their patterns, their com-
positions, were strikingly like the things children
invent in kindergartens. The insane, on the other
hand, produced the most intellectual sort of composi-
tions. I read about Laotse and Albertus Magnus and
Cagliostro and Cornelius Agrippa and Iamblichus,
each one a universe, each one a link in an invisible
chain of now exploded worlds. I came to a chart
arranged like parallel strips of banjo frets, telling off
laterally the centuries «since the dawn of civilization»
and vertically listing the literary figures of the epochs.
their names and their works. The Dark Ages stood
out like blind windows in the side of a skyscraper;

here and there in the great blank wall there was a beam of light shed by the spirit of some intellectual giant who had managed to make his voice heard above the croaking of the submerged and dispirited denizens of the marshes. When it was dark in Europe it had been bright elsewhere: the spirit of man was like a veritable switchboard, revealing itself in signals and flashes, often across oceans of darkness. One thing stood out clearly—on that switchboard certain great spirits were still plugged in, still standing by for a call. When the epoch which had called them forth was drowned out they emerged from the darkness like the towering snow-capped peaks of the Himalayas. And there was reason to believe, it seemed to me, that not until another unspeakable catastrophe occured would the light they shed be extinguished. As I shut off the current of reverie into which I had fallen a Sphinx-like image registered itself on the fallen curtain: it was the hoary visage of one of Europe's magi: Leonardo da Vinci. The mask which he wore to conceal his identity is one of the most baffling disguises ever assumed by an emissary from the depths. It made me shudder to think what those eyes which stare unflinchingly into the future had perceived....

I looked across the river to the Jersey shore. It looked desolate to me, more desolate even than the boulder bed of a dried-up river. Nothing of any importance to the human race had ever happened here. Nothing would happen for thousands of years perhaps. The Pygmies were vastly more interesting, vastly more illuminating to study, than the inhabitants of New Jersey. I looked up and down the Hudson River, a river I have always detested, even from the time when I first read of Henry Hudson and his bloody Half Moon. I hated both sides of the river equally. I hated the legends woven

about its name. The whole valley was like the
empty dream of a beer-logged Dutchman. I never
did give a fuck about Powhatan or Manhattan. I
loathed Father Knickerbocker. I wished that there
were ten thousand black powder plants scattered on
both sided of the river and that they might all blow
up simultaneously....

14

A sudden decision to clear out of Cockroach Hall.
Why? Because I had met Rebecca....

Rebecca was the second wife of my old friend
Arthur Raymond. The two were now living in an
enormous appartment on Riverside Drive; they
wanted to let out rooms. It was Kronski who told
me about it; he said he was going to take one of the
rooms.

Why don't you come up and meet his wife—you'll
like her. She could be Mona's sister.»

«What's her name?» I asked.

«Rebecca. Rebecca Valentine.»

The name Rebecca excited me. I had always
wanted to meet a woman called Rebecca—and not
Becky.

(Rebecca, Ruth, Roxanne, Rosalind, Frederika,
Ursula, Sheila, Norma, Guinevere, Leonora, Sabina,
Malvina, Solange, Deirdre. What wonderful names
women had! Like flowers, stars, constellations....)

Mona wasn't so keen about the move, but when we
got to Arthur Raymond's place and she heard him
practising, she changed her tune.

It was Renée, the younger sister of Arthur

Raymond, who opened the door. She was about nineteen, a spit-fire with heavy curly locks full of vitality. Her voice was like a nightingale's—no matter what she said you felt like agreeing.

Finally Rebecca presented herself. She was right out of the Old Testament—dark and sunny clean through. Mona warmed to her immediately, as she would to a lost sister. They were both beautiful. Rebecca was more mature, more solid, more integrated. One felt instinctively that she always preferred the truth. I liked her firm hand-clasp, the direct flashing look with which she greeted one. She seemed to have none of the usual female pettinesses.

Soon Arthur joined us. He was short, muscular, with a hard, steely twang to his voice and frequently convulsed by explosive spasms of laughter. He laughed just as heartily over his own quips as over the other fellow's. He was inordinately healthy, vital, jolly, exuberant. He had always been that way and in the old days, when Maude and I first moved into his neighborhood, I was very fond of him. I used to burst in on him all hours of the day and night and give him three and four hour résumés of the books I had just read. I remember spending whole afternoons talking of Smerdiakov and Pavel Pavlovitch, or General Ivolgin, or those angelic sprites which surrounded the Idiot, or of the Filipovna woman. He was married then to Irma, who later became one of my associates in the Cosmodemonic Telefloccus Company. In those early days, when I first knew Arthur Raymond, tremendous things occurred—in the mind, I should add. Our conversations were like passages out of *The Magic Mountain*, only more virulent, more exalted, more sustained, more provocative, more inflammable, more dangerous, more menacing—*and* much more, ever so much more, exhausting.

I was making a rapid throw-back as I stood watching him talk. His sister Renée was trying to keep up a waning conversation with Kronski's wife. (The latter always went dead on you, no matter how absorbing the theme might be.) I wondered how we would get along, the lot of us, under one roof. Of the two vacant rooms Kronski had already preempted the larger one. The six of us were now huddled together in the other room which was nothing more than a cubby-hole.

«Oh, it'll do,» Arthur Raymond was saying. «God, you don't need much room—there's the whole house. I want you to come. We're going to have a great time here. God!» He exploded with laughter again.

I knew he was desperate. Too proud, however, to admit that he needed money. Rebecca looked at me expectantly. I read very clearly what was written in her face. Mona spoke up suddenly: «Of course we'll take it.» Kronski rubbed rubbed his hands gleefully. «Sure you will! We're going to make a grand stew of it, you'll see.» And then he fell to haggling with them about the price. But Arthur Raymond wouldn't talk about money. «Make your own terms,» he said, wandering off to the big room where the piano stood. I heard him pounding the piano. I tried to listen but Rebecca stood in front of me and kept plying me with questions.

A few days later we were installed. The first thing we noticed about our new domicile was that everybody was trying to use the bathroom at once. You got to know who the last occupant was by the smell he left behind. The sink was always clogged up with long hairs and Arthur Raymond, who never owned a tooth-brush, would use the first one that came to hand. There were too many females about, for another thing. The older sister, Jessica, who was an actress, came frequently and often stayed the night. There was Rebecca's mother, too, who was always in and out of the place, always wreathed in sorrow, always dragging herself along like a corpse. And then there were Kronski's friends and Rebecca's friends and Arthur's friends and Renée's friends, to say nothing of the pupils who came at all hours of the day and night. At first it was charming to hear the piano going: snatches of Bach, Ravel, Debussy, Mozart and so on. Then it became exasperating, especially when Arthur Raymond himself was practising. He went over and over a phrase with the tenacity and persistence of a madman. First with one hand, firmly and slowly; then with the other hand, firmly and slowly. Then two hands, very firmly, very slowly; then more and more rapidly, until he reached the normal tempo. Then twenty times, fifty times, a hundred times. He would advance a little—a few more measures. Ditto. Then back again, like a crab, from the very beginning. Then suddenly he'd scrap it, begin something new, something he liked. He'd play it with all his heart, as if he were giving a concert. But maybe a third of the way through he'd stumble. Silence. He'd go back a few measures, break it down, build it up, slow, fast, one hand, two hands, all together, hands, feet, elbows, knuckles, moving forward like a tank corps, sweeping everything before him, mowing down trees, fences, barns, hedges, walls. It was agonizing to follow him. He was not playing for enjoyment—he was playing to perfect his technique. He was wearing his finger-tips off, rubbing his ass smooth. Always advancing, progressing, attacking, conquering, annihilating, mopping up, realigning his forces, throwing out sentries and sentinels, covering his rear, digging himself in, charging in prisoners, segregating the wounded, reconnoitering, ambushing his men, sending up flares, rockets, exploding ammunition plants, railway centers, inventing new torpe-

does, dynamos, flame-throwers, coding and decoding
the messages that came in....

A grand teacher, though. A darling teacher. He
moved about the room in his khaki shirt, always
open at the neck, like a restive panther. He would
stand in a corner listening, with his chin in the palm
of his hand and the other hand supporting his elbow.
He'd walk to the window and look out, humming
softy as he followed the pupil's manful attempts to
live up to that perfection which Arthur demanded
of all his pupils. If it were a very young pupil he
could be as tender as a lamb; he would make the
child laugh, would pick her up in his arms and lift
her off the stool. «*You see...?*» and he would very
slowly, very gently, very carefully, indicate the way
it should be done. He had infinite patience with his
young pupils—a beautiful thing to watch. He looked
after them as if they were flowers. He tried to reach
their souls, tried to soothe them or inflame them, as
the case might be. With the older ones it was still
more thrilling to observe his technique. With these
he was all attention, alert as a porcupine, his legs
stanced, swaying, balancing himself, raising and
lowering himself on the balls of his feet, the muscles
of his face moving rapidly as he followed with
glittering eagerness the transition from passage to
passage. To these he spoke as if they were masters
already. He would *suggest* this or that manipulation,
this or that interpretation. Often interrupting the
performance for ten or fifteen minutes at a stretch,
he would launch into brilliant expositions of com-
manding techniques, comparing one with another,
evaluating them, comparing a score with a book, one
writer with another writer, a palette with a texture,
a tone with a personal idiom, and so on. He made
music live. He heard music in everything. The
young women, when they had concluded a seance,

swooned through the hall, unconscious of everything but the flames of genius. Yes, he was a life-giver, a sun-god: he sent them reeling into the street.

Arguing with Kronski he was a different person. That mania for perfection, that pedagogic fury which was such a powerful asset to him as a music teacher, reduced him to ridiculous proportions when he launched into the world of ideas. Kronski toyed with him as a cat toys with a mouse. He delighted in tripping his adversary up. He defended nothing, except his own nimble security. Arthur Raymond had something of the Jack Dempsey style, when it came to a heated discussion. He bore in steadily, always with short, swift jabs, like a chopping block fitted with dancing legs. Now and then he made a lunge, a brilliant lunge, only to find that he was grappling with space. Kronski had a trick of vanishing completely just when he seemed to be on the ropes. You would find him a second later hanging from the chandelier. He had no recognizable strategy, unless it was to elude, to jibe and taunt, to infuriate his opponent, and then do the disappearing stunt. Arthur Raymond seemed to be saying all the time: «Put up your dukes! Fight! Fight, you bastard!» But Kronski had no intention of making a punching bag of himself.

I never caught Arthur Raymond reading a book. I don't think he read many books, yet he had an amazing knowledge of many things. Whatever he read he remembered with astonishing vividness and accuracy. Aside from my friend Roy Hamilton, he could extract more from a book than any one I knew. He literally eviscerated the text. Roy Hamilton would proceed millimetre by millimetre, so to speak, lingering over a phrase for days or weeks at a time. It sometimes took him a year or two to finish a small book, but when he was through with it he did seem to have added a cubit to his stature. For him a half dozen good books were sufficient to supply him with spiritual fodder for the rest of his life. Thoughts to him were living things, as they were to Louis Lambert. Having read one book thoroughly he gave the very real impression of knowing all books. He thought and lived his way through a book, emerging from the experience a new and glorified being. He was the very opposite of the scholar whose stature diminishes with each book he reads. Books for him were what Yoga is to the earnest seeker after truth: they helped him unite with God.

Arthur Raymond, on the other hand, gave the illusion of devouring a book's contents. He read with muscular attention. Or so I imagined, observing their effect upon him. He read like a sponge, intent upon absorbing the writer's thoughts. His sole concern was to ingest, to assimilate, to redistribute. He was a vandal. Each new book represented a new conquest. Books fortified his ego. He didn't grow, he became puffed with pride and arrogance. He looked for corroborations in order to sally forth and give battle. He wouldn't permit himself to be made over. He could render tribute to the author he admired but he could never bend the knee. He remained adamant and inflexible; his carapace grew thicker and thicker.

He was the type who, upon finishing a book, can talk of nothing else for weeks to come. No matter what one touched upon, in conversing with him, he related it to the book he had just devoured. The curious thing about these hangovers was that the more he talked about the book the more one felt his unconscious desire to destroy it. At bottom it always seemed to me that he was really ashamed of having permitted another mind to enthrall him. His talk was not of the book but of how thoroughly and penetratingly he, Arthur Raymond, had understood it. To expect him to give a résumé of the book was futile. He gave you just enough information about its subject matter to enable you to follow his analyses and elaborations intelligently. Though he kept saying to you—«You must read it, it's marvelous,» what he meant was—«You can take it from me that it's an important work, else I shouldn't be wasting my time discussing it with you.» And what he implied, moreover, was that it was just as well you hadn't read it because you would never by your own efforts be able to unearth the gems which he, Arthur Raymond, had found in it. «When I get through telling you about it,» he seemed to say, «you won't need to read it. I know not only what the author said but what he intended to say and didn't.»

At the time I speak of one of his passions was Sigmund Freud. I don't mean to imply that he knew only Freud. No, he spoke as though he had an acquaintance with the whole swarm, from Krafft-Ebing and Stekel on down. He regarded Freud not only as a thinker but as a poet. Kronski, on the other hand, whose reading was wider and deeper in this field, who had the advantage of clinical experience as well, who was then making a comparative study of psycho-analysis and not merely endeavoring to assimilate one new contribution after the other, irritated Arthur Raymond beyond words by what the latter was pleased to call «his corrosive skepticism».

It was in our cubicle that these discussions, which were not only bitter but interminable, took place. Mona had given up the dance hall and was looking about for work in the theatre. Often we all ate together in the kitchen, attempting towards midnight to disperse and reach our respective quarters. But Arthur Raymond had absolutely no regard for time; when he was interested in a subject he thought

nothing of food, sleep or sex. If he went to bed at
five in the morning he would get up at eight, if he
chose to, or remain in bed for eighteen hours. He
left it to Rebecca to rearrange his schedule. Naturally
this sort of life created an atmosphere of chaos and
postponement. When it got too complicated Arthur
Raymond would throw up his hands and walk out
on it, sometimes remaining away for days. After
these periods of absence strange rumors would come
floating back, stories which shed quite a different
lustre upon his character. Apparently these excursions were necessary to complete the physical being;
the life of a musician couldn't possibly satisfy his
robust nature. He had to get away occasionally and
mix with his cronies—a most incongruous assortment
of characters, incidentally. Some of his escapades
were innocent and amusing, others were sordid and
ugly. Brought up as a sissy, he had found it imperative to develop the brutal side of his nature. He
enjoyed picking a quarrel with some burly, bluster-
ing idiot much bigger than himself and cold-bloodedly
breaking the man's arm or leg. He had done what
so many little fellows always dream of doing—
mastered ju-jitsu. He had done it in order to have
the pleasure of insulting the menacing giants who
make up the world of bullies which the little man
dreads. The bigger they were the better Arthur
Raymond liked it. He didn't dare to use his fists for
fear or injuring his hands, but, rather meanly I
thought, he would always pretend to fight and then
of course take his adversary by surprise. «I don't
admire that in you at all,» I told him once. «If you
played me a trick like that I'd break a bottle over
your head.» He looked at me in astonishment. He
knew that I didn't care to fight or to wrestle. «I
wouldn't mind,» I added, «if you resorted to those
tricks as a last extremity. But you just want to show

off. You're a little bully, and a little bully is even
more obnoxious than a big one. Some day you'll
tackle the wrong man....»

He laughed. I always interpreted things in a queer
way, he said.

«That's why I like you,» he would say. «You're
unpredictable. You have no code. Really, Henry»
—and he would give a hearty guffaw—«you're essentially treacherous. If we ever make a new world
you'll have no place in it. You don't seem to understand what it means to give and take. You're an
intellectual hobo.... At times I don't understand you
at all. You're always gay and affable, almost sociable,
and yet ...well, you have no loyalties. I try to be
friends with you... we *were* friends once, you remember... but you've changed... you're hard inside... you're
untouchable. God, you think I'm hard... I'm just
cocky, pugnacious, full of spirits. You're the one
who's hard. You're a gangster, do you know that?»
He chuckled. «Yes, Henry, that's what you are—
you're a spiritual gangster. I don't trust you...»

It nettled him to observe the easy rapport which
existed between Rebecca and myself. He wasn't
jealous, nor had he reason to be, but he was envious
of my ability to create such a smooth relationship
with his wife. He was always telling me of her
intellectual attainments, as though that should be
the basis of attraction between us, but in a discussion,
if Rebecca were present, he behaved towards her as
if her opinions were of negligible importance. Mona
he listened to with a gravity that was almost comical.
He listened, of course, just long enough to hear her
out, saying «Yes, yes, to be sure,» but actually giving
no heed whatever to what she was saying.

Alone with Rebecca, watching her ironing or cook
a meal, I had those sort of talks which one can only
have with a woman if she belongs to another man

Here there was really that spirit of «give and take» which Arthur Raymond complained of missing in me. Rebecca was earthy and not at all intellectual. She had a sensual nature and she loved to be treated as a woman and not as a mind. We talked of the most simple, homely things some times, things which the music master found no interest in whatever.

Talk is only a pretext for other, subtler forms of communication. When the latter are inoperative speech becomes dead. If two people are intent upon communicating with one another it doesn't matter in the least how bewildering the talk becomes. People who insist upon clarity and logic often fail in making themselves understood. They are always searching for a more perfect transmitter, deluded by the supposition that the mind is the only instrument for the exchange of thought. When one really begins to talk one delivers himself. Words are thrown about recklessly, not counted like pennies. One doesn't care about grammatical or factual errors, contradictions, lies and so on. One talks. If you are talking to some one who knows how to listen he understands perfectly, even though the words make no sense. When this kind of talk gets under way a marriage takes place, no matter whether you are talking to a man or a woman. Men talking with other men have as much need of this sort of marriage as women talking with women have. Married couples seldom enjoy this kind of talk, for reasons which are only too obvious.

Talk, real talk, it seems to me, is one of the most expressive manifestations of man's hunger for unlimited marriage. Sensitive people, people who feel, want to unite in some deeper, subtler, more durable fashion than is permitted by custom and convention. I mean in ways beyond the dreams of social and political Utopists. The brotherhood of man, should it ever come about, is only the kindergarten stage in the drama of human relationships. When man begins to permit himself full expression, when he can express himself without fear of ridicule, ostracism or persecution, the first thing he will do will be to pour out his love. In the story of human love we are still at the first chapter. Even there, even in the realm of the purely personal, it is a pretty shoddy account. Have we more than a dozen heros and heroines of love to hold up as examples? I doubt if we have even as many great lovers as we have illustrious saints. We have scholars galore, and kings and emperors, and statesmen and military leaders, and artists in profusion, and inventors, discoverers, explorers—but where are the great lovers? After a moment's reflection one is back to Abélard and Heloise, or to Antony and Cleopatra, or the story of the Taj Mahal. So much of it is fictive, expanded and glorified by the poverty-stricken lovers whose prayers are answered only by myth and legend. *Tristan and Isolde*—what a powerful spell that legend still casts upon the modern world! In the landscape of romance it stands out like the snow-capped peak of Fujiyama.

There was one observation which I made to myself over and over again as I listened to the interminable wrangles between Arthur Raymond and Kronski. It was to the effect that knowledge divorced from action leads to sterility. Here were two vital young men, each brilliant in his way, and they were arguing passionately night after night about a new approach to the problems of life. An austere individual, leading a sober, modest, disciplined life in the far off city of Vienna, was responsible for these clashes. All over the Occidental world this wrangling was going on. One had to speak passionately about these theories of Sigmund Freud or not at all, so it seemed

That fact alone is of significance, of far more significance than the theories under discussion. A few thousand people—not hundreds of thousands!—would in the course of the next twenty years submit to the process known as psychoanalysis. The term psychoanalysis would gradually lose its magic and become a by-word. Its therapeutic value would decrease in proportion to the spread of popular understanding. The wisdom underlying Freud's explorations and interpretations would diminish in effectiveness with the increasing desire of the neurotic to become readapted to life.

In the case of my two young friends one of them was later to become dissatisfied with every solution to the problems of the day except that offered by Communism; the other, who would have pronounced me crazy had I then hinted at such an eventuality, was to become my patient. The music master forsook his music in order to right the world and failed. He failed even to make his own life more interesting, more satisfying, more ample. The other abandoned his medical practise and finally put himself into the hands of a quack, *yours truly*. He did it deliberately, knowing that I had no qualifications other than my sincerity and enthusiasm. He was even pleased at the result, which was nil, and which he had anticipated in advance.

It is now about twenty years since the period I speak of. Only the other day, as I was strolling aimlessly along, I ran into Arthur Raymond on the street. I might have passed him by had he not hailed me. He had altered, had taken on a girth almost commensurable to Kronski's. A middle-aged man now with a row of black, charred teeth. After a few words he began to talk about his son—the oldest boy, who was now in college and a member of the football team. He had transferred all his hopes to

he son. I was disgusted. In vain did I try to get
ome inkling about his own life. No, he preferred
o talk about his son. *He* was going to be somebody! (An athlete, a writer, a musician—God knows
vhat.) I didn't give a fuck about the son. All
 could make out of this effusive gush was that he,
Arthur Raymond, had given up the ghost. He was
iving in the son. It was pitiful. I couldn't get
way from him fast enough.

«You must come up and see us soon.» (He was
rying to hold me.) «Let's have a good old session
ogether. You know how I love talking!» He gave
ut one of those cachinating snorts as of yore.)

«Where do you live now?» he added, clutching
ny arm.

I took a piece of paper out of my pocket and wrote
own a false address and telephone number. I
hought to myself, the next time we meet it will
robably be in limbo.

As I walked away I suddenly realized that he had
vinced no interest in what had happened to me all
hese years. He knew I had been abroad, had written
 few books. «I've read some of your stuff, you
now,» he had remarked. And then he had laughed
onfusedly, as if to say: «But I know you, you old
apscallion... you're not taking *me* in!» For my part
 could have replied: «Yes, and I know all about
ou. I know the deceptions and humiliations you've
uffered.»

Had we begun to swap experience we might have
ad an enjoyable talk. We might have understood
ne another better than we ever had before. If he
ad only given me a chance I might have demon-
rated that the Arthur who had failed was just as
ear to me as the promising young man whom I had
nce idolized. We were both rebels, in our way.
nd we had both struggled to make a new world.

«Of course I still believe in it (Communism),» he
had said in parting. He said it as though he were
sorry to admit that the movement were not big
enough to include him with all his idiosyncrasies.
In the same way I could imagine him saying to himself that he still believed in music, or in the outdoor
life, or in ju-jitsu. I wondered if he realized what
he had done by abandoning one road after the other.
If he had stopped anywhere along the line and
fought his way through, life would have been worth
while. Even if he had only become a champion
wrestler! I remembered the night he had induced
me to accompany him to a bout between Earl Caddock and Strangler Lewis. (And another occasion
when we had gone together to witness the Dempsey-
Carpentier fight.) He was a poet then. He saw two
gods in mortal combat. He knew that there was
more to it than a tussle to the finish between two
brutes. He talked about these great figures of the
arena as he would have talked about the great composers or the great dramatists. He was a conscious
part of the mob which attends these spectacles. He
was like a Greek in the days of Euripides. He was
an artist applauding other artists. He was at his
very best in the amphitheatre.

I recalled another occasion, when we were waiting
on the platform of a railway station. Suddenly
while pacing back and forth, he grabs my arm and
says: «By God, Henry, do you know who that is?
That's Jack Dempsey!» And like a shot he bolt
from my side and runs up to his beloved idol.
«Hello Jack!» he says in a loud, ringing voice.
«You're looking fine. I want to shake your hand.
I want to tell you what a real champ you are.»

I could hear Dempsey's squeaky, piping voice
answering the greeting. Dempsey, who overtowered
Arthur Raymond, looked at that moment like a child.

t was Arthur Raymond who was bold and aggressive.
Ie didn't seem the least bit awed by Dempsey's
>resence. I almost expected him to give the cham-
>ion a pat on the shoulder.

«He's like a fine race horse,» said Arthur Raymond,
iis voice tense with emotion. «A most sensitive
reature.» He was probably thinking of himself, of
iow he would appear to others should he suddenly
>ecome world's champion. «An intelligent chap too.
A man couldn't fight in that colorful style unless he
>ossessed a high degree of intelligence. He's a fine
ellow really. Just a big boy, you know. He actually
>lushed, do you know that?» On and on he went,
hapsodizing over his hero.

But it was about Earl Caddock that he said the
nost wonderful things. Earl Caddock, I think, was
ver closed to his ideal than Dempsey. «The man
>f a thousand holds,» that's how Caddock was called.
A god-like body, a little too frail, it would seem, for
hose protracted, gruelling bouts which the ordeal
f wrestling demands. I remember vividly how he
>oked that night beside the burlier, heftier Strangler
Lewis. Arthur Raymond was certain that Lewis
·ould win—but his heart was with Earl Caddock.
Ie screamed his lungs out, urging Caddock on.
Afterwards, in a Jewish delicatessen over on the
Last Side, he rehearsed the bout in detail. He had
n extraordinary memory when it concerned any-
hing he was passionate about. I think I enjoyed
he bout even more, in retrospect, seeing it through
iis eyes. In fact, he talked about it so marvelously
hat the next day I sat down and wrote a prose poem
bout two wrestlers. I brought it with me to the
entist's the following day. He was a wrestling fan
lso. The dentist thought it was a chef-d'œuvre. The
esult was that I never got my tooth filled. I was
aken upstairs to meet the family—they were from

Odessa—and before I knew what was happening,
had become engrossed in a game of chess which
lasted until two in the morning. And then began
a friendship which lasted until all my teeth had been
treated—fourteen of fifteen months it dragged out.
When the bill came I vanished. It was not until
five or six years later, I guess, that we met again
and then under rather peculiar circumstances. But
of that later....

Freud, Freud.... A lot of things might be laid at
his door. There is Dr. Kronski now, some ten years
after our semantic life at Riverside Drive. Big as
porpoise, puffing like a walrus, emitting talk like a
locomotive emits steam. An injury to the head has
disregulated his entire system. He has become a
glandular anomaly, a study in cross-purposes.

We had not seen each other for some years. We
meet again in New York. Hectic confabulations.
He learns that I have had more than a speaking
acquaintance with psychoanalysis during my absence
abroad. I mention certain figures in that world who
are well known to him—from their writings. He's
amazed that I should know them, have been accepted
by them—as a friend. He begins to wonder if he
hadn't made a mistake about his old friend Henry
Miller. He wants to talk about it, talk and talk and
talk. I refuse. That impresses him. He knows that
talking is his weakness, his vice.

After a few meetings I realize that he is hatching
an idea. He can't just take it for granted that I
know something about psycho-analysis— he wants
proofs. «What are you doing now... in New York?»
he asks. I answer that I am doing nothing, really.

«Aren't you writing?»

«No.»

A long pause. Then it comes out. An exper

iment... a grand experiment. I'm the man to do it. He will explain.

The long and short of it is that he would like me to experiment with some of his patients—his ex-patients, I should say, because he has given up his practise. He's certain I can do as good as the next fellow—maybe better. «I won't tell them you're a writer,» he says. «You *were* a writer, but during your stay in Europe you became an analyst. How's that?»

I smiled. It didn't seem bad at all, at first blush. As a matter of fact, I had long toyed with the very idea. I jumped at it. Settled then. To-morrow, at four o'clock, he would introduce me to one of his patients.

That's how it began. Before very long I had about seven or eight patients. They seemed to be pleased with my efforts. They told Dr. Kronski so. He of course had expected it to turn out thus. He thought he might become an analyst himself. Why not? I had to confess I could see no reason against it. Any one with charm, intelligence and sensitivity might become an analyst. There were healers long before Mary Baker Eddy or Sigmund Freud were heard of. Common sense played its role too.

«To be an analyst, however,» I said, not intending it as a serious remark, «one should first be analyzed himself, you know that.»

«How about *you?*» he said.

I pretended I had been analyzed. I told him Otto Rank had done the job.

«You never told me that,» he said, again visibly impressed. He had an unholy respect for Otto Rank.

«How long did it last?» he asked.

«About three months. Rank doesn't believe in prolonged analyses, I suppose you know.»

«That's true,» he said, growing very thoughtful.

A moment later he popped it. «What about analyzing *me?* No, seriously. I know it's not considered a good risk when you know one another as intimately as we do, but just the same...»

«Yes,» I said slowly, feeling my way along, «perhaps we might even explode that stupid prejudice. After all, Freud had to analyze Rank, didn't he?» (This was a lie, because Rank had never been analyzed, even by Father Freud.)

«To-morrow then, at ten o'clock!»

«Good,» I said, «and be on the dot. I'm going to charge you by the hour. Sixty minutes and no more. If you're not on time it's your loss...»

«You're going to *charge* me?» he echoed, looking at me as if I had lost my mind.

«Of course I am! You know very well how important it is for the patient to pay for his analysis.»

«But I'm not a patient!» he yelled. «Jesus, I'm doing you a favor.»

«It's up to you,» I said, affecting an air of sangfroid. If you can get some one else to do it for nothing, well and good. I'm going to charge you the regular fee, the fee you yourself suggested for your own patients.»

«Now listen,» he said, «you're getting fantastic. After all, I was the one who launched you in this business, don't forget that.»

«I *must* forget that,» I insisted. «This is not a matter of sentiment. In the first place I must remind you that you not only need analysis to become an analyst, you need it because you're a neurotic. You couldn't possibly become an analyst if you weren't neurotic. Before you can heal others you have to heal yourself. And if you're not a neurotic I'll make you one before I'm through with you, how do you like that?»

He thought it was a huge joke. But the next

morning he came, and he was prompt too. He looked as though he had stayed up all night to be there on time.

«The money,» I said, before he had even removed his coat.

He tried to laugh it off. He settled himself on the couch, as eager to have his bottle as any infant in swaddling clothes.

«You've got to give it to me now,» I insisted, «or I refuse to deal with you.» I enjoyed being firm with him—it was a new role for me also.

«But how do we know that we can go through it?» he said, trying to stall. «I'll tell you... if I like the way you handle me I'll pay you wathever you ask... within reason, of course. But don't make a fuss about it now. Come on, let's get down to brass tacks.»

«Nothing doing,» I said. «No tickee, no shirtee. If I'm no good you can bring suit against me, but if you want my help then you've got to pay—and pay in advance... By the way, you're wasting time, you know. Every minute you sit there haggling about the money you're wasting time that might have been spent more profitably. It's now»—and here I consulted my watch—«it's now twelve minutes after ten. As soon as you're ready we'll begin....»

He was sore as a pup about it but I had him in a corner and there was nothing to do but to shell out.

As he was dishing it out—I charged him ten dollars a session—he looked up, but this time with the air of one who has already confided himself to the doctor's hands. «You mean to say that if I should come here one day without the money, if I should happen to forget or be short a few dollars, you wouldn't take me on?»

«Precisely,» I said. «We understand one another perfectly. Shall we begin.... *now?*»

He fell back on the couch like a sheep ready for
the axe. «Compose yourself,» I said soothingly, sitting behind him and out of his range of vision.
«Just get quiet and relax. You're going to tell me
everything about yourself... from the very beginning.
Don't imagine that you can tell it all in one sitting.
We're going to have many sessions like this. It's up
to you how long or how short this relationship will
be. Remember that it's costing you ten dollars
every time. But don't let that get under your skin,
because if you think of nothing but how much it's
costing you, you'll forget what you intended to tell
me. This is a painful procedure, but it's in your own
interest. If you learn how to adapt yourself to the
role of a patient you will also learn how to adapt
yourself to the role of analyst. Be critical with yourself, not with me. I am only an instrument. I am
here to help you.... Now collect yourself and relax.
I'll be listening whenever you're ready to deliver
yourself....»

He had stretched himself out full length, his hands
folded over the mountain of flesh which was his
stomach. His face was very pasty; it had the
blenched look, his skin, of a man who has just
returned from the water closet after straining himself to death. The body had the amorphous appearance of the helpless fat man who finds the efforts
to raise himself to a sitting posture almost as difficult
as it would be for a tortoise to right itself when it
has been capsized. Whatever powers he possessed
seemed to have deserted him. He flipped about restlessly for a few minutes, a human flounder weighing
itself.

My exhortation to talk had paralyzed that faculty
of speech which was his prime endowment. To
begin with there was no longer any adversary before
him to demolish. He was being asked to employ

his wits against himself. He was to deliver and reveal
—in a word, to *create*—and that was something he
had never in his life attempted. He was to discover
«the meaning of meaning» in a new way, and it was
obvious that the thought of it terrified him.

After wriggling about, scratching himself, flopping
from one side of the couch to the other, rubbing
his eyes, coughing, sputtering, yawning, he opened
his mouth as if to talk—but nothing came out. After
a few grunts he raised himself on his elbow and
turned his head in my direction. There was something piteous in the expression of his eyes.

«Can't you ask me a few questions?» he said. «I
don't know where to begin.»

«It would be better if I didn't ask you any questions,» I said. «You will find your way if you take
your time. Once you begin you'll go on like a
cataract. Don't force it.»

He flopped back to a prone position and sighed
heavily. It would be wonderful to change places
with him, I thought to myself. During the silences,
my will in abeyance, I was enjoying the pleasure of
making silent confession to some invisible super-
analyst. I didn't feel the least bit timid or awkward
or inexperienced. Indeed, once having decided to
play the role I was thoroughly in it and ready for
any eventuality. I realized at once that by the
mere act of assuming the role of healer one becomes
a healer in fact.

I had a pad in my hand ready for use should he
drop anything of importance. As the silence prolonged itself I jotted down a few notes of an extra-
therapeutic nature. I remember putting down the
names of Chesterton and Herriot, two Gargantuan
figures who, like Kronski, were gifted with an extraordinary verbal facility. It occurred to me that I
had often remarked this phenomenon *chez les gros*

hommes. They were like the Medusas of the marine
world—floating organs who swam in the sound of
their own voice. Polyps outwardly, there was an
acute, brilliant concentration noticeable in their
mental faculties. Fat men were often most dynamic,
most engaging, most charming and seductive. Their
laziness and slovenliness were deceptive. In the brain
they often carried a diamond. And, unlike the thin
man, after washing down troughs of food their
thoughts sparkled and scintillated. They were often
at their best when the gustatory appetites were
invoked. The thin man, on the other hand, also a
great eater very frequently, tends to become sluggish
and sleepy when his digestive apparatus is called
into play. He is usually at his best on an empty
stomach.

«It doesn't matter where you begin,» I said finally,
fearing that he would go to slep on me. «No matter
what you lead off with you will always come back
to the sore spot.» I paused a moment. Then in a
soothing voice I said very deliberately: «You can
take a nap too, if you like. Perhaps that would be
good for you.»

In a flash he was wide awake and talking. The
idea of paying me to take a nap electrified him. He
was spilling over in all directions at once. That
wasn't a bad stratagem, I thought to myself.

He began, as I say, with a rush, impelled by the
frantic fear that he was wasting time. Then suddenly
he appeared to have become so impressed by his
own revelations that he wanted to draw me into a
discussion of their import. Once again I firmly and
gently refused the challenge. «Later,» I said, «when
we have something to go on. You've only begun...
only scratched the surface.»

«Are you making notes?» he asked, elated with
himself.

«Don't worry about me,» I replied, «think about yourself, about *your* problems. You're to have implicit confidence in me, remember that. Every minute you spend thinking about the *effect* you're producing is wasted. You're not no try to impress me—your task is to get sincere with yourself. There is no audience here—I am just a receptacle, a big ear. You can fill it with slush and nonsense, or you can drop pearls into it. Your vice is self-consciousness. Here we want only what is real and true and *felt*....»

He became silent again, fidgeted about for a few moments, then grew quite still. His hands were now folded back of his head. He had propped the pillow up so as not to relapse into sleep.

«I've just been thinking,» he said in a more quiet, contemplative mood, «of a dream I had last night. I think I'll tell it to you. It may give us a clue....»

This little preamble meant only one thing—that he was still worrying about my end of the collaboration. He knew that in analysis one is expected to reveal one's dreams. That much of the technique he was sure of—it was orthodox. It was curious, I reflected, that no matter how much one knows *about* a subject, to act is another matter. He understood perfectly what went on, in analysis, between patient and analyst, but he had never once confronted himself with the realisation of what it meant. Even now, though he hated to waste his money, he would have been tremendously relieved if, instead of going on with his dream, I had suggested that we discuss the therapeutic nature of these revelations. He would actually have preferred to invent a dream and then hash it to bits with me rather than unload himself quietly and sincerely. I felt that he was cursing himself—and me too, of course—for having suggested a situation wherein he could only, as he imagined, allow himself to be tortured.

However, with much laboring and sweating, he did manage to unfold a coherent account of the dream. He paused, when he had finished, as if expecting me to make some comment, some sign of approval or disapproval. Since I said nothing he began to play with the idea of the significance of the dream. In the midst of these intellectual excursions he suddenly halted himself and, turning his head slightly, he murmured dejectedly: «I suppose I oughtn't to do that... that's *your* job, isn't it?»

«You can do anything you please,» I said quietly. «If you prefer to analyze yourself—*and pay me for it*—I have no objection. You realize, I suppose, that one of the things you've come to me for is to acquire confidence and trust in others. Your failure to recognize this is part of your illness.»

Immediately he started to bluster. He just had to defend himself against such imputations. It wasn't true that he lacked confidence and trust. I had said that only to pique him.

«It's also quite useless,» I interrupted, «to draw me into argument. If your only concern is to prove that you know more than I do then you will get nowhere. I credit you with knowing much more than I do—but that too is part of your illness—that you know too much. You will never know everything. If knowledge could save you you wouldn't be lying there.»

«You're right,» he said meekly, accepting my statement as a chastisement that he merited. «Now let's see... where was I? I'm going to get to the bottom of things....»

At this point I casually glanced at my watch and discovered that the hour was up.

«Time's up,» I said, rising to my feet and going over to him.

«Wait a minute, won't you?» he said, looking up

at me irritably and as if I had abused him. «It's just coming to me now what I wanted to tell you. Sit down a minute...»

«No,» I said, «we can't do that. You've had your chance—I've given you a full hour. Next time you'll probably do better. It's the only way to learn.» And with that I yanked him to his feet.

He laughed in spite of himself. He held out his hand and shook hands with me warmly. «By God,» he said, «you're all right! You've got the technique down pat. I'd have done exactly the same had I been in your boots.»

I handed him his coat and hat, and started for the door to let him out.

«You're not rushing me off, are you?» he said. «Can't we have a bit of a chat first?»

«You'd like to discuss the situation, is that it?» I said, marching him to the door against his will. «That's out, Dr. Kronski. No discussions. I'll look for you to-morrow at the same hour.»

«But aren't you coming over to the house tonight?»

«NO, that's out too. Until you finish your analysis we will have no relation but that of doctor and patient. It's much better, you'll see.» I took his hand, which was hanging limp, raised it and shook him a vigorous goodbye. He backed out of the door as if dazed.

He came every other day for the first few weeks, then he begged for a stagger schedule, complaining that his money was giving out. I knew of course that it was a drain on him, because since he had given up his practise his only income was from the insurance company. He had probably salted a tidy sum away—before the accident. And his wife, to be sure, was working as a school-teacher—I couldn't overlook that. The problem, however, was to rout him out of his state of dependency, drain him of every penny he owned, and restore the desire to earn a living again. One would hardly have believed it possible that a man of his energies, talents, powers could deliberately castrate himself in order to get the better of an insurance company.   Undoubtedly the injuries he had sustained in the automobile accident had impaired his health.   For one thing he had become quite a monster.   Deep down I was convinced that the accident had merely accelerated the weird metamorphosis. When he popped the idea of becoming an analyst I realized that there was still a spark of hope in him. I accepted the proposition at face value, knowing that his pride would never permit him to confess that he had become «a case».   I used the word «illness» deliberately always—to give him a jolt, to make him admit that he needed help.   I also knew that, if he gave himself half a chance, he would eventually break down and put himself in my hands completely.

It was taking a big gamble, however, to presume that I could break down his pride.   There were layers of pride in him, just as there were layers of fat around his girdle.   He was one vast defense system, and his energies were constantly being consumed in repairing the leaks which sprang up everywhere. With pride went suspicion.   Above all, the suspicion that he may have misjudged my ability to handle the «case».   He had always flattered himself that he knew his friends' weak spots.   Undoubtedly he did— it's not such a difficult thing to do.   He kept alive the weaknesses of his friends in order to bolster the sense of his own superiority.   Any, improvement, any development, on the part of a friend he looked upon as a betrayal.   It brought out the envious side of his nature....   In short, it was a vicious treadmill, his whole attitude towards others.

The accident had not essentially changed him.   It had merely altered his appearance, exaggerated what

was already there latent in his being. The monster
which he had always been potentially was now a flesh
and blood fact. He could look at himself every day
in the mirror and see with his own eyes what he had
made of himself. He could see in his wife's eyes the
revulsion he created in others. Soon his children
would begin to look at him strangely—that would be
the last straw.

By attributing everything to the accident he had
succeeded in gathering a few crumbs of comfort from
the unwary. He also succeeded in concentrating
attention upon his physique and not his psyche. But
alone with himself he knew that it was a game which
would soon peter out. He couldn't go on forever
making a smoke screen of his enormous bundle of
flesh.

When he lay on the couch unburdening himself
it was curious that no matter from what point in the
past he started out he always saw himself as strange
and monstrous. *Doomed* was more precisely the way
he felt about himself. Doomed from the very beginning. A complete lack of confidence as to his private
destiny. Naturally and inevitably he had imparted
this feeling to others; in some way or other he would
manage to so manoeuver that his friend or sweetheart
would fail him or betray him. He picked them with
the same foreknowledge the Christ displayed in choosing Judas.

What kind of drama do you want to stage?

Kronski wanted a brilliant failure, a failure so
brilliant that it would outshine success. He seemed
to want to prove to the world that he could know as
much and be as much as anybody, and at the same
time prove that it was pointless—to be anything or
to know anything. He seemed congenitally incapable
of realizing that there is an inherent significance in
everything. He wasted himself in an effort to prove

that there could never be any final proofs, never for
a moment conscious of the absurdity of defeating
logic with logic.   It reminded me, his attitude, of the
youthful Céline saying with furious disgust: «She
could go right ahead and be even lovelier, a hundred
thousand times more luscious, she wouldn't get any
change out of me—not a sigh, not a sausage.   She
could try every trick and wile imaginable, she could
striptease for all she was worth to please me, rupture
herself, or cut off three fingers of her hand, *she could
sprinkle her short hairs with stars*—but never would
I talk, never!   Not the smallest whisper.   I should
say not!   That's all there was about it....
    The variety of defense works with which the
human being hedges himself in is just as astounding
as the visible defense mechanisms in the animal and
insect worlds.   There is a texture and substance even
to the psychic fortifications, as you discover when
you begin to penetrate the forbidden precincts of the
ego.   The most difficult ones are not necessarily those
who hide behind a plate of armor, be it of iron, steel,
tin or zinc.   Neither are they so difficult, though they
offer greater resistance, who encase themselves in
rubber and who, *mirabile dictu*, appear to have
acquired the art of vulcanizing the perforated barriers
of the soul.   The most difficult ones are what I
would call the «Piscean malingerers».   These are the
fluid, solvent egos who lie still as a fœtus in the
uterine marshes of their stagnant self.   When you
puncture the sac, when you think Ah! I've got you
at last! you find nothing but clots of mucus in your
hand.   These are the baffling ones, in my opinion.
They are like the «soluble fish» of Surrealist metem-
psychology.   They grow without a backbone; they
dissolve at will.   All you can ever lay hold of are the
indissoluble, indestructible nuclei—the disease germs,
so to say.   About such individuals one feels that in

body, mind and soul they are nothing but disease. They were born to illustrate the pages of text-books. In the realm of the psyche they are the gynaecological monsters whose only life is that of the pickled specimen which adorns the laboratory shelf.

Their most successful disguise is compassion. How tender they can become! How considerate! How touchingly sympathetic! But if you could ever get a look at them—just one fluorescent glance!—what a pretty egomaniac you would see. They bleed with every bleeding soul in the universe—but they never fall apart. At the crucifixion they hold your hand and slake your thirst, weep like drunken cows. They are the professional mourners from time immemorial; they were so even in the Golden Age, when there was nothing to weep about. Misery and suffering is their habitat, and at the equinox they bring the whole kaleidoscopic pattern of life to a glaucous glue....

There is something about analysis which reminds one of the operating room. By the time one is ready to be analyzed it is usually too late. Confronted with a battered psyche the only recourse open to the analyst is to do a plastic job. The good analyst prefers to give his psychic cripple artificial limbs rather than crutches, that's about the long and short of it.

But sometimes the analyst is given no choice, as happens now and then to the surgeon on the battle-field. Sometimes the surgeon has to amputate arms and legs, concoct a new face out of an unrecognizable piece of pulp, clip the balls off, devise an ingenious rectum and God only knows what—if he has the time for it. It would be kinder to kill such a wreck off, but that's one of the ironies of the civilized way of life—you try to preserve the remnants. Now and then, in the horrible annals of surgery, you come across astonishing specimens of vitality who are

truncated and pared down to an uncouth torso, a sort
of human pear which a Brancusi might refine into an
objet d'art. You read that this human what-not
supports his aged mother and father from the earnings
of his incredible craft, a craft in which the only tool
is the artificial mouth which the surgeon's knife
carved out of a once unrecognizable face.

There are psychical specimens of this order who
walk out of the analyst's office to take their place in
the ranks of dehumanized labor. They have been
pared down to an efficient little bundle of mutilated
reflexes. They not only earn their own living, they
support their aged relatives. They refuse the niche
of fame in the hall of horrors to which they are
entitled; they elect to compete with other souls in a
quasi-soulful way. They die hard, like knots of wood
in a giant oak. They resist the axe, even when it is
all up.

I wouldn't go so far as to say that Kronski was
of this order, but I must confess that many a time he
gave me such an impression. There was many a time
when I felt like swinging the axe and finishing him
off. Nobody would have missed him; nobody would
have mourned his loss. He had got himself born a
cripple and a cripple he would die, that's how it
struck me. As an analyst I couldn't see of what
benefit he would be to others. As an analyst he
would only see cripples everywhere, even among the
god-like. Other analysts, and I had known some
personally who were most successful, had recuperated
from their crippledom, so to speak, and were of use
to other cripples like themselves, because they had at
least learned to use their artificial limbs with ease and
perfection. They were good demonstrators.

There was one thought, however, which bored into
me like a gimlet during these sessions with Kronski.
It was the notion that every one, no matter how far

gone he was, could be saved. Yes, if one had infinite
time and infinite patience, it could be done. It began
to dawn on me that the healing art was not at all
what people imagined it to be, that it was something
very simple, too simple, in fact, for the ordinary
mind to grasp.

To put it in the simple way it came to my mind, I
would say that it was like this: *everybody becomes a
healer the moment he forgets about himself.* The
sickness which we see everywhere, the bitterness and
disgust which life inspires in so many of us, is only
the reflection of the sickness which we carry within
us. Prophylactics will never secure us against the
world disease, because we bear the world within. No
matter how marvelous human beings become, the sum
total will yield an external world which is painful
and imperfect. As long as we live self-consciously we
must always fail to cope with the world. It is not
necessary to die in order to come at last face to face
with reality. Reality is here and now, everywhere,
gleaming through every reflection that meets the eye.
Prisons and even lunatic asylums are emptied of their
inmates when a more vital danger menaces the community. When the enemy approaches, the political
exile is recalled to share in the defense of his
country. At the last ditch it gets dinned into our
thick skulls that we are all part and parcel of the
same flesh. When our very lives are threatened we
begin to live. Even the psychic invalid throws away
his crutches, in such moments. For him the greatest
joy is to realize that there is something more important than himself. All his life he has turned on the
spit of his own roasted ego. He made the fire with
his own hands. He drips in his own juices. He
makes himself a tender morsel for the demons he
liberated with his own hands. That is the picture
of human life on this planet called the Earth. Every-

body is a neurotic, down to the last man and woman. The healer, or the analyst, if you like, is only a super-neurotic. He has put the Indian sign on us. To be cured we must rise from our graves and throw off the cerements of the dead. Nobody can do it for another—it is a private affair which is best done collectively. We must die as egos and be born again in the swarm, not separate and self-hypnotized, but individual and related.

As to salvation and all that... The greatest teachers, the true healers, I would say, have always insisted that they can only point the way. The Buddha went so far as to say: «Believe nothing, no matter where you read it or who has said it, *not even if I have said it*, unless it agrees with your own reason and your own common sense.»

The great ones do not set up offices, charge fees, give lectures, or write books. Wisdom is silent, and the most effective propaganda for truth is the force of personal example. The great ones attract disciples, lesser figures whose mission it is to preach and to teach. These are the gospelers who, unequal to the highest task, spend their lives in converting others. The great ones are indifferent, in the profoundest sense. They don't ask you to believe: they electrify you by their behavior. They are the awakeners. What you do with your petty life is of no concern to them. What you do with your life is only of concern to *you*, they seem to say. In short, their only purpose here on earth is to inspire. And what more can one ask of a human being than that?

To be sick, to be neurotic, if you like, is to ask for guarantees. The neurotic is the flounder that lies on the bed of the river, securely settled in the mud, waiting to be speared. For him death is the only certainty, and the dread of that grim certainty immo-

bilizes him in a living death far more horrible than
the one he imagines but knows nothing about.

The way of life is towards fulfillment, however,
wherever it may lead. To restore a human being to
the current of life means not only to impart self-
confidence but also an abiding faith in the processes
of life. A man who has confidence in himself *must*
have confidence in others, confidence in the fitness
and rightness of the universe. When a man is thus
anchored he ceases to worry about the fitness of
things, about the behavior of his fellow-men, about
right and wrong and justice and injustice. If his
roots are in the current of life he will float on the
surface like a lotus and he will blossom and give
forth fruit. He will draw his nourishment from
above and below; he will send his roots down deeper
and deeper, fearing neither the depths nor the
heights. The life thats is in him will manifest itself
in growth, and growth is an endless, eternal process.
He will not be afraid of withering, because decay and
death are part of growth. As a seed he began and
as a seed he will return. Beginnings and endings are
only partial steps in the eternal process. The process
is everything... the way... the Tao.

The way of life! A grand expression. Like saying
Truth. There is nothing beyond it... it is all.

And so the analyst says «Adapt yourself!» He
does not mean, as some wish to think—adapt yourself
to this rotten state of affairs! He means: adapt
yourself to life! *Become an adept!* That is the
highest adjustment—to make oneself an adept.

The delicate flowers are the first to perish in a
storm; the giant is laid low by a sling-shot. For
every height that is gained new and more baffling
dangers menace us. The coward is often buried
beneath the very wall against which he huddled in
fear and anguish. The finest coat of mail can be

penetrated by a skillful thrust. The greatest armadas are eventually sunk; Maginot lines are always circumvented. The Trojan horse is always waiting to be trotted out. Where then does security lie? What protection can you invent that has not already been thought of? It is hopeless to think of security: there is none. The man who looks for security, even in the mind, is like a man who would chop off his limbs in order to have artificial ones which will give him no pain or trouble.

In the insect world is where we see the defense system par excellence. In the gregarious life of the animal world we see another kind of defense system. By comparison the human being seems a helpless creature. In the sense that he lives a more exposed life he is. But this ability to expose himself to every risk is precisely his strength. A god would have no recognizable defense whatever. He would be one with life, moving in all dimensions freely.

Fear, hydra-headed fear, which is rampant in all of us, is a hang-over from lower forms of life. We are straddling two worlds, the one from which we have emerged and the one towards which we are heading. That is the deepest meaning of the word human, that were are a link, a bridge, a promise. It is in us that the life process is being carried to fulfillment. We have a tremendous responsibility, and it is the gravity of that which awakens our fears. We know that if we do not move forward, if we do not realize our potential being, we shall relapse, sputter out, and drag the world down with us. We carry Heaven and Hell within us; we are the cosmogonic builders. We have choice—and all creation is our range.

For some it a terrifying prospect. It would be better, think they, if Heaven were above and Hell below—anywhere outside, but not within. But that

comfort has been knocked from under us. There are
no places to go to, either for reward or punishment.
The place is always here and now, in your own person
and according to your own fancy. The world is
exactly what you picture it to be, always, every
instant. It is impossible to shift the scenery about
and pretend that you will enjoy another, a different
act. The setting is permanent, changing with the
mind and heart, not according to the dictates of an
invisible stage director. You are the author, director
and actor all in one: the drama is always going to be
your own life, not some one else's. A beautiful,
terrible, ineluctable drama, like a suit made of your
own skin. Would you want it otherwise? Could
you invent a better drama?

Lie down, then, on the soft couch which the analyst
provides, and try to think up something different.
The analyst has endless time and patience; every
minute you detain him means money in his pocket.
He is like God, in a sense—the God of your own
creation. Whether you whine, howl, beg, weep,
implore, cajole, pray or curse—he listens. He is just
a big ear minus a sympathetic nervous system. He
is impervious to everything but truth. If you think
it pays to fool him then fool him. Who will be the
loser? If you think he can help you, and not
yourself, then stick to him until you rot. He has
nothing to lose. But if you realize that he is not a
god but a human being like yourself, with worries,
defects, ambitions, frailties, that he is not the reposi-
tory of an all-encompassing wisdom but a wanderer,
like yourself, along the path, perhaps you will cease
pouring it out like a sewer, however melodious it may
sound to your ears, and rise up on your own two legs
and sing with your own God-given voice. To confess,
to whine, to complain, to commiserate, always
demands a toll. To sing it doesn't cost you a penny.

Not only does it cost nothing—you actually enrich others. *Sing the praises of the Lord,* it is enjoined. Aye, sing out! Sing out, O Master-builder! Sing out, glad warrior! *But,* you quibble, how can I sing when the world is crumbling, when all about me is bathed in blood and tears? Do you realize that the martyrs sang when they were being burned at the stake? They saw nothing crumbling, they heard no shrieks of pain. They sang because they were full of faith. Who can demolish faith? Who can wipe out joy? Men have tried, in every age. But they have not succeeded. Joy and faith are inherent in the universe. In growth there is pain and struggle; in accomplishment there is joy and exuberance; in fulfillment there is peace and serenity. Between the planes and spheres of existence, terrestrial and super-terrestrial, there are ladders and lattices. The one who mounts sings. He is made drunk and exalted by unfolding vistas. He ascends surefootedly, thinking not of what lies below, should he slip and lose his grasp, but of what lies ahead. *Everything lies ahead.* The way is endless, and the farther one reaches the more the road opens up. The bogs and quagmires, the marshes and sink-holes, the pits and snares, are all in the mind. They lurk in waiting, ready to swallow one up the moment one ceases to advance. The phantasmal world is the world which has not been fully conquered over. It is the world of the past, never of the future. To move forward clinging to the past is like dragging a ball and chain. The prisoner is not the one who has committed a crime, but the one who clings to his crime and lives it over and over. We are all guilty of crime, the great crime of not living life to the full. But we are all potentially free. We can stop thinking of what we have failed to do and do whatever lies within our power. What these powers that are in us may

be no one has truly dared to imagine. That they
are infinite we will realize the day we admit to
ourselves that imagination is everything. Imagination
is the voice of daring. If there is anything God-like
about God it is that. He dared to imagine everything.

15

Everybody took Mona and Rebecca for sisters.
Outwardly they seemed to have everything in common; inwardly there wasn't the slightest link between
them. Rebecca, who never denied her Jewish blood,
lived completely in the present; she was normal,
healthy, intelligent, ate with gusto, laughed heartily,
talked easily and, I imagine, fucked well and slept
well. She was thoroughly adapted, thoroughly
anchored, able to live on any plane and make the
best of it. She was everything that a man could
desire in a wife. She was a real female. In her
presence the average American woman looked like a
bundle of defects.

Her special quality was her earthiness. Born in
Southern Russia, having been spared the horrors of
ghetto life, she reflected the grandeur of the simple
Russian people among whom she grew up. Her spirit
was large and flexible, robust and supple at the same
time. She was a Communist by instinct, because her
nature was simple, wholesome and all of a piece.

Though she was the daughter of a rabbi, she had
emancipated herself at an early age. From her father
she had inherited that acumen and integrity which
from time immemorial have given to the pious Jew
that distinctive aura of purity and strength. Meekness

and hypocrisy were never the attributes of the devout
Jew; their weakness, as with the Chinese, has been
an undue reverence for the written word. For them
the Word has a significance almost unknown to the
Gentile. When they become exalted they glow like
letters of fire.

As for Mona, it was impossible to guess what her
origins were. For a long time she had maintained
that she was born in New Hampshire and that she
had been educated in a New England college. She
could have passed for a Portuguese, a Basque, a Rou-
manian gypsy, a Hungarian, a Georgian, anything she
chose to make you believe. Her English was impec-
cable and, to most observers, without the slightest
trace of accent. She might have been born anywhere,
because the English she spoke was obviously an
English she had mastered in order to frustrate all
such inquiries as relate to origins and antecedents.
In her presence the room vibrated. She had her
own wave length: it was short, powerful, disruptive.
It served to break down other transmissions, especially
those which threatened to effect real communication
with her. She played like lightning over a storm-
tossed sea.

There was something disturbing to her in the
atmosphere created by the coming together of such
strong individualities as composed the new menage.
She felt a challenge which she was not quite able to
meet. Her passport was in order but her luggage
excited suspicion. At the end of every encounter
she had to reassemble her forces, but it was evident,
even to herself, that her forces were becoming frayed
and diminished. Alone in our little room—the
cubicle—I would nurse her wounds and endeavor to
arm her for the next encounter. I had to pretend,
of course, that she had acquitted herself admirably.
Often I would rehearse some of the statements she

had made, altering them subtly or amplifying them
in an unexpected way, in order to give her the clue
she was searching for. I tried never to humiliate
her by forcing her to ask a direct question. I knew
just where the ice was thin and I skated about these
dangerous zones with the adroitness and agility of a
professional. In this way I patiently endeavored to
fill in those gaps which were distressingly blatant in
one who was supposed to have graduated from such
a venerable institution of learning as Wellesley.

It was a strange, awkward and embarrassing game.
I was surprised to detect in myself the germination
of a new sentiment towards her: *pity*. It was incomprehensible to me that, forced to show her hand,
she should not have taken refuge in frankness. She
knew that I knew, but she would insist on keeping
up pretences. Why? Why with *me?* What had
she to fear? That I had detected her weakness had
in no way diminished my love. On the contrary, it
had increased it. Her secret had become mine, and
in protecting her I was protecting myself also. Could
she not see that in arousing my pity she was only
strengthening the bond between us? But perhaps
that was not her great concern; perhaps she took for
granted that the bond would grow with the years.

To make herself invulnerable—that was her
obsessive concern. Detecting that, my pity expanded
immeasurably. It was almost as if I had suddenly
discovered that she was a cripple. That happens
now and then, when two people fall in love. And
if it is love which has united two people then a
discovery of that sort serves only to intensify the
love. One is not only eager to overlook the duplicity
of the unfortunate one, one makes a violent and unnatural effort towards identification. «Let *me* carry
the burden of your sweet defect!» That is the cry
of the love-sick heart. Only an ingrained egotist can

evade the shackles imposed by an unequal match.
The one who loves thrills at the thought of greater
tests; he begs mutely that he be permitted to put
his hand in the flame. And if the adorable cripple
insists on playing the game of pretence then the heart
already open and enfolding yawns with the aching
void of the grave. Then not only the defect, but
the body, soul and spirit of the loved one are
swallowed up in what is veritably a living tomb.

It was Rebecca who really put Mona on the rack.
Better said, she permitted Mona to put herself on the
rack. Nothing could induce her to play the game
as Mona demanded that it be played. She stood
firm as a rock, yielding not an inch one way or the
other. She showed neither pity nor cruelty; she was
adamant against all those wiles and seductions which
Mona knew how to employ with women as well as
with men. The fundamental contrast between the
two «sisters» became more and more glaring. The
antagonism, more often silent than spoken, revealed
with dramatic clarity the two poles of the feminine
soul. Superficially Mona resembled the type of the
eternal feminine. But Rebecca, whose ample nature
had no superficies, had the plasticity and fluidity of
the real female who, throughout the ages and without
abdication of her individuality, has transformed the
outlines of her soul in accordance with the changing
image which man creates in order to focus the imperfect instrument of his desires.

The creative side of the female operates imper-
ceptibly: its province is the potential man. When its
play is unrestricted the level of the race is raised.
One can always gauge the level of a period by the
status of its womankind. Something more than
freedom and opportunity are here involved, because
woman's true nature never expresses itself in demands.
Like water, woman always finds her own level. And

like water also, she mirrors faithfully all that passes in the soul of man.

What is called «truly feminine» therefore is only the deceptive masquerade which the uncreative male blindly accepts as the real show. It is the flattering substitute which the thwarted female offers in self-defense. It is the homosexual game which Narcissism exacts. It is most flagrantly revealed when the partners are extremely masculine and feminine. It can be mimicked most successfully in the shadow play of the avowed homosexuals. It reaches its blind culmination in the Don Juan. Here the pursuit of the unattainable reaches the burlesque proportions of a Chaplinesque pursuit. The end is always the same: Narcissus drowning in his own image.

A man can only begin to understand the depths of woman's nature when he surrenders his soul unequivocally. It is only then that he begins to grow and truly to fecundate her. There are then no limits to what he may expect of her, because in surrendering he has delimited his own powers. In this sort of union, which is realy a marriage of spirit with spirit, a man comes face to face with the meaning of creation. He participates in an experiment which he realizes will always be beyond his feeble comprehension. He senses the drama of the earth-bound and the role which woman plays in it. The very possessivity of woman takes on a new light. It becomes as enchanting and mysterious as the law of gravitation.

A strange four-cornered battle was going on between us, with Kronski acting as referee and goad. While Mona vainly endeavored to traduce and seduce Rebecca, Arthur Raymond was doing his utmost to convert me to his way of thinking. Though neither of us made any outright allusion to the subject, it was evident that he thought me neglectful of Mona and I thought him unappreciative of Rebecca. In all our discussions I was always championing Rebecca or she me, and Mona and he were doing the same, of course. Kronski, in the true spirit of referee, saw to it that we were kept on our toes. His wife, who never had anything to contribute, usually grew sleepy and retired from the scene as quickly as possible. I had the impression that she spent the time in bed lying awake and listening, because as soon as Kronski joined her she would pitch into him and torment him for having neglected her so shamefully. The quarrel would always end with grunts and squeals followed by repeated visits to the sink which we shared in common.

Often after Mona and I had retired, Arthur Raymond would stand outside our door, asking first if we were still awake, and talk to us through the transon. I deliberately kept the door closed because in the beginning I had made the mistake of being polite and inviting him in, a fatal procedure if one had any thought of getting a night's rest. Then I fell into another error, the stupid one of being semi-polite, of answering at intervals in drugged monosyllables—Yes...No...Yes...No. As long as he sensed the faintest stir of consciousness in his listener, Arthur Raymond would carry on remorselessly. Like a Niagara he wore down the rocks and boulders which opposed his torrential flow. He would simply drown out all opposition... There is, however, a way of protecting oneself against these irresistible forces. One can learn the trick by going to Niagara Falls and observing those spectacular figures who stand with their backs against the wall of rock and watch the mighty river shooting over their heads and falling with a deafening roar into the narrow bed of the gorge. The tingle of spray to which they are subjected acts as a stimulant to their swooning senses.

Arthur Raymond seemed to be conscious that I had

discovered some sort of protection analogous to this descriptive image. His only recourse, therefore, was to wear away the upper bed of the river and rout me out of my precarious place of refuge. There was something ludicrously obstinate about such a blind and stubborn persistence, something monumentally akin to the Gargantuan strategy which Thomas Wolfe was later to employ as a novelist and which he himself must have recognized as the defect of the «perpetuum mobile» machine in giving to his great work the title *Of Time and the River*.

If Arthur Raymond had been a book I could have tossed him aside. But he was a river incarnate, and the bed through which he pulsed like a dynamo was but a few steps removed from the ledge in which we had carved a sheltering niche. Even in sleep the roar of his voice was present; we emerged from our slumbers with the stunned expression of those who have been deafened in their sleep. This force, which no one had been able to canalize or transform, became an omnipresent menace. Thinking of him in later years, I often likened him in my mind to those turbulent rivers which slip their banks and double back on their tracks, forming mighty loops like the writhings of a serpent, seeking in vain to spend their uncontrollable energies, finishing their agony by catapulting into the sea with a dozen furious mouths.

But the force which was sweeping Arthur Raymond on to nullification was at that time, by very reason of its menacing aspect, lulling and hypnotic. Like mandragores under a glass roof, Mona and I lay rooted in our own bed, which was a strictly human bed, and fertilized the egg of hermaphroditic love. When the tingle of spray ceased to splash against the glass roof of our indifference we would gurgle from the roots with that plaintive chant of the flower which is humanized by the sperm of the dying cri-

minal. The master of the toccata and fugue would
have been appalled could he have heard the reverberations which his roar engendered.

It was only a short time after we were installed in
the Palace of Time and the River that I discovered
one morning, while taking a shower, that the head
of my cock was ringed with bleeding sores. It gave
me quite a fright, needless to say. Immediately I
thought that I had contracted the «syph». And since
I had been faithful in my way I could only suppose
that Mona had given it to me.

However, it isn't in my nature to run to the doctor
at once. With us the doctor has always been looked
upon as a mountebank if not a downright criminal.
We usually wait for the surgeon who of course is in
league with the undertaker. We always pay handsomely for the perpetual care of the grave.

«It will go away of itself», I told myself, taking
my prick out twenty or thirty times a day.

It could have been a back-fire from one of those
menstrual pea-soup fucks too. Often, in fatuous
masculine pride, one mistakes the tomato juice flow
of the period for a pre-coital flow. Many a proud
dick is sunk in this Scapa Flow...

The simplest thing, of course, was to question
Mona, which I promptly proceeded to do.

«Now listen,» I said, still in good humor, «if you've
got a dose you'd better tell me. I'm not going to ask
you how you came by it... I want the thruth, that's
all.»

The directness of this made her burst out laughing.
She laughed a little too heartily, I thought.

«You could get a dose from sitting on the toilet,»
I said.

This made her laugh even more heartily—almost
hysterically.

«Or it could be a throw-back from an old dose.

I don't care when or where it happened... *have you got it, that's what I want to know.*»

The answer was No. Emphatically No! She was sobering up now and with the change came a little show of anger. How could I think up such an accusation? What did I take her for—a trollop?

«Well, if that's the case,» said I, putting a good face on it, «there's no need to worry. You don't get a clap out of thin air. I'll forget about it...»

But then it wasn't so easy to forget—just like that. In the first place the fucking was taboo. A week had passed, and a week is a long time when you're used to fucking every night and in between a piece now and then—on the wing, as it were.

Every night it stood up like a pole. I even went to the absurd length of using a condom—just once—because it hurt like hell. The only other thing to do was to play stink-finger or suck her off. I was a little leery about the latter, despite her prophylactic protestations.

Masturbation was the best substitue. In fact, it opened up a new area of exploration. Psychologically, I mean. Lying there, with my arm around her and my fingers up her crotch, she became strangely confidential. It was as though the erogenous zone of her mind were being tickled by my fingers. The juice began to spill out.... *«the dirt»*, as she had once called it.

Interesting how women dish up the truth! Often they begin with a lie, a harmless little lie, which is just a feeler. Just to see how the wind blows, don't you know. Should they sense that you're not too hurt, not too offended, they risk a morsel of truth, a few crumbs cleverly wrapped in a tissue of lies.

That wild automobile ride, for instance, which she's rehearsing under her breath. One wasn't to think for one moment that she enjoyed going out

with three strange men—and two dopey fluffs from
the dance hall. She had only consented because at
the last minute there was no other girl to be found.
And then, of course, she may have been hoping,
though she didn't know it at the time, that one of
the men might be human, might listen to her story
and help her out—with a fifty dollar bill perhaps.
(She always had her mother to fall back on: mother,
the prime cause and motivator of all crime...).

And then, as always happens on automobile rides,
they began to get fresh. If the other girls hadn't
been along it might have turned out differently; they
had their dresses up over their knees before the car
had hardly started. They had to drink too—that
was the worst of it. Of course she only pretended
to drink... swallowed just a few drops... enough to
wet her whistle... the others gulped it down. She
didn't mind so much kissing the men either—that
was nothing—but the way they grabbed her right
away... pulling her teats out and running their hands
up her legs... the two of them at once. They must
have been Italians, she thought. Lecherous brutes.

Then she confessed to something which I knew
was a god-damned lie, but it was interesting just the
same. One of those «deformations» or «displace-
ments», as in dreams. Yes, you see, oddly enough
the other two girls felt sorry for her... sorry that
they had got her into such a pickle. They knew she
wasn't in the habit of sleeping with every Tom, Dick
and Harry. So they stopped the car and changed
seats, letting her sit up front with the hairy guy who
had seemed decent and quiet thus far. They sat on
the men's laps in the back, their dresses raised, facing
forward, and while smoking their cigarettes and
laughing and drinking, they let the men in the rear
have their fill of pleasure.

«And what did the other guy do while this was going on?» I finally felt impelled to ask.

«He didn't do anything,» she said. «I let him hold my hand and I talked to him as fast as I could so as to keep his mind off it.»

«Come on,» I said, «don't tell me that. Now what *did* he do—*out with it!*»

Well, anyway, he did hold her hand for a long time, believe it or not. Besides, what could he do—wasn't he driving the car?

«You mean to say he never thought of stopping the car?»

Of course he did. He tried several times, but she talked him out of it... That was the line. She was thinking desperately how to get round to the truth.

«And after a while?» I said, just to ease her over the rough spots.

«Well, all of a sudden he dropped my hand...» She paused.

«Go on!»

«And then he grabbed it again and placed it in his lap. His fly was open and it was standing up... and twitching. It was a tremendous thing. I got terribly frightened. But he wouldn't let me take my hand away. I had to jerk him off. Then he stopped the car and tried to push me out. I begged him not to throw me out. 'Drive on slowly,' I said, 'I'll do it... later. I'm frightened.' He wiped himself with a handkerchief and started going again. Then he began talking the vilest filth...»

«Like what? Just what did he say, do you remember?»

«Oh, I don't want to talk about it... it was disgusting.»

«Since you've told me this much I don't see why you hesitate over words,» I said. «What's the difference... you might as well...»

«All right, if you want it... 'You're just the kind
I like to fuck,' he said. 'I've been meaning to fuck
you for a long time. I like the turn of your ass.
I like your teats. You're no virgin—what the hell
are you so delicate about? You've been fucked all
over the lot—you're cunt right up to the eyes'—and
things like that.»

«You're making me horny,» I said. «Go on, tell
me everything.»

I could see now that she was only too delighted
to get it off her chest. We didn't have to pretend
anything any more—we were both enjoying it.

The men in the rear seat wanted to swap, it seems.
That really frightened her. «The only thing I could
do was to pretend that I wanted to be fucked by the
other one first. He wanted to stop at once and get
out. 'Drive slowly,' I coaxed, 'I'll give it to you
afterwards... I don't want them all on me at once.
I grabbed his prick and began to massage it. It was
stiff in a minute... even bigger than before. Jesus,
I tell you, Val, I never felt a tool like that before.
He must have been an animal. He made me grab
his balls too—they were heavy and swollen. I jerked
it fast, hoping to make him come quick...»

«Listen,» I interrupted, getting excited by the tale
of the big horse cock, «let's talk straight. You must
have wanted a fuck bad, with that thing in your
hand...»

«Wait,» she said, her eyes glittering. She was as
wet as a goose now from the massaging I was giving
her all the while...

«Don't make me come now,» she begged, «or I
won't be able to finish the story. Jesus, I never
thought you'd want to hear all this.» She closed her
legs on my hand, so as not to get too excited. «Listen,
kiss me...» and she ran her tongue down my throat.
«Oh God, I wish we could fuck now. This is torture.

You've got to get that tended to soon... I'll go crazy...»

«Don't get off the track... Now what next? What did he do?»

«He grabbed me by the neck and forced my head down into his lap. 'I'm going to drive slow like you said,' he mumbled, 'and I want you to suck that off. After that I'll be ready to give you a fuck, a good one.' It was so enormous I thought I'd choke. I felt like biting it. Honest, Val, I never saw anything like it. He made me do everything. 'You know what I want,' he said. 'Use your tongue. You've had a prick in your mouth before.' Finally he began to move up and down, to slide it in and out. All the time he held me by the neck. I was nearly crazy. Then he came—ugh! it was filthy! I thought he'd never stop coming. I pulled my head away quickly and he shot a stream of it into my face— like a bull.»

By this time I was on the verge of coming myself. My prick was dancing like a wet candle. «Clap or no clap, I'm going to fuck to-night,» thought I to myself.

She went on with the story after a lull. How he made her huddle in the corner of the car with her legs up and poked around inside of her while driving with one hand, the car zig-zagging back and forth across the road. How he made her open her cunt with her two hands and then turned the flashlight on it. How he put his cigarette inside her and made her try to inhale with her cunt. And the two in the rear leaning over and pawing her. How one of them tried to stand up and shove his prick in her mouth, but too drunk to do anything. And the girls—by this time stark naked and singing filthy songs. Not knowing where he was driving or what was coming next. «No,» she said, «I was too scared to be passion-

ate. They were capable of anything. They were
thugs. All I could think of was how to escape. I
was terrified. And all he kept saying was: 'You
wait, you lovely bitch... I'll fuck the ass off you.
How old are you? You wait...' And then he'd grab
himself and swing it like a club. 'When you get this
inside your cute little twat you're going to feel
something. I'll make it come out of your mouth.
How many times do you think I can do it? Guess!'
I had to answer him. 'Twice... three times?' I
guess you ain't ever had a real fuck. *Feel it!'* and
he made me hold it again while he jerked back and
forth. It was slimy and slippery... he must have
been coming all the time. *'How does it feel, sister?*
I can put another inch or two on that when I ram it
up that hole of yours. By the way, how would you
like it up the other end? Listen, when I get through
with you you won't be able to say fuck for a month.'
That's the way he talked...»

«For Christ's sake, don't stop there,» I said.
«What next?»

Well, he stopped the car, beside a field. No more
shilly-shallying. The girls in the back were trying to
put on their clothes, but the men shoved them out
without a stitch on. They were screaming. One of
them got a clout in the jaw for her pains and fell
like a log beside the road. The other one started
to clasp her hands, as if she were praying, but she
couldn't make a sound, so paralyzed with fright she
was.

« I waited for him to open the door on his side.»
said Mona. «Then I jumped out quickly and started
running across the field. My shoes came off, my feet
were cut by the thick stubble. I ran like mad and
him after me. He caught up with me and pulled
the dress off me—tore it off with one yank. Then
I saw him raise his hand and the next moment I saw

stars. There were needles in my back and needles in the sky. He was on top of me and going at it like an animal. It hurt terribly. I wanted to scream but I knew he would only strike me again. I lay there stiff with fright and let him maul me. He bit me all over—my lips and ears, my neck, my shoulders, my breasts—and never once did he stop moving— just fucking away like some crazed animal. I thought everything had broken inside me. When he pulled away I thought he had finished. I began to cry 'Stop that,' he said, 'or I'll kick you in the jaw.' My back felt as though i had been rolling in glass. He lay down flat on his back and told me to suck him off. It was still big and slimy. I think he must have had a perpetual erection. I had to obey. 'Use your tongue,' he said. 'Lick it up!' He lay there breathing heavily, his eyes rolling, his mouth wide open. Then he pulled me on top of him, bouncing me up and down like a feather, turning and twisting me as if I were made of rubber. 'That's better, eh?' he said. 'You work now, you bitch!' and he held me lightly by the waist with his two hands while I fucked with all my might. I swear Val, I didn't have a bit of feeling left—except a burning pain as though a red-hot sword had been thrust inside me. 'That's enough of that,' he said. 'Now get down on all fours—and lift your ass up high.' Then he did everything... taking it out of one place and putting it in the other. He had my head buried in the ground, right in the dirt, and he made me hold his balls with my two hands. 'Squeeze them,' he said, 'but not too hard or I'll lay you cold!' The dirt was getting in my eyes... it stung horribly. Suddenly I felt him push with all his might... he was coming again... it was hot and thick. I couldn't stand it another moment. I sank down flat on my face and I felt the stuff pour over my back. I heard him say *'God damn you!'* and then he must have struck me again because I don't remember anything until I woke up shivering with cold and found myself covered wih cuts and bruises. The ground was wet and I was alone...»

At this point the story went into another groove. And then another and another. In my eagerness to keep up with her flights I almost overlooked the point of the story, which was that she had contracted a disease. She didn't realize at first what it was. because it had announced itself in the beginning as a bad case of haemorrhoids. Lying on the wet ground had done that, she averred. At least that had been the doctor's opinion. Then came the other thing—but she had gone to the doctor in time and he had cured her.

To me, interesting as this might have been, considering that I was still concerned about the ringworms, another fact had emerged which transcended it in importance. Somehow I hadn't paid such close attention to the details of the aftermath—how she had picked herself up, begged a ride to New York, borrowed some clothes from Florrie, and so on. I remember having interrupted her to ask how long ago it was that the rape had occured and my impression is that her answer was rather vague. But suddenly, while trying to put two and two together, I realized that she was talking about Carruthers, about living at his place and cooking for him and so on. How had that happened?

«But I just told you,» she said. «I went to his place because I didn't dare to go home looking as I did. He was terribly kind. He treated me as if I were his own daughter. It was his doctor I went to—he took me there himself.»

I supposed from this that living with Carruthers meant that she had been living with him at the place where she had once given me the rendezvous, where Carruthers had walked in on us unexpectedly and where he had made a jealous scene. But I was mistaken.

«It was long before that,» she said. «He was living uptown then,» and she mentioned the name of some famous American humorist with whom Carruthers then shared a flat.

«Why you were almost a child then—unless you're lying about your age.»

I was seventeen. I had run away from home during the war. I went to New Jersey and took a job in a munitions plant. I only stayed a few months. Carruthers made me leave the job and go back to college.»

«So you did finish your studies?» I said, a bit confused by all the contradictions.

«Of course I did! I wish you'd stop insin...»

«And you met Carruthers in the munitions plant?»

«Not *in* the plant. He was working in a dye factory nearby. He used to take me into New York now and then. He was the vice-president, I think. Anyway, he could do as he pleased. He used to take me to the theatre and to night clubs... He liked to dance.»

«And you weren't living with him then?»

«No, that was later. Even uptown, after the rape, I didn't live with him. I did the cooking and the housework to show him that I was grateful for all he had done. He never asked me to be his mistress. He wanted to marry me... but he didn't have the heart to leave his wife. She was an invalid...»

«You mean sexually?»

«I told you all about *her*. What difference does it make?»

«I'm all balled up,» I said.

«But I'm telling you the truth. You asked me

to tell you everything. Now you don't believe me.»

At this moment the horrible suspicion flashed through my mind that the «rape» (and perhaps it hadn't been a rape!) had occured in a past all too recent. Perhaps the «Italian» with the insatiable prick had been nothing more than an amorous lumberman in the North words. No doubt there had been more than one «rape» pulled off on these midnight automobile rides which hot-blooded young girls indulge in after hitting up the flask. The image of her standing alone and naked in a wet field at dawn, her body covered with cuts and bruises, the uterine wall broken down the rectum mutilated, her shoes gone, her eyes black and blue... well, that was the sort of thing a romantic young lady might cook up to cover a careless lapse that ends wtih gonorrhea and haemorrhoids, though the haemorrhoids did seem a bit *gratuit*.

«I think we'd better go to the doctor to-morrow, the both of us, and have a blood test taken,» I said quietly.

«Of course I'll go with you,» she replied.

We embraced one another silently and then we slid into a long fuck.

A disquieting thought now asserted itself. I had a hunch that she would find an excuse for postponing the visit to the doctor a few days. In that time, if it were a disease that I had, I could have communicated it to her. I dismissed the thought as absurd. A doctor could probalby tell by examination whether she had given it to me or I to her. And how could I have caught a dose, except through her?

Before we dozed off I learned that she had had her hymen broken at the age of fifteen. That too was her mother's fault. Yes, they had been driving her crazy at home by their talk of money, money,

money all the time. So she had taken a job as a cashier in a little cage in front of a movie house. It wasn't long before the proprietor, who owned a string of movie houses throughout the country, had taken notice of her. He had a Rolls Royce car, wore the best clothes, spats lemon-colored gloves, a boutonniere and everything that goes with the part. He was rolling in money. Always peeling off hundred dollar bills from his big wad. Fingers studded with diamond rings. Nails beautifully manicured. A man of undefinable age, probably in his late forties. A highly sexed man of leisure who was always on the prowl. She had accepted his gifts of course—but no monkey business. She knew she could twine him around her finger.

But then there was the pressure at home. No matter what she threw down on the table it was never enough.

So when he asked her one day if she would like to go to Chicago with him and open up a new theatre there she consented. She was certain she could handle him all right. Besides, she was dying to get out of New York, away from her parents, and so on.

He behaved like a perfect gentleman. Everything was going beautifully—he had given her a substantial raise, had bought her clothes, had taken her to the best places, all just as she had imagined it would be. Then, one night after dinner (he had bought tickets for the theatre) he came out with it bluntly. He wanted to know if she was still a virgin. She had been only too eager to tell him yes, thinking that her virginity was her protection. But to her amazement he then began a most frank and brutal confession in which he revealed the fact that his one and only obsession was to deflower young girls. He even confessed that it had cost him a pretty penny and had got him into serious scrapes. Apparently, however,

he could do nothing to curb this passion. It was
perverse, he confessed, but since he had the means to
indulge his vice he had not bothered to cure it. He
insinuated that there was nothing brutal about his
procedure. He had always treated his victims with
kindness and consideration. After all, they might
well regard him as a benefactor later on. Sooner or
later every young woman has to surrender her
maidenhood. He would even go so far as to say
that, since it had to be done, it were better to entrust
the operation to a professional, a connoisseur, so to
speak. Many young husbands were so clumsy and
ineffectual that they often caused their wives to become frigid. Many a marital wreck might be traced
back to that first night, he insisted smoothly and
with undeniable truth.

In short, to hear her relate the incident, he was a
most excellent pleader, skilled not only in the art of
defloration but in the art of seduction.

«I thought to myself,» said Mona, «that if it was
to be just once I could let myself do it. He had
told me he would pay me a thousand dollars, and I
knew what a thousand dollars meant to my mother
and father. I felt that I could trust him.»

«So you did'nt go to the theatre that night?»

«Yes, we did—but I had already promised him that
I would go throught with it. He said there was no
hurry, I wasn't to worry about it. He assured me it
wouldn't be too painful. He said he could trust me;
he had been observing me for a long time and knew
that I would behave sensibly. To prove his sircerity
he offered to give me the money first. I wouldn't
accept it. He had been very decent to me and I felt
that I ought to go through with the bargain before
accepting his money. As a matter of fact, Val, I
began to take a fancy to him. It was shrewd of him
not to push me into it. If he had I might have hated

him afterwards. As it is I'm rather grateful to him
—though it turned out to be worse than I had imagined it would.»

I was wondering to myself what she meant by this
last when to my surprise I heard her saying:

«You see, I had a very tough hymen. Sometimes
they have to operate, you know. I didn't know
anything about such things then. I thought it would
be a little painful and bloody... a few minutes... and
then... Anyway, it didn't go like that at all. It took
almost a week before he was able to break it. I must
say he enjoyed it. And he *was* gentle! Maybe he
was just fibbing about it being so tough. Maybe that
was just a gag to prolong the affair. Then too he
wasn't so powerflly built. It was short and thick. It
seemed to me he got it in all the way, but then I
was so jittery that I really couldn't say. He would
stay in me a long time, hardly moving, but hard as
a rock and twitching like a jigger. Sometimes he
took it out and played around with it on the outside.
That felt marvelous. He could do it an ungodly long
time without coming. He said I was built perfectly...
that once the skin was perforated I would be wonderful to go to bed with. He didn't use foul language—
like that other brute. He was a sensualist. He
watched me, told me how to move, showed me all
sorts of tricks... It might have gone on much longer,
God knows, if I hadn't got terribly excited one night.
It was driving me crazy, especially when he pulled
out and started rubbing it around the lips...»

«You really enjoyed it then?» I said.

«Enjoyed it? I was wild. I know I shocked him
to death when finally I couldn't stand it any longer
and I grabbed him and pulled him down on me with
all my strenght. '*Fuck*, damn you!' I said, and I
pressed against him and bit his lips. He lost his
control then and he began to go at it with a vengeance.

Even after he had pierced it, though it hurt, I kept on pushing. I must have had four or five orgasms. I wanted to feel it penetrate all the way. Anyway, I had no shame or embarrassment. I wanted to be fucked and I didn't care any more how much it hurt.»

I was wondering if she would tell me truthfully how long this affair had lasted—after the technical side of it was over. I had my answer almost immediately. She was amazingly frank about it. It seemed to me that there was an unusual warmth about her reminiscences. Made me realize how grateful women are when they have been handled with understanding.

«I was his mistress for quite a while,» she continued. «I was always expecting him to get tired of me, because he had emphasized so strongly that he could only get passionate about a virgin. Of course I was still a virgin, in a sense. I was terribly young, though people always took me for eighteen or nineteen. He taught me a lot. I went everywhere with him, all over the country. He was very fond of me and he always treated me with the greatest consideration. One day I noticed that he was jealous. I was surprised because I knew he had had many women—I didn't think he loved me. 'But I do love you,' he said, when I teased him about it. Then I became curious. I wanted to know how long he expected it to go on, this affair. I was always anticipating the moment when he would find another girl whom he would want to deflower. I dreaded meeting a young girl in his presence.»

«'But I'm not thinking about another girl,' he told me. 'I want *you*... and I'm going to hold on to you.'»

«'But you told me...' I started to say, and then I saw him laugh.... and I realized at once what an idiot I had been. 'So that was how you got me, eh?' I said. And then I felt vengeful. It was foolish of me because he hadn't done anything to hurt me. But I wanted to humiliate him.»

«You know, I really despise myself for what I did,» she went on. «He didn't deserve to be treated that way But I derived a cruel satisfaction in making him suffer. I flirted with every man I met—outrageously. I even went to bed with some of them, and then I told him about it and gloated over it when I saw how much it hurt him. 'You're young,' he used to say. 'You don't understand what you're doing.' It was true enough, but I only understood one thing— that I had the better of him, and that even if I had sold myself to him he was my slave. I delighted in taunting him about his money. 'Go and buy yourself another virgin,' I would say. 'You can probably get them cheaper than a thousand dollars. I would have said yes if you had offered five hundred. You could have had me for nothing if you had been a little cleverer. If I had your money I'd choose a new one every night.' I would go on like that until he couldn't stand it any longer. One night he proposed marriage. He swore he would divorce his wife instantly—if I would only say yes. He said he couldn't live without me. 'But I can live without you,' I answered. He winced. 'You're cruel,' he said. 'You're unjust.' I had no intention of marrying him, no matter how sincere he was. I didn't care about his money. I don't know why I abused him so. Afterwards, after I had left him, I felt thoroughly ashamed of myself. I went back to him once and I begged his forgiveness. He was living with another girl—he told me so at once. 'I would never have been unfaithful to you.' he said. 'I loved you. I wanted to do things for you. I didn't expect you to stay with me forever. But you were too headstrong... you were too proud.' He talked to me the way my father would have talked. I felt like weeping... Then I did something I never

dreamt I could do. I begged him to take me to bed.
He was trembling with passion. He was so damned
decent, however, that he didn't have the heart to
take advantage of me. 'You don't want to go to bed
with me,' he said, 'you just want to prove to me that
you're repentant.' I insisted that I wanted to sleep
with him, that I liked him as a lover. He could
hardly resist any longer. But he was afraid, I
suppose, of what would happen to him. He didn't
want to begin craving for me again, that was it. But
I was thinking only of paying him back. I didn't
know how else to do it. I knew he loved me, my
body and everything. I wanted to make him happy,
even if it did upset him... It was all very confusing.
Anyway, we got in bed, but he couldn't get an
erection. I never knew that to happen before. I
tried everything. I enjoyed humiliating myself. As
I was sucking him off I was smiling to myself, thinking how strange it was that I had to sweat like this
over a man I despised... Nothing happened. I said
I'd come back next day and try again. He looked
at me as if he were appalled at the idea. 'You were
patient with me in the beginning, remember?' I said.
'Why shouldn't I be patient now?' It's crazy,' he
said. 'You don't love me. You're just giving yourself
like a whore.' 'That's what I am now,' I said... '*a
whore.*' He took me literally. He looked frightened,
thoroughly frightened...»

I waited to hear the rest of it. Did you go back?»
I asked.

No, she hadn't gone back. She never went near
him again.

«He must have lived on tenterhooks,» I said to
myself.

The next morning I reminded her of our proposed
visit to the doctor. I told her I would phone her
later in the day and ask her to meet me at the doctor's

office. I would have to consult Kronski about it. She was perfectly amenable. Anything I wanted.

Well, we visited the doctor Kronski had elected, we had blood tests taken, and we even had dinner with the doctor. He was a young man and not overly sure of himself, I thougt. He didn't know what to make of my cock. Wanted to know if I had ever had a dose—or the «syph». I told him I had had the clap twice. Had it ever come back? Not that I knew of. And so on. He thought it best to wait a few days before doing anything. In the meantime he'd have analyzed our blood. He thought we both looked healthy, though looks were often deceptive. In short, he talked around and about, as young doctors often do—and old ones too—leaving us none the wiser.

Between the first and second visits I had to visit Maude. I told her all about it. She of course was convinced that Mona was responsible. She had expected as much. It was laughable, really, what an interest she took in my sick dick. As though it were still her private property. I had to take it out and show it to her, b'Jesus. She handled it gingerly at first. but then, her professional interest aroused and the thing growing heavier in her hand all the while, she became less and less cautious. I had to be careful not to get too excited or I might have thrown caution to the winds. At any rate, before permitting me to shove it back in my fly she begged me to let her bathe it gently in a solution. She was sure that could do no harm. So I went to the bathroom with her, my prick stiff as a rod, and I watched her pet it and pamper it.

When we visited the doctor again we learned that the signs were all negative. However, he explained, even that didn't constitute a final proof.

«You know,» he said—evidently he had been thinking it over before our arrival—«I've been thinking that you'd be much better off if you were circumcised. When the foreskin is removed that stuff will come off too. You've got an uncommonly long foreskin—hasn't it bothered you?»

I confessed I had never given it a thought before. One is born with a foreskin and one dies with it. Nobody thinks about his appendix until it's time to have it cut out.

«Yes,» he went on, «you'd be lots better off without that foreskin. You'd have to go to the hospital, of course... it might take about a week or so.»

«And what would that cost?» I inquired, picking up the scent.

He couldn't say exactly—perhaps a hundred dollars.

I told him I'd think it over. I wasn't too keen about losing my precious foreskin, even if there were hygienic advantages attached to it. A funny thought then entered my head—that thereafter the head of my cock would be insensitive. I didn't like that idea at all.

However, before I left his office he had persuaded me to make a date with his surgeon for a week hence. «If it should clear up in the meantime you won't need to go through with the operation—if you don't like the idea.»

«*But*,» he added, «if I were you I'd have it done whether I liked it or not. It's much cleaner. »

In the interval the nightly confessions proceeded apace. Mona had not been working at the dance hall for several weeks now and we had the evenings together. She wasn't sure what she would do next—it was always the money question which disturbed her —but she was certain she would never return to the dance hall. She seemed just as relieved as I to know that her blood test had come out all right.

«But you didn't think there was anything wrong with you, did you?»

«One never knows,» she said. «That was such a horrible place... the girls were filthy.»

«The *girls?*»

«And the men too... Don't let's talk about it.» After a short silence she laughed and said: «How would you like it if I went on the stage?»

«It would be fine,» I said. «Do you think you can act?»

«I know I can. You wait, Val, I'll show you...»

That evening we came home late and sneaked quietly into bed. Holding on to my cock she began another string of confessions. She had been wanting to tell me something... I wasn't to get angry... I wasn't to interrupt her. I had to promise.

I lay there and listened tensely. The money question again. It was always there, like a bad sore. «You didn't want me to go on staying at the dance hall, did you?» Of course I didn't. What next? I wondered.

Well naturally she had to find some way of raising the necessary funds. Go on! I thought to myself. Get it over with! I gave myself an anaesthetic and listened to her without opening my trap. It was all quite painless, strange to relate. She was talking about old men, nice old men whom she had become acquainted with at the dance hall. What they wanted was to have the company of a beautiful young girl— some one they could eat with and take to the theatre. They didn't really care about dancing—or even going to bed with a girl. They wanted to be *seen* with young women—it made them feel younger, gayer, more hopeful. They were all successful old bastards —with false teeth and varicose veins and all that sort of thing. They didn't know what to do with their money. One of them, the one she was talking about,

owned a big steam laundry. He was over eighty,
brittle, blue-veined, glassy-eyed. He was almost a
child. Surely I couldn't be jealous of *him!* All he
asked of her was permission to spend his money on
her. She didn't say how much he had already forked
out, but she inferred it was a tidy sum. And now
there was another one—he lived at the Ritz Carlton.
A shoes manufacturer. She sometimes ate in his
room, because it gave him pleasure. He was a multi-
millionaire—and a little gaga, to believe her words.
At the most he had only courage enough to kiss her
hand... Yes, she had been meaning to tell me about
these things for weeks, but she had been afraid I
might take it badly. «You don't, do you?» she said,
bending over me. I didn't answer immediately. I
was thinking, wondering, puzzling over it all. «Why
don't you say something?» she said, nudging me.
«You said you wouldn't be angry. You promised.»

«I'm not angry,» I said. And then I grew silent
again.

«But you are! You're hurt.... O Val, you're so
foolish. Do you think I would tell you these things
if I thought you would be hurt?»

«I don't think anything,» I said. «It's all right,
believe me. Do whatever you think best. I'm only
sorry that it has to be this way.»

«But it won't always be this way! It's just for a
little while... That's why I want to get in the theatre.
I hate it just as much as you do.»

«O. K.» I said. «Let's forget about it.»

The morning that I was to report to the hospital I
woke up early. As I was taking my shower I looked
at my prick and by crikey there wasn't a sign of
irritation. I could hardly believe my eyes. I woke
Mona and showed it to her. She kissed it. I got in
bed again and tore off a quick one—to test it out.
Then I went to the telephone and called the doctor.

«It's all better,» I said, «I'm not going to have my foreskin cut off.» I hung up quickly in order to forestall any further persuasions on his part.

As I was leaving the phone booth I suddenly took it into my head to phone Maude.

«I can't believe it,» she said.

«Well, it's a fact,» I said, «and if you don't believe it I'll prove it to you when I come over next week.»

She seemed to want to hang on to the phone. Kept talking about a lot of irrelevant things «I've got to go,» I said, getting annoyed with her.

«Just a moment,» she begged. «I was going to ask you if you couldn't come over sooner, say Sunday, and take us out to the country. We might have a little picnic, the three of us. I'd do up a lunch...»

Her voice sounded very tender.

«All right» I said, «I'll come. I'll come early... about eight o'clock.»

«You're sure you're all right?» she said.

«I'm absolutely sure. I'll show it to you—Sunday.»

She gave a short, dirty little laugh. I hung up before she had closed her trap.

16

While the divorce proceedings were pending events rolled up as at the end of an epoch. It only needed a war to top it off. First of all the Satanic Majesties of the Cosmodemoniacal Telegraph Company had seen fit to shift my headquarters once again, this time to the top of an old loft building in the twine and paper box district. My desk stood in the center of an enormous deserted floor which was used as a drill room by the messenger brigade after hours. In the adjoining room, equally large and empty, a sort of combination clinic, dispensary and gymnasium was established. All that was needed to complete the picture was the installation of a few pool tables. Some of the half-wits brought their roller skates along to while away the «rest periods». It was an infernal racket they made all day long, but I was so utterly disinterested now in all the company's plans and projects that, far from disturbing me, it afforded me great amusement. I was thoroughly isolated now from the other offices. The snooping and spying had abated; I was in quarantine, so to speak. The hiring and firing went on in dreamy fashion; my staff had been cut down to two—myself and the ex-pugilist who had formerly been the wardrobe attendant.I made no effort to keep the files in order, nor did I investigate references, nor did I conduct any correspondence. Half the time I didn't bother to answer the telephone; if there were anything very urgent there was always the telegraph.

The atmosphere of the new quarters was distinctly dementia praecox. They had relegated me to hell and I was enjoying it. As soon as I got rid of the day's applicants I would go into the adjoining room and watch the shenanigans. Now and then I would put on a pair of skates myself and do a twirl with the goofy ones. My assistant looked on askance, unable to comprehend what had happened to me. Sometimes, in spite of his austerity, his «code» and other detracting psychological elements, he would break out into a laugh which would prolong itself to the verge of hysteria. Once he asked me if I was having «trouble at home». He feared that the next step would be drink, I suppose.

As a matter of fact, I did begin to indulge rather freely about this time what with one thing and another. It was a harmless sort of drinking, which began only at the dinner table. By sheer accident I had discovered a French-Italian restaurant in the back of a grocery store. The atmosphere was most convivial. Every one was a «character», even the police sergeants and the detectives who gorged themselves disgracefully at the proprietor's expense.

I had to have some place to while away the evenings, now that Mona had sneaked into the theatre by the back door. Whether Monathan had found her the job or whether, as she said, she had just lied her way in. I was never able to discover. At any rate, she had given herself a new name, one that would suit her new career, and with it a complete new history of her life and antecedents. She had become English all of a sudden, and her people had been connected with the theatre as far back as she could remember, which was often amazingly far. It was in one of the little theatres which then flourished that she made her entrance into that world of make believe which so well suited her. Since they paid her scarcely anything they could afford to act gullible.

Arthur Raymond and his wife were at first inclined to disbelieve the news. Another one of Mona's inventions, they thought. Rebecca, always poor at dissembling, practically laughed in Mona's face. But when she came home with the script of a Schnitzler play one evening and seriously began to rehearse her role their incredulity gave way to consternation. They foresaw nothing but disaster ahead. And when Mona, by some inexplicable legerdemain, succeeded in attaching herself to the Theatre Guild, the atmosphere of the household became supersaturated with envy, spite and malevolence. The play was becoming too real—there was a very real danger now that Mona might become the actress she pretended to be.

The rehearsals were endless, it seemed. I never

knew what hour Mona would return home. When
I did spend an evening with her it was like listening
to a drunk. The glamour of the new life had completely intoxicated her. Now and then I would stay
in of an evening and try to write, but it was no go.
Arthur Raymond was always there, lying in wait like
an octopus. «What do you want to write for?» he
would say. «God, aren't there enough writers in the
world?» And then he would begin to talk about
writers, the writers he admired, and I would sit before
the machine, as if ready to resume my work the
moment he left me. Often I would do nothing more
than write a letter—to some famous author, telling
him how greatly I admired his work, hinting that, if
he had not already heard of me, he would soon. In
this way it fell about one day that I received an
astonishing letter from that Dostoievski of the North,
as he was called: Knut Hamsun. It was written by
his secretary, in broken English, and for a man who
was shortly to receive the Nobel Prize, it was to say
the least a puzzling piece of dictation. After explaining that he had been pleased, even touched, by my
homage, he went on to say (through his wooden
mouthpiece) that his American publisher was not
altogether satisfied with the financial returns from
the sale of his books. They feared that they might
not be able to publish any more of his books—unless
the public were to show a more lively interest. His
tone was that of a giant in distress. He wondered
vaguely what could be done to retrieve the situation,
not so much for himself as for his dear publisher
who was truly suffering because of him. And then,
as the letter progressed, a happy idea ssemed to take
hold of him and forthwith he gave expression to it.
It was this—once he had received a letter from a
Mr. Boyle, who also lived in New York and whom
I doubtless knew (!). He thought perhaps Mr. Boyle

and myself might get together, rack our brains over the situation, and quite possibly come to some brilliant solution. Perhaps we could tell other people in America that there existed in the wilds and fens of Norway a writer named Knut Hamsun whose books had been conscientiously translated into English and were now languishing on the shelves of his publisher's stock room. He was sure that if he could only increase the sales of his books by a few hundred copies his publisher would take heart and have faith in him again. He had been to America, he said, and though his English was too poor to permit him to write me in his own hand, he was confident that his secretary could make clear his thoughts and intentions. I was to look up Mr. Boyle whose address he no longer remembered. Do what you can, he urged. Perhaps there were several other people in New York who had heard of his work and with whom we could operate. He closed on a dolorous but majestic note.... I examined the letter carefully to see if perhaps he hadn't shed a few tears over it.

If the envelope hadn't born the Norwegian postmark, if the letter itself hadn't been signed in his own scrawl, which I later confirmed, I would have thought it a hoax. Tremendous discussions ensued amid boisterous laughter. It was considered that I had been royally paid out for my foolish hero worship. The idol had been smashed and my critical faculties reduced to zero. No one could possibly see how I could ever read Knut Hamsun again. To tell the honest truth, I felt like weeping. Some terrible miscarriage had occurred, just how I couldn't fathom, but despite the evidence to the contrary, I simply could not bring myself to believe that the author of *Hunger, Pan, Victoria, Growth of the Soil*, had dictated that letter. It was entirely conceivable that he had left the matter to his secretary, that he

had signed his name in good faith without bothering
to be told the contents. A man as famous as he
undoubtedly received dozens of letters a day from
admirers all over the world. There was nothing in
my youthful panegyric to interest a man of his stature. Besides, he probably despised the whole American race, having had a bitter time of it here during
the years of his pilgrimage. Most likely he had told
his dolt of a secretary on more than one occasion
that his American sales were negligible. Perhaps his
publisher had been pestering him—publishers are
known to have only one concern in dealing with their
authors, namely sales. Perhaps he had remarked
disgustedly, in the presence of his secretary, that
Americans had money to spend on everything but
the things worth while in life. And she, poor imbecile, probably worshipful of the master, had decided
to avail herself of the opportunity and offer a few
crack-brained suggestions in order to ameliorate the
painful situation. She was more than likely no
Dagmar, no Edwige. No, not even a simple soul
like Martha Gude who tried so desperately not to
be taken in by Herr Nagel's romantic flights and
overtures. She was probably one of those educated
Norwegian head cheeses who are emancipated in
everything but the imagination. She was probably
hygienic and scientific-minded, capable of keeping
her house in order, doing harm to no one, mindful
of her own business, and dreaming one day of becoming the head of a fertilizing establishment or a
crêche for bastard children.

No, I was thoroughly disillusioned in my god. I
purposely re-read some of his books and, naive soul
that I was, I wept again over certain passages. I
was so deeply impressed that I began to wonder if
I had dreamed the letter.

The repercussions from this «miscarriage» were

quite extraordinary. I became savage, bitter, caustic.
I became a wanderer who played on muted strings
of iron. I impersonated one after another of my
idol's characters. I talked sheer rot and nonsense;
I poured hot piss over everything. I became two
people—myself and my impersonations, which were
legion.

The divorce trial was impending. That made me
even more savage and bitter, for some inexplicable
reason. I hated the farce which has to be gone
through in the name of justice. I loathed and despised the lawyer whom Maude had retained to protect her interests. He looked like a corn-fed Romain
Rolland, a chauve-souris without a crumb of humor
or imagination. He seemed to be charged with
moral indignation; he was a prick through and
through, a coward, a sneak, a hypocrite. He gave me
the creeps.

We had it out about him the day of the outing.
Lying in the grass somewhere near Mineola. The
child running about gathering flowers. It was warm,
very warm, and there was a hot dry wind blowing
which made one nervous and rooty. I had taken
my prick out and put it in her hand. She examined
it shyly, not wishing to be too clinical about it and
yet dying to convince herself that there was nothing
wrong. After a while she dropped it and rolled
over on her back, her knees up, and the warm wind
licking her bottom. I jockeyed her into a favorable
position, made her pull her panties off. She was in
one of her protesting moods again. Didn't like being
mauled like that in an open field. But there's not
a soul around, I insisted. I made her spread her
legs farther apart; I ran my hand up her cunt. It
was gooey.

I pulled her to me and tried to get it in. She
balked. She was worried about the child. I looked

around. «She's all right,» I said, «she's having a good time. She's not thinking about us.»

«But supposing she comes back... and finds us...»

«She'll think we're sleeping. She won't know what we're doing....»

With this she pushed me away violently. It was outrageous. «You'd take me in front of your own child! It's horrible.»

«It's not horrible at all. You're the one who's horrible. I tell you, it's innocent. Even if she should remember it—when she's grown up—she'll be a woman then and she'll understand. There's nothing dirty about it. It's your dirty mind, that's all.»

By this time she was slipping her panties on. I hadn't bothered to shove my prick back in my trousers. It was getting limp now; it fell on the grass, dejected.

«Well, let's have something to eat then,» I said. «If we can't fuck we can always eat.»

«Yes, *eat!* You can eat any time. That's all you care about, eating and sleeping.»

«*Fucking,*» I said, «not sleeping.»

«I wish you'd stop talking to me that way.» She began to undo the lunch. «You have to spoil everything. I thought we might have a peaceful day, just once. You always said you wanted to take us out on a picnic. You never did. Not once. You thought of nothing but yourself, your friends, your women. I was a fool to think you might change. You don't care about your child—you've hardly noticed her. You can't even restrain yourself in her presence. You'd take me in front of her and pretend that it was innocent. You're vile.... I'm glad it's all over. By this time next week I'll be free... I'll be rid of your forever. You've poisoned me. You've made me bitter and hateful. You make me despise myself. Since I know you I don't recognize myself any more.

I've become what you wanted me to become. You never loved me... *never*. All you wanted was to satisfy your desires. You've treated me like an animal. You take what you want and you go. You go from me to the next woman—any woman—just so long as she'll open her legs for you. You haven't an ounce of loyalty or tenderness or consideration in you.... Here, take it!» she said, shoving a sandwich in my fist. «I hope you choke on it!»

As I brought the sandwich to my mouth I smelled the odor of her cunt on my fingers. I sniffed my fingers while looking up at her with a grin.

«You're disgusting!» she said.

«Not so very, my lady. It smells good to me, even if you are a hateful sour-puss. I like it. It's the only thing about you I like.»

She was furious now. She began to weep.

«Weeping because I said I liked your cunt! What a woman! Jesus, I'm the one who ought to do the despising. What sort of woman are you?»

Her tears became more copious. Just then the child came running up. What was the matter? Why was mother crying?

«It's nothing,» said Maude, drying her tears. «I turned my ankle.» A few dry sobs belched from her despite her efforts to restrain herself. ·She bent over the basket and selected a sandwich for the child.

«Why don't you do something, Henry?» said the child. She sat there looking from one to the other with a grave, puzzled look.

I got to my knees and rubbed Maude's ankle.

«Don't touch me!» she said harshly.

«But he wants to make it better,» said the child.

«Yes, daddy'll make it better,» I said, rubbing the ankle gently, and then patting the calf of her leg.

«Kiss her,» said the child. «Kiss her and make the tears go away.»

I bent forward and kissed Maude on the cheek. To my astonishment she flung her arms around me and kissed me violently on the mouth. The child also put her arms around us and kissed us.

Suddenly Maude had a fresh spasm of weeping. This time it was really pitiful to behold. I felt sorry for her. I put my arms around her tenderly and comforted her.

«God,» she sobbed, «what a farce!»

«But it isn't,» I said. «I mean it sincerely. I'm sorry, sorry for everything.»

«Don't cry any more,» begged the child. «I want to eat. I want Henry to take me over there,» and she pointed with her little hand to a copse of wood at the edge of the field. «I want you to come too.»

«To think this is the only time... and it had to be like this.» She was sniffling now.

«Don't say that, Maude. The day isn't over yet. Let's forget about all that. Come on, let's eat.»

Reluctantly, wearily, it seemed, she picked up a sandwich and held it to her mouth. «I can't eat,» she murmured, dropping the sandwich.

«Come on, yes you can!» I urged, putting my arm around her again.

«You act this way now... and later you'll do something to spoil it.»

«No I won't... I promise you.»

«Kiss her again,» said the child.

I leaned over and kissed her softly and gently on the lips. She seemed really placated now. A soft light came into her eyes.

«Why can't you be like this always?» she said, after a brief pause.

«I am,» I said, «when I'm given a chance. I don't like to fight with you. Why should I? We're not man and wife any longer.»

«Then why do you treat me the way you do?

Why do you always make love to me? Why don't
you leave me alone?»

«I'm not making love to you, » I answered. «It's
not love, it's passion. That's not a crime, is it? For
God's sake, let's not start that all over again. I'm
going to treat you the way you want to be treated—
to-day. I won't touch you again.»

«I don't ask that. I don't say you shouldn't touch
me. But it's the *way* you do it... you don't show
any respect for me... for my person. That's what
I dislike. I know you don't love me any more, but
you can behave decently towards me, even if you
don't care any more. I'm not the prude you pretend
I am. I have feelings too... maybe deeper, stronger
than yours. I can find some one else to replace you,
don't think that I can't. I just want a little time...»

She was munching her sandwich half-heartedly.
Suddenly there was a gleam in her eye. She put
on a coy, roguish expression.

«I could get married to-morrow, if I wanted to,»
she continued. «You never thought that, did you?
I've had three proposals already, as a matter of fact.
The last one was from...» and here she mentioned
the lawyer's name.

«*Him?*» I said, unable to repress a disdainful smile.

«Yes, *him*,» she said. «And he's not what you
think he is. I like him very much.»

«Well, that explains things. Now I know why
he's taken such a passionate interest in the case.»

I knew she didn't care for him, this Rocambo-
lesque, any more than she cared for the doctor who
explored her vagina with a rubber finger. She didn't
care for anybody really; all she wanted was peace,
surcease from pain. She wanted a lap to sit on in
the dark, a prick to enter her mysteriously, a babble
of words to drown her unmentionable desires.
Lawyer what's-his-name would do of course. Why

not? He would be as faithful as a fountain pen, as
discreet as a rat trap, as provident as an insurance
policy. He was a walking briefcase with pigeon
holes in his belfry; he was a salamander with a heart
of pastrami. He was shocked, was he, to learn that
I had brought another woman to my own home?
Shocked to learn that I had left the used condoms
on the edge of the sink? Shocked that I had stayed
for breakfast with my paramour? A snail is shocked
when a drop of rain hits its shell. A general is
shocked when he learns that his garrison has been
massacred in his absence. God himself is shocked
doubtless when He sees how revoltingly stupid and
insensitive the human beast really is. But I doubt
if angels are ever shocked—not even by the presence
of the insane.

I was trying to give her the dialectics of the moral
dynamism. I twisted my tongue in the endeavour
to make her understand the marriage of the animal
and the divine. She understood about as well as a
layman understands when you explain the fourth
dimension. She talked about delicacy and respect,
as if they were pieces of angel cake. Sex was an
animal locked up in a zoo which one visited now
and then in order to study evolution.

Towards evening we rode back to the city, the last
stretch in the elevated train, the child asleep in my
arms. Mamma and Papa returning from the picnic
grounds. Below, the city spread out with senseless
geometrical rigidity, an evil dream rearing itself
architecturally. A dream from which it is impossible to awaken. Mr. and Mrs. Megalopolitan with
their offspring. Hobbled and fettered. Suspended
in the sky like so much venison. A pair of every
kind hanging by the hocks. At one end of the line
starvation; at the other end bankruptcy. Between
stations the pawnbroker, with three golden balls to

signify the triune God of birth, buggery and blight.
Happy days. A fog rolling in from Rockaway.
Nature folding up like a dead leaf—at Mineola.
Every now and then the doors open and shut: fresh
batches of meat for the slaughter-house. Little scraps
of conversation, like the twittering of titmice. Who
would think that the chubby little youngster beside
you will in ten of fifteen years be shitting his brains
out with fright on a foreign field? All day long you
make innocent little gadgets; at night you sit in a
dark hall and watch phantoms move across a silver
screen. Maybe the realest moments you know are
when you sit alone in the toilet and make caca.
That doesn't cost anything or commit you in any
way. Not like eating or fucking, or making works
of art. You leave the toilet and you step into the
big shit-house. Whatever you touch is shitty. Even
when it's wrapped in cellophane the smell is there.
Caca! The philosopher's stone of the industrial age.
Death and transfiguration—into shit! The department store life—with filmy silks on one counter and
bombs on the other counter. No matter what interpretation you put on it, every thought, every deed,
is cash registered. You're fucked from the moment
you draw your first breath. One grand international
business machine corporation. *Logistics,* as they say.

Mamma and Papa are now as peaceful as blut-
wurst. Not an ounce of fight left in them. How
glorious to spend a day in the open, with the worms
and other creatures of God. What a delightful
entr'acte! Life glides by like a dream. If you were
to cut the bodies open while still warm you would
find nothing resembling this idyll. If you were to
scrape the bodies out and fill them with stones they
would sink to the bottom of the sea, like dead ducks.

It begins to rain. It pours. Hail-stones big as bob-
o'-links bounce from the pavement. The city looks

like an ant pile smeared with salvarsan. The sewers
rise and disgorge their vomit. The sky is as sullen
and lurid as the bottom of a test tube.

I feel murderously gay all of a sudden. I hope
to Christ it will rain like this for forty days and
nights. I'd like to see the city swimming in its own
shit; I'd like to see mannikins floating into the river
and cash registers ground under the wheels of trucks;
I'd like to see the insane pouring out of the asylums
with cleavers and hacking right and left. The water
cure! Like they gave it to the Filipinos in '98! But
where is our Aguinaldo? Where is the rat who can
breast the flood with a machete between his lips?

I bring them home in a cab, deposit them safely
just as a bolt of lightning strikes the steeple of the
bloody Catholic church on the corner. The broken
bells make a hell of a din as they hit the pavement.
Inside the church a plaster Virgin is smashed to
smithereens. The priest is so taken by surprise that
he hasn't time to button up his pants. His balls
swell up like rocks.

Melanie flutters about like a demented albatross.
«Dry your things!» she wails. A grand undressing,
with gasps and shrieks and objurgations. I get into
Maude's dressing sack, the one with the maribou
feathers. Look like a fairy about to give an imper-
sonation of Loulou Hurluburlu. All flub and foozle
now. I'm getting a hard-on, «a personal hard-on», if
you know what I mean.

Maude is upstairs putting the child to bed. I walk
around in my bare feet, the dressing sack wide open.
A lovely feeling. Melanie peeks in, just to see if
I'm all right. She's walking around in her drawers
with the parrot perched on her wrist. Afraid of
the lightning she is. I'm talking to her with my
hands folded over my prick. Could be a scene out
of the «Wizard of Oz» by Memling. Time: *drei-*

viertel takt. Now and then the lightning strikes
afresh. It leaves the taste of burning rubber in the
mouth.

I'm standing in front of the big mirror admiring
my quivering cock when Maude trips in. She's as
frisky as a hare and all decked out in tulle and mous-
seline. She seems not at all frightened by what she
sees in the mirror. She comes over and stands beside
me. «Open it up!» I urge. «Are you hungry?» she
says, undoing herself leisurely. I turn her around
and press her to me. She raises a leg to let me get
it in. We look at each other in the mirror. She's
fascinated. I pull the wrap up over her ass so that
she can have a better look. I lift her up and she
twines her legs around me. «Yes, do it,» she begs.
«Fuck me! Fuck me!» Suddenly she untwines her
legs, unhitches. She grabs the big arm chair and
turns it around, resting her hands on the back of it.
Her ass is stuck out invitingly. She doesn't wait for
me to put it in—she grabs it and places it herself,
watching all the time through the mirror. I push
it back and forth slowly, holding my skirts up like
a bedraggled hussy. She likes to see it coming out—
how far will it come before it falls out. She reaches
under with one hand and plays with my balls. She's
completely unleashed now, as brazen as a pot. I
withdraw as far as I can without letting it slip out
and she rolls her ass around, sinking down on it now
and then and clutching it with a feathery beak.
Finally she's had enough of that. She wants to lie
down on the floor and put her legs around my neck.
«Get it in all the way,» she begs. «Don't be afraid
of hurting me... I want it. I want you to do everything.» I got it in so deep it felt as though I were
buried in a bed of mussels. She was quivering and
slithering in every ream. I bent over and sucked
her breasts; the nipples were taut as nails. Sud-

denly she pulled my head down and began to bite
me wildly—lips, ears, cheeks, neck. «You want it,
don't you?» she hissed. «You want it, you want
it....» Her lips twisted obscenely. «You want it...
you want it!» And she fairly lifted herself off the
floor in her abandon. Then a groan, a spasm, a
wild, tortured look as if her face were under a mirror
pounded by a hammer. «Don't take it out yet,» she
grunted. She lay there, her legs still slung around
my neck, and the little flag inside her began twitching and fluttering. «God,» she said, «I can't stop
it!» My prick was still firm. It hung obedient on
her wet lips, as though receiving the sacrament from
a lascivious angel. She came again, like an accor-
deon collapsing in a bag of milk. I got hornier and
hornier. I pulled her legs down and lay them flat
alongside my own. «Now don't move, damn you,»
I said. «I'm going to give it to you straight.» Slowly
and furiously I moved in and out. «Ah, ah... Oh!»
she hissed, sucking her breath in. I kept it up like
a Juggernaut. Moloch fucking a piece of bomba-
zine. Organza Friganza. The bolero in straight jabs.
Her eyes were going wild; she looked like an elephant
walking the ball. All she needed was a trunk to
trumpet with. It was a fuck to a standstill. I fell
on top of her and chewed her lips to a frazzle.

Then suddenly I thought of the douche. «Get up!
Get up!» I said, nudging her roughly.

«I don't need to,» she said weakly, giving me a
knowing smile.

«You mean...?» I looked at her in astonishment.

«Yes, there's no need to worry.... Are you all
right? Don't you want to wash?»

In the bathroom she confessed that she had been
to the doctor—another doctor. There would be
nothing to fear any more.

«So that's it?» I whistled.

She powdered my cock for me, stretched it like a glove-fitter, and then bent over and kissed it. «Oh God,» she said, flinging her arms around me, «if only....»

«If only what?»

«You know what I mean...»

I unglued myself and turning my head away, I said: «Yes, I guess I do. Anyway, you don't hate me any more, do you?»

«I don't hate any one,» she answered. «I'm sorry it's turned out the way it has. Now I'll have to share you... with her.»

«You must be hungry,» she added quickly. «Let me fix you something before you go.» She powdered her face carefully first, rouged her lips, and did her hair up negligently but attractively. Her wraps was open from the waist up. She looked a thousand times better than I had ever seen her look. She was like a bright voracious animal.

I walked around in the kitchen with my prick hanging out and helped her fix a cold snack. To my surprise she unearthed a bottle of home made wine—elderberry wine that a neighbor had given her. We closed the doors and kept the gas burning to keep warm. Jesus, it was quite wonderful. It was like getting to know one another all over again. Now and then I got up and put my arms around her, kissed her passionately while my hand slid into her crack. She wasn't at all shy or balky. On the contrary. When I pulled away, she held my hand, and then with a quick dive she fastened her mouth over my prick and sucked it in.

«You don't have to go immediately, do you?» she asked, as I sat down and resumed eating.

«Not if you don't want me to,» I said, in the most amiable state of acquiescence.

«Was it my fault,» she said, «that this never hap-

pened before? Was I such a squeamish creature?»
She looked at me with such frankness and sincerity
I hardly recognized the woman I had lived with all
these years.

«I guess we were both to blame,» I said, downing
another glass of elderberry wine.

She went to the ice-box to ferret out some delicacy.

«You know what I feel like doing?» she said,
coming back to the table with arms laden. «I'd like
to bring the gramophone down and dance. I have
some very soft needles... Would you like that?»

«Sure,» I said, «it sounds fine.»

«And let's get a bit drunk... would you mind? I
feel so wonderful. I want to celebrate.»

«What about the wine?» I said. «Is that all you
have?»

«I can get some more from the girl upstairs,» she
said. «Or maybe some cognac—would you like
that?»

«I'll drink anything... if it will make you happy.»

She started to go at once. I jumped up and
caught her by the waist. I raised her wrap and
kissed her ass.

«Let me go,» she murmured. «I'll be back in a
minute.»

As she came back I heard her whispering to the
girl from upstairs. She tapped lightly on the glass
panel. «Put something on,» she cooed, «I've got
Elsie with me.»

I went into the bathroom and wrapped a towel
around my loins. Elsie went into a fit of laughter
when she saw me. We hadn't met since the day she
found me lying in bed with Mona. She seemed in
excellent good humor and not at all embarrassed by
the turn of events. They had brought down another
bottle of wine and some cognac. And the gramophone and the records.

Elsie was in just the mood to share our little celebration. I had expected Maude to offer her a drink and then get rid of her more or less politely. But no, nothing of the kind. She wasn't at all disturbed by Elsie's presence. She did excuse herself for being half-naked, but with a good-natured laugh, as though it were just one of those things. We put a record on and I danced with Maude. The towel slipped off but neither of us made any attempt to pick it up. When we ungrappled I stood there with my prick standing out like a flag-pole and calmly reached for my glass. Elsie gave one startled look and then turned her head away. Maude handed me the towel, or rather slung it over my prick. «You don't mind, do you, Elsie?» she said. Elsie was terribly quiet—you could hear her temples hammering. Presently she went over to the machine and turned the record over. Then she reached for her glass without looking at us and gulped it down.

«Why don't you dance with her?» said Maude. «I won't stop you. Go ahead, Elsie, dance with him.»

I went up to Elsie with the towel hanging from my prick. As she turned her back to Maude she pulled the towel off and grabbed it with a feverish hand. I felt her whole body quiver, as though a chill had come over her.

«I'm going to get some candles.» Said Maude. «It's too bright in here.» She disappeared into the next room. Immediately Elsie stopped dancing, put her lips to mine and thrust her tongue down my throat. I put my hand on her cunt and squeezed it. She was still holding my cock. The record stopped. Neither of us pulled away to shut the machine off. I heard Maude coming back. Still I remained locked in Elsie's arms.

This is where the trouble starts, I thought to myself. But Maude seemed to pay no attention.

She lit the candles and then turned the electric light off. I was pulling away from Elsie when I felt her standing beside us. «It's all right,» she said. «I don't mind. Let me join in.» And with that she put her arms around the two of us and we all three began kissing one another.

«Whew! it's hot!» said Elsie, breaking away at last.

«Take your dress off, if you like,« said Maude. «I'm taking this off,» and suiting action to word she slipped out of the wrap and stood naked before us.

The next moment we were all stark naked.

I sat down with Maude on my lap. Her cunt was wet again. Elsie stood beside us with her arm around Maude's neck. She was a little taller than Maude and well built. I rubbed my hand over her belly and twined my fingers in the bush that was almost on a level with my mouth. Maude looked on with a pleasant smile of satisfaction. I leaned forward and kissed Elsie's cunt.

«It's wonderful not to be jealous any more,» said Maude very simply.

Elsie's face was scarlet. She didn't quite know what her role was, how far she dared go. She studied Maude intently, as though not altogether convinced of her sincerity. Now I was kissing Maude passionately, my fingers in Elsie's cunt the while. I felt Elsie pressing closer, moving herself. The juice was pouring over my fingers. At the same time Maude raised herself and, shifting her bottom, adroitly managed to sink down again with my prick neatly fitted inside her. She was facing forward now, her face pressed against Elsie's breats. She raised her head and took the nipple in her mouth. Elsie gave a shudder and her cunt began to quiver with silken spasms. Now Maude's hand, which had been resting on Elsie's waist, slid down and caressed the smooth cheeks. In another moment it had slipped farther down and encountered mine. I drew my hand away instinctively. Elsie shifted a little and then Maude leaned forward and placed her mouth on Elsie's cunt. At the same time Elsie bent forward, over Maude, and put her lips to mine. The three of us were now quivering as if we had the ague.

As I felt Maude coming I held myself in, determined to save it for Elsie. My prick still taut, I gently raised Maude from my lap and reached for Elsie. She straddled me face forward and with uncontrollable passion she flung her arms around me, glued her lips to mine, and fucked away for dear life. Maude had discreetly gone to the bathroom. When she returned Elsie was sitting in my lap, her arm around my neck, her face on fire. Then Elsie got up and went to the bathroom. I went to the sink and washed myself there.

«I've never been so happy,» said Maude, going to the machine and putting on another record. «Give me your glass,» she said, and as she filled it she murmured: «What will you say when you get home?» I said nothing. Then she added under her breath: «You could say one of us was taken ill.»

«It doesn't matter,» I said. «I'll think of something.»

«You won't be angry with me?»

«Angry? What for?»

«For keeping you so long.»

«Nonsense,» I said.

She put her arms around me and kissed me tenderly. And with arms around each other's waist we reached for the glasses and gulped drown a silent toast. At this moment Elsie returned. We stood there, naked as hat racks, our arms entwined, and drank to one another.

We began to dance again, with the candles guttering. I knew that in a few moments they would be

extinguished and no one would make a move to get
fresh ones. We changed off at rapid intervals, to
avoid giving one another the embarrassment of standing apart and watching. Sometimes Maude and Elsie
danced together, rubbing their cunts together obscenely, then pulling apart laughingly, and one or the
other making a grab for me. There was such a feeling of freedom and intimacy that any gesture, any
act, became permissible. We began to laugh and joke
more and more. When finally the candles guttered
out, first one, then the other, and only a pale shaft
of moonlight streamed through the windows, all
pretense at restraint or decency vanished.

It was Maude who had the idea of clearing the
table. Elsie assisted uncomprehendingly, like some
one who had been mesmerized. Quickly the things
were whisked to the tubs. There was a quick dash
to the next room for a soft blanket which was
stretched over the table. Even a pillow. Elsie was
beginning to get the drift. She looked on goggle-
eyed.

Before getting down to actualities, however, Maude
had another inspiration—to make eggnogs. We had
to switch the light on for that. The two of them
worked swiftly, almost frantically. They poured a
liberal dose of cognac into the concoction. As I felt
it slipping down my gullet I felt it going straight into
my pecker, into my balls. As I was drinking, my
head thrown back, Elsie cupped her hand around my
balls. «One of them's bigger than the other,» she
said laughingly. Then, after a slight hesitation:
«Couldn't we all do something together?» She looked
at Maude. Maude grinned, as if to say—why not?
«Let's put the top light out,» said Elsie, «we don't
need that any more, do we?» She sat down on the
chair beside the table. «I want to watch you,» she
said, patting the blanket with her hand. She got

hold of Maude and lifted her up and on to the table. «This is a new one to me,» she said. «Wait a minute?» She took my hand and drew me to her. Then. looking at Maude.... «May I?» And without waiting for an answer she bent forward and reaching for my cock, placed it in her mouth. After a few moments she withdrew her mouth. «*Now...* let me watch!» She gave me a little push, as if to hurry me on. Maude stretched out like a cat, her ass hanging over the edge of the table, the pillow under her head. She twined her legs around my waist. Then, suddenly, she untwined them and slung them over my shoulders. Elsie was standing beside me, her head down. watching with breathless absorption. «Pull it out a little,» she said in a hoarse whisper, «I want to see it go in again.» Then swiftly she ran to the window and raised the shades. «Do it!» she said. «Go on, fuck her!» As I plunged it in I felt Elsie slipping down beside me. The next moment I felt her tongue on my balls, lapping them vigorously.

Suddenly, utterly astounded, I heard Maude say: «Don't come yet. Wait.... Give Elsie a chance.»

I pulled out, pushing my ass in Elsie's face in doing so, and tumbling her backwards on the floor. She gave a squeal of delight and quickly sprang to her feet. Maude climbed down from the table and Elsie nimbly placed herself in position. «Couldn't you do something too?» she said to Maude, sitting bolt upright. «I have an idea...» and she sprang off the table and threw the blanket on the floor and the pillow after it. It didn't take her long to figure out an interesting configuration.

Maude was stretched out on her back, Elsie squatting over her on bent knees, her head facing Maude's feet but the mouth glued to Maude's crack. I was on my knees. giving it to Elsie from behind. Maude was playing with my balls, a light, delicate manipu-

lation with the finger-tips. I could feel Maude
squirming around as Elsie licked her furiously and
avidly. There was a weird pale light playing over
the rooom and the taste of cunt in my mouth. I
had one of those final erections which threaten never
to break. Now and then I took it out and, pushing
Elsie forward, I sank down farther and offered it to
Maude's nimble tongue. Then I would sink it in
again and Elsie would squirm like mad and bury her
nozzle in Maude's crotch, shaking her head like a
terrier. Finally I pulled out and pushing Elsie aside
I fell on Maude and buried it in her with a vengeance.
«Do it, do it!» she begged, as if she were waiting for
the axe. Again I felt Elsie's tongue on my balls.
Then Maude came, like a star bursting, with a volley
of half-finished words and phrases rippling off her
tongue. I pulled away, still stiff as a poker, fearful
now that I would never come again, and groped for
Elsie. She was terribly gooey, and her mouth was
just like a cunt now. «Do you want it?» I said,
shoving it around inside her like a drunken fiend.
«Go on, fuck, fuck!» she cried, slinging her legs up
over my shoulders and dragging her bottom closer.
«Give it to me, give it to me, you bugger!» She was
almost yelling now. «Yes, I'll fuck you... I'll fuck
you!» and she squirmed and writhed and twisted and
bit and clawed me.

«Oh, oh! Don't. Please don't. It hurts!» she
yelled.

«Shut up, you bitch you!» I said. «It hurts, does
it? You wanted it, didn't you?» I held her tightly,
raised myself a little higher to get it in to the hilt,
and pushed until I thought her womb would give way.
Then I came—right into that snail-like mouth which
was wide open. She went into a convulsion, delirious
with joy and pain. Then her legs slid off my

shouders and fell to the floor with a thud. She lay
there like a dead one, completely fucked out.

«Jesus,» I said, standing astraddle over her, and
the sperm still coming out, dropping on her breast,
her face, her hair, «Jesus Christ, I'm exhausted. I'm
fucked out, do you know that?» I addressed myself
to the room.

Maude was lighting a candle. «It's getting late,»
she said.

«I'm not going home,» I said. «I'm going to sleep
here.»

«You are?» said Maude, an irrepressible thrill
creeping into her voice.

«Yes, I can't go back in this condition, can I?
Jesus, I'm groggy and boozy and woozy.» I flopped
on to a chair. «Give me a drop of that cognac, will
you, I need a bracer.»

She poured out a good stiff one and held it to my
lips, as if she were giving me medicine. Elsie had
risen to her feet, a bit wobbly and lurchy. «Give me
one too,» she begged. «What a night! We ought to
do this again some time.»

«Yeah, to-morrow,» I said.

«It was a wonderful performance,» she said, stroking my dome. «I never thought you were like that....
You almost killed me, do you know it?»

«You'd better take a douche,» said Maude.

«I guess so,» Elsie sighed. «I don't seem to give a
damn. If I'm caught I'm caught.»

«Go on in there, Elsie,» I said. «Don't be a damned fool.»

«I'm too tired,» said Elsie.

Wait a minute,» said I. «I want to have a look at
you before you go in there.» I made her climb on
the table and open her legs wide. With the glass
in one hand I pried her cunt open with the thumb

and forefinger of my other hand. The sperm was
still oozing out.

«It's a beautiful cunt, Elsie.»

Maude took a good look at it too. «Kiss it,» I said,
gently pushing her nose into Elsie's bush.

I sat there, watching Maude nibble away at Elsie's
cunt. «It feels good,» Elsie was saying. «Awfully
good.» She moved like a belly dancer tied to the
floor. Maude's ass was sticking out temptingly. In
spite of the fatigue my prick began to swell again.
It stiffened like a blood-pudding. I got behind Maude
and slipped it in. She spun her ass around and
around, with just the tip of it in. Elsie was now
contorting herself with pleasure; she had her finger
in her mouth, and was biting the knuckle. We went
on like this for several minutes, until Elsie had an
orgasm. Then we disengaged ourselves and looked at
one another as though we had never seen each other
before. We were dazed.

«I'm going to bed,» I said, determined to make an
end of it. I started for the next room, thinking to
lie on the couch.

«You can stay with me,» said Maude, holding me
by the arm. «Why not?» she said, seeing the surprised look in my eyes.

«Yes,» said Elsie, «why not? Maybe I'll go to bed
with you too. Would you let me?» she asked Maude
point blank. «I won't bother you, she added. «I
just hate to leave you now.»

«But what will your folks say?» said Maude.

«They won't know that Henry stayed, will they?»

«No, of course not!» said Maude, a little frightened
at the thought.

«And Melanie?» I said.

«Oh, she leaves early in the morning. She has a
job now.»

Suddenly I wondered what the devil I would say to Mona. I was almost panic-stricken.

«I think I ought to phone home,» I said.

«Oh, not now,» said Elsie coaxingly. «It's so late.... Wait.»

We hid the bottles away, piled the dishes up in the sink, and took the phonograph upstairs with us. It was just as well that Melanie shouldn't suspect too much. We tip-toed through the hall and up the stairs, our arms loaded.

I lay between the two of them, a hand on either cunt. They lay quietly for a long while, sound asleep I thought. I was too tired to sleep. I lay with eyes wide open, staring up into the darkness. Finally I turned over on my side. Towards Maude. Instantly she turned towards me, putting her arms around me and glueing her lips to mine. Then she removed them and placed them to my ear. «I love you,» she whispered faintly. I made no answer. «Did you hear?» she whispered. «I love you!» I pressed her close and put my hand between her legs. Just then I felt Elsie turning round, cuddling up to me spoon fashion. I felt her hand crawling between my legs, squeezing my balls. She had her lips against my neck and was kissing me softly, warmly, with wet, cool lips.

After a time I turned back to a prone position. Elsie did the same. I closed my eyes, tried to summon sleep. It was impossible. The bed felt deliciously soft, the bodies beside me were soft and clinging, and the odor of hair and sex was in my nostrils. From the garden came the heavy fragrance of rain-soaked earth. It was strange, soothingly strange, to be back in this big bed, the marital bed. with a third person beside us, and the three of us enveloped in frank, sensual lust. It was too good to be true. I expected the door to be flung open any moment and an accusing voice scream: «Get out of there, you brazen creatures!» But there was only the silence of the night, the blackness, the heavy, sensual odors of earth and sex.

When I shifted again it was towards Elsie. She was waiting for me, eager to press her cunt against me, slip her thick, taut tongue down my throat.

«Is she asleep?» she whispered. «Do it once more,» she begged.

I lay motionless, my cock limp, my arm drooping over her waist.

«Not now,» I whispered. «In the morning maybe.»

«No, now!» she begged. My prick was curled up in her hand like a dead snail. «Please, please,» she whispered, «I want it. Just one more fuck, Henry.»

«Let him sleep,» said Maude, snuggling up. Her voice sounded as if she were drugged.

«All right» said Elsie, patting Maude's arm. Then, after a few moments of silence, her lips pressed against my ear, she whispered slowly, allowing a pause between each word: «When she falls asleep, yes?» I nodded. Suddenly I felt that I was dropping off. «Thank God,» I said to myself.

There was a blank, a long blank, it seemed to me, during which I was completely out. I awakened gradually, dimly conscious that my prick was in Elsie's mouth. I ran my hand over her head and stroked her back. She put her hand up and placed her fingers over my mouth, as if to warn me not to protest. A useless warning because, curiously enough, I had awakened with a full knowledge of what was coming. My prick was already responding to Elsie's labial caresses. It was a new prick; it seemed thinner, longer, pointed—a dog-like prick. And it had life in it, as though it had refreshed itself independently, as though it had taken a nap all by itself.

Gently, slowly, stealthily—why had we become

furtive now? I wondered—I pulled Elsie up and over me. Her cunt was different than Maude's longer, narrower, like the finger of a glove slipping over my prick. I made comparisons as I cautiously jogged her up and down. I ran my fingers along the edge and grabbed her bush and tugged it gently. Not a whisper passed our lips. Her teeth were fastened in to the hump of my shoulder. She was arched so that only the tip of it was in her and around that she was slowly, skillfully, torturingly twirling her cunt. Now and then she sank down on it and dug away like an animal.

«God, I love it!» she finally whispered. «I'd like to fuck you every night.»

We rolled over on our sides and lay there glued together, making no movement, no sound. With extraordinary muscular contractions her cunt played with my prick as if it had a life and will of its own.

«Where do you live?» she whispered. «Where can I see you... *alone?* Write me to-morrow... tell me where to meet you. I want a fuck every day... do you hear? Don't come yet, *please.* I want it to last forever.»

Silence. Just the beating of her pulse between the legs. I never felt such a tight fit, such a long, smooth, silky, clean, fresh tight fit. She couldn't have been fucked more than a dozen times. And the roots of her hair, so strong and fragant. And her breasts, firm and smooth, almost like apples. The fingers too, strong, supple, greedy, always wandering, clutching, caressing, tickling. How she loved to grab my balls, to cup them, weigh them, then ring the scrotum with two fingers, as if she were going to milk me. And her tongue always active, her teeth biting, pinching, nipping...

She's very quiet now, not a muscle stirring. Whispers again.

«Am I doing all right? You'll teach me, won't you? I'm rooty. I could fuck forever... You're not tired any more, are you? Jst leave it like that... don't move. If I come don't take it out.... you won't, will you? God, this is heaven...»

Quiet again. I have the feeling I could lie this way indefinitely. I want to hear more.

«I've got a friend,» she whispers. «We could meet there... she wouldn't say anything. Jesus, Henry, I never throught it could be like this. Can you fuck like this every night?»

I smiled in the dark.

«What's the matter?» she whispered.

«Not every night,» I whispered, almost breaking into a giggle.

«Henry, fuck! Quick, fuck me... I'm coming.»

We came off simultaneously, a prolonged orgasm which made me wonder where the damned juice came from.

«You did it!» she whispered. Then: «It's all right... it was marvelous.»

Maude turned over heavily in her sleep.

«Good-night,» I whispered. «I'm going to sleep..... I'm dead.»

«Write me to-morrow,» she whispered, kissing my cheek. «Or phone me... *promise*.»

I grunted. She cuddled up to me, her arm around my waist. We fell into a trance.

17

It was Sunday that this outing took place. I didn't see Mona until near dawn Tuesday. Not that I remained with Maude—no, I went straight to the office on Monday morning. Towards noon I telephoned

Mona and was told that she was asleep. It was
Rebecca who answered the telephone. She said
Mona hadn't been home all night, that she had been
rehearsing. «And where were you all night?» she
demanded, almost with proprietary solicitude. I
explained that the child had been taken ill and that
I had been obliged to stay with her all night.

«You'd better think up something better than that,»
she laughed, «before you talk to Mona. She's been
telephoning all night. She was frantic about you.»

«That's why she didn't come home, I suppose?»

«You don't expect any one to believe your stories,
do you?» said Rebecca, giving another low, throaty
laugh. «Are you coming home tonight?» she added.
«We missed you... You know, Henry, you ought
never to get married...»

I cut her short. «I'll be home to-night for dinner,
yes. Tell her that when she wakes up, will you?
And don't laugh when you tell her what I said—
about the child, I mean.»

She began to laugh over the telephone.

«Rebecca, listen, I'm trusting you. Don't make it
hard for me. You know I think the world of you.
If I ever marry another woman it will be you, you
know that...»

More laughter. Then: «For God's sake, Henry,
stop it! But come home to-night... I want to hear
all about it. Arthur won't be home. I'll stand by
you... though you don't deserve it.»

So I went home, after taking a nap in the roller
skating rink. I was rather exhilarated too, on
arriving, owing to a last minute interview with an
Egyptologist who wanted a job as a night messenger.
A statement he had let drop about the probable age
of the pyramids had thrown me out of the rut so
violently that it was a matter of complete indifference
to me how Mona would react to my story. There

was reason to believe, he had said, and I am sure
I heard him rightly, that the pyramids might be sixty
thousand years old—*at least*. If that were true, the
whole god-damned notion of Egyptian civilization
could be thrown on the scrap-heap—and a lot of
other historical notions too. In the subway I felt
immeasurably older than I ever thought it was
possible to feel. I was trying to reach back twenty
or thirty thousand years, some half-way point
between the erection of these enigmatic monoliths
and the supposed dawn of that hoary civilization of
the Nile. I was suspended in time and space. The
word age began to take on a new significance. With
it came a fantastic thought: what if I should live to
be a hundred and fifty, or a hundred and ninety-
five? How would this little incident that I was
trying to cover up—the Organza Friganza business—
stack up in the light of a hundred and fifty years of
experience? What would it matter if Mona left me?
What would it matter three generations hence how
I had behaved on the night of the 14th of so and so
and so? Supposing I was still virile at ninety-five
and had survived the death of six wives, or eight or
ten? Supposing that in the 21st century we had a
return to Mormonism? Or that we began to see,
and not only to see but to practise, the sexual logic
of the Eskimos? Supposing the notion of property
were abolished and the institution of matrimony
wiped out? In seventy or eighty years tremendous
revolutions could take place. Seventy or eighty years
hence I would only be a hundred or so years old—
comparatively young yet. I would probably have
forgotten the names of most of my wives, to say
nothing of the fly-by-nights... I was almost in a state
of exaltation when I walked in.

Rebecca came at once to my room. The house
was empty. Mona had telephoned, she said, to say

that there was another rehearsal on. She didn't know when she would be home.

«That's fine,» I said. «Did you make dinner?»

«God, Henry, you're adorable.» She put her arms around me affectionately and gave me a comradely hug. «I wish Arthur were like that. It would be easier to forgive him sometimes.»

«Isn't there a soul around?» I asked. It was most unusual for the house to be so deserted.

«No, everybody's gone,» said Rebacca, examining the roast in the oven. «Now you can tell me about that great love you were talking about over the phone.» She laughed again, a low, earthy laugh which sent a thrill through me.

«You know I wasn't serious,» I said. «Sometimes I say anything at all... though in a way I mean it too. You understand, don't you?»

«*Perfectly!* That's why I like you. You're utterly faithless and truthful. It's an irresistible combination.»

«You know you're safe with me, that's it, eh?» I said, sidling up to her and putting an arm around her.

She wriggled away laughingly. «I don't think any such thing—and you know it!? she burst out.

«I'm only making up to you out of politeness,» I said, with a huge grin. «We're going to have a cosy little meal now... God, it smells good... what is it? chicken?»

«Pork!» she said. «*Chicken*... what do you think? That I made this especially for you? Go on, talk to me. Keep your mind off the food a little longer. Say something nice, if you can. But don't come near me, or I'll stick a fork in you... Tell me what happened last night. *Tell me the truth, I dare you...*»

«That isn't hard to do, my wonderful Rebecca.

Especially since we're alone. It's a long story—are you sure you'd like to hear it?»

She was laughing again.

«Jesus, you've got a dirty laugh,» I said. «Well anyway, where was I? Oh yes, *the truth*... Listen, the truth is that I slept with my wife...»

«I thought as much,» said Rebecca.

«But wait, that isn't all. There was another woman besides...»

«You mean after you slept with your wife—or before?»

«At the same time,» I said, grinning amiably.

«No, no! don't tell me that!» She dropped the carving knife and stood with arms akimbo looking at me searchingly. «I don't know... with you anything's possible. Wait a minute. Wait till I set the table. I want to hear the whole thing, from beginning to end.»

«You haven't got a little schnapps, have you?» I said.

«I've got some red wine... that'll have to do you.»

«Good, good! Of course it'll do. Where is it?»

As I was uncorking the bottle she came over to me and grasped me by the arm. «Look, tell me the truth,» she said. «I won't give you away.»

«But I'm telling you the truth!»

«All right, hold it, then. Wait till we sit down... Do you like cauliflower? I haven't any other vegetable.»

«I like any kind of food. I like everything. I like you, I like Mona, I like my wife, I like horses, cows, chickens, pinochle, tapioca, Bach, benzine, prickly heat...»

«*You like...!* That's you all over. It's wonderful to hear it. You make me hungry too. You like everything, yes... but you don't love.»

«I do too. I love food, wine, women. Of course

I do. What makes you think I don't? If you like,
you love. Love is only the superlative degree. I
love like God loves—without distinction of time,
place, race, color, sex and so forth. I love you too—
that way. It's not enough, I suppose?»

«It's too much, you mean. You're out of focus.
Listen, calm down a moment. Carve the meat, will
you? I'll fix the gravy.»

«Gravy... ooh, ooh. I *love* gravy.»

«Like you love your wife and me and Mona, is
that it?»

«*More* even. Right now it's all gravy. I could
lick it up by the ladleful. Rich, thick, heavy, black
gravy... it's wonderful. By the way, I was just
talking to an Egyptologist—he wanted a job as a
messenger.»

«Here's the gravy. Don't get off the track. You
were going to tell me about your wife.»

«Sure, sure I will. I'll tell you that too. I'll tell
you everything. First of all, I want to tell you how
beautiful you look—with the gravy in your hand.»

«If you don't stop this,» she said, «I'll put a knife
in you. What's come over you, anyway? Does your
wife have such an effect upon you every time you
see her? You must have had a wonderful time.»
She sat down, not opposite me, but to one side.

«Yes, I did have a wonderful time,» I said. «And
then just now there was the Egyptologist...»

«Oh, drat the Egyptologist! I want to hear about
your wife... *and that other woman.* God, if you're
making this up I'll kill you!»

I busied myself for a while with the pork and the
cauliflower. Took a few swigs of wine to wash it
down. A succulent repast. I was feeling mellow as
could be. I needed replenishment.

«It's like this,» I began, after I had packed away
a few forkfuls.

She began to titter.

«What's the matter?   What did I say now?»

It isn't what you say, it's the way you say it.   You seem so serene and detached, so innocent like.   God, yes, that's it—*innocent.*   If it had been murder instead of adultery, or fornication, I think you'd begin the same way.   You enjoy yourself, don't you?»

«Of course... why not?   Why shouldn't I?   Is that so terribly strange?»

«No-o-h,» she drawled, «I suppose it isn't... or it shouldn't be, anyway.   But you make everything sound a little crazy sometimes.   You're always a little wide of the mark... too big a swoop.   You ought to have been born in Russia!»

«Yeah, Russia!   That's it.   I love Russia!»

«And you love the pork and the cauliflower—and the gravy *and me.*   Tell me, what *don't* you love?   Think first!   I'd really like to know.»

I gobbled down a juicy bit of fatty pork dipped in gravy and looked at her.   «Well, for one thing, I don't like work.»   I paused a minute to think what else I didn't like.   «Oh yes,» I said, meaning it utterly seriously, «*and I don't like flies.*»

She burst out laughing.   «Work and flies—so that's it.   I must remember that.   God, is that all you don't like?»

«For the moment that's all I can think of.»

«And what about crime, injustice, tyranny and those things?»

«Well, what about them?» I said.   «What can you do about such things?   You might just as well ask me—what about the weather?»

«Do you mean that?»

«Of course I do.»

«You're impossible!   Or maybe you can't think when you eat.»

«That's a fact,» I said.   «I don't think very well

when I eat, do you? I don't want to, as a matter of fact. Anyway, I was never much of a thinker. Thinking doesn't get you anywhere anyhow. It's a delusion. Thinking makes you morbid... By the way, have you any dessert... any of that Liederkranz? That's a wonderful cheese, don't you think?»

«I suppose it does sound funny,» I continued, «to hear some one say 'I love it, it's wonderful, it's good, it's great,' meaning everything. Of course I don't feel that way every day—but I'd like to. And I do when I'm normal, when I'm myself. Everybody does, if given a chance. It's the natural state of the heart. The trouble is, we're terrorized most of the time. I say 'we're terrorized,' but I mean we terrorize ourselves. Last night, for instance. You can't imagine how extraordinary it was. Nothing external created it—unless it was the lightning. Suddenly everything was different—and yet it was the same house, the same atmosphere, the same wife, the same bed. It was as though the pressure had suddenly been removed—I mean that psychic pressure, that incomprehensible wet blanket which smothers us from the time we're born... You said something about tyranny, injustice, and so on. Of course I know what you mean. I used to occupy myself with those problems when I was younger—when I was fifteen or sixteen. I understood everything then, very clearly... that is, as far as the mind permits one to understand things. I was more pure, more disinterested, so to speak. I didn't have to defend or uphold anything, least of all a system which I never did believe in, not even as a child. I worked out an ideal universe, all on my own. It was very simple: no money, no property, no laws, no police, no government, no soldiers, no executioners, no prisons, no schools. I eliminated every disturbing and restraining element. Perfect freedom. It was a vacuum—and in it I exploded.

What I really wanted, you see, was that every one should behave as I behaved, or thought I would behave. I wanted a world made in my own image, a world that would breathe my spirit. I made myself God, since there was nothing to hinder me...»

I paused for breath. I noticed that she was listening with the utmost seriousness.

«Should I go on? You've probably heard this sort of thing a thousand times.»

«Do go on,» she said softly, placing a hand on my arm. «I'm beginning to see another you. I like you better in this vein.»

«Didn't you forget the cheese? By the way, the wine isn't bad at all. A little sharp, maybe, but not bad.»

«Listen, Henry, eat, drink, smoke, do anything you want, as much as you want. I'll give you everything we have in the house. But don't stop talking now... *please.*»

She was just about to sit down. I sprang up suddenly, my eyes full of tears, and I put my arms around her. «Now I can tell you honestly and sincerely,» I said, «that I do love you.» I made no attempt to kiss her—I just embraced her. I released her of my own accord, sat down, picked up the glass of wine and finished it off.

«You're an actor,» she said. «In the real sense of the word, of course. I don't wonder that people are frightened of you sometimes.»

«I know, I get frightened of myself sometimes. Especially if the other person responds. I don't know where the proper limits are. There are no limits, I suppose. Nothing would be bad or ugly or evil—if we really let ourselves go. But it's hard to make people understand that. Anyway, that's the difference between the world of imagination and the world of common sense, which isn't common sense at all but

sheer buggery and insanity. If you stop still and look
at things... I say *look*, not think, not criticize... the
world looks absolutely crazy to you. And it is crazy,
by God! It's just as crazy when things are normal
and peaceful as in times of war or revolution. The
evils are insane evils, and the panaceas are insane
panaceas. Because we're all driven like dogs. We're
running away. *From what?* We don't know. From
a million nameless things. It's a rout, a panic.
Theres' no ultimate place to retreat to—unless, as I
say, you stand stock still. If you can do that, and
not lose your balance, not be swept away in the rush,
you may be able to get a grip on yourself... be able
to act, if you know what I mean. You know what
I'm driving at... From the time you wake up until
the moment you go to bed it's all a lie, all a sham and
a swindle. Everybody knows it, and everybody
collaborates in the perpetuation of the hoax. That's
why we look so god-damned disgusting to one another.
That's why it's so easy to trump up a war, or a
pogrom, or a vice crusade, or any damned thing you
like. It's always easier to give in, to bash somebody's
puss in, because what we all pray for is to get done in,
but done in proper and no come back. If we could
still believe in a God, we'd make him a God of Vengeance. We'd surrender to him with a full heart
the task of cleaning things up. It's too late for us
to pretend to clean up the mess. We're in it up to
the eyes. We don't want a new world... we want an
end to the mess we've made. At sixteen you can
believe in a new world... you can believe anything, in
fact... but at twenty you're doomed, and you know it.
At twenty you're well in harness, and the most you
can hope for is to get off with arms and legs intact.
It isn't a question of fading hope... Hope is a baneful
sign; it means impotence. Courage is no use either:
everybody can muster courage—for the wrong thing.

I don't know what to say—unless I use a word like
vision. And by that I don't mean a projected picture
of the future, of some imagined ideal made real. I
mean something more flexible, more constant—a
permanent super-sight, as it were... something like a
third eye. We had it once. There was a sort of
clairvoyance which was natural and common to all
men. Then came the mind, and that eye which
permitted us to see whole and round and beyond was
absorbed by the brain, and we became conscious of
the world, and of one another, in a new way. Our
pretty little egos came into bloom: we became self-
conscious, and with that came conceit, arrogance,
blindness, a blindness such as was never known before,
not even by the blind.»

«Where do you get these ideas?» said Rebecca
suddenly. «Or are you making it up on the spur of
the moment? Wait a minute... I want you to tell me
something. Do you ever put your thoughts down on
paper? What do you write about anyway? You've
never showed me a thing. I haven't the least idea
what you're doing.»

«Oh *that*,» I said, «it's just as well you haven't read
anything. I haven't said anything yet. I can't seem
to get started. I don't know what the hell to put
down first?there's so much to say.»

«But do you write the way you talk? That's what
I want to know.»

«I don't think so,» I said, blushing. «I don't know
anything about writing yet. I'm too self-conscious, I
guess.»

«You shouldn't be,» said Rebecca. «You're not
self-conscious when you talk, and you don't act self-
conciously either.»

«Rebecca,» I said, proceeding slowly and deliberately, «if I really knew what I was capable of I
wouldn't be sitting here talking to you. I feel some-

times as though I'm going to burst. I really don't
give a damn about the misery of the world. I take it
for granted. What I want is to open up. I want to
know what's inside me. I want everybody to open
up. I'm like an imbecile with a can-opener in his
hand, wondering where to begin—to open up the
earth. I know that underneath the mess everything
is marvelous. I'm sure of it. I konw it because I feel
so marvelous myself most of the time. And when I
feel that way everybody seems marvelous... everybody
and everything... even pebbles and pieces of card-
board... a match stick lying in the gutter... anything... a goat's beard, if you like. That's what I
want to write about—but I don't know how... I don't
know where to begin. Maybe it's too personal.
Maybe it would sound like sheer rubbish... You see,
to me it seems as though the artists, the scientists,
the philosophers were grinding lenses. It's all a grand
preparation for something that never comes off.
Some day the lens is going to be perfect and then
we're all going to see clearly, see what a staggering,
wonderful, beautiful world it is. But in the meantime
we go without glasses, so to speak. We blunder about
like myopic, blinking idiots. We don't see what is
under our nose because we're so intent on seeing the
stars, or what lies beyond the stars. We're trying to
see with the mind, but the mind sees only what it's
told to see. The mind can't open wide its eyes and
look just for the pleasure of looking. Haven't you
ever noticed that when you stop looking, when you
don't try to see, *you suddenly see?* What is it you
see? Who is it that sees? Why is it all so different
—so marvelously different—in such moments? And
which is more real, that kind of vision or the other?
You see what I mean.... When you have an inspiration
your mind takes a vacation; you turn it over to some
one else. some invisible, unknowable power which

takes possession of you, as we so aptly say. What the hell does that mean—if it makes sense at all? What happens when the machinery of the mind slows down, or comes to a standstill? Whatever or however you choose to look upon it, this other modus operandi is of another order. The machine runs perfectly, but its object and purpose seem purely gratuitous. It makes another kind of sense... grand sense, if you accept it unquestioningly, and nonsense—or not nonsense, but madness—it you try to examine into it with the other machinery... Jesus, I guess I'm getting off the track.»

Little by little she steered me back to the story she wanted to hear. She was avidly curious about the details. She laughed a great deal—that low, earthy laugh which was provocative and approving at the same time.

«You pick the strangest women,» she said. «You seem to choose with your eyes shut. Don't you ever think beforehand what it's going to mean to live with them?»

She went on like this for a space and then suddenly I was aware that she had veered the conversation to Mona. *Mona*—that puzzled her. What did we have in common, she wanted to know. How could I stand her lies, her pretences—or didn't I care about such things? Surely there had to be firm ground somewhere... one couldn't build on quicksands. She had thought about us a great deal, even before she met Mona. She had heard about her, from different sources, had been curious to know her, to understand what the great attraction was.... Mona was beautiful, yes—ravishingly beautiful—and perhaps intelligent too. But God, so theatrical! There was no getting to grips with her; she eluded one like a phantom.

«What do you really know about her?» she asked

challengingly. «Have you met her parents? Do you know anything about her life before she met you?»

I confessed that I knew almost nothing. Perhaps it was better that I didn't know, I averred. There was something attractive about the mystery which surrounded her.

«Oh, nonsense!» said Rebecca scathingly. «I don't think there's any great mystery there. Her father's probably a rabbi.»

«What! What makes you say that? How do you know she's Jewish? I don't even know it myself.»

«You don't want to know it, you mean. Of course I don't know either, except that she denies it so vehemently—that always makes one suspicious. Besides, does she look like the average American type? Come, come, don't tell me you haven't suspected as much—you're not as dumb as all that.»

What surprised me more than anything, as regards these remarks, was the fact that Rebecca had succeeded in discussing the subject with Mona. Not a hint of it had reached my ears. I would have given anything to have been behind a screen during that encounter.

«If you really want to know something,» I said, «I'd rather that she were a Jewess than anything else. I never pump her about that, of course. Evidently it's a painful subject. She'll come out with it one day, you'll see....»

«You're so damned romantic,» said Rebecca. «Really, you're incurable. Why should a Jewish girl be any different from a Gentile? I live in both worlds... I don't find anything strange or marvelous about either.»

«*Naturally*,» I said. «You're always the same person. You don't change from one milieu to another. You're honest and open. You could get along anywhere with any group or class or race. But most

people aren't that way. Most people are conscious
of race, color, religion, nationality, and so on. To
me all peoples are mysterious when I look at them
closely. I can detect their differences much easier
than their kinship. In fact, I like the distinctions
which separate them just as much as I like what unites
them. I think it's foolish to pretend that we're all
pretty much the same. Only the great, the truly
distinctive individuals, resemble one another. Brotherhood doesn't start at the bottom, but at the
top. The nearer we get to God the more we
resemble one another. At the bottom it's like a
rubbish pile... that's to say, from a distance it all
seems like so much rubbish, but when you get nearer
you perceive that this so-called «rubbish» is composed
of a million-billion different particles. And yet, no
matter how different one bit of rubbish is from
another, the real difference only asserts itself when
you look at something which is not «rubbish». Even
if the elements which compose the universe can be
broken down into one vital substance... well, I don't
know what I was going to say exactly... maybe this...
that as long as there is life there will be differentiation,
values, hierarchies. Life is always making pyramidal
structures, in every realm. If you're at the bottom
you stress the sameness of things; if you're at the top,
or near it, you become aware of the difference
between things. And if something is obscure—
especially a person—you're attracted beyond all power
of will. You may find that it was an empty chase,
that there was nothing there, nothing more than a
question mark, but just the same....»

There was something more I felt like adding. «And
there's the opposite to all this,» I continued. «As
with my ex-wife, for instance. Of course I should
have suspected that she had another side, hating her
as I did for being so damned prudish and proper.

It's all very well to say that an over-modest person
is extremely immodest, as the analysts do, but to
catch one changing over from the one to the other,
that's something you don't often have a chance to
witness. Or if you do, it's usually with some one else
that the transformation occurs. But yesterday I saw
it happen right before my eyes, and not with somebody else, but with me! No matter how much you
think you know about a person's secret thoughts,
about their unconscious impulses and all that,
nevertheless, when the conversion takes place before
your eyes you begin to wonder if you ever did know
the person with whom you were living all your life.
It's all right to say to yourself, a propos of a dear
friend—'he has all the instincts of a murderer'—but
when you see him coming at you with a knife, that's
something else. Somehow you're never quite prepared for that, no matter how clever you are. At best
you might credit him with doing it to some one else
—but never to you... oh dear no! The way I feel
now is that I should be prepared for anything from
those whom you're apt to suspect least of all. I don't
mean that one should be anxious, no, not that... one
shouldn't be surprised, that's all. The only surprise
should be that you can still be surprised. That's it.
That's Jesuitical, what! Oh yes, I can spin it out
when I get going.... *Rabbi*, you said a moment ago.
Did you ever think that I might make a good rabbi?
I mean it. Why not? Why couldn't I be a rabbi, if
I wanted to? Or a pope, or a mandarin, or a Dalai
Lama? If you can be a worm you can be a god too.»

The conversation went on like this for several hours,
broken only by Arthur Raymond's return. I stayed
a while longer, to ally any suspicions he might have,
and then retired. Towards dawn Mona returned,
wide awake, lovelier than ever, her skin glowing like
calcium. She hardly listened to my explanations

about the night before; she was exalted, infatuated
with herself. So many things had happened since
then—she didn't know where to begin. First of all,
they had promised her the role of understudy for the
leading part in their next production. That is, the
director had—no one else knew anything about it as
yet. He was in love with her, the director. Had
been slipping love notes in her pay envelopes for the
last weeks. And the leading actor, he too was in
love with her—madly in love. It was he who had
been coaching her all along. He had been teaching
her how to breathe, how to relax, how to stand, how
to walk, how to use her voice. It was marvelous.
She was a new person, with unknown powers. She
had faith in herself, a boundless faith. Soon she
would have the world at her feet. She'd take New
York by storm, tour the country, go abroad maybe...
Who could predict what lay ahead? Just the same,
she was a little frightened of it all, too. She wanted
me to help her; I was to listen to her read the script
of her new part. There were so many things she
didn't know—and she didn't want to reveal her
ignorance before her infatuated lovers. Maybe she'd
look up that old fossil at the Ritz-Carlton, make him
buy her a new outfit. She needed hats, shoes, dresses,
blouses, gloves, stockings.... so many, many things.
It was important now to look the part. She was
going to wear her hair differently too. I had to go
with her into the hall and observe the new carriage,
the new gait she had acquired. Hadn't I noticed the
change in her voice? Well, I would very soon. She
would be completely remade—and I would love her
even more. She would be a hundred different women
to me now. Suddenly she thought of an old beau
whom she had forgotten about, a clerk at the
Imperial Hotel. He would buy her everything she
needed—without a word. Yes, she must telephone

him in the morning. I could meet her at dinner, in her new togs. I wasn't going to be jealous, was I? He was a young man, the clerk, but a perfect fool, a ninny, a sap. The only reason he saved his money was that she might spend it. He had no use for it otherwise—he was too dumb to know what to do with it. If he could only hold her hand furtively he was grateful. Maybe she would give him a kiss sometime —when she needed some unusual favor.

On and on she ran... the kind of gloves she liked, the way to place the voice, how the Indians walked, the value of Yoga exercises, the way to train the memory, the perfume that suited her mood, the supertitiousness of theatrical people, their generosity, their intrigues, their amours, their pride, their conceit. How it felt to rehearse in an empty house, the jokes and pranks that occured in the wings, the attitude of the stage hands, the peculiar aroma of the dressing rooms. And the jealousy! Every one jealous of every one else. Fever, commotion, distracion, grandeur. A world within a world. One became intoxicated, drugged, hallucinated.

And the discussions! A mere trifle could bring about a raging controversy, ending sometimes in a brawl, a hair-pulling match. Some of them seemed to have the very devil in them, especially the women. There was only one decent one, and she was quite young and inexperienced. The others were veritable maenads, furies, harpies. They swore like troopers. By comparison the girls at the dance hall were angelic.

A long pause.

Then, à propos of nothing, she asked when the divorce trial was taking place.

«This week,» I said, surprised at the sudden turn of her mind.

«We'll get married right away,» she said.

«Of course,» I responded.

She didn't like the way I said «of course». «You don't have to marry me, if you don't want,» she said.

«But I do want to,» I said. «And then we'll get out of this place... find a place of our own.»

«Do you mean that?» she exclaimed. «I'm so glad. I've been waiting to hear you say that. I want to start a new life with you. Let's get away from all these people! And I want you to quit that awful job. I'll find a place where you can write. You won't need to earn any money. I'll soon be making lots of money. You can have anything you want. I'll get you all the books you want to read.... Maybe you'll write a play—and I'll act in it! That would be wonderful, wouldn't it?»

I wondered what Rebecca would have said of this speech, had she been listening. Would she have heard only the actress, or would she have detected the germ of a new being expressing itself? Perhaps that mysterious quality of Mona's lay not in obscuration but in germination. True enough, the contours of her personality were not sharply defined, but that was no reason to accuse her of falsity. She was mimetic, chameleonesque, and not outwardly, but inwardly. Outwardly everything about her was pronounced and definite; she stamped her impress upon you immediatley. Inwardly she was like a column of smoke; the slightest pressure of her will altered the configuration of her personality instantly. She was sensitive to pressures, not the pressure of others' wills but of their desires. The histrionic rôle with her was not something to be put on and off—it was her way of meeting reality. What she thought she believed; what she believed was real; what was real she acted upon. Nothing was unreal to her, except that which she was not thinking about. But the moment her attention was brought to bear, no matter how monstrous, fantastic or incredible, the thing became real. In her the frontiers were never closed. People who credited her with having a strong will were utterly mistaken. She had a will, yes, but it was not the will which swept her headlong into new and startling situations—it was her ever-present readiness, her alertness, to act out her ideas. She could change with devastating swiftness from rôle to rôle; she changed before your eyes, with that incredible and elusive prestidigitation of the vaudeville star who impersonates the most diverse types. What she had been doing all her life unconsciously the theatre was now teaching her to do deliberately. They were only making an actress of her in the sense that they were revealing to her the boundaries of art; they were indicating the limitations which surround creation. They could make a failure of her only by giving her free rein.

18

The day of the trial I presented myself at court in a bright and supercilious mood. Everything had been agreed upon beforehand. I had only to raise my hand, swear a silly oath, admit my guilt and take the punishment. The judge looked like a scarecrow fitted with a pair of lunar binoculars; his black wings flapped lugubriously in the hushed silence of the room. He seemed to be slightly annoyed by my serene complacency; it did not bolster the illusion of his importance, which was absolutely nil. I could make no distinction between him and the brass rail, between him and the cuspidor. The brass rail, the Bible, the cuspidor, the American flag, the blotter

on his desk, the thugs in uniform who preserved
order and decorum, the knowledge that was tucked
away in his brain cells, the musty books in his study,
the philosophy that underlay the whole structure of
the law, the eye-glasses he wore, his B. V. D's, his
person and his personality, the whole ensemble was
a senseless collaboration in the name of a blind
machine about which I didn't give a fuck in the
dark. All I wanted was to know that I was definitely free to put my head in the noose again.

It was all going like tic-tac-to, one thing cancel-
ling another, and at the end of course the law
squashing you down as if you were a fat, juicy bedbug, when suddenly I realized that he was asking me
if I were willing to pay such and such an amount of
alimony regularly for the rest of my days.

«What's that?» I demanded. The prospect of at
last encountering some opposition caused him to
brighten appreciably. He reeled off some gibberish
about solemnly agreeing to pay the sum of something or other.

«I agree to no such thing,» I said emphatically.
«I intend to pay»—and here I mentioned a sum that
was double the amount he had named.

It was his turn to say *«What's that?»*

I repeated myself. He looked at me as though I
had lost my senses, then, swiftly, as though he were
trapping me, he snapped out: «Very good! We'll
make it as you wish. It's you funeral.»

It's my pleasure and privilege,» I retorted.

«Sir!»

I repeated myself. He gave me a withering look,
beckoned to the lawyer to approach, leaned over and
whispered something in his ear. I had the distinct
impression that he was asking the lawyer if I were
in my sound senses. Apparently assured that I was,
he looked up and, fixing a stony gaze upon me, he

said: «Young man, do you know what the penalty
is for failure to meet your obligations?»

«No sir,» I said, «nor do I care to hear it. Are
we through now? I've got to get back to my job.»

It was a beautiful day outdoors. I started walking
aimlessly. Soon I was at the Brooklyn Bridge. I
started walking over the Bridge, but after a few minutes I lost heart, turned round and dove into the
subway. I had no intention of going back to the
office; I had been given a day off and I intended
to make the most of it.

At Times Square I got off and walked instinctively
towards the French-Italian restaurant over near Third
Avenue. It was cool and dark in the back of the
grocery store where they served the food. At lunch
time there never were many customers. Soon there
was only myself and a big, sprawling Irish girl who
had already made herself quite drunk. We fell into
a strange conversation about the Catholic Church
during the course of which she repeated like a
refrain: «The Pope's all right, but I refuse to kiss
his ass.»

Finally she pushed her chair back, struggled to
her feet, and tried to walk towards the lavatory.
(The lavatory was used by men and women alike
and was in the hall. I saw that she would never
make it alone. I got up and held her by the arm.
She was thoroughly potted and lurching like a storm-
tossed ship.

As we got to the door of the lavatory she begged
me to help her on to the seat. I stood her by the
seat so that all she had to do was to sit down. She
hitched up her skirt and tried to pull her panties
down, but the effort was too much. «Pull 'em down
for me, will you,» she begged with a sleepy grin. I
did as she asked, patted her cunt affectionately, and
sat her down on the seat. Then I turned to go.

«Don't go!» she whined, clutching my hand, and with that she began emptying her tank. I held on while she finished the job, Nos. 1 and 2, with stink bombs and everything. Throughout the operation she repeated over and over: «No, I *won't* kiss the Pope's ass!» She looked so absolutely helpless that I thought perhaps I'd have to wipe her ass for her. However, from long years of training she managed to do this much for herself, though it took and incredibly long time. I was about ready to throw up when finally she asked me to lift her up. As I was pulling her bloomers up I couldn't help rubbing my hand over her rose-bush. It was tempting, but the stench was too powerful to dally with that idea.

As I assisted her out of the toilet the patronne espied us and nodded her head sadly. I wondered if she realized what chivalry it took for me to perform this act. Anyway, we went back to the table, ordered some black coffee, and sat talking a little while longer. As she sobered up she became almost disgustingly grateful. She said if I would take her home I could have her—she wanted to make it up to me. «I'll take a bath and change my things,» she said. «I feel filthy. It *was* filthy too, God help me.»

I told her I would see her home in a taxi, but that I wouldn't be able to stay with her.

«Now you're getting delicate,» she said. «What's the matter, ain't I good enough for you? It ain't my fault, is it, if I had to go to the toilet? You go to the toilet too, don't you? Wait till I take a bath —you'll see what I look like. Listen, give me your hand!» I gave her my hand and she put it under her skirt, right on her bushy cunt. «Take a good feel of it,» she urged. «You like it? Well, it's all yours. I'll scrub it and perfume it for you. You can take all you like of it. I'm not a bad lay. And

I'm not a tart either, see! I got cock-eyed, that's all. A guy walked out on me, and I was crazy enough to take it to heart. He'll come crawling back before long, don't you worry. But Jesus, I did have my heart set on him. I told him I wouldn't kiss the Pope's ass—and that got him sore. I'm a good Catholic, same as he, but I can't see the Pope as Christ Almighty, can you?»

She went on with her monologue, jumping from one thing to another like a goat. I gathered that she was a switch-board operator in a big hotel. She wasn't such a bad sort, either, down under her Irish skin. I could see that she might be very attractive, once the fumes of the alcohol cleared away. She had very blue eyes and jet black hair, and a smile that was sly and puckish. Maybe I would run up and help her with her bath. I could always run out on her if anything went amiss. The thing that bothered me was that I was to meet Mona for dinner. I was to wait for her in the Rose Room of the Mc Alpin Hotel.

We got in a taxi and drove uptown. In the cab she rested her head on my shoulder. «You're awfully good to me,» she said in a sleepy voice. «I don't know who you are, but you're O. K. with me. Jesus, I wish I could take a nap first. Would you wait for me?»

«Sure,» I said. «Maybe I'll take a nap too.»

The apartment was cosy and attractive, better than I had expected it to be. She had no sooner opened the door than she kicked off her shoes. I helped her undress.

As she stood before the mirror, nude except for her panties, I had to admit that she possessed a beautiful figure. Her breasts were white and full, round and taut, with bright strawberry-colored nipples.

«Why don't you take those off too?» I said pointing to the panties.

«No, not now,» she said, suddenly becoming coy, her cheeks coloring slightly.

«I took them off before,» I said. «What's the difference now?» I put my hand on her waist as if to pull them down. «Don't, please!» she begged. Wait till I have my bath.» She paused a moment, then added: «I'm just getting over my period.»

That settled it for me. I saw the ring-worms flowering again. I got panicky.

«All right,» I said, «take your bath! I'll stretch out in here while you're at it.»

«Won't you scrub my back for me?» she said, her lips curling in that puckish smile of hers.

«Why sure I will... certainly,» I said. I led her to the bathroom, half-pushing her along in my haste to get rid of her.

As she slipped out of the panties I noticed a dark bloodstain. Not on your life, I thought to myself. No sir, not in my sound senses I don't. *Kiss the Pope's ass—never!*

But as she lay there soaping herself I felt myself weakening. I took the soap from her hand and scrubbed her bush for her. She squirmed with pleasure as my soapy fingers entwined themselves in her hair.

«I think it's finished,» she said, arching her pelvis and spreading her cunt open with her two hands. «You look... do you see anything?»

I put the soapy middle finger of my. right hand up her cunt and massaged it gently. She lay back with her hands clasped behind her head and slowly gyrated her pelvis. «Jesus, that feels good,» she said. «Go on, do it some more. Maybe I won't need a nap.»

As she got worked up she began to move more

violently. Suddenly she unclasped her hands and with wet fingers she unbuttoned my fly, took my prick out and made a dive for it with her mouth. She went at it like a professional, teasing it, worrying it, fluting her lips, then choking on it. I came off in her mouth; she swallowed it as if it were nectar and ambrosia.

Then she sank back into the tub, sighed heavily and closed her eyes.

Now is the time to beat it, I said to myself, and pretending that I was going to look for a cigarette I grabbed my hat and bolted. As I ran down the stairs I put my finger to my nostrils and smelled it. It wasn't a bad odor. It smelled of soap more than anything else.

A few nights later a private performance was being given at the theatre. Mona had begged me not to attend the performance, saying that it would make her nervous if she knew I were watching her. I had been somewhat put out about it, but finally agreed not to come. I was to meet her afterwards at the stage entrance. She specified the exact time.

I was there ahead of time, not at the stage door but at the entrance to the theatre. I looked at the announcements over and over, thrilled to see her name in bold, clear letters. As the crowd filed out I went to the opposite side of the street and watched. I didn't know why I was watching—I was just rooted to the spot. It was rather dark in front of the theatre and the taxis were all tied up.

Suddenly I saw some one rushing impulsively to the curb where a frail little man stood waiting for a taxi. It was Mona. I saw her kiss the man and then, as the taxi drove away, I saw her wave goodbye. Then her hand fell limply to her side and she stood there a few minutes as if deep in thought.

Finally she rushed back into the theatre through the main entrance.

When I met her at the stage door a few minutes later she seemed over-wrought. I told her what I had just witnessed.

«Then you saw him?» she said, clutching my hand. «Yes, but who was it?»

«Why, it was my father. He got up out of bed to come. He won't last much longer.»

As she spoke the tears came to her eyes. «He said he could die in peace now.» With this she halted abruptly and burying her head in her hands she began to sob. «I should have taken him home,» she said brokenly.

«But why didn't you let me meet him?» I said. «We could have taken him home together.»

She refused to talk about it. She wanted to go home—go home alone and weep. What could I do? I could only assent—it seemed the most delicate thing to do.

I put her in a taxi and watched her ride away. I felt deeply moved. Then I struck out, determined to bury myself in the crowd. At the corner of Broadway I heard a woman calling my name. She came up to me on the run.

«You passed me,» she said, «without recognizing me. What the matter with you? You look depressed.» She held out her two hands for me to grasp.

It was Arthur Raymond's ex-wife, Irma.

«It's funny,» she said, «I just saw Mona a few seconds ago. She got out of a cab and ran down the street. She looked distracted. I was going to speak to her, but she ran off too quickly. I don't think she saw me either... Aren't you living together any more? I thought you were all staying at Arthur's place.»

«Just where did you see her?» I wondered if she could have been mistaken.

«Why, just around the corner.»

«Are you absolutely sure?»

She smiled strangely. «I couldn't mistake *her*, could I?»

«I don't know,» I mumbled, more to myself—«it hardly seems possible. How was she dressed?»

She described her accurately. When she said «a little velvet cape» I knew it couldn't have been any one else.

«Did you have a quarrel?»

«No—o—o, not a quarrel...»

«Well you ought to know Mona by this .time,» said Irma, trying to dismiss the subject. She had taken my arm and was guiding me along, as if perhaps I were not quite in full possession of my faculties.

«I'm awfully glad to see you,» she said. «Dolores and I are always talking about you... Don't you want to drop up for a minute? Dolores will be delighted to see you. We have an apartment together. It's right near here. Do come up... I'd love to talk to you a while. It must be over a year since I saw you last. You had just left your wife, you remember? And now you're living with Arthur— that's strange. How is he getting on? Is he doing well? I hear he has a beautiful wife.»

It didn't require much coaxing to persuade me to run up and have a quiet drink with then. Irma seemed to be bubbling over with joy. She had always been very friendly with me, but never this effusive. I wondered what had come over her.

When we got upstairs the place was dark. «That's funny,» said Irma, «she said she would be home early this evening. Oh well, she'll be along in a few

minutes, no doubt. Take your things off... sit down...
I'll get you a drink in a minute.»

I sat down, feeling somewhat dazed. Years ago,
when I first knew Arthur Raymond, I had been
rather fond of Irma. When they separated she had
fallen in love with my friend O'Mara, and he had
made her just as miserable as Arthur had. He complained that she was cold—not frigid, but selfish.
I hadn't given much attention to her then because
I was interested in Dolores. Only once had there
ever been anything approaching intimacy between
us. That had been a pure accident and neither of
us had made anything of it. We had met on the
street in front of a cheap cinema one afternoon and
after a few words, both of us being rather listless
and weary, we had gone inside. The picture was
unbearably dull, the theatre almost empty. We had
thrown our overcoats over our laps and then, more
out of boredom and the need of some human contact, our hands met and we sat thus for a while
staring vacantly at the screen. After a time I slung
my arm around her and drew her to me. In a few
moments she let go my hand and placed her own
on my prick. I did nothing, curious to see what she
would make of the situation. I remembered O'Mara
saying that she was cold and indifferent. So I sat
still and waited. I had only a semi hard-on when
she touched me. I let it grow under her hand which
was resting immobile. Gradually I felt the pressure
of her fingers, then a firm grasp, then a squeezing
and stroking, all very quietly, delicately, almost as
if she were asleep and doing it unconsciously. When
it began to quiver and jump she slowly and deliberately unbuttoned my fly, reached in and grabbed my
balls. Still I made no move to touch her. I had a
perverse desire to make her do everything herself.
I remembered the shape and the feel of her fingers;

they were sensitive and expert. She had cuddled up
like a cat and had ceased to look at the screen. My
prick was out of course, but still hidden under the
overcoat. I watched her throw the coat back and
fasten her gaze on my prick. Boldly now she began
to massage it, more and more firmly, more and more
rapidly. Finally I came in her hand. «I'm sorry,»
she murmured, reaching for her bag to extract a
handkerchief. I permitted her to wipe me off with
her silk kerchief. Not a word out of me. Not a
move to embrace her. Nothing. Just as if I had
watched her doing it to some one else. After she
had powdered her face, put everything back into her
bag, I pulled her to me and glued my mouth to
hers. Then I pushed her coat off her lap, raised her
legs and slung them over my lap. She had nothing
on under her skirt, and she was wet. I paid her
back in her own coin, doing it ruthlessly almost,
until she came. When we left the theatre we had
a coffee and some pastry together in a bakery and
after an inconsequential conversation parted as
though nothing had happened.

«Excuse me,» she said, «for being so long. I felt
like getting into something comfortable.»

I came out of my reverie to look up at a lovely
apparition handing me a tall glass. She had made
herself into a Japanese doll. We had hardly sat
down on the divan when she jumped up and went
to the clothes closet. I heard her moving the valises
around and then came a little exclamation, a sigh
of frustration, as though she were calling to me in
a muted voice.

I jumped up and ran to the closet where I found
her standing on top of a swaying valise, reaching
for something on the top shelf. I held her legs a
moment to steady her and, just as she was turning
round to descend, I slid my hand up under the silk

kimono. She came down in my arms with my hand securely fastened between her legs. We stood there in a passionate embrace, enveloped in her feminine frills. Then the door opened and Dolores walked in. She was startled to find us buried in the closet.

«Well!» she exclaimed with a little gasp, «fancy finding *you* here!»

I let go of Irma and put my arms around Dolores who only feebly protested. She seemed more beautiful now than ever.

As she disengaged herself she broke out into her usual little laugh which was always slightly ironical. «We don't have to stay in the closet, do we?» she said, holding my hand. Irma meanwhile had slipped an arm around me.

«Why not stay here?» I said. «It's cosy and womblike.» I was squeezing Irma's ass as I spoke.

«God, you haven't changed a bit,» said Dolores. «You never get enough of it, do you? I thought you were madly in love with... with... I forget her name.»

«Mona.»

«Yes, Mona... how is she? Is it still serious? I thought you were never going to look at another woman!»

«Exactly,» I said. «This is an accident, as you can see.»

«I know,» she said, revealing more and more her smothered jealousy, «I know these accidents of yours. Always on the alert, aren't you?»

We spilled into the living room where Dolores threw off her things—rather vehemently, I thought, as though preparing for a struggle.

«Will I pour you a drink?» asked Irma .

«Yes, and a good stiff one,» said Dolores. «I need one. ...Oh, it has nothing to do with *you*,» she said,

observing that I was looking at her strangely. «It's
that friend of yours, Ulric.»

«What's the matter, isn't he treating you well?»
She was silent. She gave me a desolate look, as
though to say—you know very well what I'm talking
about.

Irma thought the lights were too strong; she turned
out all but the little reading lamp by the other divan.

«Looks as though you were preparing the scene,»
said Dolores mockingly. At the same time one felt
that there was a secret thrill in her voice. I knew
it was Dolores whom I would have to deal with.
Irma, on the other hand, was like a cat; she moved
about softly, almost purring. She was not in the
least disturbed; she was making herself ready for
any eventuality.

«It's good to have you here alone,» said Irma, as
though she had found a long lost brother. She had
stretched herself out on the divan, close to the wall.
Dolores and I were sitting almost at her feet. Behind
Dolores' back I had my hand on Irma's thigh; a dry
heat emanated from her body.

«She must guard you pretty close,» said Dolores,
referring to Mona. «Is she afraid of losing you—or
what?»

«Perhaps,» I said, giving her a provocative smile.
«And perhaps I'm afraid of losing *her*.»

«Then it is serious?»

«*Very*,» I answered. «I found the woman I need,
and I'm going to keep her.»

«Are you married to her?»

«No, not yet... but we will be soon.»

«And you'll have children and everything?»

«I don't know whether we'll have children... why,
is that important?»

«You might as well do it thoroughly,» said Dolores.
«Oh, stop it!» said Irma. «You sound as though

you were jealous. I'm not! I'm glad he's found the
right woman. He deserves it.» She squeezed my
hand, in relaxing the pressure, she adroitly slipped
my hand over her pussy.

Dolores, conscious of what was going on, but
pretending not to notice, got up and went to the
bathroom.

«She's acting queer,» said Irma. «She seems
positively green with jealousy.»

«You mean jealous of *you?*» I said, somewhat
puzzled myself.

«No, not of me... of course not! Jealous of Mona.»

«That's strange,» I said, «I thought she was in love
with Ulric.»

«She is, but she hasn't forgotten you. She...»

I stopped her words with a kiss. She flung her
arms around my neck and cuddled up to me, writhing
and twisting like a big cat. «I'm glad I don't feel
that way,» she murmured. «I wouldn't want to be
in love with you. I like you better this way.»

I ran my hand under the kimono again. She
responded warmly and willingly.

Dolores returned and excused herself lamely for
interrupting the game. She was standing beside us,
looking down with sparkling, mischievous eyes.

«Hand me my glass, will you?» I said.

«Perhaps you'd like me to fan you too,» said she,
as she put the glass to my lips.

I pulled her down beside us, stroking the half-
exposed limb which protruded from her dressing
gown. She too had taken off her things.

«Haven't you got something for me to slip into
too?» I asked, looking from one to the other.

«Why certainly,» said Irma, springing to her feet
with alacrity.

«Oh, don't pamper him like that,» said Dolores,
with a pouting smile. «That's just what he loves...

he wants to be made a fuss over. And then he's going to tell us how faithful he is to his wife.»

«She's not my wife yet,» I said tauntingly, accepting the robe which Irma offered me.

«Oh, isn't she?» said Dolores. «Well, then it's worse.»

«Worse, what do you mean *worse?* I haven't done anything yet, have I?»

«No, but you're going to try.»

«You mean you'd like me to. Don't be impatient... you'll get your chance.»

«Not with *me*,» said Dolores, «I'm going to bed. You two can do what you like.»

For answer I closed the door and started undressing. When I returned I found Dolores stretched out on the couch and Irma sitting by her side with legs crossed, fully exposed.

«Don't mind anything she says,» said Irma. «She likes you just as much as I do... maybe more. She doesn't like Mona, that's all.»

«Is that true?» I looked from Irma to Dolores. The latter was silent, but it was a silence which meant affirmation.

«I don't know why you should feel so strongly about her,» I hastened to continue. «She's never done anything to you. And you can't be jealous of her because... well, because you weren't in love with me... then.»

«*Then?* What do you mean? I was never in love with you, thank God!» said Dolores.

«It doesn't sound very convincing,» said Irma playfully. «Listen, if you never loved him don't be so passionate about it.» She turned to me and in her blithe way she said: «Why don't you kiss her and stop this nonsense?»

«All right, I will,» said I, and with that I bent over and embraced Dolores. At first she held her lips firmly shut, looking at me defiantly. Then, little by little, she surrendered, and when at last she pulled away she was biting my lips. As she pulled her lips away she gave me a little shove. «Get him out of here!» she said. I gave her a look of reproach in which there was an element of pity and disgust. She became at once repentant and yielding again. I bent over her again, tenderly this time, and as I slipped my tongue into her mouth I put my hand between her legs. She tried to push my hand away but the effort was too much.

«Whew! it's getting close,» I heard Irma say, and then she pulled me away. «I'm here too, don't forget.» She was offering her lips and breasts.

It was getting to be a tug of war. I jumped up to pour myself a drink. The bath robe stood out like a stretched tent.

«Do you have to show us that?» said Dolores, pretending to be embarrassed.

«I don't have to but I will, since you ask for it,» I said, drawing the robe back and exposing myself completely.

Dolores turned her head to the wall, mumbling something in a pseudo-hysterical voice about «disgusting and obscene». Irma on the other hand looked at it good-humoredly. Finally she reached for it and squeezed it gently. As she stood up to accept the drink I had poured for her I opened her robe and placed my cock between her legs. We drank together with my cock knocking at the stable door.

«I want a drink too,» said Dolores petulantly. We turned round simultaneously and faced her. Her face was scarlet, her eyes big and bright, as through she had put belladonna in them. «You look debauched,» she said, her eyes switching back and forth from Irma to me.

I handed her the glass and she took a deep draught

of it. She was struggling to obtain that freedom which Irma flaunted like a flag.

Her voice came challengingly now. «Why don't you do it and get done with it?» she said, flinging her words at us. In wriggling about she had uncovered herself; she knew it too and made no effort to hide her nakedness.

«Lie down there,» I said, pushing Irma gently back on the divan.

Irma took my hand and pulled. «You lie down too,» she said.

I raised the glass to my lips and as it was slipping down my throat the light went out. I heard Dolores saying—«No, don't do that, *please!*» But the light remained out and as I stood there finishing the drink I felt Irma's hand on my prick, squeezing it convulsively. I put the glass down and jumped in between them. Almost at once they closed in on me. Dolores was kissing me passionately and Irma, like a cat, had crouched down and fastened her mouth on my prick. It was an agonizing bliss which lasted for a few seconds and then I exploded in Irma's mouth.

When I arrived at Riverside Drive it was almost dawn. Mona had not returned. I lay listening for her step. I began to fear that she had met with an accident—worse, that perhaps she had killed herself, or tried to, at least. It was possible too that she had gone home to her parents. But then why had she left the cab? Perhaps to run to the subway. But then the subway was not in that direction. I could of course telephone her home, but I knew she would interpret that badly. I wondered if she had telephoned during the night. Neither Rebacca or Arthur ever bothered to leave a message for me; they always waited until they saw me.

Towards eight o'clock I knocked at their door.
They were still asleep. I had to knock loudly before
they answered. And then I learned nothing—they
had come home very late themselves.

In despair I went to Kronski's room. He too was
muffled in sleep. He didn't seem to know what I
was driving at.

Finally he said: «What's the matter—has she been
out all night again? No, there wasn't any call for
you. Get out of here... leave me alone!»

I hadn't slept a wink. I felt exhausted. But then
the reassuring thought came to me that she might
telephone me at the office. I almost expected a
message to be lying on my desk waiting for me.

Most of the day went by in taking cat naps. I
slept at my desk, my head buried in my folded arms.
Several times I called Rebecca to see if she had
received any message, but it was always the same
answer. When it came time to close shop I lingered
on. No matter what had happended I could not
believe that she would let the day pass without telephoning me. It was just incredible.

A strange, nervous vitality possessed me. Suddenly
I was wide awake, more wide awake than I could
have been had I rested three days in bed. I would
wait another half hour and if she didn't phone I
would go directly to her home.

As I was pacing back and forth with pantherish
strides the stairway door opened and a little shaver
with dark skin entered. He closed the door behind
him quickly as if he were shutting out a pursuer.
There was something jolly and mysterious about him
which his Cuban voice exaggerated.

«You *will* give me a job, won't you, Mr. Miller?»
he burst out. «I must have the messenger job to
complete my studies. Everybody tells me that you
are a kind man—and I can see it myself—you have

a good face. I am proficient in many things, as you will discover when you know me better. Juan Rico is my name. I am eighteen years old. I am a poet too.»

«Well, well,» I said, chuckling and stroking him under the chin—he was the size of a midget and looked like one—«so you're a poet? Then I'm surely going to give you a job.»

«I'm an acrobat too,» he said. «My father had a circus once. You will find me very speedy on my legs. I love to go hither and about with zest and alacrity. I am also extremely courteous and when delivering a message I would say, 'Thank you sir', and doff my cap respectfully. I know all the streets by heart, including the Bronx. And if you would put me in the Spanish neighborhood you would find me very effective. Do I please you, sir?» He gave me a bewitching grin which implied that he knew very well how to sell himself.

«Go over there and sit down,» I said. «I'll give you a blank to fill out. To-morrow morning you can start in bright and early—with a smile.»

«Oh I can smile, sir—beautifully,» and he did.

«You're sure you're eighteen?»

«Oh yes, sir, that I can prove. I have all my papers with me.»

I gave him an application blank and went to the adjoining room—the rink—to leave him in peace. Suddenly the telephone rang. I bounded back to the desk and picked up the receiver. It was Mona speaking, in a subdued, restrained, unnatural voice, as though she had been drained hollow.

«He died a little while ago,» she said. «I've been at his side ever since I left you...»

I mumbled some inadequate words of consolation and then I asked her when she was coming back. She wasn't sure just when... she wanted me to do her

a little favor... to go to the department store and buy
her a mourning dresse and some black gloves. Size
sixteen. *What sort of material?* She didn't know
anything I chose... A few more words and she hung
up.

Little Juan Rico was looking up into my eyes like
a faithful dog. He had understood everything and
was trying in his delicate Cuban way to let me know
that he wished to share my sorrow.

«It's all right, Juan,» I said, «everybody has to die
some time.»

«Whas that your wife who telephoned?» he asked.
His eyes were moist and glistening.

«Yes,» I said, «that was my wife.»

«I'm sure she must be beautiful.»

«What makes you say that?»

«The way you talked to her... I could almost see
her. I wish I could marry a beautiful woman some
day. I think about it very often.»

«You're a funny lad,» I said. «Thinking about
marriage already. Why, you're just a boy.»

«Here's my application, sir. Will you kindly look
it over now so that I may be sure I can come to-
morrow?»

I gave it a quick glance and assured him it was
satisfactory.

«Then I am at your service, sir. And now, sir, if
you will pardon me, may I suggest that you let me
stay with you a little while? I don't think it is good
for you to be alone at this moment. When the heart
is sad one needs a friend.»

I burst out laughing. «A good idea,» I said.
«We'll go to dinner together, how's that? And a
movie afterwards—does that suit you?»

He got up and began to frisk about like a trained
dog. Suddenly he became curious about the empty
room in the rear. I followed him in and watched

him good-naturedly as he examined the paraphernalia. The roller skates intrigued him. He had picked up a pair and was examining them as if he had never seen such things before.

«Put them on,» I said, «and do a turn. This is the skating rink.»

«Can you skate also?» he asked.

«Sure I can. Do you want to see me skate?»

«Yes,» he said, «and let me skate with you. I haven't done it for years and years. It's a rather comical diversion, is it not?»

We slipped the skates on. I shot forward with hands behind my back. Little Juan Rico followed at my heels. In the center of the room there were slender pillars; I looped in and around the pillars as if I were giving an exhibition.

«I say, but it's very exhilarating, isn't it?» said Juan breathlessly. «You glide like a zephyr.»

«Like a what?»

«Like a *zephyr*... a mild, pleasant breeze.»

«Oh, *zephyr!*»

« I wrote a poem once about a zephyr—that was long ago.»

I took his hand and swung him around. Then I placed him in front of me and with my hands on his waist I pushed him along, guiding him lightly and dexterously about the floor. Finally I gave him a good push and sent him skedaddling to the other end of the room.

«Now I'll show you a few fancy turns that I learned in the Tyrol,» I said, folding my arms in front of me and raising one leg in the air. The thought that never in her life would Mona suspect what I was doing this minute gave me a demonic joy. As I passed and repassed little Juan, who was now sitting on the window-sill absorbed in the spectacle, I made faces at him—first sad and mournful,

then gay, then insouciant, then hilarious, then
medidative, then stern, then menacing, then idiotic.
I tickled myself in the arm-pits, like a monkey; I
waltzed like a trained bear; I squatted low like a
cripple; I sang in a cracked key, then shouted like
a maniac. Round and round, ceaselessly, merrily,
free as a bird. Juan joined in. We stalked each
other like animals, we turned into waltzing mice, we
did the deaf and dumb act.

And all the time I was thinking of Mona wandering about in the house of mourning, waiting for her
mourning dress, her black gloves, and what not.

Round and round, with never a care. A little
kerosene, a match, and we would go up in flames,
like a burning merry-go-round. I looked at Juan's
poll—it was like dry tinder. I had an insane desire
to set him on fire, set him aflame and send him
hurtling down the elevator shaft. Then two or three
wild turns, à la Breughel, and out the window!

I calmed down a little. Not Breughel, but Hiero-
nymous Bosch. A season in hell, amidst the traps
and pulleys of the medieval mind. First time around
they yank off an arm. Second time around a leg.
Finally just a torso rolling around. And the music
playing with vibrant twangs. The iron harp of
Prague. A sunken street near the synagogue. A
dolorous peal of the bells. A woman's guttural
lament.

Not Bosch any longer, but Chagall. An angel in
mufti descending slantwise just above the roof. Snow
on the ground and in the gutters little pieces of meat
for the rats. Cracow in the violet light of eviscera-
tion. Weddings, births, funerals. A man in an
overcoat and only one string to his violin. The bride
has lost her mind; she dances with broken legs.

Round and round, ringing door-bells, ringing
sleigh-bells. The cosmococcic round of grief and

slats. At the roots of my hair a touch of frost, in the tips of my toes a fire. The world is a merry-go-round in flames, the horses burn down to the hocks. A cold, stiff father lying on a feather-bed. A mother green as gangrene. And the bridegroom rolling along.

First we'll bury him in the cold ground. Then we'll bury his name, his legend, his kites and race horses. And for the widow a bon-fire, a suttee Viennoise. I will marry the widow's daughter—in her mourning gown and black gloves. I will do atonement and anoint my head with ashes.

Round and round... Now the figure eight. Now the dollar sign. Now the the spread eagle. A little kerosene and a match, and I would go up like a Christmas tree.

«Mr. Miller! Mr. Miller!» calls Juan. «Mr. Miller, stop it! Please stop it!»

The boy looks frightened. What can it be that makes him stare at me so?

«Mr. Miller,» he says, clutching me by the coat tail, «please don't laugh so! *Please*, I'm afraid for you.»

I relaxed. A broad grin came over my face, then softened to an amiable smile.

«That's better, sir. You had me worried. Hadn't we better go now?»

«I think so, Juan. I think we've had enough exercise for to day. To-morrow you will get a bicycle. *Are you hungry?*»

«Yes sir, I am indeed. I always have a fabulous appetite. Once I ate a whole chicken all by myself. That was when my aunt died.»

«We'll have chicken to-night, Juan me lad. Two chickens—one for you and one for me.»

«You're very kind, sir... Are you sure you're all right now?»

«Fine as a fiddle, Juan. Now where do you suppose we could buy a mourning dress at this hour?»

«I'm sure I don't know,» said Juan.

In the street I hailed a taxi. I had an idea that on the East Side there would be shops still open. The driver was certain he could find one.

«It's very lively down here, isn't it?» said Juan, as we alighted in front of a dress shop. «Is it always this way?»

«Always,» I said. «A perpetual fiesta. Only the poor enjoy life.»

«I should like to work down here some time,» said Juan. «What language do they speak here?»

«All languages,» I said. «You can also speak English.»

The proprietor was standing at the door. He gave Juan a friendly pat on the head.

«I would like a mourning dress, size 16,» I said. «Not too expensive. It must be delivered to-night, C. O. D.»

A dark young Jewess with a Russian accent stepped forward. «Is it for a young or an old woman?» she said.

«A young woman, about your size. For my wife.»

She began showing me various models. I told her to choose the one she thought most suitable. «Not an ugly one,» I begged, «and not too chic either. You know what I mean.»

«And the gloves,» said Juan. «Don't forget the gloves.»

«What size?» asked the young lady.

«Let me see your hands,» I said. I studied them a moment. «A little larger than yours.»

I gave the address and left a generous tip for the errand boy. The proprietor now came up, began talking to Juan. He seemed to take a great fancy to him.

«Where do you come from, sonny?» he asked. «From Puerto Rico?»

«From Cuba,» said Juan.

«Do you speak Spanish?»

«Yes sir, and French and Portuguese.»

«You're very young to know so many languages.»

«My father taught me them. My father was the editor of a newspaper in Havana.»

«Well, well,» said the proprietor. «You remind me of a little boy I knew in Odessa.»

«Odessa!» said Juan. «I was in Odessa once. I was a cabin boy on a trading ship.»

«What!» exclaimed the proprietor. «You were in Odessa? It's unbelievable. How old are you?»

«I'm eighteen, sir.»

The proprietor turned to me. He wanted to know if he couldn't invite us to have a drink with him in the ice cream parlor next door.

We accepted the invitation with pleasure. Our host, whose name was Eisenstein, began to talk about Russia. He had been a medical student originally. The boy who resembled Juan was his son who had died. «He was a strange boy,» said Mr. Eisenstein. «He didn't resemble any of the family. And he had his own way of thinking. He wanted to tramp around the world. No matter what you told him he had a different idea. He was a little philosopher. Once he ran away to Egypt—because he wanted to study the pyramids. When we told him we were going to America he said he would go to China. He said he didn't want to become rich, like the Americans. A strange boy! Such independence! Nothing frightened him—not even the Cossacks. I was almost afraid of him sometimes. Where did he come from? He didn't even look like a Jew...»

He went into a monologue about the strange blood that had been poured into the veins of the Jews in their wanderings. He spoke of strange tribes in Arabia, Africa, China. He thought even the Eskimos might have Jewish blood in them. As he talked he became intoxicated by this idea of the mixture of races and bloods. The world would be a stagnant pool had it not been for the Jews. «We are like seeds carried by the wind,» he said. «We blossom everywhere. Hardy plants. Until we are pulled up by the roots. Even then we don't perish. We can live upside down. We can grow between stones.»

All this time he had taken me for a Jew. Finally I explained that I was not a Jew, but that my wife was.

«And she became a Christian?»

«No, I'm becoming a Jew.»

Juan was looking at me with big, questioning eyes. Mr. Eisenstein didn't know whether I was joking or not.

«When I come down here,» I said, «I feel happy. I don't know what it is, but I feel more at home here. Maybe I have Jewish blood and don't know it.»

«I'm afraid not,» said Mr. Eisenstein. «You're attracted, because you're not a Jew. You like what is different, that's all. Maybe you hated the Jews once. That happens sometimes. Suddenly a man sees that he was mistaken and then he becomes violently in love with what he once hated. He goes to the other extreme. I know a Gentile who became converted to Judaism. We don't try to convert, you know that. If you're a good Christian it's better that you stay a Christian.»

«But I don't care about the religion,» I said.

«The religion is everything,» he said. «If you can't be a good Christian you can't be a good Jew. We are not a people or a race—we're a religion.»

«That's what you say, but I don't believe it. It's more than that. It's as though you were a kind of bacteria. Nothing can explain your survival, certainly not your faith. That's why I'm so curious, why I get excited when I'm with your people. I would like to possess the secret.»

«Well, study your wife,» said he.

«I do but I don't make her out. She's a mystery.»

«But you love her?»

«Yes,» I said, «I love her passionately.»

«And why aren't you with her now? Why do you have the dress sent to her? Who is it that died?»

«Her father,» I answered. «But I never met him,» I added rapidly. «I've never been inside her home.»

«That's bad,» he said. «There's something wrong there. You should go to her. Never mind if she didn't ask you. Go to her! Don't let her be ashamed of her parents. You don't have to go to the funeral, but you should let her see that you care for her family. You are only an accident in her life. When you die the family will go on. They will absorb your blood. We have drunk the blood of every race. We go on like a river. You must not think you are marrying her alone—you are marrying the Jewish race, the Jewish people. We give you life and strength. We nourish you. In the end all peoples will come together. We will have peace. We will make a new world. And there will be room for everybody... No, don't leave her alone now. You will regret it, if you do. She is proud, that's what it is. You must be soft and gentle. You must woo her like a pigeon. Maybe she loves you now, but later she will love you more. She will hold you like a vise. There is no love like that of the Jewish woman for the man she gives her heart to. *Especially if he is of Gentile blood.* It is a great victory for her. It is better for you to surrender than to be the master.... You will excuse me for speaking this way, but I know what I am talking about. And

I see you are not an ordinary Gentile. You are one of those lost Gentiles—you are searching for something... you don't know what exactly. We know your kind. We are not always eager to have your love. We have been betrayed so often. Sometimes it is better to have a good enemy—then we know where we stand. With your kind we are never sure where we stand. You are like water—and we are rocks. You eat us away little by little—not with malice, but with kindness. You lap against us like the waves of the sea. The big waves we can meet—but the gentle lapping, that takes our strength away.»

I was so excited by this unexpected excursus that I had to interrupt his speech.

«Yes, I know,» he said. «I know how you feel. You see, we know all about you—but you have everything to learn about us. You can be married a thousand times, to a thousand Jewish women, and still you will not know what we know. We are right inside of you all the time. Bacteria, yes, maybe. If you are strong we support you; if you are weak, we destroy you. We live not in the world, as it seems to the Gentile, but in the spirit. The world passes away, but the spirit is eternal. My little boy understood that. He wanted to remain pure. The world was not good enough for him. He died of shame—shame for the world....»

19

Some minutes later, when we sauntered out into the violet light of early evening, I saw the ghetto with new eyes. There are Summer nights in New York when the sky is pure azure, when the buildings

are immediate and palpable, not only in their substance but in their essence. That dirty streaked
light which reveals only the ugliness of factories and
sordid tenements disappears very often with sunset,
the dust settles down, the contours of the buildings
become more sharply defined, like the lineaments of
an ogre in a calcium spotlight. Pigeons appear in
the sky, wheeling above the roof-tops. A cupola
bobs up, sometimes out of a Turkish Bath. There
is always the stately simplicity of St. Marks-on-the-
Bouwerie, the great foreign square abutting Avenue
A., the low Dutch buildings above which the ruddy
gas tanks loom, the intimate side streets with their
incongruous American names, the triangles which
bear the stamp of old landmarks, the waterfront
with the Brooklyn shore so close that one can
almost recognize the people walking on the other
side. All the glamour of New York is squeezed into
this pullulating area which is marked off by formal-
dehyde and sweat and tears. Nothing is so familiar,
so intimate, so nostalgic to the New Yorker as this
district which he spurns and rejects. The whole of
New York should have been one vast ghetto: the
poison should have been drained off, the misery
apportioned; the joy should have been communicated
through every vein and artery. The rest of New
York is an abstraction; it is cold, geometrical, rigid
as *rigor mortis* and, I might as well add, *insane*—
if one can only stand apart and look at it undaunt-
edly. Only in the beehive can one find the human
touch, find that city of sights, sounds, smells which
one hunts for in vain beyond the margins of the
ghetto. To live outside the pale is to wither and
die. Beyond the pale there are only dressed-up
cadavers. They are wound up each day, like alarm
clocks. They perform like seal; they die like box
office receipts. But in the seething honey-comb

there is a growth as of plants, an animal warmth
almost suffocating, a vitality which accrues from
rubbing and glueing together, a hope which is
physical as well as spiritual, a contamination which
is dangerous but salutary. Small souls perhaps,
burning like tapers, but burning steadily—and
capable of throwing portentous shadows on the walls
which hem them in.

Walk down any street in the soft violet light.
Make the mind blank. A thousand sensations as-
sault you at once from every direction. Here man
is still furred and feathered; here cyst and quartz
still speak. There are audible, voluble buildings
with sheet metal vizors and windows that sweat;
places of worship too, where the children drape
themselves about the porticos like contortionists;
rolling, ambulant streets where nothing stands still,
nothing is fixed, nothing is comprehensible except
through the eyes and mind of a dreamer. Hallucinating streets too, where suddenly all is silence, all
is barren, as if after the passing of a plague. Streets
that cough, streets that throb like a fevered temple,
streets to die on and not a soul take notice. Strange,
frangipanic streets, in which attar of roses mingles
with the acrid bite of leek and scallion. Slippered
streets, which echo with the pat and slap of lazy
feet. Streets out of Euclid, which can be explained
only by logic and theorem....

Pervading all, suspended between the layers of the
skin like a distillate of ruddy smoke, is the secondary sexual sweat—pubic, Orphic, mammalian—a
heavy incense smuggled in by night on velvet pads
of musk. No one is immune, not even the Mongoloid
idiot. It washes over you like the brush and passage of camisoled breasts. In a light rain it makes
an invisible aetherial mud. It is of every hour, even
when rabbits are boiled to a stew. It glistens in the

tubes, the follicles, the papillaries. As the earth slowly wheels, the stoops and banisters turn and the children with them; in the murky haze of sultry nights all that is terrene, volupt and fatidical hums like a zither. A heavy wheel plated with fodder and feather-beds, with little sweet-oil lamps and drops of pure animal sweat. All goes round and round, creaking, wobbling, lumbering, whimpering sometimes, but round and round and round. Then, if you become very still, standing on a stoop, for instance, and carefully think no thoughts, a myopic, bestial clarity besets your vision. There is a wheel, there are spokes, and there is a hub. And in the center of the hub there is—exactly nothing. It is where the grease goes, and the axle. And you are there, in the center of nothingness, sentient, fully expanded, whirring with the whir of planetary wheels. Everything becomes alive and meaningful, even yesterdays' snot which clings to the door-knob. Everything sags and droops, is mossed with wear and care; everything has been looked at thousands of times, rubbed and caressed by the occipital eye....

A man of an olden race standing in a stone trance. He smells the food which his ancestors cooked in the millenary past: the chicken, the liver paste, the stuffed fish, the herrings, the eiderdown ducks. He has lived with them and they have lived in him. Feathers float through the air, the feathers of winged creatures caged in crates—as it was in Ur, in Babylon, in Egypt and Palestine. The same shiny silks, blacks turning green with age: the silks of other times, of other cities, other ghettos, other pogroms. Now and then a coffee grinder or a samovar, a little wooden casket for spices, for the myrrh and aloes of the East. Little strips of carpet—from the souks and bazaars, from the emporiums of the Levant; bits of astrakhan, laces, shawls, nubies, and

petticoats of flaming, flouncing flamingo. Some
bring their birds, their little pets—warm, tender
things pulsing with tremulous beat, learning no new
language, no new melodies, but pining away, droopy,
listless, languishing in their super-heated cages suspended above the fire-escapes. The iron balconies
are festooned with meat and bedding, with plants
and pets—a crawling still life in which even the
rust is rapturously eaten away. With the cool of the
evening the young are exposed like egg-plants; they
lie back under the stars, lulled to dream by the
obscene jabberwocky of the American street. Below,
in wooden casks, are the pickles floating in brine.
Without the pickle, the pretzel, the Turkish sweets,
the ghetto would be without savour. Bread of every
variety, with seeds and without. White, black,
brown, even gray bread—of all weights, all con-
sistencies....

The ghetto! A marble table top with a basket
of bread. A bottle of seltzer water, preferably blue.
A soup with egg drops. And two men talking. Talking, talking, talking, with burning cigarettes hanging
from their blenched lips. Nearby a cellar with
music: strange instruments, strange costumes, strange
airs. The birds begin to warble, the air becomes
over-heated, the bread piles up, the seltzer bottles
smoke and sweat. Words are dragged like ermine
through the spittled sawdust; growling, guttural dogs
paw the air. Spangled women choked with tiaras
doze heavily in their richly upholstered caskets of
flesh. The magnetic fury of lust concentrates in
dark, mahogany eyes.

In another cellar an old man sits in his overcoat
on a pile of wood, counting his coal. He sits in the
dark, as he did in Cracow, stroking his beard. His
life is all coal and wood, little voyages from darkness to daylight. In his ears is still the ring of hoofs

on cobbled streets, the sound of shrieks and screams, the clatter of sabres, the splash of bullets against a blank wall. In the cinema, in the synagogue, in the coffee house, wherever one sits, two kinds of music playing—one bitter, one sweet. One sits in the middle of a river called Nostalgia. A river filled with little souvenirs gathered from the wreckage of the world. Souvenirs of the homeless, of birds of refuge building again and again with sticks and twigs. Everywhere broken nests, egg shells, fledgelings with twisted necks and dead eyes staring into space. Nostalgic river dreams under tin copings, under rusty sheds, under capsized boats. A world of mutilated hopes, of strangled aspirations, of bullet-proof starvation. A world where even the warm breath of life has to be smuggled in, where gems big as pigeons' hearts are traded for a yard of space, an ounce of freedom. All is compounded into a familiar liver paste which is swallowed on a tasteless wafer. In one gulp there is swallowed down five thousand years of bitterness, five thousand years of ashes, five thousand years of broken twigs, smashed egg-shells, strangled fledgelings....

In the deep sub-cellar of the human heart the dolorous twang of the iron harp rings out.

Build your cities proud and high. Lay your sewers. Span your rivers. Work feverishly. Sleep dreamlessly. Sing madly, like the bulbul. Underneath, below the deepest foundations, there lives another race of men. They are dark, sombre, passionate. They muscle into the bowels of the earth. They wait with a patience which is terrifying. They are the scavengers, the devourers, the avengers. They emerge when everything topples into dust.

20

For seven days and nights I was alone. I began
to think that she had left me. Twice she telephoned,
but she sounded far away, lost, swallowed up by
grief. I remembered Mr. Eisenstein's words. I wondered, wondered if she had been reclaimed.

Then one day, towards closing time, she stepped
out of the elevator and stood before me. She was
all in black except for a mauve turban which gave
her an exotic cast. A transformation had taken
place. The eyes had grown still softer, the skin more
translucent. Her figure had become seductively
suave, her carriage more majestic. She had the
poise of a somnambulist.

For a moment I could scarcely believe my eyes.
There was somethings hypnotic about her. She radiated power, magnetism, enchantment. She was like
one of those Italian women of the Renaissance who
gaze at you steadily with enigmatic smile from a
canvas which recedes into infinity. In those few
strides which she took before throwing herself into
my arms I felt a gulf, such as I had never known
could exist between two people, closing up. It was
as though the earth had opened up between us, as
if, by a supreme and magical effort of will, she had
leaped the void and rejoined me. The ground on
which she stood a moment ago fell away, slipped
into a past altogether unknown to me, just as the
shelf of a continent slips into the sea. Nothing so
clear and tangible as this formulated itself in my
mind then; it was only afterwards, because I re-

hearsed this moment time and again later, that I understood the nature of our reunion.

Her whole body felt strangely different, as I pressed her close. It was the body of a creature who had been reborn. It was an entirely new body that she surrendered, new because it contained some element which hitherto had been missing. It was, strange as it may seem to say so, as if she had returned with her soul—and not her private, individual soul, but the soul of her race. She seemed to be offering it to me, like a talisman.

Words came to our lips with difficulty. We simply gurgled and stared at one another. Then I saw her glance roving over the place, taking everything in with a remorseless eye, and finally resting on my desk and on me. «What are you doing here?» she seemed to say. And then, as it softened, as she gathered me up in the folds of the tribe—«*What have they done to you?*» Yes, I felt the power and the pride of her people. I have not chosen you, it said, to sit among the lowly. I am taking you out of this world. I am going to enthrone you.

And this was Mona, the Mona who had come to me from the center of the dance floor and offered herself, as she had offered herself to hundreds and perhaps thousands of others before me. Such a strange, wondrous flower is the human being! You hold it in your hand and while you sleep it grows, it becomes transformed, it exhales a narcotic fragrance.

In a few seconds I had become worshipful. It was almost unbearable to look at her steadily. To think that she would follow me home, accept the life I had to offer her, seemed unbelievable. I had asked for a woman and I had been given a queen.

What happened at dinner is a complete blank. We must have eaten in a restaurant, we must have talked, we must have made plans. I remember nothing of all this. I remember her face, her new soulful look, the brilliance and magnetism of the eyes, the translucent tone of the flesh.

I remember that we walked for a time through deserted streets. And perhaps, listening only to the sound of her voice, perhaps then she told me everything, all that I had ever longed to know about her. I remember not a word of it. Nothing had any importance or meaning except the future. I held her hand, clasped it firmly, the fingers entwined, walking with her into the overabundant future. Nothing could possibly be what it had been before. The ground had opened up, the past had been swept away, drowned, drowned as deep as a lost continent. And miraculously—how miraculously I only realized as the moments prolonged themselves!—she had been saved, had been restored to me. It was my duty, my mission, my destiny in this life to cherish and protect her. As I thought of all that lay ahead I began to grow, from within, as if from a small seed. I grew inches in the space of a block. It was in my heart that I felt the seed bursting.

And then, as we stood at a corner, a bus came along. We jumped in and went upstairs on the deck. To the very front seat. As soon as the fare had been paid I took her in my arms and smothered her with kisses. We were alone and the bus was careening over the bumpy pavement.

Suddenly I saw her give a wild look around, raise her dress feverishly, and the next moment she was straddling me. We fucked like mad in the space of a few drunken blocks. She sat on my lap, even after it was over, and continued to caress me passionately.

When we entered Arthur Raymond's home the place was ablaze. It was as if they had been expecting her return. Kronski was there and Arthur's two sisters, Rebecca, and some of her friends. They greeted Mona with the utmost warmth and affection. They almost wept over her.

It was the moment to celebrate. Bottles were brought out, the table was spread, the phonograph wound up. «Yes, yes, let us rejoice!» every one seemed to say. We literally flung ourselves at one another. We danced, we sang, we talked, we ate, we drank. More and more joyous it became. Every one loved every one. Union and reunion. On and on into the night, even Kronski singing at the top of his lungs. It was like a bridal feast. The bride had come back from the grave. The bride was young again. The bride had blossomed.

Yes, it was a marriage. That night I knew that we were joined on the ashes of the past.

«My wife, my wife!» I murmured, as we fell asleep.

VOLUME FIVE

21

With the death of her father Mona became more and more obsessed with the idea of getting married. Perhaps on his death-bed she had made a promise which she was trying to keep. Each time the subject came up a little quarrel ensued. (It seemed that I took the subject too lightly.) One day, after one of these tiffs, she began packing her things. She wasn't going to stay with me another day. As we had no valise she had to wrap her things in brown paper. It made a very bulky, awkward bundle.

«You'll look like an immigrant going down the street with that,» I said. I had been sitting on the bed watching her manœuvres for a half hour or more. Somehow I couldn't convince myself that she was leaving. I was waiting for the usual last minute break-down—a flare of anger, a burst of tears, and then a tender, heart-warming reconciliation.

This time, however, she seemed determined to go through with the performance. I was still sitting on the bed as she dragged the bundle through the hall and opened the front door. We didn't even say good-bye to one another.

As the front door slammed to Arthur Raymond came to the threshold and said: «You're not letting her go like that, are you? It's a bit inhuman, isn't it?»

«Is it?» I replied. I gave him a weak and rather forlorn smile.

«I don't understand you at all,» he said. He spoke
as though he were controlling his anger.

«She'll probably be back to-morrow,» I said.

«I wouldn't be so sure of that, if I were you.
She's a sensitive girl... and you're a cold-blooded
bastard.»

Arthur Raymond was working himself into a moral
spasm. The truth was that he had become very fond
of Mona. If he had been honest with himself he
would have had to admit that he was in love with her.

«Why don't you go after her?» he said suddenly,
after an awkward pause. «I'll run down, if you like.
Jesus, you can't let her walk off like that!»

I made no answer. Arthur Raymond bent over
and placed a hand on my shoulder. «Come, come,»
he said, «this is silly. You stay here... I'll run after
her and bring her back.»

He rushed down the hall and opened the front
door. I heard him exclaim: «Well, well! I was just
going to fetch you. Good! Come on in. Here, let
me take that. That's fine.» I heard him laugh, that
cheery, rattling laugh, which grated on one's nerves
sometimes. «Come on back here... he's waiting for
you. Sure, we're all waiting for you. Why did you
do such a thing? You mustn't run away like that.
We're all friends, aren't we? You can't walk out on
us like that....»

From the tone of his voice one would think that
Arthur Raymond was the husband, not I. It was
almost as if he were giving me the cue.

It was only a matter of a few seconds, all this, but
in that interval, brief as it was, I saw Arthur Raymond again as I had the first time we met. Ed
Gavarni had taken me to his home. For weeks he
had been telling me of his friend Arthur Raymond
and what a genius he was. He seemed to think that
he had been granted a rare privilege in bringing the

two of us together, because in Ed Gavarni's opinion
I too was a genius. There he sat, Arthur Raymond,
in the gloom of a basement in one of those solemn-
looking brown-stone houses in the Prospect Park
region. He was much shorter than I had expected
him to be, but his voice was strong, hearty, cheery,
like his hand-shake, like his whole personality. He
emanated vitality.

I had the impression instantly that I was face to
face with an unusual person. He was at his very
worst, too, as I discovered later. He had been out
on a bat all night, had slept in his clothes, and was
rather nervous and irritable. He sat down again at
the piano, after a few words, a burnt-out butt hanging from his lips; as he talked he nervously drum-
med a few keys in the upper register. He had been
forcing himself to practise because time was getting
short—in a few days he was giving a recital, the
first recital in long pants, you might say. Ed Gavarni explained to me that Arthur Raymond had
been a child prodigy, that his mother had dressed
him like Lord Fauntleroy and dragged him all over
the continent, from one concert hall to another. And
then one day Arthur Raymond had put his foot down
and had refused to be a performing chimpanzee any
longer. He had developed a phobia about playing
in public. He wanted to lead his own life. And he
did. He had run amok. He had done everything
to destroy the virtuoso which his mother had created.

Arthur Raymond listened to this impatiently.
Finally he cut in, swinging round on his stool, and
playing with two hands as he spoke. He had a fresh
cigarette in his mouth and as he ran his fingers up
and down the piano the smoke curled up into his
eyes. He was trying to work off his embarrassment.
At the same time I felt that he was waiting to hear
me open up. When Ed Gavarni informed him that

I was also a musician Arthur Raymond jumped up
and begged me to play something. «Go on, go on...»
he said, almost savagely. «I'd like to hear you. God,
I get sick of hearing myself play.»

I sat down, much against my will, and played some
little thing. I realized more than ever before how
poor my playing was. I felt rather ashamed of myself and apologized profusely for the lame performance.

«Not at all, not at all!» he said, with a low, pleasant chuckle. «You ought to continue... you have
talent.»

«The truth is I hardly ever touch the piano any
more,» I confessed.

«How come? Why not? What do you do then?»
Ed Gavarni offered the customary explanations.
«He's really a writer,» he concluded.

Arthur Raymond's eyes sparkled. «A writer!
Well, well...» And with that he resumed his seat at
the piano and began to play. A serious expression
I not only liked but which I was to remember all
my life. His playing enthralled me. It was clean,
vigorous, passionate, intelligent. He attacked the
instrument with his whole being. He ravished it.
I was a Brahms sonata, if I remember rightly, and
I had never been very fond of Brahms. After a few
minutes he stopped suddenly, and then before we
could open our mouths he was playing something
from Debussy, and from that he went on to Ravel
and to Chopin. During the Chopin prelude Ed
Gavarni winked at me. When it was over he urged
Arthur Raymond to play the Revolutionary Etude.
«Oh, that thing! Drat that! God, how you like
that stuff!» He played a few bars, dropped it, came
back to the middle part, stopped, removed the cigarette from his lips, and launched into a Mozartian
piece.

Meanwhile I had been going through internal revolutions. Listening to Arthur Raymond's playing I realized that if I were ever to be a pianist I should have to begin all over again. I felt that I had never really played the piano—I had played *at* it. Something similar had happened to me when I first read Dostoievski. It had wiped out all other literature. («Now I am really listening to human beings talk!» I had said to myself.) It was like that with Arthur Raymond's playing—for the first time I seemed to understand what the composers were saying. When he broke off to repeat a phrase over and over it was as though I heard them speaking, speaking this language of sound with which everybody is familiar but which is really Greek to most of us. I remembered suddenly how the Latin teacher, after listening to our woeful translations, would suddenly snatch the book out of our hands and begin to read aloud to us—in Latin. He read it as though it meant something to him, whereas to us, no matter how good our translations, it was always Latin and Latin was a dead language and the men who wrote in Latin were even more dead to us than the language which they wrote in. Yes, listening to Arthur Raymond's interpretation, whether of Bach, Brahms or Chopin, there were no longer any empty spaces between passages. Everything assumed form, dimension, meaning. There were no dull parts, no lags, no preliminaries.

There was another thing about that visit which flashed through my mind—*Irma*. Irma was then his wife, and a very cute, pretty, doll-like creature she was. More like a Dresden china piece than a wife. Instantly we were introduced I knew that there was something wrong between them. His voice was too harsh, his gestures too rough: she shrank from him as if fearing to be dashed to pieces by an inadvertent

move. I noticed, as we shook hands, that her palms
were moist—moist and hot. She was conscious of
the fact too, and blushingly made some remark about
her glands being out of order. But one felt, as she
said this, that the real reason for her imbalance was
Arthur Raymond, that it was his «genius» which had
unsettled her. O'Mara was right about her—she was
thoroughly feline, she loved to be stroked and petted.
And one knew that Arthur Raymond wasted no time
in such dalliance. One knew immediately that he
was the sort who went straight to the goal. He was
raping her, that's what I felt. And I was right.
Later she confessed it to me.

And then there was Ed Gavarni. One could tell
by the way Arthur Raymond addressed him that he
was used to this sort of adulation. All his friends
were sycophants. He was disgusted with them, no
doubt, and yet he needed it. His mother had given
him a bad start—she had almost destroyed him.
Each performance he had given had weakened his
confidence in himself. They were post-hypnotic
performances, successes because his mother had
willed it to be so. He hated her. He needed a
woman who would believe in him— as a man, as a
human being—not as a trained seal.

Irma hated his mother too. That had a disastrous
effect upon Arthur Raymond. He felt it necessary
to defend his mother against his wife's attacks. Poor
Irma! She was between the devil and the deep sea.
And at bottom she wasn't deeply interested in music.
At bottom she wasn't deeply interested in anything.
She was soft, pliant, gracious, willowy: her only
response was a purr. I don't think she cared about
fucking very much either. It was all right now and
then, when she was in heat, but on the whole it was
too forthright, too brutal, too humiliating. If one
could come together like tiger lilies, yes, then it might

be different. Just brushing together, a soft, gentle, caressing sort of intertwining—that's what she liked. There was something slightly nauseating about a stiff prick, especially dripping sperm. And the positions one had to assume! Really, sometimes she felt positively degraded by the act. Arthur Raymond had a short, stubborn prick—he was the Ram. He went at it bang-bang, as if he were chopping away at a meat block. It was over before she had a chance to feel anything. Short, quick stabs, sometimes on the floor, anywhere, whenever, wherever it happened to seize him. He didn't even give her time to take off her clothes. He just lifted her skirt and shoved it in. No, it was really «horrid». That was one of her pet words—«horrid».

O'Mara on the other hand was like a practised snake. He had a long curved penis which slid in like greased lightning and unlatched the door of the womb. He knew how to control it. But she didn't like his way of going about it either. He used his penis as if it were a detachable apparatus. To stand over her while she was lying abed with her legs open, panting for it, to force her to admire it, take it in her mouth or shove it in her arm-pit, was his delight. He made her feel that she was at his mercy—or rather at the mercy of that long, slimy thing he carried between his legs. He could get an erection any time—at will, so to speak. He wasn't carried away by passion—his passion was concentrated in his prick. He could be very tender too, for all his practised approach, but somehow it wasn't a tenderness that touched her—it was studied, part of his technique. He wasn't «romantic»—that's how she put it. He was too damned proud of his sexual prowess. Just the same, because it was an unusual prick, because it was long and bent, because it could hold out indefinitely, because it could make her lose

herself, she was unable to resist. He had only to
take it out and put in her hand and she was done
for. It was disgusting too that sometimes when he
took it out it was only semi-erect. Even then it was
bigger, silkier, snakier than Arthur Raymond's prick,
even when he was at white heat. O'Mara had a
sullen sort of prick. He was Scorpio. He was like
some primeval creature that waited in ambush, some
huge, patient, crawling reptile which hid in the
swamps. He was cold and fecund ; he lived only to
fuck, but he could bide his time, could wait years
between fucks if necessary. Then, when he had you,
when he closed his jaws on you, he devoured you
piece-meal. That was O'Mara...

I looked up to see Mona standing at the threshold
with tear-stained face. Arthur Raymond was behind
her, holding the big awkward bundle in his two
hands. A broad grin had spread over his face. He
was pleased with himself, terribly pleased.

It wasn't like me to get up and make a demonstration, especially in Arthur Raymond's presence.

«Well,» said Mona, «haven't you anything to say?
Aren't you sorry?»

«Sure he is,» said Arthur Raymond, fearful that
she would bolt again.

«I'm not asking *you*,» she snapped, «I'm asking
him.»

I rose from the bed and went towards her. Arthur
Raymond looked on sheepishly. He would have
given anything to be in my position—I knew that.
As we embraced, Mona turned her head and over
her shoulder she murmured: «Why don't you leave?»
His face grew red as a beet. He tried to stammer
out some apology but the words stuck in his throat.
As he turned away Mona slammed the door shut.
«The fool!» she said. «I'm sick of this place!»

As she pressed her body to mine I felt a hunger

and desperation in her of a new kind. The separation, brief as it was, had been real to her. And it had frightened her too. Nobody had ever permitted her to walk away like that. She had not only been humiliated, she had become curious.

It's interesting to observe how repetitive is woman's behavior in such situations. Almost invariably there comes the question—«*Why* did you do such a thing?» Or—«*How* could you treat me like that?» If it's the man speaking he says: «Let's not talk about it... let's forget it!» But the woman reacts as if she had been shocked in her vital centers, as if perhaps she might never recover from the mortal stab. With her everything is based on the purely personal. She talks egotistically, but it is not the ego which prompts her reproaches—it's WOMAN. That the man she loves, the man to whom she has attached herself, the man whom she is creating in her own image, should suddenly become depossessed is something unthinkable. If it were a question of another woman, if there were a rival, yes, then she might understand. But to unshackle oneself for no reason, to relinquish so easily—just because of a little feminine trick!—that mystifies her. Then everything must be built on sand... then there is no firm grip anywhere.

«You knew I wouldn't stay away, didn't you?» she was saying, half-smiling, half-weeping.

To answer yes or no was equally compromising. Either way I would only be entraining a long argument. So I said: «*He* thought you would come back. I didn't know. I thought maybe I had lost you.»

The last phrase impressed her favorably. «To lose her»—that meant she was precious. It also implied that by coming back of her own will she was making a gift of herself, the most precious gift she could offer me.

«How could I do that?» she said softly, giving me

a melting look. «I only want to know that you care for me. I do silly things sometimes... I feel as though I need proofs of your love... it's so silly.» She gripped me tight, blotting herself against me. In a moment she was passionate, her hand fumbling with my fly. «You did want me to come back?» she murmured, extricating my cock and placing it against her warm cunt. «Say it ! I want to hear you say it!»

I said it. I said it with all the conviction I could muster.

«Now fuck me!» she whispered, and her mouth twisted savagely. She lay crosswise on the bed, her skirt around her neck. «Pull it off!» she begged, too feverish to find the snaps. «I want you to fuck me as thought you never had me before.»

«Wait a minute,» I said, pulling out. «I'm going to take these damned things off first.»

«Quick, quick!» she pleaded. «Put it in all the way. Jesus, Val, I could never do without you... Yes, good, good... that's it.» She was squirming like an eel. «Oh Val, you must never let me go. Tight, hold me tight! Oh God, I'm coming... hold me, hold me.» I waited for the spasm to die down. «You didn't come, did you?» she said. «Don't come yet. Leave it in. Don't move.» I did as she wished; it was jammed in tight and I could feel the silk pennants inside her fluttering like hungry birds. «Wait a minute, dear... wait.» She was gathering her forces for another explosion. Her eyes had become large and moist, relaxed, one might say. As the orgasm approached they grew concentrated, darting wildly from one corner to the other, as though frantically seeking for something to fasten on. «Do it, do it now,» she begged hoarsely. «Go on, give it to me!» Again her mouth had that savage twist, that obscene leer, which more than the most violent movements of the body unleash the male orgasm.

As I shot the hot sperm into her she went into convulsions. She was like a trapeze artist coming off near the roof. And, as happened to her frequently, the orgasms succeeded one another in rapid sequence. I was almost on the verge of slapping her face, to snap her out of it.

The next thing was a cigarette, of course. She lay back under the sheet and inhaled deep puffs, as though she were using a pulmotor.

«Sometimes I think my heart will give out... I'll die in the midst of it.» She relaxed with the ease of a panther, her legs wide apart, as if to let the sperm run out. «God,» she said, placing a hand between her legs, «it's still running out... Give me a towel, will you?»

As I was bending over her with the towel, I put my fingers up her cunt. I liked to feel it just after a fuck. So thrilly-dilly.

«Don't do that,» she begged weakly, «or I'll start all over again.» As she spoke she moved her pelvis lasciviously. «Not too rough, Val... I'm tender. That's it.» She put her hand on my wrist and held it there, directing my movements with deft and delicate pressure of the fingers. Finally I managed to withdraw my hand and quickly glued my mouth to her crack. «That's wonderful,» she sighed. She had closed her eyes. She was falling back into the dark hollow of her being.

We were lying sidewise, her legs slung around my neck. Presently I felt her lips touching my prick. I was spreading her cheeks apart with my two hands, my one eye riveted on the little brown button above her cunt. «That's her asshole,» said I to myself. It was good to look at. So small, so shrunken, as though only little black sheep droppings could come from it.

After we had a bellyful and were lying between

the sheets softly snoozing there came a peremptory knock on the door. It was Rebecca. She wanted to know if we had finished—she was going to make tea and she wanted us to join them.

I told her we were taking a nap, couldn't say when we'd get up.

«May I come in a minute?» With that she pushed the door slightly ajar.

«Sure, come in!» I said, squinting at her with one eye.

«God, you two certainly are a couple of love birds,» she said, giving a low, pleasant, earthy sort of chuckle. «Don't you ever get tired of it? I could hear you way down the other end of the hall. You make me jealous.»

She was standing beside the bed looking down at us. Mona had her hand over my prick, an instinctive gesture of self-protection. Rebecca's eyes seemed to be concentrated on this spot.

«For God's sake, stop playing with it when I talk to you, won't you?» she said.

«Why don't you leave us alone?» said Mona. «We don't walk into your bed-room, do we? Can't one have any privacy here?»

Rebecca gave a hearty, guttural laugh. «Our room isn't as attractive as yours, that's why. You're like a couple of newlyweds: you make the whole house feverish.»

«We're clearing out of here soon,» said Mona. «I want a place of my own. This is too goddamned incestuous for me. Jesus, you can't even menstruate here without everyone knowing it.»

I felt impelled to say something mollifying. If Rebecca were aroused she could twist Mona into a knot.

«We're getting married next week,» I put in.

We'll probably move to Brooklyn, to some quiet, peaceful spot. This is a bit out of the world.»

«I see,» said Rebecca. «Of course you've been getting married ever since you came here. I'm sure we didn't prevent you—or did we?» She spoke as if she were hurt.

After a few more words she left. We fell asleep again and woke up late. We were hungry as wolves. When we got to the street we took a taxi and went to the French-Italian grocery store. It was about ten o'clock and the place was still crowded. On one side of us was a police lieutenant and on the other a detective. We were seated at the long table. Opposite me, hanging from a nail on the wall, was a holster with a pistol in it. To the left was the open kitchen where the big fat brother of the proprietor held sway. He was a marvelous, inarticulate bear dripping with grease and perspiration. Always half-cocked, it seemed. Later, after we had eaten well, he would invite us to have a liqueur with him. His brother, who served the food and collected the cash, was a totally different type. He was handsome, suave, courteous and spoke English fairly well. When the place thinned out he would often sit down and chat with us. He talked about Europe most of the time, how different it was there, how «civilized», how enjoyable the life was. Sometimes he would get to talking about the blonde women of North Italy where he came from. He would describe them minutely—the color of their hair and eyes, the texture of their skin, the luscious, sensual mouths they had, the slippery movement of the haunches when they walked, and so on. He had never seen any women like them in America, he said. He spoke of American women with a contemptuous, almost disgusting, curl of the lips. «I don't know why you stay here, Mr. Miller,» he would say. «Your

wife is so beautiful... why you don't go to Italy?
Just a few months. I tell you, you never come back.»
And then he would order another drink for us and
tell us to stay a little longer... maybe a friend of his
would come... a singer from the Metropolitan Opera
House.

Soon we became engaged in conversation with a
man and woman directly opposite us. They were in
a gay mood and had already passed on to the coffee
and liqueurs. I gathered from their remarks that
they were theatre people.

It was rather difficult to carry on a continued conversation owing to the presence of the hooligans on
either side of us. They felt that they were being
snubbed, simply because we were talking of things
beyond their ken. Every now and then the lieutenant made some dumb remark about «the stage».
The other one, the detective, was already in his cups
and getting nasty. I loathed the both of them and
showed it openly by ignoring their remarks completely. Finally, not knowing what else to do, they
began to badger us.

«Let's move into the other room,» I said, signalling
the proprietor. «Can you give us a table in there?»
I asked.

«What's the matter?» he said. «Is there anything
wrong?»

«No,» I said, «we don't like it here, that's all.»

«You mean you don't like *us*,» said the detective,
snarling the words out.

«That's it,» I said, snarling back at him.

«Not good enough for you, eh? Who the hell do
you think you are anyway?»

«I'm President McKinley—*and you?*»

«Wise guy, eh?» He turned to the proprietor.
«Say, who is this guy anyway... what's his line? Is
he trying to make a sap out of me?»

«Shut up!» said the proprietor. «You're drunk.»

«Drunk! Who says I'm drunk?» He started to totter to his feet, but slid back again into the chair.

«You better get out of here... you're making trouble. I don't want no trouble in my place, do you understand?»

«For crying out loud, what did I do?» He began to act like an abused child.

«I don't want you driving my customers away,» said the proprietor.

«Who's driving your customers away? This is a free country, ain't it? I can talk if I wanta, can't I? What did I say... tell me! I didn't say nothin' insultin'. I can be a gentleman too, if I wanta...»

«You'll never be a gentleman,» said the proprietor. «Go on, get your things and get out of here. Go home and sleep!» He turned to the lieutenant with a significant look, as if to say—this is your job, get him out of here!

Then he took us by the arm and led us into the other room. The man and woman sitting opposite us followed. «I'll get rid of those bums in a minute,» he said, ushering us to our seats. «I'm very sorry, Mr. Miller. That's what I have to put with because of this damned Prohibition law. In Italy we don't have that sort of thing. Everybody mind his own business... *What will you have to drink?* Wait, I bring you something good....»

The room he had brought us to was the private banquet room of a group of artists—theatre people mostly, though there was a sprinkling of musicians, sculptors and painters. One of the group came up to us and, after introducing himself, presented us to the other members. They seemed pleased to have us in their midst. We were soon induced to leave our table and join the group at the big table which was loaded with carafes, seltzer bottles, cheeses, pastries, coffee pots and what not.

The proprietor came back beaming. «It's better in here, no?» he said. He had two liqueur bottles in his arms. «Why you don't play some music?» he said, seating himself at the table. «Arturo, get your guitar... go on, play something! Maybe the lady will sing for you.»

Soon we were all singing—Italian, German, French, Russian songs. The idiot brother, the chef, came in with a platter of cold cuts and fruit and nuts. He moved about the room unsteadily, a tipsy bear, grunting, squealing, laughing to himself. He hadn't an ounce of gray matter in his bean, but he was a wonderful cook. I don't think he ever went for a walk. His whole life was spent in the kitchen. He handled foodstuffs only—never money. What did he need money for? You couldn't cook with money. That was his brother's job, juggling the money. He kept track of what people ate and drank—he didn't care what his brother charged for it. «*Was it good?*» that's all he cared to know. As to what they had had to eat he had only a rough, hazy idea. It was easy to cheat him, if you had a mind to do so. But no one ever did. It was easier to say, «I have no money... I'll pay you next time.» «Sure, next time!» he would answer, without the slightest trace of fear or worry in his greasy countenance. «Next time you bring your friend too, hah?» And then he'd give you a clap on the back with his hairy paw—such a resounding thwack that your bones shook like dice. Such a griffin he was, and his wife a tiny, frail little thing with big, trusting eyes, a creature who made no sound, who talked and listened with big dolorous eyes.

Louis was his name, and it fitted him perfectly. Fat Louis! And his brother's name was Joe—Joe

Sabbatini. Joe treated his imbecilic brother much as a stable-boy would treat his favorite horse. He patted him affectionately when he wanted him to conjure up an especially good dish for a patron. And Louis would respond with a grunt or a neigh, just as pleased as would be a sensitive mare if you stroked its silky rump. He even acted a little coquettish, as though his brother's touch had unlocked some hidden girlish instinct in him. For all his bearish strength one never thought of Louis' sexual propensities. He was neuter and epicene. If he had a prick it was to make water with, nothing more. One had the feeling, about Louis, that if it came to a pinch he would sacrifice his prick to make a few extra slices of saucisson. He would rather lose his prick than hand you a meagre hors-d'œuvre.

«In Italy you eat better than this,» Joe was explaining to Mona and myself. «Better meat, better vegetables, better fruit. In Italy you have sunshine all day. And music! Everybody sing. Here everybody look sad. I don't understand. Plenty money, plenty jobs, but everybody sad. This is no country to live in... only good to make money. Another two-three years and I go back to Italy. I take Louis with me and we open a little restaurant. Not for money... just have something to do. In Italy nobody make money. Everybody poor. But god-damn, Mr. Miller... excuse me... we have good time! Plenty beautiful women... *plenty!* You lucky to have such a beautiful wife. She like Italy, your wife. Italians very good people. Everybody treat you right. Everybody make friends rightaway...»

It was in bed that night that we began to talk about Europe. «We've got to go to Europe,» Mona was saying.

«Yeah, but how?»

«I don't know, Val, but we'll find a way.»

«Do you realize how much money it takes to go to Europe?»

«That doesn't matter. If we want to go we'll raise the money somehow...»

We were lying flat on our backs, hands clasped behind our heads, looking straight up into the darkness—and voyaging like mad. I had boarded the Orient Express for Bagdad. It was a familiar journey to me because I had read about this trip in one of Dos Passo's books. Vienna, Budapest, Sofia, Belgrade, Athens, Constantinople... Perhaps if we got that far we might also get to Timbuctoo. I knew a lot about Timbuctoo also—from books. Mustn't forget Taormina! And that cemetery in Stamboul which Pierre Loti had written about. And Jerusalem...

«What are you thinking about now?» I asked, nudging her gently.

«I was visiting my folks in Roumania.»

«In Roumania? Whereabouts in Roumania?»

«I don't know exactly. Somewhere in the Carpathian mountains.»

«I had a messenger once, a crazy Dutchman, who used to write me long letters from the Carpathian mountains. He was staying at the palace of the Queen...»

«Wouldn't you like to go to Africa too—Morocco, Algeria, Egypt?»

«That's just what I was dreaming about a moment ago.»

«I've always wanted to go into the desert... and get lost there.»

«That's funny, so have I. I'm crazy about the desert.»

Silence. Lost in the desert...

Somebody is talking to me. We've been having a long conversation. And I'm not in the desert any more but on Sixth Avenue under an elevated station.

My friend Ulric is placing his hand on my shoulder
and smiling at me reassuringly. He is repeating what
he said a moment ago—that I will be happy in
Europe. He talks again about Mt. Aetna, about
grapes, about leisure, idleness, good food, sunshine.
He drops a seed in me.

Sixteen years later on a Sunday morning, accompanied by a native of the Argentine and a French
whore from Montmartre, I am strolling leisurely
through a cathedral in Naples. I feel as though I
have at least seen a house of worship that I would
enjoy praying in. It belongs not to God or the Pope,
but to the Italian people. It's a huge, barn-like place,
fitted out in the worst taste, with all the trappings
dear to the Catholic heart. There is plenty of floor
space, empty floor space, I mean. People sail in
through the various portals and walk about with the
utmost freedom. They give the impression of being
on a holiday. Children gambol about like lambs,
some with little nose-gays in their hand. People
walk up to one another and exchange greetings, quite
as if they were in the street. Along the walls are
statues of the martyrs in various postures; they reek
of suffering. I have a strong desire to run my hand
over the cold marble, as if to urge them not to suffer
too much, it's indecent. As I approach one of the
statues I notice out of the corner of my eye a woman
all in black kneeling before a sacred object. She is
the image of piety. But I can't help noticing that
she is also the possessor of an exquisite ass, a musical
ass, I might say. (The ass tells you everything about
a woman, her character, her temperament, whether
she is sanguine, morbid, gay or fickle, whether she
is responsive or unresponsive, whether she is maternal
or pleasure-loving, whether she is truthful or lying
by nature.)

I was interested in that ass, as well as the piety in

which it was smothered. I looked at it so intently
that finally the owner of it turned round, her hands
still raised in prayer, her lips moving as if she were
chewing oats in her sleep. She gave me a look of
reproach, blushed deeply, then turned her gaze back
to the object of adoration, which I now observed was
one of the saints, a dejected crippled martyr who
seemed to be climbing up a hill with a broken back.

I respectfully moved away in search of my companions. The activity of the throng reminded me
of the lobby of the Hotel Astor—and of the canvases
of Uccello (that fascinating world of perspective!).
It reminded me also of the Caledonian market,
London, with its vast clutter of gimcrackery. It was
beginning to remind me of a lot of things, of everything, in fact, but the house of worship which it was.
I half expected to see Malvolio or Mercutio enter in
full tights. I saw one man, obviously a barber, who
reminded me vividly of Werner Krause in *Othello*.
I recognized an organ grinder from New York whom
I had once tracked to his lair behind the City Hall.

Above all I was fascinated by they tremendous
Gorgon-like heads of the old men of Naples. They
seemed to emerge full-blown out of the Renaissance:
great lethal cabbages with fiery coals in their
foreheads. Like the Urizens of William Blake's
imagination. They moved about condescendingly,
these animated heads, as if patronizing the nefarious
Mysteries of the mundane Church and her spew of
scarlet-robed pimps.

I felt very very much at home. It was a bazaar
which made sense. It was operatic, mercurial,
tonsorial. The buzz-buzz at the altar was discreet
and elegant, a sort of veiled boudoir atmosphere in
which the priest, assisted by his gelded acolytes,
washed his socks in holy water. Behind the glittering surplices were little trellised doors, such as the

mountebanks used in the popular street shows of
medieval times. Anything might spring out at you
from those mysterious little doors. Here was the
altar of confusion, bangled and diademed with
baubles, smelling of grease paint, incense, sweat and
dereliction. It was like the last act of a gaudy
comedy, a banal play dealing with prostitution and
ending in prophylactics. The performers inspired
affection and sympathy; they were not sinners, they
were vagrants. Two thousand years of fraud and
humbug had culminated in this side-show. It was
all flip and tutti-frutti, a gaudy, obscene carnival in
which the Redeemer, made of plaster of Paris, took
on the appearance of a eunuch in petticoats. The
women prayed for children and the men prayed for
food to stuff the hungry mouths. Outside, on the
sidewalk, were heaps of vegetables, fruits, flowers and
sweets. The barber shops were wide open and little
boys, resembling the progeny of Fra Angelico, stood
with big fans and drove the flies away. A beautiful
city, alive in every member, and drenched with
sunlight. In the background Vesuvius, a sleepy cone
emitting a lazy curl of smoke. I was in Italy—I was
certain of it. It was all that I had expected it to be.
And then suddenly I realized that *she* was not with
me, and for a moment I was saddened. Then I
wondered... wondered about the seed and its fruition.
For that night, when we went to bed hungering for
Europe, something quickened in me. Years had
rolled by... short, terrible years, in which every seed
that had ever quicknened seemed to be mashed to a
pulp. Our rhythm had speeded up, hers in a physical
way, mine in a more subtle way. *She* leaped forward
feverishly, her very walk changing over into the lope
of an antelope. *I* seemed to stand still, making no
progress, but spinning like a top. *She* had her eyes
set on the goal, but the faster she moved the farther

removed became the goal. *I* knew I could never
reach the goal this way. I moved my body about
obediently, but always with an eye on the seed
within. When I slipped and fell I fell softly, like
a cat, or like a pregnant woman, always mindful of
that which was growing inside me. Europe,
Europe.... it was with me always, even when we were
quarreling, shouting at each other like maniacs. Like
a man obsessed, I brought every conversation back to
the subject which alone interested me: *Europe.*
Nights when we prowled about the city, searching
like alley cats for scraps of food, the cities and peoples
of Europe were in my mind. I was like a slave who
dreams of freedom, whose whole being is saturated
with one idea: escape. Nobody could have convinced me then that if I were offered the choice
between her and my dream of Europe I would choose
the latter. It would have seemed utterly fantastic,
then, to suppose that it would be she herself who
would offer me this choice. And perhaps even more
fantastic still that the day I would sail for Europe
I would have to ask my friend Ulric for ten dollars
so as to have something in my pocket on touching
my beloved European soil.

That half-voiced dream in the dark, that night
alone in the desert, the voice of Ulric comforting me,
the Carpathian mountains moving up from under the
moon, Timbuctoo, the camel bells, the smell of
leather and of dry, scorched dung, («What are you
thinking of?» «I too!») the tense, richly-filled silence,
the blank, dead walls of the tenement opposite, the
fact that Arthur Raymond was asleep, that in the
morning he would continue his exercises, forever and
ever, but that I had changed, that there were exits,
loopholes, even though only in the imaginations, all this
acted like a ferment and dynamized the days, months,
years that lay ahead. It dynamized my love for her.

It made me believe that what I could not accomplish alone I could accomplish with her, for her, through her, because of her. She became the water-sprinkler, the fertilizer, the hot-house, the mule pack, the path-finder, the bread-winner, the gyroscope, the extra vitamin, the flame-thrower, the go-getter.

From that day on things moved on greased skids. Get married? Sure, why not? Right away. Have you got the money for the license? No, but I'll borrow it. Fine. Meet you on the corner....

We're in the Hudson Tubes on our way to Hoboken. Going to get married there. Why Hoboken? I don't remember. Perhaps to conceal the fact that I had been married before, perhaps we were a bit ahead of the legal schedule. Anyway, Hoboken.

In the train we have a little tiff. The same old story—she's not sure that I want to marry her. Thinks I'm doing it just to please her.

A station before Hoboken she jumps out of the train. I jump out too and run after her.

«What's the matter with you—are you mad?»

«You don't love me. I'm not going to marry you.»

«You are too, by God!»

I grab her and pull her back to the edge of the platform. As the next train pulls in I put my arms around her and embrace her.

«You're sure, Val? You're sure you want to marry me?»

I kiss her again. «Come on, cut it out! You know damned well we're going to get married.» We hop in.

Hoboken. A sad, dreary place. A city more foreign to me than Pekin or Lhassa. Find the City Hall. Find a couple of bums to act as witnesses.

The ceremony. What's your name? And *your* name? And *his* name? And so on. How long have you known this man? And this man is a friend of

yours? Yes sir. Where did you pick him up—in
the garbage can? O. K. Sign here. Bang, bang!
Raise your right hand! *I solemnly swear,* etc, etc.
Married. Five dollars, please. Kiss the bride. *Next,
please....*

Everybody happy?

I want to spit.

In the train.... I take her hand in mine. We're
both depressed, humiliated. «I'm sorry, Mona... we
shouldn't have done it that way.»

«It's all right, Val.» She's very quiet now. As
though we had just buried some one.

«But it isn't all right, God damn it! I'm sore.
I'm disgusted. That's no way to get married. I'll
never....»

I checked myself. She looked at me with a startled
expression.

«What were you going to say?»

I lied. I said: «I'll never forgive myself for doing
it that way.»

I became silent. Her lips were trembling.

«I don't want to go back to the house just yet,»
said she.

«Neither do I.»

Silence.

«I'll call up Ulric,» said I. «We'll have dinner
with him, yes?»

«Yes,» she said, almost meekly.

We got into a telephone booth together to call up
Ulric. I had my arm around her. «Now you're
Mrs. Miller,» I said. «How does it feel?»

She began to weep. «Hello, hello? That you,
Ulric?»

«No, it's me, Ned.»

Ulric wasn't there—had gone somewhere for the
day.

«Listen, Ned, we just got married.»

«Who got married?» he said.

«Mona and I, of course... who did you think?»

He was trying to joke about it, as though to say he couldn't be sure whom I would marry.

«Listen, Ned, it's serious. Maybe you've never been married before. We're depressed. Mona is weeping. I'm on the verge of tears myself. Can we come up there, drop in for a little while? We're lonely. Maybe you'll fix us a little drink, yes?»

Ned was laughing again. Of course we were to come—right away. He was expecting that cunt of his, Marcelle. But that wouldn't matter. He was getting sick of her. She was too good to him. She was fucking the life out of him. Yes, come up right away... we'd all drown our sorrows.

«Well, don't worry, Ned'll have some money. We'll make him take us to dinner. I suppose nobody will think to give us a wedding present. That's the hell of getting married in this informal fashion. You know, when Maude and I got married we pawned some of the wedding gifts the next day. Never got them back again either. We wouldn't want a lot of knives and forks sterling, would we?»

«Please don't talk that way, Val.»

«I'm sorry. I guess I'm a bit screwy to-day. That ceremony let me down. I could have murdered that guy.»

«Val, stop, I beg you!»

«All right, we won't talk about it any more. Let's be gay now, what? Let's laugh....»

Ned had a warm smile. I liked Ned. He was weak. Weak and lovable. Selfish underneath. Very selfish. That's why he could never get married. He had talent too, lots of talent, but no genius, no sustaining powers. He was an artist who had never found his medium. His best medium was drink. When he drank he became expansive. In physique

he reminded one of John Barrymore in his better
days. His rôle was Don Juan, especially in a Finchley
suit with an ascot tie about his throat. Lovely
speaking voice. Rich baritone, full of enchanting
modulations. Everything he said sounded suave and
important, though he never said a word that was
worth remembering. But in speaking he seemed to
caress you with his tongue; he licked you all over,
like a happy dog.

«Well, well,» he said, grinning from ear to ear,
and already half-cocked, I could see. «So you went
and did it? Well, come on in. Hello Mona, how´
are you? Congratulations! Marcelle isn't here yet.
I hope she doesn't come. I don't feel so terribly vital
today.»

He was still grinning as he sat down in a big throne
chair near the easel.

«Ulric will certainly be sorry he missed this,» he
said. «Will you have a little Scotch—or do you want
gin?»

«Gin.»

«Well, tell me all about it. When did it happen...
just now? Why didn't you let me know—I would
have stood up for you....» He turned to Mona.
«You're not pregnant, are you?»

«Jesus, let's talk about something else,» said Mona.
«I swear I'll never get married again... it's horrible.»

«Listen, Ned, before you get drunk, tell me something... how much money have you got on you?»

He fished out six cents. «Oh, thats' all right,» he
said, «Marcelle will have something.»

«If she comes.»

«Oh, she'll come, don't worry. That's the hell of
it. I don't know which is worse—to be broke or to
have Marcelle on one's hands.»

«I didn't think she was so bad,» I said.

«No, she isn't, really,» said Ned. «She's a darned

nice gal. But she's too affectionate. She clings. You see, I'm not made for conjugual bliss. I get weary of the same face, even if it's a Madonna. I'm fickle. And she's constant. She's bolstering me up all the time. I don't want to be bolstered up—not all the time.»

«You don't know what you want,» said Mona. «You don't know when you're well off.»

«I guess you're right,» said Ned. «Ulric's the same way. We're masochists, I guess.» He grinned. He was a little ashamed of using a word like that so readily. It was an intellectual word and Ned had no use for things intellectual.

The door-bell rang. It was Marcelle. I could hear her giving him a smacking kiss.

«You know Henry and Mona, don't you?»

«Why sure I do,» said Marcelle brightly. «I caught you with your pants down... you remember? That seems a long time ago.»

«Listen,» said Ned, «what do you think they did? They got married... yeah, just a little while ago... in Hoboken.»

«That's wonderful!» said Marcelle. She went up to Mona and kissed her. She kissed me too.

«Don't they look sad?» said Ned.

«No,» said Marcelle, «I don't think they look sad. Why should they?» Ned poured out a drink for her. As he handed it to her he said:

«Have you any money?»

«Of course I have. Why? Do you want some?»

«No, but *they* need a little money. They're broke.»

«I'm so sorry,» said Marcelle. «Of course I have money. What can I give you—ten, twenty? Why certainly. And don't pay it back—it's a wedding present.»

Mona went over to her and took her hand. «That's awfully good of you, Marcelle. Thank you.»

«Then we'll take *you* to dinner,» I said, trying to express my appreciation.

«No, you're not,» said Marcelle. «We're going to make dinner right here. Let's settle down and get comfy. I don't believe in going out to celebrate.... Really, I'm very happy. I like to see people get married—and stay married. Maybe I'm old-fashioned, but I believe in love. I want to stay in love all my life.»

«Marcelle,» I said, «where the devil do you hail from?»

«From Utah. Why?»

«I don't know, but I like you. You're refreshing. I like the way you hand the money out too.»

«You're joshing me!»

«No, I'm not. I'm serious. You're a good woman. You're too good for that bum over there. Why don't you marry him? Go on! It would scare the life out of him, but it might do him a lot of good.»

«Do you hear that?» she gurgled, turning to Ned. «Haven't I been telling you that all along? You're lazy, that's what. You don't know what a prize I am.»

At this point Mona had a fit of laughing. She laughed as though her sides would burst. «I can't help it,» she said. «It's too funny.»

«You're not drunk already, are you?» said Ned.

«No, it's not that,» said I. «She's relaxing. It's just a reaction. We put it off too long, that's what's the matter. Isn't that it, Mona?»

Another peal of laughter.

«Besides,» said I, «she's always embarrassed when I borrow money. Isn't that so, Mona?»

There was no answer—just another explosion.

Marcelle went over to her, spoke to her in a low, soothing voice. «You leave her to me,» she said.

«You two get drunk. We'll go out and get some food, won't we, Mona?»

«What made her so hysterical?» said Ned, after the two had left.

«Search me,» I said. «She's not used to getting married, I guess.»

«Listen,» said Ned, «what ever made you do it? Wasn't it a little impetuous?»

«You sit down,» I said. «I'm going to talk to you. You're not too drunk to follow me, are you?»

«You're not going to give me a lecture, are you?» he said, looking a little sheepish.

«I'm going to talk turkey to you. Now listen to me.... We just got married, didn't we? You think it's a mistake, eh? Let me tell you this.... I never did a better thing in my life. I love her. I love her enough to do anything she asks of me. If she asked me to cut your throat... if I thought that would make her happy... I'd do it. *Why was she laughing so hysterically?* You poor bugger you, I don't know what's the matter with you. You don't *feel* any more. You're just trying to protect yourself. Well, I don't want to protect myself. I want to do foolish things, little things, ordinary things, anything and everything that would make a woman happy. Can you understand that? You, and Ulric too, thought it quite a joke, this love business. Henry would never get married again. Oh no! Just an infatuation. It would wear off after a time. That was how you looked at it. Well, you were wrong. What I feel for her is so damned big I don't know how to express it. She's out in the street now, Mona. She could be run over by a truck. Anything could happen. I tremble when I think what it would do to me, to hear that something had happened to her. I think I'd become a stark, raving lunatic. I'd kill you right off the bat, that's the first thing I'd do...

You don't know what it means to love that way, do
you? You think only of the same face for breakfast every day. I think how wonderful her face is,
how it changes every minute. I never see her twice
the same way. I see only an infinity of adoration.
That's a good word for you—*adoration*. I bet you've
never used it. Now we're getting somewhere.... I
adore her. I'll say it again. *I adore her!* Jesus, it's
wonderful to say that. I adore her and I prostrate
myself at her feet. I worship her. I say my prayers
to her. I venerate her.... How do you like that?
You never thought, when I first brought her up here,
that I was going to talk this way some day, did you?
Yet I warned you both. I told you something had
happened. You laughed. You thought you knew
better. Well, you know nothing, neither of you.
You don't know who I am or where I came from.
You see only what I show you. You never look
under my vest. If I laugh you think I'm gay. You
don't know that when I laugh so heartily sometimes
I'm on the verge of despair. At least it used to be
so. Not any more. When I laugh now I'm laughing,
not weeping inside and laughing outside. I'm whole
again. All one piece. A man in love. A man who
got married of his own free will. A man who was
never really married before. A man who knew women, but not love.... Now I'll sing for you. Or
recite, if you like. *What do you want?* Just name
it and you'll have it.... Listen, when she comes back
—and God, just to know that she *will* come back,
that she didn't walk out of that door and disappear
—when she comes back I want you to be gay... I
want you to be *naturally* gay. Say nice things to
her... good things... things you mean... things you find
it hard to say usually. Promise her things. Tell
her you'll buy her a wedding gift. Tell her you hope
she'll have children. Lie to her, if you must. But

make her happy. Don't let her laugh that way again, do you hear me? I don't want to hear her laugh like that...*never!* *You* laugh, you bastard! Play the clown, play the idiot. But let her believe that you think everything is fine... fine and dandy... and that it will last forever....»

I paused a moment for breath and took another swallow of gin. Ned was watching me with mouth wide open.

«Go on!» he said, «keep it up!»

«You like it, do you?»

«It's marvelous,» he said. «Real passion there. I'd give anything to be able to get worked up to that pitch... Go ahead, say anything you want. Don't be afraid of hurting my feelings. I'm nobody....»

«For God's sake, don't talk like that—you take the steam out of me. I'm not putting on an act... I'm serious.»

«I know you are—that's why I say *go ahead!* People don't talk this way any more... leastways not the people I know.»

He rose to his feet, slipped an arm in mine, and gave me that charming Klieg-light smile of his. His eyes were big and liquid; the eyelids were like chipped saucers. It was amazing what an illusion of warmth and understanding he could give. I wondered for a moment if I had underestimated him. Nobody should be spurned or rejected who gives even the illusion of feeling. How could I tell what struggles he had made, and was still making perhaps, to rise to the surface? What right had I to judge him —or anybody? If people smile at you, take your arm, give off a glow, it must be that there is something in them which responds. Nobody is altogether dead.

«Don't worry about what I think,» he was saying

in that rich, pastoral voice. «I only wish Ulric were here... he would appreciate it even more than I.»

«For Christ's sake, don't say that, Ned! One doesn't want appreciation... one wants a response. To tell you the truth, I don't know what I want of you, or of anybody, for that matter. I want more than I get, that's all I know. I want you to step out of your skin. I want everybody to strip down, not just to the flesh, but to the soul. Sometimes I get so hungry, so rapacious, that I could eat people up. I can't wait for them to tell me things... how they feel... what they want... and so on. I want to chew them alive... find out for myself... quick, all at once. Listen...»

I picked up a drawing of Ulric's that was lying on his table. «See this? Now supposing I ate it?» I began to chew the paper.

«Jesus, Henry, don't do that! He's been working on that for the last three days. That's a job.» He tore the drawing from my hand.

«All right,» I said. «Give me something else then. Give me a coat... anything. Here, give me your hand!» I made a grab for his hand and raised it to my mouth. He pulled it away violently.

«You're going nuts,» he said. «Listen, hold your horses. The girls will be back soon... then you can have real food.»

«I'll eat anything,» I said. «I'm not hungry, I'm exalted. I just want to show you how I feel. *Don't you ever get this way?*»

«I should say not!» he said, baring a fang. «Christ, if it got that bad I'd go to a doctor. I'd think I had the D. T.'s, or something. You'd better put that glass down... that gin isn't good for you.»

«You think it's the gin? All right, I'll throw the glass away.» I went to the window and threw it into the courtyard. «There! Now give me a glass of water. Bring a *pitcher* of water in. I'll show you... You never saw anybody get drunk on water, eh? Well, watch me!»

«Now before I get drunk on the water,» I continued, following him into the bathroom, «I want you to observe the difference between exaltation and intoxication. The girls will be coming back soon. By that time I'll be drunk. You watch. See what happens.»

«You bet I will,» he said. «If I could learn to get drunk on water it would save me a lot of headaches. Here, take a glass now. I'll get the pitcher.»

I took the glass and swallowed it down in one gulp. When he returned I swallowed another in the same fashion. He looked on as if I were a circus freak.

After five or six of these you'll begin to notice the effect,» I said.

«Are you sure you don't want a wee drop of gin in it? I won't accuse you of cheating. Water is so damned flat and tasteless.»

«Water is the elixir of life, my dear Ned. If I were running the world I'd give the creative people a bread and water diet. The dullards I'd give all the food and drink they craved. I'd poison them off by satisfying their desires. Food is poison to the spirit. Food doesn't satisfy hunger, nor drink thirst. Food, sexual or otherwise, is only satisfying to the appetites. Hunger is something else. Nobody can satisfy hunger. Hunger is the soul's barometer. Ecstasy is the norm. Serenity is the freedom from weather conditions—the permanent climate of the stratosphere. That's where we're all headed... towards the stratosphere. I'm already a bit drunk, do you see? Because, when you can think of serenity it means that you've passed the zenith of exaltation. At one minute past twelve noon night begins, say the

Chinese. But at zenith and nadir you stand stock
still for a moment or two. At the two poles God
gives you the chance to leap clear of the clock-work.
At the nadir, which is physical intoxication, you
have the privilege of going mad—or of committing
suicide. At zenith, which is a state of ecstasy, you
can pass fulfilled into serenity and bliss. It's now
about ten minutes after twelve on the spiritual clock.
Night has fallen. I am no longer hungry, I have
only an insane desire to be happy. That means I
want to share my intoxication with you and everybody. That's maudlin. When I finish the pitcher
of water I'll begin to believe that everybody is as
good as everybody else: I'll lose all sense of values.
That's the only way we have of knowing how to be
happy—to believe that we are identical. It's the
delusion of the poor in spirit. It's like Purgatory
equipped with electric fans and streamlined furniture.
It's the caricature of joyousness. Joy means unity;
happiness means plurality.»

«Do you mind if I take a leak?» said Ned. «I
think you're getting somewhere now. I feel mildly
pleasurable.»

«That's reflected happiness. You're living on the
moon. As soon as I stop shining you'll become
extinct.»

«You said it, Henry. Jesus, having you around is
like getting a shot in the arm.»

The pitcher was almost empty. «Fill it up again,»
I said. «I'm lucid but I'm not drunk yet. I wish
the girls would come back. I need an incentive.
I hope they didn't get run over.»

«Do you sing when you get drunk?» asked Ned.

Do I? Do you want to hear me?» I began the
Prologue to Pagliacci.

In the midst of it the girls returned, loaded with
packages. I was still singing.

«You must be high,» said Marcelle, glancing from one to the other of us.

«He's getting drunk,» said Ned. *«On water.»*

«On water?» they echoed.

«Yes, on water. It's the opposite of ecstasy, he says.»

«I don't get you,» said Marcelle. «Let me smell your breath.»

«Don't smell mine... smell his. I'm satisfied to get drunk on liquor. Two minutes after twelve it's night time, says Henry. Happiness is only an air-conditioned form of Purgatory... isn't that it, Henry?»

«Listen,» said Marcelle, «Henry's not drunk, you're the one who's drunk.»

«Joy is unity; happiness is always in the majority, or something like that. You should have been here a little earlier. He wanted to eat my hand. When I refused to oblige him he asked for a coat. Come on in here... I'll show you what he did to Ulric's drawing.»

They looked at the drawing, one corner of which had been chewed to a frazzle.

«That's hunger for you,» Ned explained. «He doesn't mean ordinary hunger—he means spiritual hunger. The goal is the stratosphere where the climate is always serene. Isn't that it, Henry?»

«That's it,» I said, with a grave smile. «Now Ned, tell Mona wha* you were telling me a moment ago...» I gave him a hypnotic blink and raised another glass to my lips.

«I don't think you'd better let him drink all that water,» said Ned, appealing to Mona. «He's finished one pitcher already. I'm afraid he'll get dropsy—or hydrocephalis.»

Mona gave me a searching look. What's the meaning of this act? it said.

I put my hand on her arm, lightly, as if I were

laying a divining rod on it. «He has something to say to you. Listen quietly. It will make you feel good.»

All eyes were focused on Ned. He blushed and stammered.

«What is this?» said Marcelle. «What did he say that was so wonderful?»

«I guess I'll have to say it for him,» I said. I took Mona's two hands in mine and looked into her eyes. «This is what he said, Mona... 'I never knew that one human being could transform another human being as Mona has transformed you. Some people get religion; you got love. You're the luckiest man in the world.'»

Mona: «Did you really say that, Ned?»

Marcelle: «How is it I haven't transformed *you?*»

Ned began to sputter.

«I guess he needs another drink,» said Marcelle.

«No, drink only satisfies the lower appetites,» said Ned. «I'm searching for the elixir of life, which is water, according to Henry.»

«I'll give you your elixir later,» Marcelle rejoined. «How about some cold chicken now?»

«Have you any bones?» I asked.

Marcelle looked perplexed.

«I want to eat them,» I said. «Bones give phosphorus and iodine. Mona always feeds me bones when I'm exalted. You see, when I'm effervescent I give off vital energy. You don't need bones—you need cosmic juices. You've worn your celestial envelope too thin. You're radiating from the sexual sphere.»

«What does that mean in plain English?»

«It means that you feed on seed instead of ambrosia. Your spiritual hormones are impoverished. You love Apis the Bull instead of Krishna the charioteer. You'll find your Paradise, but it will be on the lower level. Then the only escape is insanity.»

It's as clear as mud,» said Marcelle.

«Don't get caught in the clock-work, that's what he means,» Ned volunteered.

«What clock-work? What the hell are you talking about, you two?»

«Don't you understand, Marcelle? I said. «What can love bring you that you haven't got already?»

«I haven't got anything, except a lot of responsibil-ities,» said Marcelle. «*He* gets it all.»

«Precisely, and that's why it feels so good.»

«I didn't say that! ...Listen, what are you talking about? Are you sure you're feeling all right?»

«I'm talking about your soul,» I said. «You've been starving your soul. You need cosmic juices, as I said before.»

«Yeah, and where do you buy 'em?»

«You don't buy them... you pray for them. Didn't you ever hear of the manna that fell from the sky? Ask for manna to-night: it will give tone to your astral ligaments...»

«I don't know anything about this astral stuff, but I do know something about ass,» said Marcelle. «If you ask me, I think you're giving me the *double entendre*. Why don't you go to the bathroom for a little while and play with yourself? Marriage has a queer effect on you.»

«You see, Henry,» Ned broke in, «that's how they bring things down to earth. She's always worrying about her nookie, aren't you, dear?» He stroked her under the chin. «I was thinking,» he continued, «that maybe we ought to go to the burlesque to-night. That would be a novel way to celebrate the occasion, don't you think? You know, it gives you *i*-deas.»

Marcelle looked at Mona. It was obvious they didn't think it was such a hot idea.

«Let's eat first,» I suggested. «Bring that coat in, or a pillow... I might want something on the side. Talking about ass,» I said, «did you ever take a good bite... you know, *a real bite?* Take Marcelle, for instance... that's what I call a tempting piece of ass.»

Marcelle began to titter. She put her hands behind her instinctively.

«Don't worry, I'm not biting into you yet. There's chicken first and other things. But honest, sometimes one does feel like tearing a chunk out, what! A pair of teats, that's different. I never could bite into a woman's teats—*a real bite*, I mean. Always afraid the milk will squirt into my face. And all those veins... Jesus, it's so bloody. But a beautiful ass... somehow you don't think of blood in a woman's ass. It's just pure white meat. There's another delicacy just below the crotch, on the inside. That's even tenderer than a piece of pure ass. I don't know, maybe I'm exaggerating. Anyway, I'm hungry... Wait till I drain some of this piss out of me. It's given me a hard-on, and I can't eat with a hard-on. Save some of the brown meat for me, with the skin. I love skin. Make a nice cunt sandwich, and slap a little cold gravy over it. Jesus, my mouth's watering...»

«Feel better nov?» said Ned, when I had returned from the bathroom.

«I'm famished. What's that lovely puke over there—in the big bowl?»

«That's turtle shit with rotten eggs and a bit of menstrual sauce,» said Ned. «Does that whet your appetite?»

«I wish you'd change the subject,» said Marcelle. «I'm not overly delicate but puke is one thing I don't like to think about when I'm eating. If you have to talk dirt I'd rather you talked sex.»

«What do you mean,» said Ned, «is sex dirt? How about that, Henry, *is sex dirt?*»

«Sex is one of the nine reasons for reincarnation,» I answered. «The other eight are unimportant. If we were all angels we wouldn't have any sex—we'd have wings. An aeroplane has no sex; neither has God. Sex provides for reproduction and reproduction leads to failure. The sexiest people in the world, so they say, are the insane. They live in Paradise, but they've lost their innocence.»

«For an intelligent person you do talk a lot of nonsense,» said Marcelle. «Why don't you talk about things we all understand? Why do you give us all this shit about angels and God and the booby-hatch? If you were drunk it would be different, but you're not drunk... you're not even pretending to be drunk ...you're insolent and arrogant. You're showing off.»

«Good, Marcelle, very good! Do you want to hear the truth? I'm bored. I'm fed up. I came here to get a meal and borrow some money. Yeah, let's talk about simple, ordinary things. How was your last operation? Do you like white meat or dark? Let's talk about anything that will prevent us from thinking or feeling. Sure, it was damned nice of you to give us twenty dollars right off the bat like that. Mighty white of you. But I get itchy when I listen to you talk.. I want to hear somebody say something... something original. I know you've got a good heart, that you never do any one harm. And I suppose you mind your own business too. But that doesn't interest me. I'm sick of good, kind, generous people. I want a show of character and temperament. Jesus, I can't even get drunk—in *this* atmosphere. I feel like the Wandering Jew. I'd like to set the house on fire, or something. Maybe if you'd pull your drawers off and dip them in the coffee that would help. Or take a frankfurter and diddle your-

self... Let's be simple, you say. Good. *Can you let
a loud fart?* Listen, once I had ordinary brains,
ordinary dreams, ordinary desires. I nearly went
nuts. I loathe the ordinary. Makes me constipated.
Death is ordinary—it's what happens to everybody.
I refuse to die. I've made up my mind that I'm
going to live forever. Death is easy: it's like the
booby-hatch, only you can't masturbate any more.
You like your nookie, Ned says. Sure, so does every
one. And what then? In ten years your ass will be
crinkled and your boobs will be hanging down like
empty douche bags. Ten years... twenty years... what
difference? You had a few good fucks and then
you dried up. So what? The moment you stop
having a good time you grow melancholy. You don't
regulate your life—you let your cunt do it for you.
You're at the mercy of a stiff prick...»

I paused a moment to get my breath, rather surprised that I hadn't received a clout. Ned had a
gleam in his eye which might have been interpreted
as friendly and encouraging—or murderous. I was
hoping somebody would start something, throw a
bottle, smash things, scream, yell, anything but sit
there and take it like stunned owls. I didn't know
why I had picked on Marcelle, she hadn't done anything to me. I was just using her as a stooge. Mona
should have interrupted me... I sort of counted on
her doing that. But no, she was strangely quiet,
strangely impartial.

«Now that I've gotten that off my chest,» I resumed, «let me apologize. Marcelle, I don't know what
to say to you. You certainly didn't deserve that.»

«That's all right,» said she blithely, «I know something's eating you up. It couldn't be *me* because...
well, nobody who knows me would ever talk that
way to me. Why don't you switch to gin? You see
what water does. Here, take a good stiff one...» I

drank a half glass straight and saw horse shoes pounding out sparks. «You see... makes you feel human, doesn't it? Have some more chicken—and some potato salad. The trouble with you is you're hypersensitive. My old man was that way. He wanted to be a minister and instead he became a book-keeper. When he got all screwed up inside my mother would get him drunk. Then he beat the piss out of us—out of her too. But he felt better afterwards. We all felt better. It's much better to beat people up than to think rotten things about them. He wouldn't have been any better if he had become a minister: he was born with a grudge against the world. He wasn't happy unless he was criticizing things. That's why I can't hate people... I saw what it did to him. Sure I like my nookie. *Who don't?* as you say. I like things to be soft and easy. I like to make people happy, if I can. Maybe it's stupid but it gives you a good feeling. You see, my old man had the idea that everything had to be destroyed before we could begin to have a good life. My philosophy, if you can call it a philosophy, is just the opposite. I don't see the need to destroy anything. I cultivate the good and let the bad take care of itself. That's a feminine way of looking at life. I'm a conservative. I think that women have to act dumb in order not to make men feel like fools...»

«Well I'll be damned!» Ned exclaimed. «*I* never heard you talk this way before.»

«Of course you didn't, darling. You never credited me with having an ounce of brains, did you? You get your little nookie and then you go to sleep. I've been asking you to marry me for a year now but you're not ready for that yet. You've got other problems. Well, some day you'll discover that there's only one problem on your hands—*yourself.*»

«Good! Good for you, Marcelle!» It was Mona who suddenly burst out with this.

«What the hell!» said Ned. «What is this—a conspiracy?»

«You know,» said Marcelle, as though she were speaking to herself, «sometimes I think I really am a cluck. Here I am waiting for this guy to marry me. Suppose he does marry me—what then? He won't know me any better after marriage than before. He's not in love. If a guy's in love with you he doesn' worry about the future. Love is a gamble, not an insurance racket. I guess I'm just getting wise to myself.... Ned, I'm going to stop worrying about you. I'm going to leave you to worry about yourself. You're the worrying kind—and there's no cure for that. You had me worried for a while— worrying about *you*, I mean. I'm through worrying. I want *love*—not protection.»

«Jesus, aren't we getting rather serious?» said Ned, baffled by the unexpected turn the conversation had taken.

«Serious?» said Marcelle mockingly. «I'm walking out on you. You can stay single for the rest of your life—and thrash out all those weighty problems that bother you. I feel as though a big load had been taken off my shoulders.» She turned to me and stuck out her mitt. «Thanks, Henry, for giving me a jolt. I guess you weren't talking such nonsense after all....»

22

Cleo was still the rage at the Houston Street Burlesk. She had become an institution, like Mistinguett. It's easy to understand why she fascinated that audience which the enterprising Minsky Brothers gathered every night under their closed roof garden. One had only to stand outside the box office of a matinee, any day of the week, and watch them dribble in. In the evening it was a more sophisticated crowd, gathered from all parts of Manhattan, Brooklyn, Queens, the Bronx, Staten Island and New Jersey. Even Park Avenue contributed its clientele, in the evening. But in the bright light of day, with the marquee looking like the aftermath of small-pox, the Catholic Church next door so dingy, woe-begone, so scroungy-looking, the priest always standing on the steps, scratching his ass by way of registering disgust and disapprobation. It was very much like the picture of reality which the sclerotic mind of a sceptic conjures up when he tries to explain why there can be no God.

Many's the time I had hung around the entrance to the theatre, keeping a sharp eye out for some one to lend me a few pennies to make up the price of admission. When you're out of work, or too disgusted to look for work, it's infinitely better to sit in a stinking pit than to stand in a public toilet for hours—just because it's warm there. Sex and poverty go hand in hand.

The fetid odor of the burlesque house! That smell of the latrine, of urine saturated with camphor balls! The mingled stench of sweat, sour feet, foul breaths, chewing gum, disinfectants! The sickening deodorant from the squirt guns levelled straight at you, as if you were a mass of bottle flies! Nauseating? No word for it. Onan himself could scarcely smell worse.

The décor too was something. Smacked of Renoir in the last stages of gangrene. Blended perfectly with the Mardi Gras lighting effects—a flushed string of red lights illuminating a rotten womb. Some-

thing disgracefully satisfying about sitting there with
the Mongolian idiots in the twilight of Gomorrah,
knowing all too well that after the show you would
have to trudge it back home on foot. Only a man
with his pockets cleaned out can thoroughly appreciate the warmth and stench of a big ulcer in which
hundreds of others like himself sit and wait for the
curtain to go up. All around you overgrown idiots
shelling peanuts, or nibbling at chocolate bars, or
draining bottles of pop through straws. The Lumpen
Proletariat. Cosmic riff-raff.

It was so foul, the atmosphere, that it was just
like one big congealed fart. On the asbestos curtain
remedies against venereal diseases, cloak and suit ads,
fur trappers, tooth-paste delicacies, watches to tell
time—as if time were important in our lives! Where
to go for a quick snack after the show—as if one
had money to burn, as though after the show we
would all drop in at Louie's or August's place and
look the girls over, shove money up their asses and
see the Aurora Borealis or the Red, White and
Blue.

The ushers... Ratty, jail-bird types, if male, and
floozy, empty shits, if the other sex. Now and then
an attractive Polish girl with blonde hair and a
saucy, defiant mien. One of the dumb Polaks who
would rather earn an honest penny than turn up
her ass for a quick fuck. One could smell their
filthy underwear, winter or summer...

Anyway, everything on a cash and carry basis—
that was the Minsky plan. And it worked too. Never
a flop, no matter how lousy the performance. If you
went there often enough you got to know the faces
so well, not only of the cast but of the audience too,
that it was like a family reunion. If you felt disgusted you didn't need a mirror to see how you
looked—you had only to take a glance at your neigh-

bor. It should have been called «Identity House».
It was Devachan hindside up.

There was never anything original, never anything
that you hadn't seen a thousand times before. It
was like a cunt you're sick of looking at—you know
every liverish crease and wrinkle; you're so god-
damned sick of it that you want to spit in it, or
take a plunger and bring up all the muck that got
caught and the larynx. Oh yes, many a time one had
the impulse to let fire—turn a machine gun on them,
men, women and children, and let 'em have it in
the guts. Sometimes a sort of faintness came over
you: you felt like sliding to the floor and just lying
there among the peanut shells. Let people walk over
you with their greasy, smelly, shitty shoes.

Always a patriotic note too. Any moth-eaten cunt
could walk out front-and-center draped in the American flag and by singing a wheezy tune bring down
the house. If you had an advantageous seat you
could catch her wiping her nose on the flag as she
stood in the wings. And the sob stuff... how they
liked the mother songs!

Poor, dopy, dog-eared saps! When it came to home
and mother they slobbered like wailing mice. There
was always the white-haired imbecile from the Ladies' Room whom they trotted out for these numbers. Her reward for sitting in the shit-house all
day and night was to be slobbered over during one
of the sentimental numbers. She had an enormous
girth—a fallen womb most likely—and her eyes
were glassy. She could have been everybody's
mother, so goofy and docile she was. The very picture of motherhood—after thirty-five years of child-
bearing, wife-beating, abortions, haemorrhages, ulcers,
tumors, rupture, varicose veins and other emolu-
ments of the maternal life. That nobody thought of

putting a bullet through her and finishing her off always surprised me.

No denying it, the Minsky Brothers had thought of everything, everything which would remind one of the things one wanted to escape. They knew how to trot out everything that was worn and faded, including the very lice in your brains—and they rubbed this concoction under your nose like a shitty rag. They were enterprising, no doubt about it. Probably Leftwingers too, even though contributing to the support of the Catholic Church next door. They were Unitarians, in the practical sense. Big hearted, open-minded purveyors of entertainment for the poor at heart. Not a doubt about it. I'm sure they went to the Turkish Baths every night (after counting the money), and perhaps to the synagogue too, when there was time for it.

To get back to Cleo. It was Cleo this night again, as it had been in the past. She would appear twice, once before the intermission and a second time at the end of the show.

Neither Marcelle nor Mona had ever been to a burlesk before; they were on the qui vive from start to finish. The comedians appealed to them; it was a line of filth they were unprepared for. Yeoman work they do, the comedians. All they need are a pair of baggy trousers, a piss-pot, a telephone or a hat rack to create the illusion of a world in which the Unconscious rules supreme. Every burlesque comedian, if he is worth his salt, has something of the heroic in him. At every performance he slays the censor who stands like a ghost on the treshold of the subliminal self. He not only slays him alive for us, but he pisses on him and mortifies the flesh.

Anyway, Cleo! By the time Cleo appears everybody is ready to jerk off. (Not like in India where a rich nabob buys up a half dozen rows of seats in

order to masturbate in peace.) Here everybody gets
to work under his hat. A condensed milk orgy.
Semen flows as freely as gasoline. Even a blind man
would know that there's nothing but cunt in sight.
The amazing thing it that there is never a stampede.
Now and then some one goes home and cuts his balls
off with a rusty razor, but these little exploits you
never read about in the newspapers.

One of the things that made Cleo's dance fascinating was the little pom-pom she wore in the center
of her girdle—planted right over her rose-bush. It
served to keep your eyes riveted to the spot. She
could rotate it like a pin-wheel or make it jump and
quiver with little electric spasms. Sometimes it
would subside with little gasps, like a swan coming
to rest after a deep orgasm. Sometimes it acted saucy
and impudent, sometimes it was sullen and morose.
It seemed to be part of her, a little ball of fluff that
had grown out of her Mons Venus. Possibly she had
acquired it in an Algerian whore-house, from a French
sailor. It was tantalizing, especially to the sixteen-
years olds who had still to know what it feels like to
make a grab for a woman's bush.

What her face was like I hardly remember any
more. I have a faint recollection that her nose was
retroussé. One would never recognize her with her
clothes on, that's a cinch. You concentrated on the
torso, in the center of which was a huge painted
navel the color of carmine. It was like a hungry
mouth, this navel. Like the mouth of a fish suddenly
stricken with paralysis. I'm sure her cunt wasn't
half as exciting to look at. It was probably a pale
bluish sliver of meat that a dog wouldn't even bother
to sniff. She was alive in her mid-riff, in that
sinuous fleshy pear which domed out from under the
chest bones. The torso reminded me always of those
dressmaker's model whose thighs end in a framework

of umbrella ribs. As a child I used to love to run my hand over the umbilical swell. It was heavenly to the touch. And the fact that there were no arms or legs to the model enhanced the bulging beauty of the torso. Sometimes there was no wickerwork below—just a truncated figure with a little collar of a neck which was always painted a shiny black. They were the intriguing ones, the lovable ones. One night in a side show I came upon a live one, just like the sewing machine models at home. She moved about on the platform with her hands, as if she were treading water. I got real close to her and engaged her in conversation. She had a head, of course, and it was rather a pretty one, something like the wax images you see in hairdressing establishments in the chic quarters of a big city. I learned that she was from Vienna; she had been born without legs. But I'm getting off the track.... The thing that fascinated me about her was that she had that same voluptuous swell, that pear-like ripple and bulge. I stood by her platform a long time just to survey her from all angles. It was amazing how close her legs had been pared off. Just another slice off her and she would have been minus a twat. The more I studied her the more tempted I was to push her over. I could imagine my arms around her cute little waist, imagine myself picking her up, slinging her under my arm and making off with her to ravish her in a vacant lot.

During the intermission, while the girls went to the lavatory to see dear old mother, Ned and I stood on the iron stairway which adorns the exterior of the theatre. From the upper tiers one could look into the homes across the street, where the dear old mothers fret and stew like angry roaches. Cosy little flats they are, if you have a strong stomach and a taste for the ultra-violet dreams of Chagall. Food and bedding are the dominant motifs. Sometimes they blend indiscriminately and the father who has been selling matches all day with tubercular frenzy finds himself eating the mattress. Among the poor only that which takes hours to prepare is served. The gourmet loves to eat in a restaurant which is odorous; the poor man gets sick to the stomach when he climbs the stairs and gets a whiff of what's coming to him. The rich man loves to walk the dog around the block—to work up a mild appetite. The poor man looks at the sick bitch lying under the tubs and feels that it would be an act of mercy to kick it in the guts. Nothing gives him an appetite. He is hungry, perpetually hungry for the things he craves. Even a breath of fresh air is a luxury. But then he's not a dog, and so nobody takes him out for an airing, alas and alack. I've seen the poor blighters leaning out of the window on their elbows, their heads hanging in their hands like Jack-o'-Lanterns: it doesn't take a mind-reader to know what they're thinking about. Now and then a row of tenements is demolished in order to open up ventilating holes. Passing these blank areas, spaced like missing teeth, I've often imagined the poor, bleeding blighters to be still hanging there on the window-sills, the houses torn down but they themselves suspended in mid-air, propped up by their own grief and misery, like torpid blimps defying the law of gravitation. Who notices these airy spectres? Who gives a fuck whether they're suspended in the air or buried six feet deep? The show is the thing, as Shakespeare says. Twice a day, Sundays included, the show goes on. If it's short of provender you are, why stew a pair of old socks. The Minsky Brothers are dedicated to giving entertainment. Hershey Almond Bars are always on tap, good before or after you jerk off. A new show every week—with the same old cast and the same old jokes. What would really be a catastrophe for the Minsky gents would be for Cleo to be stricken with a double hernia. Or to get pregnant. Hard to say which would be worse. She could have lockjaw or enteritis or claustrophobia, and it wouldn't matter a damn. She could even survive the menopause. Or rather, the Minskys could. But hernia, that would be like death— *irrevocable.*

What went on in Ned's mind during this brief intermission I could only conjecture. «Pretty horrible, isn't it?» he remarked, chiming in with some observation I had made. He said it with a detachment that would have done credit to a scion of Park Avenue. Nothing anyone could do about it, is what he meant. At twenty-five he had been the art director in an advertising concern; that was five or six years ago. Since then he had been on the rocks, but adversity had in no way altered his views about life. It had merely confirmed his basic notion that poverty was something to be avoided. With a good break he would once again be on top, dictating to those whom he was now fawning upon.

He was telling me about a proposition he had up his sleeve, another «unique» idea for an advertising campaign. (How to make people smoke more— without injuring their health.) The trouble was, now that he was on the other side of the fence nobody would listen to him. Had he still been art director everybody would have accepted the idea immediately as a brilliant one. Ned saw the irony of the situation, nothing more. He thought it had something to do with his front—perhaps he didn't look as confident as he used to. If he had a better wardrobe, if he could lay off the booze for a while, if he could work up the right enthusiasm.... and so on. Marcelle worried him. She was taking it out of him. With

every fuck he gave her he felt that another brilliant
idea had been slaughtered. He wanted to be alone
for a while so that he could think things out. If
Marcelle were on tap only when he needed her and
not turn up at odd hours—just when he was in the
middle of something—it would be ducky.

«You want a bottle opener, not a woman,» I said.

He laughed, as though he were slightly embarrassed.

«Well, you know how it is,» he said. «Jesus, I
like her all right... she's fine. Another girl would
have ditched me long ago. But—.»

«Yes, I know. The trouble is she sticks.»

«It sounds rotten, doesn't it?»

«It is rotten,» said I. «Listen, did it ever occur
to you that you may never again be an art director,
that you had your chance and you muffed it? Now
you've got another chance—and you're muffing it
again. You could get married and become... well,
I don't know what... any damned thing... what difference does it make? You have a chance to lead a
normal, happy life—on a modest plane. It doesn't
seem possible to you, I suppose, that you might be
better off driving a milk wagon? That's too dull for
you, isn't it? Too bad! I'd have more respect for
you as ditch digger than as president of the Palm
Olive Soap Company. You're not burning up with
original ideas, as you imagine, you're simply trying
to retrieve something that's lost. It's pride that's
goading you, not ambition. If you had any origin-
ality you'd be more flexible: you'd prove it in a
hundred different ways. What gripes you is that you
failed. It was probably the best thing that ever
happened to you. But you don't know how to exploit
your misfortunes. You were probably cut out for
something entirely different, but you won't give
yourself a chance to find out what. You revolve

about your obsession like a rat in a trap. If you ask me, it's pretty horrible... more horrible than the sight of these poor doomed bastards hanging out of the windows. They're willing to tackle anything; you're not willing to lift your little finger. You want to go back to your throne and be the king of the advertising world. And if you can't have that you're going to make everybody around you miserable. You're going to castrate yourself and then say that somebody cut your balls off....»

The musicians were tuning up; we had to scoot back to our seats. Mona and Marcelle were already seated, buried in a deep conversation. Suddenly there was a full blare from the orchestra pit, like a snarl of prussic acid over a tight tarpaulin. The red-haired fellow at the piano was all limp and boneless, his fingers falling like stalactites on the keyboard. People were still streaming back from the lavatories. The music got more and more frenetic, with the brass and the percussion instruments getting the upper hand. Here and there a switch of lights blinked, as if there were a string of electrified owls opening and closing their eyes. In front of us a young lad was holding a lighted match to the back of a post-card, expecting to discover the whore of Babylon—or the Siamese twins rolling in a double-jointed orgasm.

As the curtain went up the Egyptian beauties from the purlieus of Rivington Street began to unlimber; they flung themselves about like flounders just released from the hook. A scrawny contortionist did the pin-wheel, then folded up like a jack-knife and, after a few flips and flops, tried to kiss her own ass. The music grew soupy, alternating from one rhythm to another and getting nowhere. Just when everything seemed on the verge of collapse the floundering chorines did a fade-out, the contortionist picked

erself up and limped away like a leper, and out
mped away like a leper, and out came a pair of
congruous buffoons pretending to be full-blown
chers. The back curtain drops and there they are
anding in the middle of a street in the city of
kutsk. One of them wants a woman so bad his
ngue is hanging out. The other one is a con-
isseur of horse flesh. He has a little apparatus,
sort of Open Sesame, which he will sell to his
iend for 964 dollars and 32 cents. They compromise
a a dollar and a half. Fine. A woman comes walk-
g down the street. She's from Avenue A. He
lks French to her, the fellow who bought the
paratus. She answers in Volapuk. All he has to
o is turn on the juice and she flings her arms around
m. This goes on in ninety-two variations, just as it
d last week and the week before—as far back as
e days Bob Fitzimmons, in fact. The curtain drops
d a bright young man with a microphone steps out
the wings and croons a romantic ditty about the
roplane delivering a letter to his sweetheart in
aledonia.

Now the flounders are out again, this time disguised
Navajos. They reel about the electric camp-fire.
he music switches from «Pony Boy» to the «Kashmiri
ng» and then to «Rain in the Face». A Latvian
rl with a feather in her hair stands like Hiawatha,
oking towards the land of the setting sun. She has
stand on tip-toe until Bing Crosby Junior finishes
urteen quatrains of Amerindian folklore written by
cow-puncher from Hester Street. Then a pistol
ot is fired, the chorines whoop it up, the American
g is unfurled, the contortionist somersaults through
e block-house, Hiawatha does a fandango, and the
chestra becomes apoplectic. When the lights go
t the white-haired mother from the lavatory is
nding by the electric chair waiting to see her son

burn. This heart-rending scene is accompanied by a
falsetto rendition of «Silver Threads Among the
Gold». The victim of justice is one of the clowns
who will be out in a moment with a piss-pot in his
hand. He will have to measure the leading lady for
a bathing suit. She will bend over obligingly and
spread her ass so that he can get the measurement
absolutely correct. When that's over she will be the
nurse in the lunatic asylum, armed with a syringe
full of water which she will squirt down his pants.
Then there will be two leading ladies attired in
negligee. They sit in a cosy furnished flat waiting for
their boy friends to call. The boys call and in a few
moments they start taking their pants off. Then the
husband returns and the boys hop around in B. V.
D's, like crippled sparrows.

Everything is calculated to the mminute. By the
time 10:23 strikes Cleo is ready to do her second and
final number. She will have just about eight and a
half minutes to spare, according to the terms of the
contract. Then she will have to stand in the wings
for another twelve minutes and take her place with
the rest of the cast for the finale. Those twelve
minutes burn her up. They are precious minutes
which are completely wasted. She can't even get into
her street clothes; she must show herself in all her
glory and give just one little squirm or two as the
curtain falls. It burns her up.

Ten twenty-two and a half! An ominous decres
cendo, a muffled two-four flam from the drums.
All the lights are doused except those over the Exits.
The spot-light focuses on the wings where at 10:23
to the dot first a hand, then an arm, then a breast will
appear. The head follows after the body, as the aura
follows the saint. The head is wrapped in excelsior
with cabbage leaves masking the eyes; it moves like
a sea urchin struggling with eels. A wireless operator

s hidden in the carmined mouth of the navel: he is
a ventriloquist who uses the deaf-mute code.

Before the great spastic movements begin with a
drum-like roll of the torso, Cleo circles about the stage
with the hypnotic ease and lassitude of a cobra. The
supple, milk-white legs are screened behind a veil of
beads girdled at the waist; the pink nipples are
draped with transparent gauze. She is boneless,
milky, drugged: a medusa with a straw wig undulat-
ing in a lake of glass beads.

As she discards the tinkling robe the pom-pom
becomes the tom-tom and the tom-tom the pom-pom.

And now we are in the heart of darkest Africa,
where the Ubangi flows. Two snakes are locked in
mortal combat. The big one, which is a constrictor,
is slowly swallowing the smaller one—tail first. The
smaller one is about twelve feet long—and poisonous.
He fights up until the last breath; his fangs are still
spitting, even as the jaws of the big snake close about
his head. A siesta in the shade now follows in order
to give the digestive processes full sway. A strange,
silent combat produced not by hatred but by hunger.
Africa is the continent of plenty in which hunger
reigns supreme. The hyena and the vulture are the
referees. A land of chilly silences split by furious
snarls and agonizing screams. Everything is eaten
warm and uncooked. Life so abundant whets the
appetite of death. No hatred, only hunger. Hunger
in the midst of plenty. Death comes quickly. The
moment one is *hors de combat* the process of devora-
tion sets in. Tiny fishes, mad with hunger, can
devour a giant and leave him a skeleton in a few
minutes. Blood is sucked up like water. Hair and
skin are instantly appropriated. Claws and tusks
makes weapons or wampum. No waste. Everything
eaten alive amidst blood-curdling snarls and screams.
Death strikes like lightning through forest and river.

The big fellows are no more immune than the little
ones. All is prey.

In the midst of this ceaseless tussle the remnant
of the human kingdom stage their dances. Hunger
is the solar body of Africa, the dance is the lunar
body. The dance is the expression of a secondary
hunger: sex. Hunger and sex are like two snake
locked in mortal combat. There is no beginning nor
end. One swallows the other in order to reproduce
a third: the machine become flesh. A machine which
functions of itself and to no purpose, unless it be to
produce more and more and thus create less and less
The wise ones, the renunciators, seem to be the
gorillas. They live a life apart: they inhabit the
trees. They are the most ferocious of all—more
terrible even than the rhino or the lioness. They
utter piercing, deafening screams. They defy
approach.

Everywhere throughout the continent the dance
goes on. It is the ever-repeated story of dominion
over the dark forces of nature. Spirit working
through instinct. Africa dancing is Africa trying to
lift itself above the confusion of mere reproduction

In Africa the dance is impersonal, sacred and
obscene. When the phallus becomes erect and is
handled like a banana it is not a «personal hard-on»
we see but a tribal erection. It is a religious hard-on
directed not towards *a* woman but towards every
female member of the tribe. Group souls staging a
group fuck. Man lifting himself out of the animal
world through a ritual of his own invention. By his
mimicry he demonstrates that he has made himself
superior to the mere act of intercourse.

The hoochie koochie dancer of the big city dance
alone—a fact of staggering significance. The law
forbids response, forbids participation. Nothing is
left of the primitive rite but the «suggestive» move

ments of the body. What they suggest varies with the individual observer. For the majority, probably nothing more than an extraordinary fuck in the dark. A dream fuck, more exactly.

But what law is it that keeps the spectator rigid in his seat, as though shackled and manacled? The silent law of common consent which has made of sex a furtive, nasty act to be indulged in only with the sanction of the Church.

Observing Cleo, the image of that Viennese torso in the side-show reverts to mind. Was Cleo not as thoroughly excommunicated from human society as that seductive freak who was born without legs? No one dares to pounce upon Cleo, any more than one would dare to paw the legless beauty at Coney Island. Though every movement of her body is based on the manual of earthly intercourse no one even thinks of responding to the invitation. To approach Cleo in the midst of her dance would be considered as heinous a crime as to rape the helpless freak of the side-show.

I think of the dressmaker's model which was once the symbol of feminine allure. I think how that image of carnal pleasure finished off below the torso in an airy skirt of umbrella ribs.

Here's what's passing through my head....

We are a community of seven or eight million people, democratically free and equal, dedicated to the pursuit of life, liberty and happiness for all—*in theory*. We represent nearly all the races and peoples of the world at the height of their cultural attainments—*in theory*. We have the right to worship as we please, vote as we please, create our own laws, and so forth and so on—*in theory*.

Theoretically everything is ideal, just, equitable. Africa is still a dark continent which the white man is only beginning to enlighten with Bible and sword.

Yet, by some queer, mystical agreement, a woman
called Cleo is performing an obscene dance in a
darkened house next door to a church. If she were
to dance this way in the street she would be arrested;
if she were to dance this way in a private house she
would be raped and mangled; if she were to dance
this way in Carnegie Hall she would create a
revolution. Her dance is a violation of the Constitution of the United States. It is archaic, primitive,
obscene, tending only to arouse and inflame the base
passions of men and women. It has only one honest
purpose in view—to augment the box office receipts
for the Minsky rothers. That it does. And there
one must stop thinking about the subject or go crazy.

But I can't stop thinking.... I see a mannikin who
under the lustful gaze of the cosmopolitan eye has
assumed flesh and blood. I see her draining the
passions of a supposedly civilized audience in the
second biggest city in the world. She has taken on
their flesh, their thoughts, their passions, their
lascivious dreams and desires, and in doing so has
truncated them, left them with stuffed torsos and
umbrella ribs. I suspect that she has even robbed
them of their sexual organs, because, if they were
still men and women, what would hold them to their
seats? I see the whole swift performance as a sort
of Caligari séance, a piece of deft, masterful psychic
transference. I doubt that I am sitting in a theatre
at all. I doubt everything, except the power of
suggestion. I can just as easily believe that we are
in a bazaar in Nagasaki, where sexual objects are
sold; that we are sitting there in the dark with rubber
sexes in our hands and masturbating like maniacs. I
can believe that we are in limbo, amidst the smoke
of astral worlds, and that what passes before the eye
is a mirage from the phenomenal world of pain and
crucifixion. I can believe that we are all hanging by

the neck, that it is the moment between the springing of the trap and the snapping of the cerebro-spinal cord, which brings about the last most exquisite ejaculation. I can believe that we are anywhere except in a city of seven or eight million souls, all free and equal, all cultured and civilized, all dedicated to the pursuit of life, liberty and happiness. Above all, I find it most difficult to believe that I have just this day given myself in holy wedlock for the third time, that we are seated side by side in the darkness as man and wife, and that we are celebrating the rites of spring with rubber emotions.

I find it utterly incredible. There are situations which defy the laws of intelligence. There are moments when the unnatural commingling of eight million people gives birth to floral pieces of blackest insanity. The Marquis de Sade was as lucid and reasonable as a cucumber. Sacher Masoch was a pearl of equanimity. Blue Beard was as gentle as a dove.

Cleo is becoming positively luminous in the cold radiance of the spotlight. Her belly has become a swollen, sullen sea in which the brilliant carmine navel tosses about like the gasping mouth of a *naufragé*. With the tip of her cunt she tosses floral pieces into the orchestra. The pom-pom becomes the tom-tom and the tom-tom the pom-pom. The blood of the masturbator is in her veins. Her teats are concentric veins of stewed purple. Her mouth flashes like the red sear of a tusk ripping a warm limb. The arms are cobras, the legs are made of patent leather. Her face is paler than ivory, the expressions fixed, as in the terra cotta demons of Yucatan. The concentrated lust of the mob invades her with the nebulous rhythm of a solar body taking substance. Like a moon wrenched from the fiery surface of the earth, she disgorges pieces of blood-soaked meat. She moves without feet, as do the freshly amputated victims of the battle-field in their dreams. She writhes on her imaginary soft stumps, emitting noiseless groan of lacerating ecstasy.

The orgasm comes slowly, like the last gouts of blood from a geyser in pain. In the city of eight million she is alone, cut off, excommunicated. She is giving the last touches to an exhibition of sexual passion which would bring even a corpse to life. She has the protection of the City Fathers and the blessings of the Minsky Brothers. In the city of Minsk, whence they had journeyed from Pinsk, these two far-sighted boys planned that all should be thus and so. And it came about, just as in the dream, that they opened their beautiful Winter Garden next door to the Catholic Church. Everything according to plan, including the white-haired mother in the lavatory.

The last few spasms.... Why is it that all is so quiet? The black floral pieces are dripping with condensed milk. A man nammed Silverberg is chewing the lips of a mare. Another called Vittorio is mounting a ewe. A woman without name is shelling peanuts and stuffing them between her legs.

And at this same hour, almost to the minute, a dark, sleek chap, nattily attired in a tropical worsted with a bright yellow tie and a white carnation in his button-hole, takes his stand in front of the Hotel Astor on the third step, leaning his weight lightly on the bamboo cane which he sports at this hour of the day.

His name is Osmanli, obviously an invented one. He has a roll of ten, twenty and fifty dollar bills in his pocket. The fragrance of an expensive toilet water emanates from the silk kerchief which cautiously protrudes from his breast pocket. He is as fresh as a daisy, dapper, cool, insolent—a real Jim Dandy. To look at him one would never suspect that he is in the pay of an ecclesiastical organization, that his sole mission in life is to spread poison, malice, slander, that he enjoys his work, sleeps well and blossoms like the rose.

To-morrow noon he will be at his accustomed place in Union Square, mounted on a soap box, the American flag protecting him; the foam will be drooling from his lips, his nostrils will quiver with rage, his voice will be hoarse and cracked. Every argument that man has trumped up to destroy the appeal of Communism he has at this disposal, can shake them out of his hat like a cheap magician. He is there not only to give argument, not only to spread poison and slander, but to foment trouble: he is there to create a riot, to bring on the cops, to go to court and accuse innocent people of attacking the Stars and Stripes.

When it gets too hot for him in Union Square he goes to Boston, Providence, or some other American city, always wrapped in the American flag, always surrounded by this trained fomentors of discord, always protected by the shadow of the Church. A man whose origin is completely obscured, who has changed his name dozens of times, who has served all the Parties, red, white and blue, at one time or another. A man without country, without principle, without faith, without scruples. A servant of Beelzebub, a stooge, a stool pigeon, a traitor, a turncoat. A master at confusing men's minds, an adept of the Black Lodge.

He has no close friends, no mistress, no ties of any kind. When he disappears he leaves no traces. An invisible thread links him to those whom he serves. On the soap box he seems like a man possessed, like a raving fanatic. On the steps of the Hotel Astor, where he stands every night for a few minutes, as though surveying the crowd, as though slightly

distrait, he is the picture of self-possession, of suave,
cool nonchalance. He has had a bath and a rub-
down, his nails manicured, his shoes shined; he has
had a sound nap, too, and following that a most
excellent meal in one of those quiet, exclusive restaurants which cater only to the gourmet. Often he
takes a short stroll in the Park to digest his repast.
He looks about with an intelligent, appreciative eye,
aware of the attractions of the flesh, aware of the
beauties of earth and sky. Well read, travelled, with
a taste for music and a passion for flowers, he often
muses as he walks on the follies of man. He loves
the flavor and savour of words; he rolls them over
on his tongue, as he would a delicious morsel of food.
He knows that he has the power to sway men, to stir
their passions, to goad them and confound them at
will. But this very ability has made him contemptuous, scornful and derisive of his fellow-man.

Now on the steps on the Astor, disguised as a
boulevardier, a flaneur, a Beau Brummel, he gazes
meditatively over the heads of the crowd, unperturbed
by the chewing gum lights, the flesh for hire, the
jingle of ghostly harnesses, the look of absentia-
dementia in passing eyes. He has detached himself
from all parties, cults, isms, ideologies. He is a free-
wheeling ego, immune to all faiths, beliefs, principles.
He can buy whatever he needs to sustain the illusion
that he needs nothing, no one. He seems this evening
to be more than ever free, more than ever detached.
He admits to himself that he feels like a character
in a Russian novel, wonders vaguely why he should
be indulging in such sentiments. He recognizes that
he has just dismissed the idea of suicide; he is a little
startled to find he had been entertaining such ideas.
He had been arguing with himself; it had been quite
a prolonged affair, now that he retraces his throughts.
The most disturbing thought is that he is unable to

recognize the self with which he had discussed this question of suicide. This hidden being had never made its wants known before. There had always been a vacuum around which he had built a veritable cathedral of changing personalities. Retreating behind the façade he had always found himself alone. And then, just a moment ago, he had made the discovery that he was not alone; despite all the change of masks, all the architectural camouflage, some one was living with him, some one who knew him intimately, and who was now urging him to make an end of it.

The most fantastic part of it was that he was being urged to do it at once, to waste no time. It was preposterous because, admitting that the idea was seductive and appealing, he nevertheless felt the very human desire to enjoy the privilege of living out his own death in his imagination, at least for an hour or so. He seemed to be begging for time, which was strange, because never in his life had he entertained the notion of doing away with himself. He should have dismissed the thought instead of pleading like a convicted criminal for a few moments of grace. But this emptiness, this solitude into which he usually retreated, now began to assume the pressure and the explosiveness of a vacuum. The bubble was about to burst. He knew it. He knew he could do nothing to stay it. He walked rapidly down the steps of the Astor and plunged into the crowd. He thought for a moment that he would perhaps lose himself in the midts of all those bodies but no, he became more and more lucid, more and more self-conscious, more and more determined to obey the imperious voice which goaded him on. He was like a lover on his way to a rendezvous. He had only one thought—his own destruction. It burned like a fire, it illumined the way.

As he turned down a side street, in order to hasten to his appointment, he understood very clearly that he had already been taken over, as it were, and that he had only to follow his nose. He had no problems, no conflicts. Certain automatic gestures he made without even slackening his pace. For instance, passing a garbage can he tossed his bank roll into it as through he were getting rid of a banana peel; at a corner he emptied the contents of his inside coat pocket down a sewer; his watch and chain, his ring, his pocket knife went in similar fashion. He patted himself all over, as he walked, to make sure that he had divested himself of all personal possessions. Even his handkerchief, after he had blown his nose for the last time, he threw in the gutter. He felt as light as a feather and moved with increasing celerity through the sombre streets. At a given moment the signal would be given and he would give himself up. Instead of a tumultuous stream of thoughts, of last minute fears, wishes, hopes, regrets, such as we imagine to assail the doomed, he knew only a singular and ever more expansive void. His heart was like a clear blue sky in which not even the faintest trace of a cloud is perceptible. One might think that he had already crossed the frontier of the other world, that he was now, before his actual bodily death, already in the coma, and that emerging and finding himself on the other side he would be surprised to find himself walking so rapidly. Only then perhaps would he be able to collect his thoughts ; only then would he be able to ask himself why he had done it.

Overhead the El is rattling and thundering. A man passes him running at top speed. Behind him is an officer of the law with drawn revolver. He begins to run too. Now all three of them are running. He doesn't know why, he doesn't even know that some one is behind him. But when the bullet pierces the

back of his skull and he falls flat on his face a gleam
of blinding clarity reverberates through his whole
being.

Caught face downward in death there on the sidewalk, the grass already sprouting in his ears, Osmanli
redescends the steps of the Hotel Astor, but instead
of rejoining the crowd he slips through the back door
of a modest little house in a village where he spoke
a different language. He sits down at the kitchen
table and sips a glass of buttermilk. It seems as
though it were only yesterday that, seated at this same
table, his wife had told him she was leaving him.
The news had stunned him so that he had been unable
to say a word; he had watched her go without making
the slightest protest. He had been sitting there
quietly drinking his buttermilk and she had told him
with brutal, direct frankness that she never loved
him. A few more words equally unsparing and she
was gone. In those few minutes he had become a
completely different man. Recovering from the
shock, he experienced the most amazing exhilaration.
It was as if she had said to him: «You are now free
to act!» He felt so mysteriously free that he wondered
if his life up to that moment had not been a dream.
To act! It was so simple. He had gone out into the
yard and, thinking; then, with the same spontaneity,
he had walked to the dog kennel, whistled to the
animal, and when it stuck its head out he had
chopped it off clean. That's what it meant—to act!
So extremely simple, it made him laugh. He knew
now that he could do anything he wished. He went
inside and called the maid. He wanted to take a look
at her with these new eyes. There was nothing more
in his mind than that. An hour later, having raped
her, he went direct to the bank and from there to the
railways station where he took the first train that
came in.

From then on his life had assumed a kaleidoscopic pattern. The few murders he had committed were carried out almost absent-mindedly, without malice, hatred or greed. He made love almost in the same way. He knew neither fear, timidity, nor caution.

In this manner ten years had passed in the space of a few minutes. The chains which bind the ordinary man had been taken from him, he had roamed the world at will, had tasted freedom and immunity, and then in a moment of utter relaxation, surrendering himself to the imagination, had concluded with pitiless logic that death was the one luxury he had denied himself. And so he had descended the steps of the Hotel Astor and a few minutes later, falling face downward in death, he realized that he was not mistaken when he understood her to say that she had never loved him. It was the first time he had ever thought of it again, and though it would be the last time he would ever think of it he could not make any more of it than when he first heard it ten years ago. It had not made sense then and it did not make sense now. He was still slipping his buttermilk. He was already a dead man. He was powerless, that's why he had felt so free. But he had never actually been free, as he had imagined himself to be. That had been simply an hallucination. To begin with, he had never chopped the dog's head off, otherwise it would not now be barking with joy. If he could only get to his feet and look with his own eyes he would know for certain whether everything had been real or hallucinatory. But the power to move has been taken from him. From the moment she had uttered those few telling words he knew he would never be able to move from the spot. Why she had chosen that particular moment when he was drinking the buttermilk, why she had waited so long to tell him, he could not understand

and never would. He would not even try to understand. He had heard her very distinctly, quite as if she had put her lips to his ear and shouted the words into it. It had travelled with such speed to all parts of his body that it was as though a bullet had exploded in his brain. Then—could it have been just a few moments later or an eternity?—he had emerged from the prison of his old self much as a butterfly emerges from its chrysalis. Then the dog, then the maid, then this, then that—innumerable incidents repeating themselves as if in accordance with a pre-established plan. Everything of a pattern, even down to the three or four casual murders.

As in the legends where it is told that he who forsakes his vision tumbles into a labyrinth from which there is no issue save death, where through symbol and allegory it is made clear that the coils of the brain, the coils of the labyrinth, the coils of the serpents which entwine the backbone are one and the same strangling process, the process of shutting doors behind one, of walling in the flesh, of moving relentlessly towards petrifaction, so it was with Osmanli, an obscure Turk, caught by the imagination on the steps of the Hotel Astor in the moment of his most illusory freedom detachment. Looking over the heads of the crowd he had perceived with shuddering remembrance the image of his beloved wife, her dog-like head turned to stone. The pathetic desire to overreach his sorrow had ended in the confrontation with the mask. The monstrous embryo of unfulfillment blocked every egress. With face pressed against the pavement he seemed to kiss the stony features of the woman he had lost. His flight, pursued with skillful indirection, had brought him face to face with the bright image of horror reflected in the shield of self-protection. Himself slain, he had slain the world. He had reached his own identity in death.

Cleo was terminating her dance. The last convulsive movements had coincided with the fantastic retrospection on Osmanli's death....

23

The incredible thing about such hallucinations is that they have their substance in reality. When Osmanli fell face forward on the sidewalk he was merely enacting a scene out of my life in advance. Let us jump a few years—into the pot of horror.

The damned have always a table to sit at, whereon they rest their elbows and support the leaden weight of their brains. The damned are always sightless, gazing out at the world with blank orbs. The damned are always petrified, and in the center of their petrifaction is immeasurable emptiness. The damned have always the same excuse—the loss of the beloved.

It is night and I am sitting in a cellar. This is our home. I wait for her night after night, like a prisoner chained to the floor of his cell. There is a woman with her whom she calls her friend. They have conspired to betray me and defeat me. They leave me without food, without heat, without light. They tell me to amuse myself until they return.

Through months of shame and humiliation I have come to hug my solitude. I no longer seek help from the outside world. I no longer answer the door-bell. I live by myself, in the turmoil of my own fears. Trapped in my own phantasms, I wait for the flood to rise and drown me out.

When they return to torture me I behave like the

animal which I have become. I pounce on the food
with ravenous hunger. I eat with my fingers. And
as I devour the food I grin them mercilessly, as though
I were a mad, jealous Czar. I pretend that I am
angry: I hurl vile insults at them, I threaten them
with my fists, I growl and spit and rage.

I do this night after night, in order to stimulate my
almost extinct emotions. I have lost the power to
feel. To conceal this defect I simulate every passion.
There are nights when I amuse them no end by
roaring like a wounded lion. At times I knock them
down with a velvet-thudded paw. I have even peed
on them when they rolled about on the floor convulsed with hysterical laughter.

They say I have the makings of a clown. They say
they will bring some friends down one night and
have me perform for them. I grind my teeth and
move my scalp back and forth to signify approval.
I am learning all the tricks of the zoo.

My greatest stunt is to pretend jealousy. Jealousy
over little things, particularly. Never to inquire
whether she slept with this one or that, but only to
know if he kissed her hand. I can become furious
over a little gesture like that. I can pick up the
knife and threaten to slit her throat. On occasion I
go so far as to give her inseparable friend a tender
jab in the buttocks. I bring iodine and court plaster
and kiss her inseparable friend's ass.

Let us say that they come home of an evening and
find the fire out. Let us say that this evening I am
in an excellent mood, having conquered the pangs of
hunger with an iron will, having defied the onslaught
of insanity alone in the dark, having almost convinced
myself that only egotism can produce sorrow and
misery. Let us say further that, entering the prison
cell, they seem insensitive to the victory which I have
won. They sense nothing more than the dangerous

chill of the room. They do not inquire if I am cold, they simply say—it is cold here.

Cold, my little queens? Then you shall have a roaring fire. I take the chair and smash it against the stone wall. I jump on it and break it into tiny pieces. I kindle a little flame at the hearth with paper and splinters. I roast the chair piece by piece.

A charming gesture, they think. So far so good. A little food now, a bottle of cold beer. So you have had a good evening this evening? It was cold outdoors, was it? You collected a little money? Fine, deposit it in the Dime Savings Bank to-morrow! You, Hegoroboru, run out and buy a flask of rum! I am leaving to-morrow... I am setting out on a journey.

The fire is getting low. I take the vacant chair and beat its brains out against the wall. The flames leap up. Hegoroboru returns with a grin and holds the bottle out. The work of a minute to uncork it, guzzle a deep draught. Flames leap up in my gizzard. Stand up! I yell. Give me that other chair! Protests, howls, screams. This is pushing things too far. *But it's cold outdoors,* you say? Then we need more heat. Get away! I shove the dishes on to the floor with one swipe and tackle the table. They try to pull me away. I go outside to the dust-bin and I find the axe. I begin hacking away. I break the table into tiny pieces, then the commode, spilling everything on to the floor. I will break everything to pieces, I warn them, even the crockery. We will warm ourselves as we have never warmed ourselves before.

A night on the floor, the three of us tossing like burning corks. Taunts and gibes passing back and forth.

«He'll never go away... he's just acting.»

A voice whispering in my ear: «Are you really going away?»

«Yes, I promise you I am.»

«But I don't want you to go.»

«I don't care what you want any longer.»

«But I love you.»

«I don't believe it.»

«But you *must* believe me.»

«I believe nobody, nothing.»

«You're ill. You don't know what you're doing. I won't let you go.»

«How will you stop me?»

«Please, please, Val, don't talk that way... you worry me.»

Silence.

A timid whisper: «How are you going to live without me?»

«I don't know, I don't care.»

«But you need me. You don't know how to take care of yourself.»

«I need nobody.»

«I'm afraid, Val. I'm afraid something will happen to you.»

In the morning I leave stealthily while they slumber blissfully. By stealing a few pennies from a blind newspaperman I get to the Jersey shore and set out for the highway. I feel fantastically light and free. In Philadelphia I stroll about as if I were a tourist. I get hungry. I ask for a dime from a passerby and I get it. I try another and another— just for the fun of it. I go into a saloon, eat a free lunch with a schooner of beer, and set out for the highway again.

I get a lift in the direction of Pittsburgh. The driver is uncommunicative. So am I. It's as though I had a private chauffeur. After a while I wonder where I'm going. Do I want a job? No. Do I

want to begin life all over again? No. Do I want
a vacation? No. I want nothing.

Then what *do* you want? I say to myself. The
answer is always the same: Nothing.

Well, that's exactly what you have: Nothing.

The duologue dies down. I become interested in
the cigarette lighter which is plugged into the
dashboard. The word cleat enters my mind. I play
with it for a long time, then dismiss it peremptorily,
as one would dismiss a child who wants to play ball
with you all day.

Roads and arteries branching out in every direction.
What would the earth be without roads? A trackless
ocean. A jungle. The first road through the
wilderness mut have seemed like a grand accomplishment. Direction, orientation, communication. Then
two roads, three roads... Then millions of roads. A
spider web and in the center of it man, the creator,
caught like a fly.

We are travelling seventy miles an hour, or perhaps
I imagine it. Not a word exchanged between us. He
may be afraid to hear me say that I am hungry or that
I have no place to sleep. He may be thinking where
to dump me out if I begin to act suspiciously. Now
and then he lights a cigarette on the electric grill.
The gadget fascinates me. It's like a little electric
chair.

«I'm turning off here,» says the driver suddenly.
«Where are *you* going?»

«You can leave me out here... thanks.»

I step out into a fine drizzle. It's darkling. Roads
leading to everywhere. I must decide where I want
to go. I must have an objective.

I stand so deep in trance that I let a hundred cars
go by without looking up. I haven't even an extra
handkerchief, I discover. I was going to wipe my
glasses but then, what's the use? I don't have to see

too well or feel too well or think too well. I'm not going anywhere. When I get tired I can drop down and go to sleep. Animals sleep in the rain, why not man? If I could become an animal I would be getting somewhere.

A truck pulls up beside me; the driver is looking for a match.

«Can I give you a lift?» he asks.

I hop in without asking where to. The rain comes down harder, it has become pitch black suddenly. I have no idea where we're bound and I don't want to know. I feel content to be out of the rain sitting next to a warm body.

This guy is more convivial. He talks a lot about matches, how important they are when you need them, how easy it is to lose them, and so on. He makes conversation out of anything. It seems strange to talk so earnestly about nothing at all when really there are the most tremendous problems to be solved. Except for the fact that we are talking about material trifles this is the sort of conversation that might be carried on in a French salon. The roads have connected everything up so marvelously that even emptiness can be transported with ease.

As we pull into the outskirts of a big town I ask him where we are.

«Why this is Philly,» he says. «Where did you think you were?»

«I don't know,» I said, «I had no idea... You're going to New York, I suppose?»

He grunted. Then he added: «You don't seem to care very much one way or another. You act like you were just riding around in the dark.»

«You said it. That's just what I'm doing... riding around in the dark.»

I sank back and listened to him tell about guys walking around in the dark looking for a place to

flop. He talked about them very much as a horticul-
turist would talk about certain species of shrubs. He
was a «space-binder», as Korbyski puts it, a guy
riding the highways and byways all by his lonesome.
What lay to either side of the traffic lanes was the
veldt, and the creatures inhabiting that void were
vagrants hungrily bumming a ride.

The more he talked the more wistfully I thought
of the meaning of shelter. After all, the cellar hadn't
been too bad. Out in the world people were just as
poorly off. The only difference between them and
me was that they went out and got what they needed;
they sweated for it, they tricked one another, they
fought one another tooth and nail. I had none of
those problems. My only problem was how to live
with myself day in and day out.

I was thinking how ridiculous and pathetic it would
be to sneak back into the cellar and find a little
corner all to myself where I could curl up and pull
the roof down over my ears. I would crawl in like
a dog with his tail between his legs. I wouldn't bother
them any more with jealous scenes. I would be grateful for any crumbs that were handed me. If she
wanted to bring her lovers in and make love to them
in my presence it would be all right too. One doesn't
bite the hand that feeds one. Now that I had seen
the world I wouldn't ever complain again. Anything
was better than to be left standing in the rain and
not know where you want to go. After all, I still had
a mind. I could lie in the dark and think, think as
much as I chose, or as little. The people outside
would be running to and fro, moving things about,
buying, selling, putting money in the bank and taking
it out again. That was horrible. I wouldn't ever
want to do that. I would much prefer to pretend
that I was an animal, say a dog, and have a bone
thrown to me now and then. If I behaved decently I

would be petted and stroked. I might find a good
master who would take me out on a leash and let me
make pipi everywhere. I might meet another dog.
one of the opposite sex, and pull off a quick one now
and then. Oh, I knew how to be quiet now and
obedient. I had learned my little lesson. I would
curl up in a corner near the hearth, just as quiet and
gentle as you please. They would have to be terribly
mean to kick me out. Besides, if I showed that I
didn't need anything, didn't ask any favors, if I let
them carry on just as if they were by themselves.
what harm could come by giving me a little place in
the corner ?

The thing was to sneak in while they were out, so
that they couldn't shut the gate in my face.

At this point in my reverie the most disquieting
thought took hold of me. What if they had fled ?
What if the house were deserted ?

Somewhere near Elizabeth we came to a halt.
There was something wrong with the engine. It
seemed wiser to get out and hail another car than to
wait around all night. I walked to the nearest gas
station and hung around for a car to take me into
New York. I waited over an hour and then got
impatient and lit off down the gloomy lane on my
own two legs. The rain had abated; it was just a
thin drizzle. Now and then, thinking how lovely it
would be to crawl into the dog kennel, I broke into a
trot. Elizabeth was about fifteen miles off.

Once I got so overjoyed that I broke into song.
Louder and louder I sang, as if to let them know I
was coming. Of course I wouldn't enter the house
singing—that would frighten them to death.

The singing made me hungry. I bought a Hershey
Almond Bar at a little stand beside the road. It was
delicious. See, you're not so badly off, I said to
myself. You're not eating bones or refuse yet. You

may get some good dishes before you die. What are
you thinking of—lamb stew? You mustn't think
about palatable things... think only of bones and
refuse. From now on it's a dog's life.

I was sitting on a big rock somewhere this side of
Elizabeth when I saw a big truck approaching. It
was the fellow I had left farther back. I hopped in.
He started talking about engines, what ails them, what
makes them go, and so on. «We'll soon be there,»
he said suddenly, apropos of nothing.

«Where?» I asked.

«New York, of course... where do you think?»

«Oh, New York, yeah. I forgot.»

«Say, what the hell are you going to do in New
York, if I ain't getting too personal?»

«I'm going to rejoin my family.»

«You been away long?»

«About ten years,» I said, drawing the words out
meditatively.

«Ten years ! That's a hell of a long time. What
were you doing, just bumming around ?»

«Yeah, just bumming around.»

«I guess they'll be glad to see you... your folks.»

«I guess they will.»

«You don't seem to be so sure of it,» he said, giving
me a quizzical look.

«That's true. Well, you know how it is.»

«I guess so,» he answered. «I meet lots of guys
like you. Always come back to the roost some time
or other.»

He said roost, I said kennel—*under my breath*, to
be sure. I liked kennel better. Roost was for
roosters, pigeons, birds of feather that lay eggs. I
wasn't going to lay no eggs. Bones and refuse, bones
and refuse, bones and refuse. I repeated it over and
over, to give myself the moral strength to crawl back
like a beaten dog.

I borrowed a nickel from him on leaving and ducked into the subway. I felt tired, hungry, weather-beaten. The passengers looked sick to me. As though some one had just let them out of the hoosegow or the alms house. I had been out in the world, far, far away. For ten years I had been knocking about and now I was coming home. Welcome home, prodigal son ! *Welcome home!* My goodness, what stories I had heard, what cities I had seen! What marvelous adventures! Ten years of life, just from morn to midnight. Would the folks still be there ?

I tiptoed into the areaway and looked for a gleam of light. Not a sign of life. Well, they never came home very early. I would go in upstairs by way of the stoop. Perhaps they were in the back of the house. Sometimes they sat in Hegoroboru's little bedroom off the hall where the toilet box trickled night and day.

I opened the door softly, walked to the head of the stairs which were enclosed, and quietly, very quietly, lowered myself step by step. There was a door at the bottom of the steps. I was in total darkness.

Near the bottom I heard muffled sounds of speech. They were home ! I felt terrifically happy, exultant. I wanted to dash in wagging my little tail and throw myself at their feet. But that wasn't the program I had planned to adhere to.

After I had stood with my ear to the panel for some minutes I put my hand on the door knob and very slowly and noiselessly I turned it. The voices came much more distinctly now that I had opened the door an inch or so. The big one, Hegoroboru, was talking. She sounded maudlin, hysterical, as though she had been drinking. The other voice was low-pitched, more soothing and caressing than I had ever heard it. She seemed to be pleading with the big one. There were strange pauses, too, as if they were embracing. Now and then I could swear the big one gave a grunt, as though she were rubbing the skin off the other one. Then suddenly she let out a howl of delight, but a vengeful one. Suddenly she shrieked.

«Then you do love him still ? You were lying to me!»

«No, no! I swear I don't. You *must* believe me, *please*. I never loved him.»

«That's a lie!»

«I swear to you... I swear I never loved him. He was just a child to me.»

This was followed by a shrieking gale of laughter. Then a slight commotion, as if they were scuffling. Then a dead silence, as if their lips were glued together. Then it seemed as if they were undressing one another, licking one another all over, like calves in the meadow. The bed squeaked. Fouling the nest, that was it. They had gotten rid of me as if I were a leper and now they were trying to do the man and wife act. It was good I hadn't been lying in the corner watching this with my head between my paws. I would have barked angrily, perhaps bitten them. And then they would have kicked me around like a dirty cur.

I didn't want to hear any more. I closed the door gently and sat on the steps in total darkness. The fatigue and hunger had passed. I was extraordinarily awake. I could have walked to San Francisco in three hours.

Now I must go somewhere ! I must get very definite—or I will go mad. I know I am not just a child. I don't know if I want to be a man—I feel too bruised and battered—but I certainly am not a child !

Then a curious physiological comedy took place. *I began to menstruate.* I menstruated from every hole in my body.

When a man menstruates it's all over in a few minutes. He doesn't leave any mess behind either.

I crept upstairs on all fours and left the house as silently as I had entered it. The rain was over, the stars were out in full splendor. A light wind was blowing. The Lutheran Church across the way, which in the daylight was the color of baby shit, had now taken on a soft ochrous hue which blended serenely with the black of the asphalt. I was still not very definite in my mind about the future. At the corner I stood a few minutes, looking up and down the street as if I were taking it in for the first time.

When you have suffered a great deal in a certain place you have the impression that the record is imprinted in the street. But if you notice, streets seem peculiarly unaffected by the sufferings of private individuals. If you step out of a house at night, after losing a dear friend, the street seems really quite discreet. If the outside became like the inside it would be unbearable. Streets are breathing places...

I move along, trying to get definite without developing a fixed idea. I pass garbage cans loaded with bones and refuse. Some have put old shoes, busted slippers, hats, suspenders, and other worn-out articles in front of their dwellings. There is no doubt but that if I took to prowling around at night I could live quite handsomely off the discarded crumbs.

The life in the kennel is out, that's definite. I don't feel like a dog any more anyway...I feel more like a tom-cat. The cat is independent, anarchistic, a free-wheeler. It's the cat which rules the roost at night.

Getting hungry again. I wander down to the bright lights of Borough Hall where the cafeterias blaze. I look through the big windows to see if I can detect a friendly face. Pass on, from shop window to shop window, examining shoes, haberdashery,

pipe tobaccos and so forth. Then I stand a while at
the subway entrance, hoping forlornly that some one
will drop a nickel without noticing it. I look the
news stands over to see if there are any blind men
about whom I can steal a few pennies from.

After a time I am walking the bluff at Columbia
Heights. I pass a sedate brown stone house which I
remember entering years and years ago to deliver a
package of clothes to one of my father's customers.
I remember standing in the big back room with the
bay windows giving out on the river. It was a day
of brilliant sunshine, a late afternoon, and the room
was like a Vermeer. I had to help the old man on
with his clothes. He was ruptured. Standing in the
middle of the room in his balbriggan underwear he
seemed positively obscene.

Below the bluff lay a street full of warehouses.
The terraces of the wealthy homes were like overhanging gardens, ending abruptly some twenty or
thirty feet above this dismal street with its dead
windows and grim archways leading to the wharves.
At the end of the street I stood against a wall to take
a leak. A drunk comes along and stands beside me.
He pees all over himself and then suddenly he dou-
bles up and begins to vomit. As I walk away I can
hear it splashing over his shoes.

I run down a long flight of stairs leading to the
docks and find myself face to face with a man in
uniform swinging a big stick. He wants to know
what I'm about, but before I can answer he begins to
shove me and brandish his stick.

I climb back up the long flight of stairs and sit on
a bench. Facing me is an old-fashioned hotel where
a school-teacher who used to be sweet on me lives.
The last time I saw her I had taken her out to dinner
and as I was saying good-bye I had to beg her for a
nickel. She gave it to me—just a nickel—with a

look I shall never forget. She had placed high hopes in me when I was a student. But that look told me all too plainly that she had definitely revised her opinion of me. She might just as well have said: «You'll never be able to cope with the world!»

The stars were very very bright. I stretched out on the bench and gazed at them intently. All my failures were now tightly bound up inside me, a veritable embryo of unfulfillment. All that had happened to me now seemed extremely remote. I had nothing to do but revel in my detachment. I began to voyage from star to star...

An hour or so later, chilled to the bone, I got to my feet and began walking briskly. An insane desire to repass the house I had been driven from took possession of me. I was dying to know if they were still up and about.

The shades were only partially drawn and the light from a candle near the bed gave the front room a quiet glow. I stole close to the window and put my ear to it. They were singing a Russian song which the big one was fond of. Apparently all was his bliss in there.

I tiptoed out of the areaway and turned down Love Lane which was at the corner. It had been named Love Lane during the Revolution most likely; now it was simply a back alley dotted with garages and repair shops. Garbage cans strewn about like captured chess pieces.

I retraced my steps to the river, to that grim, dismal street which ran like a shriveled urethra beneath the overhanging terraces of the rich. Nobody ever walked through this street late at night —it was too dangerous.

Not a soul about. The passageways tunneled through the warehouses gave fascinating glimpses of the river life—barges lying lifeless, tugs gliding by

like smoking ghosts, the skyscrapers silhouetted
against the New York shore, huge iron stanchions
with cabled hawsers slung around them, piles of
bricks and lumber, sacks of coffee. The most poi-
gnant sight was the sky itself. Swept clear of clouds
and studded with fistsful of stars, it gleamed like the
breast-plate of the high priests of old.

Finally I made to go through an archway. About
halfway through I felt a huge rat race across my
feet. I stopped with a shudder and another one slid
over my feet. Then a panic seized me and I ran
back to the street. On the other side of the street,
close to the wall, a man was standing. I stood stock
still, undecided which was to turn, hoping that this
silent figure would move first. But he remained immobile, watching me like a hawk. Again I felt
panicky, but this time I steeled myself to walk away,
fearing that if I ran he would also run. I walked
as noiselessly as possible, my ear cocked to catch the
sound of his steps. I didn't dare to turn my head.
I walked slowly, deliberately, barely putting my heels
down.

I had only walked a few yards when I had the
certain sensation that he was following me, not on
the other side of the street, but directly behind me,
perhaps only a few yards away. I hastened my steps,
still however making no sound. It seemed to me
that he was moving faster than I, that he was gaining
on me. I could almost feel his breath on my neck.
Suddenly I took a quick look around. He was there,
almost within grasp. I knew I couldn't elude him
now. I had a feeling that he was armed and that he
would use his weapon, knife or gun, the moment I
tried to make a dash for it.

Instinctively I turned like a flash and dove for his
legs. He tumbled over my back and struck his head
against the pavement. I knew I hadn't the strength

to grapple with him.   Again I had to move fast.   He was just rolling over, slightly stunned, it seemed, as I sprang to my feet.   His hand was reaching for his pocket.   I kicked out and caught him square in the stomach.

He groaned and rolled over.   I bolted.   I ran with all the strength I had in me.   But the street was steep, and long before I had come to the end of it, I had to break into a walk.   I turned again and listened.   It was too dark to tell whether he had risen to his feet or was still lying there on the sidewalk.   Not a sound except the wild beating of my heart, the hammering of my temples.   I leaned against the wall to catch my breath.   I felt terribly weak, ready to faint.   I wondered if I would have the strength to climb to the top of the hill.

Just as I was congratulating myself on my narrow escape I saw a shadow creeping along the wall down where I had left him.   This time my fear turned my legs to lead.   I was absolutely paralyzed.   I watched him creeping closer and closer, unable to stir a muscle.   He seemed to divine what had happened ; his pace never quickened.

When he got within a few feet of me he flashed a gun.   With that I instinctively put up my hands. He came up to me and frisked me.   Then he put his gun back in his hip pocket.   Never a word out of him. He went through my pockets, found nothing, cuffed me in the jaw with the back of his hand and then stepped back towards the gutter.

«Put your hands down,» he said, low and tense.

I dropped them like two flails.   I was petrified with fright.

He pulled the gun out again, levelled it, and said in the same even, low, tense voice : «I'm givin' it to you in the guts, you dirty dog !»   With that I collapsed.   As I fell I heard the bullet spatter against the

wall. It was the end. I expected a fusillade. I
remember trying to curl up like a fœtus, crooking my
elbow over my eyes to protect them. Then came the
fusillade. And then I heard him running.

I knew I must be dying, but I felt no pain.

Suddenly I realized that I hadn't even been scratched. I sat up and I saw a man running after the
fleeing assailant with a gun in his hand. He fired a
few shots as he ran but they must have gone wide of
the mark.

I rose to my feet unsteadily, felt myself all over
again to make certain that I was really unhurt, and
waited for the guard to return.

« Could you help me,» I begged, «I'm pretty
rocky.»

He looked at me suspiciously, the gun still in his
hand.

«What the hell are you doing here this hour of
the night?»

«I'm weak as a cat,» I mumbled. «I'll tell you
later. Help me home, will you?»

I told him where I lived, that I was a writer, that
I had been out for a breath of fresh air. «He cleaned
me out,» I added. «Lucky you came along...»

A little more of this lingo and he softened up
enough to say—«Here, take this and get yourself a
cab. You're all right, I guess.» He thrust a dollar
bill in my hand.

I found a cab in front of a hotel and ordered the
driver to take me to Love Lane. On the way I
stopped to get a package of cigarettes.

The lights were out this time. I went up by the
stoop and slid lightly down to the hallway. Not a
sound. I put my ear to the door of the front room
and listened intently. Then I stole softly back to
the little cell at the end of the hall where the big
one usually slept. I had the feeling that the room

was deserted. Slowly I turned the knob. When I had opened the door sufficiently I sank to all fours and crept in on hands and knees, feeling my way carefully to the bed. There I raised my hand and felt the bed. It was empty. I undressed quickly and crawled in. There were some cigarette butts at the foot of the bed—they felt like dead beetles.

In a moment I was sound asleep. I dreamt that I was lying in the corner by the heart, with a coat of fur, padded paws and long ears. Between my paws was a bone which had been licked clean. I was guarding it jealousy, even in my sleep. A man entered and gave me a kick in the ribs. I pretended not to feel it. He kicked me again, as though to make me growl—or perhaps it was to make me let go of the bone.

«Stand up!» he said, flourishing a whip which had been hidden behind his back.

I was too weak to move. I looked up at him with piteous, bleary eyes, imploring him mutely to leave me in peace.

«Come on, get out of here!» he muttered, raising the butt end of the whip as if to strike.

I staggered to all fours and tried to hobble away. My spine seemed to be broken. I caved in, collapsed like a punctured bag.

The man coldly raised the whip again and with the butt end cracked me over the skull. I let out a howl of pain. Enraged at this, he grasped the whip by the butt end and began lashing me unmercifully. I tried to raise myself but it was no use—my spine was broken. I wriggled over the floor like an octopus, receiving lash after lash. The fury of the blows had taken my breath away. It was only after he had gone, thinking that I was done for, that I began to give vent to my agony. At first I began to whimper; then, as my strength returned, I began to scream and

howl. The blood was oozing from me as if I were
a sponge. It flowed out in all directions, making a
big dark spot, as in the animated cartoons. My voice
got weaker and weaker. Now and then I let out a
yelp.

When I opened my eyes the two women were bending over me, shaking me.

«Stop it, for God's sake, stop it!» the big one was
saying.

The other was saying: «My God, Val, what's
happened? Wake up, wake up!»

I sat up and looked at them with a dazed expression.
I was naked and my body was full of blood and
bruises.

«Where have you been? What happened?» Their
voices now chimed together.

«I was dreaming, I guess.» I tried to smile but
the smile faded into a distorted grin. «Look at my
back,» I begged. «I feels broken.»

They lay me back on the bed and turned me over,
as if I had been marked «fragile».

«You're full of bruises. You must have been
beaten up.»

I closed my eyes and tried to remember what had
happened. All I could recall was the dream, that
brute standing over me with a whip and lashing me.
He had kicked me in the ribs, as if I were a mangy
cur. («*I'll give it to you in the guts, you dirty dog!*»)
My back *was* broken, I remembered distinctly. I had
caved in and sprawled out on the floor like an octopus.
And in that helpless position he had lashed away
with a fury that was inhuman.

«Let him sleep,» I heard the big one say.

«I'm going to call an ambulance,» said the other.
They began to argue.

«Go away, leave me alone,» I muttered.

It was quiet again. I fell asleep. I dreamt that

I was in the dog show; I was a chow and I had a blue ribbon around my neck. In the next booth was another chow; he had a pink ribbon around his neck. It was a toss-up which of us would win the prize.

Two women whom I seemed to recognize were bickering about our respective merits and demerits. Finally the judge came over and placed his hand on my neck. The big woman strode away angrily, spitting in disgust. But the woman whose pet I was bent over and, holding me by the ears, raised my head and kissed me on the snout. «I knew you would win the prize for me,» she whispered. «You're such a lovely, lovely creature,» and she began stroking my fur. «Wait a moment, my darling, and I'll bring you something nice. Just a moment...»

When she returned she had a little package in her hand; it was wrapped in tissue paper and tied with a beautiful ribbon. She held it up before me and I stood on my hind legs and barked. «Woof woof! Woof woof!»

«Take it easy, dear,» she said, undoing the package slowly. «Mother's brought you a beautiful little present.»

«Woof woof! Woof woof!»

«That's a darling... that's it... easy now... easy.»

I was furiously impatient to receive my gift. I couldn't understand why she was taking so long. It must be something terribly precious, I thought to myself.

The package was almost unwrapped now. She was holding the little gift behind her back.

«Up, up! That's it... *up!*»

I got to my hind legs and began prancing and pirouetting.

«Now beg! Beg for it!»

«Woof woof! Woof woof!» I was ready to jump out of my skin with joy.

Suddenly she dangled it before my eyes. It was a magnificent knuckle bone, full of marrow, encircled by a gold wedding ring. I was furiously eager to seize it but she held it high above her head, tantalizing me mercilessly. Finally, to my astonishment, she stuck her tongue out and began to suck the marrow into her mouth. She turned it around and sucked from the other end. When she had made a clean hole through and though she caught hold of me and began to stroke me. She did it so masterfully that in a few seconds I stood out like a raw turnip. Then she took the bone (with the wedding ring still around it) and she slipped it over the raw turnip. «Now you little darling, I'm going to take you home and put you to bed.» And with that she picked me up and walked off, everybody laughing and clapping hands. Just as we got to the door the bone slid off and fell to the ground. I tried to scramble out of her arms, but she held me tight to her bosom. I began to whimper.

«Hush, hush!» she said, and sticking her tongue out, she licked my face. «You dear, lovely, little creature!»

«Woof woof! Woof woof!» I barked. «Woof! Woof, woof, woof!»